On Black Wings of Vengeance

Part Two of the
Chain of Shadows -
Begun in 'Halo of Thorns'

Drew Bryenton

On Black Wings of Vengeance
Drew Bryenton

This edition Copyright © 2015 by Oxford eBooks Ltd.
Published under the sci-fi-cafe.com imprint.
www.oxford-ebooks.com
Story Copyright © 2014 by Drew Bryenton

The right of the author to be identified as the author of this work
has been asserted in accordance with the
Copyright, Designs and Patents Act 1988.

All rights reserved.
No part of this publication may be reproduced, stored in a retrieval system, or
transmitted, in any form or by any means, electronic, mechanical, photocopying,
recording or otherwise, without the prior permission of the copyright owners.

ISBN 978-1-910779-10-1 (Paperback)
ISBN 978-1-910779-09-5 (ePUB)
ASIN B015WKCVF4 (Kindle)

Cover artwork by Jim Ellis

Book design and typesetting by
Oxford eBooks Ltd.
www.oxford-ebooks.com

sci-fi-cafe.com

One

Blood on Glass

"Three hundred years from the fall of dark
Urexes, and see how far we have come! It is no
longer feeble superstition or brutal subjugation
which govern our lives. It is peaceful co-operation,
reason, and science which now rule a more rational
world. Across the whole of Sarem, kingdoms
once at war, or dragged down under the Imperial
yoke, now enjoy a renaissance of art, literature,
artifice and trade. We thank the Aemortarch, in
his solitude, for this mercy. And for his sake, we
worship the memory of no other."

Ghuram Legate M'aat Segaar, on the opening of the Seven
Kingdoms Parliament, 309 Anno Occultis

SUMMER WAS SHORT in the North – a brief season of warmth and light squeezed tight between what seemed like eternities of cold. But it was all the more glorious for its brevity, and on a day like this, it was hard to even imagine the ice-flurries of winter, only a few months away.

The taste of them was on the air though, even as the sunlit meadows unfurled before Suul Anvhaur. A patchwork of clouds dappled the green, and swallows flitted after insects in the long grass, following the path of a second rider, perhaps a league ahead. Suul grinned to himself, standing high in the stirrups.

She was playing the old game, then – but tellingly, she wasn't playing to win. Tessira, the daughter of the village smith, eighteen years old and in love with Suul's wild tales as much as with his looks… her roan gelding had left a broad trail of crushed grass behind her as she struck off into the wildlands, no doubt watching intently to see if he still followed.

There was no chance that he would falter. This was the first time that the lovely half-Ontokhi lass had agreed to meet him anywhere away from her father's watchful eye – not to mention his huge and callused fists. Suul remembered what had befallen his sometimes-friend Dalmar when he'd dared too much at the harvest dance… and that Dalmar's nose now covered half his face. Tessira's father was quick to anger, and days working the forge had left him with a right hook that could drop the Aemortarch himself, Ark take him!

Suul spurred his own horse down the shallow slope from the

copse of poplars where he'd stopped to rest, coming up to a trot as they moved into the stirrup-high grass of the plainsea. Of course, it helped that this time the girl was more than willing, and he had his own bastard ancestry to thank for that. Lamenter's grief, that being a half-blood Khytein could actually be *useful* for something! Then again, Tessira's love of history was almost equal to his lust for her. A couple of stories about the barrowlands and she'd been more than keen to ride with him.

Suul thought he felt a drop in the temperature as he passed the first of the blue-grey standing stones which ringed the old necropolis, but of course that was foolish. Whatever had happened here (and he'd made damned sure that Tessira thought his great-great granddaddy had been a big part of it) had happened long ago. There was nothing under the warm summer earth but rotten bones and old armour. None of it was *alive* – not any more.

Three hundred years had smoothed over the grassy hillocks and mounds of the necropolis, turning it into nothing but a jumble of low hills, their flanks nodding with wildflowers. If the old campfire tales were to be believed, a thing called Sothara had built this place for one of the stupid gods his grandmother still sometimes mumbled about over her porridge. But the Aemortarch had come, and tricked him, and stolen his power – at least, that's what Brother Falmius had taught him, back when he attended the Tabernacle School.

Years ago. A superstition built on a fable, built on a probable lie. What was real was the glimpse of pale blonde hair reflecting the sun only half a league distant – that, and the dull, pleasant ache between Suul's legs as he made his secret plans.

For today, he wasn't the miller's boy in a tiny Kaltensund village. For these few sunlit hours he was a warrior of the old Vhaur, the people who had given him his family name, and who had vanished along with their pagan gods three centuries ago. He was playing the game they used to call the Dance of Theyr, the ritual in which a young Khytein brave would ride down his intended bride. If she was willing and he was skilled, he could be assured of a day to remember. If he was a fool or she spurned his advances, he'd feel the caress of nothing but thorns and brambles.

Tessira had listened to his story of the old rite with a twinkle in her pale blue eyes. She'd sprung up from the hay-bale where she sat, slapped him across the back of the head with her short riding whip, and turned at the barn doorway, smiling with coy innocence.

"I suppose you'll have to try to catch me then!" she'd said, igniting a fire in Suul's belly – and points south. He'd never run to the stableyard so fast, or cinched a saddle-girth so quickly.

Now Tessira's big roan was tired, huffing its way up the slope of a tall barrow as her hair streamed out behind her in the wind. Suul didn't think he'd ever seen anything so lovely. Especially as his own mount showed no signs of slowing down.

He dug his heels in, urging the pale grey mare into a canter and then a gallop. They pelted along an avenue between two rows of drunken, leaning obelisks, the runes on their surfaces worn smooth by years of ice and rain.

Suul let out a whooping war-cry as he saw Tessira turn in the saddle, and his heart leaped in his chest as he saw her laughing in reply, urging her horse to the very crest of the barrow. He hit the slope hard, and his horse didn't falter at all – perhaps, he thought, there was really a little Vhaurish blood in those veins after all. The forgotten races of the Khytein had been beastmasters in their day, with gods made from wolves and bears and crows…

He reined in at the top, next to Tessira, and he didn't even wonder for a second why she had stopped. The young miller's boy launched himself from the saddle in an arc of taut muscle and flying dark hair, wrapping his arms around the girl he was fairly certain he loved and carrying them both down to land amid the wildflowers.

He rolled to take her weight in the fall, and only realised the hubris of his action when he heard Tessira's squeal of outrage. A second later a hand slapped him hard across the face, making his ears ring. Surely *this* wasn't part of the old Khytein ritual… what was supposed to happen next was more about pleasure than pain!

"You idiot, Suul!" said Tessira, sitting astride him like a victorious wrestler. She was sucking on the fingers of her left hand – the one she'd used to numb the entire side of his face. "What in the Ark's name do you think you're *doing?*"

A wave of fiery embarrassment roiled up inside him. He was sure that his face was turning beetroot red, which hardly fit the cool demeanor of a plainsea warrior. Surely, thought a part of Suul's mind, this entire game of chase and catch was designed so that he didn't have to make his intentions plain in words…

Then Tessira's hands were woven in his hair, and she leaned over him to plant a kiss directly on his lips. Outrage turned to confusion, and then melted away all in one tinderburst moment.

"There'll be plenty of time for *that*, Suul Anvhaur. That and more. But look! Down there, in the valley."

Suul didn't really want to move. The delicious feeling of Tessira's ample bosom against his chest pinned him down just as surely as her father's anvil would have done. But he struggled up onto his elbows – mainly to show willing – and squinted past the golden curtain of her hair.

What he saw brought back the image of sour-faced old Brother Falmius, his punishment switch clutched in one liver-spotted hand.

Oh yes! I told you so! I told you all the fables of Our Watchful Lord, and about his battles with the dark empire. Ark take you, boy, you should have paid attention! Do you really think a booze-addled old sot like me could make up stories like that?

Down the far side of the barrow, in a crater at least as wide as miller Yarbrough's homestead farm, lay the remains of an arrowhead-shaped wedge of stone, bigger than a castle. Now admittedly, Suul had only seen one castle in his lifetime, and that only the Wayfort at Candleford town. This was ten times the size, and carved with runes as tall as houses. For all that it was broken-backed and crumbled, overgrown with moss and creepers, the young Kaltensunder could well imagine it riding the clouds, armed with deadly sorceries and manned by the dreaded Faceless in their bone-white armour.

"It's one of their Keels," breathed Tessira, rolling off him and rising to her feet. "So this must be the Black Pyramid. There… that's where the Silence fell, and there, under the wreck…"

"The Aemortarch himself fought Endsong," breathed Suul, all thoughts of lust driven away before holy terror. "This is sacred ground. And under our feet…"

"He's long dead! Don't you remember the catechism? The Lamenter and the Dark Lady tricked him, and he tore himself apart."

"Then her brother died here. The Wolfchild. And she herself… not ten feet from where we're standing…"

"Look!" cried Tessira, suddenly darting down the slope. A cloud of wildflower petals tumbled in her wake.

"There, Suul! A piece of… Oh!"

Her cry of pain got the halfblood Vhaur moving faster than any revelation could. This was a forbidden place, after all, and if there really was good reason to shun the old barrowlands, then the pair of them could be in terrible danger. If Tessira was badly hurt, the truth could come out as well – and then it wouldn't be ghosts and monsters

Suul had to worry about. It would be a blacksmith's hard right hand…

He found her kneeling amid the knee-high flowers, the tip of one finger in her mouth. A bright bead of blood trickled from between her lips, then splashed to the ground.

There was a humming sound, right at the very edge of perception. Suul looked down, and saw that the blood had fallen on the very thing which had cut Tessira in the first place – a three-foot long shard of grey glass, rising like a spine of bedrock from the loam. Its edge sparkled with tiny points of light, and it was *resonating* – humming like a lyre-string at full tension.

"Glass?" he asked, instinctively pulling the girl away from it. "But they said Sothara's age was one of iron and stone. At least, Brother Falmius…"

Tessira pulled her fingertip from her mouth and inspected it. A tiny, razor-thin cut dimpled the whorled flesh, but it was nothing more.

"You really *didn't* pay attention, did you?" she said, slipping out of his protective grasp. "There was a verse in the Book of Ascendancy which they kind of hurried past… as though perhaps the Prophet who wrote it was a little bit mad. It said that one of the Bards of the Ancients turned to glass here, and grew to the size of a mountain, and cast down the serpents of death-in-winter."

The words were indeed familiar. But young Suul had been anything but a studious religious scholar. When poor old Falmius was explaining the meaning of the Errata (visions, metaphors, moral allegories and the like, apparently), he had been flicking dried-up snot at the back of Nathum Grenley's head.

Tessira gathered her skirts around her and kneeled. She tugged the yellow Ontokhi scarf from her neck and wrapped it around her hands, reaching out for the shard again.

"You probably shouldn't…" began Suul, but then the vision descended on him, with all the weight of a hammer. The clouds above them spun and twisted into a lighting-shot vortex, and darkness spread is wings over the barrowlands. The cold assailed him in waves as realities sheared and shattered, the past rising up from cracks in the earth like mist.

Tessira had fallen back, the scarf in her hands bloody. The shard of glass had tugged itself from the earth and now rose, spinning, to head height, glittering flashes of sorcery licking across its surface.

"Oh, Lamenter's pain! Look, Suul! Look!"

She didn't have to tell him.

Below, in the basin of the valley, the bulk of the Keel had taken on the glassy, unreal transparency of a phantom. In the space where that wreck of jumbled stone had stood a battle was being fought.

At the centre stood a great armoured phalanx of Imperial soldiers, with their proud tall helms and their crescent-moon shields. Their ranks bristled with spears, fanned out into a deadly array.

But against them came a horde of the dead – half-rotten things with eyeless skulls and jaws hanging askew, dragging rusted iron swords and axes as they clambered from gaping holes in the ground.

The soldiers of the Empire held fast as the wave of undead stumbled up to the charge, bellowing a cry like the wind through an endless graveyard. Then they struck, and Suul saw spears go reaming in, shattering ribcages, skewering skulls, punching through paper-thin mummified flesh. A horn-blast from the Imperial ranks issued an order, and the desperate men of the front line locked shields, pushing forward, trying to stem the tide.

But they were too many. Corroded blades rose and fell in a spray of crimson. Armour crushed and buckled as the ravenous dead lapped around the flanks of the phalanx, tearing holes in the tight-leaved shield wall, dragging men screaming from among their comrades to be torn limb from limb in the mud.

Then light bloomed in silence, right at the heart of the Imperial line. A starburst of radiance, narrowing to a killing beam – it blasted clean through ten ranks of living men from behind, reducing them to windblown ashes. Then it ploughed on through the insatiable dead, detonating their bones with furious heat.

They were dry, those tomb-things. They burned. In an instant a whole swathe of the undead army was afire, though they fought on, grim and determined, until their lifeless flesh carbonized and crumbled. Many a man was locked in the death-embrace of a fleshless ghoul, roasted alive in his armour as he faced down a blackening, skeletal grin…

It was all too much for Tessira. She turned her head away, sobbing, and clung to Suul like a drowning child. But he was unable to look away. Because the source of that terrible power could see him. Even across the gulf of centuries, the thing which had wielded that deadly light met his gaze.

Endsong.

The Aemortarch's nemesis was – as the Good Book said – a thing of beauty. Androgynous and pale, he was clad in a robe of seamless white, belted with cloth-of-gold, and his hair was a whipping tangle of silver, streaming away from his face in the backwash of sorcery. That face was slim and fey, with eyes as dark as the void, and lips peeled back in a cruel smile.

"Suul Anvhaur," purred a sweet, cloying voice inside his head. *"Run home, little boy. Leave this place. And should you ever return…"*

The ancient demigod raised his hand, and force collected in his palm, flowing inward like trickles of quicksilver. He pointed one finger directly at Suul, his smile becoming a demon mask of unholy glee…

And the vision collapsed. It fell with a sound like breaking glass, whole fractured panes of sky tumbling down, the cries of the dying fading into the distance, the cold blown away by a warm eddy of summer wind.

The sky was blue again. The grass was green. The broken remains of a Keel Suul had just seen hanging motionless in the air…

He found himself on the ground, his head haloed by wildflowers. He promptly rolled over and threw up his breakfast, groaning with the pain of it.

"Did you see her?" asked Tessira, her voice so real and familiar that Suul almost broke down in tears. Her hand rested lightly on his shoulder.

"Her? No. Just *Him*. Just… oh, Ark's fury, it's all *real*. I saw… I saw Endsong. He *talked to me!* He said…"

Tessira rolled him over onto his back. Her father wasn't the only one who worked the forge, and there was a deceptive strength in those long, lean limbs. For the first time since the vision broke, Suul caught a glimpse of her eyes. And what he saw there both excited and horrified him, because they were no longer cornflower blue.

They were violet, and they blazed with a mixture of religious zeal and lust. The colour of the haloed nimbus of a lightning bolt, and *far*, far more frightening than the empty black pits of Endsong's stare.

"He doesn't matter. He was cast out long ago. But I saw *Her*. The Dark Lady. The Maiden of Sorrows. She told me not to be afraid. She told me… what we have to do."

It was everything that Suul had wanted. But it was nothing like he had imagined. Tessira straddled him and tore his shirt open, scattering bone buttons like hail.

"In the old ritual," she said, in a voice thick with desire, "The women of the Vhaur would hold a knife to their chosen's throat, after the chase was done." She leaned down to kiss him, and for the second time that day all confusion and doubt was burned away. Something of the divine madness which had taken Tessira entered him, and Suul wrapped his fingers in her hair, arching his back against the weight of her. They broke apart, and she looked down at him, a flush of bright red high on each cheek.

"If they weren't satisfied, they cut the poor man's throat when he was helpless, afterward." She smiled. "Though I can already tell *that* won't be a problem…"

The nightmare vision of Endsong was gone. Now there was just the summer sunlight, the smell of wildflowers, and the thunder of his heartbeat in his temples. He gave in to it, and the world blurred red…

He only remembered one thing from the frenzied two hours which followed. Surfacing for a moment from the depths of raw sensation and dark communion, he looked over Tessira's bare shoulder, over the deep claw-tracks his fingernails had made against her pale white skin.

The shard was watching them.

It hung in the air, a three-foot sliver of grey, flecked with motes of starlight. And it turned, slowly, still wrapped in a bloody scrap of Ontohki silk.

Then the rapture took him again, and he was lost.

But under the warm summer soil – directly beneath the young lovers – a teardrop-shaped bead of glass, about the size of a clenched fist, began to crack and unfurl. Petals bloomed deep in the musty darkness, and tendrils quested blindly upward, toward the light.

Suul Anvhaur didn't even feel them as they pierced his spine, each one slimmer than the finest human hair. Tessira was equally oblivious to the message the tendrils carried. But then again, she was aflame with the desire of a long-dead sorceress, utterly consumed by the endless moment…

Three hours later, they would ride home, frightened by what had happened to them and between them.

Three months passed, and the results of that summer afternoon could no longer be kept from the village blacksmith, Garald. The fearsome old man was actually not too displeased – his daughter needed a husband, not a succession of lusty boyfriends, and the lad would, after all, one day be part-owner of a very fine mill. In the meantime there was extra work to do around the forge – the lad looked tough enough, and the Lamenter knew that Garald himself wasn't getting any younger…

Suul got away with no more than a fairly desultory backhand (you had to keep up appearances), and was only missing two teeth when he stood before the magistrate and the Holy Brother to pledge his marriage vows. Tessira smiled throughout the ceremony like a kitten who had just upended a cream churn.

Six months later, the happy couple were delivered of a healthy, squalling baby girl. Her hair was black as coal-dust, and her eyes were the deep, deep violet of the last flicker of dusk.

The three-foot long shard of glass which was, in a very real sense, the reason for her being, was tucked away in the back of a cupboard in their new home, a cottage beside the millpond.

Tessira told Suul that her name was Siara – and not in a tone which brooked any argument. Suul, who had learned very quickly when to simply nod and smile and allow his wife her eccentricities, did just that.

Ten years later, when word came from the far south of the dead walking, the miller of Cross Corners thought nothing of it. Probably just some trader-talk nonsense, and no more than that. He certainly didn't recall the vision he'd suffered, back on one short-summer day in his youth, on a day far more noteworthy for pleasure rather than fear.

And he, like nearly everyone else in all of Sarem, believed that sorcery still slept – the dying sleep of a frail old man. The Gods were dead, the Aemortarch watched over their corpses, and the new age was one of peace and reason. So all right-thinking folk held true.

All, that was, except his daughter Siara.

Who was really not *his* daughter at all…

Part Two

The Doom of Oram

Histories from that time are biased at best, garbled nonsense at worst - but we know this for a fact. The one we now worship as the Aemortarch, the great balancing force who has brought peace through terror for the last three centuries, was indeed a real man. It was always assumed that casualties during his overthrow of the White Empire were absolute, but obviously there were survivors, and witnesses to his feats. Otherwise we must posit that the Prophets who wrote the Book of Ascendancy - and raised the Tabernacles - were either fools or liars...

Solgren Kern, High Historian of the Guild of Chains

I HARDLY REMEMBERED myself.

Three hundred winters, and I had aged not a single day.

But the years had taken their toll in other, more insidious ways. The face which stared back at me from the tarnished silver mirror in my lair (for what else could you call this shadowed, book-lined room?) was all but unfamiliar. The mind behind it… ahh, well. I supposed time would tell.

The lines and fractures on my face were nothing compared to the fissures clawed out of my memory, especially since I had cut myself off from the best part of my power.

This much I knew.

I was named Kuhal Da'Hurik Moer, son of the wild north, and I was a necromancer.

Perhaps not by choice, and certainly without the blessing of the God my little tribe had worshiped as ruler over death – but a necromancer nonetheless. A very misunderstood profession, mine. Hardly the type to encourage visitors, which was why I had spent several hours this day learning how to make appropriate facial expressions again. Smiling is *hard*. More so, when you have very little reason to do it.

But I was learning about myself anew, as I ran my fingers over the unfamiliar face in the glass. Already I had discovered a breathtaking lack of humility, a quick temper, and a streak of melancholy which would better befit a poet than a hard-bitten barbarian tribesman[1].

---

1 Sad but true – I was indeed born of the kind of people who wear uncured furs, sword-

They were traits which I hoped I had actually earned… arrogance without power, in my experience, being like a brandished sword-hilt without a blade.

The figure which looked back at me through the cobwebs and grime was utterly unlike the young man who had come down out of the wildlands years ago. *He* was all spite and vengeance, the puppet of mad divinities and those who would supplant them. I would love to say that the years had mellowed his sharp and unlovely features, but they hadn't. All they had done was bleach his mane of unruly hair bone white, leaving a single hank of black to spill down over my forehead.

I sighed, and took stock. Again.

My eyes were dark and sunken, ringed with bruise-purple bags. The mageblight – that disease of the flesh and soul peculiar to sorcerers – had woven a web of faded scars across my cheeks and down my forearms. My hands, which at one time had seethed with city-shattering might, were stained black, jagged lightning-bolts of darkness following my veins in tangled confusion almost to the elbows.

I looked nineteen summers old, going on a thousand.

Would I pass for mortal? Perhaps. With the leather longrider's gloves I slipped on, and the wide-brimmed hat of a pilgrim on my head, with smoked glasses and a cassock which looked just a little too priestly for my liking… I would pass muster.

So long as I didn't forget myself.

The habit of absolute power is a hard one to break, for any aspirant Lords who are listening. I would have to learn to be slightly more human again – at least, I thought with a smirk, unless I was set upon by bandits. That might prove… entertaining.

I'd given up on the concept of traveling Sarem as a beggar, because there is such a thing as too much humility. It was a quality I didn't really care to cultivate, even if it *had* taken me three hours to master an expression of servile good humour. No – I would go forth as a wandering Magus, of the kind who used to trek from cairn to barrow across my native land, muttering under their breaths and following the path of powers they could dig up and enslave. Three hundred years

---

belts and not much else – who quaff ale like they want to drown the man behind them, and who make up countless entertaining lies about themselves, their relatives and their ancestors striding about with not much on, slaying huge monsters and, of course, anyone queer and sickly enough to become a craven sorcerer instead of a proper, meat-headed warrior.

or not, there would still be such men abroad – charlatans, mostly, but feared enough by the peasantry to allow me safe passage.

Just because I could flay the flesh from the bones of whole armies didn't mean I *wanted* to. Or – perhaps closer to the truth – I didn't want the undue attention such a display would call down.

Why leave my tower at all, you might ask?

A fine question. I'd asked myself the same thing all through the lengthy and tedious process of disengagement, the stripping down of my great Incantus to a few strands of power wrapped around a single soul. It was hard for me to answer, but the need to be out in the world again, and soon, tugged at something deep in my mind. My thoughts returned to that need like a tongue probing at a rotten tooth, relishing the pain of knowing that everyone I had fought against was long gone to worm-food.

Morbid, perhaps. But then… Necromancy is no art for the squeamish. I sighed, resting my forehead against the cool glass of the mirror. Around me lay a drift of discarded and rejected clothes, from black, ornate Ghuram plate armour to the white robes Jerrold Sinder had once worn, back when he was still my enemy.

I looked like a sickly, poppy's-blood-addicted priest from some puritan death-cult. But it was the best I was going to do.

And I knew *why*, deep in my withered and unreliable old heart. I knew why I had to leave, perhaps never to return.

Over the last few years I had felt the Gods I had imprisoned growing weaker. Down in the Capitoline Deep, a straight mile beneath my feet, poor mad Zael and the insufferable, martyred Esau kept each other from the world of men, balanced in perfect hatred.

But they were failing. It shouldn't have been possible. It *scared* me, which is quite something – it's hard to frighten a man who is reviled across seven cultures as the very apogee of wickedness.

Because I knew that I needed the power of the Aziphem – the old Gods at the heart of the world – to bring back the only other person I had ever loved. Witch, demoness, Nameless One of the infernal Coven of Nine – and the sweetest girl ever born of the Khytein Vhaur.

I had her soul, wrapped up in the black jade amulet around my neck. Her body was taken by Zael in a cataclysm which had brought down an empire, but I had amassed scrolls and tomes of great antiquity during my self-imposed exile, using agents as varied as Zengaji assassins and Ghuram trademasters to bring me the knowledge required to give her life.

All I needed was power.

Not the power of my chained and bleeding Gods – any shift in their balance would lead to an age of madness. No… I needed another power entirely. And if the force of the Aziphem was passing from the world, I had precious little time left to find it…

Hence my somewhat frenzied preparations. Hence the Zengaji killer who had replaced me on the throne in the Capitoline Deep, his ravaged flesh now the focus for titanic energies. *I* had been the one who paid his Clanfather to send him. His mission had been to kill me. His test – that he had almost succeeded.

A nice word, 'almost'. How it puts a positive spin on abject failure…

I didn't have any minions to wish me well. I didn't have any servants who I could entrust with the keys to my awful dark tower, a spike of obsidian rising from the ruins of the Urexian Plain.

All I had was a pouch of ancient, tarnished coins, the amulet around my neck, and a sword called Cryptfeeder, cunningly re-worked from the immense metal slab it once was into a basket-hilted sabre, in the style of an Ontokhi duelist.

I took one last look in the mirror.

The hat, the cassock, the glasses, the long, elbow length gloves…

I looked like a fool. But I had no choice.

It was time to see what the people of Sarem had done with the three hundred years of peace I had bought them.

And if they knew what was good for them, it was time for them to pay me back.

The pogroms were, if anything, more vile, brutal and disturbingly honest than the tyranny they were enacted to overthrow. The cult of the Aemortarch in its ascendancy burned so many heretics, it's said, that whole forests were razed just to build their pyres. We know this much, at least. None of the Sacred Blood, the noble-born of Anganesse, survived that zealous uprising. The kingdom whose fields are now made fertile by the ashes from those fires is called Angenstrand, and it wears the hollow echo of its former greatness like a scar on a courtesan's face...

Histories of Near Antiquity
Redactor-General Orsin Cawel of Saradrim

IF I WAS a grandiose idiot – like a vast percentage of those who grow ancient with power – I would have stormed from my tower astride an undead draken, borne on black wings of dread. I would probably have whipped up an unnatural storm as well, just to set the scene.

But I'd seen the price of such theatrics. I'd burned Gods down to wreckage in chains thanks to their love of theatre. I'd learned subtlety from their mistakes.

So I left the black tower by a small and cunningly concealed postern door, without fanfare, on foot. Thousands of spans of tortured rock reared up above me, like the gnomon of a mad giant's sundial. Would I miss the old place? Unlikely. It was cold in winter, stifling in summer... better suited to a hive of termites than a single sorcerer.

But we are of a kind, we who are shot through with the 'blight. An old sailor friend of mine (long gone to dust, I supposed) had once told me of a kind of soft-bodied crab which inhabits the shells of dead things on the ocean floor. How like that pulpy little morsel I felt as I left the place of my exile! The place where I had spent long decades on my throne, sending my mind wandering the world instead of my frail, unsteady flesh.

The Angans[2] would have laughed to see their conqueror now. They would have laughed even harder when they saw the mule I brought with me. No draken. No mythic beasts. Not even a midnight-black stallion.

We trudged along, raising a rooster-tail of fine white ash, both laden down with packs of provisions and books, blankets, water-skins, and alchemical apparatus. I showed admirable restraint in not blasting the dumb beast with sorcery. The mule showed far less restraint in biting any appendage which came too near to his snaggle-yellow teeth.

The Desolation was vast, and it took us most of a day to cross it. The sun beat down on a shattered plain of broken glass, a crust of soil blasted beyond endurance by elder sorcery. I could hardly complain about the heat, or the oppressive silence – for I had helped to bring it about, three hundred years ago. Here and there tangles and clusters of bleached bone humped up through the glass and ash, alongside rusted weapons, battered, dented armour and empty helms. The remains of two immense armies, joined together in death. Pieces of Urexes' huge stone walls were strewn across the plain like children's blocks, some of them burned black with the shadows of the dead. Hands and arms raised up to ward off a terrible, killing light…

Before the sun hoisted itself to noonday I had decided two things. Firstly, that I would call my mule Bastard. And secondly, that marching through a dry-bone desert in high summer was work for young men and fools, along with all other saga-song conceits like 'heroism' and 'regular exercise'. Oh, I still had the body of a lean, fit Khytein youth – it's just that it was webbed and calcified with the 'blight, making my limbs feel as heavy as waterlogged wood.

No power, you see. Torn away from the wellspring of my bleeding gods, I was like a poppy-addict bereft of his pipe and coals. And this was just the first day of my odyssey! Zael, who had used me, was crucified in the Deep. Anghul, another facet of the same shard of the Divine, turned his face away. If it wasn't for the power coiled and stored in the artefacts I kept about my person, I would be – and I shuddered to think it – merely a *mortal man*.

The day dragged on toward dusk, and at last I could see the low incline which formed the edge of the desolation – the crater-rim

2. Anganesse was once an immense, powerful, civilized and utterly rotten theocracy which ruled all of Sarem. It will spoil nothing in this narrative to tell you that it worked out very, very badly for them. Turns out the Holy Word is not, in fact, mightier than the Sword.

of pumice, bone, glass and soil which had been flung up by the detonation of so much elder sorcery. Bastard balked at the foot of the hill, and I was drawing back my riding crop to deliver a much-deserved thrashing when I paused, listening.

Something was out there. The mule heard it, and now so did I.

It was a sound I was all too familiar with – steel and chain, leather and harness… the sound of an army on the march. Just beyond the ridgeline, soldiers were moving into position, wagons wheels were creaking, and muttered oaths and blasphemies given vent.

Perhaps they had seen my dust, and guessed at the identity of the only man likely to come walking out of the Desolation? Perhaps a band of Angenstrand patriots wanted to carve off a slice of revenge for their long-dead grandsires?

I paused. It didn't *sound* like an ambush. And surely, if an army was coming to face me, they would have had the tactical wherewithal to line the ridge with archers. A sorcerer – *any* sorcerer – is more than the match for a sword-gristle warrior. But a sky full of arrows doesn't discriminate.

Of course, in my weakened state, even one woodsman with a good length of yew could pin me screaming to the dust. My only hope was that they'd skewer Bastard first.

Paranoia, I muttered, belting on my sword. *Stupidity!*

I was out here to set the world right, not shit myself at shadows. So I left the mule behind and went scrambling up the incline, feeling a little more like the child of the North I had once been, and less like a sorcerous cripple.

The sight which met my eyes at the ridge's crest knocked that conceit out of me – and hard.

The land beyond the Desolation was once a wildflowered steppe, traversed by migrating herds of bison. In the last three centuries it had been tamed, and then, apparently, abandoned. Down the incline lay the log fences and cultivated fields of a little farm, though it had long gone to ruin. A scarecrow hung like carrion amid a riot of weeds, crops gone to seed and untended. The thatched roof of the farmer's cottage had fallen in, and his barn was a bleach-wood tumble, brought down by storms.

But this wasn't the fact which gave me pause. The cornfields, radiating out from the homestead in wild, tangled fans, were *moving*.

They were aswarm with the dead.

Haggard, grey-skinned shapes tottered through the chest-high corn, some wearing scraps of armour, some naked and bloody, some in peasant smocks and leathers, others in ragged finery. There were women, children… even cloven, hacked-open things which could have been either, but which now determinedly pulled themselves forward with their bodies scraggling away to trailing rot, the stumps of spines and femurs glistening.

There must have been *hundreds* of them, and each one was armed, carrying the most crude and motley assortment of weapons I had ever seen. Wheat flails and billhooks, clubs and maces, sickles and pitchforks, even two-handed greatswords which must have been relics in my youth. These blank-eyed, stumbling things had no ranks, no grace, and no co-ordination, but they had a purpose, and it was horribly clear.

There was blood - and worse - crusted around the mouths of every one. They wanted to *feed*.

And I couldn't feel them. The tangle of souls, struggling to escape their flesh… they weren't there at all.

For a moment I thought it all a dream. Some fevered, sun-baked hallucination. A flashback to the horrors I had raised in my younger days… But no. Not even the most wild imagination could bring to life that *smell* - the reek of putrefaction which hung over the ghouls like a cloud.

There must have been scarcely a hundred soldiers there in the stableyard, but they showed no fear. Indeed, they formed up in ranks behind a row of unlimbered wagons as though this kind of battle was a dreary chore, rather than a waking nightmare. The walls of the high-sided wagons clanged down to form sloping palisades, covered with barbs. Arbalests in the wagon beds were loaded by siege gunners, two-man teams ready to turn their wooden cranks. And amid the shouts and curses, as banners were raised and spears bristled, strode a man who was almost familiar – for his air of swaggering command if not for his face, which was hidden beneath a half-helm of riveted steel.

"Come on, you whoremasters! You should be quicker with those damned Spitters than you are in bed, Ilwen! Gorsk, hold that bloody halberd like you mean it, man! It's not your limp bloody cock!"

Within the space of a sixty heartbeats the little company had formed a square inside the confines of the wagons – one which would funnel any attackers in to the centre, where they could be hacked to bloody offal. I was smiling with the recognition of a job well done as the first of the dead shambled up to a run, voicing a mournful howl.

But centuries of invulnerability had made me foolish. I was still out in the open.

"There! On the hill! That's one of them!"

An armoured figure pointed, and one of the huge repeating siege-bows rattled around to face me.

"A Taken priest! Eyes of the Thane!" bellowed the man I'd marked, his face between his helm and his forked, grey-streaked beard splitting in a wide grin. "Snare me that one, Ilwen, and the Tabernacle will be kissing our arses for forgiveness, not the other way round!"

There's nothing better than the handspan-wide iron arrow of a ballista to focus one's resolve. Despite the fact that a cassock is not the best vestment in the world for athletics, I scrambled down the incline and toward the stableyard, waving my hands over my head.

"Don't shoot! I'm alive, dammit! I'm *alive!*"

Ilwen looked more than a little disappointed. But off to my left the first ranks of the dead were streaming around and through the wreck of the cottage, and the Commander of this warband had made his decision.

"Come on then, you foolish God-botherer! Get in among us! If you have any prayers for your precious Aemortarch, grovel to the bastard now!"

I pushed through the thicket of spearheads, helped along by rough, chain-mailed hands. Halfway through being manhandled to the centre of the square the Commander's gauntlet snagged my collar, and he hauled me the rest of the way in a single heave. One of those men even slapped my arse! *Me!* The Dark Lord, who had once been every living man's nightmare!

"Lamenter's balls!" spat the Commander. "What a sorry sight you are!" He grinned. "I suppose Deacon Fell sent you to spy on our little expedition? How are you liking it so far?"

Up close, the man's similarity to Elion Morekh was… *uncanny.* Like the old pirate, this soldier was wiry and filled with wild-spark energy. Unlike him, he still had all his own teeth, and his hair was bundled back into huge, fat, Akhazi-style dreadlocks, each one woven about with steel rings. They burst out from under the lip of his helm like serpents.

I climbed to my feet, a little unsteady. My black cassock was covered in dust, and my hat was askew on my head.

"I have no idea," I said, in as icy a voice as I could muster, "What a *Deacon Fell* is, or what business it has with you and yours. But I assure you, I…"

The Commander clapped me on the shoulder and smiled all the more widely.

"No time for that now," he said. "They're on us! If you survive, we'll talk about it later."

And with that he was off, unsheathing a pair of great crossed sabres from his back and leaping up to the bed of one of the wagons.

"Hold! Hold until you can smell their ruptured guts, damn you! There's a Thane in this horde, mark me, and *I will have its bloody head!*"

Then the wave of the dead struck, and the clash of steel on steel rose to fill the world.

The men I had raised, all those centuries ago… they had fought in silence, and they had done so with the memory of battle still upon them. These things came on as if they were lashed with invisible whips, moaning and flinching, throwing themselves on the spears and pikes of the living with doomed resignation. Black, tarry blood fanned and spattered. Limbs, hands and heads flew wide, hacked from the press of greying flesh. It seemed that whatever cold intellect commanded these wretches, it would swamp the soldiers' position through sheer weight of numbers.

But then the arbalests spoke, and black iron spears began to spit from their draken-carved snouts. Each six-span length of wood and metal carried a clay cylinder, a sputtering fuse whipping through the air behind it…

The detonations ripped through the ranks of the dead like a red-hot chain, lashed down across the stableyard by the hand of a God. Bodies vaporized as bone fragments whickered through rotting flesh, cutting down twenty, forty, a hundred ghouls. The stench was mephitic. The sound – like thunder and tearing meat.

Still they came.

Now the Commander himself joined the fray, leaping down from his perch beneath a flashing silver arc. A ghoul's head was chopped into three clean chunks by his downswing, blades driven down as far as its fluid-choked lungs. Those twin blurs of steel sliced left and right, unsplicing muscle and bone. Behind him rallied his troops, loosing a lusty battle-roar, and now the flanks were unfolding, the centre moving forward, butchering their way against the tide.

"Gahhh, you cockless freaks! Taste steel! You, and your ugly mothers!"

Surely, though, this blood-drunk hero was insane. Surely even *he* couldn't stand against the drooling, snapping throng who hemmed him in on all sides, groping and clawing even as they were hacked apart.

Down he went under a pile of bodies. I waited for the crunches, the screams…

But then a blast lifted a handful of the dead away, shredding through them in a cone of dirty fire. Another explosion, and the Commander staggered to his feet, something clicking and whirring on his forearm, clockwork mechanisms interlocking. A giant ghoul came pelting at him, dragging behind it a cleaver the size of an alehouse table, furrowing the dry-packed earth. Before it could swing, the Commander cocked back his forearm. A tube snapped forward over the back of his fist.

And, as the giant brought its rusted meat-chopper up and over, he delivered a solid punch to the thing's gut.

Fire flared, and the ghoul seemed to fold in on itself, its weapon spinning away. Then it was blown in half, entrails uncoiling, the look on its face one of bemused stupidity. Smoke billowed from the tube as the Commander reclaimed his fallen sabre and pushed back the visor of his helm.

"It's in the farmhouse, men! Come on! Volunteers! Who wants a story for the wenches that isn't all booze and buggery?"

A ragged cheer went up. A proud few saga-heroes bulled their way to the front, their tabards drenched in black gore.

"It'll be a big one, so keep your wits about you. Samel, you and Greith circle around the back. Narven, you and I go in the front. And the rest of you, pile in through the windows. Hack until the wretch stops moving, and we might get out of this with no worse than a few bloody nightmares."

There were more of the dead coming, though. Whatever commanded them – and I still couldn't pin down its mind, even though it was just behind the walls of that tumbledown cottage – had called for aid. The corn thrashed with unseen ranks and legions, eerie in the deep-shadow dusk.

I had to do something.

Now, the habit of being a sorcerer is a hard one to break. With the power of a God on his side – a facet of one of the Shards of the Divine – a sorcerer wields powers most petty tyrants would envy, and has little use for the thrusting and grunting of swords and meat. I'd seen

Corvo of Ontokh master entire storms with the aid of his God. I'd watched Tishande the Erysan conjure a sky full of draken, breaking men's minds like matchwood.

So I leaped up beside Ilwen at his arbalest and cast my arms up high, in the classical gesture for calling power. I had no God to aid me – the Shard of Death spurned me as an enemy of the Divine – but I did have a black onyx ring on my little finger, its jewel guttering with inner fires.

"S'chardith Kialtu Hamazesh!" I shouted, giving voice to the Ritual of Injunction. Invisible forces built between my hands, then released in a rolling wave, striking sparks from every sword-blade and spearhead. The tangle of hooked magick rushed down on the dead, loaded with the force of my will.

And nothing happened.

Men around me looked bemused, horrified, and – worst of all – *pitying*.

"His mind's gone," said a voice from in the press of bodies. "Poor bastard."

"Get down, you stupid priest!" yelled another. "Unless you want to join the fucking ghuldren for dinner!"

Hands tugged at my cassock. I snarled.

But I was secretly terrified. What I had just unleashed – the Ritual of Injunction – came from the wisdom of old Korisal, and it should have brought every ghoul within a league's span under my control. That tide of grey flesh still surged toward us, threatening to drown the Commander and his bravos at any second. And it meant that things in the wider world were sicker than they seemed.

But there was another way.

"Hands off, if you want to keep them," I growled, throwing back my robe to reveal the hilt of Cryptfeeder. I drew the sword with an oily rasp, and was further horrified to find that I almost couldn't lift it. The runes of featherlight and wind-swift refused to glow. The edge of the blade failed to hum and blur with eager bloodlust.

In other words, the saga-sword of legend was now just a big, cold lump of steel.

This was going to cost me.

I drilled down into the second ring on my left hand – a cluster of rubies imbued with the fires under the earth. This time I felt a tingle of force. It wasn't the storm-surge of fury it should have been (I had forged the ring myself, in caverns so deep and hot that only draken and their ancient Sire could walk there unprotected) – but it was enough.

Cryptfeeder howled. I joined in. Then I was free of the grasping hands, off and running toward the cottage, even as the dead came hording and bulking around its flanks, milky eyes filled with murder.

"He's mad," said a voice behind me.

"Should we…"

"And kill ourselves, too? Fuck off!"

"What will the Tabernacle..?"

"Shit on the Tabernacle! If they send a mad priest to spy on Feurio's Company, he's not our responsibility!"

Some of them actually *laughed*.

Then I was face to face with the dead, and my blade sang butchery. Some things you don't forget.

I had never been a great warrior; not by the savage standards of the Khytein Moer. But a snake-quick, iron-fisted bastard called Ulkar Jaerl had beaten swordplay into me three centuries past, and since then I had picked apart the minds and souls of a good many battle-striding killers.

It helped, of course, that these things were woeful fighters.

Cryptfeeder lopped the arm off one wight, then sheared backhanded through the torso of another, spraying thick, greasy blood in a black rain. Hands reached out for me, and fingers flew, severed. Gaping mouths moaned, tongues lolling from between broken teeth, and I carved through them, shortening a whole rank of ghouls by half a head. Stinking brain matter slopped to the parched ground. The dead quailed back, then staggered toward me again, driven by those invisible whips of force.

They came, and they died. I pushed through an abattoir of corpses until the ground was slick underfoot. Around the corner of the cottage, and to a staved-in door, from behind which…

The soldier called Samel came flying in two pieces. Left and right, as through some impossibly sharp blade had taken him from crown to crotch in a single swing. He flew in a flat trajectory until his remains struck the tumbledown barn, exploding crimson. Ghouls turned away from their charge to slop at the wreckage, keening their hunger. I noted with disgust that quite a few were children - that one was in fact half an infant, carried by a mother with her lower jaw missing.

Screams came from within the cottage. The stone walls shook, letting out a puff of dust.

"Under the thatch!" came the Commander's voice – the man I guessed was Feurio. "Mangle it down! Hack it ragged!"

High strategy, then. But I could hardly blame the man when I saw exactly what he faced.

The Thane, as promised, was a big one. Back in my questing days I had called up such things, and called them Slaughterborn.[3] But this – this was sicker by far than those patchwork horrors. The Thane was a soft, melted tangle of flesh, a slubbering mound of torsos and faces, eyes rolling and lips drooling as it crabbed its way out from under the fallen thatch on a horrorworks of arms and legs. Cold radiated from the thing – a deep, sorcerous chill which I felt in my soul. Its hunger was absolute, deep and ravenous as oceans.

"Join. Merge. Consummate." it grated, in a voice like a tortured choir. *"Resist not. Fear not. Embrace."*

There was little chance of that. As the thing revealed itself, the warriors Greith and Narven plunged screaming to the attack, one with a bearded axe, the other with a spiked mace. Both were fearsome weapons, and both men were bull-necked brawlers, their arms as thick around as my thighs.

Both men died.

The Thane moved with insect swiftness for all its shuddering bulk, unfolding a pair of many-jointed limbs which seemed all knees and elbows. Sharp horns and spikes of bone studded these fleshy flails, but it was the hands at the tip of each one which brought Greith and Narven low. Sorcery flared as those hands bit home, mismatched numbers of fingers sinking through armour and leather like suet. The air glittered as sheets of ice formed, pure geometrical planes of the stuff, neatly bisecting each man.

Now I knew what had happened to poor, doomed Samel.

"See? Futile! Come. Join. Partake. We love…"

Its eyes made it a liar, though. There was nothing in that constellation of blinking, shivering whiteness but pain. Something was controlling this thing, and it wanted very, very badly to die.

Feurio tried to give it its wish.

The Commander had lost his helm, and his dreadlocks whipped out

---

3. Recipe for the Slaughterborn – Find a mass grave, left over from some hideous massacre. These are all too easy to unearth, which says more about human nature than it does about necromancy. Next, use the latent rage of the dead to bind all of them into one huge, wallowing, rotten creature. Such a thing goes through castle walls like damp parchment. Unfortunately, it also smells exactly as you would imagine.

behind him as he leaped across an overturned table, sabres singing. He lopped off one of the Thane's killing limbs with a twin-bladed scissorcut, then rolled and dodged the other meat-flail, coming in close to the thing's lumpen body. One sabre went in deep, wrenched from his grip. The other flew backhand – and I swear the man *didn't even bother to turn and look* as he hacked off another striking tentacle.

Tubes whirred and clicked on Feurio's forearms as he rammed the point of his second sabre into a moaning, gibbering mouth. The Thane lurched forward, trying to crush its assailant with sheer bulk.

"Any time you want to help, priest," he puffed, still smiling his reckless grin. "And perhaps… this time… not just a sermon on peace?"

That got me moving. That… and the power which radiated from the body of the Thane, a visible knotwork of tendrils at its core. I may have been cut off from the source of my necromancy, but energies consecrated to death seethed inside it. And I had remade Cryptfeeder to suck such wellsprings dry.

Feurio was rammed up against the cottage's soot-black hearth by the bulk of the Thane as I attacked. The problem, I found, with assaulting a beast with more eyes than testicles, is that there's no element of surprise to speak of. Thick, whiplike tongues lashed at me, tipped with what appeared to be scorpion stings. Arms and legs, repurposed as tooth-studded clubs, hammered against my defences. I was forced to hold the flat of Cryptfeeder's blade in my left and its hilt in my right, forming a roof of steel overhead. Nameless, flaccid appendages spent their fury on the sharp edge of the blade, chopping themselves to ribbons.

I bought the Commander time. I saw him slap each of his forearms in turn, making three tubes lock into place across the back of both fists. Then, with a roar of wordless rage, he jammed one arm into a snapping mouth on his left, and the other into a less identifiable orifice (though still one with *teeth*) on his right.

I had barely enough time to step back, bringing Cryptfeeder up in front of me, point first, like a duelist's rapier.

Then the strange mechanisms which Feurio wore cut loose, and the whole mass of the Thane seemed to swell, ballooning out to twice its size. A wall of barbed, eye-studded grey flesh rushed up at me. But only for an instant.

A heartbeat later, the whole gruesome mess of the thing exploded outward, some weakness in its form giving way. A storm of burning offal swept past me. If I wasn't more mageblight than skin and bone, I may very well have been battered to a pulp by explosive innards.

As it was, the empty sac of the Thane skewered itself on my blade, while ragged flaps of the rest of it painted the entire inside of the farmhouse stinking black. Long ago, Elion Morekh had told me about the octopus of the shallow sea – a creature which I still believed must be mythical. Morekh said that the little beast sprayed a toxic black ink when threatened. I felt like a sailor who had dared such a creature and lost.

I must have made quite a sight, because when the ringing in my ears faded all I could hear was Feurio's laughter. The soldier was dripping from head to toe with gore, but his smile was wide and white.

"Do you want to know the irony, priest?" he asked, sliding down the filth-slick wall. "I said I'd have its Gods-damned head. But… but the fucking thing was *too ugly to have one!*"

I'd stood on plenty of battlefields. I'd heard the hysterical laughter of men about to lose their minds. This wasn't the same. For all Feurio seemed to care, he could be telling the same bad joke in a tavern taproom somewhere.

"Suppose you'll have something nice to tell your Deacon, then. I hope he appreciates our efforts."

"I don't have a Deacon," I replied. To my surprise, I was panting with the effort as I lifted Cryptfeeder over my shoulder and stepped up to the corpse. "But this thing *does* have a head. Of sorts…"

Feurio looked at me quizzically, as if actually seeing me for the first time.

"You don't, do you? What are you then? Some kind of renegade? A preacher who fights the ghuldren instead of just bemoaning our sins? You're not going to be popular. Not on either side!"

I kicked aside a tattered flap of hide, exposing a ball of bone-ribbed tissue. *Brain* tissue. This thing, whatever it really was, had grown its own damned Incantus.

"I'm a… scholar. Of elder sorcery. The resemblance to a holy man is purely co-incidental, I assure you."

Feurio tore his sabres loose with a hideous sucking sound.

"And I'm the virgin queen of Ythe. You may not be a priest, but no ink-fingers scribe fights like that."

I slipped the ruby ring from my finger and slotted it into the pommel of Cryptfeeder. Hidden vice-jaws snicked tight.

"Have you ever *seen* a scholar of elder sorcery?"

"No. I've seen what passes for mages and conjurers, though. They're usually drunk, and more often than not they're slowly going mad with syphilis. I don't see you asking a pox-raddled tavern crowd to pick a card, boy."

I reversed my grip and rammed the blade home. Sickly green lightning sizzled up the fuller as arcane mechanisms I had devised sucked the Thane dry. Now the ring blazed with power again.

"I don't even do wedding parties," I said, scabbarding the sword. The ring went back on my finger, fire dancing within it once more.

Feurio stepped closer.

"I'm going to guess a little more, then," he said. "I'm going to guess that you have *no idea* what just happened here. That you'll tell me you've been away for a while, or traveling, or some other pretty lie."

There was still a smile on his face, but there was undeniable menace in his voice.

"How pretty do you want it?"

Now Feurio was eye to eye with me, staring at his own reflection in my blood-spattered smoked glasses.

"How about the truth, hmm? You don't look Akhazi, but some of the guildbrothers have been... *speculating*. Nothing like the Doom comes out of nowhere. And if I was going to curse an entire continent, I'd be wanting overseers to give me the good news."

I was very, very tempted to step back. A droplet of gore dripped pendulously from the Commander's nose, in a fashion which was almost mesmerizing.

"Are you from the Protectorate? The Sorathi Isles? Hmai?" He punctuated each exotic place-name with a prod of one armoured finger.

There was no use denying it. Sooner or later, someone would have to know my true name.

"I'm from... from the *Desolation*. I'm Kuhal Moer, the Lamenter, Lord of Ashes, Grandfather Despair. I've decided to walk the world again, and I'm searching for the reason the Gods are fading."

Feurio regarded me from scant inches away, unblinking. There was no way to read the look on his face.

Then he clapped me on the shoulder, threw back his head and laughed uproariously – just as a trio of his men came bursting into the cottage.

"You hear that? This sickly young book-grub is the Aemortarch himself! Oh, Ark's grief! That's a good one!"

He slung an arm around my shoulders and presented me to the row of helmed and chain-coifed faces now packing the windows of the hovel.

"Boys, this here is Kuhal, the Nightmare Lord, come down from his tower to shit lightning and fart thunder at the bloody ghuldren for us! No… no…" He wiped away a tear with the ragged edge of his tabard. "I'm sure he has a good reason to hide his real name. Perhaps even a *few* good reasons, all keen to call him the father of their children, eh?" This provoked a gale of laughter. "But even if he looks like a dust-mumbling clerk, he's fought with the Guild of Chains this day, and done us proud. So I propose we call him *Brother!*"

The cheering was all but deafening. In the midst of it, for a brief moment, I felt Feurio tighten his grip around the back of my neck.

"I still have no idea what you *really* are, Brother mine," he whispered, so only I could hear, "But I plan on keeping you close until we can have a little talk. So you'll join us on the road back to Oram, and we'll get to know each other better. There hasn't been sorcery in this land for three lifetimes, lad, and I don't see it starting with you."

We came out through the cottage's door and into the last light of dusk – the purple hour when the sun has set but its light still veils the western sky. Torches had been lit, and I could see that this 'Guild of Chains' had been brutally efficient when it came to mopping up the last of the dead.

"I… I have a mule." I said, still a little dazed. Going from power to effective imprisonment in the course of a day had taken a lot out of me.

Feurio looked at me quizzically, then laughed again, holding up my hand like that of a champion gladiator.

"Looks like he's also brought us dinner, lads! Ilwen, light the fires. Narth, circle the wagons! There's a spit to be roasted, and hungry ghuldren in the dark!"

Men broke away, forming up their camp for the night. I didn't know if Feurio was joking about eating Bastard, but I had my suspicions. And, let's face it, it was more than the beast deserved.

"We will share a cup of wine, and talk at length about our past and our options," said the Commander of the Guild of Chains, leading me through the bustle of busy soldiers to where a folding wooden table and a pair of saddle-chairs had already been set up.

"Tonight, you are my guest. Tomorrow… well, that all depends on whether I like what I hear, stranger."

I would have been much, much happier had he not looked out

across the piles of flamelit corpses, then. I would have felt far more secure had I possessed even a fraction of the power which had earned me the name this man didn't believe in.

But for now, I had little choice.

I was the honoured guest of Feurio Zahfrey, and his five score hard-bitten soldiers would see to it that I stayed that way.

It is nothing but peasant superstition that the bite of the ghuldren can Turn one of the living. It takes far more than just a single bite to make one of the Taken. But a bite will fester, and unless the affected limb is amputated and burned, the flesh cauterized, then death of a more prosaic kind will soon follow. This fact reveals two important truths. Firstly, that when the victims of the Doom are close enough to get their teeth into a person, it is often already too late to save them. And secondly, that such medical niceties are of little comfort should a man be bitten on an area which cannot be safely amputated - such as the head or neck...

Loremaster Gaius Seddow, master of the cutters in Oram's Tabernacle

WE TRAVELLED THROUGH a landscape in ruins. Or at least a landscape under siege, adjusted to the cruel dictates of what Feurio called the Doom.

THERE WERE NO smallholdings and farmsteads. Now the only cultivated land was cut from the wilderness in wide circles, surrounding stone towerkeeps. These squat, ugly fortifications glowered from every hilltop, and the peasants in the fields were forced to huddle behind their walls by night, when the ghuldren roamed the land. Livestock was herded into cavernous basements or high-fenced corrals. The rest – crops, orchards, vines – went untouched by the hungry dead. After all, according to the wisdom of the Guild of Chains 'if it don't scream, they ain't hungry for it'.

We sheltered like the rest, pulling our train of armoured wagons into filthy courtyards to be greeted by starvelings, hollow-eyed, full of prayers but little else. By day the company made as many miles as we could, and I rode along with them, perched on the buckboard of a wagon, a loaded crossbow in my hands.

After all, as Feurio said, they didn't *always* come by night. And every man was needed. No idle hands ever earned a full belly in the Guild. They really had eaten Bastard, too. Even in death the mule had proved stringy and somewhat nauseating.

For my part, I found it easy to keep my head down. Without power, the 'blight in me weighed heavy. I was forced to tap into my precious store of sorcery just to keep from falling torpid as the wagon jolted and creaked its way north, away from the Desolation. I told Feurio my 'real name' was Rhul – and he was ignorant enough not to know that this was simply the Khytein word for 'nobody'.

The lying was easy. The truth became harder by the day. Because it was painfully apparent that these people *worshiped* me. Not in any real or useful sense – I had to wipe my own arse, wash my own pots and fetch my own water. But their god was the *idea* of the all-seeing Aemortarch, vigilant in his tower, the deity who had cast down the White Empire. And who was widely reputed to have visited the Doom on a sinful world.

The credulous believed. Feurio Zahfrey, half-Faeroan mercenary captain and sworn sword of the Guild of Chains, did not. I learned that he believed in his own capacity for killing, in money, and in strong liquor, in that order.

He was drunk by noon on the third day after the battle near the Desolation. I could smell the coarse red wine on his breath as he brought his horse up next to my wagon, reining in with a jingle of harness.

"So, how are you enjoying life on the road?" he asked, swinging across from his saddle to the buckboard. He passed me the wineskin and I took a swig – more to wash the taste of dust from my throat than for anything else.

"The truth? This land is dying, and its people don't deserve it," I said.

Feurio tried to look sly. He managed to look like a pederastic uncle.

"So if you really *were* the Aemortarch, you wouldn't send a curse like the Doom against them?"

I grimaced. Some of it was due to the foul taste of the wine.

"If I *was* the Aemortarch, I'd find there was precious little I could do to enact even the most feeble curse. I doubt that I... that is *he*... could so much as curse the lice out of your beard, with the way the Gods have turned their back on Sarem."

"Perhaps we have turned our backs on *them*, hmm?" He belched, weighing the wineskin in his hand. "That old revenant in his tower is the only thing we've seen fit to worship in centuries. Can't blame the Gods for being a little pissy about such neglect, can we?"

Indeed, I thought. But where had all of that belief gone? I had seen the worship of men fill Dirge to bursting point with power, once – and that was only in an instant, as he hung in the sky above Urexes. If offerings had been made, temples raised...

"Why has no one tried to tell him?" I asked.

"What?" Feurio looked at me sidelong, his leering wink turning into a spasmodic twitch of one eyelid. "They've gone, all right. Gone into the meat-grinder of the Desolation and never come back. The Tabernacle sends emissaries of priests every year, and they all know it's a death sentence."

True, perhaps. Not all of the bones in my domain had been old and dry, I will admit. The things I had set to guard my solitude had been anything but discerning. Just *hungry*.

"And your prayers..?"

Feurio laughed.

"Now I'm sure you really *are* a stupid young preacher. He's deaf to them. Deaf, or he just doesn't care. Ha! I'm sure it suits his Hierarchs and Deacons to keep us thinking he'll answer, so long as we pay to be absolved of our sins."

He dangled the wineskin again, but when I reached for it he snatched it away and took a long swallow. He waggled a finger mockingly.

"I'm guessing you're really from Kanelon. They got... got cities carved from ice in Kanelon, and beasts as big as houses, with tusks like... like..." He trailed off into silence. "Been there once. Through the wall, over the gap. Back in my wild days. Seen my share of Yrde, and I know people are the same the world over." He rocked his head back against the wagon, letting it roll with the movement of the wheels. "I've decided I don't care, though. You're not a bad bastard, even if you are a bit strange in the head. I won't be the one to call you a spy."

I nodded, and took the wineskin. It tasted no better the second time.

"They still have sorcerers, then?" I asked. "In Kanelon?"

Feurio laughed.

"I was sixteen summers old, Rhul. Sixteen, and running away with a company of mercenaries rather than face the father of a girl I've all but forgotten. They had mages, aye... iceshapers, wind-walkers, ones what talked to the minds of those shaggy great beasts, and the wolves, and the bears. Hmai have their wizards, and the Sorath, and even the bloody Akhazi, for all I know. But there's none left here. And that... that's how I know you ain't from any of the seven lands of Sarem, boy."

"Why not?"

"Because the Tabernacle have been killing them out for three hundred years! Because anyone who can do more than rig a game of find-the-lady in a stinking dockside tavern gets put up on the pyre, and gets shown their guts before the torches go in. *That's* why."

He leaned in close, and I could smell the harsh fumes of liquor on his breath as he put one fingertip to his lips.

"That's why you should shut up about being a bloody scholar when we get to Oram. The pike up Deacon Fell's arse has... has a pike up its arse about heresy. And the Guild. And a certain handsome, dashing Commander in particular." He burped again, but this time he tried to hold it in. I suspected there was more than just foul air in his mouth as he swallowed, looking slightly green.

"Stick close to me, Rhul. Tell 'em... tell 'em you were part of a merchant caravan that got butchered. Still *some* what try. Tell 'em you're Kaltensunder blood, 'cause Lamenter knows you're pale and lanky enough to pass for a Northman. They got all kinds of weird monasteries up there too, in the lands where the old bonebag used to live. Kid with a big fancy sword, of course you'd want to join up with heroes like us, eh?"

Then he proceeded to fall off the wagon. He hit the mud with a crunch of armour and mail. I shook the reins and drove on, trying not to think too deeply on what Feurio had told me. Or the fact that all our lives were in the hands of a raging alcoholic.

At least the powers woven into my rings, my amulet and my clothes were working. The old bastard could get away with calling me 'lad' for as long as he liked, because it meant that I still looked passably like the nineteen-year-old Khytein youth who had given himself over to power three hundred years before. Subtle glamours hid the fact that my face looked like cracked marble, and that my eyes were those of an ancient, dying greybeard. The 'blight works slow, but its work is long, and very thorough. I'd never grow old, but I had already grown *ancient*.

Feurio had the good fortune of most happy drunkards, and he was hardly injured by his fall. Our procession crept onward, and the men of the Company made very little attempt to pry into my past. Perhaps it was because most of them appeared to be rogues, vagabonds and thieves themselves – more than a few of them wore old brands and tattoos denoting their crimes. We kept the cautious distance of soldiers, who know that the man they share ale with tonight may be the bloody corpse they have to bury tomorrow.

So went the days. Creaking wagon wheels, sunlight, dust, and the sight of weed-choked ruins where villages had once stood. We crossed a branch of the lower Iceflood at a ford protected by two towerkeeps, an armoured mill squatting in the lee of the west bank. Peasants huddled under its muddy palisade, hoping for a ration of flour.

By night we sheltered behind walls of stone. When we couldn't – when we were too far from the nearest holdfast, and dusk was drawing in – that was the only time Feurio put down his bottle and picked up his blade. I sensed a terrible contradiction in the man. He wanted to die, gloriously, in battle. But when he faced the enemy he couldn't fight with anything less than utter, deadly grace. As I watched him shake off the blurry-eyed stagger of a drunk and take command of his men, I wondered exactly what he had done to hate himself so much.

The dead always came, on those nights.

We squared the wagons, wooden walls studded with metal blades forming a chest-high barricade. We allowed ourselves no fires, because the ghuldren were drawn to light and heat. Instead we shivered through the watch-bells of night wrapped in blankets, men standing ready on the arbalests, until something came crashing through the undergrowth, moaning a one-note song of hunger.

Then the horns rang out. Then the fuses were lit.

Often it was only a solitary ghoul, and arrows tipped with the alchemist's thunder blew it to foul tatters. At other times a whole shambling horde descended on us, and it was pikes over the palisade, crossbows at point-blank range, milky eyes reflecting moonlight like opals as we hacked and grunted, breath steaming in the cold.

We never met another Thane. Dalross, the guild alchemist, told me that the hideous things were rare, but that without them the ghuldren were disorganized, more like wild beasts than men. With a Thane, they were faster, more savage, and possessed of at least rudimentary tactics. I was helping him grind charcoal in a pestle at the time, and my mind must have wandered, thinking of Sothara and his leathery-skinned, yellow-boned warriors. The sorcery was similar, but what God would weave such a curse? And *why*? I knew each facet of the Shard of Death, and none of them were strong enough, now, to raise up another Necromancer like him...

"If you hold that any closer to the flame," said Dalross, breaking my trance, "we'll all be getting scraped into a shallow grave, son."

I looked down at my hand. I was holding one of the alchemist's little bags of black powder up to the lamp, staring at the skull and crossed bones on its side. I smiled weakly.

"Reminded me of someone," I mumbled, bending back to the pestle and mortar.

"Aye," said the round little 'chemist, with a very nervous grin. "I know a few too many people who ended up looking like that. Think we all do. But there's such a thing as too soon and too sudden, Rhul."

Days passed. Miles unrolled behind the Guild of Chains. I convinced myself that I was playacting at being powerless – which was much more comfortable than admitting the truth. Every night – at least those nights when we weren't fighting off grey, slack-faced ghuldren – I went to sleep with one hand clasped around my black amulet, feeling the flicker-flame of Makara's soul inside. I told myself it wasn't growing weaker. I told myself a lot of things... but most of them were just to put my mind at ease.

Lies, then.

I was a power in the hidden realms! I was the vanquisher of a mad God! I was worshiped, feared...

I was a beardless boy named Rhul, a nobody from Kaltensund, with a fancy sword they all knew I'd looted from a rich man's corpse. I'd done something so horrible that even I didn't want to remember it. And if I'd come dressed as a preacher, it was because I'd found one dead and stolen his robes, hoping the simple folk would spare me a meal or two in exchange for my prayers.

Stories build reality. These stories my fellow Guildsmen believed. Not the musty old chapters and verses of the *Book of Ascendancy.*

The day before we reached Oram we found the remains of a trader's caravan. Six wagons, each one bigger than ours, and half-eaten bullocks barded in leather and spiked plate. Each wagon had wheel scythes and wooden sides studded with arrowheads, but they had done them no good at all. Three of the six were toppled, broken open to reveal their cargo of wool, silk, spices and flour. Two more were burned down to their axles. The last was still upright, but its timbers burst outward as though it had been peeled apart, and the whole wreck of it was slick with blood. Flies swarmed in buzzing clouds.

"That was the one they thought was safest," said Feurio, riding up beside me. "See? They'd hammered a whole lot of metal flat and nailed it to the walls. Armour, platters, cooking pots... no use, really." He shrugged. "This lot had a Thane with them, and it took matters personally. The merchants and their families ran for the strongwagon..." he pointed with one finger. "Their guardsmen tried to stand, but they were outnumbered. Eaten." Feurio gestured to a welter of mud, stained red, where scraps of cloth and chainmail littered the ground. "Then they got to work on the other wagons. There were passengers, too – not just trade goods."

Now we were close enough to see the truth of Feurio's grim account. Gnawed bones and bloodied clothes. Children's toys trampled into the mud. There, a little leg, its foot still stuffed into a knitted woolen slipper...

"The Thane's a smart one, as those things go. Some of its ghouls used fire, which for them is akin to scholarship in the ancient magicks. Then it paid a visit to the strongwagon, personally... and well, you can see the results."

We passed by slowly. The insides of that shattered wooden cage were a charnel-pit, crimson from end to end. Black, clotted chunks were plastered to the walls. A ribcage glistened wetly behind a veil of flies.

I could imagine all too well the piss and panic of those huddled merchant families, feeling the weight of the Thane bearing down, its bulk cracking the timbers which they had thought impregnable...

"Are we going after it?" I asked.

"*Us?* Ark's shadow, you must think I'm stupid as well as drunk! This one's got an army, and we all know its name. The Guildmaster in Oram will chalk this up as another victory for Slaughtermaw, and then he'll hide up in his tower and shit his britches. Deacon Fell will say a few pretty prayers, but he won't stop the traders from trying to leave. I reckon the withered old bastard wants to keep the ghuldren fed – then they won't try to take the city again."

I looked away from the carnage, though not for the reasons Feurio likely assumed. Such a scene of death would once have appeared to me as a tangle of witchfire, the threads of unspliced souls. But this place was cold, barren – those who had died here hadn't been set free. They had simply been *obliterated*.

"Then... why are you out here at all? If you aren't going to fight those creatures, why risk going all the way to the edge of the Desolation?"

The look Feurio shot me was innocently sly. He leaned a little closer.

"We heard that there'd been watchmen killed. Those young fools the Tabernacle have staring out across the Desolation, on the pretence of keeping folks away. Fell's oracles got a message from the last one alive – a whole clan of Zengaji came out of the south, knifed their way through, and disappeared into the ash wastes. Two days later, the bloody Aemortarch's tower lit up like a witch on a pyre. You see any of that?"

I licked my lips with a tongue that had suddenly gone very, very dry.

"No. Can't say that I did. But then again..."

"Then again, you were nowhere near the place, were you... *Rhul?* The nobody from nowhere, who managed to trek from Lamenter-knows-how-far, when an armoured caravan of traders like those bastards - " he gestured over his shoulder " - got hacked to mincemeat in a few short leagues. No, I suspect you didn't see a *fucking thing.*"

I quietly re-evaluated my opinion of Feurio's vocabulary. And his perception.

"I killed them all, Commander. Twenty-six of them. Then the last one replaced me on the throne in the Capitoline Deep, and I walked out across the Desolation to meet you. Is this starting to make sense yet? Are you inclined to believe me?"

Feurio whistled through his teeth.

"One Zengaji is bad enough. Anyone who can get rid of twenty-seven... well, he'd have to be quite something. You, on the other hand... well, you're *something*, but not exactly enough to earn the 'quite.'"

I rolled my eyes.

"So you went to see what all the fuss was about? A five-day ride, through open country, just because of some *pretty lights?*"

The Commander spat.

"Because of what those oracles *said*, boy. The last survivor of that Zengaji attack, he was raving – what they call God-taken. Possessed. And he said that something was coming." He looked ahead, his face grim, and it was only when he moved his hands that I noticed the dagger clenched in his fist. It must have been close to kissing my left kidney.

"*He comes. He rises*" grated Feurio. "*To break the doom or seal it. The Stormreaper. The Blade of the Void. The Song for the Ending of All Things Under Light...*"[4]

It was a litany – spoken from rote. I wondered how many nights those words had been chasing each other through Feurio's drunken dreams, taunting him.

"And then there you are. With a Thane sniffing after you, too – they only come to power, to relics... ask Dalross. He has a book about them." The Commander sighed. "I didn't know *what* to expect. You sure ain't no Aemortarch I ever prayed to. But you're a loose thread, and that means something is going to unravel. And going by the ravings of

---

4. My opinion of prophecy is as follows – It is, without exemption, either a plot device used by the most mentally deficient bards, or the divine equivalent of a full bucket perched over an outhouse door. The difference, of course, is that it's a merry jest to fill such a bucket with night-soil. The Gods would use live scorpions, or molten brass.

that priest, the Stormreaper herself might be interested, too. Gives us a shot at her, for what it's worth."

I wasn't going to ask. Not now, when Feurio's mind was rocking on the knife-edge of belief. The fact that he'd given Dirge's full name, though... that sent fresh splinters of fear through my soul.

"When we get to Oram, then?"

"When we get to Oram, you're still Rhul, the wastrel from the North, and any man who asks too many questions about you will be found short of a head," said Feurio. "If the Stormreaper wants you, she'll have to come through eighty span of stone and iron, not to mention me and mine. And after *that*... well, that's up to you."

So, I was to be used as human bait. After seeing the work of Slaughtermaw, I could only guess at the horrors this Stormreaper had in store for me. And if she was Dirge's creature... if that deathless bastard had somehow slipped the bonds of the Outer Dark...

We'd have much more to worry about than the walking dead, that was certain.

"I'll go north," I said. "North, into Rasuul, and into the Hiledoran. There's a valley up there, and in that valley a cave, and in that cave..."

"The Archaeon. Father of Draken." Feurio laughed. "You know, just when you've *almost* got me convinced you're telling the truth, you come out with some faery-tale hogwash and strike me sane again. The Archaeon! Ark's shadow! I hope the Stormreaper really *does* come for you... the bitch could probably do with a good laugh!"

It's acutely embarrassing when most of your life's memories make up the bulk of another man's religion. It's even worse when things you recall more vividly than taking a piss that morning have crumbled into parables and myths. Makes a person feel *old*.

"Come to think of it," I said, "The Archaeon could use a bit of levity himself. Do you want to come with me? A good freak-show is always worth a chuckle..."

The scar-faced old Commander grinned, tucking his dagger away beneath his tabard.

"There? See? There's nothing holy about you, boy. When you finally get knocked on the head and lose your delusions, you're welcome in the Guild of Chains. Hells, I might even do you a favour and knock you on the head myself!"

I laughed as he reined in and fell back along the convoy, bellowing orders and slapping at the wagons with the flat of his sword. But only on the surface. Only for appearances.

Oram was on the horizon, a vast, dirty jumble of stone towers squatting beneath a pall of smoke. Tall holdfasts jutted like rotting teeth from the plain surrounding it, connected to its battlements with strands of wire. Even from here, where the ridge we were on dropped down a hundred spans to the plain, I could see great metal wheels turning atop skeletal gantries, flames belching from chimneys, and soot-blackened steeples clawing at the clouds.

The Tabernacle there was meddling with oracles. They had – and I shuddered – resorted to *prophecy*. When madmen babble in the voices of the divine, the Gods are laughing.

But this little joke didn't sound like the gallows-humour of Anghul, or any of the other Facets in death's Shard. It sounded much more like the kind of subtle snare Jerrold Sinder would have wrought, if he wasn't a long-dead monster, banished to darkness and madness.

Whoever this Stormreaper was, I hoped she was smart enough to be cynical.

And I prayed, to any Gods with life enough left to hear me, that she didn't take the bait...

It seems that no matter how far back we go - or how deep we dig - the remains we find, of every civilization, have all been fatally compromised by religion. Before the ages of ice, when our distant forefathers huddled in stone brughs and crofts, whittling spears out of the tusks of nameless beasts, they still did so under the watchful gaze of Gods. Gods who have long since died. Which begs the question - can such beings ever truly perish? Or do the shreds of old superstitions bind them to us even now, shadows raving and gibbering at our backs for sacrifices we will never make again?

Theological Redactor Tallis De'Thrial,
Saradrim philosophical cadre

ORAM WAS NO prettier close up. The city was surrounded by a moat filled with sewage and oil, a rainbow-sheened cesspit in which the corpses of dead livestock bobbed and bloated. As we approached the city a huge drawbridge was loosed, slamming into the mud like a giant's palm. Behind it rose three portcullis gates, all of them studded with barbs. Soldiers peered red-eyed at us from murder-holes in the gatehouse ceiling, while repeating arbalests covered the killing field before the walls.

The real cost of the Doom began exactly within bowshot of those thirty-span bulwarks of stone. A path had been cleared – *ploughed* would be a better word – between a slurry of black, churned mud, decomposing flesh and bones. Ghouls who came too close were cut down, it seemed… and their remains swarmed with clouds of biting flies, sending up a stink which was part cesspit and part charnel-house drain.

Feurio seemed undaunted by this gruesome reception. I'm sure he was happy enough that someone had dropped the drawbridge at all.

Our pennants and banners unfurled, we rumbled across the bridge and into the slums of Oram. Shadows coiled in that close-packed maze of narrow streets and near-permanent fog, where the wooden houses leaned together like drunkards, climbing the spiral road up toward the twin bastions of the Tabernacle and the Guildhouse. It stank. It was cold. But its walls were thick, and that, it seemed, was all that mattered.

The square beyond the gatehouse keep had once been a marketplace – now it was a shantytown of crude huts, cookfires, and washing lines strung between dry fountains and the statues of ancient heroes. At least one of them was supposed to be me, and another was clearly the old Ontokhi rogue Vyrim Chaar. They'd remade the bandy-legged little bastard into a musclebound hero, and as for their image of the Aemortarch…

Suffice to say that nobody was going to recognize me from *that* likeness. Stern, noble, cowled and caped, with a great iron ball in one hand which must have been the sculptor's image of the Incantus Instrumentorum. My statue glowered down on the Guild of Chains company – and on the rider who came galloping into the square to greet us, his red tabard emblazoned with the three linked rings of the order.

His horse's hooves slithered and clattered on garbage-slick cobbles. He turned his look of wide-eyed fright into a bluster of anger.

"Hell's grief, Zahfrey! If you'd been gone any longer the Lord Marshall would have been sizing up your boots! You're commanded to take these men to the Guildhall immediately – speak to no one, stop for nothing!"

"Good to see you too, Artaun," drawled Feurio, casting the man a mocking salute. "Has our Guildmaster managed to find himself a cock and balls since we were gone? Or can we expect to be peeling potatoes for the next few week instead of putting ghuldren back in the ground?"

The rider glowered – I got the impression that he fancied himself far more important than a mere soldier.

"A couple of weeks? Potatoes? For this one, Faeroan, you'll likely be polishing boots with your tongue until the Lamenter returns!" He turned to ride away, in what was supposed to be a gesture of contempt, but his horse reared, tangling his arm in a string of filthy laundry.

Feurio looked at me sidelong, then grinned.

"We may not be waiting long, then. I have news."

The rider swore, tearing down a whole slew of smocks, trousers and assorted undergarments. They draped across his horse's rump like carnival barding.

"It better be good, Zahfrey! The Tabernacle are talking treason, and that's only one step away from witchcraft. Fell would *love* to see you up on a pyre…"

"And so would you, Artaun. But then who would keep your sister, you mother and your daughters entertained?"

Artaun's hand went to his sword hilt before his brain thought better of it.

"Brave words, Graverobber," he grated. "Let's see how your men like being sent down the mines for a month or two. Will they love you then, for all your bloody jokes?"

His eyes, hard as flint, flickered over the rest of the company for the merest trace of laughter. There was none. At least, not until he wheeled about and spurred his horse away, into the narrows streets and out of sight.

"I wasn't actually joking…"

"Worried, sir?" called a voice from back in the ranks. Feurio smiled.

"Oh, Ark's shadow *yes*. I think one of his daughters has the lice!"

"If she doesn't, she'll have 'em by tomorrow morning!" shouted another solider. There was a murmur of laughter. Feurio held up his hand.

"Don't fear the Marshall's judgment. All you did was follow orders. To a soldier, that is bread, butter, ale and gospel all in one. *I* was the one who asked you to follow. I will accept the consequences."

The Commander sat higher in his saddle, reaching out to grasp a pennon-tipped lance from its holder on one of the wagons.

"Guild of Chains, Oram Thirteenth – form up!"

Suddenly they were soldiers again. Men who had drunk and diced and cursed with their Commander, wearing rags over their armour, mud-smeared and unshaven – that one order had them ranked up in neat lines, pikes and halberds high. Soot-smeared faces peeked out of windows at us – some smiling, others dour and hard.

"By the left! Graverobbers – MARCH!"

And march they did. I kept to my perch atop the lead wagon as the scruffy, rusty-armoured column of Guildsmen paraded through Oram, their Commander riding ahead with all the pomp and arrogance of a conquering prince. Perhaps he was going to face demotion or worse, but he was doing it with the same reckless bravery with which he hacked apart ghuldren. I caught myself thinking that the Lord Marshall, whoever he was, would be mad *not* to let Feurio Zahfrey lead these men.

And, perhaps, even crazier to let him…

We toiled our way up the hill, ascending steep switchbacks between greasy, tumbledown houses stacked three or four storeys high. These

were the dwellings of the comfortably well-off, by Oram's standards –
this was a city of mines and forges, with twin seams of iron ore and
coal below. The truly wretched lived and worked in the undercroft
levels, in endless galleries and shafts, each with its own taverns and
Tabernacles, brothels and infirmaries. Hence the wheels and gantries,
the oxen counting out their days on the great wooden treadmills, the
iron stacks and stand-pipes combusting noxious gases to light the
night.

At last we clattered our way through the gates of the Guildhouse,
a stocky, squat fortress planted four-square across from the baroque,
many-steepled opulence of the High Tabernacle. I cast a look over
one shoulder at the great dark building before the Guildhouse gates
rumbled shut.

"They really think their Lord wanted them to raise a church like
that?" I asked Dalross, who sat beside me on the buckboard, holding
the reins. "Aren't they supposed to feed the poor, help the sick… that
kind of thing?"

The alchemist shot me an incredulous glance.

"Poor, naïve lad," he chuckled. "Maybe in Kaltensund. Though I'm
sure even there they'd rather spend their alms on pretty robes and
golden candlesticks. No, dear old Fell thinks that letting the poor
starve just sends them to the embrace of the Deadfather sooner. It's
likely a spiritual burden to be so fat and comfortable."

I was framing a bitter retort when we passed from the shadow of the
gatehouse, out into the castle's main square. But it died in my throat,
becoming nothing but a gurgling rasp.

The walls of the inner court were ringed with archers. Crossbowmen
knelt on the bowman's walks before them, so two ranks of arrowheads
and quarrels glinted in the pale sunlight, a noose of thorns hemming
in Feurio's company. There must have been a thousand of them –
more, if the shadowed arrow-slits of the main bastion were manned.
I was certain they were.

Have I mentioned before that sorcery is little protection against a
storm of arrows? It seems worth saying again.

The company came to a ragged halt, muttering their anger, and I
knew that one sudden move would see us ripped to bloody shreds.
Silence unwound, sharp and thin as wire.

Then the doors of the bastion creaked open, two storeys tall and
bound in iron-studded bronze. A figure came limping out from
between them, followed by a scurrying bevy of scribes and a pair of

mail-clad bodyguards, so overburdened with steel that they could barely waddle along behind. Artaun came last, bearing a battle standard in red – crossed skeletal forearms over the black outline of a coffin.

"Zahfrey! Zahfrey, you poxy bastard! If you think you're going to be anything more than an armour-scrubbing squire-boy in this Guild ever again, you had better have a *damn* good explanation for this outrage!"

The man who walked out onto the blood-red cobbles of the yard was ancient – dried out, stick-thin, trembling with rage. He wore a surcoat of mail which dragged on the ground behind him, and over it a belted red tabard, blazoned with the three linked rings of the Guild of Chains. His face was hawklike, sharp-nosed and sunken-eyed, but those eyes were blazing black, filled with righteous fury.

"Give me *one* reason – one good reason not to cut the lot of you down where you stand! Mutineers have been flayed for less!"

The old man reached Feurio's horse, and stood glaring up at him for a heartbeat until his bodyguard caught up. Then he snapped his fingers imperiously, and the armoured thugs dropped to their hands and knees, allowing him to step up level with the Commander.

"My Lord, we were bound by honour to…"

The ancient didn't let him finish. His hand, heavy with golden rings, connected with Feurio's face in a vicious backhand slap, almost sending the man reeling from his saddle. On the battlements, a thousand archers drew their bowstrings a little tighter. Men of the Thirteenth gripped their pikes and halberds with white knuckles.

"Don't shit on the concept of *honour* by speaking the word out loud," slurred the old man, his voice thick with rage. "I know what you did. I know what you were after. *Glory*. That, and a chance to get your hands on this, when the Aemortarch finally takes me!"

Gnarled, gold-heavy hands clutched at a thick rope of steel chain – a chain from which hung a huge and weighty medallion.

"My Lord, we received word that another Thane was bringing its horde to join Slaughtermaw. Our vows…"

"Your vows are to *me*, Feurio Zahfrey! *To me!* And to the Guild. I know about the mad priest too, soldier. I know why you had to disobey me and scuttle off on your stupid quest. Thought you'd be the one to take down the Stormreaper, did you? Or perhaps try and take that witch to your bed?"

"My apologies, Lord Geran. But I promised to protect the common people from the Doom and its servants. That doesn't sit well with *cowering behind stone walls while they get eaten alive!*"

Geran looked about ready to burst. I believe he would have given the order to fire, then – and never mind that he would have been skewered with the rest of us – had it not been for the intercession of more rational voices.

"Good Brother, a second of your time?"

I looked away from Feurio and Geran (one icy calm, eyes unwaveringly focused on a point in the distance, the other snarling mad, his liver-spotted fist clenched to deliver a blow), across to the doors of the bastion. Two more men had appeared beneath the arch, one even older than the Lord Marshall himself, the other as grossly fat as it is possible to be without the full-time aid of a palanquin and bearers.

It had been the fat man who spoke, and I swear even his *voice* was greasy, dripping with wry obsequiousness.

"Far be it for me to interrupt in what is clearly an internal, *disciplinary* matter, Brother mine," he purred. "But the outright butchery of so many... ahem... able-bodied soldiers would seem to be a tactical error. Especially in the present crisis."

Geran scowled, lowering his fist.

"It's more than this one deserves, Rancilo. If I can't beat respect into him, I can at least beat the life out of him!"

The greybeard at Rancilo's side quailed back, muttering. A stocky guildsman in white robes steadied him with both hands, while another rummaged in his satchel among handfuls of tiny blown-glass bottles.

"Peace, please! Look what you've done to Lord Artificer Quenlon! *Surely* you can see the value in our Brother Feurio's... ahem... rather rash actions. Considering our noble Deacon's recent... requests?"

"Fell and his dry-cocked eunuchs can all go and fuck themselves," snarled Geran, rounding on Rancilo. "If they don't think these walls can hold, they'd be better off praying than trying to tell me how to run my army. I didn't see a single choirboy lift a *finger* to raise those defences, and now..."

"The situation is somewhat... unprecedented," wheezed Rancilo, all smiles. A bead of sweat tracked its way across the broad topography of his pate, glistening wetly.

"As is a third of my damned heavy infantry haring off across the countryside after a bloody myth!"

Quenlon gave a sudden groan. One of his minders wrapped him

bodily in his arms, while the other forced a spoonful of something foul-smelling between his lips.

"All I'm saying," sighed Rancilo, "Is that the contents of Feurio's head might be of more use to us than that same head on a spike. Nobody else has been so far outside the walls in months!"

Geran seemed to visibly sag, as if the rage had suddenly dropped out of him, replaced by the weight of his years.

"You're right, of course," he said, stepping down stiffly from the backs of his retainers. "Hah! Perhaps Fell can let his inquisitors ask you a few questions, Feurio? I'm certain they'd love to accommodate you. Plenty of room in the dungeons…"

My eyes narrowed. I'd caught a subtle eddy of power there, just as the Lord Marshall changed his tune. Someone was using sorcery to draw the poison from the old man's mind. Could it be Feurio himself? His face betrayed nothing as he dismounted and knelt, offering both his sabres hilt-first.

"My Lord, I accept your judgment. I sought only to prove myself worthy of my vows. These men…"

"Are guilty only of an excess of loyalty." smiled Rancilo. "Even a *civilian* such as myself can see that they are soldiers of integrity. As for my charge amongst them – Brother Dalross is rarely happy unless he's blowing something to pieces. Better that it were ghuldren than my other alchemists!"

"Nevertheless," scowled Geran, "Punishment accrues. For each of the sergeants of the Thirteenth, two weeks extra labour in the kitchens. For every corporal, one week. For the enlisted men and officers both, dawn parade in full battledress every morning for a month."

A groan rose from the ranks of the Graverobbers, swiftly cut short by Feurio.

"The Lord Marshall will be obeyed!" he bellowed, leaping to his feet. "And by the Ark's shadow, each and every one of those parades will see us fucking *gleaming*, you hear me!"

"There's such a thing as overdoing it," murmured Dalross.

"There's such a thing as not trying for *two* months," I replied. Enough of the dead I'd raised had been soldiers for me to know exactly how army life worked.[5]

Atop the battlements, the archers stood down. The tension in the air

---

5. From the oldest tribal warband to the most modern legion, it's basically shouting, peeling vegetables, keeping your boots clean, jokes about penises, and killing people, in roughly that order of proportion.

relaxed, along with their creaking bowstrings.

"Commander, you will tell your men to report to the barracks, launder themselves, tend to their armour and weapons, and then form up here again at ten bells. None of us are likely to get much sleep tonight."

Geran turned, chains clinking, and addressed Artaun.

"Strike their colours, Steward. And then we'd best prepare for the Deacon's little party."

Smirking, the Steward of the Watch untied a cord, letting a plain black flag fall in front of the Thirteenth's battle-standard. He turned, saluted with pompous gravity, then marched back into the bastion.

"So now the whole of Oram will know we've been shamed," sighed Dalross. "Oh well. At least old Rancilo didn't have any punishment detail lined up for me!"

But the fat alchemist did have one last item on his agenda.

"Brother Geran," he said, clutching at the old man's mail-clad sleeve as he walked past. "A moment?" The Lord Marshall seemed ready to spit flame at this touch, his eyes widening and his lips compressed to a bloodless line. Then I felt another gentle stir of sorcery, and all defiance drained out of the ancient's face.

"Yes, Lord Alchemist?"

"We must report to the Deacon with all due haste, but it occurs to me... poor Lord Artificer Quenlon is in no fit state to help in our proceedings. Commander Zahfrey, however..."

The old man blinked, peering back over his shoulder at Feurio and his company.

"Hmmm... could give us some kind of tactical advantage. If things go bad, we'll need the church and all its resources."

"Precisely," purred Rancilo, all smiles. "Let dear Brother Quenlon rest, and we will take care of this delegation ourselves."

The grossly fat Brother reached out and patted Quenlon's cheek, while his two white-robed minders held him upright. The Artificer tried to twist away, moaning with apparent horror.

"Zahfrey! You have half a bloody bell to get changed out of that reeking armour. You're coming with us to the cathedral!"

The fire came back into Geran's voice as soon as he strode back toward the company, brandishing his finger like a loaded weapon.

"And for the love of the Dark Lady, bring someone who's passingly literate this time. Your field notes look like the scratchings of a drunken pigeon... or something it shat out!"

Feurio saluted, then turned to address his men.

"Thirteenth! Fall out! I expect the lot of you back here at ten bells, looking less like the dead men we're supposed to be fighting!"

Dalross flicked the reins, setting our wagon creaking into motion, but the Commander singled me out as we passed him.

"You! Kaltensunder Can you read and write?"

"Four languages," I lied. It was closer to seventeen, most of them long dead.

"Then we're getting you a proper tabard, and you're coming with me. Seems that old Fell wants to know how bad it's gotten outside the walls. You might have something to add to that discussion."

I nodded, then swung down from the wagon. Feurio wrinkled his nose.

"You might want to take a bath, too. Dalross will tell you where to go. And Rhul..?"

I looked up, and caught Feurio's gaze. He was smiling, a mischievous twinkle in his eye.

"Remember where you're *from*, lad. Not a word about sorcery. The inquisitors are always eager for fresh meat."

I couldn't help smiling back, despite the danger. What if the priesthood *could* skry out the truth? What if they saw right through my veils and glamours? Something told me they wouldn't welcome a pretender to the Aemortarch's throne with open arms… unless those arms were holding chains and torches.

But curiosity has always meant more to me than caution. I simply had to see what the pious fools had wrought in my name. So I threw Feurio a salute – with just enough calculated sarcasm to make him chuckle – then followed after Dalross on his wagon, losing myself in the maze of the Guildhouse Bastion.

This was no exaggeration. It was *easy* to get lost in that cold, draughty labyrinth. My dark tower had been vomited out of the Urexian plain in a single great orgasm of sorcery, and even its web of tunnels and corridors made more sense. Here, three orders – the Militants, the Artificers and the Alchemists – had all had their own ideas about the perfect castle. No attempt had been made to compromise. The result was less architecture than a battle of wills cast in stone.

If it wasn't for Dalross and his near-infinite patience – not to mention his easy way with the guards and sentries, quartermasters and armourers – I might never have found my way back to the courtyard, let alone within half a bell's time.

With the florid little 'chemist's help I was plunged into a huge cedar tub, scrubbed mercilessly (thankfully being allowed to keep my amulet), then outfitted in a knee-length coat of ringmail, a red, belted tabard, and a pair of tall leather boots. Standard Guild of Chains weaponry – a short, broad-bladed gladius – was belted at my hip, opposite the jewelled basket-hilt of Cryptfeeder. I suspect they burned my cassock and preacher's hat, still crusted with the residue of black blood. The smoked glasses, however, I kept. They may not have been uniform, but they hid the terrible, ancient depths of my eyes.

For the second time in a month I was forced to confront myself in a mirror. This time I was anxious to see if my charms of concealment were working properly – and the results were surprising.

The story I had woven about myself was written in my face, wrapped tight around the truth. I was a nineteen-year-old boy from Kaltensund, with white-blonde hair tied up in a loose braid – a youth as lanky and awkward as I had once been, three hundred years ago.

To be honest, it made me uncomfortable. My young years had been anything but spun-sugar and sunshine, and I had no urge to revisit them. There was another problem, too, my considerable pride had made sure I was just a little too handsome, a little too fine-boned and fey to ignore. If the question of young love arose, how would I tell some poor girl that I secretly desired no other but a dead and disembodied witch?

If it was any consolation, none of the other members of the guild delegation looked any happier than I did. A steady, drizzling rain had begun to fall on Oram as the day failed, and the two Masters of the Guild and their entourage of scribes, standard-bearers, retainers, heralds and assorted menials were trying to huddle in on themselves as they waited in the courtyard, their horses stamping and whickering impatiently.

It was, predictably, Rancilo who was missing.

"Ah! I see they've tried to make a soldier of you, Rhul," grinned Feurio Zahfrey, looking out of sorts in a red leather rain-cape and woollen robes. He would probably have been more comfortable in his filthy armour. "*Tried*, of course, being the operative word. Still, you'll do. All you have to wield this evening is a quill..."

"Don't be so sure, pup," growled Geran, looking up into the clouds. "I'm pretty certain of why those bloody priests finally want to talk, and it ain't about the finer points of theology."

"No? I had brushed up on some very novel arguments..."

"Lamenter forefend." Geran scowled. "No – this storm is by no means natural. Not here, and not for this time of year. Things are happening under its cover, you mark me."

"The ghuldren?"

"Aye, and in force. Why do you think I ordered you to stay here, Zahfrey? Because I needed someone to massage my aching feet? All the time you've been gone, they've been restless. And we haven't seen old Slaughtermaw in weeks."

I remembered the wreck of that trader caravan, and shuddered. Soul-stripped, bloody bones… there are some things too awful for even a necromancer to contemplate.

"I say! I say! Sorry to be late, fellows, but… well, I did want to look my best!"

The Marshall and the Commander of the Thirteenth both turned to watch Rancilo approach out of the rain. The look on Feurio's face was one of disgust, while that of his master… there was contempt there, certainly – but also a hint of fear.

True to form, the fat alchemist preferred a sedan chair, borne by four burly, hooded porters. Rain pattered off a canopy of hide, dribbling down the poor wretches backs.

"Certainly, there was room for… improvement," said Zahfrey, with a curl of his lip. "But now we are assembled, shall we?"

Rancilo smiled back, but his eyes were flinty and hard. If he'd had the muscles to match his girth, I'm sure he would have struck the Faeroan down.

"If you would be so good to lead on then, Commander," he drawled. "And make sure to keep your fascinating new friend close. There's many a priest who'd *love* to have a handsome lad like that as their… well, as a *personal aide.*"

Feurio nodded. I got the feeling that a mark had been made on some kind of grim, internal tally-board. One day, the Commander intended for the fat old 'chemist to pay. For my part, I was hard pressed not to laugh. Any doddering cleric who wanted *this* young man as his catamite would find some grim surprises in store…

The gates rumbled open. Chains clattered as the iron portcullis was raised. Alchemical fires blazed from metal pipes, lighting up the whole gatehouse orange and red.

And our little procession made its way across the square on Oram's hilltop, huddled beneath the grumble of thunder, lit up by flames and the flicker of lightning out of the west.

The doors of the cathedral were open, but there was no-one there to greet us. Instead a single lantern creaked in the rising wind, casting a swaying pool of light. The statues flanking the door were more idealized images of the Aemortarch – aquiline figures holding books carved in stone. I'm certain I never made such a face in my life, unless I was hideously constipated at the time.

"They must be short on servants," sniffed Geran, swinging down from his saddle. "Shame, really. All this trouble to ride a few spans – and nobody here to appreciate how stern and mighty we look."

Rancilo laughed nervously. Now that I looked closely, there was a sheen of sweat plastered across his pink forehead, despite the cold.

"No doubt we come during evening prayers," he said, wringing his meaty hands together. "For which we can surely forgive them. Gentlemen?"

We left our horses outside, under an overhanging canopy, and entered the vast, echoing nave on foot. Feurio took the lead. Rancilo brought up the rear… his porters must have been glad that the journey was ceremonial rather than protracted. They flanked the alchemist once they had helped him from his padded chair, carrying pennants on long spear-shafts, and all four were breathing heavily inside their cowls.

The cathedral was empty. An immense stone cavern of a place, cold and tapestry-hung, lit up by banks of guttering candles. I saw that my old companions had been afforded the status of saints – small altars billowed with incense, honouring idols of Makara, Vyrim Chaar, Corvo… even Elion Morekh's giant first mate Soap was now in the company of angels, despite the fact that he was a bawdy and unrepentant pirate.

But there was more darkness than light under the vaulted triple-dome of my church. A gaggle of stalking shadows followed our little party as we shuffled down the red-carpeted aisle, between heavy hardwood pews, toward a pool of warm, yellow radiance.

A long chain suspended a globe within the transept, crafted to resemble the sphere-within-a-sphere of the Incantus. The very core of this globe was fashioned from stained glass, and hidden lamps within threw a circle of light around the high altar, where Deacon Fell was waiting for us.

The tall, thin man was knelt at prayer, his severe black robes pooled around him in a shimmering satin slick. At the sound of our footsteps he rose and turned - smiling like a week-old corpse.

"Ahhh. My good Brothers of the Guild. *So* pleased you could join me. We have so much to discuss."

I'd heard a voice like that before – the smug, self-congratulatory tone of the Angan priest Ulan Veth – just before he had tried to open my throat.

"Some hospitality," snarled Geran, advancing like a one-man siege. "Every feast day I count about a hundred of your black-clad ravens flapping about the high table. Were they all busy washing their robes tonight?"

Fell laughed, dismissing Geran's anger with a gesture.

"My dear Lord Marshall! Such fire! It's no wonder your soldiers have held off the ghuldren so well… until now. No, my holy brethren are somewhat *indisposed*. We have had a day of revelations, after all. And we, like good soldiers, must also prepare for the coming battle."

Feurio's hand went to the hilt of his gladius – perhaps without any conscious thought.

"What battle? What do you know, Fell?"

The archpriest raised a single eyebrow, as if waiting to see if Geran would allow his pet thug such insolence. When it became apparent that the Lord Marshall would do just that, he spread his hands in supplication.

"I see. I see. I had thought your Guild possessed of certain… *instrumentalities*, which perhaps you lack. The strategic situation has changed, gentlemen. Not just for the church, or for your threefold order. But for all of Oram. Look."

Fell raised his hand, and the great globe began to descend on its chain, the lights within it beginning to spin and pulse. Now I caught the scent of sorcery in the air – a cold, metallic tang like blood and ice. Some base instinct, 'blight-deep, told me to look away from the false Incantus, but it was too late. My eyes were mesmerized by its dancing, shifting hues, as were those of every man present.

Deacon Fell smiled, and it was a leer of triumph. His fingers twitched, releasing power.

Darkness rushed in at the corners of my vision. I heard Feurio's shout, and the oily rasp of his sword being unsheathed – then the clatter of metal on the marble floor. Something slippery and hooked slithered down my spine, recoiled for a second from the black amulet at my throat, then plunged deep into my chest.

And then…

I was atop the spire of the cathedral, the rain lashing down in curtains now, the lightning walking from cloud to cloud around me in crooked arcs. Thunder grumbled and boomed as my vision narrowed, an invisible beam sweeping the landscape like the beacon-light on a Faeroan breakwater.

And there they were.

Silent, drenched by the pouring rain, an army of ghuldren surrounded the city of Oram. Their pallid grey skin was slick with the downpour, their eyes, dark pits reflecting the stuttering lightning. On every side they stood, each one perhaps a span apart from the next, immobile as statues.

There were millions of them.

The plains which cupped Oram in their fertile palm were thick with motionless corpses – men, women, children, infants, even wild animals, half-chewed and ragged, ribs showing through torn flesh, black blood crusted on muzzles, lips, chins, hands…

My vision swung around again, a ponderous blade of thought quartering the night. For leagues out they stood, waiting, watching… but for what?

This time I saw it.

A hunched, bestial shape, crouched under the lash of the rain – a thing which on the first pass I had discounted as a small hillock or a barrow-grave. Slaughtermaw was bigger than the Thane we had faced, in the same way that death is more final than sleep. It crouched on one knee, head bowed, and I could see that the lumpen dome of its skull was studded with eyes and horns, the antlers of a hundred beasts erupting in tangled profusion from between ridges of slick grey flesh. Each of the thing's arms was a ropy conglomeration of limbs, straked and banded with bone, and a row of twisted spinal columns stood proud from the curve of its back, tight sails of skin stretched between them.

The creature must have felt the weight of my gaze, because it looked up, a constellation of dead eyes blinking in the rain. And I saw how the damned thing had got its name as it rose to its feet, hefting a gigantic iron mace which had once been the ram of a war-galley.

Slaughtermaw's chest – from its throat to its belly – was one huge, vertical gash. Thousands of teeth – the teeth of every kind of wild beast, and human teeth besides – studded that lipless chasm, and swollen nodules all down its length burst with rolling, black-pupiled eyes. A tongue like a rope of rancid meat lashed out, twenty spans if it was a fingerlength, its tip a ball of spiked and studded bone.

Then the vile thing bellowed, its voice louder than the storm, and its army picked up the song, moaning their hunger to drown out the roll of thunder.

The vision collapsed. I found myself slumped against the altar, lights swinging and shifting around me. Somewhere close by Feurio Zahfrey was being noisily sick, and I saw Lord Marshall Geran flat on his back, his lips pulled back from his teeth in a snarl.

"So you see!" crowed Deacon Fell, swinging one slippered foot to kick the prone Guildmaster in the ribs. "A *tactical situation*, indeed. One which calls for new plans, and bold strategies!"

He capered a little. His liver-coloured lips twitched into a merry smile.

"Of course, you're all going to die. But look on the bright side – you won't be lonely!"

I lurched to my feet, my hand darting to Cryptfeeder's hilt, but arms wrapped me up from behind, pinning me in place. I saw Feurio make a lunge for his own gladius, but Rancilo's foot came down hard on his wrist, with all of his flaccid weight on top of it. Bones creaked. The fat man giggled, grinding with his heel.

Fell ignored him. He was staring at *me*, and I knew for a fact that those beady dark eyes had torn my wardings and veils to tatters.

"Oh yes… we know who you are as well, *My Lord*. Forgive me if I don't fall to my knees – you must allow an old man at least *some* decorum."

I struggled, but it was no use. The hands which held me were cold, under a layer of crusted bandages. Rancilo's porters – the cowled ones. No wonder they hadn't wanted to show their faces.

"You really think you can defeat a God?" I snarled, bluffing outrageously. "I am terrible in my wrath, yea, and…"

Fell laughed – a sound so unhinged that I knew he was a long bowshot from sanity.

"A *God?* Dear me, no! You were the puppet of Gods, at best. And now we have neatly removed them. Thank the Guild and its science for that! We made you a myth, then just a story, and then…" he snapped his fingers. "There are philosophers here in Oram who congratulate each other on how little they believe in you. You have been *diminished*, Aemortarch Kuhal Moer. Now the power you have so jealously guarded belongs to…"

The thunder roared directly overhead, shaking the cathedral from steeple to crypt. Blue-white light flared, illuminating the shadowed vault of the nave.

There were the other priests of my temple – for all the good they'd do me. Fell and Rancilo – and whatever coven they belonged to – had hung the lot of them from glistening metal hooks, a chained multitude swaying from the rafters. Most were stripped naked to the waist, hideously scarred, and the runes carved into their flesh were sickeningly familiar…

"Dirge," I said. "You miserable *fools*. I doubt you ever actually had the pleasure of his company. He was quite insane. Smelly, too. Poor personal hygiene. It's the first thing that goes…"

Deacon Fell delivered a backhand slap, rattling my teeth in their sockets. I spat. Compared to some I'd met, the withered old priest hit like a dying woman.

"Father Endsong told us all about you and your *lies*," he hissed. "You denied us the rapture of a world beyond flesh! You brought down the Doom on us by bleeding Zael and Esau dry! Now we have you, and your precious tower stands unguarded. When Slaughtermaw embraces you, you will know the true face of our master!"

I tried to struggle against the wight who held me, but the thing may as well have been carved from iron. All I managed to do was loosen one of the rings on my finger – the one which contained the power of the dead Thane.

"I've *seen* his face. I wouldn't recommend it. By the end he was one ugly piece of meat. Then again, by that point the outside and the inside matched."

Fell swung his hand back to strike me again, and a flickering stutter of lightning painted him as a stick-thin shadow, his eyes ablaze. I knew the scent of his sorcery now – old, dry cinnamon, congealed blood, sun-baked clay and copper. He spoke of Dirge, but this was the blessing of the Outer Dark itself.

Fell smiled, all condescension.

"You think your sorcery will save you? Those pitiful remnants you have on your fingers and at your throat?" Fell dropped his hand, and picked up a serpentine dagger from the altar. The blade made a slick grinding sound as it slithered across the marble. "*Our* power comes from an eternal wellspring, Lamenter. When your fingers are dripping stumps, and your throat a bloody smile, you'll see. You'll see."

What Fell *hadn't* seen – or Rancilo, for that matter – was the glance which passed between Feurio Zahfrey and his Lord Marshall. Perhaps the old man's heart really *had* stopped when he was plunged into the vision-trance. Or perhaps he was a much better actor than I would have believed. It scarcely mattered. Because while Geran and Feurio agreed on very little, both men were soldiers down to the bone and gristle. They knew a diversion when they saw one.

Feurio's free hand came up in a blurring arc, connecting between the fat alchemist's thighs with a sick, meaty crunch.

Not a eunuch, then. Up until that moment I wouldn't have laid odds – but the look of utter agony on the man's wide face spoke volumes.

Only for an instant though.

Then I heard a clicking, whirring noise from under Feurio's long leather gloves, and the oily snick of one of those short iron tubes slotting into place. Rancilo just had time to turn pale and sickly-looking before the Commander of the Thirteenth grinned up at him.

"Your pardon, sir… but it seems that you've put your foot somewhere it doesn't belong."

The detonation shook the cathedral at the same time as another rolling peal of thunder, but it was localized, *concentrated.*

I watched, in the blue-white flare of the lightning, as a tongue of flame punched clear through Rancilo's leg at the hip, transmuting a sickening weight of flesh into a cloud of bone-chips and gore. The entire ball-joint at the top of his femur sailed clean across the nave to land in the baptismal font.

At the same time Geran was rising to his feet, far too quick for a man of his years. Under that mottled-parchment skin his muscles were corded like wires, beaten tough as leather by a lifetime of swordplay. And the old bastard kept his weapons *sharp.* Two of Rancilo's porters were chopped off at the waist before Geran had even cleared a crouch, and as he rose to his feet his gladius licked out to the right, blocking the blurred arc of the third ghoul's quarterstaff.

"Fatty's all yours, whelp. I'll carve my due out of this God-baiting sack of shite."

He turned to point at Fell, while his sword hand snapped from one defence to the next, parrying a blur of quarterstaff strokes.

Fell screamed.

It wasn't a coherent sound – the sound of a man pushed beyond the bounds of rage. It was a sound like metal being twisted in an over-stoked furnace – the kind of noise which made miners and engineers run in the opposite direction.

He drew down power from the very stones, cracking them with frost. Statues of saints shattered, spilling candle wax and incense dust. A tracery of fractal ice crawled across every surface – and I understood.

I was the benevolent Father in this little pantheon. The kind and caring one, who ushered the worthy to their eternal reward. But Dirge – he'd become the axeman, the one who held the blade over the necks of sinners. And everyone *was a sinner. No-one measured up. My heaven was empty, but Fell, and men like him, had blithely kept Endsong's hell filled to bursting.*

Sorcery lashed out, twin snarls of thorny tendrils bursting from Deacon Fell's hands. They ripped out through the flesh of his palms and forearms in a gruesome tangle, shredding him to the bone, but his scream was one of ecstasy. The thorns picked up Feurio and flung him aside, a rag-doll spinning through the darkness to collapse whole rows of pews. Geran was slammed up against the wall as the hooked and gnarly vines wrapped him tight, wringing him out with a series of dry-stick snapping sounds – his bones shattering one by one.

"To think we bothered with subtlety!" roared Fell. "Rancilo, you fat fool! Can you feel it! From Endsong's blackened Shard, to the roots of your soul! The *power!*"

The vines had all but mummified Geran now, and they pumped and twisted obscenely as blood rained down, leaking from between their coils. Some of those thorns were as long as my thumb, ivory pale, and serrated like knives. I prayed the old man's death had been swift.

Rancilo wasn't answering. He lay on the floor in a spreading puddle of his own arterial blood, trying to clamp his fat fingers around the ragged stump of his leg. It was simply too wide for him to manage – and he rocked there, mewling in terror, as the life spurted out of him.

"Master! Master Fell! I...."

The archpriest turned from his slaughter, eyes blazing. His mouth was twisted into a sneer of contempt.

"Pathetic! Our Lord has no use for your weakness, alchemist. But your *power...*"

Rancilo had barely time to squeal as ropes of thorn slithered across the flagstones toward him. They tore into his wound with a sound like grinding meat, erupting in a spray of crimson from his belly, his throat...

It was all over in an instant. But it bought me enough time to palm the ring from my finger, unlocking the spark within.

My head lolled to one side. My eyes rolled back, sightless. And I sent my will spearing down through the marble floor, hoping that this cathedral they'd raised in my name was the same as all those other holy sites I'd desecrated…

It was.

Beneath the cold stone were layers of crumbled masonry. Rune-carved slabs defaced, obliterating the name of Esau. Useless. A God chained, deep beneath the Desolation – he couldn't save me now.

Deeper still, and I tasted the cold iron and crusted blood of Zael's conventicle, cast down during the Angan civil war. He, too, was a powerless prisoner, his martial cult scattered ten centuries hence.

I went deeper, prying into crevices and cracks, peeling back layers of dusty years.

And I found what I was looking for.

Light wove patterns in silence, budding and unfurling the past. My mind fell into its webs and knotworks, collapsing away from the now. No sun, no moon – just *stars*, an endless spiral skein of them, chill and indifferent in their wheeling cascade.

The cold reached out to grasp me like an armoured fist.

And antiquity came with it.

Dare not go up to the Shadowed Heath,
Where the Old God's stones stand like rotted teeth
In the howling wind, in the wintery rain
You'll hear the sound of the Ancient's pain
Dead or sleeping, or both the same
A nameless grave for a graven name
For now only shadows and echoes dwell
Where the last, lost vengeance of Kharnath fell.

Angenstrand folk rhyme,
concerning the site of the fallen city of Oram.
Appended to this text by Envigilator Parvan Kalmaat, Ghuram
Chamber of Enlightenment, Scribe Grade III

IN MY MIND I stood atop a wind-blasted hillock, within a circle of hand-hewn trilithons. Crude fetishes of bone and feathers spun in the blast from off the distant sea, while torches streamed sideways, glowing sickly green. The ghost-forms of shamen priests, dressed in antlered finery, passed through and around me, carrying obsidian adzes, blood-dripping bowls of stone, and dragging between them the limp bodies of sacrificial victims.

At the centre – beneath an altar grooved with steaming blood-channels – flickered the wraith of a God almost forgotten. Some brother of Anghul, his Facet and Shard diminished to a mere splinter, but holding on to reality through grim determination. Perhaps, I thought, the poor doomed thing didn't even know that its time was finished. Its ghostly priests mumbled and hacked eternally, bowing in the same place where, in later years, Zael's armoured acolytes would pray, then Esau's chosen, then the satin-robed ministers of my own misbegotten faith.

The God saw me.

"Who comes to the sacred stones of Kharnath? Without reverence, without sacrifice… who, after all these cold centuries disturbs my sleep?"

Kharnath. A name I had read only in the most mouldering, brittle scrolls. From before the age of Zael, when the men of Anganesse had dragged themselves from out of caves and earth-roofed hovels to forge themselves a first link to the Divine. They had made Kharnath, the Father Beneath, from a fear of death and a wonder at the starry arc of the heavens. Every other holy site built atop his circle of stones had fed him power… just enough to keep him suspended in a kind of senile madness.

"An emissary," I said, choosing my words carefully. "From your brother in the North. From dread Anghul, the Antlered One, master of the Hunt. I come to offer you a sacrifice."

The old God laughed, and I saw the mist of its being swirl, tattered and indistinct. A face, all sunken eyes and tribal war-paint, coalesced above the altar.

"You think me a fool, do you? Thirty thousand years, and no-one has remembered the rites. I stand on the threshold of the Outer Dark, and I can feel your precious Anghul standing beside me. You are no acolyte of his, for all that you have his stink on you!"

"Nevertheless," I said. "I know you, Kharnath. And the sacrifice I bring you comes with a choice."

The swirling smoke flared, baring teeth.

"What do *you* know of choice? Or indeed, of sacrifice? Pinned under these chains of stone and faith, mortal, I have endured countless winters. What *choice* do I have, whose people have forgotten me? Whose tribes have been scattered, their blood diffused to water?"

"You can choose *revenge*… and then oblivion," I said. "The sacrifice I offer is final. The casting down of the holy places which bind you. The death of those who imprison you."

The God's laugh was a storm of knives, ice-cold and mirthless.

"This is all you can offer? After so many centuries…"

"Look at me, old one! I am a vessel for power. You always told your children to seek death in battle – to die with a blade in their hands, and the words of their slaying song on their lips. All I ask of you is the courage to do the same."

Kharnath swelled like a thunderhead, shot through with crawling filaments of witchfire. His eyes blazed black, flames boiling out from them in slow motion.

"I see you for what you are, Son of Shadow. And I see what you have done. You have the mark of a Godslayer. Would you have me as another notch in your sword-grip?"

I reached into my mind, invisible fingers closing on a skein of memory. Ripped it loose, with a savage jolt of pain. And offered it up in my hands, a bleeding sacrifice to this ancient, hungry God. Tendrils of mist coiled, evaporating the tattered soul-stuff from between my fingers.

Kharnath saw Zael crucified. He saw Esau weeping black tears, nails driven through his hands and feet. His spectral eyes widened.

"Enemy of my enemies!" he hissed. "Perhaps... perhaps you *can*, then. Perhaps... it is better to burn for one last, glorious moment. Not to grind out years of dust, unknown..."

I had him, then. I raised my head, defiant, my long, bleached-white hair whipping out behind me in a tangle.

"I *promise* you, ancient. This hill will be a sacred place forever. A place of dread and awe. When they see the vengeance of Kharnath, the Father Beneath, generations yet unborn will tremble."

Saga-story nonsense, I know. But this was the way the forsaken God's old, old mind worked. He had become the echo of bards' songs, epics carved on antler and bone in runes none alive could read. A voice muttering in the crypts and dungeons of other Aziphem's temples.

"Very well," he rumbled, sparks now rising through the swirling mist of his form. "Burn with me then, mortal. One last time. Once, and the Dwellers in Darkness *will choke on my ashes!*"

My eyes snapped open. Only seconds had passed, and Deacon Fell was still drinking in the life's-blood of poor, fat Rancilo – now a leathery husk of his former self, his face a taut-skinned skull.

The cathedral began to shake.

And the power!

It coursed through me in such a heady, orgasmic rush that I almost screamed. I had cut away so much of myself, disengaging from my throne in the Deep. I had almost forgotten how it felt to brim with energy, to wield a crackling nimbus of force. The mageblight was no longer a cold and aching weight inside me – it was a marbling of pure fire through my flesh, and its touch was simply too much for the ghoul who restrained me. Its bandages caught flame, then the dry, grey skin beneath, sending it staggering back, ablaze.

They say that a warrior – backed into a corner, pierced by arrows and dripping blood from his wounds – is far more dangerous just before he dies. Wild, reckless butchery often follows.

I was suffused with the death-energy of a God in just such a state – a faded, tattered God, but a true Facet of divinity nonetheless.

In that moment I had Deacon Fell's undivided attention. Thick, bloodied skeins of thorns slipped back into the wide sleeves of his cassock, collapsing into tangles of shadow.

"Well. *This* is an unwelcome development," he said, his eyes bright with madness. "I had expected you to go quietly, Kuhal. But Endsong always told us you were a man of... hidden depths."

I rose to my full height, drawing Cryptfeeder with my right hand

and my Guild-issue gladius with my left. A poor attempt at becoming a warrior, and far too late – but the spirit of Kharnath approved.

"You've read my holy book?" I asked, taking a step toward the altar. The cathedral pitched beneath my feet, as though the whole great pile was a ship riding out a hurricane.

"Of course. Slander and lies, all of it. Quite poetic, though."

"Quote me a verse about my righteous wrath, then," I said, advancing grimly. "Or just get down on your knees and pray." I crossed my swords before me, and fire rippled out across the steel, blue-green and hungry. I smiled – the kind of smile they should have carved on all my Gods-damned statues. "Because it's time to pay your penance…"

Perhaps he really *should* have believed more of what the scriptures said about me. But perhaps… well, there was no true way around it. Half of my posturing was empty bravado.

For Deacon Fell was also suffused with power. He had spent countless years drawing it down into the stones of my cathedral – stolen sorcery, but no less deadly for that fact. Now he stood revealed atop the altar, Dirge's creature through and through.

His face was a death-mask stretched tight over muscles and tendons which *writhed*, tearing loose from the bone. Darkness spilled from the hem of his cassock in an inky pool, smoking around the edges, and wrist-thick ropes of thorns came questing up from within it. More coiling lashes of shadow erupted from his wide sleeves, and each one plucked a weapon from the walls. It seemed that my dogma was hardly one of peace – Fell brandished two score pitted, rusty swords, axes, and maces as his laughter rattled the nave.

"So, you've found some kind of will to fight, have you?" he said. "A little splinter of a flaw in the Shard? Some echo of a dead God? Lord Endsong has *become* death, mortal. You *literally* don't have a prayer!"

The eruption of force around Fell drove me back, swords raised before me. I gritted my teeth as the swirling penumbra of power expanded, igniting pews and tapestries with its touch. A deep bass thrum pulsed through the stone.

"You're forgetting something…" I said, forcing myself forward. Pieces were spiralling up from the floor now, chips of marble torn from the altar in a whirling gyre. My tabard began to smoulder. I smelled singed hair and fingernails.

"Oh, really?" asked Fell. "Here I thought it was *you* who had forgotten. How I crushed your people. How I butchered your father and his pathetic nobles. *How I cored out the feeble husk of your*

Vhaurish witch!" There was far too much of Dirge in his voice now for this to be anything less than total possession. "Please *enlighten* me, Lamenter. Before I feed you to my pets out there, and The Darkness takes your captive Aziphem. There may even be some scraps left for the Coldblood!"

I could feel the wellspring of Kharnath's power running dry. Almost all that remained of the Elder One was within me now, and my vision blurred and cracked, swarming with ghostly images of obsidian knives. *I smelled woodsmoke and fresh blood, heard priests chanting red-eyed behind their antlered masks.*

"The Coldblood?" I took one more step into the whirlwind. Fell was like a writhing tree of tentacles at its heart, outlined in stuttering lightning. His body was distorted and broken now – bones warped and split, flesh roasting as the power of Dirge violated him. "What does that vile thing have in common with you? Other than its *embarrassingly.*" Another step. "*Obvious.*" And one more… "*Insanity?*"

Dirge's laughter unhinged the Deacon's lower jaw, and it sloughed away, crumbling to dust in the flux of power. More dripping pseudopods erupted from his throat, swelling it obscenely. I heard vertebrae separating, and winced.

"All will be made apparent when we feed on Zael and Esau," came the mocking reply. "You'll be there to watch, after all. One Facet of one Shard is all we need, and we will be among the Divine. We will be the infection which hollows out the husk of their broken corpse – this whole worthless world!"

"Ahh," I said, forcing myself a final step closer. My tabard was ash now, my leather gloves and boots crisping and smoking. "That's *two* things you've forgotten, then."

Now Deacon Fell turned his eyes on me, and there was only the chaos of the Outer Dark at their centres. *Things like parasites and mountains, flesh and fire, writhing in the throes of fatal copulation* – a reality skinned over Fell's own torment.

"What have I overlooked then, little savage? Enlighten me!"

I was almost close enough to touch him now. The will of Kharnath pressed up from below my feet, urging me to let go. He knew what to do, and how this would end. After all, I had made him a promise…

"*Never tell me your plans, Dirge*[6]," I grated, forcing my swords out

---

6. True villains always want to talk about just how very clever they are. That's what makes them so much less dangerous than heroes. If a hero doesn't need to know the intricacies of your grand plan to take over the kingdom, he will just kill you then and

to my sides. The splayed blades burned with witchfire, tiny sparks tumbling away as sheer sorcerous energy abraded the steel. "Haven't you noticed? I have a nasty knack for survival. And then your elaborate little schemes get smashed to matchwood..."

"No Zael to save you this time, Kuhal. And the ragged thing you've dragged up from the dirt hasn't got a thousandth part of his power. He's already wrung dry!"

The tentacles came hissing in without warning, a dozen on each side. My swords swept left and right in a blur, shattering old, time-gnawed steel with a sound like breaking harp-strings.

"*Second,*" I panted. "and even more importantly..."

I looked into Fell's eyes. Saw the pain there, the fraying away of his soul before the blowtorch of Dirge's possession. The *betrayal...*

"Deacon Fell, for all your sins, you are not Jerrold Sinder. *You are not Dirge. You are not your master.*"

The man behind that stretched and writhing mask blinked at me for an instant. I could feel him trying to push Dirge out, but it was like trying to will away a cancerous growth. All I could do was use that instant of confusion to strike. I hoped that some Divinity would have mercy on Fell's soul...

Because I had neither the halo, the inclination, or the power.

Silence bloomed as I released a blast of sorcery. Statues of battle saints exploded as the candles before them tapered up into forked tongues of fire.Serpents of light sizzled out from my hands, plunging down through the floor, coursing across the walls, converging on the great slab of stone which held the holy book of my church.

Kharnath, Father Below, was inextricably tied to his altar... the prison of his sacred memory. The old God couldn't harm Fell directly. But his *cathedral...*

That was another matter entirely.

I raised my hands, and Kharnath's standing stones came up through the floor, rising like monsters from an abyssal trench. The stone was old, hard granite, burning with runes and spattered with fresh blood. Rusted chains clattered and chimed as they exploded through the marble flagstones, some of them still gripped tight around skeletal wrists and arms.

---

there. But a proper villain doesn't want violence. He wants *conversation.* Leading me to believe that most of the world's truly evil beings are starved of intelligent discourse, and that a chess league for wicked sorcerers and transcended demons would save the wretched masses no end of suffering.

A large part of the thing which had once been Deacon Fell – but which was now a seething anemone of tendrils – was within the stone circle. Ghostly obsidian blades whirled through his flesh, but not one of the thorny whips recoiled.

"See!" crowed Dirge, riding the remnants of Fell's mind into ruin. "Powerless! You were always a fool, Kuhal Moer! Without the hand of a God up your arse you're *worse than pathetic!*"

The sentinel stones ground to a standstill, leaning in a drunken ring. For an instant the smoke from the burning Tabernacle was gone, cleared in a swirling vortex, and I could smell the clean scent of a frosty morning, of dew on grass, of fresh arterial blood…

"Oh, *fuck off,*" I slurred, drunk with power.

Then I blew the cathedral to pieces.

Stone remembers. Sand recalls the dreams of mountains. In its slow cycle of lava-heat and granite-shear, stone speaks of the Dawn Times, before even the Archaeon and the Coldblood, when Yrde was a seething ball of molten rock, unriven by the hubris of the Divine.

And this stone held more recent memories, too. It was the blink of an eye, in geological terms, since every block and column, gargoyle and flagstone which made up the Aemortarch's temple had been part of Kharnath's barrows, Kharnath's sacred places, Kharnath's domain.

Lazy, you see. Why quarry, when ruins lie right under your feet?

Deacon Fell had been leaching power into the stones of my cathedral for decades. But the Father Below had been worshiped on this bleak hilltop for *thirty thousand years* before Zael came blustering and raving across this land, his faith taught on the edge of Imperial swords.

The stone came to Kharnath's call like a hound to its master. And, in a moment of painful, needle-bright clarity, I saw how each and every brick fit together. How arches took the load of vaulted ceilings, how buttresses bore up spires…

It was the work of an eyeblink to simply *move* all of those component pieces, causing the entire great twin-spired edifice to explode.

But not far. The whole tumbling mass only flew apart by a few spans, then began to rotate, in a gyre which mirrored the storm above. The hammering rain came down on us, extinguishing the fires with an angry hiss. Thunder boomed and grumbled. Lightning reflected off rain-slick blocks of flying stone.

Dirge may have been a deathless sadist, but he was no fool. The heartbeat of power I had unleashed shook him loose from Deacon

Fell's soul, leaving that poor deluded puppet bereft. He was a husk –
but Dirge had burned one final command into the rotting slush of his
brain.

"Heretic! Defiler! YOU MUST PERISH!"

He howled like the dead beyond the walls, lost and hungry.

And then he came down on me, tendrils tearing through the rain,
his eyes blank and unblinking.

Tens of thousands of tons of stone answered him.

Huge blocks of masonry had been torn loose from the crown of
the hill, like teeth from a broken jaw. They spun away from the cloud
of stone, whirling in as if they were attached to Fell by tethers. They
met an instant before he reached me, impacting with a terrible, final
crunch – the sound of a cockroach under a soldier's boot. A thin spray
of blood squirted from between the cracks.

Then the lightning flashed, and I saw a figure rising from the
churned mud which had once been marble flagstones. It was crooked
and bedraggled, but it was laughing.

Feurio Zahfrey.

"Are you going to try to put this damned thing back together
anytime soon? Begging your pardon, *My Lord.* It's just that it's rather
cold out here in the rain!"

I turned, holding my hands up over my head. Lumbering, hundred-
ton foundation stones carved spiral grooves in the dirt around the
hilltop's crown. Gargoyles went sailing past, leering. High above, a
storm of flettons and tiles scudded like windblown birds.

"This is nowhere near as easy as I'm making it look," I grated. "But
if I let it fall…"

Feurio looked out over the rain-lashed rooftops. There were
people in the streets, tiny lanterns and torches bobbing, reflected in
overspilling puddles. Some were pointing. Most, however…

The horns rang out from the gatehouse, first one, then a whole
mournful chorus of them splitting the night. Low and thrumming,
their dire warning sent the anthill of Oram into panic. Even such
wonders as a cathedral-sized gyre of flying stone were forgotten.

"The ghuldren…" whispered Zahfrey. "Fell's warning. It's coming
true. They're coming! *Now!*"

The drifting curtains of rain obscured most of the city walls, but it
was easy to tell where the sound of the horns was coming from. There
was no time for plans – no time at all, as the power of Kharnath was
draining out from my fingertips, leaving me with only the echo of his

laughter.

"Yes! Kill the vile things for me! This hilltop will bear my crown of stones until Yrde cracks and crumbles, mortal. Now – make them remember my name!"

I felt the last lurching gasp of the God, then. The last vestige of his memory, uncoiling from the bones of the hill, stained red with seeping sacrificial blood. Just enough power to gather up in my arms, grit my teeth – and *heave.*

The slowly tumbling storm of stone became a horizontal hail. A fan of tiles, columns, statues and bricks flew just above the rooftops of Oram, clipping off weathervanes and shattering chimneys.

Then the whole rough-edged, chisel-hewn mess arced down over the walls, into the field of grey flesh beyond. I had seen millions out there – whole nations and tribes reduced to slack-faced ghouls. The populations of entire cities, shambling forward under Slaughtermaw's command.

Oh, the bastard felt this one.

There was a link between them, the ghuldren and their Thane.

Twisted like wire through the meat of them, through the great Incantus which pulsed like an obscene heart in Slaughtermaw's chest…

My storm of stone did more than pluck those strings. It sheared them through, *a thousand at a stroke, ten thousand* – stones skipping and pulverizing, sliding through blood-slick mud, cartwheeling end over end through motionless ranks of the dead. Bones shattered like green twigs. Bodies were macerated, smeared into chunks, clotted filth spraying wide. Tiles hissed in like shuriken, merciless, lopping off heads, torsos, limbs, carving through soft tissue and rotten skin…

I watched as a statue of Elion Morekh rolled lengthwise, the two-storey pillar of granite grinding a hundred lifeless things under before it shattered. Morekh's smiling face was smeared with mud and gore, his stone cutlasses snapped off at the hilts. I think he would have appreciated the show.

I staggered. Blood was leaking from my eyes and from my nose, a thin, trickling runnel of the stuff. Funny – my heart hadn't actually beaten for over three hundred years. Feurio had collapsed to his knees in the rain, laughing. A flashburst of lightning illuminated him, sparking from the steel rings tied up in his hair.

"Oh, to think that I called you Rhul," he said. *"Nobody!* Ha! All I feared about your bloody cult come true, and I can't even sit here as an atheist and mock your non-existence…"

I smiled, but it was a fragile thing. My head hung down in the rain, my hair lank and dripping as my shoulders heaved. There was a pain in my chest – a burning fist clenched about my heart.

"Gods don't feel this awful after crafting their miracles." I stood, pushing my hair back from my eyes. "Or at least, if they do, the condition of godhood is *extremely* overrated."

Feurio came to help me stand, and by Anghul, I needed it.

"That *was* pretty impressive, though. I don't think Fell will be getting up from whatever you just did to him"

"Not me," I grimaced. "The other one. If I'm your precious Aemortarch, then it follows, surely?"

Feurio's eyes widened.

"Endsong. The Pale Tyrant. Thought he was more of a bullshit faery-story than you were – pardoning your presence, Lord."

"You can stop with the *Lord* nonsense," I said. "And let's get out of the rain. Just because I'm technically dead doesn't mean I want to catch a chill."

"We'll want good stone between us and those ghuldren, in any case," said Feurio, pulling a red-wrapped tube from his belt. "I think you got Slaughtermaw's attention, boy."

"*Boy?*"I chuckled. It hurt. "I preferred your false piety, Commander. Remember, I was ancient when you were just a bad idea at the bottom of your father's ale-cup."

Feurio held the tube up over his head and pulled a string which coiled down from inside it. A whoosh of sparks spiraled up into the heavens, bursting into a red star as it rose.

"We're not going to get dry tonight, in any case" he said, casting the empty flare aside. "The ghouls are at the walls, and I don't think they realise their traitorous friends are gone. We have to rally the Thirteenth, and every other man who can swing a sword."

Ahhh – *swords.* Of course. The cold steel weight of them was gone from my hands, though I couldn't remember dropping either Cryptfeeder or my gladius. Then again, with the power of Kharnath wrung out of me, I would be hard-pressed to…

Then I felt it. A sensation which began as a crawling flare of gooseflesh up my forearms and spine, prickling the hairs at the back of my neck. It rose as the red light above us bloomed huge and bloody, painting my shadow across the low stormclouds – and casting it huge and jagged against the white curtain-wall of the Guild Bastion.

Belief.

Down in the streets of Oram the bells were ringing, the minehead flares guttering in the gale. And people had stopped in their panic, pointing, some collapsing to the mud on their knees, hands clasped in prayer.

They were praying to *me.*

I knelt and scooped up my gladius. It suddenly felt feather-light, as did the curved, basket-hilted bulk of Cryptfeeder. The gems on my knuckles and at my throat thrilled with power, winking incandescence.

"Aye," said Feurio, watching me unfold from a crippled hunch. "I thought as much. Too long they've believed in Fell, and that bloody great monument you've just toppled. Now they've seen something worth kneeling to." He clapped me on the shoulder, grinning as the sound of trumpets rung out from the Bastion. "Not me, of course. I'm far too much of a cynic to pray. But the rest of these bastards would likely follow you merrily into Hell."

"Hell's just a pretty piece of theology, Zahfrey. What's out there..."

He lofted one eyebrow.

"Leave the tactics to me, then. I've been fighting the ghuldren for as long as I can remember. All *you* have to do is be seen."

Belief filled me up. It gave me back a little of the person I had once been, for one grim season in my youth. Once again, through the distorting mirror of faith, I was the Lord of the Graveyard Ark, the force of nature which had come reaping a path out of the North to the gates of Anganesse. Sparks crackled in a halo around me as I lifted my blades high, whispering words of power I'd learned from Maegister Corvo Azrai.

"Being *seen* isn't going to be a problem, Commander," I said, as clouds boiled and clotted above me. "In fact, I think there's a few things out there I'd rather have stayed hidden from. But – oh well..."

The power was building fast. And it was far from being a one-way flow. I could feel the onrush of Slaughtermaw's horde, a tide of rotting flesh surging like the waves of an ocean against Oram's high walls. Where I had scourged them back the ghuldren were slow to recover, but they massed in their hundreds of thousands, clawing their way up on the backs of their brothers and sisters where they piled up against the ramparts. Those at the bottom were crushed, twitching, as more and more piled on, fingers scrabbling bloody against the stone.

"To the Hangman's Gate!" yelled Feurio – and I realised he was rallying his men. The hilltop behind me was suddenly full of milling

Guildsmen, rain hammering itself to spray against their armour as they poured out of the Bastion's arch. Summoned by their Commander's flare… and all, it seemed, itching for a fight.

"Silbern, you and your Greatswords will escort Rhul here to the top of the wall. Lieutenant Berun, I'll take you and your pikemen to the gateyard, and prepare a little surprise for our guests when they break through. Dalross, you command the archers. Shafts and quarrels don't mean shite to these gravespawn – not without a little alchemy to add some spice. I hope to any Gods foolish enough to listen that you have enough powder to last the night."

Dalross came squelching forward through the rain, his long green robes soaked through and dragging behind him across the cobbles.

"Sir, we have all of thirty thousand men at our command. The city watch and the council militias will be expecting Geran, but I suspect you will do at a pinch. The wires are all live, and the defence awaits your orders."

Feurio sagged for a second, looking out across the crowd of red-cloaked and chain-armoured Guildsmen. I could see that he had no desire to be a general, or a strategist in some high tower. He wanted to be ankle-deep in gore, swinging his sword through flesh and bone. Not for the first time, I wondered exactly what fearsome fire had been the crucible for Feurio Zahfrey.

"Any voice which shouts loud enough will be obeyed right now. Any voice which doesn't smell of piss and fear. Dalross – you know what I would do. *You* man the wires. Tell them to abandon the outer barbicans, and concentrate on the walls themselves. When the ghuldren break through, we'll stage a fighting retreat, street by street, house by bloody house. We make them pay for every step. And when we lure Slaughtermaw inside the walls, we try out the Artificers' little toy. I hope they've actually finished working on the damned thing!"

The little 'chemist smiled wryly.

"Lamenter knows I'm grateful for a posting in out of the rain, Commander. But…"

"But *nothing*," growled Feurio. "Now, where's my standard? That slippery bastard Artaun was so pleased to see me this morning – he can carry the banner of the Thirteenth with us to the walls!"

The luckless herald was prodded forward – perhaps with more than just boots and spear-shafts – and the crossed-bones and coffin of the Graverobbers was raised, flapping like a broken wing in the storm. Behind us, the bare, churned earth where the cathedral had stood was painted flickering green, in the light of a ring of standing stones.

"Brothers of the Guild of Chains!" bellowed Feurio. "Men of the Ninth, of the Eleventh, of the Twenty-First companies! Men of the glorious Thirteenth! Tonight, the treachery of the Tabernacle has been made clear. Lord Marshal Geran has died defying its corruption! And we have found an unexpected ally in our fight – this… this *sorcerer* from out of the North."

He had their attention now – not just his own sworn brothers, but the commanders of the other Guild Legions, too – they, and the hard-bitten veterans who followed them.

"All our lives, men like Deacon Fell and his ilk have told us that sorcery is corrupt, or weak, or *unnatural*. But tonight I ask you – who among you could cast down an entire cathedral with your will alone? Who among you can crush *ten thousand ghuldren with a single blow?*"

There was a murmur of unease from the crowd, rising above the staccato hammering of the rain.

"Fell was a traitor, as was our own Lord alchemist Rancilo. I saw both taken by demons – aye, real demons! Not some storybook nonsense, boys, but fucking horrors, walking! And it was Rhul here who put them down. Hard. So I ask you this." He paused, slowly sweeping the tip of his gladius across, to point down into the city. "Do you want to see such power unleashed on these undead bastards? Do you want to *fight?* Or do you want to curl up into a whimpering ball and shit yourselves right here? I know I've made my decision."

He turned away, sheathing his sword, and the murmur from the crowd rose to an angry rumble. I heard words like 'heresy' and 'blasphemy' among the tumult – not the kind of terms a necromancer feels comfortable with. While I'd appreciate the irony of being burned for destroying my own church, there'd be precious little to laugh about when the pyre started to catch…

So I finished the cantrip Corvo had taught me. A lance of blue-white lightning came down from the clouds, splitting into a forked tangle to lick the tops of the standing stones. Ancient runes spit sparks. Totem-skulls exploded.

"The Commander speaks the truth," I growled, in my best battlefield voice. I'll freely admit that I was trying as hard as possible to sound like my long-dead father. "Fell was a traitor. *But I am not.* I'll make you a deal, all of you. Let us fight the ghuldren together, tonight – and if you still feel like burning me in the morning, well…" I smiled, lacing my hands together and cracking my knuckles. "You can try."

A little nervous laughter. The mass of fighting men wavered, uncertain…

But then the horns droned out again, a flat, heavy sound in the rain. Feurio didn't look back to see if I was going to be followed for crucified. He just started pelting down the slope of the hill, his sword out, heading for the breach.

"You heard the man!" bellowed one of the other Legion Commanders, a woman with iron-grey hair cut close to her scalp. "Greatswordsmen, accompany our new ally! Pikemen of the Eleventh, with me! You others, look to your squad sergeants, and rally those damned militiamen! Come on!"

The crowd shook itself, like a great shaggy beast with pikes and spears for quills. Then soldiers were running, wagon wheels creaking, oxen lowing as whips cracked in the rain. Men of the Thirteenth streamed after their leader, carrying Artaun and the crossed-bones banner bodily amongst them. He seemed to be protesting as the black flag of shame was ripped away – but then it was stuffed into his mouth, silencing him.

Within a hundred heartbeats the square was all but empty. Stewards and white-robed artificers laboured to secure a sailcloth over the single huge wagon which remained, tying down ropes which whipped in the wind. Alchemists rolled wax-sealed barrels out from the Bastion's gates, tallying them on abaci.

And striding toward me across the square came my honour guard.

They were armoured from head to toe in soot-blackened steel – perhaps not the wisest form of raiment during a thunderstorm, but one which lent the little group of sword-bearers a grim, almost funerary air. Lashing rain pelted itself against the steel blades and spikes which protruded from every pauldron, vambrace, greave and riveted plate, while the intermittent flickers of lightning illuminated all those razored edges – but could not reach inside the roughspun black cowls they wore. Not a man among them was shorter than two and a half spans, though part of this was down to their shrouded helms and great cleated boots.

Now they approached – and I wondered, for a second, if this was an execution squad rather than an escort. For the smallest of the group – still half a head taller than me – now looked me eye to eye. Lightning and firelight glittered off the mask within that deep cowl. It was a silver-plated skull, a death's-head grin cunningly etched into jointed steel. In place of its eyes were two lenses of smooth-ground crystal.

There was no scabbard in all of Sarem big enough to sheathe the blade this apparition carried across one shoulder – rippled, blued steel in a tapered triangle two spans long, three thumb-width fullers straked down its length. It was made of metal so thin and sharp that its edge seemed transparent; it hummed in the rain, like a wickedly lethal tuning fork.

There was a muffled click from within the skull-faced helm, and the lower jaw hinged down and away, the rest of the face splitting along invisible lines to swing outward.

"Do all sorcerers stare like that, or were you dropped on your head as a child?" asked a sweet, Ontokhi-accented voice. It took me a few heartbeats to realise that the person inside this horrorworks of ironmongery was in fact a tall and statuesque woman.

I must have been staring for a little too long – but the contrast between that blue-eyed, dimpled face (with a strand of honey-blonde hair tucked behind one ear) and the nightmarish black armour was strangely fascinating.

"Dropped right on an anvil," she said. "*Obviously*. But if Zahfrey says you can fight, I'll humour him. And having that cathedral gone will make for a better view." She extended one gauntleted hand, smiling. "I'm Silbern Chaar. These are the Greatswords of the Thirteenth. We go where you go tonight, Northman."

I grasped her hand in the Ontokhi fashion – forearm to forearm – and she raised an eyebrow.

"Chaar? As in…"

"As in the battle saint, yes," she said, clearly embarrassed. "And yes, I forgive you for desecrating his likeness. So long as that smug-looking statue hit a few ghuldren on the way down, I'm sure he'd forgive you too."

I remembered Vyrim Chaar – a thieving, rapacious and good-natured killer from the city of Almerre. Looking at what must be his great-great-great granddaughter – a few more times removed – I recalled that it had been more than three centuries since I had lain with a living woman. The reason, of course, was apparent in all the modifications her armourer had been required to make. Something about a curvaceous, blonde beauty who slays ghouls with a broadsword… *well*. Even with no heartbeat, it was still possible for me to turn slightly red.

"*Ahem*…Well met then, Silbern. I hope your Commander's faith in me is well founded. We have butcher's work to do tonight, if we want to see the morning."

One of the other greatswords grunted, his helm latching open with a snick of hidden clasps.

"Never seen sorcery in battle. They say we used to have mages ride with us, back in the old days. Ice-callers, storm-masters… is that your power?"

Well, I had to admit that I hadn't really given my tactics much consideration. Old Corvo would have lashed the ghouls with splinters of razor ice, it's true. Tishande, despite being a hallucinomancer, still possessed a few slaying spells to her name. But I had always relied on raising the dead – an easy enough feat for a necromancer in the heat of battle. Raw Materials being plentiful and all…

This time, the dead were the enemy. And my arts were useless. Better to piss into a firestorm.

"I'll try to impress," I said, feeling the mageblight within me crawl with power. Half of Oram believed that the Aemortarch himself had come down to aid them, and as the focus of that faith I was operating on borrowed time. If they began to falter, if their faith turned to despair… well, I would be nothing but a very weak, unnaturally old fool with a sword he could hardly lift. No time to waste, then.

"Feurio wants me on the walls," I said. "Atop the Hangman's Gate. Though I've never actually been to Oran before – I'd be glad of an escort."

Silbern laughed, slamming her skull-faced visor closed.

"Then allow us to give you the guided tour, sorcerer. And don't worry about those pious fools who would see you burn. My glorious ancestor Vyrim walked with the Aemortarch himself, and *he* was a force in the Unmanifest. Besides…" She winked at me, a shutter of articulated silver rasping across one crystal eye. "If they look like they're too serious, you can always drop another church on them."

I decided I liked Silbern Chaar. There was a lot of her long-dead grandsire about her.

As well as a figure mere plate-mail could not hide.

"Lead on then," I said, drawing Cryptfeeder. I let a little shimmer of sorcery lick down the blade – more to convince the greatswords of my credentials than for any real purpose. "If we stand out in this rain much longer, My Lady, then the whole sorry lot of us will rust solid."

Down below, I heard the sound of screams, over the leaden bray of the horns. Explosions tore through the night, lighting up the top of the curtain-wall.

There, cresting the merlons like a gruesome wave, came the ghuldren. A mass of them, slick and writhing beneath the downpour, their eyes as pale as quartz in the lightning-flash.

Soon we would be amongst them.

I prayed – to myself, I suppose, in the absence of any other shred of Divinity – that the belief of Oram's citizens would hold.

"I know we have the remnants - the *ruins*, really, for they were fortresses, those Keels. Things which had no right to be airborne, even with the sorcery of countless dead souls to send them skyward. But standing amid the shattered towers, or staring up at the sheared cliff-face of a Keel snapped in half, looking into galleries and corridors like the tunnels in a termite's nest... I still can't make my mind believe that they once flew."

'Aeronautica Obscuris Occultae'
Sathandris the Elder

IN RASUUL, WHERE the fields of wheat grow in rolling, golden waves from horizon to horizon, there are artificers who build machines for the harvest. Great six-wheeled wagons, pulled by teams of oxen, with a brace of spinning scythes underneath. These reaping engines can mow down grain in great swathes, faster than any army of peasants, allowing the Rasuuli to bring in the harvest before the storms of autumn roll in off the Ythean Steppe, stripping them down to the stalks with hail.

That was how Silbern Chaar and her dozen greatswords waded through the ghuldren as we fought our way to the top of the wall. Wide-spaced, feet planted square, their blades gripped by the handle and by a cross-brace set at right angles from the hilt – they sliced and butchered tirelessly, steel blurring in the rain. Soon the ramp leading up to the battlements flowed with inch-deep black blood, and severed limbs slithered down the gutters, still twitching.

We had reached the guardhouse at the Hangman's Gate to find all the defenders dead. Ghouls raved and clawed at the portcullis, packed into the gateway arch like bream in a fisherman's net. This was the inner gate which led to the top of the wall – beyond it a ramp curved upward over a moat of spikes, even now filling up with groaning, impaled ghuldren.

Silbern didn't stop. Her men strode forward, and their unnaturally sharp blades sheared through muscle, flesh and iron, dropping the portcullis grating back onto the mass of ghouls. The greatswords marched over the dead, crushing them, stabbing down between the fallen grating with grim accuracy. I could only follow, struggling to weave power, wishing that I had brought with me at least some of the webwork of my Incantus. Swords hacked into an almost solid wall of grey flesh, sending gobbets of filth flying.

Once again, I was assailed by the terrible, soulless chill of the ghuldren – the antithesis of true necromancy. The dark arts ultimately free the dead, promising release to trapped and wrathful spirits. Battlefields and mass graves make for rich pickings. Even those who are snared by a necromancer in open war are granted respite, once their work is done.

But these ghouls were not animated by anything so pure as vengeance. Honour, oaths, or misbegotten faith had not kept them chained to their flesh. Their essence had been *devoured*, sucked down into the maelstrom of the Outer Dark, and what remained made my Dark Sight recoil, unwilling to comprehend such horror.

"I hope you've got something spectacular up those sleeves, conjurer!" panted Silbern Chaar, turning from the slaughter. She ripped her sword clear of a ghoul's shattered ribcage, twisting it as it sheared loose. "We can take care of mere thousands of these things, but this attack… they've never assaulted in such numbers. I fear that if you hadn't come this night, we would all have been in the Lamenter's Halls by morning."

Aye… my empty, powerless halls. Likely as not, this whole night of madly pealing bells, screams, rain and murder was my fault in any case…

"I have an idea." I said, swallowing my fears. "Something which might even the odds. But tell me… if we survive, do you prefer red wine or white? I have some very charming vintages in my cellars – fit for a Thearch, in fact, and…"

Silbern shot me a look of scornful amusement.

"I thought you mages took a vow of chastity?"

"It's not at all mandatory. Not even a guideline, really. And, well, it's been…"

The gem at my throat suddenly weighed as much as worlds. Its chain bit into my neck, almost choking me.

If I was not Makara's – body and soul – then what was I? The echo of my past deeds, cast as huge and insubstantial shadows? I would be nothing but Rhul, a stray from the Northlands. And Rhul was powerless. He was literally nobody. He was, in fact, already dead.

Silbern saw right through me.

"Were it not for the other woman in your eyes, sorcerer… then perhaps. Although you look like you might break quite easily. Better you concentrate on your spells – and staying alive!"

She turned away, her face sealed tight beneath a silvered death-grin, and her sword misted the falling rain as she limbered up her swing. She was right. The weak thump and surge of blood through my body was awakening more than just misplaced lust. I was, for the first time in centuries, genuinely afraid to die.

So, against my better judgment, I began crafting incantations from the lore of Zael. I knew there would be bleed-over – and that the chained God would be laughing in his prison as I drew on the symmetries of his Shard of War. But it could not be helped. Zael's cadres had forged the old Angan empire with sorceries of fire and iron, and such spells would serve me better, here and now, than trying to raise things which were both more and less than corpses.

Spike-armoured soldiers drove forward in a rush, heaving the last of the dead from the ramp. Down they went, to impact with the bladed thicket below. Silbern unlatched her skeletal visor, her voice rising above the rumble of the storm.

"We've driven them back! Make for the battlements, men! Get our friend Rhul into position, and we'll see these bastards burn!"

I smiled weakly at Silbern's fury. Such faith! Twisting the skeins of belief into sorcery was far more difficult than I would have liked the lass to believe. There was a weight of inertia to what the pious of Oram thought their Aemortarch could do. Diverting that power to another God's lore made the 'blight in me ache, blurring my vision. Indeed, the slog up the ramp, over still-twitching corpses, had taken on the timbre of a nightmare.[7]

"If… if Slaughtermaw is here… then we'll have some fun…" I slurred, tasting blood at the back of my throat. "These others… just chaff. No challenge. I can…"

Silbern's hulking great lieutenant caught me by the arm as I slumped to my knees. His boot came down on a severed ghuldren head, its jaws still snapping for my flesh. The damned thing exploded like a rotten melon.

---

7. Obviously, the fact that we were wading through the living dead would have been a nightmare for most of you in any case. But necromancers don't have bad dreams about corpses, any more than bakers have bad dreams about bread. My nightmares were filled with images of endless, unrolling screeds of accountancy, quill pens and uncomfortable chairs. My other dreams, from that night on, would feature prominently the image of rain glistening on Silbern Chaar's steel-armoured cleavage.

"You don't get to die yet," he growled, in thickly accented Ontokhi. "We were promised a slaughter, such as the Aemortarch himself would have delivered. If you die now, I'm going to have to kill you."

I laughed, but it seemed a faraway sound. In my vision the shards of the Aziphem danced, spinning on the axis of the Divine's shattered mind. Lines and arcs of fire linked the facets of Anghul and Zael. Power surged between them, flickering like razorcuts of lightning, earthed through the mageblight in my hands.

My leather gloves burst into flames. Ashes spiralled out, and my fingers were revealed, crooked black claws dripping with amber energy.

"Point me at the bastard, Ontokhi," I rasped, struggling to my feet. "I'm ready. This is going to hurt, but damn you, *I'm ready.*"

At the top of the ramp the wall flared out into a wide, cobbled expanse – a empty trebuchet platform between the twin towers of the Hangman's Gate. I could see how that grisly edifice had earned its name – a scaffold ran between the towers, and the time-gnawed remains of criminals swung in the gale, a dozen or more. There were ghuldren here, a snarling pack of them, jumping like over-eager hounds to scrabble at the hanged men's feet.

"Rotten meat," drawled Silbern. "These things are less than discerning, it seems. Rhul – make them burn."

No time for foreplay, then. Zael's sorcery felt like oily glass in my chest, heavy and unnatural. But it was writhing to be let loose, and the weight of Oram's prayers was building up behind the wall of my willpower like water behind a dam.

I clenched on hand into a fist, pointed it at the ghouls, and screamed.

Flames roared out in an almost solid rod of force, licking across the horde of the dead like drakenfire. Where the white-hot plume struck home grey flesh boiled and smoked, sloughing away from glistening bones. Eyeballs burst, and marrow sizzled. Sparks blew back in a swirling cloud, hissing in the rain. The whole shuddering mass of ghuldren staggered back, keening in agony, and a score plunged over the merlons, to slither and roll down a ramp of their fellows.

Oh, there was pain – but not from the dead, who were blasted to ashes in their hundreds. Agony whipsawed through the mageblight inside my chest. The laughter of Zael had *teeth*, and it ripped into my sanity, assailing me with images I prayed were false.

They were of Makara – or of the creature she had become, after Urzen the Mad had remade her as a demoness. I had her soul, trapped in the amulet around my neck. But Zael had her physical body, and the things he showed me – well, they blurred the line between torture and pleasure, each image driven home like a rusty nail. The scream I let out as I wielded the chained God's sorcery was one part battlecry and nine parts suffering.

Because as the nails went in, I lost true memories. I felt them being torn away, ablating into nothing, and I knew I would never get them back.

At the core of my soul, the linchpin. A single night of passion I had shared with Makara, half a world away and three hundred years ago. We had taken what solace we could from each other before fate overcame us. And now... now that most precious of my recollections was being laid bare, Zael's incorporeal fingers scrabbling for it like a ghoul ripping into a dead man's ribcage.

I wouldn't let him have it. Too long had I held the old God of Anganesse a prisoner. I wasn't about to allow him the satisfaction of revenge.

No, I said, and no, and no, and NO...

The furnace-blast tapered off, spluttering to red and dirty orange before it died. I was reeling on my feet, my mind in tatters, images of horror and ecstasy crowding behind my eyes. My temples throbbed, and I tasted blood on my tongue.

I was Kuhal. Kuhal, the Lamenter, the Lord of Ashes... I was ambushed by the ghuldren, when my family were traveling down from Kaltensund. I was... no! Not Rhul! I was...

A heavy, gauntleted hand clapped me on the shoulder, almost making me vomit. I managed to crush down the feeling of sickness and anger, and turned to see Silbern's Lieutenant standing over me.

"That's about what I expected," he said. His scarred, stubbled face split into a smile. "I'm not a pious fool like some of the others. I wish we had more like you, and a long time ago."

I felt that this was probably the best compliment I was likely to get this night.

"What do they call you, soldier?"

"My parents called me Ashren. But the boys – they know me as Mouse."

Army humour. The man was three spans tall, and held his greatsword in one ham-sized fist.

"My thanks then... Mouse. But we're far from done. This one gatehouse, it's..."

"One of seventeen," said Silbern, striding over the cooling cobbles.

"Hangman's, Bell Tower, the Oubliette, Rosechurch Deep, the Shadow Gate… all are under assault. Make no mistake – we need Slaughtermaw dead if this city is to stand."

I dragged myself up on Mouse's spiked vambrace, looking out over the wall and into the night. Lightning split the clouds, illuminating the churned mud of the Oramun Plain.

It was just as bad as I had feared.

The ghuldren didn't attack like an army – there was no discipline to their advance, no tactics. The most ragged of them staggered forward in the vanguard, to be shot full of quarrels and arrows from the defenders lining the wall. Most of the bowman's walks and arbalest platforms were overrun already, but a few desperate militiamen had managed to barricade themselves in towerholds, and they rained down steel on the grey-skinned horde, barely slowing their advance. Alchemical munitions cracked and flared here and there, ripping knots of ghuldren to shreds. But for every one which fell there were dozen more, drooling and moaning, dragging themselves forward to the moat and the wall.

Where they plunged into the oil-slick water, disappearing below the surface. One after another, bodies on top of bodies, gnarled, half-chewed fingers sinking into necrotic flesh… they filled the moat and began to ramp up against the walls, the sheer weight of rotting meat crushing those beneath them.

Up this grisly siege-ladder came those ghuldren who were still whole enough to wield weapons – decomposing peasants with pitchforks and scythes, things in rusted armour with notched and pitted axes, wild men carrying the thighbones of cattle and horses as crude clubs. They came in their thousands, and more than once I saw a ghoul literally fall apart halfway through its climb, rotted tendons and muscles giving way to send the creature slithering down the charnel-heap, trampled underfoot.

To the east, and then to the west – the entire arc of the city wall was besieged. Ours seemed to be the only section of battlements free from the walking dead, who were tumbling from the walls into the inner moat, choking its spiked depths with even more bodies. Soon they would be in the city itself, and Feurio's promise of grim house-to-house fighting would come true. The losses amongst the folk of Oram would be catastrophic.

I croaked a curse, thankfully in a language over a thousand years dead. I realised, in the silence between the thunderclaps, that all of

Silbern's greatswords were waiting for me to lead them.

"Very well. If you want a general, I'll be one. Just don't ask about my last command." A score of expressionless silver skulls stared back at me. "First… first we have to get the ugly bastard's attention." I pointed, staggering toward the parapet. Spike-armoured, black-cowled warriors fanned out on either side of me, hacking into the ghouls who were now regrouping, clawing their way back between the merlons. "Then… then I can stand to be a little less subtle. But no more from you, Zael. No more of your lies and tricks. This will only need a little of Corvo's finesse, and then we can finish Slaughtermaw the Khytein way…"

Silbern was at my side, her blade a shimmer of silver-blue death. Slick dead hands which groped toward me were lopped off clean from their wrists, heads split, necks severed with a sound like tearing silk.

"Whatever you have planned, make it quick, wizard!" she panted. Her facemask was open now, and I could see the strain in her eyes. The greatswords had been swinging those immense two-handed blades for an hour or more, and it was beginning to show.

"*Conjurer* I could take. Mage… at a pinch. But *wizard?* This is no faerytale, Miss Chaar. If it was, I wouldn't be telling you that my plan involves charging down that slope, then cutting a path through an army of corpses."

Silbern's eyes flashed defiance – exactly the same flinty stare which had made her ancestor Vyrim a battle saint.

"Where you go, we go… *wizard.* If that means the Lamenter's cold halls, then so be it. I'll take you up on your offer when we meet beyond his gates."

"Then you know…"

"That we're likely not coming back? Aye. What of it? What *I* want to know is how you're going to win us a chance at the Thane in the first place!"

There would be no need for Zael's insidious power this time. The storm still raged and blustered above the creaking tenements of Oram, and it was pregnant with lightning. I would never be able to call lightning from empty skies, but I was skilled enough to coax a bolt or two from those belly-heavy clouds.

"The sheen I saw on the moat. What is it?" I asked, peering squint-eyed up into the storm.

"Leachings from the mine slag. Poisonous. The alchemists say it's better out there than in our drinking water, though I'm certain the ale here is worse."

I looked sidelong at Mouse, who shrugged.

"Only saying. *I'll* still drink the stuff."

I knew little of mining, and less of its by-products. But I'd seen that rainbow-hued stain floating atop water before, in the swamps of the Khytein Marches. One careless spark…

"You all might want to stand back," I muttered, weaving power into a lightning-snare. I let the coiled ball of forces loose, and it dropped like a sycamore seed, spiraling down into the moat between buttress-roots of live, writhing ghuldren.

I may have miscalculated.

The bolt of lightning which came searing down from the clouds was as thick around as a ship's mast, incandescent white shading to summer-sky blue. It threw the lot of us from our feet, sparks snapping and twisting from every spike on the greatswords' ornate platemail.

The world held its breath for an instant.

And then flame roared up in answer, a curtain topping the wall by twenty spans, furiously hot and shot through with twining threads of purple and green. Whatever vile processes the alchemists of Oram used had blended into an explosive soup, one which no amount of rain would quench.

The fire spread around the ring-wall of the city; faster than a charging war-horse under the spurs, raising a hell-chorus of moans and screams from the ghuldren. They were incinerated in their tens of thousands as the flames took hold, roasting their squamous flesh from their bones. Tottering ramps and towers of dead things cracked and fell, an image from some madman's apocalypse. In some places – the gatehouses, where the press of Slaughtermaw's thralls was at its thickest – blackened frameworks of bone stood stick-thin and skeletal against the conflagration, fused together into tangled geometries.

The defenders took it as a sign. Bones burning, consumed with sorcerous flame – it was the work of their misbegotten God, and the weight of belief came down on me like a millstone, the size of mountains. An insectile hum of prayers blurred in behind my aching eyes.

Oh, there was temptation in that power. All that swirling, devouring fire… with the lore of Zael I could make it live, shape it into golems of pure slaying heat and rage, send them wallowing through the dead in a walking auto-de-fe. That was assuredly what the Chained One wanted. But cowering before that firestorm was the snowflake of my memory – the last few shreds of a centuries-old devotion. That which made me Kuhal Moer.

Not the Aemortarch the people of Oram needed.

Not Rhul, the nameless sorcerer, who Feurio's men were willing to follow.

No. Just the child of a dead tribe, whelped by a barbarian bastard, raised on sagas of glory and then made into a monster.

If the fire lived, then he would die. And then, what purpose was there to my years of hollow, empty life? I would forget Makara, forget myself, and become once again nothing but the pinch in the hourglass – a conduit for power. To burn for a second, and then to blow away as ash…

I saw Kharnath's warpainted face in my mind – infinitely ancient, infinitely sad. The fact that he had chosen oblivion told me all I needed to know about power and its price.

So I held back. As the fire guttered and sunk beneath the top of the wall, I drew Cryptfeeder from its scabbard, channelling power into the familiar forms and weavings of battle. This wasn't sorcery stolen from Zael, or learned piecemeal from teachers like Corvo or Tishande. It was the spirit of the Wild Song, that elder magick of the Khytein Moer, and it came down from antiquity to resonate in my mageblighted bones, plucking my tendons like lyrecaster strings.

"He sees us!" I shouted, more than a little mad with battle-lust. Such base and bloody urges had lain dormant in me for far too long. "We'll make that shambling flesh-pile rue that day it was spawned! You hear me, Dirge? Sinder? Mock me by making me a God, would you? I'll see you chained up with the other two, you arse-born whoremonger! Now! CHARGE!"

There must have been enough fire in my eyes for Silbern and her veterans to take me seriously. *I* would have been more skeptical. But then again, I was never meat-headed enough to become a solider.

"You heard the spellweaver! Over the wall, and the Ark take the hindmost!"

Out in the rain-lashed dark, beyond the circle of firelight, Slaughtermaw bellowed. The unholy thing had come to itch at the source of its frustration, honing in on the scent of sorcery. Of course, I was a fool to believe I could cut down such a beast, even with twenty hard-bitten warriors at my back. But then again, it is a peculiar twist of the Wild Song that makes fools into heroes. The Gods shared our perverse sense of humour, I supposed.

It was only as I flung myself from the parapet, pale hair streaming out behind me, that I realised the whole Khytein pantheon were likely ghosts in the Outer Dark by now. There would be no-one to laugh at the pale and sickly son of Hurik the Scalptaker as he plunged to his doom down a pile of blackened bones, screaming his father's war-cry.

For that's just what we landed in. I struck the scree of smoking bodies hard, rolling and sliding, the chainmail of my hauberk soaking up the impact of carbonized ribs and femurs. Mouse plunged straight through, starting a minor avalanche of ghuldren debris. As for the rest – I think we lost three of our number just in that first suicidal plunge, dragged down by their armour, never to resurface. There were *things* left alive in the depths of the pile, after all – things which were half-cooked and hungry.

The stench of burned meat and charred hair assailed me as I rolled to a stop, plastered in ashes and mud. The Hangman's Gate was where the most fierce assault had fallen, and bones filled the still-guttering moat, preventing any of us from drowning. Though the broth which now slopped against Oram's walls seemed repulsively thick…

I shuddered, picking myself up. A second wave of the dead were advancing, lumbering with terrible speed, some scrabbling on all fours like beasts. Silbern Chaar was at my side, her mask hinged back and her sword held high. Not for three hundred years had I seen a sight so beautiful as this Ontohki battle-maiden, smiling like a wolf, her spiked armour dripping with gore.

"I can feel the Thane's footsteps drawing closer, little wizard. So, what's your plan?"

Now that Silbern mentioned it, I *could* feel the ground shaking with a rhythmic tremor. A mindless bellow split the night behind it.

"Ummm… we kill it, I suppose. Slaughtermaw. Once it's dead, the rest of these things…"

She rolled her eyes.

"I meant, are you going to call lightning? Open a pit in the earth? Summon demons to tear its flesh from its bones? Anything the rest of your little entourage might want to know about?"

I hefted Cryptfeeder – one of the few times in its long, long history that the legendary battle-blade of Sothara Roege had looked slightly inadequate.

"I thought we might just cut the damned thing to pieces, lass. That often seems to work."

To her credit, the look of horror which flickered across Silbern's face lasted only for an instant.

"I thought wi… *sorcerers* didn't fight," she said, turning to face the onrushing wall of ghuldren. They were close enough now that I could pick out their milky eyes, the strands of drool stretched taut between their blackened teeth…

"That's sort of like the vows of chastity. Not even a guideline," I replied, bracing myself for impact. Behind the cresting wave of ghouls I saw the silhouette of their master, wading through the press of bodies like a fisherman through the surf. The battle-ram clenched in the Thane's hand swept down, making the mire heave beneath us.

Then there was no time for thought, no time for strategy. The dead were upon us, and all was lost under the flare of the Wild Song.

Usually it takes a lyrecaster to weave Khytein magick. But I used the tuning-fork hum of those seventeen battle-blades, rising and falling like the teeth of some nightmare machine. Rippled skeins of witchfire bloomed, binding up armoured limbs, stealing tendrils between muscle and bone. Weariness melted away like hot grease on a hearthstone. Swords, already a silvery blur in the rain, became mere contrails of reflected lightning, too fast for the eye to follow.

And Slaughtermaw's minions died.

I plunged amongst them too, not at all immune to the song I had woven. Cryptfeeder's edge was unstoppable, flaring with cold pale flame, and it hacked through steel, wood, bronze, bone and flesh with equal fervour, dismembering ghuldren left and right. I had the power within me now to recall those terrible incantations I had spoken on the plain before Urexes, and I added them to the knotted vortex of magick which surrounded me.

"Aligning the seal of the Black Gate. Balancing the vitae flow to the seven cardinal sigils. Cerebrex bindings locked by the praxis of the Horned Eye, with restraint now unlimited to the second level…"

They fell in their thousands. A spume of black gore rose thirty spans in the air, pattering down across the heaving throng as they bulled forward, trampling each other in their hunger. Only to be met by the implacable threshing engine of Silbern Chaar's greatswords. The restraints of the second level made the 'blight in me burn, fresh tendrils drilling through uncorrupted bone and flesh. But they gave me the collective memory of hundreds of dead Zengaji, that cult of assassins who were said to be able to slice a man's soul from his shadow, ten minutes before he knew he was dead. Centuries ago they had bound their lore – the Way of the Killing Strike – into my bones, and now I unleashed it, moving even faster, until the world became blue and cold, glassy as an illusion. In that fugue the ghuldren moved with glacial slowness, each raindrop hanging crystalline in the air.

I watched those drops shatter to mist against Cryptfeeder's blade as I spun and whirled, ducking low to sever legs at the knee, rising to tear through spines, ribs, necks...

And came face to face with Slaughtermaw.

I hadn't heard the gates behind us open, but they had. Feurio Zahfrey was with us, two thousand soldiers of the Thirteenth in a sortie at his back, as we hacked down the last of the ghuldren and confronted their master.

Too late, I realised exactly what the bloated Thane was doing. Too late to rein in the Wild Song, to snuff out the candle-flame of my sorcery....

Which was being devoured by the undead beast. Sucked down into the Incantus in its chest. Light flared blue to red. Time came back, with an echoing roar of screams and crunches.

We hadn't defeated an army to reach Slaughtermaw. *It had cleared a path for us.*

It wanted to fuel those fires of pious belief which gave me strength – because the Thane was an *Occultiphage*[8], an eater of the Unmanifest. I felt the mageblight grow cold and heavy within me, Cryptfeeder a dead weight in my hands. The animating force which had pushed Silbern Chaar and her men beyond endurance withered away, leaving them aching, fallen to their knees in the mud...

And Slaughtermaw laughed.

My vision of the ghuldren's master had been from afar, and even then it had seemed the size of a burial mound, a barrow made of knotted, lumpen flesh, Seeing it up close...

The beast was terrible in its vast bulk. It was a sheer wall of scabrous grey skin, screaming faces stretched tight over slabs of decaying muscle. Patches of leather, iron, fur and pebbly drakenskin were stitched atop it in overlapping plates, and a whole meatworks of knives, hooks and skewers pierced the folds and flaps of its ill-fitting hide, glittering in the rain. The mace gripped in Slaughtermaw's wagon-sized fist was an

---

8. Occultiphages are rare, dangerous, and very hard to either create or control. After all, what sorcerer would willingly give life to a thing which will awaken hungry - with its hapless creator the nearest source of food. In this case, the answer was, of course, a mad, unhinged, undead spawn of the primordial Chaos. But we will hear more of Dirge Endsong later...

obelisk of brass, twenty spans if it was an inch.

And then there were the eyes. Countless squinting, greeding dark eyes, all of them fixed right on me. Slaughtermaw's pumpkin-shaped head had no mouth – that was the vertical gash between its ribs. But I was certain it was smiling nonetheless.

One great flat stump of a foot came down on a Greatsword, pulverizing armour and flesh. Then an overhand blow of that mace swept into the line, lifting men from the mire, sending them flying. Mouse lurched to his feet, hacking at Slaughtermaw's wrist, but the thing's off-hand plucked him away, fingers woven from whole arms and legs clenching, crushing… the huge Ontokhi had barely time to scream. The Thane stuffed him halfway into its gaping chest, and Mouse was torn in half with a sick, wet crackle of gristle.

"Fall back!" shouted Feurio, dragging me by the collar of my hauberk. "To the gates!"

Hopeless. The dubious safety of the city wall was too far away. Slaughtermaw wallowed forward, mace raised up for another devastating blow, and four more greatswords were obliterated, driven into the mud like nails into rotten wood. The pikemen of the Thirteenth wavered. Curses and prayers were drowned beneath the Thane's triumphant bellow.

Silbern Chaar bought us enough time to flee.

The captain of the Greatswords should not have been able to *stand*, let alone match Slaughtermaw's fury. But stand she did, meeting the next swing of that huge battle-ram with her sword. It should have crushed her like a rag doll, shattered her blade to splinters – but impossibly, she held. A flare of sparks scattered where brass met steel, and the warrior maiden was driven knee-deep into the mud. She screamed – but it was defiance, not terror in her voice. And she heaved the mace aside, dragging one armoured boot and then the other from the earth.

I saw Slaughtermaw's galaxy of eyes widen, suddenly terrified. Then the Thane's chest creaked open, and its muscle-knotted tongue lashed out, slippery and spiked. The knout of bone and teeth at its end whipped sideways, a crushing blow…

Only to fly severed, hacked from its roots by Silbern's blade.

"Run! Run, you fools! I can't do this forever!"

Her words goaded Feurio and his men back to life. What would have been a deadly rout became an ordered retreat, ashen-faced soldiers streaming back toward Oram's gates. Neither I nor the Commander could look away, though.

Slaughtermaw drew itself up over Silbern Chaar like a cresting wave, lightning flickering around its crown of horns. It drew back its huge, heavy mace, double-handed, prepared to crush her utterly.

Then a stuttering roll of detonations tore apart the night. Slaughtermaw twisted sideways, huge chunks blown from its glistening hide. The thing which Dirge had crafted to entrap me staggered, tried to right itself – and a second battery of explosions ripped it ragged, staving in its head, almost severing one of its lumpen arms. The mace spun away into the dark, plucked from the Thane's bloodied fingers.

Feurio wasted not a second. He plunged forward into Slaughtermaw's shadow, wrapping one arm around Silbern Chaar. The Ontokhi had dropped to her knees in resignation, awaiting a killing blow which never came. Now the Commander dragged her bodily from the field – just as Slaughermaw collapsed to one side, falling with bone-jarring impact. A heartbeat later, and Silbern would have been lost beneath that shuddering bulk.

"Whatever that was, it won't kill the bastard!" panted Feurio, shaking the Greatsword back to some semblance of clarity. "We have go go! Now! Before..."

Behind us, the Thirteenth had all but reached the gates. Ghuldren were staggering in on all sides, sluggish and dazed by their master's sudden fall. But it seemed that the Thane was indeed far from finished. As I watched, the immense beast drove its hands into the piles of slaughtered dead, opening its hollow chest to unleash a mass of coiling tubes. Rain-slick grey flesh flowed into Slaughermaw in waves, those tubes pumping obscenely, and the Thane began to knot back together, its head bulging out with a crack and grind of bone.

Its eyes opened. It narrowed them, all at once, in a look of pure hate. We ran.

I don't know if any of the others thought to look skyward, or even to question where our reprieve had come from. Enough, perhaps, that they walked in the footsteps of a sorcerer, where inexplicable and violent destruction was as natural as breathing. But I looked. Even as I pelted across the gore-slick mud, dragging Cryptfeeder behind me, I couldn't help but feel something pressing heavy on the world.

There, wheeling against the roiling wall of stormclouds. An arrowhead shape, slicing through the rain under a cloud of taut sailcloth. Smoke drifted from a row of open ports across its flank, and tiny figures swarmed its decks, hauling on ropes and reloading black iron cannon. For an instant I thought it was stone – a Keel of Anganesse – but such things had been purged from the world centuries ago.

It was a ship – but none such as had ever sailed the Shallow Sea. Wood and copper plating, canvas and hempen rope, all brought together into the form of my own poor Graveyard Ark. It flew before the gale faster than my vessel ever had, tacking and wheeling to present a second broadside to the ghuldren horde. Detonations shattered the night, and a thousand walking corpses were swept away, macerated by chainshot and shrapnel.

I must have croaked a warning as the spectral ship swung low over the Oramun Plain, because Feurio turned, just inside the gate. He squinted up through the rain as the drawbridge began to rumble closed.

"Perhaps that mad priest wasn't so crazy after all," he spat. The great iron portcullis rattled and slammed down behind us. "That's the Stormreaper, lad. The *witch*. As if we didn't have enough to worry about tonight!"

A thunderous blow shook the raised drawbridge. Wood splintered, and iron-headed nails flew past us like hail, driven from the boards. Outside, Slaughtermaw bellowed, a sound of utter, mad frustration.

"The enemy of our enemy, Feurio Zahfrey?"

Stone dust sifted down as the Hangman's Gate shook to its foundations.

"For what it's worth, Northman," he said. "But that ain't much. You probably haven't heard the stories, but she's more than just a shadow to frighten children. I've seen the *pieces*…"

My smile, in the gloom of the shuddering gatehouse arch, was terrible to behold.

"I've been the villain in a few stories myself, Zahfrey. The important part – the part which sorts out the revered from the reviled…" I lifted Cryptfeeder over my shoulder. It took nearly all the strength left in me. "Is who's left to tell them."

Beyond the gate, Oram was in chaos. Bells pealed madly, people screamed and fought and scrabbled in the mud, killing each other over rags and scraps of food. The faith of this city was shattered, and with it the source of my power.

If there was to be anything left of Oram come dawn, we would need all the help we could muster.

The Burning Dark was grievously wounded
before the battle of Urexes - deployed by
Endsong against the power of the Coldblood.
When it arrived, too late to stem the tide of the
Aemortarch's armies, it was already weakened,
and as soon as its master was distracted it made
use of its abilities to escape. The Hanged Man, by
comparison, never crossed swords with a single one
of the Lamenter's undead. Some would call such
a decision *cowardice*, but considering the utter
destruction of Sister Pain, That Which Walks and
the Black Shepherd on that fateful day, others
might call it pragmatism. Certainly, there are no
further horror-tales of the other seven. But in
far-flung, forsaken places, stories still emerge of
atrocities perpetrated by the last of the Nine...

Tractatorus Philisophico Lex Daemonae
Kulain the Blasphemous, the Mad Monk of D'arvonne

THE NIGHT SEEMED endless. The rain came down relentlessly, hammering on the rooftops of Oram, overflowing the gutters and churning the streets to mud. And through it all came the resurgent assault of the ghuldren – too many to stop, too hungry and driven to throw back, an army which cared not for casualties or morale.

We fought them house to house, street to street, just as Feurio had promised. Townsfolk filled the gaps in the lines of the Thirteenth, taking up bloodied pikes and notched, blunted halberds. Women and children reloaded crossbows behind the lines, tying alchemical munitions to the shafts with numbed fingers.

The carnage was brutal. I burned up the power in all eight of my rings holding the line, swinging Cryptfeeder again and again until my arms were dead weight, my shoulders aching, my back a solid rod of pain. I was painted black with undead gore, plastered with gobbets of flesh, hair and skin, and so were the haggard-faced defenders who stood shoulder to shoulder with me, dying one by one.

I never learned their names. They fought with grim ferocity, beyond words, snarling their defiance as waves of shambling horrors broke against us again and again. They died so that I may live, anticipating another firestorm of sorcery.

I didn't have it in me. Some of those Guildsmen turned to me as the blades went in, as teeth closed around their throats, and I saw mute betrayal in their eyes. *More reasons for me to hate Dirge and his masters. More reasons for me to hate myself.* I fought on, retreating tenement by tenement, street by street, leaving the dead to be devoured.

We fired the mines as our band of defenders shrunk, retreating up the hillside toward Kharnath's ring of standing stones. Firedamp and poisonous gases blazed from a thousand throats of stone as Dalross and his men rolled barrels of blackpowder down into the dark, making chimneys burst and opening fissures in the streets. Whole neighbourhoods tottered and fell, dragging thousands of ghouls down into a subterranean hell.

It was too good for them. And it wasn't nearly enough.

Above us, the Stormreaper's ship ruled the air for a time, pouring chainshot into the ghuldren as they topped the walls. But then Slaughtermaw himself intervened, tearing the immense steeple bell from a slumside chapel and hurling it skyward. The hole it punched through the Stormreaper's Keel blazed with green witchfire, and the ship crabbed sideways through the air, smoking, narrowly missing the towers of the Bastion as it lost control. The last I saw of the witch and her crew they were limping away to the north, sails furled, great bat-wing rudders almost ploughing the Oramun Plain.

We were on our own, outnumbered, and all but doomed. Silbern and Feurio were everywhere in that last grim hour, as the grey light of dawn cracked the horizon. They were the ones who rallied the last of the living, herding us into the Guild Bastion while the weary heavy infantry of the Ninth fought a suicidal rearguard action, dying within sight of the walls.

The city seemed to hold its breath as the sun crested the eastern hills. The portcullis was slammed shut, the courtyard cleared, and Slaughtermaw's horde skulked out of bowshot, heaping up barricades just under the brow of the hill. I knew they were just waiting for their master – that this final push to cleanse Oram of life was too sweet a victory for the Thane to miss. This fact alone convinced me that Dirge saw through the creature's eyes. *He would want me to be the last one taken, alive, entombed in the spiked womb which was Slaughtermaw's chest...*

Hardly a cheering thought.

We mustered as the rain faded to a drear, grey drizzle. It was a sorry sight indeed.

Barely two thousand soldiers were left standing – with three times that number wounded or dying. The caves which honeycombed the Bastion's hill were crammed to bursting with refugees, the dispossessed and the hopeless. If – *when* – the walls came down, they would be nothing but a captive feast for the dead.

Despite my sorcerous impotence, I was still summoned to the command tent which had been pitched in the central bailey – dragged there by a glum and battered Artaun, who still held the banner of the Thirteenth, his other arm wrapped in a sling.

"They're talking about a final stand," said the herald, wincing with pain. "Which is not the kind of thing I really need to hear this morning. When all you can hope for is to take a few of the enemy with you, you start to wonder why you joined the army in the first place…"

I managed a wan smile in return.

"*I* never did. At least you must have gotten a few paychecks out of the Guild, Artaun."

He sniffed.

"If you could call them that. Still, my father died of the Black Lung. My uncles all died in a cave-in. At least I'm going to die in the open air."

I decided that I'd quite changed my opinion of the Lord Marshall's Herald.

"I always thought I'd die on a battlefield," I said. "With a Vhaurish long-knife through my guts. At least these ghuldren won't let any part of us go to waste, eh?"

Artaun chuckled.

"If we meet up in the horde, I'll make sure to save you some nice livers and lungs. Suppose we'll get to like the taste."

I followed behind Artaun to a red-striped pavilion, where a knot of broken-looking people warmed themselves over an iron brazier. These were the last few officers of the Guild and the Militia, their scarred and dented armour testament to a long night's fighting. Most looked as grey and dead as the ghouls they had been routed by.

I had barely pushed through the tent flap when a gauntleted hand had me by the throat, lifting me bodily from my feet. I'm no heavyweight, but the arm which bore me up was built like a chain of hams, clad in white-enameled armour and leather. It was connected to a face which was literally steaming with anger.

"Feurio's worthless sorcerer! This is all *your fault!* You desecrate our Lord's cathedral, and expect to take us all down to the Hells with you?" I couldn't breathe. Fingers bit into my windpipe, rendering an erudite counter-argument pointless. "He says that Fell was a traitor, but is it any co-incidence that these hellspawn have come for us now? The first time we let a heretic live, and they assault us as never before!"

It was Silbern Chaar who saved me. Not with words, but with a straight cross to the burly knight's jaw, rocking him back on his feet. Anyone else would probably have been knocked sprawling, but my captor simply let me fall, then massaged his stubbled jaw until it clicked back in place.

"My vows forbid me to strike a lady, Mistress Chaar. Or else…"

"Or else *what*, choirboy? In case you haven't noticed, I'm no lady. Take your best damned shot!"

The white-armoured thug closed his eyes, muttering a prayer under his breath. I felt it tingle, like iced water trickling down my spine. *Great – he was one of mine.* I had had quite enough of irony for one night.

Feurio Zahfrey stepped between the pair of them before another blow could be struck – because it seemed that Silbern wasn't about to wait for an invitation.

"Lieutenant! Stand down! And you…" he rounded on the knight, teeth clenched with fury. "Comport yourself with some damned *dignity*, Paladyne Uveryn. Not *every* fucking problem can be solved by *burning people alive*, you know!"

The Paladyne shot me a sour look as I dragged myself back to my feet, trying to claw together the scraps of my pride.

"The things we burn aren't *people*, Zahfrey," he snarled. "Witches like that cowardly Stormreaper. Scum who belong in Endsong's hells. Heretics like this one – they are better off as ashes. Aemortarch have mercy on us all for letting him live!"

"And has he ever shown the least shred of mercy before?" I asked, drawing a saddle-chair up to the pavilion's central table. "When you light the pyre under innocent wise-women and harmless lunatics? No. I'm fairly certain he's silent."

I still had enough power left in me to flay this pompous sword-swinger to the bones. Oh, how sweet it would have been! Unfortunately, it would also have precisely proven his point. And, in my present state, quite possibly killed me.

"Feurio said *enough*, and I second his motion," said the grey-haired warrior-woman who I'd seen before, marshalling the troops of the Ninth. "By arguing amongst ourselves we only strengthen Slaughtermaw…"

"As if the beast needs *strengthening*, Coryne!" put in a florid-faced man in muddied furs. "The ghuldren have us, and even if they don't…"

"Oram is finished," said a morose, leather-clad greybeard wearing a pair of multi-lensed brass goggles. "I won't dispute that we had to fire the mines, but getting that inferno under control… it's all but impossible. Those coal seams will burn until doomsday, and it's more than my lanternmen can do to quell them."

"There's still a way to get these people to safety," said Feurio. "The tunnels beneath the Bastion Rock run deep – there are hidden exits on the moors. We can…"

"We can let the noble-born scurry for those exits first, perhaps, while the poor become a feast for the dead. And when those wretches are out under the stars? Slaughtermaw isn't the only Thane in Sarem, Commander."

This from the white-armoured Paladyne again, his craggy face curled into a sneer. I was beginning to truly detest the man – and the detestation of a necromancer is hard currency indeed.

"*What we will do*," said Feurio, fists clenched, "Is shepherd the women and children out first. Noble blood means nothing in such grim straits. Gold means even less – your pardon, Vaultmaster Jorin." The fat, fur-clad banker shut his mouth, his outstretched finger wilting. "And we'll bring down the tunnels in controlled deadfalls behind our retreat. Varlo's lanternmen can take command of that detail."

"So we run?" asked Silbern. "Don't sit right with me, that notion. Too many dead…"

"And you want to join them? I'm sure they'd love the company!"

Uveryn snorted, collapsing onto a wooden trestle. It creaked alarmingly under his weight.

"For once the wench is right. I took holy orders to *destroy* those things. Scurrying away with shit in our britches is not what the Aemortarch expects of us."

"And where can we run *to?*" asked Jorin. "Cyvenne is the closest city, but by all accounts they have their own woes. If we turn up begging at their gates, we'll be treated no better than…"

"Than the poor of your own city, Vaultmaster?" snarled Varlo. "Too long you've had my bondsmen by the balls with your ledgers and your gold. If I'm going to die today, I'll die having called you a pox-raddled shite to your face! Usurer!"

"Peasant!"

"*Leech!*"

"*Whoreson!*"

The miner and the merchant were more than ready to come to blows. Both were held back, one by Feurio, the other by his fellow Guild commander, her face sick with disgust.

But there was a reason I had kept silent through all of this pointless wrangling.

"I know how to kill them all," I said. Quiet words, but my voice carried, sharp as winter. All eyes in the command tent turned toward me – the rake-thin, white-haired Northerner with the blackened, burned hands.

"Forgive me, Sir Paladyne, but your Deacon was possessed by a terrible evil. I hold that each man has the right to his faith, and so I apologize for casting down your very fine cathedral. A small price to pay, I'm sure you agree, to destroy a pair of *actual demons.*"

Uveryn's cheeks reddened, but he nodded, a tight little gesture which made his stubble rasp against the lip of his iron gorget.

"*Real* demons. Not old women who collect herbs and mix ointments. Horrors from out of your Book of Ascendancy, the equal of the Nine Now Nameless. But there was a greater power hidden under their feet. A God named Kharnath."

"Heresy!" spat Uveryn. "I know that name! We were taught the signs and perversions of the false Gods in battle seminary. Kharnath is an unclean idol! One of Endsong's dark pantheon!"

"And yet, when Deacon Fell *grew tentacles and thorns*, it was Kharnath who crushed him like a cockroach," I said. "Curious." I raised a hand as the white-clad knight began to rise from his seat, and a snap of sparks stunned him into silence, sizzling between my fingers. Anghul help me, but even such a minor glamour *hurt.*

"Curious… but immaterial. The reason for Kharnath's presence – for the altar his followers raised here, thirty thousand winters past, is *far* more interesting."

Now I had them. Uveryn's histrionics and Varlo's cold anger hadn't been enough to focus our little gathering of the condemned. But a shred of hope…

"There is fire under the earth. Rivers, arteries and veins of fire, liquid rock heated to boiling by the presence of the Divine. One such upwelling lies beneath us, and it is this source of power which Kharnath was drawn to. If I can unleash it, Slaughtermaw and his ghuldren will burn."

"Lies!" sputtered the Paladyne. "This poxy spellweaver has already doomed us. Now he spins us wild stories about fire underground! Have you never snuffed out a candle, then? Kicked earth over a hearth to quell the embers?"

Varlo turned a look of scorn on the white-clad knight.

"And have *you* ever been in the deep delvings, Urveryn? It's mighty hot down there – aye, a mile deep, and my engineers have to work in their loincloths alone, such is the sweat and boil of it. That's not all, either. We come across tunnels, sometimes – *old* tunnels, dug long before there was a city of Oram, or a cathedral perched on top of it. There's bones down there, wrapped in old, old hides, covered in beads and feathers. Some of them tunnels turn into drop-shafts, and some of them drop-shafts have light coming up out of 'em. Red light. *Fire*light."

"And why wasn't the Tabernacle told?" grated Urveryn.

Silbern answered for the engineer, smiling sweetly.

"Because you have a habit of burning the messenger, Sir Knight?"

"Those corpses should have been shriven! Purified! It's our holy duty to…"

"It's your holy duty to *shut up*," said Feurio. He turned to me, leaving Uveryn seething. "What do you need, Rhul, to spring your trap?"

I licked my lips, wondering just that. My plan hinged on power, and this ever-so-pious city would have precious little to spare. 'Shriven and purified' long ago, no doubt.

"Relics," I said. "Anything entwined with the legend of the Aemortarch. Books, bones, weapons…"

"Unthinkable!" said Uveryn. He looked almost physically sick. "Unclean hands can never touch it! The pyx of Saint Acanthes must never be opened by the likes of…"

Feurio and his co-commander shot each other a meaningful glance. Mistress Coryne nodded, then stepped out of the tent, the hint of a smile on her lips. Wonders, I supposed, would never cease.

"Acanthes," I said. "Can't say I've heard the name. What was he famous for? Some gruesome martyrdom, no doubt? Involving fire, perhaps?"

Uveryn clenched his fists, his face an ever deeper shade of red, but Silbern Chaar was already behind him. Her immense broadsword rasped across his chestplate as she settled it in the hollow of his throat, gripping it tight by both hilt and blade. Feurio's alchemical gauntlets clicked, and he pointed one short black tube right at the Paladyne's face.

"He was a farmboy, Rhul," said the Faeroan halfblood. "At least, until he found something out here, after the Desolation. A relic which gave him holy visions, through the Aemortarch's eyes. He recounted ninety-nine scrolls, despite being an illiterate serf – he even has his own gospel. What he found was put into a small stone chest, then entrusted to a chapel…"

"Until finally, a pig-headed bunch of knights – who should have been protecting the living – dragged it all the way up this very hill, in the middle of a pitched battle, simply because it seemed like the godly thing to do," finished Silbern. "Isn't that right, Uveryn?"

The Paladyne would have murdered the lot of us with the fury in his eyes alone – if he'd been any kind of sorcerer. As it was, his ruddy face trembled with barely controlled wrath.

"Twenty men died to protect the holy pyx, *heretic*," he whispered, all cold iron. "Don't mock their sacrifice. Don't give in to this monster."

"Can you really do what you claim?" asked Feurio.

"Given enough power. Aye."

"Then the *monster* gets what he wants. I'd tell you, Uveryn, why this stranger from Kaltensund deserves a little more of your respect. But I don't think you could handle the truth of it. Not tonight, in any case."

"Then I have failed," said the Paladyne, his anger turning grim. "The last of my order, and our vows are to be shattered by those we sought to protect. Let me go, then, Zahfrey. I want no part of your dark alliance."

"You think him a fool?" asked Silbern. "As soon as I let you out of this chair…"

It had taken me this long to notice it, but there was something in the Greatsword's voice when she talked about her Commander. The way she flicked a glance at him, eyes sparkling blue… Oh, by all the Gods and demons! I wondered if Feurio Zahfrey was even capable of comprehending feelings beyond rage and guilt.

"As soon as you take your sword from my throat, lady, I will seek redemption. I will walk amongst the ghuldren, and take as many of them to the Lamenter's Gates as I can, before the end. At least *their* motives are pure."

Feurio buried his face in his blood-crusted gauntlets.

"Fine. *All right.* But don't think I didn't warn you." He looked up, grinning madly, and pointed one armoured finger at me. "That's your Aemortarch. *There's* no such person as Rhul the Kaltensunder! That's

Kuhal Moer, son of Hurik the Scalptaker, Doom of Urexes, Lord of Ark's Shadow, the Lamenter in Bones and Ashes. *Him*. And you know the best part? *I don't even believe in him!*"

Everyone in the tent looked at me, goggle-eyed.

I shrugged.

"I came out of the Desolation for… for reasons of my own. But your need is great. Your worship has wrought things wrong in the world. Endsong lives, and I must, it seems, dig his grave a little deeper."

"This? THIS?" Uveryn was back to his usual boiling point of rage. "Twenty of my sworn brothers died this night, for *this thing*? Your jest is in poor grace, Zahfrey! I should…"

"The contents of the pyx, Paladyne. Have they ever been revealed?"

Uveryn looked at me, his lip curled into a sneer of contempt.

"Only to my brotherhood. But I won't speak of powers you cannot comprehend, impostor. I'm not as easily duped as your drunken Guildmaster!"

Silbern cursed. Her sword pricked a razor line of blood from Uveryn's throat.

"Within the stone box," I said, "Is a small rabbit-skin pouch. About the size of a skirmisher's sling-bag. And within the pouch lie the bones of a domestic cat – a Khytein snow-lynx, to be precise. His left front fang is chipped. The bones seem polished smooth, as if by flowing water."

Uveryn made a strangled choking sound. I'm sure it had nothing to do with Silbern's blade.

"How…"

The truth was, I could feel the presence inside Saint Acanthes' Pyx, even as Guild Commander Coryne carried it into the pavilion. Meteoric iron calls like to like, shards of metal pulled together by unseen forces. So it was with my familiar and I, who had been missing each other for three long centuries.[9]

I never got a chance to explain.

The horns bellowed their bleak warning even as I felt tiny claws scrabbling at the underside of the pyx's lid. Silbern and Feurio looked at each other and nodded, grim-faced.

---

9. I had tried to find Sei, of course. I had sent out shades and wraiths, things like clouds of smoke with only one thought in their gaseous little heads. But this explained my lack of success. The poor feline had been wrapped up in rune-carved stone, the relic of an idiot saint. Even things made of shadow and memory can't insinuate their way past brute, stupid faith.

"They're coming. The final attack. We need to start moving those civilians!"

But it wasn't the one-note blare of the horns which drove me to my feet. Uveryn clutched at the sleeve of my tabard as I passed, his face white as whey.

"Forgive me, Lord! I have failed you! I have…"

"Then this is your penance," I snarled. "No glorious suicide for you! You will obey Feurio Zahfrey to his merest whim. You will hold the rearguard, until those tunnels come down. And you will survive this battle, for I have need of men like you. Tell me – is Oram the only city where I am worshiped?"

"No, Lamenter! Your faith has spread far and wide! All of Sarem…"

I groaned a curse in Old Korisali. Decades ago, it would have blistered the varnish on the table. Now… nothing.

"We will talk soon, Paladyne. Do not fail me again!"

All those chapels, all those cathedrals, all those monasteries and shrines… were they all as corrupt as the Tabernacle of Oram? Were men like Deacon Fell coiled like maggots at the heart of all my holy places? It would make sense, if Dirge had orchestrated the entire farce. All of Sarem! And all, no doubt, suffering the Doom of the ghuldren as well.

The presence which weighed heavy on my thoughts all but confirmed it. It blazed with dark unlife, a twisted web of geometric patterns, threads of fire wrapped around toothed wheels, pain and duty bound around a core of cruelty…

I pushed past Silbern, Feurio and Coryne, out into the courtyard of the Guild Bastion. Just in time to see the wall of clouds to the north part, ripped top to bottom like a curtain. The Stormreaper's ship slipped through that boiling wound in the sky, slick as an assassin's knife, sails bellying tight against the wind. Whatever damage Slaughtermaw had wrought was repaired, and the witch's crew now swarmed the rigging, trimming sail to bring the whole great wooden edifice in low over the city.

It was the thing perched upon the bowspirit which drew my gaze, though, narrowing it down to a dark tunnel of horror. Robed and hooded in pale, creamy-coloured leather, belted with chain… a tall, thin figure framed by a pair of draken wings, flared wide from its shoulders. It was armed with a pair of flails, and as it raised them to the heavens I saw the red blaze of its eyes, deep within a ragged-edged cowl.

If I had thought the Stormreaper our ally, all such hopes were crushed. If I had discounted rumours of her infamy as mere superstitious ignorance, then I was thoroughly re-educated.

For the thing which now leaped from the bows of the Stormreaper's ship was known to me. I had read the Tomes of Making, deep in the forges of Urzen the Mad. I had witnessed the undoing of fully seven of this creature's kin.

The black jewel at my throat pulsed with power. It seemed it wasn't just my familiar's soul which called like to like.

"What in all Hells…." breathed Silbern, watching the figure fall. Its wings unfurled with a double crack of leather, sending it wheeling over the ruined jumble of tenements in the shadow of the walls.

My voice was hollow as I answered.

"One of the Nine, Silbern Chaar. Something I thought long dead. Makara wounded it at the battle of Urexes, but it seems to be hale enough."

The cold, doomed hatred of the demon churned my stomach. It was seeking, seeking… and the horror it would unleash when it found its prey would be *apocalyptic*. This latter age had not witnessed such vile sorcery.

"One of the *Nameless?* I thought…"

"This one lives. And now we are damned in truth. I'm afraid our friend the Stormreaper has brought us the attention of the Burning Dark."

Up above us, the draken-winged demon screamed – a sound like saws cutting bone. From the city below, Slaughtermaw's bellow answered it.

Perhaps, I thought, Paladyne Uveryn's idea of noble suicide was the best any of us could hope for.

Perhaps we would have little choice.

You know, they used to have cannons which were primed with the sacred bones of dead men. Back in olden times, when sorcerers wandered about, making such things. Foolish, really. Cannons exist to make the dead men - not to use them up!"

Master gunner Harlaw Chaldonis,
Artificer of the Guild of Chains.

KTH'ALA VRYESSE. CONSECRATED *Instrument of Aesurn, Herald of the Solar Halo, the Right Hand of Flame* – these were the Burning Dark's names before its fall. Taken by the legions of Anganesse, forced to watch his priesthood crucified, the great Ziggurat of the Eclipse in Rasuul's capital torn down by Keels... the Consecrated One was dragged to Korisal in a casket of bronzewood and lead, his power shackled by a whole chantry of Esau's faithful.

There, Urzen the Mad subjected him to experiments which would one day find their fullest fruition in the creation of That Which Walks. Experiments of flesh and fire which left him both more and less than human.

Which is not to say that poor Consecrated Instrument Vryesse didn't suffer. Oh no.

His suffering was *legendary*, even in a land of such creative brutality as old Sarem. Flayed and bound in sorcerous stasis, the poor doomed wretch was a walking illumination of anatomy, a crusted scab with pain-filled eyes the colour of blood. And that was *before* Urzen began augmenting him for demonhood. Before he became the last conduit to the dying fires of Aesurn, a sun-God without worshipers, scrabbling against the terminal dusk of the Outer Dark...

The Shard of the Sun is powerful indeed. In other lands, in other times, Aziphem aligned to the solar halo have utterly dominated the pantheon. But now Aesurn was just an echo, a lost sacred name, his betrayed fury channelled through the form of the thing which swept down on us, alighting atop the Guild Bastion with a clap of vast black wings.

Soldiers atop the wall were already firing wildly into the onrushing ghuldren. But I didn't take my eyes off the flail-wielding Nameless as I scaled the spiral stair to the battlements. I didn't have to. The very presence of the Burning Dark made Makara's soul-gem seethe with energy, stabbing filaments of power clear through my chest. I drew on

110

it, and freed my familiar from his tomb.

Behind me, a resounding crack was followed by some very creative Faeroan swearing. I surmised from this that Feurio's father had stayed sober long enough to teach him the rudiments of their language. And that my little pet, Sei, had decided the pyx of Saint Acanthes was a mite too restrictive.

The Burning Dark looked down at me as Sei's tiny sharp claws skittered across the courtyard and up the stairs. He pointed at me with one flayed, bloody finger.

"Kuhal Moer. My mistress has need of you. Alive. Come with me now, and there will be no need for... unpleasantness."

Sei scrambled up to my shoulder, hissing, arching his clean-picked spine. The thing's voice twisted in my mind like fish-hooks, dry and cold as hoarfrost. I nodded.

"Well, seeing as *you're* here, Nameless, things are quite unpleasant enough. I can't see how they could get much worse…"

Fate made a fool of me again. Slaughtermaw must have reached the Bastion's iron-banded doors, for a shuddering impact rocked the entire castle, sending men scrambling forward with baulks of timber.

"Your capture cannot be risked, necromancer. Endsong's shard must not be made whole. I ask you again – will you spare me the need for slaughter?"

There was no way I could strike the horror down. At the height of my powers, clad in armour of bone and wielding the full might of the Incantus, I had barely managed to defeat its lesser sibling, the scourge called Sister Pain. But that didn't mean I couldn't bluff outrageously.

"You do what you have to do, demon," I growled, raising Cryptfeeder to guard. I prayed the Nameless One couldn't see the trembling in my hands. "And as for my *capture* – between yourself and dear old Slaughtermaw, I'm not sure who I'd rather choose."

The Burning Dark had attracted some attention, perched with one fist clenched around the Bastion's highest flagpole. Some sword-saga hero came charging up onto the roof, blade held high, and the demon didn't even grace him with a glance as it swung its flail, utterly macerating the man from the waist up. Crossbow quarrels punctured its pale leather robes, but they burst into flames as soon as they struck home, flashing into ashes. A pair of legs tottered on the edge of the turret, then fell, trailing smoke.

"You always were a cruel one, Khytein. Very well. I will try to make this as quick as possible. Then you will come to kneel before my mistress.

This I can assure you."

"Kuhal!" shouted Feurio from the courtyard below. "How do we kill it? Come on, lad, there has to be a way!"

Ghuldren were scaling the parapets now. Grey, rotting hands scrabbled at the merlons as soldiers hacked and cursed. The inner walls were dripping black blood, pattering from between the boards of the bowman's walks. Muffled screams came from under the Bastion, as thousands of panicked refugees were herded lower, into the secret reaches of the Guild's labyrinth.

Then Slaughtermaw took his mace to the gates again, splintering the half-span-thick timbers. Prayers scattered like snowflakes before a gale.

I closed my eyes tight, casting my senses out, searching for power. *Anything.* Any shred…

But there was nothing. Without sacrificing Makara or Sei, there was nothing I could do. And without them, without a thread back to my past…

The Burning Dark stepped off its tower perch, wings spread wide to bathe us all in shadow. Now I could see with my own eyes the horrors which Urzen's tomes spoken of. The fallen sorcerer's robes were not pale leather, but *human skin* – his own flayed and cured hide, stitched up with the tattooed backs, arms and chests of his inner coven. His cowl was fashioned from eyeless, empty faces, and beneath this grisly raiment he was utterly naked – peeled and bleeding, each ligament and tendon as fresh as meat on a butcher's slab of ice. The wings which flared from his shoulders punched out through ragged tears in his robe of skin – draken wings shorn from an adolescent, for those of a full-gown sire would have been far too large. The flails in his hands were the ceremonial instruments of Aesurn, heavy brass handles with triple-chained, octagonal heads, each one glowing white-hot.

He was a man no more. *He* was an *it* – a weapon of sorcerous destruction.

As the demon's shadow fell upon me, I consigned myself to death. If not in a sudden, incinerating rush, than surely at the leisure of the Stormreaper… for a witch in Dirge's service was not likely to have a working grasp of mercy.

But the death-blow never came. The Burning Dark swooped low over the courtyard – just out of the reach of Silbern Chaar's sword – then alighted atop the wall, wings flared out behind it in a scaled half-dome. Kth'ala Vryesse turned his head left, then right, and the Guild soldiers who had been working up the courage to charge him wavered into full-blown retreat.

Wings curved into a dish-shaped shield, facing down the hill into the ruins of Oram. The golden chain slipped loose from around the demon's waist...

And I suddenly remembered why Urzen had used the wings of draken to build this monstrosity. *Beasts immune to fire...*

I threw myself to the ground at the last instant, leaving Sei to witness what happened next.

The inside of the Nameless One's robe was utterly black. But this was not the darkness of the void – the terrible, hungry emptiness which had been at the heart of That Which Walks. This was a hot, seething blackness, like the sun at its eclipse – shadowed, but ravenous. A furnace which burned light itself, leaving only invisible heat to lash out in waves.

A firestorm assailed the ghuldren and their master. Shimmering, shadowy waves of force came rippling out from the inside of Kth'ala Vryesse's raiment to crack the cobblestones, evaporating puddles to superheated steam. Ghouls caught in the beam of sunfire simply froze where they stood before their flesh detonated from their bones, swirling away as a cloud of sparks and ashes. Then even those fused, blackened twigs cracked and scattered, thrown back as a hail of charcoal.

Slaughtermaw caught a flickering eddy of heat and curled up into a ball, flesh blistering even as the Thane tried to scramble for cover. Its roar of outrage became a squealing scream as it burned, but it reached a barricade of toppled stone, crabbing over it beneath a pall of smoke.

The Burning Dark swept its hatred across the hillside in a single cataclysmic outpouring of power, combusting the ruins as far away as the city walls. Any survivors under that blowtorch would have at least known swift mercy, I supposed.

When the demon finally furled its wings, letting the blast falter and die, the winding road to the Bastion was gone. Kharnath's ring of trilithons stood at the top of a perfectly smooth slope of glass, crazed and cracked with shadows. I realised, with dread and awe, that these were the final despairing poses of a hundred thousand ghuldren, their hands thrown up to protect their sightless eyes.

"It... it's on our side, then?" asked Feurio, picking himself up from the courtyard. "The damned thing is one of *ours*?"

I grimaced.

"Not one of ours, Zahfrey. The Nine are no friends of… well, of *anything*, to tell it true. I suspect they would even have butchered Dirge, given half the chance."

"So we try to kill it, then?" Silbern sounded almost eager.

"We could try to *run*, I suppose. But the fact that it used those wings to shield us from the backdraft – that suggests an uncharacteristic shred of mercy. I think we should let it try Slaughtermaw on for size, and then…"

"I won't even look back," said the Guild Commander. "But *you* – you're the one it's here for."

"Then I suppose I'm with Uveryn in the rearguard." I shrugged my shoulders. Sei wrapped his tail around my neck, purring. "He'll hate that, of course. Which makes it all the more important that I survive."

The Burning Dark stood atop the wall, still as an oversized gargoyle. I realised, piecing together scraps of memory from Urzen's tomes, that it was *cooling* – that if it moved too suddenly after such an unveiling it would likely crack and shatter. Most of its bones had been replaced with rods of steel and copper, after all.

Feurio thrust his sword between the cobbles and reached under his tabard. His hand reappeared holding a leather bottle, marked with a surprising number of skulls and bones.

"The hells with it all, then." he said, pulling the cork with his teeth. "I never wanted to feel what it was like to be fifty, in any case. Aching joints, greying hair… the sages can keep their wisdom." He held the bottle out to me, and against my better judgment I took it. One swig, and I was sure that my back teeth had been stripped of all enamel. Two, and I ceased to care.

"You're not serious."

"Deadly," he replied, knocking back a draught. It took a couple of wild swings for him to find the hilt of his sword.

Silbern Chaar looked at both of us as if we'd gone insane.

"It *would* give them all the best chance to escape. But…"

"Just take the bottle, girl. You want to become a sad old crone? Or do you want to die killing something worthwhile?"

The Ontokhi lass looked about ready to slap Feurio's head from his shoulders. But then she grabbed the leather bottle and took a heroic swallow.

"Lamenter's balls!" she sputtered. "Your pardon, of course… But what in the name of all Hells did you *distill* that from, Zahfrey?"

"Credit to Mister Dalross for that, Silbern. I gather you're with us?"

I hefted Cryptfeeder. With Sei awake and at my side, I had a little of my old vigour back. Enough to be as hale as a normal, mortal man, at least. Which gave me pause. I had seen what Slaughtermaw had done to thousands of hale and normal men. The results had been… graphic.

All this time the Burning Dark had been perched above us on the wall, watching the ruins. Now it turned to regard us, its red eyes smouldering.

"While I find your conversation entertaining," it said, *"Your deliberations are pointless. I have decided that thing you call Slaughtermaw offends me. I will finish it, and then you, Warlock, will come with me. There can be no argument."*

"No argument." I nodded. "But how about a *deal*, demon? Let's put all our cards on the table. I'm betting you gave that motherless bastard everything you had. And it's *still alive*. So here's my offer. Give me enough vitae to fight beside you, and give me the Thane's heart when we tear it down. *Together*. Then I'll come with you willingly."

Both Silbern and Feurio looked ready to protest, but I simply shook my head.

"We still have to save those townsfolk, Commander. Even if our friend here destroys Slaughtermaw – and that's a *big* if – Oram is rife with ghouls. Better it were their pyre than their stronghold."

The Burning Dark flexed its wings with a creak of desiccated tendons.

"What gives you such faith in the beast, Warlock? What do you know that my mistress does not?"

I looked deep into the Nameless One's eyes, feeling the amulet at my throat thump like a living heart.

"Don't you taste it, Nameless? The spoor of your old master? Jerrold Sinder rides Slaughtermaw's soul, and his is a power which you cannot face alone."

The Burning Dark trembled, licking its flayed lips.

"That name, Kuhal Moer! Long years have passed since I have heard it. And still the hatred burns in me. If you lie…"

"About this? Please! He was my foe while you still licked the shit from his boots, Kth'ala Vryesse. No vengeance falls on him or his without my blade blooded."

I held that red and sullen gaze. All eyes were on me as the soldiers of the Guild waited for me to break. But I had stared down horrors worse than the forsaken priest of Aesurn.

"Very well. I acknowledge your right. But if you fall, know this. My mistress can make use of you, dead or alive. Dead… may simply prove considerably less comfortable."

I swallowed, hard. Comfort is often a relative term. But the thing addressing me had been bloody and skinless for well over three hundred years. There was no time for fear. No time, even, for its shadow. I crushed my horror down deep, and I grinned.

"Enough empty threats. Do we have a pact, Nameless? By the anvil of Korisal which birthed you, and the hands of Urzen which gave you life?"

The Burning Dark flinched as if struck when it heard those names. But it hissed, wing-scales clattering, and it extended its hand, letting one of its flails fall.

"Take this weapon, Lamenter. Wring it dry. We will butcher Dirge's beast, and then we will talk again. Now, the time for words is finished."

I stooped to pick the heavy flail up. Little sparks of power sizzled up my arms, making the hairs on the back of my neck stand to attention.

The Nameless One was right. The time for words was definitely over.

From beyond the walls came a rumbling bellow of rage – then a howl, torn from hundreds of thousands of decaying throats. Slaughtermaw lived, and it had tasted pain. All the beating had achieved was to make the Thane angry.

"Soldiers of the Guild!" roared Feurio, brandishing his blade. "I vow to finish this, once and for all! When those gates open, who will stand with me?"

Earlier, Zahfrey had joked about the men of the Thirteenth following us into the Hells. Now, when he asked the last defenders of Oram to do just that, he was met with a battle-shout which drowned out the ghuldren's fury. That – and a strangled fit of laughter.

"Oh, we'll follow you, Feurio Zahfrey," came a dry, cracked voice. A gaggle of white-robed artificers parted, letting an ancient greybeard totter forward. He leaned heavily on a long brass staff, wincing. "Most of these men have families below, you know. Either that, or they *had* families down in the lower city. Vengeance or pragmatism. Either will do at a pinch."

With a start I realised that this was Master Quenlon – the man who I had last seen choking down calming tinctures in the grasp of his minders. Now there was a spark of defiance in his eyes, and his wits had been gathered afresh. He pointed up at the Burning Dark, his lips pulled back from a set of yellowed ivory dentures.

"Nice trick, son. Very… hmm… *focused* display of thermodynamics. But sloppy. Wasteful. What you do with sorcery, we can achieve with science. Ought to make those ghuldren think twice, eh?"

Even the Burning Dark looked shocked. Perhaps because nobody had called the Nameless thing 'son' for more than seven lifetimes.

"Bold words, ancient. But it was the Old Science of Korisal which made me. Do you think yourself the equal of Urzen the Mad?"

"Anyone who got 'the mad' tacked onto his name can't have been all that bright," cackled Quenlon. "Come on then lads! Throw off those sailcloths! Let them see our handiwork! The masterpiece of Quenlon the Crazed!"

Artificers swarmed over the huge covered wagon I had seen earlier, loosing ropes and stays. Layers of oiled canvas slithered to the cobbles, revealing a many-barrelled iron monstrosity, its six muzzles forged in the image of draken skulls.

"The steam pressure is optimum, Lord," said one of the white-robed men. "Temperature is holding. We are ready on your mark."

"Open the damned gates then, Zahfrey!" said Quenlon, hobbling forward. His staff chimed against the wet stones as he made for the wagon, then clambered up a series of ladders to a padded banker's chair atop the hissing, rattling engine. "Come on, man! Some of us might die of old age if you keep us waiting!"

"Does anyone know what it *does?*" hissed Silbern under her breath.

"No idea" shrugged Feurio. "But at this point, does it matter? I gather it's supposed to kill people. That's good enough for me."

The howl of the ghuldren was rising. Men on the walls readied their crossbows, lighting the fuses on the few alchemical munitions we had left. The ground trembled as Slaughermaw lumbered up to the charge, giving vent to his own mindless roar.

"*Soldiers of the Guild, form up!*" shouted Feurio. A straggle of tired, scorched and bloodied veterans surged forward, shields up, blades flashing in the chill dawnlight. "Lock shields to the fore. Pikemen to the second and third ranks. Sergeants of the Ninth and Eleventh, take your orders from Coryne, and hold the left. The rest of you, with me on the right. Give Quenlon's Artificers a clear line of fire…"

I could hear the meaty thumps of ghuldren throwing themselves against the bastion walls now. Ranks closed around me, and I was surprised to see that the man at my shoulder was Dalross, his green hood thrown back, a long spear clenched in his hands.

"Out of powder, Rhul," he said, by way of explanation. "Have to do this the hard way. All the times that bastard Zahfrey made me practice with this thing, I never thought…”

“Oh aye,” I replied. “And if you had seen this mess coming, would you have signed up for the Guild at all?”

The little ’chemist grinned.

“It wasn’t a case of *signing up*, Northman. It was a case of collapsing number three shaft in the Long Hallows mine with a little youthful experimentation…”

Men were at the gates now, wrapping lengths of wrist-thick chain around their forearms. Bolts slid and locked, priming the huge oiled hinges.

“FOR ORAM! FOR VENGEANCE! RELEASE THE GATES!”

The bolt came loose with a clang like the door of Anghul’s oven. And they were upon us.

Slaughtermaw came in swinging wild, a two handed sweep of its mace which would likely have shattered the gates to matchwood. But the great Thane wasn’t ready for them to be thrown open. It stumbled, off-balance, reeling into the space between the two wings of Guildsmen. The great brass ram scored a deep groove in the cobbles, throwing up a sheet of sparks. Around the Thane, between its tree-trunk legs, the ghuldren surged forward, gibbering and moaning, hands crooked into claws.

They charged the muzzles of Artificer Quenlon’s engine, as ignorant of its purpose as were the rest of us. At least, until the madly cackling old greybeard threw some terminal lever, setting gears and belts into motion. Then…

I have seen the cataclysmic unleashing of sorceries, fit to level whole cities. I have witnessed the madness of Gods, and the horrors of genocidal war. But the thunder of Quenlon’s six-barreled cannon in the narrow confines of the Bastion court was perhaps the most bowel-loosening experience of my long, long life. A good thing, then, that I was technically dead – and as such, had needed neither privy nor chamber-pot for centuries.

The barrels spun, and as they reached the top of their rotation they were met by spring-loaded hammers. Each hammer-blow loosed a red-hot blast of metal shards, an overlapping storm of shrapnel fanning out to rake the courtyard clean. The cobblestones were chewed to fragments as the old Artificer turned a hand-crank by his side, tracking upward – then the ghuldren which had crowded in around Slaughtermaw were simply *gone*, scythed away by a hideous tearing wind. Black blood painted the inner walls ten spans high, and still the guns ground on, steam hissing and governor-valves spinning. Now that devouring storm tracked up the Thane's legs, flaying them raw. Now it gnawed at its belly, sending the creature stumbling back. Through it all, the soldiers of the Guild of Chains simply stared slack-jawed – and I believe that the Burning Dark did too. Here was a power which surpassed that of its long-dead brothers. *Here was an end to sorcery as the prime force in the nations of Yrde...*

At least, until the mechanism jammed.

A spring cut loose, shearing some vital bolt. Cogs meshed, screaming. Steam popped rivets with backed-up pressure.

"Oh, shi..." began Master Quenlon – but he never got to finish.

Slaughtermaw reached out with one hand, mashing a pile of shredded ghuldren between its fingers. It was already rising as it stuffed them whole into its chest-gullet, and its flesh and skin were stitched up in a web of scars as it brought its mace back over its head, hundreds of eyes blazing.

The mace came down in an unstoppable arc. Quenlon stood from his chair, defiant in its shadow.

"Do it then, you dead bastard! You think I'm young enough to fear you?"

Then the Burning Dark was between them, moving so fast that it seemed to flicker into existence right atop the smoking barrels of the gun. Kth'ala Vryesse held but a single one of his flails, but that was enough to check the arch-ghoul's swing, sending a radial shockwave of power tearing across the courtyard. The whole bastion shifted. Stone ground on stone. Men were thrown from their feet, cursing.

"This engine is for the future, grave-spawn," spat the Nameless. *"For tomorrow. But for you – thereis no tomorrow. Just now. And now... you die!"*

A backhand blow deformed Slaughtermaw's antlered skull. The whole great bulk of the Thane spun on its axis in the air before it slapped the cobbles, hard.

I felt the other sacred flail of Aesurn grow warm in my hand. *Heavy*, somehow, as if the consecrated metal was weighed down with the chains of the setting sun. Visions exploded behind my eyes, filling the empty spaces inside me, where the power of Zael Kataphraxis had once burned.

I saw a figure in armour of gold, a great white jade disc bound to his brow, hanging by his fingertips over a dark abyss. Things seethed and coiled down there, thousands of spans below, and they were things which I recognized. The nightmares of the Outer Dark.

There were no words. The fallen God looked at me, eyes filled with pain. I saw the coils of thorny black vines which punched through his chest, straggling down into the darkness. I felt the power which they poured into Kth'ala Vryesse, the Burning Dark. And I watched as Aesurn slowly, painfully unhooked one hand from the lip of the fall. How long he had held himself there I could not know, but there were four finger-sized grooves in the stone, and dried runnels of blood stained the lip of the precipice.

That gnarled hand clutched thorns. Spikes of glistening darkness punched through wrist and palm. Eyes widened with pain, blazing like the halo of the sun at its eclipse.

I saw the shard itself, at the last, as Aesurn tore a serpentine snarl of thorns from his own ribcage. Clotted, unformed chunks of flesh came with them, blood gouting crimson, feathered away to mist as it fell. *The shard of the sun, and one facet of it, shrunken to a sliver... closing...*

We struck at the same time – the very instant my eyes snapped open. I found myself already committed to a wild, reckless leap, the triple-head of Aesurn's flail scoring razorcuts of white across the world behind it.

"When you are done... kill it. Kill that thing which was once my favoured son. Please..."

The words of a dying Aziphem echoed in my mind for the second time that day. Grim tidings, indeed. And an even more grim task before me...

The flails struck home with a detonation which drove Slaughtermaw back against the bastion's gatehouse, smashing the stones asunder. The crack of hundreds of bones breaking at once rang out as the Thane's shoulder exploded, spraying rotting tissue. I swung low, pulverizing its left knee, ripping the joint to ruin, and the arch-ghoul bellowed, thrashing as it fell.

But its children surged forward, clambering over its fallen bulk, and now Feurio and Coryne loosed their legions, closing the trap with a rippling flash of steel. Battlecries turned to screams. My ears rang with the aftershock of alchemical explosions. The air was full of blinding, choking dust, smelling of shit, brimstone and blood.

I was left shaken by the power of Aesurn. Power not so much given as *forced through* me, the only available conduit. And had my ally, the demon, heard the price his God had demanded?

Apparently not.

"*Before it heals, Khytein.*" it grated. "*We press our attack. I will scourge it with fire, and you… weave your necromancy. Take it apart from within.*"

There was no time to explain my sorcerous impotence. Or, indeed, that an unveiling of such power would only heal the beast. The Nameless leaped into the air, wings thrashing through a pall of dust. As Slaughtermaw tried to rise it threw back the folds of its flayed-skin robe, and a shimmering bolt of heat licked out, furious and raving. The Thane squealed, writhing in pain. But it was healing even as it suffered, drinking in the power from the Nameless One's attack.

This close, it's occultiphage hunger was stronger.

And there was *nothing I could do*. I waded toward the fallen beast, cursing in dead tongues, my borrowed flail battering back scores of ghouls, reducing them to charcoal and ashes with each swing. But sorcery – *my* sorcery – was woven from the witchfire of souls. And Slaughtermaw's puppets had none.

Feurio, Silbern and their men couldn't help me. Tens of thousands of ghuldren swarmed the bastion from all sides now, and the last few defenders fell behind me, far away, a half-circle of steel around the keep's inner doors. Through them, down in the serpentine maze of the rock's labyrinth, the last survivors of Oram were packed tight, a jostling, praying throng fleeing through darkness.

If I faltered now, they all would die.

So I did the one thing I could. I reached out to Zael again, hearing his ghostly laughter, feeling his armoured talons clench deep into my mind.

And I wove the fires lit by Kth'ala Vryesse's fury, swirling them up into whirlwinds of flame. Hungry firespouts tore through the close-packed ghuldren, whipping them up into the air as they disintegrated. Stones cracked and melted to magma under the lash of this unveiling. I balanced the desperate extremity of Aesurn on my left with the vengeful hate of Zael on my right, and their coming together put the Burning Dark to shame.

I'm told I screamed the whole time, like a man under the torture irons. I'm told that even the ghuldren tried to run from that lost, forsaken sound.

I stood at the centre of a red-hot maelstrom, hands outstretched and blazing until I could see the bones within them. Blood-red energy sizzled and arced, mocking the purity of lightning.

"You are mine now, little mortal!" gloated the God chained beneath my tower. "Mine! *And the facet you stole from me will be mine as well, as soon as you* burn!"

I forgot a hundred years of study and solitude as the curtain-wall of the bastion ceased to exist. On either side of Slaughtermaw twin pyroclasms burst out, stone turned to liquid and driven like horizontal sleet through an army of corpses. I lost the better part of my short and squalid childhood to Zael's hunger, sending one whirlwind lashing through the Thane's icy wards, drilling toward its heart. He took the names of my brothers. He took my loneliness and my pride. Decades of lovelorn occult research went up in smoke, forged into a hell-storm around me. But the foul thing *choked*. Too much power. Even occultiphage demons have their limits, after all.

I felt the years blazing like paper in a forge, memories blackening around the edges and bursting into flames. The fire skipped ahead of me, gleefully tearing into my mind, threads of liquid radiance dripping and pooling, surrounding the inviolate core of my self.

(eyes, her eyes burning, her eyes melting her face charred and blistered, smiling)

I only just managed to stop it.

The final wards broke just as the firestorm blew apart, and I stood at Slaughtermaw's feet, his body stretched prone before me on a bed of blackened stone. The Burning Dark knew no hesitation – it folded its wings and stooped into a dive, flail hissing through the air…

Only to be met by the half-melted, red-hot bulk of the arch-ghoul's mace.

It swept the Nameless One from the sky, crushing him to the ground with a sickening crack. I knew just how strong those forge-crafted bones were, and I winced. Slaughtermaw roared. It struggled to sit upright, but its flesh had fused to the stone in healing, melting and knitting into a half-cooked, blistered web of skin and muscle. It raised its mace again, then brought it down, driving the Burning Dark into the dirt, three spans deep.

Slaughtermaw had drunk Urzen's creation dry. It had nothing left with which to save itself.

Best that it had ignored me, then. Just one of those blows would have snuffed out my life in an instant. I was reeling on my feet, spots of darkness swimming behind my eyes. I felt like a full-body bruise – like the centuries-old corpse I was.

I let the flail of Aesurn fall from my numbed fingers – spent. I tried to draw Cryptfeeder, but I couldn't even jerk the steel clear of its scabbard. There was power in me, certainly – power raging and churning, like liquor in a drunkard's guts – but my flesh had simply given up. The mageblight in me throbbed, driving me to my knees.

It was not really the best place to fall.

I heard a sick, wet cracking sound as the Thane's belly split. Tendrils of flesh snapped taut as its mouth gaped, jagged with teeth. Then the thing's tongue came slithering toward me, its lopped-off stump budding with eyes.

What could I do but die? *I was Rhul, the orphan of a trader clan, a lost Kaltensunder child fallen into horrors. I was thirteen-year-old Kuhal Moer, a feckless youth whose father despaired, shamed by his son's lack of muscle and fury. I was confused, and lost, and as that writhing tongue came coiling around my leg, I couldn't even remember the name of the girl I was about to die for.*

For some reason, that made me extremely angry.

I reached out and grabbed the Thane's tongue with both hands, snarling. Out of the boiling soup of my mind came a single memory – one which shattered even as the image formed in my head. It was a picture of a ghostly cat, its eyes like liquid amber, its body picked out in blue-green fire. *Once, long ago, I had known this creature's name. Once, it had sat on my chest and spoken to me, in the voice of a long-lost Warbard of my people. Aeron... Esric... his name was...*

"Aerik Stormsong," I slurred. "And *your* name was Sei. I called you *vengeance*. They made a holy relic out of you! Oh, the shame of it!"

Slaughtermaw's tongue twitched in my hands, trying to reel me in. But I dug my fingernails in hard, pricking blood from the corded rope of muscle. Sei was at my shoulder, a tiny, perfect skeleton outlined in wisps of green light. He rubbed his smooth skull up against my cheek, then leaped down, feather-soft, to land between my hands.

Slaughtermaw thrashed, pulling its belly-tongue tight. And that was all the invitation Sei needed.

The little cat skittered along its fleshy tight-rope, quick as an arrow from a bow. Before the fallen Thane could react he had slipped between a double row of teeth and eyes, plunging into the cavity of Slaughtermaw's chest.

But not to be devoured. Oh no.

Zael Kataphraxis may have been able to push his bloody thumbs through the meat of my brain, but the instincts of my familiar were unerring. Sei knew all about the Incantus Instrumentorum – that intricate caging of iron and gold which I'd used to animate hundreds of dead men at once. The knot of power at Slaughtermaw's heart was a mockery of the Incantus, grown like a tumour within. Tiny teeth and claws gouged and shredded. Ligaments snapped, destabilizing forces bound in blood.

And I saw.

Through the welter of ruin inside the Thane, I saw how the Doom had been created. Not by binding the souls of the dead back to their bones, then incanting pacts of servitude and release – for all its horror, such necromancy was *clean*. This... this was partly the artifice of Urzen, and partly a twisted mockery of Death's Shard. Tens of thousands of souls... flayed, stripped and woven together, into a mindless, hungry melange – a microcosm of the Outer Dark. That was the heart of Slaughtermaw, and spectral chains burst forth from it like spiderwebs, plunging into wounds in reality, barbed hooks twitching at their ends.

Those hooks were anchored in the flesh of the ghuldren.

Now the whole shuddering mound of the Thane was coming apart. Rotting bodies sloughed away from where they had been bound into Slaughtermaw's form, bones reshaped and tangled like the branches of graveyard trees. Crudely stitched flaps of hide split at their seams, leaking foul fluids. And still Sei worried and gnawed at the roots of the Thane's heart. The rope of muscle and sinew I held came loose in my hands, tearing off at the roots.

"What's the matter," I asked nobody in particular. "Cat got your tongue?"

I laughed at my little joke, and realised that I was balanced on the knife's-edge of hysteria.

I tottered to my feet. One step, and my whole leg disappeared in the dissolving stew of Slaughtermaw, all the way to the knee. The next step was like walking through noisome quicksand, and black, putrid filth slopped away in my wake.

I pushed apart a thicket of chalk–brittle ribs. There was Sei, bloodsoaked and grinning, perched atop a two–span–wide ball of brain tissue, laced with scars. The effect was like some deep–sea coral enfolding a sponge – but one which seethed with barely suppressed power.

I was dimly aware of battle–cries shouted joyously behind me. Trumpets blared, and steel clashed, roaring far away.

I reached out with one finger to touch the Thane's heart. I released the souls of the Ghuldren to oblivion.

The shock of it threw me backward. I tumbled end over end, helpless, until I struck the wall of the inner bastion upside down, driving the air from my lungs. Gasping, all but unconscious, I slithered to the rain–slick cobbles, curled up around my pain.

But the ghuldren fell. I blinked back tears, scrabbling to prop myself up against the wall, and I watched the vengeful solders of the Guild butcher the last of Slaughtermaw's horde, hacking them down without mercy. Not that they would have accepted any. Their eyes were blank, and they stood dazed, uncomprehending as they were taken apart.

Sei found me, what seemed an eternity later. When the sound of metal on meat had faded, and all that remained was the ringing silence of the aftermath. The little skeletal cat came and curled up on my lap, suffused with power, and he tugged at my tabard with his tiny needle teeth.

A shadow fell over me. It was Silbern Chaar, covered head to toe in black blood, her skeletal mask cracked and hinged open.

"So… you survived, then," she said. Her smile was a sad, pale thing. "I thought… but no, of course you didn't. You and your demon friend did what we mortals never could."

There was bitterness in her words, and in her eyes – but fool that I was, I didn't quite grasp the reason why.

"That thing… no friend of mine, Silbern. In fact…" I tried to stand. One of my legs simply wouldn't support my weight, and I slumped back against the wall, biting back a scream. "Could you..?"

The Ontohki greatsword slung my arm around her shoulders, and heaved. I was dragged upright, and I could finally see what remained of Oram's hilltop.

The Bastion's outer ward was in ruins – the wall blown apart, molten twists and jags of stone frozen like fangs where they had cooled. They all pointed outward, like the barbs of some broken crown. The gatehouse was non–existent. What remained of Slaughtermaw smoked and bubbled in a slew of scattered bricks, while the gates themselves were long gone to ashes. And the dead…

"How many?" I croaked, blinking the dust from my eyes.

"Better to ask how many are *left*, wizard," he said. "The Ninth are entirely wiped out. The Eleventh…" she gestured, and I saw a tangled mass of fused, blackened armour, bones still smoking. I groaned, shuddering in her grasp. They had been caught up in my unveiling. Collateral damage – a concept as old as war itself. Not that the fact made me feel any better.

"Coryne died bravely. She held the standard of the Guild against a hundred ghouls. But in the end… well, there is only so much steel and muscle can achieve. You…".

I pushed away from her side, swaying for a moment. My vision reeled, blurring the grey–skinned bodies of the ghuldren, the crimson–spattered armour of the guildsmen…

"And Feurio?" A chill stole up my spine. "What of the Thirteenth?"

Silbern couldn't meet my eyes.

"Gone to join his family, Kuhal Moer. Gone to his long rest. He never believed in you, but if any part of your Book is true, then…"

Sometimes the truth is hard. Other times, it's damned near *impossible*.

"My enemies seem to think I have my own Shard. They think that I've Transcended, but the truth is – well, look around you."

Silbern stiffened, her face growing cold and remote.

"So it was all lies. Hymns and chants and empty words…"

"Perhaps," I sighed. "But… I think there is one who would welcome him."

The Ontohki turned to where I pointed, and her shoulders sagged. The huge, blue-steel blade slipped from her fingers, clattering to the ground. I'm sure she would never forgive me for saying so, but I believe the warrior-maiden was crying. I'll admit I was close to tears myself, though my eyes had dried to the consistency of marble centuries ago.

Transcendence… and perhaps, redemption.

Above Kharnath's ring of standing stones the air boiled and seethed, thousands of pinprick lights dancing like fireflies in a gale. One by one they alighted on the glowing stones, sinking into the swirls of runes carved there. The Old God's passing had left a gateway open, a conduit to the Primordial Shard which was his demesne, and the souls of the dead were pouring through, finding their level like water.

"Kharnath's people believed in an afterlife of plenty," I said. "Feasting, hunting, following the herds – they taught that great warriors would find peace in that shadow realm. And the Primordial Shard is inviolate. The petty wars of lesser Aziphem cannot touch it."

There would be an empty throne within that fragment world now. An endless plain under an older, warmer sun – a world which wrapped around itself, never ending, never beginning. Kharnath's people may just, I mused, have found themselves a new king. One who cared less for bloody sacrifices than the old one.

Silbern turned back to me. Her eyes were red-rimmed, but they blazed with sudden anger.

"The petty wars of the Aziphem? Is *that* all this was? A whole city doomed, thousands dead… and all for a power you claim you *don't even have.*" She spat. "If that's the price of immortality, you can keep it. That and your sordid faith."

I opened my mouth to speak as she walked away, but there was nothing I could say to make things right. Deep down I knew that I had brought this ruin to Oram – simply for the crime of my existence. Not for the first time, I wondered if I had finally become the monster which Dirge had tried to make me.

Sei rubbed up against my leg, mewling.

Ahh, yes. The monster had one last bargain to fulfil.

I hardly remember staggering across the battlefield to where the Burning Dark had fallen. Providence fend, but the unnatural thing had managed to throw aside the bulk of Slaughtermaw's mace, heaving it up and out of the trench where it lay. Had it not, I'm certain there was no way I could have lifted it.

Kth'ala Vryesse was a wrecked and ruined thing – smashed like a spider under a steel-shod boot. The Nameless One's wings were broken and torn, its flayed body half flattened and leaking pale, colourless fluids. When it saw me approach it tried to hold out one hand, fingers all twisted at nightmare angles, but even this entreaty was too much. Its head lolled back, bone and riveted steel exposed, and its eyes flickered shut.

"*I know what Aesurn asked of you,*" it rasped. "*And all I beg of you is this.* Make it quick. *Please. Hold to your bargains, Khytein. Honour is all we take with us into the dark.*"

I unbelted Cryptfeeder, letting the scabbard fall away as I hefted the blade. My fingers fumbled to slot a ring of power into its hilt.

"No regrets, Nameless?" I asked, gently setting the point of the sabre on the demon's sternum. It laughed, coughing up a mixture of blood and alchemical balm.

"*Too many to mention. But my God calls me home, Kuhal Moer. He would choose oblivion rather than madness. And oblivion… is a gift I excel at delivering.*"

I leaned down on the blade's guard. Bone creaked, and the tip of the sabre sunk an inch into Kth'ala's chest. A sound, half a sigh, half a moan escaped from the thing's skinless lips.

"For what it's worth…" I began.

"*No need for apologies, Lamenter,*" it chuckled. "*You will keep your word. My mistress awaits you. And you* will *go to her…*"

I leaned all my weight into the point of Cryptfeeder, until finally something within the Nameless gave way, and the runic steel ran it through. The thing arched its back, broken fingers scrabbling at the hem of my surcoat… and then it was silent.

Power trembled up the fullers of the sword, filling the gem at its hilt with fire. Deep inside that captive flame, I saw the face of the Sun's Shard shift, planes interlocking to erase a single tiny facet.

"What makes you think," I asked the Burning Dark's corpse. "That I have any intention of bowing before your damned witch now?"

Because – well. There is honour… and then there is being a thrice-damned fool.[10]

The answer came from behind me – from within my own shadow. It came with an oily, self-congratulatory little chuckle, a second before I felt ropes bind my arms to my body, and a cruel garrotte pull tight against my throat.

"*Trust is a fine thing, Lamenter, as my poor dead brother has just professed. But alas, it is so lacking in this latter age.*" I could *feel* the thing rising up out of the pool of darkness behind me, forcing itself into the world with a noise like a fingertip on glass. "*When one wants surety… when one needs guarantees… then it is always best to plan ahead. Don't you think?*"

I knew that voice. The dry, cynical tones of an assassin, so inured to death that it had become just another amusement. A thing crafted by Urzen not for main force, but for subtlety, for stealth…

"*That's right,*" said the Hanged Man, last of the Nine Now Nameless. "*The Stormreaper really does want to talk to you very, very badly. So be a dear, and don't struggle. I'm informed she'd like you in one piece.*"

Well, struggling was out of the question. But there was enough air left in my lungs for one last, hopeless shout…

"Silbern Chaar! For the love of your grandsire's name! Help me!"

The Nameless One snarled. I felt the ropes cinch tight around me.

Silbern turned, her eyes widening with horror. She went from a dead stop to a pelting sprint faster than even poor dead Vyrim could have done. In fact, her fingers almost grasped the collar of my tabard as I fell back into my own shadow, the Hanged Man's arms wrapped tight around me.

---

10. What did you expect? I'm a *necromancer*, not a hulking pile of meat, neuroses and sacred oaths like the Paladyne!

Darkness leaped up to blot out the world.

I was falling.

The last thing I heard was a dwindling, despairing scream –

Then the darkness closed its fist on me, and consciousness was snuffed out.

Part Three

Lord of the
Drowned

Even when a God is dead - his temples toppled,
his priesthood slain, his holy relics ground to dust
- there is a brief twilight, a *fading away*, during
which a conquered people turn their old religion
into folk tales, superstitions and childrens' stories.
A God deposed lives on in this state for so long
as the credulous have but a shred of faith. He
lives, not as a potent Facet of his Shard, but as a
mere echo, a thing half-glimpsed in dreams and
nightmares... a ghost deity, his power welling up
in strange places to fit the forms of superstitious
whisperings...

'The Conquest of Nations -
a treatise on the persecution of cultural warfare'
General Yarisch Nolane,
Anganesse Tactical and Strategic Command.

I DREAMED I fell through fire.

Whole suspended oceans of it, where flames licked out it all directions, fluid as water, scalding as regret. I dreamed of the void at the cracked heart of Yrde – the hot, dense core which had split the planet into fragments, then held them in place with a skein of unspeakably potent geomancy.

I dreamed of the Shards.

They orbited the core in a glittering halo – some merely the size of mountains, others bigger than the cold face of the moon. Translucent, sheened over with licks and jags of rainbow light, they tumbled in silence, beams of radiance snapping between facets as they aligned in their endless dance. They were, or so Urzen's books had told me, the fragments of the mind of the Divine, who had sundered himself to pieces in order to give life to a barren world.

An intellect which made mine seem like that of a mayfly, broken...

What remained was shaped by the fears and dreams of the living. Shards for the archetypes of Gods, and Facets for their many masks.

In my old village, in the Stormwood of Khytein, there had lived an old warrior, Eivann, – one of the berserkers we called the Touched. In a battle before I was born, a Vhaurish mace had caved in his right temple, giving his face a leering, lopsided cast. It had also awakened four other personalities inside his fractured skull – one who claimed to be a Warbard, one a little boy, one a foul-mouthed old crone, and the last a Rasuuli trader from the south.

Aerik Stormsong – our tribe's *real* Warbard – told us that these four were ghosts, brought back from the edge of Anghul's realm when Eivann lay wounded.

By his decree my father, the Scalptaker, had granted the old warrior a stipend, and named two of his own wives to care for him when the spirits raved and gibbered. We children had watched through a knothole in the wall of his hut, horrified, pitying and fascinated. The sight of Eivann in full possession had the sick allure of an open wound.

That was the entirety of my frame of reference regarding the Gods. Not much, I suppose, but how can the mind of a mayfly contemplate that of a man? How else to reason with the fact that each Shard bound together up to a score of distinct Aziphem, often warring among themselves… but that each Facet stood alone, possessed of its own personality, its own face?

Such were questions for theologians, philosophers… and drunkards. People with more time left than I.

Because even through the dream-haze I knew where I was going. The Shard of Death spun huge and cold before me, weathered like rotten ice, glittering along its myriad edges with the fire of trapped stars. A vast fragment of the Divine, this… for who cannot wonder at what awaits beyond mortality? Even Kharnath had a place among the Facets here, though if that ancient thing was still sane and whole, its domain would have waned to a tiny sliver.

For the face of each Shard was not immovable. Some Gods waxed potent with belief, while others dwindled into voices on the wind. As they did so…

The breath caught in my throat as the tumbling monolith spun a new face toward me. *Surely not.*

But yes.

This was the reason my dreaming mind had brought me here.

This… *abomination.*

Nearly a whole quarter of the great Shard was diseased – cracked through as if with the blow of a hammer. A web of fissures crawled out from that scarring, webbed across the blighted Facet in a pattern like frozen lightning. To one side they bled darkness – a busy, teeming shadow which seemed to swarm with insects, carrion-flies on the corpse of a God. To the other, the cracks were painted over a sickly curdling of the light, a glow like corpse-worms and fungus.

Around it, other Facets had been edged out, eroded away until they were tiny things, flakes chipped from the face of a mountain. Within them raged the images of Gods all but forgotten.

The eyes of my mind narrowed, and I fell closer still to the cold face of the Shard. Close enough to touch, until I could see the hatred in the eyes of those diminished Gods, see their accusing fingers pointing...

Anghul, the antlered lord, his crown of thorny bone weighed down with antiquity. The Harvestman, his skull beneath its moth-eaten cowl riddled with worms, cracked and yellowed. The Lady of Storms, seaweed tangled in her hair, her drowned flesh as grey and lifeless as that of the ghuldren.

They swept by in silence – all of Sarem's faces of death. All reduced to ruin, their Facets shrunk down to mere slivers, bordering a sheer cliff of darkness and disease.

For this was *my* Facet – the one which all my enemies had been scrabbling and clawing for. It was hardly a thing to covet, however. And when I looked below that broken surface...

The face there was not my own. It was the cold, smug graven image of the statues I'd seen in Oram. A sculptor's imagining of a stern and frosty Lord of Death.

But that wasn't the worst part. Oh, no. Not by a long way. Artists had gotten my portrait wrong before, and it hadn't spawned a cancer in the heart of the Divine.

No – the true horror was this. *I wasn't the darkness. I was the* light. The *lesser* of two evils. Which meant...

I have no idea who decided to throw a bucket of iced water over me at this point, but whoever it was, I owe them a debt of gratitude. No doubt waking up spluttering and cursing was far preferable to seeing the leering face of Dirge, pushed up through that swarm of buzzing black motes, his hands reaching out for me in broken-clawed hunger.

Consciousness exploded behind my eyes as I rolled onto my side, retching. My fingers scrabbled against a floor of varnished timbers, and I heard the creak and shudder of wood under strain; smelled wet canvas, tar and salt.

The sea. I *hated* the sea.

There was no question as to whose ship I sailed on, either. Not even a sliver of hope. Mentally, I checked my wrists and ankles for the weight of chains, but there were none. Just a blur which I blinked from my eyes, resolving itself into a circle of worn sea-boots, one set more than three times the size of the rest.

"Torture me if you wish," I croaked, collapsing onto my back. "I'll tell you anything you want to hear. The pain might even prove *interesting...*"

A rumble of laughter, like stones being ground together underwater.

"Away, thralls! Nibs, Callow – back to the galley! Talleq, take your men aloft and see to those sails. They sound as loose as a whore's underthings!"

Boots shuffled away, leaving only the oversized, hobnailed pair. Just my luck.

"We can arrange some nice tortures if you want, Lamenter," said that deep-gravel voice. "Thumbscrews, aye... we could fashion a lovely rack, I suppose. Hot irons, and pincers – of those we have a few. But I thought you might like a bowl of soup instead."

Lamenter. They called me *Lamenter.* Surely that meant something important. But even my dream was fading now, and all I was left with was a jumble of disjointed memories. Fear gripped me.

"What... what's my name? Where am I?"

A rumble of concern.

"Your *name?* You really have had a hard night, boy. Captain says you're Kuhal Moer, Lord of the Dark Tower. Last of our crew. And as to where – we're just out of Oram, heading south over the Shallow Sea. You're aboard the *Sorrow's Vengeance*, a guest of the Stormreaper herself. Now... about that soup?"

Hands the size of shovel blades lifted me up, depositing me in a wooden chair. A bowl of something hot and fragrant was set down in front of me, and a spoon folded gently into my fingers.

Kuhal Moer. A familiar name. But not mine, surely? A brother, perhaps? A cousin? It was a Kaltensunder name, indeed, and I was Rhul, son of... son of...

"Don't worry," said my captor. "Despite what you may have heard, it's just pork, onions, garlic and carrots. I haven't actually eaten anyone for months."

That made me blink the last of my sleep away, fast. The insinuation of cannibalism will do that to a person.

I almost spilled my soup when I saw the face of my host.

Well – not just his face. The whole impression, really...

A giant, malformed head, with wisps of orange hair sprouting from beneath a stained chef's toque. An apron made of blood-spattered leather, belted with anchor chain, and clattering with a horrorworks of knives, cleavers and forks. Trousers crudely sewn from sealskin, those boots a man could drown in… and straining the seams of this whole nightmare ensemble, a humanoid beast with ruddy, leather-thick skin, a broken hump of a nose, tiny dark eyes and stubbled jowls. Its arms were all out of proportion, knuckles dragging the floor, and each tattooed bicep was bigger than a fat man's torso.

"You… you're an…"

"Oh, go on. Say it. Either word is just as hurtful, but if you must get it out of your system…"

"Ogre! A bloody *ogre!* Urzen said you'd been extinct for centuries!" My captor nodded, a sad look in his eyes.

"*Extinct.* Yes. That's what the Mistress says as well. But we ogres and our troll kin are not just things of flesh. When the Divine gave life to Yrde, we were born of stone. I'm told I slept for a whole age, half buried in a hillside. Some of my family were… *quarried.*"

Now, I'm no stranger to the impossible. But ogres and trolls are things out of faery stories – not creatures you expect to wax mournful as they serve you bowls of soup. The look on this one's face was like that of a kicked puppy.

"My apologies, sir ogre," I said, tentatively stirring my meal with the tip of my spoon. "But what should I call you then?"

"My sire named me Gryst," sniffed the ogre. "And as to my people – we were called the Suudarach, in the times before men drove us out. We were the First Builders, and we shaped stone for the Sauren, the Archaeon's children. Now…"

I mustered up my courage, and took a mouthful of soup. It was, perhaps, the very best I'd ever tasted.

"Now you're working for a witch? Seems sort of… stereotypical, to me."

Anger flared in the huge creature's eyes.

"Our culture is dead. Replaced by the stories of men. *You* are the ones who made us eat your children, human – you, with your fears leaching down into the stone! They taste TERRIBLE!"

I held up my hands in placation.

"Hold now, Gryst. I'm not one to judge. If I really am the Lamenter, then I'm a grave-robbing lich with the blood of millions on his hands. We're both monsters together, or not at all." I lifted the bowl to my mouth, and drank hungrily. I couldn't quite recall, but it seemed I had eaten nothing for… well, surely it couldn't be *centuries.* Perhaps a day or two, then.

"You like the soup, then?" asked Gryst, wringing his chef's hat in his hands.

I smacked my lips.

"Perfection. I just hope it isn't my last meal…"

Gryst grinned. His teeth were blue-grey granite, knapped to sharp points.

"Oh no, Kuhal Moer. I wouldn't waste my arts on the condemned. Usually they just go over the side. You're to see the Mistress as soon as you can stand – that's why I put a little blindflower and bonebark in the pot. Wake the dead, or so they say."

And well it could have. Before long I almost felt alive again, and rational enough to wonder who Urzen was – the authority I had quoted on the extinction of ogres. Not that it mattered, for there was one thing I assuredly did recall. It was that the Stormreaper, mistress of this latter-day Keel, was a figure of darkest dread, and likely another of the murderous fools who thought me some kind of God.

Gryst gave me very little choice in the matter, though. When a half-ton butcher with granite teeth asks you to walk, you walk. I took in the sights and sounds of *Sorrow's Vengeance* as I was marched up stairs, abovedecks to my doom.

My first impression of the Stormreaper's ship was of sheer size. Though nowhere near the bulk of an old Angan war Keel, the *Vengeance* was much larger than any seagoing craft I had ever seen – three times the length and twice as broad across the beam as Elion Morekh's *Shadow of Blades*. I noted with interest that the timbers beneath my feet were Stormwood oak, and the masts were hewn from single great trunks of ghostleaf – trees which grew only in the wilds of the north.

The second thing I noticed was the crew. All of them were soldiers, it appeared, clad in a motley assortment of uniforms. They came from every tribe and nation – Sedrekan fisherfolk from southern Ghuram next to pale-skinned Ytheans, dark-haired Ontokhi heaving at the ropes beside Faeroans… the only thing they had in common was their unnatural silence. A closer look told me why they didn't swear, sing, curse or expectorate like the sailors I'd known before. Every one of them had his lips sewn shut, bound together with thin leather strips. And their eyes… as we passed a trio of men, heaving at a capstan's handles, I saw nothing but blank, glistening darkness where pupil and sclera should have been. These men were *enchanted*, and the sorcery which bound them reeked of Urzen's work. That name again!

I shuddered.

"Pay them no heed," rumbled Gryst, as if reading my thoughts. "What she's done to them is far kinder than what they deserve. Men who have tried to kill us, one and all. Once our quest is done, the mistress even says she'll set them free."

A memory swum into focus, sending needles of ice through my head. *I'd freed my own thralls, eventually. Death is a kind of freedom, you must admit.* It was not a thought which inspired confidence.

I kept such thoughts to myself as we made our way astern. Below us the clouds were an unbroken blanket of white, the sun cold and remote, veiled in ice crystals. I suppose if I was truly living I would have felt the wind which filled the *Vengeance's* sails – three masts rigged with acres of canvas, pennants snapping from the stays. We climbed the first tier of the sterncastle, past rows of brass-bound portholes, and I caught a glimpse down through the heart of the ship, through the well which, had this been a true Keel, would have seethed with trapped souls.

Aboard this vessel, the chasm was wood instead of stone, sheathed in plates of copper, and a curved limb of ghostleaf curved out above it. Hundreds of thin silver wires trailed down into the empty air, like a harp without a frame.

"She calls it the Focus," said the ogre, stopping to prod me along as I peered over the railing. "We call it the Soulharp. Don't know how it works. Don't care, neither. So long as it gets us where we're going."

Things were beginning to add up in my mind, skewed as it was by the caress of Zael Kataphraxis. First, the word 'quest'. That didn't bode well. A saga word, if ever I heard one. A word for bards, to make young fools all starry-eyed and, ultimately, make them worm fodder. Then that subtle insinuator, 'we'. As if *I* was being included in such a grandiose and doomed venture…

Such concerns would have to wait. Because now Gryst herded me to the top of a final curving staircase, and we came to a canvas-shaded deck, wider than the top of Oram's Bastion. The ship's wheel stood here, manned by a tall, thin figure robed in black. Loops of cord were wrapped around its narrow waist, and coiled around both shoulders.

It was the Hanged Man – the demon which had abducted me. But my horror at seeing it, as it were, face-to-cowl, was overshadowed by the rest of the Stormreaper's crew. A more motley and sinister collection of villains I hadn't seen since I'd assembled my own undead army.

And I had. I remembered. Once, I sat on a throne of bones, my black cape rippling out on the wind, an army of dead men following me into darkness…

They lounged on a half-circle of velvet couches, arranged about a roaring brazier. A low table between them held silver platters of fruit, roasted goose, sea bass, buttery Ghuram flatbread, pitchers of chilled wine and bowls of candied almonds. Censers wafted cloying smoke, while one of the crew – a dark-haired beauty in an utterly inappropriate red satin gown – plucked the notes of a sad old Rasuuli folk song on a balalaika.

To be fair, I probably seemed just as fey, wild and alien as any of those there assembled – with my hexagonal smoked glasses hiding my eyes, my mane of white hair whipping in the wind, and the remains of my Guild armour hanging from my bony frame. But even more powerful than the impression of otherworldly *strangeness* was the reek of power in the air. These were sorcerers, every one, and each one more potent than I.

"Ahh!" said a man all in motley furs, leaping up from his divan. "Our guest awakens! Come, sit! Have you tried Gryst's soup? Yes? Then perhaps you'd like a cup of wine to get the taste out of your mouth?"

The ogre growled, but there was laughter behind it.

"The last thing *you* cooked belonged in a chamber pot, Seventails! Now, where is the Mistress? I have work to do – unlike you lazy sods!"

The one called Seventails threw back the hood of his patchwork cloak, and I realised with a shock that he was Khytein. We had the same pale skin, the same broad, high cheekbones and slanted eyes… he was of the Roege, the tribe who had lived in the far north of the Stormwood.

"Aye, one of yours, Lamenter," he said, his grin wide and white. "We still exist, though the old ways may be dying. Kaltensund and its rules and laws and *commerce* aren't for everyone…"

He clasped my forearm, in the traditional Khytein greeting, almost grinding the bones to splinters. Gods, the *strength* of this man! He would have put old Hurik himself to shame.

"Your sorrows to be short, and your glory long, then," I replied – the traditional formal greeting of my long-dead race. Seventails smiled even more broadly, clapping me on the shoulder. Any harder, and I would have been driven to my knees.

"See, Rasq? Another one of us! Why, our culture is in a state of renaissance!"

I bowed to the Zengaji, hoping that certain of my other acts among the Skyborn were forgotten.

"If that is our path, then I walk it willingly," I replied, dredging up from some mental recess the words of the draken-cult's language. Urmokh grinned.

"It's been *years* since I've heard one of you lowlanders butcher my native tongue! Ahhh, the scrolls were right about you, Deadfather. I can't wait until my soul-brother Scarwing shares your scent."

"You're *not* letting that thing land here," growled Gryst. "You know how long it took to cook all of this? That damned lizard will have it gobbled up in a heartbeat!"

Seventails looked a little pale.

"And as for me, Skyborn – have you explained about… you know? The bloody thing was trying to eat *me*, and…"

Urmokh was laughing, along with both Issara and Kell. Rasq winked at me, one shaggy great eyebrow dipping low.

"Come on now, you two! I quite like the little fellow. And his skill at chess far surpasses your own. I think we should invite him down!"

They could only mean one thing – Urmokh was soul-bound to a draken of the high Hiledoran, a saurian beast the size of a longship, with a temper like a swarm of hornets. Though I'd never heard of one of the great predators playing *chess* before…

A pillar of darkness rose up behind the Skyborn, unfurling into what appeared to be an empty, rope-coiled cowl. It was the Hanged Man, last of the Nine, and the thing was steaming with cold from its journey through the Unmanifest.

"*The Mistress has informed me that if you bring your pet aboard while we're flying, she will have me throttle it to death. Not that I feel any malice, you understand. Orders. She says it makes the Focus impossible to control. Ancient sorcery. Before the time of the Aziphem. Not good for keeping us airborne.*"

Urmokh didn't seem to move, but suddenly two long-bladed knives were crossed through the Nameless One's chest. It didn't seem to feel them. The Skyborn didn't comment – he hardly needed to. Instead he reached out, plucked an apple from a silver platter, and leaned back on his divan, taking a juicy bite.

"*Very mature, mortal. Very professional.*" The Hanged Man's tone was withering. It pulled the blades out with a dry-paper rasp, letting them clatter to the deck. "*I suppose you have completed your introductions? We are about to touch down, and then the Mistress and*"

I thought the… *thing*… Seventails addressed was huddled on a fur-draped throne. But it wasn't. It unfolded – and unfolded, and unfolded – until it was sitting cross-legged on the deck, nearly as tall as Gryst.

"*We* were never Khytein, skinwalker. At least, not in human recollection. Not that I don't welcome our guest, of course. But don't expect any enthusiasm for folk songs and war dances, Seventails."

"You? *Dance?* I'd rather watch Gryst perform a strip-tease."

The ogre snorted.

"You're not my type, Seventails. Now, if you were some jade-toothed beauty from the Ghuram mountains…"

Rasq extended a long, long arm to grasp me by the hand. He didn't squeeze – thank the Gods.

"Welcome to this ship of fools, Kuhal Moer. I'm sure you'll feel right at home."

I noted the pale blue-grey skin of the creature as it looked up at me, eyes glittering black beneath a mane of white hair. Rasq's face was all but obscured by a bushy, grey-white beard, knotted with bird skulls, tiny, rune-carved bones and shark teeth. Standing, I guessed he'd be a lanky three spans tall.

"An ogre," I said. "A skinwalker…" A nod at Seventails, who bowed mockingly. "And now one of the Yheti of the frozen wastes. What's next? Faeries? Goblins? Magical flying ponies?"

Rasq laughed, a sound like icebergs grinding together.

"I told you he'd fit right in! Son, I'm no mythical beast. If Yheti ever lived, they died long ago."

Gryst put up his hand.

"I think I may have eaten one, once."

"There? You see? I come from a place where you are remembered, Kuhal. An island of ice, pulled through the winter seas by leviathenes…"

The memory struck me like a slinger's stone between the eyes. *Milky seafood broth. Sealskins and firelight. Gernish Maudrin's black bearskin coat wrapped around me, as I stood on a cliff of ice, watching a thousand great, broad-fluked beasts haul at their leather traces.*

"But… those folk… and you…"

Rasq smiled, but it was a sad and lonely thing.

"All of us here have been *changed*," he said. "And all of us were different inside, even before that change began. You Khytein aren't supposed to look like half-drowned albino weasels, either – and yet here you stand."

Seventails chuckled.

"Not one for the social niceties, is he? Still, I am. And so – allow me to introduce the rest of your traveling companions."

He gestured to the tall, raven-haired lady with the balalaika.

"Issara of Rasuul. Or, to be more precise…"

"Oh, I'll tell him," she sighed. "He makes it sound so *sordid!* I'm the Curse of Er'kesh, the terrible blood-drinking horror…" she laughed. "Funny how the common folk make such a fuss about a few dead bodies, isn't it?"

I'd heard of this one. In fact, I'd sent my undead spies out, to see if intervention was needed. If this really was Issara, Countess of Spirefend, then she'd literally bathed in blood to stave off the effects of the 'blight – and of mortality.

"You… and the silver bath? The pitchers full of virgin's blood?"[11]

"Oh *yes*… and how hard is it, do you think, to find that many virgins? In a rural backwater with no real forms of entertainment?" She grinned, exposing a mouthful of delicately pointed teeth.

"Thankfully, the Mistress has helped me with my addiction. Like dear old Gryst, I'm no longer in the business of eating people alive."

I sketched a little bow, blackened fingertips touched to my lips and then held out, in the courtly Rasuuli fashion.

"Don't think that I'm any one to judge, Milady," I said, hoping that the blood-mage really couldn't read my thoughts. "As I've told your worthy cook here, we're all monsters together, or not at all."

Seventails coughed nervously.

"And the other lady amongst our company is Kell Du'ath, from Ythe."

He gestured to a slight, pale figure who had – literally and figuratively – been in Issara's shadow this whole time. It was with some concern that I noted the *shape* of that shadow – for while the Rasuuli countess was curvaceously and unquestionably female, her shadow was a spiked and bat-winged terror.

"I saw your stand against the ghouls," said Kell, in a voice not much more than a whisper. She was dressed entirely in white – lacy, many-

11. So the legends go - Issara, widow of Count Albrecht Van Gristaal-Karkovic of Spirefend, bathed in the blood of virgins to remain young and beautiful. The truth, however, was far more prosaic, and less messy. As a blood-mage, it was the 'blight which kept her alive. Glamours like my own made her appear young and beautiful. And the blood which gave her strength didn't have to come from virgins. It was simply a very convenient line for young Rasuuli men to use on impressionable girls - convincing them that after this night, they would have nothing to fear from the Red Countess again...

layered Ythean wedding robes slightly yellowed with a[ge] folded white silk scarf covered her eyes. "But then, th[at] ago. I was once an Oracle, you see – one of the Silent Sis[ters] Goddess of the crescent moon. That was before…"

Before she died, I realised. Because as Kell Du'ath tur[ned] toward the light I saw that she was nothing but pal[e] mageblight, through and through. How old must th[e] wondered, for the web of sorcery to have snared her [ ] thousand years? Two thousand? I suddenly felt very, ver[y] foolish.

"As one who shares your… condition, Lady Du'ath, y[ou] be embarrassed on my account. Being dead is hardly th[e] once was, after all."

The ancient oracle smiled, a mere twitch of her opal-sh[ ]

"Oh, I don't mourn for myself, necromancer. Not any[ ] has been most… supportive." One of her tiny, marble-[ ] reached out to clasp that of the countess. "But poor Nyal[a] fragments of vision, all I hear now is her weeping."

A flicker of sadness passed over the whole group like [ ] seemed that the Ythean oracle wasn't the only one feelin[g] their soul-bound Aziphem. Seventails broke the gloom [ ] smile.

"And thus to the last of us – but by no means the least.[ ] brothers Urmokh and… well, you have already met the [ ] He's hardly the talkative type."

Urmokh was clearly Zengaji, but of the old cadre – S[ ] like the lowlander clansmen I had so recently slaughtere[d] other men assembled in the Stormreaper's crew, he wa[s] and trim, his skin tattooed with red sigils from the top[ ] hair at his crown to his bare chest and belly. Points furthe[r] not care to speculate about. As the Skyborn fixed me wi[th] glare, I noticed that one of his eyes was dark, almost black[ ] other was yellow and slit-pupiled – the eye of a Draken.

"The Archaeon sees you and greets you, Deadfather,[ ] grim formality. "He bids me ask you if you're ready to e[ ] begun three hundred years past, on the Urexian Plain."

Well, if this dour little man spoke for the Archaeon,[ ] only be one thing he was alluding to. An apocalypse of [ ] which had all but crippled the Coldblood. Not many now [ ] possibly know about that epochal act of sorcery.

her helmsman will attend."

"What about Harlaw?"

"Harlaw's below. I think he's jealous of that bloody engine the Oramun built. Trying to weld some cannon together, probably."

"Harlaw," said Issara, with an icy tone of command, "Is *always* below. And in any case – alchemy is not sorcery. He has no place in our counsels."

"How typically aristocratic," sneered Seventails. "I don't see you complaining when his guns do the work your blood-magick can't handle!"

"Hah! If I had enough blood we wouldn't need his blackpowder, peasant! *Your* veins would do nicely!"

"They used to be…" whispered Gryst, behind one callused hand.

"*You're all fools,*" rasped the Hanged Man. "*But She needs you alive, more's the pity. I was sent to tell you to brace for landing. The Faeroan Gates are held against us, and the Mistress commands you to prepare yourselves for battle.*" The rope-hung spectre extended a withered finger toward me. "*That means you as well, Kuhal Moer. We have corpses on which you can… practice. Those we face are Sorathi, and their fear of undeath is legendary.*"

I smiled nervously. One ring left, filled with the power of the Burning Dark. Enough to animate a corpse or two, surely? Then again…

I blinked, cold sweat prickling my brow. I reached out for my little familiar, Sei – but met only the sensation of coiled, contented sleep, the sound of spectral purring at the edge of hearing. No help there, I supposed.

Oh, no. The sick, chained, divine *bastard!* He couldn't have! How…

"No need to worry!" said Gryst, slinging a comradely hand around my shoulders. My neck fit like a twig in the hollow between his thumb and fingers. "It may have been a few hundred years, but it will all come back to you."

"Easy for you to say," I muttered. "I suppose you're a very demon in battle."

The ogre looked shocked for a second, his craggy brows lifting.

"Oh no. Not me. I'm just the cook. I'm a pacifist."

Fragments of memory blurred past. The sensation of knowledge on the tip of my mental tongue was infuriating. But…

"*I can't remember how,*" I whispered. "He's taken it all."

Issara and Seventails were still bickering. Rasq, Urmokh and Kell seemed content to watch the show. But Gryst had heard me.

"Can't remember what, Lamenter?"

No use trying to hide it, I supposed.

"I can't remember how I did it. Not even that first time. *I can't remember how to raise the dead!*"

And it was true. I had wondered, as I slept, why Zael hadn't simply torn away my last memories of Makara – the most cruel thing the chained God could have done. Now I knew. And this was, in truth, much worse. Now I knew that the trapped soul in the amulet around my neck belonged to the woman I loved… but I had no practical way to bring her back.

Gryst frowned.

"Better learn quick, then. We're coming down. And then the Mistress is going to want a demonstration."

I licked my lips, suddenly as dry as tomb-dust.

"And… supposing I fail?"

The ogre laughed.

"Don't worry, Kuhal Moer. I told you, I don't eat people anymore! No – you'll just get tossed over the side. She don't like dead weight – pardoning the pun, of course."

A bell began to chime, high and urgent. Wood creaked and canvas cracked as the *Sorrow's Vengeance* angled sharply downward, its bows knifing through the clouds. I grabbed the rail with both hands, Gryst's huge fingers knotted in the back of my ragged tabard.

I was hanging half-over the wooden beam when the clouds feathered away, revealing a shimmering, copper-coloured expanse of water, lit by the rising sun. Far below us bulked the shadow of the Faeroan city of Coramis, a floating mass of platforms, ships and wooden towers. Ahead, leagues distant, twin coastlines of pale white sand came curving together to the rocky pinnacles of the Faeroan Gates, where the famous Colossus stood waist-deep in the whirlpool-wracked brine.

Flocks of seabirds wheeled and cried below us as we fell. I could pick out tiny fisherboats now, pennants snapping from the masts and towers of Coramis as it slipped into our wake…

Then the water was rushing up fast, a rumpled, beaten-metal plain, reflecting splinters of sunlight as it raced under our keel.

"Retract the rudders!" yelled a voice. "Stabilizers down! Brace for impact!"

As it was, the *Vengeance* barely kissed the wavetops, sliding across the surface of the Shallow Sea like a razor across soapy skin. We hung suspended for an instant, then the Stormreaper must have let her Focus go. The whole immense bulk of the ship seemed to pause in midair, before settling with a splash into the foam. Spray drenched me from the waist up as Gryst hauled me back on board.

"We won't have you going over yet, Lamenter" he chuckled. "There's sharks down there, you know! Good eating."

Above us, thralls swarmed in the ratlines and rigging. Canvas bloomed in new, more nautical configurations. And with a shudder, the *Sorrow's Vengeance* began to make headway, a ship thrice as large again as any in the fleet of Coramis, scudding before a gentle wind like a nobleman's pleasure-skiff.

The bell had stopped ringing. But now came a high-pitched whistle – two notes which drilled into my mind like the echo of the Wild Song. I couldn't help but look.

"Captain on deck!" shouted Gryst. I ducked as his huge hand came up into a salute, almost knocking me over the rail. Even Issara and Seventails fell silent, keeping a prickly distance as they turned to face the sterncastle. In fact they were *all* standing – and any mark of mutual respect from such a crew made me decidedly nervous.

There was an ornate bronzewood door set into the sloping face of the sterncastle – the upper level which hung over the transom of the Keel. Now it creaked open, and for a heartbeat or two the gloom within seemed impenetrable. Then the bobbing light of a lantern appeared, and behind it a huge, stoop-shouldered shape, caped in ragged canvas over the remains of an admiral's uniform. On the thing's head…

I felt physically sick for a second. If it was possible, I would dearly have loved to pass out. But I saw the face of the Stormreaper's helmsman with horrible clarity, underlit by a sputtering hurricane lamp, and then thrown into hideous relief by the sun.

It was Elion Morekh. The gold-brocaded tricorne hat had been a dead giveaway – and *dead* was clearly the operative word. Three hundred years of unlife in a salty climate had all but mummified the old pirate, and his hands, neck and face were covered with stitches, holding him together. There was no way to tell if his blank, milky eyes either saw or recognized me. At least, I thought, someone had replaced that bloody hook…

Then the witch herself came through the door, and such trivialities were blown away.

I had expected a withered hag – or some fey sorceress of Issara's cast, a witch-queen from the fables. I was not prepared for what I saw.

The Stormreaper was small and trim, clad in black leather scale armour, her face hooded and a pair of slim duelling knives belted at her waist. When she threw back that hood I staggered, the gem at my throat seething with power.

That heart-shaped face. Those violet eyes, like the corona of summer lightning. That shimmering fall of black hair, tucked behind one ear – just as I remembered.

It was impossible. I knew her to be gone, subsumed by the spirit of Zael. I had nailed her to a cross with my own hands, the vessel to chain a mad God. And yet…

"You look like you've seen a ghost," smiled the Stormreaper, beckoning me closer. My feet stumbled forward of their own volition. "But that shouldn't be any great problem for the likes of you, I should imagine…"

Even the voice. Even the sparkle in the depths of those mesmerizing eyes…

The captain of *Sorrow's Vengeance*, the witch feared by all of Sarem – It was Makara.

Far away, on the gold-edged horizon, the people of Coramis shuttered their windows and locked their doors as they heard the echo of my scream.

It was Elion Morekh who rushed to catch me as I fell. Something had burst inside my brain, I was sure, and triple-images of Makara's face spun before me, haloed in rainbow light.

"Khytein!" rasped the ancient Captain. "Khytein, it's all right!" he turned back over his shoulder to the Stormreaper. "I *told* you this would happen! There's plenty wrong with this one, but hate ain't the beginning or the end of it. You're the spit and image of your mother, girl, and he…"

Leathery claws cradled my head down to the deck. I struggled to rise, tasting blood on my tongue. Deep in my chest, where no such organ had any right to be, I felt my withered heart thump once… twice… then fall still.

"Morekh…" I whispered. "You old bastard! How did you… the wreck of the Ark… I saw it fall…"

My old friend smiled, a crinkling of salt-crusted lips and cured-hide skin. His teeth had entirely been replaced with scrimshawed ivory. "They… they found you a new hand, too. That hook was… a bit too much."

"You don't get to be an *old* pirate captain if you don't know when to jump, Kuhal," he said. "And don't worry. The years have been kinder to me than you may imagine. I have my own legends now. Stories about the Ghost Captain and his crew of the damned… some of the folk songs are actually bearable."

Gryst and Seventails helped Morekh heave me to my feet. Sometime during this process, my mental faculties caught up with the whirring engine of my panic.

"Her *mother*? But how?"

Elion nudged me in the ribs.

"You're three hundred and twenty, lad. Hasn't anyone told you about the… you know…"

The Stormreaper rolled her eyes, in a gesture I found heart-rendingly familiar.

"Spare us your lewd gestures, helmsman. I think we can clear this up quite easily."

I still wanted to turn away. Looking at her face *hurt*. But the young sorceress cupped my chin in her fingers, plucking the smoked glasses from the bridge of my nose with one hand.

"Yes," she said. "You're just like he said you'd be. Although I'm glad I take more after the Vhaur…"

The Stormreaper peered at me intently for a long moment, then planted a chaste little kiss in the middle of my forehead.

"Aside from the usual… well, those things which dear old Elion was so vigorously alluding to… my mother was indeed Makara, Lady of Sorrows. My father was supposed to be Gernish Maudrin, last Warbard sworn to Theyr. Suffice to say that my real parents – the ones of flesh and blood – chose an interesting place to… enjoy each others' company."

She held out her hand, and Elion passed her a canvas-wrapped bundle from under his cape. Carefully unwound, it proved to be a long blade of glass, knapped along both edges to fashion a crude, prehistoric sword. A very modern hilt, grip and pommel had been affixed to this relic, which sparkled and danced with inner radiance.

Somehow, that smoky grey glass seemed familiar…

"*The Necropolis*," I said, disbelieving. "Aerik Stormsong. He broke the covenant, and unveiled himself in flesh like this. But the child… Makara's child…"

"Endsong killed it. Or so he thought. Your Warbard saw that Maudrin's seed was usurped, however. Another life entirely grew within his young apprentice. And so your enemy's wish – that the child of Gernish Maudrin should die – was misdirected. Aerik hid the soul of that unborn life deep, but some twenty-three years ago…"

"It *is* nice to get out of doors sometimes," put in Issara. "Beds only offer so many possibilities…"

Seventails looked more than a little embarrassed, but held his peace.

I, on the other hand, could only gurgle mindlessly. Sometimes you wish that the mental wheels would just stop turning. Sometimes, the truth you feel dawning in the back of your mind is so awful in its magnitude that you wish for poppy's blood, or strong drink, or a merciful blow to the head.

"Then who…" I croaked, already knowing the answer.

"If my advisor tells me true – and he usually does – Makara was sworn to Gernish Maudrin. She ritually foreswore any…ah, *relations* with other men. Apart from one."

I was dumbstruck. Flashes of light ignited inside my eyes as this witch – this living image of my long-dead love – wrapped her arms around me and squeezed. I had not been hugged for so many centuries that I took a moment to realise just what she was doing. Gods help me, I thought a knife was going to plunge into my back at any second.

"Welcome to the *Sorrow's Vengeance*, Father," she said, stepping back and cuffing at her eyes with the back of one hand. "I hope you like it."

The Kothrai -
A race of reavers and raiders, populating the Cold
Isles to the utter south of Sorath. For centuries
they waged a campaign of banditry, rape and
plunder on the more prosperous, weaker Tarkhand
to the north, sowing terror and fear. Their
longships travelled immense distances, striking as
deep into Tarkhanden territory as Sunder's Reach,
Bilrath and Quaziir.

With the rise of the united Tarkhanden
Trade Alliance, however, the Kothrai have been
increasingly marginalized - the remnant of a
darker history, subjugated not by the sword
but by economics. Many proud Kothrai tribes
have become dissolute, prey to drunkenness and
addiction to poppy's-blood. Others have died out
altogether, or migrated to Tarkhanden cities to
become an undercaste of vassals and wretches.

The fear of the Council of Seven, of course, is
that a unifier will arise among the Kothrai, rousing
them to dreams of former glory. Such a cultural
renaissance would surely prove a dire thorn in the
side of Tarkhand - though the sheer seapower
and sorcerous might of the Council would likely
mean such an uprising was only fatal for one of the
cultures involved...

Angan historical illuminus Nath Uldara Brecayne,
'A tactical overview of the nations of Sorath, Hmai and Akhaz'

SIARA ANVHAUR. HER name was Siara Anvhaur.

I learned this later, of course – long after the battle we were just
about to fight, and the first time I came face to face with Grennen
Vhul and his dark sorcery. At that moment, as the Stormreaper (my
daughter! Makara's daughter!) stepped out of the numbed circle of
my arms, the first thought which came to me was a monstrous one.
How easy it would be, hissed a seductive voice in my head, *to take this
body, to infuse it with the soul which hung heavy on a chain around my*

neck...

She mistook the pained expression on my face for a much purer emotion. And so she smiled – this girl who had been raised by a miller and his wife in Kaltensund, under the shadow of the old Necropolis. In a village which was now a blackened wreck, a haunt of the ghuldren.

"I… I know this must be quite a shock," she said, biting her lip in the same heart-rendingly vulnerable way her mother had done. "But those are Kothrai raiders ahead of us. We don't have time for a proper family reunion. Take the sword, and Aerik will tell you what to do."

"Aerik *Stormsong?*" I asked. "You mean the dead warbard? The one who I watched shatter into a million pieces?"

She arched an eyebrow.

"This, from a three-century-old talking cadaver? Come on, Father – this isn't, as the Rasuuli say, your first harvest dance." She smiled, presenting the hilt of the glass blade in the old Khytein style, the flat of the sword laid across her left forearm. "For me?"

All eyes were on me. I tasted salt on my tongue, spray hissing past as we closed with the little fleet of raiders. Horns blared out, and canvas snapped, tilting the deck beneath us. I hesitantly extended one hand, and touched the copper-bound grip of the sword.

Music jangled up my arm, kicking through my long muscles like a physical shock. Along with it came laughter, and a subtle blurring of the world around me – rope, canvas, wood and sunlight bending around a prismatic disturbance, a form coalescing…

"Ohhh, he's used you sorely lad. Zael Kataphraxis looks like he'd make a terrible master and a worse lover, if what's left of you is anything to go by."

I hadn't heard that voice for… well, for *centuries*. A permanently amused drawl, kindly and just a little mocking – the voice of a Warbard, all liquid honey and razors.

Aerik Stormsong flickered into existence next to Siara, tall, grey-haired and robed in blue, a silver foxfur collar clasped at his neck with a brooch in the shape of a harp. His great double lyrecaster was strapped to his back, and his long-stemmed pipe was in his hand, sending out a curling tendril of smoke.

"We're sorry about Urexes, son. Though, given the recent familial revelations being thrown about, I must tell you that I use 'son' only in the broadest sense. I was never fool enough to dip my ladle into Hurik Moer's soup, after all."

I squinted. The ancient Bard was vaguely transparent, and motes of starlight whirled inside him, like fireflies in smoke.

"So, you're really dead this time?" I asked. "And as for 'sorry about Urexes' – you *thorough, rotten, corpse-raping old bastard!* Did you know about Zael all along?"

Aerik shrugged. Behind him I could see my daughter commanding her crew, sending them off to sharpen their blades and focus their powers for the coming battle. An ember of pride stirred, flared... and was snuffed out by guilt.

"Would you believe me if I told you we didn't? The Archaeon was fixated on the threat of the Coldblood. We – myself and Maudrin – just wanted the Thearch toppled, and as for you... well, boy, you can't say that by the end it wasn't your fight as well. You did what you had to. Hells, you *enjoyed* it."

"If you hadn't died, Stormsong, I could perhaps be just *slightly* more irate."

"Good! Then all is forgiven!"

"*I didn't say that!* It's very, *very* hard to be more irate than I am right now. A *daughter*, Warbard? And don't look down your pipe at me, either. Three hundred years I've studied sorcery, and I'm your equal. In fact..."

"Three hundred years you can't remember! I heard what you said to the Ogre."

Aerik took a long drag on his pipe. I retracted my trembling finger from beneath his nose.

"Yes. You have a daughter. Someone *did* explain to you about the... you know?"

I sighed.

"Yes. The *'you know'* isn't the question. The question is..."

"Dirge lives," said Aerik, cutting directly past my tangled mess of accusations and fears. "The Doom was his idea. If he – or his masters in the Outer Dark – are denied Sarem due to sorcery, then they will reduce the Gods to nothing, and bleed sorcery from the land. In many ways, the Doom is a gift for you. Tailored precisely to render you helpless. A physical invasion of the whole continent is more than the Coldblood will risk again – and Dirge doesn't have an army of his own."

I blinked, barely catching up.

"For which all sane men are thankful," I risked. "And a few of the rest of us, too."

Aerik frowned.

"He's *building* one. This war has spread, Kuhal, and our side is not faring well. The Celestial Guard of Hmai have invaded Akhaz, taking terrible losses. We have no idea what's going on in the entire bloody Protectorate, but Tsargon Urd and his legions must be after something. They're only expected to hold out another few months, after which they will have to retreat back across the Chasm. It's likely that the Protectorate's armies will follow."

I knew little of Hmai – a cold and ancient land far to the south, peopled by (if the legends were to be believed) men with yellow, feline eyes and an unquenchable lust for jade. If they had roused themselves to fight the Coldblood then their courage must be at least as great as their avarice.

"Dirge has set his sights on Sorath, and the reaver nation of the Kothrai. He…"

"Kothrai," I said. "The ships which block our path. The *same* Kothrai?"

Aerik shot me a withering look.

"You always were a slow student, Moer. Of *course* there's only one kind of Kothrai. And they – for reasons I can only assume are base, vile, seditious and venal – are working for Dirge."

"Does he seek to slay their gods, too?"

Aerik nodded, lifting his pipe to his lips again.

"Perhaps not so slow after all," he said. "The Doom was indeed intended to reduce the old Gods of Sarem – to replace them with… well, with *you*. And, as you had taken it upon yourself to sulk in your tower like a lovesick calf, for that power to flow directly into the one they call 'Endsong'. Our old friend Dirge, again. How else do you think he could return from where Zael sent him?"

This was beginning to sound horribly familiar.

It was all my fault; I was a well-meaning but incompetent child; only the sage advice of an older, wiser mind could soothe my shame and set me on the path to redemption. In short, Aerik Stormsong in full flight.

I was having none of it.

"I won't do it again. There's no way. Not you, or the Archaeon, or any number of Gods and demons can make me…"

"If you don't, she'll die," said Aerik.

Simple as that. Cold as a blade of ice straight through the sternum.

"*All of them* will. They're misfits and freaks. The by-blows of sorcery welling up to fill the places where the Gods have faded. They're no match for Dirge, or for his ally Grennen Vhul. A proper necromancer, that one."

"And what's *that* supposed to mean?"

"He does it right. Skulls, black armour, a coven of demons… not moping about in silks writing bloody poetry."

"Hey! You're a *bard*, Stormsong! And who says I'm not a real necromancer? I…"

His look of smug self-assurance drew me up short. But not soon enough.

"Anghul, lad. *He* says you're not. But he can help you. He can show you the way…"

"Another destitute God. No thank you. I've had enough of them for one lifetime."

"In Sorath, he was worshiped as Urghal, Herald of Abyssus. Not the lord of death, but a passable substitute. Abyssus, sadly, hasn't been heard of for some time. But his herald… well, people *are* still dying. Anghul has a little power, bled over from the symmetry in his Facet. And with Zael gone from within you…"

I don't know if the feeling which gripped me then was Aerik's work, or an unfolding of memories long held dormant. But I saw my mind cast wide in a shimmering web, binding up the bones of the dead. I drank down the pure, vengeful chill of their desire. I felt the power I had once commanded, the thrill of exultation as I stood at the very bow of the Graveyard Ark, black cape blowing out behind me like a thundercloud. The earth below trembled to the relentless march of a hundred thousand armoured wights, as much a part of me as my own pale flesh.

It called to me, like the lure of poppy's blood in the fevered mind of an addict. I couldn't hide the twitch which tugged at the corner of my eye, or the tiny smile which bared my canine teeth.

Oh, I wanted it back. *All of it.* It was the fear of what I had become which locked me away in my tower – fear, and the vigil I kept over a pair of broken Gods. But there was a greater fear. I had seen how easily history could write out the truth, replacing it with holy lies.

"It slipped away so slowly that you never felt it leave," said Aerik, his voice a rough whisper. "Take the word of one who has been… *reduced*. I am a mere shadow, Kuhal, and every word I speak comes from within you. There is nothing I can tell you which you don't already know."

It was true. In reality, I knelt on the salt-crusted deck of Sorrow's Vengeance, cradling a sword in my hands. The crew had left me, but

Elion Morekh had taken the helm, and his milky-eyed, stitch-crazed face was somehow reassuring.

"She'll die if you don't, boy," said the shade. But I needed no more convincing.

"What do I do?" I asked.

Aerik's smile was as bright and broad as the sunrise.

"Go and give you daughter back her blade. I must advise her further. She is in possession of certain… means… which will draw the Antlered One closer."

He was already beginning to fade. Whatever sorcery bound the remains of the Stormsong's soul to his blade of glass, they must have been taxed to breaking point to sustain him for so long.

"Wait!" I shouted, holding out my hand. It passed through the weave of Aerik's robe, feathering the wool away into smoke. "This time, no tricks, Warbard. This time… there will be a price."

Aerik's eyes, and the outline of his face, seemed to sink away, dissolving into a pattern of light and shade on the dappled bronzewood deck. But there was still enough left of both for me to see him smile.

"We know your price, Kuhal Moer. We've *always* known. If you succeed in this, then Makara will live again. We promise."

I scrabbled at the phantom Warbard, my hands trailing through swirls of mist.

"You know a way, then?"

"Let us just say… we know of a way more honourable than the one you've so recently contemplated." He grimaced. "We offer you something you've taken away from so many others, necromancer. We offer you a family."

Aerik's eyes blinked closed, then vanished. The shadows snapped taut, swept away by an invisible gale, and shimmering sunlight played across the glass blade in my hands. Then a huge, callused paw settled on my shoulder.

"Enough talking to the spirits, Deadfather," rumbled the glacial voice of Rasq. "*We* know you're not mad – at least by the standards of this crew – but mumbling to yourself like that does raise a few questions."

I stood, shaking, the feeling of dark exultation still casting its echoes inside my skull.

"Where's Siara? I have… *news* for her. And her blade, of course."

"She'll need it," grunted the Shamen. "Four Kothrai warships. Four! They've never crossed over in such numbers before!"

I smiled grimly.

"Then it's all the more important that I'm ready to fight. Lead on, Rasq, and we'll show these outlanders a proper welcome."

We found Siara atop the forecastle of the *Vengeance*, squinting through an ornate brass spyglass at the Kothrai fleet. A heavy wooden table was bolted to the deck beside her, and the sailcloth which covered it did little to mask the shape of a huge and hulking corpse. One hairy-knuckled hand hung down from below the sheet, slowly dripping blood.

My daughter snapped the spyglass closed, and turned to me with a brittle smile.

"I take it he told you, then? If not everything… then at least enough?"

I nodded. I was still, to be honest, a little dumbfounded by this fey, dark, and unspeakably powerful young girl who claimed to be my kin.

"There's more," she said. "But it can wait until we've dealt with our uninvited guests. The Kothrai have raided here before… the Faeroans have legends about green-eyed demons from the sea carrying off their women. This is the first time we've faced so many, though. We think it's because they know you're here."

"For all the good I'll do," I said. "You were there in Oram, girl. I was hardly a battle-striding colossus that night."

"I saw you use yourself as a conduit for power," she replied, all coldly rational. It seemed my daughter shared her mother's disdain for melodrama. "*Any* power. The *wrong* powers, of course – but then again, none which resonated with the 'blight inside you were available. Your whole escapade was akin to playing an air on a badly tuned lyrecaster."

"Hey! I didn't see *you* stepping in to help! People *died*, girl! Good people…"

She looked at me for a long moment, anger and disbelief warring in her eyes.

"People died in Almerre, and Cyvenne, and Urexes, too. People died because of the Doom. The parents who raised me, for instance. People die *all the damned time!* I sent you the Burning Dark – which, by the way, cost me dearly to bind and master. If you'd heeded its words, we could have saved a *lot more* of those people. But you had to stand and fight!"

"Excuse me if I place little faith in demons," I said, curling my lip in a snarl. "And as for the Doom…"

I was ready to argue my case until all Yrde ground itself to dust on its axis. But Siara shut my mouth with one fingertip, a fragile little smile on her face.

"No," she said. "There's no time for this. I know we have a whole lifetime of silly arguments to catch up on, Father, but what we need now isn't about who's right. Though, of course, it's obvious ..."

"Captain!" shouted Rasq, from his perch out on the bowspirit. "They're changing tack! Looks like they're going to cut across our starboard quarter. Sorcery's building – I think they'll try to weather the broadside, then close to grappling distance."

Siara wrinkled her nose.

"See? We need the *Aemortarch* now, Father. We need these reavers to see that they've woken the terrible beast of Sarem, the thing which has the Coldblood skulking scared."

"That 'beast', child – and how flattering a term it is – was half Zael Kataphraxis, and half my own madness. Aerik said something about Anghul's power, some bleed-over from Sorath, but..."

Her eyes twinkled.

"These fools are *from* Sorath, Lamenter. They believe that Urghal guides the drowned down to the halls of Abyssus, to judgment. Just a touch of necromancy, and they'll be leaking in their britches. After all, their own master commands the dead. But the way he does it..."

"I've seen how the Doom works," I grated. "Vile sorcery. Such perversions have no place in this world."

"Good!" she said. "Get mad about it! A little righteous fury! Then, all you have to do is drink Sothara's blood..."

"Wait! What? There's no way that..."

"Oh, don't be a big baby," said the Stormreaper. "Just a little more won't hurt you."

"*More?* When have I ever..."

"What did you think was really in Gryst's damned soup? Bonebark and blindflower wouldn't have brought you back anywhere *near* so fast."

I felt slightly ill. My memories of Sothara da'Urgon Roege were hardly pleasant, and, as every warlock knows, blood has terrible power. Power which cuts both ways.

"Don't fret, Father. He's very, very dead. But Anghul is bound by rituals, and blood is one of the oldest...

"No pressure whatsoever," rumbled Rasq. "But those black ships are moving fast. Take my advice and *drink*, Khytein. What have you got to lose?"[12]

I thought about the way in which Sothara had tried to entrap me once before, and I shuddered. But Siara was right. They needed the Aemortarch now, not a feeble, hesitant old coward. I held out my hand, and she pressed a slim crystal phial into my palm, wrapping my fingers around it.

I held my breath, pulled the stopper, and threw it back, feeling it burn down my throat, slithering as it went.

It came on hard, like the rush of bladeleaf venom. I gurgled, sparks popping inside my eyes. Visions from the darkness of my tribe's memory spun at me out of nowhere – autumn leaves spattered with blood, dolmen stones arrayed with grinning skulls, twisted oaks hung heavy with rusted chains…

And the form of a robed and hooded creature, squatting on a throne of weathered granite, its claws bound with iron knives. A pair of immense, spreading antlers reared up from within its cowl, tangled in thorns.

But the shadowed glade where it sat was overgrown, the ground beneath the throne boggy and sinking. Skeletal hands clawed up from stagnant pools, while flies and other crawling things scuttled across Anghul's body, swarming in clouds from the open folds of his robe. Death had come to the Lord of Death himself, and the only spark of sentience in his moss-hung frame was the sparkle of fire in his eyes.

Those eyes held me, though. I imagined I heard a leathery creaking, as lips long mummified split in a ghoulish grin.

"Punish them, my prodigal," sighed the Khytein God of Corpses. **"Seek Abyssus. I will be the key, but he is the gateway…"**

With those cryptic words, Anghul's image blurred and faded. Power rushed into me, cold and sweet as meltwater, making the mageblight in me come alive.

She was right. It *resonated* – a low hum, a tuning-fork echo which felt *right* – not like the mental violation of Zael, or the crippling death-agony of Aesurn. Not even like the despairing last gasp of Kharnath. No. This was *necromancy*, and it fit me like a spiked black gauntlet, oiled and lethal. The sight which returned to my eyes was not of the sun and spray of the shallow sea, but a shadow-realm of darkness,

---

12. The phrases which have preceded some of Yrde's greatest disasters are, in order of hubris - 'What have you got to lose?', "What could possibly go wrong?" and "Hey! Watch this!" Those in my trade will also recognize - "Foolish mortals! I am invinci… *(gurgling, chopping sounds of decapitation)."*

where witchfire seethed and crackled, painting all life as a scrawl of emerald flame.

I staggered to the table, looking down at my hands. A little focus, and they brimmed with pale green fire, dripping as slow as mercury. A moment's hesitation, and I thrust them both down through the ragged sailcloth, through dented armour, through flesh, through ribs…

I clutched the dead man's heart, and I knew him.

Paladyne Samek Uveryn, lately of the White Brotherhood, protectors of the Pyx of Saint Acanthes. Now just a slab of meat and gristle, his soul bound to his dead flesh by strings of light.

I didn't have to remember anything. No rune, nor song, nor incantation. Anghul's gift flowed through me as intuitively as the pump and surge of blood through a living man's veins. I carefully knotted those threads, twisting them into a compacted star of power. I pushed it into the cold meat of his heart with my thumbs, and felt the muscle kick between my fingers, slippery and vital.

His scream shocked me back into the world of light. Bellowing what was surely the second half of some terrible death-curse, the Paladyne jack-knifed upright, one huge fist catching me squarely on the jaw. I spun away and Rasq caught me, laughing.

Still the scream went on. Through a haze of red I saw Uveryn throw off the sailcloth, exposing the ragged tear in his armoured cuirass, the bloody wound where a ghuldren blade had hacked open his guts. Now they slopped out in a slithering rope, and he clawed them back in, howling.

I clicked my jaw back into place, shrugged Rasq off, took two tottering steps, and backhanded the undead knight, hard.

"Shut up!" I shouted, the Cold Voice slicing into his mind like razors. "So you're *dead!* There's no need to carry on about it! I told you I had need of you, Uveryn."

"Dead?" rasped the wight. He tried, half-heartedly, to stuff his entrails back through the rent in his armour. "Then you really *are* the Lamenter. This is a blessing, Lord! I only ask…"

"Oh, be quiet!" I snarled. "You don't *ask*, Uveryn. Not any more. And for the record, you were just the first fresh meat my darling daughter found for me." I pointed at Siara, who was grinning with smug self-satisfaction. A little too much like Aerik for my liking, in fact.

"Tell your pet ogre that the sharks are going hungry." I sketched a mocking bow. "*Necromancy*, milady. Though why you couldn't have just carried on the family tradition without me…"

"I take after Mother," sighed the Stormreaper. "So my talents lie in other areas, alas. But *this*…"

"I'm glad you're so impressed. We must hope your Kothrai friends are equally credulous. You!" I swung around to level a finger at Uveryn. "Stop playing with your filthy guts! Either bind them in or rip them out, dead man. Gastric processes won't feature highly in the rest of your existence."

The look on Uveryn's face was almost pathetically grateful.

"I am one of yours in truth, then? Lord, what would you have me do?"

"Decompose quickly," I snapped. "And make sure your tongue is the first thing to fall off."

Too harsh, perhaps. The hulking great dead man looked pitifully sad. "Oh, very well. Find a sword, and use it better this time than you did the last. You can be my bodyguard."

Siara cleared her throat.

"Ummm… actually, Father, there's already somebody who wants to take that role…"

A flicker of movement caught my eye, and I looked up, out over the sea, just in time to watch Urmohk's soulbound Draken skim the wavetops with the clawed tip of one wing. The beast was immense – a young sire, all bronze and black, its fangs bared in an exultant grin as it rolled and climbed. The Zengaji on its back looked like a frail little stick-doll perched in the stirrups, but I knew just how deadly the combination of Draken and rider could be. Those Kothrai were going to wish they had never come to Sarem – and that was before they'd even met *me* face to face.

I heard armoured bootsteps behind me as I leaned out over the rail, breathing in the clean scent of salt and sky. It would be Elion, I thought – him, or that sentimental fool Seventails, who thought that a little shared blood gave us a culture…

But it wasn't.

"You brought back Uveryn," said a voice I hadn't, until that instant, realised I missed. "I don't know whether to curse you or kiss you for that, Lamenter. And as for dragging me along on this little cruise…"

It was Silbern Chaar, clad in her nightmare armour, and the look on her face was one of little sleep and even less solace. She tried bravely to smile, but I could see the corpses reflected in her eyes. Feurio Zahfrey's stood foremost among them.

"I'm sorry, then. Not for Uveryn – though I'm sure he'll feel sorry enough for himself after not too long."

"Don't be." She took my daughter's tiny hand in one great black gauntlet. "Siara has told me everything. And I've decided that this is the best way to grieve for Oram. We'll strike back at the ones who did this, Kuhal Moer."

Siara smiled.

"And Silbern can make sure you don't get cut to pieces on the way. Isn't that nice?"

The Ghuram have a saying. "When a woman talks *to* you, smile, nod, and say nothing foolish. When two women talk *about* you, smile, nod… and plan your escape." I wondered what these two had planned for me – and decided it was probably some variation of 'Silbern will keep the fool well supervised'.

"Do you really think," I asked, "That these Kothrai will have any respect for a deathless, necromantic tyrant protected by a mere *woman?*"

They looked at each other, then back at me – a withering stare. My attempt at chauvinistic outrage withered and died.

"If the great-granddaughter of Vyrim Chaar is a 'mere woman', then I'll eat Elion's hat," said Siara. "And in any case, Kothrai is a matriarchal society. They worship the trinity of the divine feminine."

"If that doesn't work, I can always cut a few of them in half," grunted the sword-maiden. "Horrible violence tends to garner a fair amount of respect."

I knew when I was beaten. But I still had some ragged dignity left.

"Remember what happened to everyone else who tried to help me, lass," I said – to neither one of them in particular. "There are small blackened patches of dirt out in the Desolation which record their noble sacrifice."

"Boundless gratitude," smirked Siara. "Another of his many qualities."

Silbern chuckled.

"Just try to keep up, Ontohki," I grated, feeling the blood of Sothara Roege kick and squirm inside of me.

His Facet may have been diminished, but the Shard of Death was strong here, where the Shallow Sea foamed around the waist of the great Colossus, and the pillars of the gates stood gaunt and black, circled by flocks of white-winged gulls. Down below us, the seabed was a graveyard of wrecked and broken ships, many of them tangled up with the bones of the drowned. Tendrils of witchfire quested up toward the light like saltwrack, calling to the power which lay dormant in my belly.

"As you like it, Father. Four ships, then. You and your bodyguard – Silbern and your ghoul – take the one on the starboard point. There – the sail marked with the weeping eye. I will take the Hanged Man and destroy their flagship. Seventails and Rasq, the trireme with the swordfish ram. That leaves the last one for the ladies. Agreed?"

The Stormreaper must have been in contact with them all through some sorcerous means, because she grinned, loosing the peace-knots from the twin long knives at her hips.

"They're expecting a show, Father. I'd suggest you deliver. Issara was quite fixated on drinking Sothara's blood herself, rather than giving it to a dried-out old has-been."

I raised an eyebrow – the perfect image of Aerik himself.

"Her words. Not mine."

"And to think, I never sent Zengaji to murder her in her sleep. *Gratitude*, hmm?"

"It's scarce in this world," said Silbern, unlimbering her greatsword. She shot me a certain look.

The Kothrai ships were close enough now that I could see the men crowding their beams, round shields held high, weapons glittering in the spray as they tacked in. They would indeed scythe past our bows, daring a broadside from the cannon at barely twenty span's distance. A shimmer of sorcery coiled around the low, sinister raidercraft, whose oars churned the water to foam, pulled hard to the thud of hidden drums.

"And allegedly one of my many qualities," I muttered, striding toward the bowspirit. Rasq was already away, swarming up the ratlines like a some gigantic spider. I held myself steady, a rope clenched in one fist, and teased at those drowned threads of witchfire, calling to them, promising release…

It was time to take the measure of these Kothrai. But it seemed that our as-yet unseen master gunner, Harlaw, would have the first strike.

I was forced to hold tight as Elion Morekh spun the ship's wheel hard, presenting our flank to the onrushing quartet of raiders. Long iron guns were run out by an army of thralls, and as the spellweavers aboard the Kothrai galleys babbled and raved Harlaw ordered the tapers pressed to one hundred and forty fuses.

The broadside began near the stern, then rippled forward in a wave which trembled the *Sorrow's Vengeance* to her keel. Stabbing fingers of fire and clouds of smoke, a ringing noise in my ears as though the world had become one vast cathedral bell…

And then came the splintering of wood, the screams and curses from the Kothrai as they died. Perhaps, across the divide from their native land, the power of their wards and bindings was weakened. Certainly, it couldn't stop iron cannonballs. Not such a storm of them…

Harlaw's battery of solid shot tore into their ships like some vast invisible flail, snapping off masts, shearing away whole banks of oars, and wreaking a terrible toll among the warriors tight-packed on their boarding decks. I watched cannonballs the size of men's heads skip and bounce through the press, tearing black-clad Kothrai away in a spray of blood and gristle. Others were cut down as their allies exploded around them, lacerated by chips and shards of bone. Wooden splinters flew, impaling, slashing. Fires guttered to life, rippling across the fallen sailcloth.

The drums fell silent for a moment. Then their strident beat came pounding through again, as new oars were run out. Whips were cracking belowdecks, I was sure, as Kothrai slavemasters tried to close the gap. One of the ships – the one marked with a great weeping eye – was wallowing in the swells, holed below the waterline, and the only hope for survival for those crowded atop her was to board the *Vengeance*. If not, their heavy furs and chain would drag them to the bottom.

As had happened to so many others.

Others who I now mastered, thanks to the power of Anghul.

It occurred to me, as I let my will spear down into the icy depths – down to where sunlight was a blurred memory, and eyeless fishes gnawed on a feast of bones – that I would soon need a new Incantus. Without one, I was reduced to commanding a mere handful of undead, and even that burden was enough to sorely tax my brain. Still, it was immaterial. The dead below were eager to rise from their silty grave, hungry for warmth and light and release. They obeyed me without question.

The ship we had marked struck home, timbers splintering and grinding against the copper-sheathed hardwood of the *Vengeance's* hull. But before grappling lines could bite, and black-swathed Kothrai begin their assault, I loosed the dead under my command, letting some collapse into salt-bleached bones as their power was passed on, redoubled…

An anchor broke the surface at the stern of the Kothrai vessel, arcing up from out of the sea in a spray of brine and rotting kelp. A long, rusted chain flew behind it. Now another and another burst from the swells, corroded and massive, biting into the timbers of the raidercraft with a terrible, final sound.

The spellcaster aboard the galley pointed, screaming. He was a pale, stick-thin man wrapped in soiled red robes, his face painted chalky grey and daubed with runes.

Symbols I'd seen before. On the dripping bodies of a score of butchered priests, swinging from the rafters of a dark cathedral…

He belonged to Dirge, and I snarled, levelling one gnarled finger in his direction. From deep below I fished up the memory of a drowned man, his lungs filling with water, his vision blurring to black as terrible pressure embraced him…

That was the sensation which I drove into the Kothrai mage's mind – a mind which seemed foul to the touch. Suddenly he was bent double, retching, turning purple… his brain yammering in terror that we was sinking, drowning, pressure building…

The man's eyes collapsed into his skull with a wet double pop. Then his ribs caved in, a bundle of wet twigs snapping. Blood spumed from between his lips.

And the dead pulled their anchor-chains tight.

Without ceremony, the entire Kothrai ship was torn in half, timbers shearing and splintering as skeletal hands took up the strain. Water swirled in and men began to scream, scrabbling at the smooth side of the *Vengeance* for grip. A sorry few made it and began to climb, but the rest –

Down into a whirlpool they went, armour and furs and weapons useless, dragging them under to a nether-realm of wrecks and bones. Those who looked down as they drowned would have seen a hundred empty-eyed skulls grinning up at them, and a thicket of fleshless hands groping toward them, eager for the warmth of blood.

Uveryn and Silbern Chaar were waiting at the rail for the rest. Fingers which wrapped around the polished bronzewood were unceremoniously hacked to stumps. The undead paladyne's boot connected with a man's face, all but crushing his skull. Swords flashed, misted red, rose and fell…

And we were done. I completed the ritual with a gesture and a word, releasing the souls of the drowned. Motes of witchfire floated up from the churning wrack, fraying apart in the low sunlight. I don't know where those poor souls went, but it was surely a better place than the clammy grip of sea-bottom mud.

And my allies had only just begun to fight.

Silbern Chaar stumbled back from the rail, her armour spattered with gore. She drew a silken cloth from one of her belt loops to clean her great three-span broadsword, letting the rippled steel wink in the sun.

"That was a foul business, Lamenter," she said, not able to look me in the eye. "I counted four hundred men, gone to their doom without even lifting a blade."

"And I counted four hundred rapists and murderers, about to do the bidding of that bastard you call Endsong. Would you rather have offered them guest right?"

Silbern scowled.

"You know what I mean. There were honourable warriors among them. It seems… *wrong* that they were so cruelly slain. Drowning is a bad death."

"I know," I said – and there was true conviction in my voice. The price of necromancy is to know the doom of all those you raise. Taking the burden of their last moments, their final pain… that is what unpicks the knots in that witchfire web.

"Three hundred and eighty-two dead men were released from these waters today," I said, trying to make her understand. "Honourable men, no doubt. Sailing to conquest, most of them. Their ships were smashed to matchwood by Faeroan seige-engines. Some have been down there for hundreds of years. Unconsecrated, unmourned… trapped. Was it a foul business to set them free?"

Silbern's face became blank and cold – the practiced, emotionless mask of a soldier.

"Forgive me my questions, then, Lord. There is much, it seems, I do not understand about the wars of the Unmanifest." She turned to walk away.

"Oh no." I said. "Not yet. You want to learn? Then *watch!* Three more ships, Silbern Chaar. And I don't think our new friends are inclined to give any quarter…"

Urveryn gurgled, swaying, his broadsword clenched in one pale fist. Silbern's sidelong glance at his slack face could very well have been one of envy.

"For Oram, then," she said – and the unspoken fate of Feurio Zahfrey hung in the air between us. "Your daughter called her ship the *Sorrow's Vengeance*. Let us make it a worthy name."

Grappling hooks bit. Timbers crunched. Horns blared out.

Somewhere high above, Urmokh's draken screamed, a long, high, predatory howl.

Now she would see sorcery turned to war. My own efforts were merciful, compared to some which I had witnessed. But there is a certain cruel joy to be had in watching naivety crushed. A flaw in my character, perhaps – but such hard lessons had defined my entire childhood.

I looked out across the canted decks of the three remaining Kothrai raiders, at their ineffectual spellweavers, at the grizzled veterans and the beardless boys gripping their axes tight…

And I knew they were all doomed.

"Knee-deep in the ocean
Ankle-deep in bones
Souls becoming water
Guard our hearths and homes"

This Faeroan rhyme, regarding the Colossus which
stands at the mouth of the Shallow Sea, hints at
the sheer number of enemy ships which have tried
to invade the domain of the Floating Cities and
failed. It's estimated that, from the legendary (and
likely grossly overstated) grand fleet of Prince
Obermarche to the conquering Third Nautical
Arm of the Angan Empire, over thirty-two
thousand individual vessels, ranging in size from
raider longships to three-masted quinquiremes
have been destroyed by the massed trebuchets
and flame ballistae of the Faeroan Gates. Indeed,
the fabled Colossus must stand ankle-deep in the
bones of dead sailors.

'Folk Rhymes of Faeros and Angenstrand' - third edition
Compiled by Yalder and Owynn Greyth

IT SEEMED, HOWEVER, that the fierce sea-reavers did not agree.

The Kothrai were worked up into a frenzy of battle, immune to
the fears which would have unmanned a lesser host. Drum-beats
pounded frantically, accompanied by the rough clatter of axe-hafts
against round wooden shields. All three low-slung galleys struck the
flank of the *Vengeance* hard, and men clad in furs and mail began to
swarm up the grappling lines, a motley assortment of blades in their
hands and clenched between their teeth.

"Come on!" I shouted, slapping Uveryn's broad back as I ran past
him. Where were the others? I did not think for an instant that Rasq,
Seventails, Issara or Kell were cowards – and of course, the Hanged
Man had no concept of mortal dread. But in their absence the terrible
black-armoured axemen were storming the decks… and they were
not short on numbers.

The three of us rushed toward the place where the nearest Kothrai
ship had hammered home – the trireme with the swordfish-shaped

ram. As we went, I reached out for the drowned warriors I had so recently slain. Soul-stuff twisted away from the hooks of my will, swirling through the water in frenzied eddies.

Once again, I tried to call out to Sei – because the little skeletal snow-lynx was often able to seek out threads of witchfire too fine for my coarse human mind. But while he was close, it seemed he was still sleeping. And trying to command a cat, as most of you will know first-hand, is like trying to put out a volcano by pissing in its crater. Futile.

"The hard way, then," I panted, loosening Cryptfeeder in its scabbard. Anghul's power would help me little if it came down to steel on steel, but there seemed to be no choice.

Then a huge, shaggy-grey shape plunged down past us from above, hammering into the Kothrai where they swarmed up over the rail. It was a stormwood bear, one of the Sons of Theyr, ten times the bulk of a man and with claws as long as daggers. Its sheer mass and fury flung a dozen reavers aside, though they surged forward again, axes and swords flashing, battlecries ringing out…

And they died. Paws battered them to a pulp, while yellowed fangs ripped chunks free, spattering gore. Armour crumpled and collapsed, skulls cracking and bones shattering within. A score of Kothrai plunged over the rail, some living, some dead - all doomed. But there were more of them, and their frenzy brooked no fear.

They were no fools, either. They brought long spears to the fore, hunting lances with cross-barred tips.

At the very moment when the beast seemed overwhelmed it reared back, roaring defiance. It rolled clear just as a rain of ice tore through the Kothrai - jagged knives of it, two spans long. Rasq fell from the rigging behind the storm, a staff of bone in one hand, a stone-bladed maul in the other. Deadly force licked out, and I watched spear-wielding Kothrai freeze solid with the chill of sorcery, their eyes frosted over. When the shamen's maul followed through, they simply shattered, steaming fragments flying wide.

The great bear's form blurred, and now I was looking at Seventails, his patchwork cloak besmirched with blood. A wink, and a nod to the ice-shamen, and then he shifted again – a sickening moment of inside-out flesh and bone, then a brief popping sound, the iron scent of sorcery…

A satin-black Ghurami hunting cat crouched in his place, a sash of furs and hides cinched tight about its broad neck. With no surprise I noticed that one of the patches was pale human skin.

"These ones are ours," rumbled Rasq, looking like the mythical yheti in truth. Seventails yowled, glowering down at a boatload of Kothrai warriors. They hammered their weapons against their shields and shouted taunts in their own rough language, raising a thicket of spears.

"If you're sure you don't need the help…" I shrugged.

The Northman bared his teeth. *Changed*, he had said… and he was already three quarters the legend his sorcery had made him. As for Seventails - he was every peasant herder's nightmare made flesh. I wondered what form his other five skins gave him.

"After months of indolence, Deadfather, you must allow my friend and I some exercise. Go and assist the ladies. They may find your efforts chivalrous, at least."

With that, both Seventails and Rasq leaped over the side, plunging in amongst the milling Kothrai warriors with a bellowed war-cry. Spear shafts snapped. Flat, thin planes of ice flickered out, bisecting a ring of men at the waist. Then came the crunch of bones, the piteous screams of the disemboweled…

I turned away. Silbern looked almost as pale as Uveryn as she caught up with me.

"What *are* these people, Lamenter?"

"The kind of sorcerers who came before pointy hats and scrolls," I said, furrowing my brow. Try as I might, the souls of the dead Kothrai escaped me, plunging down into the salty water like coils of ink. No matter. There were clean-picked bones aplenty here in the shadow of the Colossus. If it came to it, I would raise skeletons crusted with barnacles and weeds.

"They… they're *monsters!*"

"And my dear daughter is a *witch*, Silbern. Our friend the paladyne wasn't entirely wrong about such matters. The fact is, we *need* to be monsters. Light don't beat darkness, lass. It takes a deeper dark to snuff it out."

Now we approached the midships of the *Vengeance*, where the rail swooped low to the water. Through a combination of luck and seamanship, the captain of the smallest raidercraft had hauled to at a place where his men could swarm aboard – and they awaited no invitation. Siara's thralls fought ineffectively to stem the tide, for the Kothrai were skilled warriors, and their long-bladed axes made short work of the mute, dazed crewmen. Blood slopped through the scutters, making the surface of the shallow sea boil with predatory life.

"Here, then!" I shouted. "A chance to test their honour, mistress Chaar!"

She didn't need to answer. For the first time this day, Silbern was smiling.

We utterly blindsided them – a suicide charge of three against five-score Kothrai, with yet more swarming up the ladders and planks lashed between our ships. Disbelief turned to amusement. Amusement to bloodlust. The black-clad men nearest to us brandished their weapons, lumbering forward into a ragged charge…

And I cast out my will, snaring the souls of a handful of thralls, binding them tight to their twitching flesh. Men who had thought their foes dead, sagging from spear-shafts and split by blades, suddenly found teeth around their throats, fingers gouging into their eyes…

A momentary fugue – a thrall hacked apart, his head and one arm flopping on a twist of muscle and shattered spine, crabbing sideways across the deck to tackle his murderer. Dead fingers forced open the Kothrai's jaws until bone and gristle snapped…

Then we were on them, and my two bodyguards closed in, left and right, greatswords swinging. Chainmail parted, links flying like hail. Once, twice, great butchering strokes unspliced entrails and innards, and four Kothrai went down, flopping and bucking like gutted trout. I darted between them, Cryptfeeder a blur, but I was blocked by a crossed pair of axes. The Kothrai warrior who gripped them was fast, snarling – he moved from defence to attack, forcing me to parry left, feint right… then gather up the death-agony of one of his fallen comrades, driving it through his forehead like a spike. The green-eyed axeman gurgled, struck dumb, then toppled forward to be spitted on my blade. A stroke of luck – for I, too was somewhat distracted, by the tooth-pulling sensation of raw necromancy.

I staggered back, gasping for breath. All our little sortie had achieved was to raise the ire of the three hundred remaining Kothrai.

Urveryn had taken the thrust of a short-sword through the chest, but he didn't even look at the bone-hilted steel as he strode forward, moaning. Silbern Chaar's spiked armour dripped with crimson, and her silver mask was closed, breath hissing from between its fangs as steam.

"Did you have an actual *plan* this time, Kuhal?" she asked, her voice muffled. "Or are you going to make me slap you, once this is over?"

"Same as last time, lass. We cut them to pieces. They die. And if I can just pin down one of their slippery damned souls…"

"I'll leave the sorcery to you," she growled. "But leave the killing to me. That last axeman almost had you, Lamenter. Magick makes you sloppy."

Now a figure draped in bearskins pushed through the ranks of the Kothrai, holding his brothers back. He carried a double-bladed axe and a round, spiked shield, and his helm was adorned with raven wings.

"You fight well, Sarem'ec," he growled. "But I would take your scalps this day. One at a time or all three at once, it is all the same to Hithar Drahl."

I chuckled. This huge oaf and my father would have had much to talk about. In another time and place, the glorious fools would have been fast friends.

Hithar Drahl levelled his axe.

"You think this is *funny*, pale one? You will be first to taste my steel!"

Yes indeed. They would probably both have died in some roistering ale-quaffing contest, their livers pickled in their chests...

"Abyssus will be pleased to meet you," I said, bringing Cryptfeeder up to guard. The words seemed to have little effect.

But then I noticed the beads of blood quivering on the edge of my blade. Tiny droplets of crimson dripped upward from each spike of Silbern Chaar's armour, running like quicksilver against the pull of gravity. Threads of blood twined skyward, drawing my gaze...

And I saw Issara in all her beauty and horror, naked as the day she was born, held aloft by wings of shadow. A thick, rippling skein of blood coiled and spun around her, protecting what little modesty the Rasuuli witch cared to keep. *Strategic*, I noted, but hardly puritanical.

"Boys!" purred Issara, descending to land lightly atop the prow of the Kothrai raider. "So pleased to see you. And now that a little blood has been spilled, I fancy we should give it some company!" Hithar Drahl hefted his axe, his craggy brow furrowing into a frown.

"This is no place for women, wench," he growled. "Await the doom of your men, and I will be sure to rape you later. It is a mark of honour to be so chosen."

Issara laughed, a sound like crystal bells.

"And who's to say I don't want to rape *you* right now, you big ugly lump of beef?"

It's likely that the huge Kothrai would have been outraged. Had he lived.

As it was, he only had time to draw a final breath as Issara gestured with one finger, sending a liquid scrawl of blood through the air toward him. It burrowed between his thick belly-plate and his chainmail kilt, hissing.

Issara turned her palm up, fingers spread. Hithar Drahl groaned, his face turning a paler shade of white. Sweat beaded his forehead, and he dropped his axe.

"What's that? Is my grip a little too tight? Cutting off blood from your brain, perhaps? Or just that other thing you think with?"

Her fingers snapped shut. There was a horrible, wet popping sound, and the Kothrai collapsed to his knees, mouth open in a mute scream of agony. Even I, dead as I was, could feel the ghost of his pain. Every man there imagined it all too well.

"Kell!" shouted the blood-mage. "We feed!"

Then Issara wrapped her pale left hand around the clenched fist of her right. With a violent gesture she brought her hands apart, and blood fountained from Hithar Drahl's every orifice, hot and steaming, coiling through the air in spirals and jags. Blood from the decks joined it, and the tide plunged down throats and into eyes, burrowing into ears and up noses… as well as finding other, unspeakable forms of ingress. What horrors it wrought inside the Kothrai I do not know – suffice to say that they dropped to the deck like puppets with cut strings, leaking bile and gore. Ten died under the first rush of demonic blood, then twenty more, as the liquid tendrils leaped and danced, hungry for fresh victims. As for Hithar Drahl himself – he was wrung dry, a husk collapsed to nothing but bones and leather inside his armour. The look of suffering on his face had been shrivelled up into a horror-mask, wrinkled as a walnut.

Archers at the stern of the Kothrai raider were forming up, cranking back heavy crossbows. They took aim at the madly laughing witch perched atop their figurehead, but not one was quick enough to reach the trigger. Kell Du'ath appeared among them in a flash of ghostly light, her hands clasped together in prayer. Axes sliced at her, and spears stabbed down, but they broke and bent against her stone-hard skin, throwing sparks. Then her hair blew back in an invisible wind, strands whipping and flailing and *growing…*

Her eyes were utterly black. Black enough to fall into forever. Black enough to drown in.

Each single hair was pure mageblight, and they sizzled with power. Grown men in full chain and plate ran from this tiny girl – and were plucked from their feet, wrapped and bound by crystal-bright filaments, dragged screaming from the deck to hang like flies in a spider's web. Raving fire crackled, throwing the world into sharp-edged monochrome. Then there were no men left at all – just blackened bones tumbling away, red-hot armour hissing as it was swallowed by the sea.

"I see you. I'm watching. One, two, three..."

Rarely have the words of a nursery rhyme seemed so terrifying.

Silbern, Uveryn and I plunged into the fray behind Issara's wave of death, brutally hacking into those who the sorcery had missed. It was desperate fighting, for the Kothrai realised their doom, backed into a corner by blood and blades. I used the Dark Sight to skry out their weaknesses, dodging and parrying far more blows than I actually struck. When I did see an opening I darted the heavy sabre in and out like a serpent's tongue, piercing hearts and opening veins, slicing hamstrings an putting out eyes. But still the souls of the Kothrai eluded me.

"We have them now!" shouted Issara, tendrils of living blood whipping out from her fingertips to pierce a dozen men. "Go forward! The flagship awaits!"

Kell Du'ath was among the archers, her hair streaming out in a terrible halo to bind them up. The cloth was torn away from her empty eyes as well, and tiny spiders were swarming out from those blackened sockets, scuttling down the web of mageblight toward their prey.

"What Milady means," said the dead seeress "Is that she doesn't want to share our feast with you, necromancer. A rare display of good manners, I think... and one which you should probably heed."

"Oh yes," said Issara, smirking as she ripped the entrails from a fleeing swordsman's throat. "This is going to get a lot messier before it gets clean. Your lady friend there already looks fit to lose her breakfast."

In truth, Silbern was less green than ash-grey. Uveryn looked far healthier, though now two entire Kothrai spears and a small throwing axe were buried in his flesh.

"Lead on, then," she rasped, looking away as Kell's killing light flared. "We'll see what horrors your daughter can teach us, shall we? What's next? Men turned inside out? Slow flaying? Molten lead in their bones?"

Issara cooed.

"I *like* this one, Lamenter. Tell me, are you of a mind to share?"

I started walking away before Silbern could answer.

"I know," I hissed under my breath. "*Monsters*. Judge ye not, lass, as my bloody holy book says. Just remember that these Kothrai wrought the Doom."

"What?" she asked, as we left the sound of screams and cries behind us. "The fifteen-year-old boys? Or was it that sorcerous genius Hithar Drahl? *He* looked like an archmage, if ever I saw one."

"The archmage," I said "Is still ahead of us. I can feel his power... Hells, I can all but *taste* it."

"A match for Siara?"

I frowned.

"He... no. Not alone. His mind is... *deformed*. Stunted. But there's something coming up from below him. Something in the water. He's..."

An immense impact threw me from my feet before I could finish speaking, let alone skry out the sorcerer's intent. Something huge scraped its way along the *Vengeance's* keel, making the timbers quake beneath me as I struggled to rise.

I looked down toward the ship's sterncastle, to where the Kothrai flagship had rammed home, rusted grapples pulled taut. And I watched, horrified, as the water around the raidercraft turned black as night, oily and swirling, tapering up into pillars laced with foam. Two of the pillars merged together, twining into one appendage... and then this whole vast mass came crashing down across our decks, sweeping a score of thralls overboard. Bones and fragments of armour swirled in the inky darkness, scraps of mail and fur – and I realised, with a jolt, just what had happened to the souls of the Kothrai slain.

"A *sacrifice*," I cursed. "Thrown against us to die. And now..."

Silbern Chaar hauled me to my feet, just as a second pillar of black water came curving in, driving through the upper decks of the *Vengeance* like a battering ram. A fierce, malign will burned within that focused torrent, and its wellspring was aboard the Kothrai flagship.

Where Siara Anvhaur had gone, alone but for a single demon of the Nine.

"She needs us, Lamenter," said Silbern, reading the look on my face. "Witch or mortal, that's no power to face without steel at your back."

I nodded, reaching down into the deeps for the dead. But the darkness spread like a stain, blunting the force of my will, causing me to recoil in agony. It was like the sickness of the Doom – utterly polluted.

"Come on then," I gasped, propping myself up on Cryptfeeder. "And forget your conceits of honour, lass. This time it will be butchery."

The Kothrai warriors aboard the flagship had made no attempt to board us – they were gathered on the triple-tiered decks of their own vessel, silently watching the duel which unfolded amidships. There knelt my daughter, the Stormreaper, holding her pair of long-bladed knives, each one split like a tuning fork and humming with power. I recognized the blades – Jerrold Sinder's own, bound with sorceries to shatter bone. They seemed to have availed her little.

For the monster which faced her was the source of the dark Kothrai magick – a huge man clad in salt-crusted black scale, a draken-hide robe flying out behind him as he worked his will. His head was entirely hidden by a rusted, eyeless, bell-shaped helm, from which a pair of immense, chain-hung horns branched out. But his hands were the focus of that foul energy – oil-black skeletal claws, seething with darkness. The halo around his fists was not true fire – it was a smouldering hole in the world, punched clear through to the Outer Dark.

As I watched, the Kothrai brought his left hand high, then swept it down in a chopping arc. A pillar of black water reared up from between the two ships, swords and axe-blades spinning inside it. Then it curved over, spearing down toward the Stormreaper. She seemed too weak and dazed to stop it.

I screamed, forcing my will down through layers of silty blackness. Down into the mud and marl of the seabed, where ancient bones stirred, hands clenching the rusted stumps of swords…

I knew I'd be too late.

But the Hanged Man was there before I could even call the first of my wights to battle. It reared up out of the shadow of the Kothrai's mast, blood-soaked ropes snapping out to bind the sorcerer's wrists. Where they touched they burst into flame, and Urzen's creation howled. But – and all credit to the wretched thing – *it didn't let go.*

Not even when the seething tip of the waterspout hammered directly into its cowl, exploding into a thunderhead of steam. Little traceries of lighting danced within the cloud for an instant as the Nameless One's scream clawed its way up the scale and out of human hearing.

Then came a clear, distinct cracking sound, as of a crystal goblet tapped with a hammer.

The steam blew away in a great spiral, revealing the Kothrai raider's decks again, the ranks of black-clad warriors standing silent…

But the Hanged Man was gone.

All that remained of the last of Urzen's demons was a fluttering heap of rags – and as I watched, even these dissolved into a puddle of black water, writhing and twisting until they were utterly devoured. The dark liquid slithered across the deck to its master, running uphill into his cupped palm. Then it sunk into his pores, like rain on a parched desert. The huge, bell-shaped helm tilted upward, and though it was utterly expressionless, I knew the thing within it was smiling.

I could only stare in shock.

The Hanged Man was one of the lesser Nameless, true – but this Kothrai had just reduced it to ruin in a single instant. I remembered the Devouring Wind, and how it had torn down Corvo of Ontokh, himself a power in the Unmanifest. I recalled the difficulty I myself had faced, dismembering Sister Pain… and that had been at the height of my strength.

"This is bad, isn't it?" asked Silbern Chaar.

Uveryn cleared his throat - a singularly horrible sound.

"To use the correct theological terminology, milady," he rumbled. "We are *utterly fucked*."

The figure in the bell-shaped helm stood tall, his hands held high. Twisting spouts of darkness reared up on either side of him, taller than the masts of his ship, and now the Kothrai on the decks began to stamp their feet, setting up a slow, ponderous cadence.

"*Vuhl! Vuhl! Vuhl! Vuhl!*"

Chains jingled and clattered as he pointed at the Stormreaper.

"Give him to me, witch," said the sorcerer, in a voice which seemed more tired and sad than angry. "You know what we want. When my master feeds on him, your sorrows will be over. Is it really worth so much pain to let the old fool live?"

"You're wasting you time appealing to my better nature, Grennen Vuhl. I can't afford to have one. And as for the Lamenter… I fear you have underestimated my father, just as your pathetic master once did."

If only that were true! Beneath the Kothrai flagship my wights were rising, bone clasping bone as they clambered over each other's fleshless backs toward the light. The dark water swirled around them, trying to pluck them away from me. But I forced them on, teeth clenched tight with the strain of it.

"*Underestimated?*" asked Grennen Vuhl. "I think not. Neither he nor your other foolish vassals can save you now, Siara Anvhaur. Where are they, in any case? Your ragged little band of superstitions?

No stomach for a real fight?"

Siara smiled, and I was reminded afresh of her mother, the soul I kept trapped in the stone at my neck. Raw emotion clawed inside my chest.

"I have no vassals, Kothrai. I have *friends*. And something else you'll never comprehend, as well. I have a *strategy*."

Hell was unleashed inside the next few heartbeats. It began with a long, red-fletched arrow which caromed off Grennen Vuhl's helm, sending him staggering sideways. The clay ball behind its head split on impact with the deck, and draken vitriol spewed out, sending flames slithering across the polished hardwood. Then Urmokh was there, his mount folding its wings to slip between the Kothrai flagship's masts, faster than the bolt from a seige-bow. Talons struck, wrapping around the sorcerer and plucking him away into the air. A few scales of salt-rimed armour clattered to the deck forlornly.

"Now?" asked Silbern, slamming her skeletal visor shut. I nodded.

"Now. And spare no one."

She didn't hesitate, grabbing Uveryn and leaping over the rail. At the same time I felt hundreds of bony fingers scrabbling against the keel of the Kothrai raider, and I urged my undead to *climb*. They hooked their talons into the barnacle-crusted wood, scuttling up the sides of the ship hand over hand.

Grennen Vuhl wasn't about to be simply dismembered without a fight, though. Even as the draken lofted him skyward, he stabbed up at it with one of his waterspouts. An almost solid fist of darkness battered Scarwing from the air. I heard hollow bones snap and wing membranes tear, and the beast let out an agonized scream, dropping the Kothrai like a hot stone. A second pillar of foam-flecked darkness slammed into Urmokh from the right, tearing him from the saddle.

Siara leaped up to meet Grennen Vuhl as he fell, blades crossed. But the Kothrai had unshipped his own sword – a vast and jagged scimitar seemingly hammered from a cooled splash of iron – and he met her with a great double-handed blow, all his momentum behind it. Siara was thrown back in a detonation of raw magick, striking the ship's deck with enough force to crack the timbers. I was airborne myself, over the rail and falling as I watched Scarwing and Urmokh splash down, spinning and tumbling until they struck the surface of the ocean.

Then my dead men were amongst the Kothrai, coming up over the sides of the raidercraft all seaweed-hung and dripping. Bony hands throttled and ripped. The rusted stubs of swords sawed through pale white flesh, spilling blood…

Which rose into the air, droplets coalescing into strands, strands braiding into thick, barbed skeins…

Issara appeared amongst the Kothrai warriors in their confusion, her magick whipsawing through a dozen before they could even raise their axes. She nodded to me, licking her fingers clean of gore, and then drew a brace of daggers, blurring as she engaged a dozen more.

Rasq slammed into Grennen Vuhl next – he caught the armoured sorcerer just as he pushed off the mainmast with his boots, nimble as a Zengaji assassin. There were no eye-slits in Vuhl's rusted helm, but I could imagine him narrowing them as he fell toward his prey, scimitar above his head…

The shamen's arm was as long as Grennen Vhul was tall, an immense cantilevered mass of muscle and bone. It drove a fist the size of an ale-barrel into the Kothrai's chest, and three hundred stones-weight of angry shamen was enough to slam him back into the mast - and hard enough to make its stout timbers splinter and groan.

A second later Rasq's other fist connected with that bell-shaped helm, and ropes snapped, unraveling. The mast fell, even as the sorcerer summoned up a looping coil of dark water, tearing Rasq away. Throttling fingers missed his throat by a whisper.

My dead men were making short work of the Kothrai, backed up by Issara and Kell, Silbern and Uveryn. A swathe of black canvas settled gently over the afterdecks, muffling the screams and cries of the dying.

On the deck below, the Stormreaper had tottered to her feet, slotting her twin blades together. She gripped a double-ended instrument of bone – a half-span handle inset with tiny holes which she brought up to her lips…

But Grennen Vhul was far from dead. He arose just in time to watch a mob of his Kothrai axemen charge at Siara, shields held high. A sound – less a noise, more a flurry of unseen blades – shredded them in mid-stride, bones shattering as the song ran them through. My daughter's lips barely touched the bone-pipes of Jerrold Sinder, but their terrible keening set up dark harmonics in femurs and spines, skulls and ribs, cracking them to the marrow. The disjointed remains of ten men thudded to the deck around her, eyes wide in horror as they gasped and died.

Grennen Vuhl was not impressed.

"I tire of your games, witch," he growled, striding forward. He gestured with his hands, and twin spires of darkness punched up through the deck behind him, liquid fingers binding up Issara and Kell. Both struggled for a moment, and then they were sucked down through a ruin of timber and salt, their magicks flickering and dying. "Give him to me now, or your friends will perish slowly. My master can *devour*, Sarem'ec... or he can savour his repast. Pray you never live to feed his hunger."

Seventails was on him almost before he finished speaking – a silver-grey wolf with slavering jaws, emerald eyes flashing murder...

The Kothrai slapped him aside with a fist of darkness, breaking bones and shattering fangs. He had barely needed to twitch one finger.

"Very well. If that's your answer... we end this now." He raised his hands, runes glowing lambent red against the rusted iron of his helm.

The whole ship lurched as something vast was shat into life in the waters below it. Coils and eddies of dark water became horribly solid, slippery and thorned, bursting through the timbers to crush and snatch away my wights. Those on the seabed below looked up with empty eyes, showing me a vision of a huge and nebulous thing... a black anemone embracing the ship from bow to stern.

Uveryn hacked at a waist-thick tentacle of the stuff, but it simply engulfed his sword, tugging it from his hands. Then the foul appendage split open, gaping to swallow him whole. The paladyne struggled, but it was no use. I could see through the gelatinous flesh of the thing, and I watched my undead thrall melting like wax, his face turning to liquid. At once the tentacle snapped back, squeezing itself through a jagged hole in the ship's deck, and Uveryn was gone.

So were my drowned foot-soldiers – every one of them torn apart. The Kothrai's flagship was listing now, pulled down into the black water. Around us loomed a cage of twisting spires, studded with the flash of broken steel, poised to break over the decks and take us to the bottom.

"You'll never have him, Vuhl," said my daughter, spinning her bladed flute between her fingers. With her other hand she reached behind her back and drew forth a glass sword – one which was milky grey, shot through with the flicker of dying stars. The last fragment of Aerik Stormsong. "You don't understand what the Lamenter *is*, do you? His great-grandsire Sothara was a mere puppet-master of bones and flesh. But Kuhal Moer has raised dead *Gods*. Think on that, while you still struggle to raise the shade of a mad aspirant."

The Kothrai chuckled.

"An *aspirant*? My master is more than that, as you know too well. As for raising dead Gods – he's simply snuffing out the last of their power. Each facet which dies helps to feed Lord Dirge. All *you* are doing is prolonging the inevitable."

All this time I had watched Siara and her foe from atop the ship's bows, perched on a blood-slick bowman's walk. From here I had commanded the dead – but they were gone, and nothing stood between my daughter and the Kothrai warlock.

"You'll never defeat him, you know," she said, carefully wrapping her fingers around the hilt of her blade. Her feet shuffled into a fighting stance – one which my old swordmaster Ulkar would have approved of. "If Dirge couldn't, and the Angan Thearch… what hope for a drowned rat like you?"

"Oh, enough of your foolishness, girl," said Vuhl. "I've felt his power. A trifling amount of necromancy, bled over from some soul-rotten Shard. Whatever he *was*, he has been reduced. The Doom has done its work."

And with that, Grennen Vuhl brought his hands together, fingers interlaced. Spires of roiling darkness bent at right-angles, hissing in from either side. Siara sliced left and right with her ensorcelled blade, hacking the first two tentacles apart. But there were more. Ever more, and they came crowding in like the fingers of a closing fist, blotting out the light…

Now, I knew very little about family. The ties which bind kin and clan were as alien to me as the courtly manners of Ghuram, for I had been raised as a bargaining tool, the lesser son of a drunken warlord, and I had been universally reviled by my warrior brothers. Three hundred years in a cold spire, custodian to two mad Gods, had not taught me any rudiment of warm compassion.

But when I saw Grennen Vhul laughing, reaching out to slay my only child, I suddenly understood what all those bards and poets had meant. I suddenly knew why the most grizzled Khytein hunters, men who would joyfully tackle a stormwood wolf with their empty hands, would go out of their way to avoid a wild sow with piglets.

It was a feeling beyond anger. It came straight from the most primal, knotted core of my hindbrain, painting the world in a haze of crimson. *This was the kind of emotion which bound souls to their long-dead bones. This was the force of rage which dragged centuries-old wights from their graves, seeking bloody vengeance.*

Perhaps my insight was what bridged the gap. Because suddenly the voice of Anghul was there again, inside my head. Rage fueled my will, sending barbed tendrils of thought down into the inky waters, seeking out whole sunken graveyards worth of bones.

"No," said the shade of the Antlered Lord. **"Not that way. Do you remember Urexes, child? Do you remember the coming of Zael Kataphraxis?"**

The moss-hung old skeleton on its monolithic throne laughed, a sound like the winter wind through dead leaves. And I saw his plan – one which would tax his power and mine to their very limits.

I saw my daughter's face. There was fear there – the dawning of the realization that she was about to die. And in her eyes… the fear of her mother, the betrayal of a possessed and abused creature of the Nine…

"Very well," I grated, clenching my teeth. The vast wheeled engines of my will began grinding all that rage into pure necromancy. "We do it your way, Anghul. But the soul of this one… he belongs to *me*."

They called 'im Urzen the Mad, right? But yer
don't have to be mad to create demons. To trust
'em, sure. To expect 'em to keep their faith,
hold to their bindings, not chew your face off at
the first opportunity... for that, yer have to be
mad. But to create them? Nah. That's just a bit
eccentric."

The considered opinion of Rath Drullen,
servant to Kulain the Blasphemous during his exile in the
Hiledoran. Drullen transcribed large portions of Kulain's De
Occultae Erotica and Grimoire Obscuris before being hunted down
by Tabernacle witch-finders and burned.

I PITCHED MYSELF over the side of the Kothrai flagship before I could think better of Anghul's scheme – for it was utter madness. In my long, long life I had seen many dark and dire visions, but what the Antlered God proposed... well, all that commended it as a battle strategy was the fact that I could think of nothing better.

Cold, gelid darkness slithered across my skin, tendrils trying to force their way into my nose, between my lips... but the dead men below were eager to earn their freedom. They were not about to let their liberator share the fate of poor Uveryn, floating in the belly of the Kothrai's beast. An anchor chain came surging up out of the deep, and I wrapped my fingers around two curving flukes of iron, letting it pull me clean through the dark water. Down, to the salty gloom of the seabed.

It was a good thing that I was dead already – the pressure was crushing down there, and the light a mere memory. I used my Dark Sight to take in a field of broken and rotting ships, layer on layer, whole strata of them charting centuries of foolhardy attempts to break the seapower of Faeros. Among their timbers were entombed tens of thousands of dead men, all of them feeling the hooks of my will in their souls. All of them heeded the call of Anghul. They swirled up around me in an eruption of silt and bone, seaweed and broken shells, blotting out the last vestiges of light.

I felt us rising, tugging whole sheets of rotten canvas behind us, ropes and chains pulled taut as spiderwebs. I felt bone binding tight to granite, woven together like the Pale Armour of Sothara... though this time it did not cover warm, living flesh.

I was held within the embrace of salty bones, arms outstretched like a man crucified. Tendrils of witchfire snapped taut, seething with power. They picked out a form the same shape as my own, except *huge*, cold, filled with the memory of raging storms and crashing waves.

Behind the sullen chill of the drowned, the mind of the Colossus rose like an island from a stormy sea, indomitable and jagged, fed by the belief of generations of sailors.

This was why Anghul had told me to remember Urexes. There, Zael Kataphraxis had animated a huge statue of himself, striding across the burning city clothed in stone. *This* statue – this immense, guano-streaked wonder of Sarem, helmed like a Faeroan warrior – was an image of Erhaal, Lord of the Drowned. An aspect of death. A Facet, indeed, which shared the same geometry as Urghal, Herald of Abyssus. And with the Antlered One on his forest throne…

I opened my eyes, and found myself two hundred spans above the ocean, looking down on the *Sorrow's Vengeance* and the Kothrai. I blinked, and I heard stone grate on stone as the Colossus began to awaken. Down there, the surface of the water was heaving and dancing. Tottering spires of darkness arched and collapsed as I gritted my teeth, tearing one immense foot loose from its iron mountings.

The Colossus walked.

Dear Gods and Hells, it took nearly all my strength to force that single step. The entire great statue was sheathed in barnacle-crusted bones, draped with ragged sailcloth and chains, but it took all of Anghul's will and my own to give it the semblance of life. *One single step*, and then we stooped down, fingers cracking and scattering shards of granite…

A Kothrai raider – so recently made a charnel-house by Issara and Kell – collapsed like matchwood between those fingers. I crumbled it to ruin as I forced the Colossus to stand, driving my will into its stony heart.

These were the raiders and reavers you were forged to stand guard against. These are the nightmares from the stories of your people. Now – destroy them! Protect Faeros!

Anghul was laughing as we took a second step, a hacking, coughing laugh which sounded more like dying than mirth. With both hands we swept up Grennen Vuhl's flagship, peering down at him from the eye-slits of that stone-plumed helm. Sticky strands of darkness attenuated and snapped as the keel of the ship broke loose from the waves. A sad few Kothrai threw themselves clear, some gripping barrels and planks.

Another handful managed to cut one of the ship's longboats free, and their oars churned the water as they lit out for the horizon.

"YOU SEEK THE BEAST OF SAREM?" boomed the voice of the Colossus – or rather, a cantrip which was more theatre than sorcery. "YOU SEEK TO MOCK THE LAMENTER, LORD OF BONES AND ASHES? I AM YOUR DESPAIR, KOTHRAI – JUST AS I WAS THE DOOM OF YOUR MASTER."

For the first time I saw Grennen Vuhl's confidence waver. He flinched back, raising an arm above his head as if mere flesh could protect him from thousands of tons of stone. But there is no room for cowardice in a mind gone mad. I am certain that it was Dirge who goaded him to his feet then, whispering threats and promises. In retrospect... who knows. Grennen Vuhl was at least as twisted as the thing he followed.

"Ahhh," he said, in a voice which I could hear even over the creaking of timbers and the cries of the dying. "The creature lives. I had thought you were ashamed to show yourself, Kuhal Moer."

There was fresh defiance behind that eyeless helm. The Kothrai's hands blazed with busy darkness, tugging and kneading the flow of vitae in the waters below us. But I was out of my mind with power, and the pain of wielding it. I laughed, and the Colossus laughed with me, a sound like iron on stone.

"I HAVE NAUGHT TO BE ASHAMED OF, MORTAL. *YOU* ARE THE ONE WHO SERVES A SHIT-CAKED MADMAN, AFTER ALL..."

The Kothrai sketched a little bow.

"I assure you, Lamenter – there is none more pure or sane than my Lord. It is this world of filth and unreason which he wants to do away with."

I could have ended it there. Perhaps I should have – and been the heartless monster they all called me. One thought, and my vast hands of stone would have come together, obliterating the Kothrai ship and every living thing still clinging to its timbers. But that would mean the end of Silbern Chaar, of Seventails and Rasq... of the Stormreaper herself.

Who chose that very instant to play the heroine.

While Grennen Vuhl stared up at me she lunged forward, her sword a blur, trying to run the sorcerer through. It should have been a killing strike – and there were none left to save the Kothrai, his minions slaughtered to a man by Siara's fearsome crew.

Yet he had seen it coming. And he knew, somehow, that I lacked the cold resolve to sacrifice my only child.

There was a flare of power, and the Kothrai's sea-draken cape seemed to turn in on itself, black smoke coiling out. Then Siara was past his guard, her sword piercing nothing but salt-crusted hide. Leathery strips bound up the blade as Grennen Vuhl re-appeared behind her, one arm around her throat, his free hand gripping a serrated dagger.

"He devours them, you know!" shrieked the sorcerer, as my stony fingers gripped tight. The whole ship twisted in my grasp, nails popping from its timbers. "Dirge. Endsong. He will be reborn, Kuhal Moer, but only through the death of the Aziphem's chosen. Do you think you're the only one who can bind souls into pretty jewels?"

The dagger pricked a line of blood from Siara's throat. She clawed at the Kothrai's armoured hands, but they may as well have been forged from the same iron as his blade.

"LET HER GO!" I raged, the Colossus trembling against my back. I was held cruciform against its chest, walled in behind bones, and I could hear a ghostly heartbeat thundering within the stone.

"Or *what?* You'll kill us both? Go ahead, if you dare! Your daughter claimed I had no sense of strategy, Lamenter, but I know this much – I should not have chosen to face you on your own terms. Now… now you must come to me, and I will be waiting. *Dirge* will be waiting. And together, we will finish what he began."

I could feel the mind of the Colossus slipping away from me, as my anger overruled reason. Anghul alone could not animate the huge creature of stone – I could sense the old God fading, his power barely as deep as that of poor, lost Kharnath. And so I drew as much vitae as I could from the bones around me, bursting from their calcified embrace. The Kothrai ship slipped from hands suddenly cold and lifeless as I flew, Cryptfeeder swinging, and we all fell as one – the Colossus toppling backwards, ropes and timbers in free-fall, Grennen Vuhl with Siara in his grip…

The raider's keel snapped as it struck the ocean, a heartbeat before I followed through with my swing, throwing all my momentum and wrath behind it. It should have cut the sorcerer clean in half, from his helm to his boots in a single strike, but he landed an instant before me, rolling backward, and all I managed to catch was the very edge of that great horned and armoured bell.

Steel shattered, shards of red-hot metal punching through my skin in a dozen places. Grennen Vuhl shrieked, recoiling – but he kept his grip on the Stormreaper, kept the knife to her throat. She cried out as its serrated edge cut in, and I felt the jewel at my throat convulse. Phantom pain needled through me. Two great hunks of iron clanged against the timbers.

"Last chance," I grated, steadying myself on the canting deck. "I'll let you leave this place alive, Kothrai, if you at least *pretend* to have some mercy."

Then I saw the face which had hidden behind that helm, and I knew I asked too much.

Grennen Vuhl was a pale-skinned, black-bearded warrior, his hooked nose criss-crossed with scars. One side of his face was hashed with runic tattoos, a web of them radiating out from his left eye. But the other… the other was simply *gone*. It was as if someone had scooped a double handful of bone, flesh and brain from the right side of the Kothrai's skull, the wound still slick and raw. Perhaps, I thought for an instant, I had done this myself, when I shattered his helm. But no – for there was an *eye* floating unsupported in that grisly hollow – an emerald-green eye connected to no shred of sinew or flesh. It turned to look at me, and I saw a nimbus of dark flames boiling around it – a cold fire I had seen before.

"*The Nine*," I breathed. "Dirge has been busy…"[13]

Grennen Vuhl laughed.

"Aye, Kuhal. That he has. Unlike your poxy Sarem'ec demons, though, my lord's new coven have chosen their fate willingly. I was the first reborn, but there are others. Not nine – not yet. But it will amuse my master to make a new vessel from the Stormreaper here. Like mother, like daughter, hmm?"

The ship was sinking fast. Whatever sorcery Grennen Vuhl had laced through the water to turn it black was gone, and soon we would be ankle-deep in sharks. The *Sorrow's Vengeance* was underway, tacking against the wind toward us, but even all her banks of cannon would be no use now. It was up to me.

"If you seek to provoke me into a foolish, headlong attack, Kothrai,

---

13. The original Nine Now Nameless were horrors created by the Angan church, at the hand of Pontifex Jerrold Sinder and a mad, ancient creature known as Urzen of Korisal. Their task - to stalk the seven lands, providing massacres and other atrocities which the church could blame on 'demons'. Thus ensuring the obedience of their flocks… for, of course, those who heeded Mother Church were spared the attentions of the Nine. Despite their title, many of their names were known, at least to me. Alas, unlike real demons, knowing their true and former names gave me no power over them.

you may just get your wish." Empty words… but they bought me a few heartbeats of time. I slotted a ring of power into the hilt of my blade, not daring to look at my own trembling hands. That ring contained the dying fire of Kth'ala Vryesse, the Burning Dark – and if Vuhl was of the same ilk as the Nine, its power would cut his soul to the quick.

"Father! No!" said Siara, twisting in the sorcerer's grasp. "He…"

I thought she meant that the vile thing would truly open her throat – but I was past such niceties. I didn't plan on giving Vuhl time to so much as twitch.

But it seemed that I wasn't the only one who had been stalling.

The deck between us erupted in a slash-cut line of splintered timbers. A wall of glistening darkness punched through, cutting me off from the Kothrai sorcerer. I hacked at it with Cryptfeeder, but the darkness was sticky as tar, knitting back together even as I struggled, cursing.

"Come and find me, Lamenter!" cackled Grennen Vuhl. "I'll be waiting for your company!"

And then, gripping my daughter tight, the Kothrai leaped from the deck. His draken-skin cloak spread like a pair of ragged wings as he sprung to the top of the aft-mast. I leveled a finger at him, loosing a bolt of dead men's pain. But the searing jag of sorcery missed, shattering a spar below him.

The deck heaved beneath me. Darkness surged away, as if the whole squirming mass in the waters below us was simply the Kothrai's shadow.

Then came a thunderclap of inrushing air, a skin-prickling surge of sorcerous power…

And Grennen Vuhl was gone.

Ahh, yes. Of course. Like the Eyeless and the Devouring Wind before him, this new demon of Dirge's creation could *fly*.

This time my curse had power behind it. The timbers of the sinking raider charred black for three spans around me, smouldering. But it was too late.

My horrific new enemy had fled, leaving hundreds of his men to their fate. Even now, a fresh harvest of corpses was drifting to the bottom of the Faeroan Sea, covering the Colossus where it had fallen. The immense statue had collapsed onto its back, so that now, where once a granite warrior had stared out across the Gates, only a pair of grasping hands broke the waves.

He had taken Siara.

That was the thought which consumed me as the wreck I was standing on gave one last shuddering gasp and began to founder. I was still staring up at the sky, to where they had disappeared, as the water rose up around my boots, around my waist – and finally closed over my head.

The next thing I recall is hands reaching down for me. Fingers clenched around my arms, fingers knotted in my hair… Then a gasping rebirth into light, my dead lungs bubbling with salt water as it streamed from between my teeth. I blinked in the sunlight, feeling warm timber against my back, and I saw the faces of Elion Morekh and Gryst, peering down at me.

"He lives," rumbled the ogre. "For which we must at least be thankful."

Elion smiled – a horrible sight for one just regaining consciousness.

"He hasn't *lived* for centuries, Suudarach. But he's back with us. And we have work to do."

I sat up, belching another bucketful of seawater. Never let any man tell you that the dead can't feel! At that moment I felt heartily, wretchedly sick.

"He has Siara …" I mumbled, trying to stand. My legs would not support me, and I wondered, for an instant, why the power of Anghul had left me. "We have to…"

"We have to walk blithely into his trap, just like we did in Korisal for her mother?" asked Elion. "Not again, Khytein. This leathery old hide is the only one I've got."

This time I managed to totter to my feet. Gryst slung an arm around me, giving me something to lean on.

And there they were – the ragged, bedraggled and dispirited little band who had gathered to my daughter's banner. Seventails, looking like a flood-drowned rodent. Rasq, one of his arms slung in bloodied sailcloth. Issara, less regal and proud than I could have imagined for such a creature. Even Kell Du'ath seemed pale and sickly. Urmokh leaned on a spear-shaft crutch, the left side of his body one solid purple-black bruise.

"No," I said, as I saw the look in their eyes. "Oh no. I won't. I can't…"

Silbern Chaar pushed her way forward, wrapped up in what appeared to be one of Gryst's aprons, twenty sizes to large. Oddly, it seemed to cover far less than it should. But of course… her spiked armour would be at the bottom of the Shallow Sea by now, sunken amid the bones.

"You've already saved us once, Kuhal," she said – as an utterly, madly inappropriate twinge of desire sparked through me. "When the Kothrai sank, you kept us from the sharks. Look…"

I followed her pointing finger, off the beam of *Sorrow's Vengeance*, and I saw a tangled thicket of bones rising clear of the water, binding up the two shattered halves of Grennen Vuhl's flagship. Skeletal forms twined and twisted together – thousands upon thousands of them, holding the broken raider up above the waves. Without an Incantus, without even being *conscious*…

Now I knew why my power had ebbed so low. Such a working should have been far beyond me, even with Anghul's aid.

"So, you owe me your lives? Good! Use them wisely. Don't follow me where I'm going. I can't promise to save you again."

"And who will save *you*?" asked Kell, her voice barely a whisper. "You are the key to the unraveling of this world, Lamenter. We cannot let you throw your life away."

"I've fought worse!" I snarled. "Hells, I *am* worse. This Kothrai will find himself chained next to Esau and Zael for what he's done. I…"

"You'll fail," said Elion. "Just as Dirge wants you to. And in your despair, he will have your soul. I see no choice, old friend. We have to hold to our course."

"It's what she would have wanted," put in Seventails. "Even if…"

"*Don't you dare try to make this a funeral!*" I caught myself up, sawing at the bridle of my rage. My voice dropped to a whisper. "She's still alive. Powers below, she has to be. I…"

"The Helmsman is right," said Rasq. "Siara Anvhaur had a purpose for you, Lamenter. We should see it through."

"And leave her to that monster?"

Elion Morekh placed one stitch-scarred hand on my shoulder, his eyes brimming with pain.

"Don't think you are the only one who cares, Kuhal. Family is family, and I know you see her mother in her. But we… we have stood by the Stormreaper through good times and bad. She didn't get that name by being weak, or frightened. Have faith."

There was something in the dead Captain's eyes which I recognized. Something which seemed out of place in a face all salt and bone.

"You love her, then? All of you?"

Elion's stare turned flinty.

"Like the father she never had, Khytein."

I winced.

"Enough, then. I will follow. To the ends of Yrde, if I have to. And…
I'm sorry. I'm sorry I'm not the terrible power you needed."

I hung my head, eyes closed. Rarely has a creature of my antiquity
and reputation felt so humbled.

Kell's gasp brought me back to myself.

"The jewel! Look!"

I scrabbled at my throat, but the black amulet was gone. Panic
gripped me for an instant, until I saw where the seeress was pointing
– to a small gathering of artifacts, salvage from the Kothrai's wreck.
Siara's glass blade was there, along with the two halves of Grennen
Vuhl's helm, and atop a black wooden chest -

Makara flickered into existence as if walking through a haze of mist,
her features seeming to flow from the shadows around her. If I were a
mortal man my heart would have stopped in my chest, I suppose – as
it was I felt the withered old thing thump once, spasming against my
ribs.

*Oh, she was beautiful. Three centuries had not so much as touched
her, and her violet eyes still held the depths of the dusk sky at its zenith,
lit by the first scattering of stars…*

"You always were a fool, Kuhal Moer," she said – though there
was a certain sad kindness in her voice. "Power isn't what matters
now. Power is where we find it. What matters is the truth. She is *our
daughter*, Khytein. Even you can feel it, in your dry old bones. She is
the best of both of us, and that alone is reason for Grennen Vuhl to
fear."

"But… I never… she was…"

Makara laughed.

"I never loved you for your eloquence, Kuhal. Thank the Gods! But
I *have* been with you, all these centuries. I've seen you devour yourself
with guilt. Please… leave it behind. She needs you now, more than I
ever did. But not as some saga-song hero. That's never ended well for
you."

I smiled, rueful and bitter.

"No… it never has. I'll rescue you yet though, princess. Some day
soon…"

"Our book will burn long before the story ends, and you know it,"
she said. "Now – Aerik has only lent me enough life to ask you one
more time. Will you be what these people need you to be? What *Siara*
needs you to be?"

"I told you! I'm no great power! I am… *reduced.* I'm just Kuhal

Moer, son of Hurik, and I can't seem to save…"

Her kiss was ghostly, but it burned - right in the middle of my forehead. A whisper of black hair fell across my face like a breath of air.

"And I never loved you for your power either, you sweet old fool," she said. "Power kept us apart. Just be Kuhal Moer, son of Hurik, as hard as you can. That will be enough."

I didn't see the shade of Makara disappear. I don't think my soul could have endured watching her fade away. But when I opened my eyes the Stormreaper's crew were circled around me, looking down at me expectantly.

"Grennen Vuhl is a dead man," I said, a wild grin twitching at the corners of my lips. "Of that, you can be assured. But my daughter had a plan to destroy him, and Endsong as well…"

"We sail for Tarkhand, then," rumbled Rasq. "Zamara. We seek the Maelstrom."

At the time they were words without meaning. I had yet to see the fabled minarets of the Eternal Harbour, or stare into the eye of Abyssus. But at that moment, Rasq could just as easily have told me we were sailing to the gates of the Outer Dark, and I would have gleefully assented.

"Elion Morekh?"

"Yes?"

"Do nautical things. Set sails, and such. Silbern?"

"Yes?"

"Please, put on some real clothes. That armour of yours hid far too much, if you understand me…"

The Ontohki reddened, then for no discernible reason slapped Seventails in his grinning face. Issara raised one eyebrow.

"The rest of you, we have much preparation ahead of us. The Kothrai may have beaten us once, but we Khytein have an old saying on the arts of war…"

"We do?" asked Seventails, rubbing at his face. He was still smiling.

"Oh yes. 'Any fight which don't leave you dead is a fight you've won'. Because no matter if it comes the next day or a decade hence, your enemy will have to face you again. And now you know he can't kill you, see?"

Barbarian logic, perhaps. The kind of thinking which had doomed my people to an eternity of hardscrabble feuds and warfare.

But if I was to lead these people – these saga-song villains and children's nightmares – then the only example I had was my dead, drunken father. Hurik the Scalptaker was probably looking down at me from some ale-sodden afterlife, laughing fit to split his guts.

Elion Morekh took the wheel, bringing us around hard to slip between the grasping hands of the fallen Colossus. Ahead of us, the water faded from sky-blue to deep aquamarine, dead through the gates and out into the open sea.

Soon we would be leaving Sarem altogether. Soon, we would enter the realm of Sorath, where, if anything, Grennen Vuhl would be even more powerful.

It didn't matter. Aboard this ship were gathered the darkest stories of a whole continent, led by a tyrant who could once again raise the dead. And the Kothrai had woven himself into our tale, abducting the maiden, becoming the monster…

I smiled, watching Elion line up the *Vengeance's* bowsprit with the shimmer of the sun on the waves.

Makara's daughter and mine. Gods and demons! Dirge's thrall had assuredly bitten off more than he could swallow…

Part Four

His Dark Reflection

As the mind of the Divine was shattered to give life to all things on the surface of Yrde, so too was the world itself shattered by that great outpouring of Elder Sorcery. So it is that a globe torn apart by the awesome power of the Father of Aziphem is held together - even to this latter age - by His will. Some say that the great progenitor could re-assemble the Shards and Facets of His sundered soul, were it not for His constant vigil; the endless task of keeping Yrde from flying to pieces in the void...

Morune Salayne,
the hermit of Frostreach - Meditations on the nature of the Divine

WE SET OUT across the Sunrise Ocean, driven before a focused gale of Rasq's creation, clouds of canvas bellying taut against the wind. The mood was bleak, but resolute. We would hold to my daughter's path, until fate or cataclysm forced our hand.

A week out from land, with leviathenes riding our bow-wave, Elion's unnaturally sharp eyes caught sight of the Chasm, that world-spanning wall of sorcery which marked the very limit of Sarem. Soon we were close enough to see the rising sun come swimming up through the sheared-off edge of the ocean, glassy geomancy holding back league upon league of water.

Across the Chasm was Sorath, Grennen Vuhl's homeland. But there was no way we could tell just where in the great archipelago we would emerge if we sailed through the Chasm blind. There were places marked on Elion's dusty old maps which showed safe crossings – places where a ship could be counted on not to simply plunge into the sundered heart of Yrde, or find itself emerging a thousand spans below the waves.

Needless to say, we left the ancient Faeroan to his calipers and compasses, trusting he would see us through. For days before we crossed we ran a course parallel to the Chasm wall, looking out across a gulf to the continent of Sorath on the other side. From the deck of the *Vengeance* we could see the ocean, its surface perhaps a clear mile higher than that on our side of the divide. Then the silty layers of the seabed, fading to rock, which plunged down into a red-tinged abyss. Vast, ancient bones were trapped in that layered crust, hinting at beasts the size of the Archaeon, and even older. The fractured globe we lived upon was a wonder and a terror, indeed.

Not that I had much time to admire the secrets of creation. No – I was engaged in a grislier pastime. Before we set out, we had commanded a small army of thrall sailors to bring aboard the dead Kothrai from the wreck of Grennen Vhul's ship. Their souls may have fed the demonic shadow at his command, but their flesh… well, most of it ended up as chum in our wake, or attached to the oversized hooks which Gryst used to angle for sharks.

The rest, however…

The soft tissue of their brains was sawn and scooped from their lifeless heads, encysted in a noxious broth of alchemy, and forged into the core of a new Incantus.[14] Thankfully, the Stormreaper's ship contained both a forge and a laboratory; the first lifted in its entirety from her surrogate grandfather's workshop in Kaltensund, the last courtesy of Harlaw, for whom I developed a deep and abiding respect.

The little engineer still wore his Guild of Chains whites, along with an apron sewn with so many pockets it was a wonder he could find his tools at all among them. We very quickly reached the kind of working friendship in which very few actual words are spoken – all our plans were sketched out with fingertips on sooty bench-tops, or scratched in chalk on any available surface. He learned of Urzen's works – what little I could recall – and I learned more in those two weeks about the principles of metalcraft than I had gleaned in the past three centuries. Alas, I would never have the arms or hands of a blacksmith… unless I resorted to certain necromantical experiments which Harlaw seemed awfully keen to try.

As for the rest – they healed, for the most part, and trained, with a certain grim determination. Urmokh tended to Scarwing, who had been grievously broken by his fall, hollow bones snapped in so many places that Harlaw was forced to join many of them with metal staples. Seventails paced, brooding as his wounds healed, for he could

14. Put simply, the Incantus Instrumentorum is a prosthetic mind. As you will know, if you have ever tried to wield a Zengaji battle staff or its like, it's often hard to make your body obey perfectly sensible commands from your brain. Now imagine commanding ten thousand, a hundred thousand bodies with that one grapefruit-sized pudding of grey flesh. It hurts. Right to the roots of your teeth. So necromancers create ways to spread the load. The best way is to use human brain tissue itself, artfully crystalised to prevent that curdled smell. The legends about groaning dead men searching for fresh brains are often down to the poorly phrased orders of a trainee necromancer.

not shape-shift while so badly hurt. He told me, in the long watches of the night, that he missed the clean sharp senses of his animal forms, the veils of scent which defined the world of the wolf and bear.

Issara and Kell Du'ath would not talk about their ordeal in the heart of Grennen Vuhl's shadow-beast. One had saved the other from grisly dissolution, this much we could glean. But what they had seen within the thing's maw… Kell whispered of a leering face the size of a moon, cast against a starless black sky, a face comprised of seething insects devouring each other even as they gave birth to more and more. I was willing to wager whose face it was, and the thought did more than just trouble me.

So I threw myself into my work, enduring countless little failures and celebrating innumerable small triumphs. My Incantus was made whole, and with it, the means to once again command the dead. Urmokh led all of us in drill after drill with swords, spears, shields, maces, daggers… I thought I was back in the nightmare of my squalid youth, destined to become a warrior for a very short and painful interlude. But the Zengaji Skyborn was a far kinder teacher than Ulkar Jaerl had ever been, and the humiliation we all felt at our defeat spurred us to train even harder.

That fact hung over the *Sorrow's Vengeance* as we sailed north, seeking the place which Elion called the Boneclaw Reef. We had failed Siara, and worse, we had let her be taken by Grennen Vuhl himself. Perhaps the imagination of what the Kothrai was doing to her was worse than the reality – but somehow I thought not. Over the chasm and over the horizon, Vuhl and his master were busy with their knives and tomes, constructing a new coven of man-made demons to replace the Nine Now Nameless…

I tried not to dwell on what that meant. I wished for poppy's-blood, or bladeleaf, or anything else which would steal such visions from my mind. But it was no use. Sickness churned with anger in my soul. The only cure would come with the Kothrai's death.

And so I waited, watching the flat, hammered-silver ocean slip away behind our keel.

We reached the Boneclaw Reef at dawn on the eighth day, after a night spent hanging at anchor in a thick fog. Rasq sat up with me by lantern light, reminiscing about his icy home and playing a hand or two of cards.[15] Of all Siara's crew, the shamen from the north was the

---

15. The deck, popular in Angan times, now contained the Incantus, Priest, Sorcerer, Witch and Aziphem instead of the old arcana. The Sorcerer, a crude picture of a robed

one most changed by the upwelling of magick – the filling up of the hollow places in men's souls with superstition.

"It began when I was just a lad," He said, leaning back against the rail, an earthern jug of Gryst's frankly suicidal rotgut in one hand. "Chosen to be apprentice to the Windcaller, sent out into the ice-wastes to slay one of the great white bears… I was lost in a blizzard. Trapped for days in a little snow-cave I dug with my hands. Voices came to me, in that white oblivion. Voices coming up through the ice, distorted… like seeing a familiar face through deep water. They said the land was awakening. The old guardians were needed again, for the new ones were failing."

He took a deep swallow of grog, wincing at the taste. His face crinkled up like leather between the shaggy white mass of his bone-hung beard and his matted hair.

"What choice did I have? I let them in. And I didn't feel the cold, after that. I found my white bear… oh yes! But it rolled on its back as soon as it saw me – an ice-crusted little urchin, blue-skinned and black-fingered, and it showed me its belly. I brought it back to the frozen shore alive, on a length of leather trace, and the old Windwalker dropped to his knees when he saw me. Said he could teach me no more. And that the change would come…"

He flexed his immense fingers, his pale blue eyes filled with sadness.

"O'course, you know all about that, Lamenter. We all change, when the power takes us. For all their morality and goodness, the Gods are selfish shits. We become like them, and they feel a little bit of life and sunlight through us. Parasites sucking on each other's blood, we are. And now you have to change again, you poor dead bastard." He chuckled, taking another swallow of moonshine.

"You mean… Siara? I have to be family to someone, after all this time? Well, northman, I can only try. Here… pass me that damned bottle."

Rasq held out the bottle to me, and I took a long gulp of the fiery liquor.

"No, no…" he said. "For the *plan*. Archaeon's plan. Him… him and that old Khytein demon in the sword. They said we'd go and get you, pluck you outta your tower like… like a grub from out a rotten log." He hiccuped, a most alarming vision. "Then… then we get you and what's left of old Anghul together. Fool those Tarkhanden, the

---

man with antlers sprouting from his brow, held a flaming spiked-metal ball in one hand and a sword in the other. Behind him capered grinning skeletons.

pompous bastards. You have to be the Herald of Abyssus, lad. Gotta play the part, all the way to the hilt." He looked down at his hands. "Just like I did, Khytein. Let the voices in. Be the monster. Ride the bloody story, because there's power in it."

I felt a chill shiver down my spine. The Archaeon and its cabal had used me before, twisting me into a weapon against Anganesse. But this time there would be no subtle manipulation. I promised myself that I was old and cynical enough after three hundred years to bend their schemes to my will. After all, my purpose had become horribly simple.

If Grennen Vuhl was creating his own Coven of Nine, he would have the arcane mechanisms and the raw power needed to enact a soul-binding – to give Makara new life. But before I stole his sorcerous toys, I was going to break my own oldest rule. I would treat the bastard to the most exquisite tortures I could imagine…

"That's it," cackled Rasq, reading the grim look in my eyes. "Oh, the change has been a long time coming to you. But come it will. Grennen Vuhl's become the villain, Lamenter. He's usurped your throne. Now you're the righteous one, and I'll tell you something…" He leaned in, all conspiratory, reeking of fish oil, wax and rotgut liquor. "They like it best when the scary monster turns on some bastard what deserves it." He winked, haltingly, his massive teeth grinning yellow from the thicket of his beard.

"They? Who's watching, Rasq?"

"The *Gods*, Khytein. You don't know that already? Why did the Divine shatter his mind to pieces? Why bring life to Yrde at all? He was bored, and lonely… lonely and bored…. sick of tedious planets in their damned circles, I suppose. We call what they feed on *worship*, those Aziphem which are what's left of him. But it's all just stories."

"Stories?"

"And religion's just a faerytale in a big impressive book, lad. Look at yours. Bears about as much resemblance to the truth as I do to lady Issara. I tell you, Kuhal Moer – stories have *power*, because they tell the Gods what to be. How me, and Seventails, and all those others ended up like they are. You think Gryst is really an Ogre? Hah! You stay entertaining, and you find the thread in the tale which can pull you along, and you'll stay lucky. Might even stay alive."

I was too sober for such philosophy. Too sober by far. But I was just drunk enough to see the light around the edges of what Rasq was saying. A kind of symmetry – the Divine created life, life shaped the

Aziphem. And sorcerers balanced on the tenuous place in between…

We sailed through the maze of the Boneclaw Reefs the next morning, while Rasq snored off a hangover and Elion Morekh barked orders, taking soundings every few spans. The reefs were curved tusks of coral, grown huge and twisted with their proximity to the Chasm. As the tide fell they rose up out of the water like the rib-cages of drowned beasts, marking our passage toward the shimmering wall at the edge of Sarem.

It reared up before us, taller than clouds – in fact, fluffy cumulonimbus passed directly through it, blown through from Sorath on a warm wind. At last we maneuvered the huge bulk of the *Vengeance* into position, her bowspirit aimed at the void. Then Elion cast off the sea-anchors, and we surged ahead, the wall rushing up at us with a backdrop of stars behind it.

The ship disappeared when it struck that barrier. I braced myself as the glittering curtain rushed toward me, but when it passed through me I felt nothing but a deep throbbing sensation in my 'blight-cored bones, like the toll of a temple bell. I found that I had closed my eyes tight, and when I opened them…

"All hands to battle stations! Unknown ships incoming! Hard a'port, and trim the sails for speed, you dogs!"

The deck lurched beneath me, and a curtain of spray whipped up over the rail to drench me head to foot. The air smelled different here – subtly spiced with the aroma of distant islands, I supposed. And the sun seemed brighter, too – buttery yellow, like beaten gold. None of this mattered, however, compared to the fleet of red-sailed ships bearing down on us, their decks bristling with armed marines.

These were no Kothrai raidercraft, though – they were double-hulled, with triangular sails, and rows of oars thrashing the waves to foam. Bright banners streamed and cracked from their mastheads, bearing the sign of a star and crossed anchors.

"Who are they!" I shouted, grabbing at the first crewman I could reach. This turned out to be Urmokh, and his sharp-toothed smile was more than a little unnerving. He seemed feverish, and even more thin and wiry than usual, pallid beneath his tattoos.

"Tarkhanden! Grand Fleet – a bunch of pompous bastards, but not actually our foes. Come on! We have to get you below!"

"Why?" I asked, as the Skyborn hustled me in through a hatchway and down a winding stair. "Do they behead sorcerers on sight? Do they know about… well, about what I've done to Sarem?"

"*What you've done,*" said a voice from out of the gloom, "*Is nothing. That's rather the point. Boy, they don't know you from a ripe turd, and that's the way we mean to keep it.*"

A lantern flame kindled into life, and I found myself in a long, low store-room, facing a bronzewood table. Seated at its far end was the oracle, Kell Du'ath, and balanced atop the boards…

"Aerik Stormsong. Of course. Even as a particularly primitive-looking sword, you still find ways to insult me!"

"All part of the Stormreaper's plan," said Kell. "And, Gods willing, the undoing of Grennen Vuhl."

"*You have to become something they fear and worship, boy. Can't you feel it? The Shard of Death is strong here, and Abyssus is the name of its avatar. You… you can become his Herald, and steal a whole damned nation for us.*"

I looked at the only other item of furniture in the room, then back at the glass blade, balanced on its point. Flecks of light inside the glass seemed to glitter like the old warbard's eyes. Across the table from Kell stood a stout, iron-banded chair, bolted to the deck. Leather straps and buckles were secured to its arms and legs.

"If you think…" I began – but that was when I felt a hot, sharp pain in the side of my neck, followed by a spreading numbness. Urmokh took my weight as my legs buckled beneath me.

"Sorry, Deadfather," he whispered, gentling me down to the boards. "Just a little something to take away the pain. You are not betrayed… at least, not by us."

I felt them manhandle me into the chair. I felt the belts and buckles cinch tight. The room began to waver and dim, as if seen through a thick mist. The mageblight in my bones tingled, while my eyes grew heavy with sleep.

The last thing I remember, before delirium took me, was Kell Du'ath setting out a black velvet roll of tools on the tabletop – tiny hooks and knives, a silver saw, fine-threaded bolts…

That, and the cold regard of Aerik Stormsong, the living blade of glass turning to follow me as Kell approached, a scalpel in one pale hand, reaching out with the other to steady my face.

"*Don't even think to complain,*" said the sword, as I felt my skin unspliced. Steel against bone. Machinery whirring and grinding, far away. "*I have spent three centuries as a gods-damned piece of cutlery for this, Kuhal. You, at least, are being made into something terrible…*"

I felt a great weight on my brow. I felt threads of mageblight stitching through my skin and muscles, binding something tight to the bone of my skull. And I felt the straps loosen, strong hands holding me up, stripping away my robes, replacing them with something soft and dark.

Then a second spike of pain. Sensation blossomed through me like slow fire, and I tottered, staggering to my feet. I pushed Urmokh away and groped with my hands, up across my face…

I felt lines of ritual scarification. Mageblight sculpted into a skeletal mask beneath my skin, making my cheekbones stand sharp and angular. Lines cut down across my cheeks, picking out the shape of a ghoulish grin, obscuring my lips. Further… I pushed back the velvet cowl they had dressed me in, and reached my forehead. My fingertips encountered what felt like cold, old scar tissue, and then…

"Oh, you bastards," I croaked. "You *utter bastards*. Get me a mirror!"

They must have been prepared. Kell threw open a cupboard, revealing a floor-length sheet of beaten silver. I noticed, remotely, that her hands were covered with blood.

"We thought we'd have time to tell you. We thought we could explain it all before we reached Zamara. *Belief*, Khytein, will do more than just let you raise the dead. It will give us a whole nation of the living as well! Tarkhand worships the Black Herald, and now…"

Well, now I was surely his living image. 'His Dark Reflection,' as the Kothrai would come to call me, in the war we had just begun.

They had given me horns.

Not, thank providence, the huge spreading antlers of Anghul's idols – I would scarcely have been able to lift my head. No, these were pale and curving tines of ivory, reaching up from my temples to almost brush the ceiling. So much for my careful efforts at looking human! My face was a gaunt and deathly mask, hollow-cheeked and grim.

"Time to tell me! I suppose you thought I could be convinced to willingly join your charade, then? What happens if these Tarkhanden have any low doors I have to duck through?"

Seventails chose that moment to throw open the door of our room – one, I noted, which was barely high enough for his own head.

"No time!" he hissed. "They are here! Elion has raised the white banner, and they're coming aboard. Is he..?"

"*He* has been thoroughly molested," I growled. "And, master Stormsong, you were quite correct. There is power here – enough for me to well and truly curse the lot of you. I suppose you want me to show these Sorathi a display befitting my new guise?"

"No!" shouted the glass blade, Urmokh and Kell at once.

"We'll claim to be your acolytes. An emissary from Sarem. It will soothe their substantial pride to learn that their own Black Herald is the very same monster who is said to rule there."

"So they'll fall to their knees, just like that?"

Kell shook her head.

"It could never be that simple, I'm afraid. These men are High Tarkhanden – worshipers of the Twins. The god and goddess of the sea and storms. But they will take us seriously. We'll be afforded safe passage to…"

The *Sorrow's Vengeance* shuddered as another ship ground along her flank – the Tarkhanden flagship heaving to. Up above, I heard the muffled sound of Elion Morekh bellowing orders, and a hundred dead-eyed thralls scurrying to obey.

"How else are we to explain our odd little crew?" shrugged Seventails. "The mistress had it all figured out. We need to get you to the temple of Abyssus, and then… well, what happens there will give us ample room for negotiation."

I scowled. With my new, frightful face, it was a most convincing look.

"My devoted acolytes all," I said. "Sworn to obey my every order. Don't be surprised if I'm forced to be rather… *humiliating* with you, then. It's only to keep in character!"

The sneer worked, too. Rasq had been right. Sometimes there is a perfect place where you can fit into the story, and wear it like armour about your soul.

"Now!" said Aerik Stormsong. "Pick me up! And when you greet the Saltmaster, be sure to behave like a demigod. The Herald of Abyssus carries the power of death's Shard, after all."

"If this Abyssus is so mighty," I grated, gathering up the robes they'd dressed me in, "Why doesn't he simply get off his omnipotent arse and cast down Grennen Vuhl himself?"

Despite having no eyebrows (a defining characteristic of swords the world over), Aerik managed to give the impression that one of his was arched ironically.

"Abyssus is no Aziphem, boy! He's… look, there's no time to explain. Just be haughty and vague if their damned Saltmaster asks about your supposed Lord. And for the sake of all our lives, don't make a mess of this! I can feel the power of the mages they've brought with them, and it's enough to send us all to the seabed!"

I took the glass blade in my hands, feeling an unpleasant jolt of power.

"If we're all here, who in the Hells is welcoming this bastard aboard?" I asked, as Kell belted an ornate black scabbard around my waist.

"Issara and Rasq," she said. "Oh. I see…"

There was a rather undignified rush for the door. As predicted, I had to duck my head to let my new pair of horns clear the lintel.

"*Remember*," said the somewhat muffled voice of Aerik Stormsong. "*Cold, proud, and unspeakably powerful. But recall that these Tarkhanden are too…*"

We formed up into a little formal party at the top of the stairs – Kell Du'ath in front, Seventails and Urmokh on either side. The Skyborn had produced from Gods-knew-where a kind of black, tasseled shade – a small portable tent which he and the skinchanger erected over me, shielding me from the harsh Sorathi sunlight.

It didn't matter how foolish I thought I looked. Because, as we proceeded out onto the upperdeck, I was able to see that these Tarkhanden were even more outlandishly arrayed.

The last of them were just wobbling their way across the gangplank between our ships – their galley very much the smaller of the two, despite its double-hulled design. The Saltmaster – the man at the very fore of their delegation, clad in a white leather greatcoat and an outrageously plumed helmet – apparently traveled with no less than four banner-bearers, two scribes, a sword-boy, and an immense, turbaned eunuch carrying what appeared to be a solid gold anchor. Facing this bizarre array of Sorathi were Elion Morekh, who knelt, his tricorne cap in one hand, Rasq and Gryst, both clad in motley armour and black capes, and Issara, who was wrapped, as usual, in skin-tight red satin, one hand on her hip and the other holding a long-stemmed silver tobacco pipe.

All eyes turned toward us as we approached. The choreography must have been planned well in advance – Kell had found a basket full of black, dead flower petals, and she scattered them before me as I advanced, trying to keep from laughing. *Perhaps such lunacy is the linchpin of all diplomacy*, I remember thinking. *Whole gruesome wars held back only by the ability of delegates to avoid insulting each others' foolish costumes…*

"Ahhh – here is my sweet Prince Consort now!" purred Issara, exhaling a chain of linked smoke rings. "The poor dear. I've kept him up half the night, but… you don't care for such intimate details, do you, Saltmaster Meracq? I'm sure you boys have weighty matters to discuss…"

The witch blew me a kiss. Sorcery skittered through the air after it, letting me feel the brush of lips against my cheek. I forced myself to smile.

"Ohhh… come now, sweetness! I'm certain that our guest would rather hear tales of love than war. Were it not for these troublesome Kothrai…"

I arched an eyebrow. The very spit and image of Aerik Stormsong. Meracq blushed, crimson as a lobster between his helmet and his forked orange beard.

"Troublesome indeed," he managed, regaining his composure. "And worse by the day. Which is why the Eighth Fleet has been tasked with closing the border to Sarem. We have heard dire tales of that land."

I studied the Saltmaster more closely as I approached – at the same time letting him take in a good look at my scarified face. He was a man of middle years, broken-nosed, scarred across his right cheek with the clean cut of a rapier, and his bristling beard and mustache were pointed with scented wax. A soldier, then, before he was a diplomat.

"Tales of war, perhaps? Of armies of the dead walking? Flying ships, burning cities, the Lamenter re-awoken?"

He nodded.

"And the Kothrai sail between the realms at will. We fear that all of Sarem is lost to our mutual foe. Thus…"

I stopped him, raising one hand. At once I felt the prickling caress of sorcery, prying to discover the depths of my power. Aerik was quicker than I ever could have been, wreathing the shallow wellspring of Anghul's vitae in veils and wards.

"Thus, you are only doing your duty when you tell us to turn back? How trite…" He stiffened, eyes growing hard. "I tell you we *cannot*. Do you know before whom you stand, Saltmaster of Tarkhand?"

Aerik had warned me about the pride of these people. The Saltmaster drew himself up to his full height, hand held out for his ceremonial sword. The boy who bore it bent on one knee, presenting its ornate basket hilt.

"And do *you* even care what my title means, Sarem'ec? I am the youngest scion of Zamara ever to command a fleet. I have cut whole Kothrai galleys from bow to stern with this blade. Do not give me reason to draw it!"

"And force me to send you early to my master's embrace? There is no need for such woe to befall your family. We are emissaries from Sarem, and we come to offer our aid in destroying the pretender. This… *Grennen Vuhl.*"

That name caused Meracq to think twice. His fingers trembled, poised over the hilt of his sabre.

"You know the title of our grief, then," he said. "So speak. Who are you, and why should we do anything but send you back to the Deadlord's lands?"

This called for a little theatre – and Aerik was happy to oblige. He had always been one for illusions and glamours, a sorcerous discipline which I could never quite perfect. Hence my need for smoked glasses and a cassock, I supposed.

I raised my head, and the wily old warbard made my eyes blaze. I seemed to grow in stature as an unseen wind whipped back my cloak, revealing armour of interleaved bones.

"Because I *am* the Deadlord, to give me your vulgar Sorathi name! The Lamenter has indeed awoken, and even now the men of Akhaz flee from my numberless hordes of corpses! I am Kuhal Moer, Lord of Bones and Ashes, the Herald of Abyssus returned to *call my master to war!*"

Meracq's eunuch must have been the religious type, because he dropped his gilded anchor and began praying, right there on the deck. Men aboard the Tarkhanden ship were pointing and shouting, some clutching for their weapons, some for the rosaries of shell beads which were the fetish of the Twins.

But Saltmaster Meracq didn't so much as blink. His smile was a tiny twitch of his mustachios, accompanied by merest relaxation of his guard.

"Prove it," he said.

I may have hesitated, then, were it not for Silbern Chaar. During our voyage she had adapted a suit of plate to her very particular curves, and now appeared as a warrior-maiden of death, a silver-inlaid skeleton inset into the steel of her armour. She unwrapped a cloth from around the bundle she held in her arms, throwing it to the deck.

"Proof enough, Tarkhanden? This is the helm of Grennen Vuhl, is it not? The fool dared to trespass, and it was only through cowardice that he escaped the full fury of our master's wrath."

It was a good speech. Obviously Silbern had been practicing. But it was more than her words which hooked Meracq's attention. As I've said before, even in armour the Ontokhi sword-maiden had curves to make a courtesan jealous.

"And you are..?" he drawled.

"The Herald's mortal instrument," she replied, letting a cascade of honey-gold hair fall from her skeletal helm. "Commander of his living armies. Of course, my Lord needs no such hierarchy among the countless dead."

Meracq nudged the cloven helm with his toe. His retainers were muttering and whispering, casting furtive glances at me as I smirked.

"An *emissary*, you say? Very well. You will accompany me to Zamara, where the Council will receive you. But I caution you – these are dark times. Try to leave the protection of the Eighth Fleet, and I will be forced to destroy you, despite your credentials."

Elion Morekh and Harlaw the gunnery master were standing at the back of our little delegation, but the undead Captain couldn't help himself. His muffled laughter caused Meracq to fix him with a steely glare.

"Deadlord, would you care to inquire of your slave *what in all hells is so funny?*"

I inclined my head, gesturing regally with one hand.

"Morekh?"

"My… apologies, Lord. It's just that… well, there's only four of them. Tiny little boats, too. It wouldn't even be target practice for my old mate here…"

This time Saltmaster Meracq's smile spread slowly across his face, until his mustachios could barely contain it.

"Such bravado! This must be the famed Faeroan sense of humor. Good to see that our cousins across the divide still have the heart to jest. But the fault is mine. We are but the 'advance guard', as you say. The swiftest of my command, noble Lamenter. My flagship, the *Ironheart*, and the Eighth Fleet's order of battle should be hoving into view… ahh!"

Meracq snapped his fingers. Gold rings clacked together. The sword-boy knelt next to him fumbled for a long, thin rod of ivory, passing it to his master.

"There! Now, know you the glory of Tarkhand!"

I couldn't help but look. None of us could.

On the horizon bristled a thicket of masts, a storm-wall of sail. The great maritime dreadnaughts of the Tarkhanden Eighth Fleet came bellying through the waves toward us with all the bulk of the floating cities of Faeros, a seaborne nation bristling with guns and aflutter with pennants. Troop transports, boarding craft, fortress-ships bearing four rows of iron cannon, catapult carriers with their giant mangonels, ramming galleys carrying great circular mechanical saws and spiked drills…

Ahead of them skipped the forms of what I took to be porpoises, until one of the great grey beasts lifted itself from the water, opening a pair of fins which spread like wings. It was a shark the size of a whaler's skiff, and it snapped a mouthful of silver bream from the foam of the bow-wave before it knifed back into the sea.

"… So you can see why I find it so bizarre that Grennen Vuhl himself would dare the crossing with only four small ships…" continued Meracq. "His Black Fleet has all but wiped out the Tarkhanden Fourth – enough sails, they say, to darken the very sun. The fool must have had some reason to think you *weak*, my Lord."

So – the fop was sharper than he appeared.

"Who can fathom the mind of a madman, Saltmaster?" I managed. "Vuhl's desire to face a man who slew his master must have overbalanced his reason, such as it is."

Meracq nodded.

"Desperation can make fools do the *strangest* things, can't it? Still, we would hear more of this master of Vuhl's. No doubt the Council will have some rather penetrating questions to ask you, Lamenter. *Especially* as you come to us as the Herald of Abyssus. I had no idea the position was available."

"You would have liked to volunteer?"

"Not at all. I just like to know that the people I kill are in good hands." He smiled coldly. "But come now! We are all allies here! Enjoy our voyage to Zamara – and I insist that you, My Lord, your charming concubine and your *lovely* Mortal Instrument join me aboard the *Ironheart* this evening at the captain's table."

He winked at Silbern. Winked! She looked ready to gut him for such outrage, but also strangely amused.

"Until then," I said, keeping calm composure.

"Until then, Lord Herald," said the Saltmaster, turning to leave. "One last thing. Two days ago, I had a man keelhauled for stabbing another sailor over a game of tiles. Did you see him down to the halls of Abyssus in good order? What with being in Sarem, and all?"

I clenched my fist around the grip of my glass blade, hoping for some wisdom from Aerik Stormsong. I got nothing but a nasty static shock.

"All they have to do is *sink*, Tarkhanden," I said, with what I hoped was icy disdain. "I'm not required to wield the power of the Shard unless one tries to get away. Your poor wreckage of barnacle-flayed meat found the seabed – as did sixteen hundred Kothrai. Which do you think my Master craves more of?"

Meracq nodded, seemingly satisfied. I hoped I had been vague and haughty enough for Aerik's liking.

The Tarkhanden delegation trooped back across their gangwalks, leaving us alone on the decks of the *Vengeance*. Suddenly the immense war-keel didn't seem quite so formidable – not with the Eighth Fleet encircling us in a wall of wood and canvas.

"We sail for Zamara, then," shrugged Elion Morekh. "He shouldn't feel so damned smug. We were going there anyway…"

"Aye," spat Rasq. "But this way, we're going as the dear old Saltmaster's prisoners. A subtle distinction, but not one I really care for."

I just watched Meracq and his entourage disappear from view, my mind turning over the man's words.

"The fool must have had some reason to think you weak, *my Lord."*

Oh, I was certain. The Saltmaster of the Eighth knew far more than he was letting on.

But it would avail me nothing to know his mind. Meracq was just the hound at his masters' feet.

And the Council of Seven would no doubt be even sharper than he…

You are all accused of madness - not a crime, *per se*, but a regrettable condition nonetheless. The kind ministrations of the Sisters of the Calm Seas should help you see out the rest of your days with the minimum of gibbering and self-mutilation. I believe that they sometimes even allow visitors!

In this case, however, we believe that that privilege can be waived.

The basis of my judgment is as follows...

Counsel for the defence, you will stop that wailing *this instant!* It is *most* irritating and, if I might add, unbecoming of a gentleman of law.

Now - where was I?

You were seeking, according to the documents provided and the witnesses brought forward by the Trade Guild Collective, to provision, crew and commission a journey to the mythical island of Dath N'kaal - a place only mentioned in children's stories of the very worst character.

Any man who believes that a place - as fictional as the Rum-fountain of the Temple of Ten Thousand Whores - can be reached by means of *conventional navigation* is surely mad. And any man who signs up to crew with him, or who provides him with maps, or who is so cruel as to goad on his madness with whispers and the jingle of coins... well, he is a wicked soul as well.

The city of Zamara commits you, Captain Lysenne, along with the defrocked priest Namat Grael, the merchant traders Othos and Glisk Sumansis, and seventy-seven other men to the care of the Pale Sisters. Accordingly, the Council of Seven also grants a construction stipend, one-hundred and ninety-three cartloads of bricks, the services of eighteen masons and a yearly requisition for grain to the Calm Seas Sanitorium to ensure that you are all never heard from again by sane society.

Counsel for the defence to be incarcerated with his clients.

Case closed!

The judgment of Magistrate Jackan Z'evecq,
First Lord of the Balance, Zamaran Judiciary Hierarchy
In the case of 'The Council vs Lysenne, Grael and Co.'

DEATH FLOWED THROUGH this realm. Sorath, the million isles – where the hungry sea had shaped the superstitions of hundreds of tribes and nations, creating the image of the Black Herald, His Dark Reflection. And Abyssus himself, the dweller beneath – depicted only as an eye set among a swirling starburst of tentacles.

I studied the beast to whom I was supposed to play gatekeeper, and even probed the depths with my will, seeking him out. To no avail. The throne of the Herald was indeed empty, and belief came leeching into me as I slept, stoking the slow fires of my power.

I began to feel every shipwreck we passed over, eyeless skulls rolling in the deep to track the keel of the *Sorrow's Vengeance* above, flanked by one hundred and sixty two men o' war from the Zamaran Eighth Fleet.

Anghul and the Herald, facet to facet, bound back to back. But one was a true God, however different from the Aziphem of Sarem. While the other was a mortal, chosen to wield the power of death's Shard. A grim suspicion haunted me – that the longer I played at being the hand of Abyssus, the less it would be an act at all.

Thrones, like graves, are hungry. They need filling.

We weathered storms. We were becalmed. We fought off guts-ache and calenture, picked weevils from our hardtack and endured interminable dinners with the officers of the Eighth Fleet, around the ornate wooden table of Meracq D'avarian. His board was sumptuous; the hardtack was often preferable. Meracq himself was all needles and sly sarcasm, while most of his captains were the kind of military aristocrats whose idea of 'natural leadership' is based mainly around having an impressive mustache. Diplomacy stretched to its breaking point.

My crew trained, and healed and waited with little patience.

I learned that the winged sharks of the Sorathi Seas – those sleek, grey-skinned killers which haunted our wake – were known as Skarne.

Hunters of flying fish and of seals, feared by the Tarkhanden sailors as the vengeful avatars of the Twins.

I meditated for long hours, attuning the mageblight in my bones to the eddies and swirls of death-energy in the oceans below me. Vast, inky currents of power moved there, fueled by war. Necromancy binds souls, but it also frees them. Sometimes the soul itself sees the binding as a penance. Sometimes a simple hunger for vengeance ties spirit to bone, and one last, defiant gesture is enough.

Here, there were no tombs, no barrows. The dead were given to the sea, one way or another. And so we sailed across a cauldron of dim and diffuse power, tiny whispers scratching at my skull when I slept. *For those who were bound, His Dark Reflection brought freedom.* It was right there in writing, in the holy book Rasq dug out of the ship's library for me.

It's not many a man who can say he has been the focus for two great heavy tomes of superstition, lies and madness. I choked down the precepts of my new faith, finding them just as infantile as the last ones.

It was no wonder, then, that I turned to the poppy's-blood. Two weeks of sighing, bubbling voices, calling out for mercy, freedom, absolution? I began to understand how the Gods went mad. Hells take me, I even began to have some sympathy for Zael!

I needed sleep. But what came to me was a dream – one which I realised had been scrabbling and clawing at my mind for ingress for many nights.

It was Sei.

I had thought that the tiny skeletal cat was somewhere aboard – snubbing me for the indignity of three centuries in a stone box. There were rats aplenty in the *Vengeance's* bilges, and some of them would give my undead familiar a tussle worth at least a short saga-song. With my mind otherwise occupied, I had been content to leave him to his own amusements. After all, I could feel him clearly enough; a small, warm presence in the corner of my mind's eye.

That night I barely had time to set down my jade pipe before my eyelids flickered closed. Whorls and drifts of heavy, scented smoke filled my cabin, where tomes and scrolls were stacked on every surface, held down with a collection of skulls, clay tablets, candles and surgical tools. Awake, I was trying to research the creation of the Nine. But asleep – or at least in the blissful slumber of the poppy…

I was inside a stinking drain. A stone pipe, slippery with ooze and smelling of rancid sewerage. Claws where my fingers had been, skittering over rock as I wriggled through a tight space, then up a shaft, past drop-holes letting in rays of light…

Up again, claws finding purchase in the splintered stone, and out through a plughole set in a slab of granite. A charnel-room, windowless, lit by torches. A hunch-backed shape clad in stinking furs whistled to itself, swinging a cleaver. Human bodies lay in piles, hacked limb from limb. The butcher never saw us pass, and we went slinking through the shadows and the blood, strange scents coiling and twisting low to the ground.

Through a crack in the door, and out into a long, dark corridor, hung with smoke-fouled tapestries. Iron bars slipped by to our right, and slit windows to our left – the smell of shit and fear from behind those barred doors, whimpering and prayers in the darkness.

A prison, then. A place of death.

Sei shivered as he felt my revulsion, the image of the Angan 'processing camps' welling up fresh and raw in my mind. I do not torture. What use is a broken thrall, in any case? No – like gloating, a lust for torment is the sign of a sick mind. Such cruelty is a petulant tantrum, a mask for weakness…

Ahh. A *mask*, indeed.

I thought about a face all hollowed out and bloody, like an autumn solstice gourd carved to resemble a demon. What kind of citadel would the owner of that face construct?

Something dark, and predictable, and daunting enough to cow a nation of superstitious bullies, no doubt. This was Grennen Vuhl's stronghold.

And Sei… *must have come here with Siara.*

The little skeletal cat leaped up to a window ledge, then picked his way along a narrow wooden beam – a support bolted to the rotten stone to keep this wall from tumbling into the ocean. We were high above a turbulent sea, near the tip of a crag carved and shaped into a tower.

Another dark tower! Grennen Vuhl was either madder than I thought, or Dirge was trying to mirror my own black spire, in a form of sympathetic magic. I hoped it was the latter. Otherwise next would come the unhinged laughter and the endless sermonizing, neither of which I cared for.[16]

---

16. NEVER chain your enemy up in an elaborate death-trap, and then give his friends plenty of time to overpower your thick-headed guards while you rattle off your master plan. A true Dark Lord always says "I'm sorry, Sir Knight, but the Dark Summoning

Sei reached a particularly hideous gargoyle, and hopped up atop its head. From the thing's shark-toothed maw depended a length of chain, one of two supports for a hanging bridge. This swayed out above the whitecaps, leading to a lone barbican. Sullen red light shone out from within, and Sei set out along the chain toward it with a cat's characteristic fearlessness. The wind plucked at us, skirling through his empty little ribcage. But there is nothing more sure-footed than a feline who is already dead. We reached the tower's window and dropped lightly into the room, curling up in the shadow of a wooden workbench.

Red light suffused the chamber, painting the vast, domed space as a blur of crimson and black. It flickered in globes suspended from chains and inset in the walls, illuminating a combination of laboratorium and prison – an airy space centred around a stone dais, benches and bookshelves leaning drunkenly together all around.

The prisoner in this tower was Siara Anvhaur, the Stormreaper. Chained by a single leg-iron to a solidly carved bedframe, my daughter was reading by candlelight, poring over a great musty grimoire while seated at a lectern. Within reach of the chain were a washstand, a table set with the remains of a princely meal, a stack of similar tomes, and a circle of rice-paper screens. Sei's inexplicably acute sense of smell informed me that these concealed a chamber pot.

I saw no despair. I saw no sense of defeat. Pride stirred within me, only to be smothered by horror a moment later.

"Have you anything?" grated a voice from out of the darkness. "I am not famed for my patience, you know, and I'm beginning to think that your father isn't too worried about your fate…"

Invisible hairs prickled along Sei's spine. I knew that voice, and so did my familiar.

Jerrold Sinder, Pontifex of Anganesse, lately known as Dirge, Lord Endsong, the champion of the Dwellers in Darkness.

Siara hissed with frustration.

"Your mind-games are as crude as they are useless, creature," she spat. "Uncle Aerik always said you had all the subtlety of a hammer to the face, but still…"

"Spare me the platitudes," growled Dirge. From our position we couldn't see the deathless sorcerer, but his voice seemed to echo from the dais at the centre of the room. "Just get me results! The only reason

---

happened hours ago. Your castle is already a very scenic ruin. So I'm just going to efficiently and quietly cut off your head."

you're not under dear old Grennen's knives right now is that *I* know what you were questing for. *Questing!* Hah! An absurd conceit! The age of heroes is over, girl!"

"And overblown, pantomime villains?"

Her voice was sweet and sharp-edged, and I smiled. Dirge laughed – a sound no less pleasant now than it was three centuries ago.

"A curious side-effect of the Doom, child. Alchemists and artificers will soon make the idea of one man with a magic sword obsolete. Villainy will die with heroism. People like me – like Grennen Vuhl, and indeed, like your father could have been – will simply be painted as pragmatists, forced to do regrettable things in the name of policy."

"And your policy is still to pitch all of Yrde into the abyss? Forgive me for not considering that too pragmatic…"

Another oily chuckle.

"Now, now! I'll be the one to ask the questions, miss Anvhaur. After all, who wears the chains here? Suffice to say – and so long as Grennen's wardings give us privacy – that I have enjoyed the hospitality of the Dwellers in Darkness for three hundred years. Their promised world is as shallow as a madman's wish. No… for all their power, my masters have underestimated me. The Coldblood, however, is far more earnest. Thick-headed lizard that it is."

An intake of breath. Pages rustled and dust swirled up before the crimson light as Siara slammed her book closed.

"Why now? Why risk telling me…. oh."

I could imagine Dirge's knowing leer.

"Because we both know you aren't going to leave this place, *Stormreaper.* Such a silly name. Part of the old saga-song tradition, alas. So soon lost to us…"

The balefire reflected from two tear-tracks, sliced like scars through the dust on my daughter's face. I screwed up my rage, crushing it into a tiny hot pinpoint inside Sei's skull.

"He'll come…" she whispered. And then straightening, strengthening, digging deep for iron resolve – "You need the Void Heart to kill it, then. One man and a magic sword."

Dirge's laugh was a hacking rasp this time.

"Oh, it will be *such* a shame to lose you. But needs must…"

"And you need my father to steal a shard."

"Hah! As if I would leave such a thing to that bilious old wyrm!"

"So that you can be just like Abyssus and his Herald. Good to know why you chose Sorath, Dirge."

"Such a fine mind! Yes, the Lord of the Drowned has my particular admiration. I would be forced to wield the Void Heart against him as well, were he not already conveniently compromised. To be a God, without the terrible hunger of the Aziphem. Real, without belief! And look at what belief has made me…"

There came a grinding sound from the dais – the scrape of metal on stone. Pale, ghostly witchfire sprung up from the scribed lines of a pentacle, illuminating a twisted construct of iron.

Dirge was stretched across it. What was left of him, at least – hanging like the tattered ruin of a painting's canvas from its frame. The aspirant was little more than a dripping hide – a flayed skin to which his pale face was melted like wax. His cheek was split by a jagged rent, all the way from one corner of his mouth to the edge of the frame, where ensorcelled hooks pulled him tight. Arms and legs – indeed, his lacerated manhood, too – were ragged flaps of skin, dripping the stuff of the Outer Dark.

"Beautiful, isn't it? Grennen Vuhl would tell me so, the sycophant. But I can tell by the revulsion in your eyes that you share you mother's opinion of me."

The hooks and chains jingled as Dirge twisted, little gobbets of black ooze pattering from the back of him.

"You think that little of your host?"

"He has power," shrugged the flayed sorcerer – a revolting gesture from a thing with no bones. "And he obeys. What more could an aspirant ask? There is a reason why I haven't just devoured his essence to make myself whole again, Siara."

She shuddered. Obviously, Dirge had made it clear that that honour would be hers, one day soon.

"The Void Heart, then. I… I need more time. These books are vague, muddled up with superstition, and…"

"And *I* taught your foolish father how to lie, girl. Don't think you can hide the truth from me."

"I just…"

"You just thought that so long as I need you, you will be safe from my… appetites. So *wrong*. I could tear the truth from your living brain right now, for all your conceits of power."

Something crystalized into anger within her. Siara slammed her fists down on the lectern, raising twin plumes of dust.

"*Why don't you, then?* You're full of brave words, demon. But I can sense your fear. He's coming, Jerrold Sinder. And he'll make you wish you were never reborn."

This time the thing's laughter trailed off into madness, an utterly unhinged giggle of delight.

"Because this is just so much more *delicious*, girl! Come now. Co-operate. This way you stay out of poor Grennen's clutches another day, and I get to watch you twist out that fragile little thread of hope. *He's coming! He'll get you!*" His voice was a falsetto sing-song. "How many stupid children have cried the same stupid curse? And how many have been raped and burned and sold into slavery while their parents… *Just. Fucking. Watched!*"

Mirth screwed up Dirge's shredded face, his lips tugging at the hooks. One of his eyes, I saw, floated just behind its socket, while the other was an empty gash, seething with light.

Siara bowed her head, and levered the book open again.

"These sages – the Covenant of the Dark Mirror – didn't know how the Void Heart came to be. We can fill that in from Angenstrand folk tales, eyewitness accounts of the battle of Urexes…"

"Yes, yes… get on with it!"

"It seems that Zael Kataphraxis was able to summon a piece of… *somewhere else*. When the Divine fragmented, the part which became Zael remembered, I think, where it had come from."

"Somewhere *else*? What nonsense are you talking, witch?"

Siara growled, turning over a handful of pages.

"Are you familiar with the skryer's deck?"

"The cards hags use to dupe the brain-damaged? Of course."

"Imagine that Yrde is an image on the top card. Your precious *masters* in the Outer Dark are the image on the back of the same card."

"Go on…"

"Now imagine driving a nail clean through the deck. Down to the tenth card, or the thirtieth, or right to the bottom. All those cards represent worlds which came before this one. Worlds where things fell apart, things like *distance* and *time* and *weight*. Worlds which collapsed in on themselves, and became inimical to life."

Dirge nodded, slowly, his face hanging slack on its frame.

"Perhaps the Divine was fleeing from such a world. But the sages of the Dark Mirror – and the philosopher Saro K'ruin, and the court astrologers of Hmai, not to mention several passages in Kulain's *Tractatorus Philisophico Lex Daemonae*…"

"Yes, yes… get to the point, damn you!"

"They all agree that the Void Heart – the blade which Zael

summoned – is a two-dimensional fragment of a dead creation. It landed here, in Sorath, in a place called Dath N'kaal. Although that's simply old Tarkhanden for 'cursed isle', so we can assume…"

"Enough! Have you located this *Dath N'kaal?*"

Siara's hands scrabbled among layers of parchment, papyrus and vellum. I was struck by the impression, in a sudden moment of clarity, that my daughter didn't really care that she was unraveling this mystery for a twice-dead monster. The challenge itself was enough, the sense of victory just as sweet…

"It was expunged from all the maps. The Council of Seven made sure of it. Sea lanes were moved, trade routes shifted, new reefs, whirlpools and seamounts charted to steer sailors away. I think somebody must have *touched* the thing, considering the horrors attributed to it. But… yes. I have found a suspiciously empty quarter on several maps. Tectonics and geology indicate that the tail of the Tayak archipelago should continue all the way to this trench… here. But it doesn't. Instead, both the Kothrai's maps, and those of the old Tarkhanden Imperial Survey *and* the Trade Guilds Navigator's Conventicle… they fill this stretch of water with outlandish pictures of Skarne and serpents. This is the most likely location of Dath N'kaal. Find the island, find the sword. Find the sword, truncate the Coldblood. And then… oh."

Dirge chuckled.

"So very sharp, Siara Anvhaur. But now I sense that you've cut yourself. Never mind."

In a single horrifying instant, the entire frame which held Dirge screwed itself around, grinding metal on stone. His one good eye stared directly into Sei's, and his ravaged lips split in a hideous grin.

"Wheels within wheels, Lamenter! Games within games! Now you know! And now you get to choose. Go after the Void Heart yourself, and leave Siara to Grennen Vuhl's tender mercies. Fulfill your child's silly faith in you, walk into my trap, and let Grennen take the sword. Or, let your new friends the Tarkhanden collect the blade, and they can kill Vuhl's new coven without you. Including, of course, the thing that used to be your daughter."

Sei arched his back, hissing and spitting. But the Stormreaper was quicker.

As her captor laughed she launched one of the heavy iron-bound tomes from her lectern at him, catching Dirge on what, for want of more definitive anatomy, I suppose I must call the side of his head.

Pale skin stretched and tore, hooks pulling loose with the sound of plucked lyre strings.

"Go! Find the blade, Father! This rotting thing holds no fears for me!"

It was a brave lie. Dirge coiled in sorcery, making the air glitter with frost. A spiral wind stretched him hideously taut on his frame before all those fine chains and sharp hooks slipped loose, allowing his flayed form to rise, hovering in the air.

"No fears? *No fears?* Impertinent bitch!" he lashed out with sorcery, throwing my daughter from her feet. She fetched up at the very end of her chain, slamming into the bedstead. "Fear is *exactly* what I deliver, Siara Anvhaur! And if you think that a noble death will be any release from it, you are wrong! Perhaps both you and your idiot father could do with a *demonstration...*"

The wind kept rising, until Sei was forced to grip the floorboards with his needle claws. Books flapped and flew as the gyre quickened, bearing Dirge aloft at its centre. His hands – one instant boneless, ragged flaps of skin, the next filled out around a skeleton of raw power. His fingers gripped the edges of a raw gash across his chest, unlacing a row of rawhide stitches.

"Fear is what they have given me, Kuhal. The mind is free to dream horrors, adrift in the Outer Dark. And from its primordium, from chaos... I can bring forth the flesh of those dreams. How else do you think I keep Vuhl and his savages in line?" He chuckled, fingers twisting deep, pulling the wound open. "No..." he gasped. "I show them their deepest fears, and promise them an oblivion where such things cannot find them. Now..." He looked right at me, leering.

"Now it's your daughter's turn."

Siara tried to form the words and gestures of a spell, but the chain around her ankle flared with lightning, earthing the forces before she could shape them. Then invisible hands picked her up again, slamming her back against a bookshelf. She snarled in defiance, but Dirge's sorcerous grip was too tight. And now his hands had stretched his own chest open wide, revealing a sucking vortex of darkness. Things swum in that seething gyre – things both tiny and far away and huge and immediate, heaving with eyes and teeth.

"Go! *Now!* You can't help me, Father! Find the Void Heart! Make him..."

An invisible slap rocked her head to one side, spraying blood. Sei growled, ready to pounce, but to let go now would be to be torn to pieces in the relentless wind.

"Don't think of anything! Clear your mind! If he can't find your fears, he can't…"

But it was too late.

With a cracking, slithering rush, something dark and gelid was shat into the world, heaved out of the wound in Dirge's chest. It split open like some vile organ-sac, revealing grey, pallid arms, a misshapen head…

It was one of the ghuldren, half its face eaten away, and as it lurched to its feet I saw that it was dressed in blood-smeared leathers, a full-length apron hanging ragged from its chest. The thing moaned as it uncurled to its full height, the wind whipping its straggle of grey hair out sideways. In one hand – a hand the size of a shovel blade – it dragged a heavy sledgehammer. In the other, fingers blackened and chewed down to the bone were knotted through the hair of a woman's severed head, still dripping blood.

In a way, I was almost disappointed. I had assumed that the darkest fear of a witch – indeed, a witch who was the daughter of an avowed Evil Lord – would be somehow more horrific. Certainly *bigger*. But this thing…

It flared its nostrils, taking a shuddering breath. Then it turned its dead eyes on Siara, issuing that low ghuldren moan as it tottered forward. Dirge was laughing again, a sound of madness cut to ribbons by the wind. Books flew by, pages torn free. And Siara screamed.

"Grandfather! Mother! No!"

The apparition grinned, revealing a mouthful of blackened, cracked teeth. It lifted the severed head and took a ragged bite out of its face, crunching through bone and tearing loose threads of muscle. Siara tried to look away, but Dirge clamped an invisible hand around her skull, prying her eyelids open…

And it *was* her grandfather. The Kaltensunder smith who had raised her. *A hulking ghoul, clumsy fingers mauling the remains of her mother's face.* A memory made real again, a nightmare dredged up from when my daughter was just a little girl, and the Doom I had called down on Sarem had come staggering fly-blown into her village. I had no doubt that this scene had really happened, and that the hammer which the creature now hefted was equally real.

The ghoul staggered toward Siara, drooling. Little bubbles of blood and spit foamed from the corners of its mouth. It raised the hammer over its head, prepared to crush her utterly…

And then it was gone. The wind fell away, letting books, candlesticks, parchment and scrolls drop to the floor. My daughter slid down the bookshelf, where she curled up in a ball, sobbing. The memory had done far more damage than that hammer-head ever could.

I caught a glimpse of something black and slithering, sucked back through the hole in Dirge's chest as he settled onto his frame, hooks and chains reaching out for him hungrily. The flayed sorcerer regarded Sei with a smirk as the cat picked his way over to where Siara lay, tiny fangs bared.

"*Fear*, Lamenter. At the core of it, fear is the one and only human emotion. Even conceits like love and honour are just the masks it wears – they hide the terror of dying alone, of being outcast, of being proven a coward. But we are *all* cowards at heart. Even you." he smiled. "*Especially* you, Kuhal Moer. When it comes time for me to reveal your greatest fears, what fun we'll have!"

I wanted to rip out his throat, but practical considerations intervened. At the moment, Dirge hardly had one. And Sei's claws were not nearly sharp enough.

"Sermonizing prick," mumbled Siara. She lifted her head just enough for me to glimpse her eyes, behind a tangled curtain of black hair. "Was he always so full of himself?"

Dirge couldn't see it, but there was a fragile little smile on her face. I felt her press a folded square of paper into Sei's mouth, hiding it in his hollow skull.

"He's always been an idiot," I said – fully cognizant that I was only dreaming, and that my words would be lost in the ether. I don't think she was expecting an answer.

"Go!" hissed my daughter, stroking the little cat's skull with one fingertip. "You have what you need now. I can keep this creature occupied. Come and find me when you want to destroy him… together."

Sei backed away a couple of steps, hesitant… just as the door of the tower slammed open, revealing the tall, wild-eyed shape of Grennen Vuhl. Rain swirled in around him, pattering against the mess of open books and strewn papers.

"Master! I heard the noise! And I *felt him*. The Lamenter! Has he come to…"

The ruin of the laboratorium finally sunk into the Kothrai warlock's brain. Dirge, smug and hideous on his rack. Siara, curled up in what appeared to be catatonic terror. A gruesome slick of blood stretching from the centre of the room out toward her, dark with muddy boot-prints.

"Just a little entertainment, Vuhl. Though I find your concern quite touching. When Kuhal Moer finally arrives, you will not be able to mistake it. He is a fool, but his power is – unpredictable."

Vuhl nodded, his half-face twisted into a smile. His floating eye boiled with unnatural fire – what I supposed passed for a wink.

"And the bitch? Broken yet? Are you ready to let me ply my art, Lord Endsong?"

Dirge grimaced.

"You sound more like a back-alley rapist than a sorcerer, Grennen. Remember, we serve pure reason! I won't allow my great work to be sullied by your sickness!"

The Kothrai quailed back, as if expecting the blow of a whip, and I was reminded, just for a second, of the ghuldren under Slaughtermaw's command. Then Dirge laughed, drawing veils of darkness in around himself. Soon the dais at the centre of the room was once more cloaked in shadow.

"One day soon, my disciple. *Very* soon. When I grow tired of sharpening my fears on a mind that still resists."

His contempt was plain, and Grennen Vuhl twitched. Imagining, I supposed, the horror which his Lord had manifested just for him…

"I swear I can smell him, though. He was watching. He was *here*… ahhhh."

The Kothrai had seen Sei. His hands brimmed with witchfire as he leveled them at the little skeletal cat, muttering a curse.

"Not in here, you fool!" howled Dirge. But it was too late. A crackling arc of sorcery lashed out, earthing itself against a dozen grimoires and other wells of arcane vitae. Sparks fountained from Dirge's frame, spitting actinic white.

I didn't wait for the second salvo – and neither did my familiar. With a skitter of claws we were off, leaping up to a tabletop, running along the edge of a bookcase, and then down, between the warlock's legs and into the rain-lashed night. A burst of arcane fire followed, melting a patch of stone at our heels.

"He's escaping!" roared Vuhl. Dirge just screamed, the force of his rage distorting the entire island. Stone cracked and shifted, and for an instant Sei was pulled backward, toward the immense gravity of the Angan's wrath. Then came a great silent explosion which tore the hanging bridge away from under our paws, sending us cartwheeling through darkness. I saw foaming breakers and jagged rocks spinning end over end, growing ever closer…

Then Sei took control, spearing a tendril of will out from his forehead and into the night. Somewhere below something answered it – but the croaking, cawing sound of its awakening was lost behind the double-whipcrack of sorcery. Grennen Vuhl screamed, not in rage, but in pain. It seemed that Dirge's discipline was swift.

"No! Master! Not that! Please…"

The tower shuddered. I only hoped that Siara had managed to crawl to safety – or, indeed, that she was able to use this spat between our enemies to win her freedom.

Too much to hope for, perhaps. And now the hungry ocean was there to swallow us up…

Something huge and dark blotted out the light. The smell of moldering feathers enfolded Sei as strong talons gripped clean through his ribcage, carrying him up into the storm.

It was a scavenger gull – black and oily, reanimated by my little cat's will. Either the hook-beaked old corpse had been resurrected just in time, or this was how my familiar had followed the Stormreaper in the first place. Now it bore us aloft, sinews creaking, dead eyes picked hollow by crabs. We were soon up above the clouds, drifting beneath a starlit sky.

"That was unexpected," I murmured, letting my newfound respect for Sei colour my thoughts. The skeletal cat purred contentedly, hanging loose between the scavenger gull's claws. "And yes, it's good to see you again, little friend. I take it you approve of my long-lost daughter?"

Sei's purr deepened. I sensed that I had basically lost him, then – he was Siara's creature, through and through. Cats are fickle, I know, but somehow the thought didn't hurt as much as I thought it should.

"Follow me back, then," I muttered, stirring in my sleep. "By dawn we'll see just what my daughter has risked her life for…"

And indeed we did. None of the Tarkhanden noticed the black-winged shape come scudding out of the clouds as the sun rose, but Rasq was there to catch Sei as he dropped to the deck of *Sorrow's Vengeance*. I was there too, bleary-eyed with the after-effects of poppy's-blood, but too alert and on edge to rest. My familiar coughed out the folded square of paper and I opened it with trembling hands, trying to explain what my wandering mind had seen.

It was a map. The hidden island of Dath N'kaal, along with a scrawl of runes, crabbed, hand-written notes stolen from a dozen tomes, and the image of a sword, utterly black, speckled with stars. Its handle was forged in the form of a pair of intertwined serpents, and its pommel bore the mark of Zael.

"The Void Heart," breathed Issara, pressing up far too close to me for comfort. Seventails grimaced.

"And a hard choice, if what you tell us is to be believed."

Rasq and Urmokh looked equally grim. It was an impossible judgment – go to the aid of my poor, tormented daughter, their captain… or claim the relic which could end this war.

"If I know Dirge – and, to my sorrow, I know him like no other – he wants us to go for the sword. Perhaps he thinks it is guarded. Perhaps he hopes we will die questing for it. The Tarkhanden didn't name its resting place the 'cursed isle' for its pleasant weather and tropical beaches, I suppose."

"And the Stormreaper?"

My knuckles went white where I gripped the map.

"Dirge is no fool. And he knows we suspect a trap. But I know his mind well enough to tell you this…"

"He won't actually try to kill her unless you are there to watch," said Kell, her voice barely a whisper. "Otherwise, where is the sport? Where is the jest?"

I nodded.

"Either way, there will be a reckoning. And, as I've told you, Grennen Vuhl is kept well under the Angan's thumb. For now, Dirge's spite is all that protects Siara. But that spite has brought down empires. It will hold."

Disparate mutterings from the crew. I felt that I was about to lose control, and have the lot of them fall to arguing in circles. But then bells rang out from the Tarkhanden fleet around us, and the crack of blackpowder cannon split the dawn. The ragged apparition which was Elion Morekh came hurrying down from the wheeldeck to us, waving his tricorne in the air.

"Save your counsels, all! This is something you have to see!"

Urmokh immediately reached for his knives. Seventails' cape swirled up around him like a pair of mantled wings, ready to enfold him in sorcery.

"Are we attacked? The Kothrai? Already?"

Morekh laughed, stretching the stitches at the corners of his mouth.

"Nothing anywhere near so boring, Skinchanger," he said. The sound of bells was all around us now, shimmering off the surface of the ocean. It was joined by the sporadic pop and snap of small-arms fire, and the cheering of hundreds upon hundreds of Tarkhanden sailors.

"They have sighted the spires of Zamara! One of the wonders of Yrde, Kuhal Moer. If you live another three hundred years, you will not see its equal. Come! We must make ready to cross the harbour. Let's give these Sorathi dogs a look at how we sail in Sarem!"

The sounds of celebration washed over me. I stood there, hearing none of it, staring down at the scrap of parchment in my hands. Below all the arcana – below the runes and the glyphs, the diagrams and the maps, my daughter had scrawled a final message, intended only for me.

"*The Void Heart can destroy him utterly,*" she had written, in a neat and scholarly cursive. "*If he asks you to trade it for my life, I am ready. Strike him down instead.*"

I wondered if her hands had been shaking as she took up the quill. I wondered if she was still alive right now.

Then, with a terrifying effort of will, I compacted everything I felt down into a hard, white-hot core of rage inside me. One day soon, it would be unleashed. And when it was…

Elion Morekh looked back at me, waving.

I carefully folded the parchment, closed my fist around it, and followed the rest of the crew up to the wheeldeck. It was time to take the measure of my enemy's enemies.

Hmai -
(the Cold Land, the Empire of Jade and Steel)

Ruler - Tsargon Urd V, ninth scion of the Urd Dynastic Cycle. Son of the Empress Lirani Urd, age 46.

Temperament - frosty at best, murderous at worst. Would like to be remembered as 'firm but fair' despite a penchant for the mass impalement of pirates, brigands, tax defaulters and rapists.

Economy - Determinedly feudal, with an emerging merchant class bound to labyrinthine laws of title, inheritance and heraldry.

Main staple crop - maize. Main artisan craft - the intricate working of jade and other semi-precious stones into implements of sorcery. The Hmai are also known for their fine silks, hand-glazed pottery and unspeakably sharp weapons forged by an arcane process utilizing vulcanism.

Strategic Situation - Currently fighting what Hmai generals call 'a well ordered retreat' but what the rank and file call 'an insane death march' out of the jungles and swamps of southern Akhaz, after a punitive expeditionary force was sent to match strengths with the Coldblood and halt that beast's machinations of power.

Sameth Raal,
Strategic Ethnologist of the Guild of Chains
"Nations of Yrde"

MUCH HAS BEEN written about Zamara, capital of Tarkhand. Sameth Raal, for example, gave it two pages, most of which was, to put it frankly, horseshit.

Poets call it the Eternal Harbour, and architects studiously copy its towers and minarets in pale imitation. Seeing it for the first time, behind the flickering, mother-of-pearl curtain of geomancy which enfolded it, I was moved by admiration – despite the repellent smugness of Saltmaster Meracq D'avarian.

I could forgive him a little pride, though. His people had wrought wonders.

The whole fleet fell silent with awe as we approached the outer pinnacles, their arching bridges seeming as thin and light as gossamer against the bulk of the towers supporting them.

Sorrow's Vengeance sailed beneath, a toy afloat amid the castles of giants. We surged between two octagonal pillars of stone which reared up ten times higher than our masts, watching fires blaze from their crowns – signal flames for navigation by night. The bridges which curved inward from these bastions passed *through* the wall of geomancy above us, becoming distorted and skewed, like reeds pushed into clear water. The city beyond was a mirage, crystalline and indistinct.

Because the outer wards of Zamara were built in Sorath – but the city itself was not.

Here, as nowhere else, a vast plug of stone had been forced up from the core of Yrde, forming a separate island, as distinct from the Million Isles as Sarem is from Hmai. The ancient Tarkhanden had built clear across the chasm, linking two fractured fragments of the globe. And in doing so they had created a naval citadel impregnable in its might – one with the Chasm of the open void protecting it. The only way to sail from the Sorathi side to Zamara itself was between these mighty bastions, for to broach the wall of geomancy elsewhere would simply send our ship tumbling into the abyss, a tiny speck plunging down into the world's core.

Circling Skarne and ironhead sharks patrolled the gates, feeding on scraps hurled from the towers above.

"It's incredible!" breathed Issara – for once visibly impressed.

"I liked the colossus better," shrugged Seventails, with badly feigned nonchalance.

Harlaw was scribbling formulae on a pad of paper, squinting up at those bridges, where tiny, bright-armoured figures moved like burnished insects. Rasq simply chuckled to himself, shaking his head, and folded his immense form up on the deck to wait.

"So, this is what the Kothrai face," I said. "Ambitious bunch, hmmm? Has anyone ever actually breached the inner harbour?"

Meracq regarded my slyly, stroking his beard.

"None, Lord Herald. Save for your presence, of course. We all know that guards, gates and locks are no protection against the icy grip of mortality!"

"A poet, this one," smirked Issara. "Unfortunately, about as bad as Gryst. Where *is* the ogre, in any case?"

The Saltmaster flinched just a little at the mention of our granite-toothed friend. Silbern Chaar had indeed accepted Meracq's invitation to dinner – but she had taken the ogre with her as a chaperone. Not only had the huge creature's rumbling growl been enough to defuse the Tarkhanden's amorous attentions, Gryst had also spent most of the meal delivering a pointed, highly accurate critique of the culinary skills of the Saltmaster's chefs. A return invitation aboard the *Vengeance* had been as frosty as a Kaltensund winter morning, as three very highly paid Tarkhanden gourmands mournfully tasted the best soup ever concocted, and were then informed it had been made entirely of the meager pickings from our stores.

"I think he's preparing a list," said Elion Morekh, standing at the wheel. Tiny alteration to the ship's heading kept his eyes on the Zamaran signal-flags, herding the fleet into a long serpentine formation. We were approaching the arch of silver and marble which was the final gate – the 'needle's eye' as the Tarkhanden sailors called it. It was big enough to accommodate the *Sorrow's Vengeance* three times over. "Resupply. Never fear, Lord Saltmaster. We promise not to bargain *too* hard."

Saltmaster D'avarian just smiled. It was ever so slightly unsettling.

"Prepare yourselves, then. We are about to enter the Eternal Harbour."

The wall loomed up over us now, chains hung with banners piercing its nacreous surface. One each, or so I was later told, for each of the Trader-Captains of Zamara, the backbone of the fleets. Behind the swirling veils of geomancy the towers and domes of the Tarkhanden capital were a hazy mirage, but as we passed through the wall they blurred into focus, tier upon tier of them, mounting one atop the other in a web of buttresses and supports, zig-zagging staircases and aqueducts.

"Not enough room," muttered Harlaw. "The whole island can only be about twenty old Imperial Chains in diameter. No room to build out, like we did in Sarem. They built *up*."

And indeed they had. The island of Zamara was shaped like a crescent moon, twin arms encircling the harbour itself. At each tapering point rose immense towers, like those Meracq called the Sunrise Gates. Arching gossamer bridges swept out from them, piercing the wall and disappearing. The city itself rose from behind the flat silver mirror of the harbour, a jumble of domed white buildings stacked up in what seemed to be geometric confusion. I realised the scale of it all as we approached the hundreds of piers and wharves encircling the inner harbour, and reasoned that there would be whole warrens in the bowels of this place where the wretched never saw the sun.

"*This* is what Grennen Vuhl faces, Lord Herald. Even without your master Abyssus, and without the legions of the dead who you command – in Sarem, of course," (he raised one eyebrow) "We are still most confident of victory. See there? Our shipyards are well stocked with timber from the east of Qauziir. We commission a new dreadnaught every three weeks, and a war-galley each day."

"It's not how many you build," muttered Elion. "It's how many the Kothrai *sink*, captain."

The Saltmaster bristled. I have often heard the expression, but this was a physically visible effect.

"Few enough that we don't call on the aid of our Faeroan cousins, creature."

"And yet, here we are. Never let it be said that Faeros was ungenerous!"

"Two thousand years is a bit long between visits, if you want to discuss generosity," said Rasq, shifting slightly and shielding his eyes with one great callused hand. "But you two surely act like cousins. I ought to knock your empty heads together."

He was smiling when he said it, though Meracq D'avarian's anchor-bearing eunuch made to step in front of his master. The Tarkhanden waved him aside.

"Don't fret, northman. This is a day for celebration, not petty rivalry. Not only do we welcome a most singular delegation from our friends in Sarem… we are able to reunite His Dark Reflection with the acolytes of Abyssus, as well. Most auspicious."

There was no mistaking the temple of my supposed Lord. As we furled sails and slipped into the harbour (to be met by a frenzy of pilot boats, lamp-bearers, customs-and-excise skiffs and rafts displaying living advertisements for Zamara's houses of ill repute), the immense stone structure loomed grim and grey off our port bow. The temple of Abyssus took the form of ten twisted spires, fashioned in the shape of tentacles. They reached toward the sun in a spiral, around a central dome, and I could see smoke rising from its hollow heart – some sacrifice, no doubt.

"Matters of faith can wait, Lord D'avarian," I said, trying my very best to sound pious. "Matters of state must prevail. Are the Council of Seven prepared to meet with us?"

"They are already in conclave, Lord Herald," said the Saltmaster, nodding to a bright chain of banners high on the slopes of the city. "Messenger gulls have brought them news of your arrival, and your offer of alliance. We will be met at the dockside by crowds, I am sure. Though not all will be pleased to see us, I'm afraid."

"Trouble in paradise?" sneered Elion.

"The kind of dissent a free nation must endure, noble cousin. We can't all be ruled by a tyrant – no offense meant, Lord Lamenter."

"Of course," rumbled Rasq. "You Tarkhanden practice that fool system they call *democracy*. Everyone gets to *choose* the members of the Council, and after three years, out they go!"

"Surely they might choose a tyrant, were he rich enough to bribe the mob with wine?" asked Seventails.

"Well… they could, I suppose. But we are not *imbeciles*. The mad cannot vote. Neither can women, slaves, prisoners, the poor, the sick, foreigners, pirates, priests, children, domestic animals or sodomites. It's a very fair system."

"And the current councilmen?"

"Returned, by the people's acclamation, for six consecutive terms."

"Then why are the mob so restless now?"

"The war against the Kothrai is unpopular. Too many mothers have sent their sons down to Abyssus. Though of course, *you* would know the exact figures, My Lord."

Again, that knowing little smile. I was sure my playacting was convincing enough… after all, I had *horns*, for the Divine's sake. Still…

"Do they really think they can broker a peace with Grennen Vuhl?"

The Saltmaster nodded.

"There is a faction within the council who think it possible. They have spread the word about your coming, Lamenter, and whipped up the mob. We face one necromancer, they say – even less reason to ally with another such abomination." He quickly held up his hands. "Their words, I'm afraid. Not mine."

"Reasoning with Vuhl – and with the one he serves – is as pointless as reasoning with the rising tide, D'avarian. What do you propose we do?"

"In the first instance," said the Saltmaster, just as *Sorrow's Vengeance* slid up against the dock, lines thrown wide and pulled taut – "Don't kill any of them with sorcery, even if a bit of rotten produce does come our way. Look dignified. Eyes ahead. And remember, these people are *afraid*. Not just of Vuhl – but of *you*. You *don't* want to know the stories we have about Sarem here."

"One big graveyard?" asked Issara.

"One big graveyard." confirmed Kell. Meracq nodded.

"You can fill in the more prurient details yourself. Suffice to say – well, you might not want to listen to what they're chanting."

I could hear them now.

Whichever faction in the Council of Seven thought (madness!) that they could broker a deal with Dirge, they certainly new how to turn out a crowd. The dockside strand was packed ten deep with angry plebians, citizens of Zamara's Low Town dressed in the belted tabards and canvas leggings which constituted Tarkhanden national costume. Many also wore the round leather cap of sailors, while others were obvious veterans – amputees with crusted bandages and clattering medals. The mob was held back by a thin line of soldiers, many of whom were decidedly half-hearted in their defence of the Great Beast of Sarem. Effigies were hoisted, burning. Placards named me a warmonger, among other less wholesome epithets. The traditional rancid produce pattered on the cobbles, though we were well out of range.

"This is it..." hissed Seventails, moving in to form one half of my honour guard. Silbern Chaar came up on my left, sword bared. Behind me, Rasq lofted a banner showing the arms of Sarem – a fanciful creation featuring far too many skulls for the present mood of the crowd.[17] There were loud catcalls, and more than one pithy curse as it caught the breeze.

But the threat of the soldiers' muskets and pikes kept the crowd at bay. Spit, invective and last week's vegetables were all that assaulted our delegation as we descended the gangway and ducked inside a large black carriage, pulled by a team of silver-horned oxen.

"No horses on the island, of course," reasoned Harlaw, ducking a well-aimed pomegranate. "What would they do with all the manure? At least you can *eat* oxen, aye?"

The carriage ride was smooth, the windows shut tight, and all we

---

17. Those arms were a snow-lynx skull, saber-fanged on a silver shield, barred with black. Praying human skeletons supported this device, which was topped with a seven-pointed black crown. The motto read - 'Quare Eligere Minus Malum'. In the old Ythean, of course. It means, in crude translation to the Guildspeil of Angenstrand 'Why Choose the Lesser Evil'..

had to contend with was the smell of Rasq and Seventails in a confined space. Several times we stopped, only to be lofted several hundred spans at a leap by elevating platforms, powered, so D'avarian told us, by armies of condemned prisoners turning capstans underground. The carriage windows were thrown open. Breathtaking vistas unfolded one after another, until I was heartily sick of them.

At last the carriage rocked to a halt, and we were ushered to the end of a long, royal-blue strip of carpet, traversing a balcony so high and immense that Urmokh (were he here) would have guessed he was back in the hidden aerie of the Archaeon. Soldiers in immaculate whites lined the way to a door as high and ornate as any in my own dark tower, and as we approached they raised trumpets to their lips, pealing a deafening blast.

Ears ringing, we were herded into a vast, domed hall – a space in which the high table of the Council was all but lost.

Seven tired-looking old men crouched in their ermine and silks behind it, dwarfed by the space around them. The scratch of quills on paper sounded like woodworm feeding.

One among them – a tall, severe ancient with a nose like a ship's rudder and a towering powdered wig – stood as we entered. A leader, then – for he cradled an immense black gavel in both hands. His colleagues looked in order sickened, drunken, enraged, sad, remorseful and avid as they looked up from their scrolls, but he appeared simply *exhausted* – dead on his feet as he rose to greet us.

"Welcome, emissaries of Sarem. We understand you have traveled far to join us this day. And so… I am deeply sorry."

The avid councilman – an ancient in a black mitre emblazoned with crossed anchors – actually chuckled. And the gavel came down, along with a great iron portcullis, sealing our escape.

"Kuhal Moer, otherwise known as the Lamenter in Bones and Ashes, the Beast of Sarem, Lich-lord of the Dark Tower, you are hereby placed under arrest to await trial. The charges are many, but all relate to bringing strife to our nation in a time of war."

"Treachery!" shouted Rasq, leaping toward the council table. His lips were pulled back from his impressive dentition in a snarl, his staff clattering with bones as it swung…

But no sorcery lashed out from it. A sputter of blue light crackled and faded from the bird's skulls and shark's teeth, and the temperature dropped perhaps half a degree. I felt it too – a blanket of potent anti-magick, falling as soft and silent as snow across us all.

"D'avarian!" shouted Silbern Chaar, sword in her hands. The upper chamber of the hall was filling with musketeers, matchlocks smoking as they aimed at our party.

"I didn't know!" growled the Saltmaster, drawing his own sabre as we pressed in back to back. Seventails could not shift into one of his primal forms – instead he held out a hand to Silbern, who slapped a dagger into his palm.

"He tells the truth, Sarem'ec," said the head of the Council. "We could not risk you staying away, Lamenter. You see, rendering your person unto Grennen Vuhl is one of the key conditions of his surrender."

I was more restrained than Rasq. I noted the blue-robed clerics among the Tarkhanden soldiers – men and women with vellum pages from the holy book of the Twins sewn to their cassocks. Silan and Suramaei, Aziphem of the Calm and Storms… they had consecrated this place as holy ground. Even the power I'd stolen from Abyssus would be useless here.

"You betray us all!" shouted Meracq D'avarian, pointing at his city's rulers with his sabre. "Have any of you withered old men actually *faced* the Kothrai? Have you any idea what they are?"

"They are men like you and me, Saltmaster." replied another of the Council – the one I'd dubbed enraged. His jowls quivered with anger as he hammered the table with one gold-crusted fist. "Men who also regret these foolish hostilities. Now they have seen the folly of war, and they desire peace."

"There is no word in their language," spat Meracq, "For *peace*. A fact you would know if you'd stood blade to blade with their bloody axemen!"

"Then it devolves to us, as the civilised men we are, to *teach them*," said the leader of the Council. We have voted, son of house D'avarian. Were your father still sat among us…"

"And we have other reasons," put in the drunken councilman. "That Herald of yours… he's got a few answers to cough up, don't he?"

The Saltmaster glared daggers at his rulers for a moment, then seemed to sag, his sabre dropping to his side.

"Aye. You are right, My Lords. Forgive the ardour of a warrior who has seen too many friends fall. I will leave diplomacy to my betters, First Democrat Berolde."

Berolde smiled, stroking his gavel.

"Good. We would not want to strip you of your commission, dear boy. Not when the Kothrai are but *one* of the threats at our borders."

He turned an icy stare on me.

"In my experience, necromancer, like sticks with like. Crows flock with crows, and gulls with gulls. Fish swim in shoals, and thieves and whores drink with other thieves and whores. Your dark arts may have subdued Sarem, but we are free men here. And we know much of your power. It is the same as Grennen Vuhl's, is it not?"

He didn't give me time to protest. Not that arguing my case would have done any good. My mind and my will were engaged solely in self-preservation, as the choking weight of anti-magick threatened to snuff me out.

"His emissaries have told us much, as we prepare a framework for peace. How you once both served the same master – the one called Endsong. How you colluded to steal the power of Abyssus – the very reason why Vuhl commands the Elder One's shadow. *And of your treachery.* Yes… even our darkest enemy is wary of you, Beast of Sarem. Is there even a single living man, woman, or child left in your graveyard realm? Barring, of course, these monsters who attend you."

"I never served Endsong! Never! And as for Sarem…"

"Give it up!" slurred the drunken councilor. "We know you're lying. 'Bout Sarem. Sent ships there. Whole place crawling with the dead. 'Bout Endsong. You was the one who delivered him to Urzen the Mad. An… an the other thing. *Abyssus.* You never knelt before his altar in your life. Come on! We're *politicians*, boy. Don't try to lie to the liars!"

Foolishly, I decided that perhaps the time *had* come for the truth.

"Grennen Vuhl is your true enemy," I began. "Sarem *is* in the grip of a terrible curse. I came here to break it. As for Abyssus – the Kothrai and I never colluded in any plot to steal his power. I wouldn't know where to begin!"

"Aha!" shouted the sick-looking councilor – a jaundice-eyed mummy in cloth-of gold robes. "So, so you *admit* that you are no true Herald. That the land where you rule is cursed. And yet you still expect our sympathy – let alone our aid? We want no part in a squabble between warlocks!"

I drew breath to explain, to refute, to argue… but I saw the self-satisfied little smile on First Democrat Berolde's face, and I held my tongue. Parchment, ink and whispers had achieved what ships and soldiers could not. We were undone.

"Take them, Saltmaster," said Berolde, with a desultory twitch of his gavel. "We will interrogate the impostor Herald, then turn him over to the Kothrai delegation. As for the rest – they are unclean creations, born of dark sorcery. Shrive them, then burn them. Feed them to the Skarne in the harbour, for all I care. The Twins will take their souls, now that Abyssus is cleansed from Tarkhand."

Those white-suited soldiers who had trumpeted our arrival now streamed into the room, carrying chains inscribed with holy words. Others hefted long spears, nets and iron-banded clubs. Meracq D'avarian looked sincerely sorry.

"You can appeal to the law, of course," he said, edging away as the soldiers closed in. "I'm sure that a good barrister could have your sentence reduced to exile…"

Rasq was having none of it.

The wild shaman saw the nets and chains coming for him, and something snapped inside his mind. Sorcery may have been impossible under the deadening influence of the Tarkhanden priests, but even without it the northman was a gangly nine feet of muscle and bone. I felt like cheering as his fist caught Saltmaster Meracq D'avarian a solid blow to the jaw, lifting his boots from the floor and sending him flying.

Then the huge and hairy creature was amongst the Tarkhanden soldiers, and the hall turned to chaos. Seventails leaped for the council table, his dagger flashing, only to be taken down by a trio of woven wire nets. But Rasq was unstoppable, shrugging off lengths of entangling chain and splintering bones left and right. He picked up one luckless soldier like a club and swung him in a whistling arc, scattering assailants left and right. Silbern Chaar pushed me to the ground and swung her greatsword, snarling a challenge. Harlaw produced a double-barreled pistol, but before he could fire, the master gunner was mobbed, buried under a pile of swearing, struggling marines.

Then the priests of the Twins redoubled their efforts, making the very air squeeze in like the jaws of a vise. The mageblight inside me suddenly felt as cumbersome as lead, and I could not have risen to fight, even if I thought it would make a damned bit of difference.

For, just as Rasq gripped his living cudgel by the neck and tore him in half, First Democrat Berolde chopped down with his gavel, giving his men the order to fire.

The first volley of musket balls made Rasq twitch and snarl, but failed to slow him down. He was pouring blood as he strode toward the council table, throwing two mangled halves of a white-clad corpse to the ground.

The second volley cracked out through a pall of smoke – but this, too, proved not enough to halt the northman's inexorable advance. He walked through the assault like a man battling an arctic gale, fist-sized chunks of flesh torn away, his eyes flashing murder.

Seventails screamed as soldiers mobbed him, clubs rising and falling until he was silenced. Silbern Chaar dropped her sword, hands held high, a look of disgust on her face.

And the third volley dropped him.

One last step from the table, venal old men scrabbling away from their chairs, Berolde's smug grin turned to a mask of horror. Now came the meaty thwack of lead on flesh, the crack of impossibly strong bones, pieces of scalp and hair torn away…

A lucky shot caught Rasq high on the temple, shearing off a quarter of his skull. He wavered for a second, reeling like a drunkard. Then his lips parted in a hideous grin and he took that final step, picking up the council table in both hands. Lead shot cracked against the ancient polished oak, but it had the consistency of stone. Another musket ball shattered Rasq's leg as he tottered forward, every muscle straining, and brought the immense tonnage of wood up over his head.

I saw his eyes, blazing blue-white. I saw the frost radiating in fractal whorls across the oak, out from his fingers, digging an inch deep into the table's edge. I saw the Tarkhanden priests falling, clutching their heads, screaming as their anti-magick overloaded, feeding back in a flurry of whipsawing energies.

Then a final shot struck the shaman between the eyes, and his head was erased in a spray of crimson. He staggered, already dead, hefting a table four times his size…

And he threw it.

With terrible accuracy.

First Democrat Berolde was already backing away, slack-jawed with horror. When he saw the table take flight he turned and ran, but he was too old and far, *far* too slow.

The double impact silenced everyone in the great hall. All fighting ceased as that impossibly heavy slab came down on the leader of the Council, like a brick crushing a blowfly. Not one part of him protruded from beneath its upended bulk – nothing but a trickle of blood. The second impact was the sound of Rasq's mangled body collapsing to the floor, headless and cold.

Saltmaster D'avarian staggered to his feet, rubbing at the purple bruise which covered half his face. He spat out a tooth, grimacing.

"Hold! Hold, all of you! Enough!"

The soldiers hesitated – but he was a battlefield commander. Something in his tone hearkened back to every drill-yard sadist who has ever flogged a raw recruit.

"Don't be fools, Sarem'ec! Berolde's edict of death flouted the law – but as we can all see, he has paid dearly. There will be no more killing this day."

The other members of the Council were ashen-faced, darting glances at the table which had become their master's tombstone. I received a distinct impression that many of them were secretly pleased that he had been so neatly squashed… and that all were planning their political gambits to replace him.

"Lamenter, you will be taken to the temple of Abyssus. Holy ground. If he is truly your Lord, he may show you a way to leave this place, board your ship, and never return. I will see to it that you sail from here unopposed."

I stood – hesitantly, for I ached bones-deep – and nodded.

"I can't say I think much of your hospitality, Saltmaster. But you are right. More death would prove… superfluous, even to a *necromancer*." This last with no small amount of venom, aimed at the cowering Council of Six-still-alive.

"Will you go in peace?"

"Aye. Though if you ever meet Mistress Chaar here in a dark alleyway…"

"Bugger *that* with a bargepole," spat the Ontokhi. "I'll slit his guts in broad daylight, Kuhal Moer."

"She means it," I said, smiling. "But not now, Silbern. We have come all this way by the will of Abyssus. Let us at least see his temple before we go."

I rested a calming hand on the sword-maiden's shoulder, but she shrugged me off, stooping to retrieve her blade.

"Your company was vile, your attentions noisome, and your charm non-existent," said Silbern. "But I *do* look forward to the next time we meet, Meracq D'avarian."

He bowed, looking tired and more than a little sad.

"My masters hold my honour cheap, it seems. I pray you will not do the same, dear lady. Now – Captain Galayne?"

A slightly powder-burned marine in ceremonial whites stepped forward and saluted.

"I will take these four to the temple. Have Magister Verlocke seal the wardings behind them. And signal their ship. There are two very, very dangerous young ladies aboard, along with a thing that looks like it could chew boulders. Tell them that there is contagion loose in the city, and they must await our plague doctors in the outer harbour. Tell them that their friends are in isolation, but safe."

Would Elion and the witches believe it? And why had Meracq said nothing of the ravenous, ship-length draken we had in our hold? I struggled to remember whether he had ever actually *seen* Scarwing, who was mending admirably thanks to the sorceries of his human brother Urmokh.

I could not answer myself, so I simply concentrated on sweeping out of the council chamber with as much dignity as my splitting headache allowed. Tarkhanden soldiers hustled to form up on either side of our sad little party, making this look more like an arrest and less like an escape. We passed by the upended table, and the huddled knot of Zamaran elders, and I gave a smug little nod, the merest shadow of a bow.

"Pray for your colleague, gentlemen," I murmured, just loud enough for the Councilmen to hear. "I may be a false Herald, but I know enough about Abyssus to recognize a candidate for the Hell of the Hooks when I see one…"

They flinched, like children under crossbow fire. But petty mind-games were of little comfort. We were bundled into another ox-cart, many flights of stairs below, wards and sigils deadening the flow of vitae all around it.

"Was this one just for me?" I asked, as Meracq D'avarian swung up onto the footplate. I peered out at him though an iron grille in an iron door, carved deep with the Dead Zero and the Rune of Null. "I can only assume," said the Captain, tight-lipped and tense. "Honestly, Lamenter, I don't know how long my authority is going to last. We have to get you to the temple before one or another of those factions shakes off its torpor. Both will want you dead now."

"Both?" asked Silbern, getting comfortable on a pile of dirty straw. The whips cracked, and the wagon began to roll, creaking from side to side. It must have weighed several tons.

"The pacifists – Berolde's backers – will still want to hand you over to the Kothrai. The others, who want to crush Grennen Vuhl, will want to string you up to placate the mob. One of your men killed our First Democrat, you recall."

"It was self defence. Clear case."

"It was assault with a deadly table, and technically an act of war," said Meracq. "By most of the old statutes, Sarem is now on the same side as Kothrai. Burning the evil necromancer of *one* enemy army will be good for morale – it makes it seem far more plausible that we'll burn the other one soon."

Seventails regained consciousness with a prolonged, unwelcome retching sound.

"Lovely," said Silbern. "How long is this hayride, anyway?"

"Clear across Zamara," said Meracq. He wasn't smiling. "And we can't outrun the semaphore. If either of the factions takes control back there, they can have barricades up and muskets aimed right down the Avenue of Glass to stop us.

"Can we go any faster?" asked Harlaw. I could tell he was performing mathematical calculations behind me – the sheer pressure of cognition made the hairs on the back of my neck itch.

"Oxen, I'm afraid. They're mainly acting as a brake, though – it's all downhill from here."

"Then why..?"

"The *sudden stop*, Mistress Chaar. Otherwise…"

The conversation took this opportunity to become thoroughly academic. Because as we pulled out of the tapering shadow of the Council tower, a whole battery of cannon began to fire on us from every arch and window of that great marble edifice. It seemed that negotiations had only taken a short time – likely backed up with some quick stiletto work. Meracq D'avarian was more than likely out of a job.

And out in the open, too.

The heavy iron carriage protected we four inside from the crack and whine of shrapnel, but the driver was not so lucky. Those were deck-clearing munitions, hollow cannonballs packed with powder and nails, and they shredded the cobblestones, shattering windows and roof tiles as they rained down.

Whoever had commanded this barrage was indiscriminate. People who had come out of doors to see the grim black wagon roll past were cut down, bloodied, screaming. The driver toppled from the buckboard and rolled under the wheels, his cry cut off by a hideous crunch.

"Meracq!" I shouted. "Cut the traces! We have to get out of range!"

The Saltmaster looked at me as if I was mad.

"Did you not hear me mention the sudden stop, Lamenter? I…"

Another shell whistled and cracked, shrapnel scoring a line across the Tarkhanden's cheek. He cursed.

"Wait here," he said – as if I had any choice.

From the front of the wagon came the sound of a sword being unsheathed, then a sharp crack. The carriage lurched left. A second splintering sound, and a pained lowing of oxen… then we shuddered to the right. And began picking up speed.

Meracq swung back down to the footplate, a bunch of keys between his teeth. He selected one, then threw the door open, breaking the wardings.

"I'll need one of you to steer, and the others to pray," he said, smiling grimly. "This is going to be a bumpy ride. Come on!"

Silbern pushed past me, and swarmed up the ladder to the wagon's roof after Meracq. I found myself praying that she wouldn't just give in to her cravings and twist his foolish head off. Harlaw went next, and I followed, almost getting my horns tangled in the bars. Cosmetic drama! There's more than one Dark Lord who's died because his billowing black cape got snagged at the wrong moment…

I braced myself in the doorframe, just in time to watch the oxen fall away behind us. Cannons were still booming and spitting from the tower, but at this range their aim was abysmal. A water trough, two pots of flowers, one of the wandering oxen and a statue of the Twins were obliterated, while we clattered up to a running pace, the wagon's leaf-springs creaking and jangling.

By the time I reached the roof, we were rolling faster than a horse can trot. By the time I slid onto the buckboard next to Harlaw, it was more of a flat-out, red-eyed gallop.

And I could see why.

Between the Council Tower and the Temple of Abyssus, the road followed the spine of Zamara, paved along the razorback ridge with buildings falling away on either side. The priciest real estate on the island flanked this avenue, and at strategic places whole bastion towers straddled the road, plunging it into darkness as it pierced their foundations. If this had been old Urexes, the Anganesse would have laid out the plans for the avenue with a steel ruler, then whipped a million slaves to death making nature conform. The happy-go-lucky engineers of Tarkhand, on the other hand, would rather be designing boats. They simply ordered an industrial quantity of hexagonal cobbles, then paved what must have been a goat-herder's track in days of yore. The result was steep, winding, and fraught with curves. We were in a two-ton wagon with no functional brakes, and steered by Meracq D'avarian, perched on the hub of the wagon's front wheels, holding a spar of timber which had been jammed in as a kind of tiller.

Silbern Chaar was on the other side of it, and I was pleased to note that the simple problem of staying alive had overridden her hatred. Between them they heaved and hauled on the makeshift tiller, wrestling the wheels of the carriage around as we crested a shallow rise, coming into the first corner. Its iron-shod rims sparked as we went into a four-wheel drift, the footplate neatly decapitating a row of ornamental shrubs by the roadside. But we made it. And still we were gaining speed.

Harlaw was smoking a vile roll-up which he had manifested out of nowhere, while inspecting the innards of a long, blue-steel musket.

"Interesting. Revolving mechanism. Hand-loaded paper cartridges go *here*... rifled barrel. This is quite a work of art, m'lord. Nine shots, then you have to slide in another of these little brass drums."

I looked at the small metal log he held up for my inspection. It was a better view than the blurred facades of housed whipping past us. "They must have some kind of workhouse packing these things. Precise work. Little fingers. Probably orphans."

Now the street had straightened out, and the wagon really began to shake itself loose. Every pebble and bump caused us to lift a wheel off the ground, sometimes gliding in a shallow trajectory before impacting with a smash of iron on stone. Like everyone else on board, I could feel my spine being vibrated into nerveless jelly. I had to keep my mouth slightly open, to save my teeth from cracking together.

While ahead of us, the semaphore flickered a message of alarm. A barricade was forming up, sawhorses and pikemen, musketeers pointing and shouting...

"Can you *fire* it, Harlaw?" I asked, over the sound of the wagon's breakneck passage. It sounded like cutlery being rolled in a barrel down stairs.

"Oh aye, m'lord. Thing like this, you don't have to ask me twice..."

The first shot took off a sword-brandishing officer's head as he bellowed some heroic speech or other. Harlaw levered the handle, rolling the brass drum around. A second shot felled a pikeman, bone splinters slicing through the comrades who stood on either side. I thought it likely that, given enough time, Harlaw could calculate a tailored trajectory to put a musket ball through the chest of every one of them, mathematical formulae collapsed into the crack and thud of lead against bone.

But time was something we didn't have. The barricade rushed up at us, pikes dropping into a shimmering wall…

Thankfully, we had sorcery.

Not much – *you* try manipulating two tons of cold iron inscribed with the bloody Dead Zero! But enough for what I had planned. This road, like any other feat of empires, was paved not just in stone, but in the blood of countless labourers. Slaves, this time. They had been interred beneath the cobbles[18], and it only took a moment to reach out ahead of the speeding wagon, calling to a rich strata of trapped souls pressed under the gravel and clay.

I held my palm upward, and spoke a Word. I raised my open hand, chanting, and held on tight…

The road just in front of the barricade suddenly erupted, chips of stone and dust blasting out as if it had been struck by a cannonball. The cobbles grated together with a terrible grinding sound, forced skyward by a tectonic shrug of underlying mud and stone. It was as if an invisible hand had sunk its fingers into the avenue, then peeled up a slice of it, forming a sharply angled ramp to nowhere.

The wagon hit the ramp even as the barricade behind it toppled. Dust swirled as our spoked wheels churned through clouds of it, springs compressing with a howl like tortured angels. Then we were airborne, all weight fallen away, Harlaw grabbing for the rail as his cigarette turned end over end, shedding sparks…

The tips of pikes flickered by below us. Muskets tracked the belly of the wagon. I could have spit down into the gaping mouths of a hundred Zamaran guardsmen.

Then came the impact, the shock of it trying to hammer my spinal column out the top of my skull. Both Meracq and Silbern clung grimly to the tiller, and I saw his hand shoot out to grasp hers, saving her from what would have been a fatal fall. In the back, Seventails was loudly sick. Musket shot spanged impotently off the rear armour of the wagon as we leaned into a wicked left-hander, going up onto two wheels before we rushed through the yawning arch of a bastion tower, scattering beggars and whores.

Darkness and light. Darkness and light. The three other towers

---

18. It is said that this practice is to ensure good fortune - though obviously not for the slaves, for whom it comes a bit too late. Even Khytein villages had bound captives interred alive beneath their longhall thresholds, in the belief that no traitor could enter, being warned away by he contrite soul of the buried foe.

passed us by like pickets on a fence. Even flying on Drakenback, I had never experienced such speed. And now we were aimed down the gullet of the Avenue of Glass, facing the gates of Abyssus' temple. They had had more time to prepare for us here. Before us the cobbled road was split by a long, mirror-bright pool, an ornamental pond designed to reflect the temple's spires. Fountains hissed and spumed along its length, forming a beautiful and culturally interesting counterpoint to a wall of spiked and smoking death.

There must have been three hundred soldiers being bawled and kicked into formation, behind overturned wagons and carts. Blue-robed acolytes of the Twins swung censers, preparing to call forth their spells. This time it wouldn't be anti-magick… oh no. This time it would be the full elemental fury of their patron Aziphem, and as I had seen before, the elemental Shards command horrifying levels of power.

"How in the *hell*, shouted Harlaw, "Are we going to get through that?"

At least he must have shouted – any noise quieter than a bellow would simply have been whipped away and chopped to ribbons in our slipstream. It hardly mattered, though. I had no answer for him. Just the grim certainty that we were all about to die.

That is, until I felt the voice of Aerik Stormsong in my mind.

"*A mess you've made of things as usual, boy,*" he grumbled.

"Well, it's all thanks to your assistance… as usual," I snarled. "I don't know why I bother lugging you around with me, when all you can do is play the critic."

"*I do what I can,*" said the voice from the glass sword, and I detected a certain sense of smugness in its tone. "*Such as remembering who you are supposed to be, here and now.*"

"The Herald of Abyssus? Aye, well, they were *onto that one.* I would have been better to dress in drag, Aerik, and claim to be the Virgin Queen of Ythe."

The Stormsong chuckled. That same dry, mocking laugh, even as we bore down on a wall of steel and wood and sorcery. I could actually hear the drone of the chantries now, and feel the hair-raising prickle of elemental sorcery.

"Lightning. They'll bloody well do lightning. Show me an elemental mage who doesn't like to throw lightning about, and I'll show you a craven neophyte…"

"*Focus!*" barked Aerik. "*You always were a slow child, Kuhal Moer.*

Now, there was a reason we dressed you up in all that silly black velvet. The Herald's throne really is vacant. The fact that you're a poor imitation might just be good enough."

"You've got about twelve seconds left in which to explain," I grated, watching a hundred musketeers lift their smoking matchlocks. We were listing to the right, and now fountains were flickering by on our left in a haze of rainbows – one every second or so, counting down to the end of the ornamental pool.

"Rasq. His soul. I have it. He's angry, Kuhal."

"Oh."

"Yes, oh. Do you think you can unsheathe me, then? Those bloody elementalists are sure to want lightning, and that means they'll first have to saturate the air. Feel that humidity?"

I certainly did – though I'd passed it off as terror-sweat. The air was growing slippery and hot with magick as the covens of the Twins worked, and now we were barreling down the final straight to meet them, iron rims sparking, springs screeching, Seventails choking on his own breakfast in the back…

Meracq D'avarian looked over his shoulder at me.

"A good day to die, Lamenter. Perhaps I will see you in the afterworld."

"The hells you will!" snarled Silbern. "*I* get to kill you – not these Tarkhanden fops of yours!"

Harlaw shrugged, then began taking shots with his musket, standing up on the buckboard.

But I drew the glass blade of Aerik Stormsong, with a sound like a soapy finger on the rim of a goblet. It flashed in the light, motes of silver swimming deep inside.

"All of you, listen to me," I said. And I proceeded to recount a plan of such stunning insanity that only a disembodied Warbard could have conceived it.

They stared at me, wide-eyed. The vile roll-up dropped from Harlaw's open mouth.

"We are agreed, then?"

I didn't wait for an answer. Instead, Aerik let what remained of Rasq free.

There is usually no need for a Herald of Death to guide the deceased. But Rasq was not as normal men. He had been taken and *changed* by the wild magick of the utter north, knapped and sharpened until his soul fit the shape of a legend. The part of him which Aerik had snared was the essence of ten thousand years of campfire stories, told by hunters as they huddled in their furs. He was the shadow of the white bear, the howl of the wolf, the horns of the crescent moon…

But above all, he was *ice*. Bone-snapping, utter, relentless cold; the stealer of breath, the taker of children, a thing we all saw unfurl from the blade in a moment of soul-deep shock.

It was taller than cathedrals. Its body was a swirl of frosty air, condensing every drop of moisture into a boiling fog. It's teeth were three-foot icicles, and its eyes were the blue-green of calving glaciers.

This vision flew ahead of us, borne on a blizzard wind. But it was only a spirit, in truth. I watched it reach the Tarkhanden barricade and flow through a thousand men, extinguishing the burning tapers of matchlocks, painting frost across armour and blades.

But it could not kill. For all its rage, it was just a memory – a last howl of defiance feathering away into nothingness.

What it left behind it, though…

Visibility dropped to near zero as fog filled the avenue. Out of the swirling grey came a rattling, sparking monstrosity – the remains of a secure carriage, etched with the Rune of Null and the Dead Zero.

The Tarkhanden were merciless. Bolts of incandescent lightning flew from the hands of their sorcerers, tearing off both front wheels in a spray of molten metal. Wood combusted, charring. Then the guns opened up, and huge holes were punched through the rolling wreck, which began to tumble end over end as it slid along on the stubs of its ruined axles. Flailing, cartwheeling, shedding doors and spokes and bolts and beams, the carriage became a burning iron box, dented and scarred, red-hot in places, smoking, grinding toward the barricade until it collapsed onto its roof and slowly, sadly fell apart.

Soldiers rushed forward, pikes and halberds down, a rough warcry echoing in the fog. Metal rang on metal. Curses and shouted orders.

"Sarge! Sarge, it's empty!"

"There's nobody there!"

"You think the mages burnt 'em to ashes? Wouldn't there be bones?"

I was the first one out of the water, punching through a thin crust of ice to emerge, dripping and bruised. Traveling at that speed, the surface of the ornamental pool had felt like solid marble. The fog wrapped us up, playing tricks with sound, so that the belching, cursing, scrabbling and sloshing of my companions was strangely intermingled with the bawling and cussing of three hundred Tarkhanden guards lost in the same pale grey world.

I tottered across the cobbles, leaving a trail of icy water behind me. My robes were far more ceremonial than practical – another reason why a true Dark Lord should always wear trousers. Robes might look sinister… but have you ever tried running in them after an unplanned swim? These are the things which we in the Evil business must consider.

"Come on!" Hissed Meracq. "One, two, three – and a pleasure to have you awake and back among us, Mister Seventails. I *do* hope it tasted better going down than coming up, by the way."

I heard the skinchanger groan, and followed the sound into an alcove, part of the immensely ramified baroque frontage of some noble house. Silbern's armoured hand slid into mine, and we staggered like blind beggars through a milky haze, emerging into a cloister which connected with the temple grounds.

"Right around them. Classic flanking technique," said Meracq. He seemed to have quite forgotten that we were his prisoners – but I have found this to be true of most military men. Put an enemy in front of a soldier, and anyone helping him kill that enemy is suddenly a sworn brother.

"Holy ground, then?"

"Consecrated to Abyssus," grinned the Saltmaster. "And that means no help from the Twins. They'll think twice about baiting a necromancer here."

"And we'll have to think even harder if we mean to get out. Bottled like rats in a trap, we are."

D'avarian smiled down at Harlaw, who was cradling his newfound repeating musket like a mother does her child.

"Why do you think, my Sarem'ec friend, that I didn't tell them about the draken?"

That raised eyebrow would have done Aerik Stormsong proud.

Not long after, we slipped through an open door and into the echoing vault of the temple of Abyssus. Tentacular carvings and maps of the stars were all around us – heavy and dark in the gloom. The whole temple seemed to have been carved, without joints or mortar, from a single great excrescence of gold-flecked jade, sullen evergreen in colour and warm to the touch.

But of the Elder One's priesthood we saw nothing. No acolytes rose from their prayers to greet us. No monks tended the enclosed gardens with their beehives and vines. Kitchens, refectories, cells and studies – all were empty.

Until at last we crept – for something about temples seems to force whispering and creeping on mortals – into the great central nave of the place. A dusty shaft of light speared down through a hole in the dome of this inner sanctum… a space big enough to engulf the entire village of my childhood. At the very centre, a bonfire burned, heaped high with charred logs and drifts of ash.

Ash… containing a jumble of cracked and blackened bones.

At the instant I noticed this grisly truth, I heard the sound of swords unsheathing in the dark. We were surrounded on all sides by a constellation of glowing yellow eyes, slit-pupiled and wicked.

"I *told* you it was good day to die," sighed Meracq D'avarian, drawing his sabre.

"And I told you that killing you was *my* privilege," hissed Silbern. "When are you going to just accept the inevitable?"

A figure stalked forward out of the gloom, dressed in long black robes. In one hand this stranger carried a sickle-shaped sword, apparently forged from brass. In the other, an ornate and multi-barreled pistol, which caught Master Gunner Harlaw's undivided attention.

Everyone else – myself included – was far more fixated on the horns.

Twinned with my own – a pair of slim, curved tines sweeping back from the forehead of a golden-eyed woman who also shared my pattern of ritual scars and tattoos.

"You didn't… ahhh… have any *other* daughters you didn't tell us about, Lamenter?" asked Seventails, stepping in close to me as the circle of warriors drew tight. "It's just that…"

"Oh, I think not, Skinchanger. Even *one* I didn't know about was one too many."

The woman laughed, a sound which seemed far too free and wild for the smoky vault we stood in. Then she spun her sword up over her shoulder, securing it to a hidden sling. The pistol dropped to a holster at her hip, and she extended her empty hands, palms out, in a gesture of welcome.

"Well," she said. "I can see why they caged us up in here, then. You folks have one of your own."

She was looking at me as she spoke, her words sharp and crisp with the inflection of someone reading from a translator's scroll.

"One *what?*" I managed, dragging my gaze away from those deep, honey-gold eyes. I swear I could hear Makara's laughter, echoing from somewhere far away.

"Why, one of you, of course. A necromancer. An *impostor*."

"I assure you," said Seventails, coming to my aid. My tongue felt like a solid wad of salted meat, too huge and clumsy for my mouth. "Lord Kuhal, the Lamenter is every inch a true necromancer. I've seen him raise the dead myself."

The woman smirked, those hypnotic eyes sparkling.

"Every inch, eh? I'd believe it. We can sense each others' power, those in our profession..."

I would have blushed crimson, had I been technically alive. I had not even tried to sense this outlander witch's aura, let alone taste its depth and colour. Now I did – and the chill, flickering halo of it lit up my dark sight in waves. I realised, with a start, that there were certain protocols and traditions which I was supposed to follow at a time like this.

"Well met, then, sister in shadow. I am Kuhal da'Hurik Moer, born of the Khytein, heir to Sothara the Bone Collector, and chosen of Anghul. We... well, we're from Sarem. There's a fellow named Dirge who wants to destroy the world, and we were..."

"I know all about the one who styles himself Lord Endsong," said the sorceress, gently folding back the cowl of her robe. Her face was heart-shaped and elfin, her hair bound up in twin coils and the same shade of red as arterial blood. I have heard people called 'red-headed' who are merely tawny orange – this woman's tresses were utterly scarlet, and bound with clasps of ivory and jade.

"I was sent here to discover what I could about him – and then to cut his heart out."

"Won't work," I said. "I tried that myself. He's come back form the Outer Dark, and there's not much left of him in the way of... well, internal organs, for starters."

"So you sailed in to Zamara, tried to forge an alliance, and got given a one-way passage to this cheerful little prison of ours?"

"How did you know?"

At least she had the good grace to look embarrassed.

"The truth? The same thing happened to us. But please. You have given me the courtesy of your name – allow me to do the same."

Now I could clearly see the coterie of warriors who accompanied this lady. They were, all of them, slim and leather-armoured slayers, armed with sickle-blades and flintlocks, marked with tattoos across half of their faces like spiral knotwork. I noticed them – but my eyes were drawn back to the sorceress herself.

"I am Kayan Orsii, court astrologer and spiritsinger to the court of the Jade Emperor, Tsargon Urd of Hmai. Lately a delegate for my Lord and Master… and the apparent Herald of Abyssus."

Meracq groaned. Seventails cursed. I found my mind utterly clear and blank, scintillating with points of light.

"That'll be why they didn't believe us, then," drawled Harlaw.

"You think?" asked Silbern, sheathing her sword with a huff of disgust.

"Precisely," said Kayan Orsii, clapping her hands together in a businesslike manner. "Well, at least it wasn't my abysmal playacting. I never could get the hang of that icy, cold hauteur…" She grinned, a thoroughly disarming deployment of twinned dimples. "Now… Lamenter. Or can I call you Kuhal?" I nodded. It was probably beyond me at that point to form cogent sentences.

"Good! We can get down to strategy, then. I trust you have a cunning, potent, fiendish and foolproof plan to escape from this carcass of a place?"

I smiled, weakly, like a noviate priest beset by the parish widows.

"We're doomed," whispered Seventails to Harlaw, just loud enough for me to hear. I prayed that Kayan Orsii couldn't read lips.

Because, unfortunately, the reeking, fur-clad barbarian was probably right.

The Way of the Tempest -
Of all the old arts of the founding families of
Zamara, this martial discipline - allegedly lost
in far antiquity - is the most rumored, most
whispered about, most claimed and least defined.
    Gifted, it is said, by the twin Aziphem known
as Silan and Suramaei, the Lord of Storms and
the Lady of Tranquility, this technique allows the
wielder to harness the forces of the Elemental
Shard, focusing, for example, the entire wild fury
of a hurricane through the edge of a single blade.
    Whether or not a present-day son or daughter
of the first families is pious enough to be chosen
is irrelevant. For to learn the Way one would have
to study beneath a living Grand Master, and then -
even more difficult, perhaps - actually find, steal,
forge or scavenge a blade finely balanced enough
to survive the unleashing of such savage forces.
    In short, then, this is likely nothing more than
another myth from our rich and storied heritage.
Please discourage the sons of noble houses from
trying to learn more about this fruitless technique
- a good brace of pistols will achieve more in battle
than wild tales ever will.

Saltmaster Noxis Calthe
"Treatise for the preparation of scholars as instructors to the
Academy Martial"

WE TALKED LATE into the night, Kayan Orsii and I. A strange, stilted,
tenuous conversation, prickly with suspicion at first, and laden with
any number of misunderstandings which could have been the result
of poor translation... or clumsy efforts at charm.

    Did I feel anything for this strange, fey woman? Perhaps. But then,
I had little recollection of feeling anything natural at all, except for
anger.

    And guilt. Seething, dark guilt, which had me clutching the black
jewel at my throat as I finally drifted off to sleep, wrapped in the

blankets of dead monks, trying to conjure Makara's face.

Like called to like, that was all. Poor old First Democrat Berolde had been right. Gulls flock with gulls, and crows with crows. Perhaps it was only vanity, at seeing my own image reflected in the Hmai sorceress' face, which drew me back to those tawny yellow eyes, that sardonic little smile…

I muttered to myself like a penitent, trying to pierce the haze of years and forgetfulness. The best that I could do was to recall that Makara looked just like her daughter, the Stormreaper – and then my guilt swelled and redoubled, remembering that I had left *her* locked up in Grennen Vuhl's tower.

I had not expected to sleep easy in that haunted place. And my dreams, when they came, did not disappoint.

I found myself in a sunken city, a drowned place built on a cyclopean scale. Towering monoliths of stone loomed up out of the silty water, graven with the images of some long-dead people. Scaled faces, immense, jeweled eyes, many-jointed limbs and spiny fins… the kings and heroes, I supposed, of a race who had lived and died in some elder aeon.

They had wrought mightily, these spawn of the deep. But it had availed them nothing. Down here at the bottom of some ocean trench sickly phosphorescence picked out their temples and avenues, leading me on through ruins. My dream-self could feel the crushing pressure of all that dark water above me, but I moved through the city like a ghost, half expecting to be joined by the spirits of those who had perished here.

Instead, as I came to a vast and open hollow at the city's heart, I saw a flickering outline ahead of me. A human form, perched on the lip of a well of stone. Peering through the murk, I saw that this figure was turned away from me, keeping a vigil on the edge of the pit.

I drifted closer, drawn in by the flickering green glow which haloed the stranger, picking out a ragged cloak, the shape of a long-necked Khytein lyrecaster hanging on chains…

"You took your time," said Makara, turning to face me. Her dark hair coiled in the water, each strand limned in witchfire. "But you always were running to catch up, weren't you? She seems nice, by the way."

I recoiled, like a murderer faced with the blood-caked evidence of his crime.

"The Hmai? She… that is, we were just…"

Makara's laugh seemed tiny, swallowed up by the dark and pressure of this lifeless place.

"Oh, come on, Kuhal Moer! We both know that I'm already dead. I wouldn't have been able to lead you to this place otherwise."

My hand went instinctively to the black jewel at my throat, scrabbling against cold, dead skin. It was gone.

"*No!* I have translated the Black Incantations of Aziman Kanesh. The alchemists of the third Toluran dynasty knew of methods which I have pieced together. You can live again! All I need is…"

Her hand cupped my cheek and brought my face around until I was looking into her eyes. The yawning pit behind her, carved from the seabed, was nowhere near as deep.

"And have you thought about what *I* need, necromancer? When you bind the dead, they only ask for one thing, don't they?"

I nodded.

"*Freedom.* They want to leave this world. But they are just bones, Makara! Just bones and memories. You…"

"I'm even less. The echo in a black gem. Some fraying recollections in the mind of one man. And, ironic as it seems, dear one, *you're* the one who has to live. Do you ever wonder why the dark lords in stories go mad? Why they want to destroy the world?"

I shook my head, reaching up to grasp her fingers.

"Power corrupts. And they are all fools. We aren't stories, Makara. We are *real*. And I can bring you back."

"Wrong. Wrong as usual, you sweet, deluded idiot." Her smile was tiny and fleeting, lost down here in the darkness. "They lost touch with the world, and when they found out that it had left them behind, they felt *betrayed*. You're in danger of losing touch as well. Which is why I'm still here. I read all those dusty old texts too, you know. Right over your shoulder. And the alchemists, the incantors – they're all the same. What you'd create is no better than what Urzen made of me."

"I didn't care," I said, stepping back with her hands clasped in mine. "I didn't give a damn what Dirge and the Korisali made you. I loved you just the same."

This time there was real pain in her eyes. That, and no small amount of regret.

"I know, she whispered. "Why do you think I'm still here? But I *suffered*, Kuhal. I wouldn't want to live like that again. Not now that I know…"

"Know *what?*" I began – but I was cut short by a tectonic upheaval from below. Tons of dense, silty water shifted, pistoning up from the well to blast out through the ruins in a radial shockwave, stripping centuries of slime from monoliths and obelisks. A mass of gelatinous flesh came questing out of the darkness, slapping down onto the flagstones in silence. Instead, the shock crumbled the ancient architecture, sending cracks skittering across every surface. Silt spun past and through my dream-self in clouds, making me grit my teeth and shield my eyes – all unnecessary, of course.

"Him!" shouted Makara, now outlined against a black and thrashing wall of tentacles. "Abyssus! The ancient one! He was the first…"

There was a heaving, sucking sound. There was a terrifying pressure-shift, as countless gelid tentacles braced themselves on the lip of the chasm and *heaved*. And then…

"The first… and soon to be the last, little son of the Shard," said a voice like creaking, waterlogged timber. It echoed directly into my mind, deep and somehow sad. **"I was ancient when the Archaeon and the Coldblood were young. I was the first to weave the raw life-force of the Divine into mortal form, cell by cell. Before me, they were eternal, those tiny things. But mindless. Oh, even more mindless than *your* idiot race, Kuhal Moer."**

Abyssus rose up above the great central plaza of his temple-city, a starburst of black tentacles sheathed in segmented armour. Eye-stalks as tall as longship's masts protruded and twitched, bearing jeweled orbs filled with ghostly fire. Lithe, whiplike secondary tentacles lashed the water, each one tipped with a hook of bone. And on the creature's back bulked a coiling, spiral shell, crusted with overlapping panels of stone and gold, carvings and stelae, bones and chains, gemstones and mosaics hashed out in a dizzying profusion. The worship of numberless centuries, turned to an armoured hide.

"Yes – even the Archaeon and his doomed nation. Even the Coldblood itself, curse it. I made life *complex*, so it could see this world through other eyes, and tell the Divine which shapes to walk it in. *I* created the Aziphem, for what they are worth. Devourers of stories. They would have starved without me. But complexity falls apart. Hah! Look around you! This was once the greatest citadel Yrde had ever seen! Now gone. All gone. Complexity…"

"Demands *death*," I breathed, struggling to comprehend the cope of this ancient thing's existence. "Bodies are just engines… like Urzen's creations. But minds grow weary. Souls -"

"Yes… For want of a better word, human. *Souls* must carry what

they have learned back to the source. All but mine, of course. I fear I am the keystone in the arch, Kuhal Moer. If I give in to my weariness, all life may unravel and collapse, just as my poor children's temple here has done."

"You could rebuild! The Tarkhanden worship you, and with reason! If what you say is true…"

"You misunderstand," sighed the beast. "This is the thirty-ninth such temple I have had the misfortune to see ruined. I am quite content to simply wait for the end of the great cycle. One day the Divine will call all the scraps and shreds of his being home at once. Then I will be free."

"Unless the Coldblood's minions slay him first," said Makara. "They are abroad in Sorath right now. While you have slept, they have perverted the law of death itself."

"My Herald?"

"Slain. And your shadow stolen from him. This is not just a petty war of men, Abyssus. I have brought you this one so that you may see."

"Wait!" I said. "You've *what?*"

But it was too late. Thin, whiplike tentacles hissed in from every angle, reminding me of the chains which bound up the wreckage of Dirge. I screamed as they plunged into my flesh, but it was only the stuff of dreams – there was no real pain. Instead, images unfurled like cold fire from within me, a blur of them flickering through my entire life. Shards of memory, some of which I had assumed forgotten forever, sleeted across my vision and into the mind of Abyssus, which hung over me like the bulk of a dead star, massive, hungry and eternal.

At last he let go, leaving me to drift to the silty seabed like a scrap of ragged sailcloth. I drew my mind together and stood, grimacing with imagined pain.

"He's weaker than I would have liked," rumbled Abyssus. "But any weapon is better than an empty … what do you call those things? Hand. An empty hand. He will have to do."

Makara nodded.

"The dead which you have gathered – those who have chosen to sleep rather than be reborn. You will give him their command?"

There was a pause, while Abyssus made complex twitching and chewing motions with his unspeakable mouthparts.

"Very well. But you must come to me. Here – to the Maelstrom which churns above us. This is just an illusion we share, and the mantle of His Dark Reflection can only be granted in the flesh."

"Where..?" I croaked, as unsteady on my feet as a shade has any right to be.

"The one you name Meracq D'avarian knows," replied the ancient thing. "But you must hurry! The Kothrai are already upon you, and the time grows short."

Makara suddenly turned, looking up through the swirling silt to the ocean's surface.

"Damnation! He's right, Kuhal. You didn't carry anything of Grennen Vuhl's through the Zamaran gates, did you?"

I thought of the cloven iron helm we'd boxed up to present to the Council of Seven, and I winced.

"Perhaps…"

"Then we have no time left at all. Abyssus! Grant your chosen a taste of your power, that he may come to find you!"

The great beast was sinking now, stuffing its gelatinous bulk back into the chasm from whence it had come.

"Oh, you mortals! Take, take, take! Very well. For the love my child Anghul bears you, Kuhal Moer. Use it wisely…"

The mageblight in my bones burned suddenly incandescent. I woke, screaming, back arched, sparks crackling from my fingertips and arcing between my teeth.

The sunken city was gone. This darkness was the smoky vault of Abyssus' temple, and the face leaning over me was…

"Makara?"

Blood-red hair brushed against my cheek.

"I'll ask who *she* is later," hissed Kayan Orsii. "But quickly! There's something afoot! We have to…"

The Hmai sorceress looked down at me – at the crawling blue sparks popping from every joint under my skin.

"Do you always wake up so…*potent*, Lamenter?"

"Oh… umm… that's nothing personal, I assure you. Just - "

"I meant the *power*, fool! Do you meditate on the balance in your *sleep?*"

"That… that was Abyssus, I fear. He said that the Kothrai may be…"

But the Kothrai had stolen a march on us while I dreamed. The Kothrai were already here.

I'm not certain if any of you have been besieged before. And, of those, how many have been inside a building when it's struck by a flaming ball of Ythean fire.[19]

Suffice to say, it's rather noisy.

First came a whistling sound, building to a howl. Then a staggering detonation, lurching the very stones beneath our feet. The dome of the temple cracked like an eggshell, dripping flame through a web of fissures. Barely had we begun to scramble clear when a second hammer-blow fell, splattering a swathe of the nave with fire.

"I think their intentions are rather clear, Kuhal. Now – about that plan of yours?"

All around us Kayan's warriors were calmly and methodically breaking camp, checking their weapons, loading pistols and tightening the buckles on their armour. Silbern Chaar emerged from the Abbot's cell, sliding her skull-faced helm down over her braids of golden hair.

"It's Oram all over again," she growled, pausing to glare at us before taking the stairs to the temple's roof two at a time. Another shuddering crack rocked the building as the Kothrai trebuchets thudded and creaked.

"This time there's no Slaughtermaw!" I shouted, as falling dust obscured her.

"Aye," said Harlaw, appearing at my side, his repeating musket slung over one shoulder. "This time it's Grennen bloody Vuhl himself. And who knows what demons he's called?"

Kayan, as befitted her royal appointment, was all business.

"I'll not ask how you got to Abyssus first, Sarem'ec. But I will ask you this. Has your new patron granted you enough power to get us out of this mess?"

I grimaced.

"We are yet to discover, Mistress Orsii, exactly how deep this mess is."

"Sewer deep and sinking," grinned Seventails, clapping me across the shoulder as he passed. He and Meracq D'avarian were also headed for the roof, following after Silbern and Kayan's Hmai warriors.

"Let me put it this way," said the sorceress. "I've had eyes above

---

19. The 'Unquenchable Fire of Ythe' is first described in the works of the ancient alchemist and savant Septimus Kraaste. It was devised from a mixture of ammoniac salts, pitch, naptha, mineral oil and draken's venom during the wars between the Old Ythean Republic and the Magocracy of Crethys. Suffice to say, we have heard little about the Magocracy for these past few thousand years, primarily because the 'Unquenchable Fire' proved to be quite the potent weapon of war. Septimus, we are told, intended it to be used for metalworking and in heating bathwater.

since that rude awakening of yours – nothing too grandiose, just a dead sparrow. It's black sails, bloody murder and the gates torn down, Lamenter."

There was a kind of grim excitement in her voice. Kayan Orsii looked at me as if I was a barrel of black powder with a hissing fuse, waiting to see the devastation it would cause. It occurred to me, then, that my legend had outgrown me by several orders of magnitude.

But, like Rasq - like Seventails and Issara and Kell - perhaps my soul had twisted and grown to fit that legend. There was no time like the present to find out.

"Stories have power. Find the place where you can fit in, and ride them..."

A whisper, under my breath. A half-remembered drunken conversation with the ice-shamen. Kayan looked at me as if I had gone mad. Perhaps I had, for a moment, in fact gone *sane*.

"To the roof! I don't want to try this indoors..."

The Hmai witch rolled her eyes.

"That sounds promising, Kuhal Moer. In the meantime, I can make use of these poor dead acolytes. The Kothrai are trying to land, and this temple will be the first place they come knocking."

"Because of us?"

"Sweet boy! No, we're not *that* important. Because of the shadow of Abyssus. Grennen Vuhl's unwilling weapon. Only the ancient beast itself can claim it back, and the chances of him awaking are..."

"More than fair," I said. "If we can get to a place called the Maelstrom..."

"Hidden depths," she said, with a demure little smile. "But go! Now! My chantry will assist you as they can. You must win clear, to your ship. I know that design, and I know the working of the Soulharp. Zamara may well fall, but we can still reach Dath N'kaal - and the Maelstrom – before our enemies."

I paused at the foot of the stairs, letting the hell-chorus of pealing bells, bellowing trumpets, screams and the crackle of flames wash over me. The sound took me back to Oram - back to Urexes the fair, when a necromancer from the wild north had torn it down, three hundred years ago.

"Never again," I whispered, clenching my fists tight. I shot one last glance at Kayan, then ran up the stairs, feeling the building shudder and lurch as Ythean fire rained down.

How did the Kothrai see me? What was my place in their story?

"Long, long ago," they would tell their children. *"There lived a wicked king named Grennen Vuhl. He was mighty and proud, but in his pride he could not stand to have an equal. He set out to make war on another ruler from across the sea – a terrible, powerful old lich-king who ruled over a court of skeletons. But King Grennen had no honour – he stole the Lich-king's daughter, and imprisoned her in a tall tower, seeking to force her father's surrender..."*

This was belief. Not dressed up in the false philosophies of religion, but raw, stark faith. The songs and stories of children, feeding the Aziphem, weaving the illusions which lurked in the back of mortal minds. There was a loop which bound together the world of flesh and the Shards of the Divine. A place where, like the centre of the Dead Zero, absolute balance became absolute power.

"The Lich-king's anger was terrible to behold. He gathered up a crew of nightmares and set out to avenge himself on wicked Lord Grennen..."

I emerged onto a broad balcony, and witnessed what Kayan Orsii had seen through the eyes of her dead sparrow.

The great cannons and siege-mortars of Zamara boomed and flamed like earthbound thunder, thrashing the harbour to foam in the cold dawn light. Waist-thick chains had been pulled taut between the breakwater piers, holding back the Kothrai fleet, but the sorceress was right – the gates were down, and the wall of mother-of-pearl geomancy was twisted and torn, warped into a tunnel of nacreous fire. As I watched, one of the slim, arching bridges which linked the mainland to the Sunset Gates was torn away, tiny figures plunging down amid a storm of shattered stone. A never-ending rain of Ythean fire, boulders and casks of arrows arched in from the spearhead of the Kothrai fleet – three hundred strong, jammed like logs in a spillway. It looked possible to ride a horse from one curving horn of the Zamaran isle to the other across the decks of black galleys and dromons. Fire-arrows in swarms and clouds traced mad, intricate threads of light as they rose from the Kothrai decks, plunging down amid the Tarkhanden defenders on the shore, who bore their brunt on heavy shields and mantlets covered in wet leather.

"The Eighth! We are ruined!" shouted Meracq D'avarian, his great sabre clenched in one fist. He leaped up to the parapet, steadying himself on the shoulder of a half-human statue.

"Never mind your fleet, Saltmaster," growled Seventails. The skinchanger looked half wild already, hunched and bulky in his robes, his eyes red with the rising sun. "How did they get through so *fast*? We had no warning – none!"

I was still staring into the tunnel of geomantic force which had pierced the gates.

"Your precious Eighth may still be afloat, Meracq," I said. "Look – there! What holds that portal open?"

Down the gullet of sorcery, where the waves were churned to foam by a glut of Kothrai warships, I could see a webwork of darkness pushing the walls apart. Vast, gelid tentacles, seething with power – the shadow of Abyssus, put to monstrous use.

"Grennen Vuhl only needed the correct degrees of navigation," I said. "He's opened a bridge between Zamara and Sorath which passes the Gates entirely. With luck, your sailors will be the hammer to our anvil, Saltmaster!"

"There are demons among them," warned Silbern. "We have seen them. Things like your Burning Dark, and worse."

"And what of the *Sorrow's Vengeance?*"

Silbern looked at me with a wry smile, as though shrugging off news of hell-fiends was admirably insane. She nodded.

"Elion Morekh made it beyond the chain. Kell and Issara are holding the wardings firm. I doubt she's going anywhere, but mere fireballs and rocks won't send her to the bottom."

There - I picked them out. The water of the inmost harbour was aswarm with boats, some burning, some wallowing as they foundered in the shallows. But among them, dwarfing them in their panic, the *Sorrow's Vengeance* rode at anchor, protected behind a shimmering curtain of sorcery. Kell Du'ath stood before the ship's wheel, her hands outstretched, weaving a mesh of wardings which rippled and sparked when the Kothrai's stones and arrows struck them. Issara stood behind her, hands on her shoulders, her head thrown back and her eyes blazing. Blood magick poured from her into the Ythean seeress, but it could only last so long.

"Demons, you say?" I grinned at Silbern Chaar, wild and reckless. An image had blurred into focus in my mind – the face of the Kothrai's fears. And, as the people of Zamara died, crushed and immolated in their falling towers, the power of death had begun to suffuse the air, turning the whole city into a pale, grey-green pyre in my Dark Sight.

"Aye. *Demons*. At least three of them. Those few Tarkhanden ships which tried to stem the tide – all were destroyed. Now the fiends prepare to make landfall."

Below us on the strand, Kothrai boarding barges dug their bows into the shingle. Beneath the temple precinct on its hill the city straggled away to a shantytown. Crude fisher's huts and upturned boats on frames, awaiting the ministration of pitch-daubers and hullwrights...

The cowering fisher-folk hiding there began to scream as the Kothrai's boarding ramps clattered down, and black-clad axemen surged forth, roaring drunkenly. Led by musclebound, iron-clad thugs the size of Hithar Drahl, they crashed through whole hovels and shanties, swinging their double-headed axes in reaping arcs. I saw men die valiantly there, on that pebble beach. Men armed with gaff-hooks and staves, looking back once at their fleeing families, then turning, grim-faced, to be hacked apart...

"We have demons of our own, Silbern Chaar. And I have been granted power such as I haven't known for centuries. Now," I smiled, gallows-grim. "Shall we take a little walk?"

"Where to?" she asked, slamming her skeletal visor shut. Behind their crystal lenses, her eyes were wide and blue, twinkling with anticipation.

"Where else, dear lady? Our ship awaits. Having enjoyed the hospitality of the Tarkhanden, I am suddenly overwhelmed with a desire for good, honest Sarem'ec hardtack. Maggots and all."

"Spoken like a true necromancer," grunted Seventails.

"Then you'll be glad to fight at my side, Khytein. Abyssus is generous, and we'll have no shortage of blood and souls..."

I could feel the power growing, fueled by the slaughter unfolding around us. It resonated in my blighted bones, finding its level like water, filling up an image which the Kothrai's fear had defined.

Hah! Thank all things wicked for survivors and their whispered tales...

Kayan Orsii was not to be left behind, however. Frost spread across the parapet beneath my fingers as she unleashed a terrible, potent working. The wall of the temple bulged outward, grinding stone on stone. Cracks radiated from amid a spray of fractured marble, and an inhuman scream stopped the Kothrai in their tracks.

There were *knuckle-prints* driven through the wall. Something with fists the size of logging drays was desperate to win free.

"I think we'd better..." began Meracq D'avarian – before the entire balcony fell away, plunging us all down the bluff amid a slew of rubble. Through the pall of dust stalked an immense figure, outlined in flame, flanked by flitting wraiths in black. Pale hands reached down amid the tumble of stone, dragging me to my feet.

"*Try* to keep up, Lamenter. I know you're old enough to be my grandsire, but please - this is a *battle*, after all."

It was Kayan Orsii herself, and her blood-red tresses were unbound, twin swords riding at her hips. As she brushed the grit from my shoulders a Kothrai warrior loomed up behind her, and she spun with lithe grace, parrying his axe-blow and neatly beheading him. I hardly saw the swords leave their scabbards – but I heard them click back into place, oiled with blood.

"What… what *is* that thing?" I asked, as another scream echoed across the harbour. A brief, ruddy flare of fire followed it, and I heard the sound of men's dying agony, suddenly cut off by the crunch and snap of timbers.

"It wasn't us who massacred the Abyssal Priests," said Kayan – as if the thought had not been preying on my mind. "It was the peace faction – those who would have tried to treat with Grennen Vuhl. Their dying anger gives them strength. They have become… *Sian' ku Talat*. How do you say… *Pyreborn*. Burned bones and ashes, given life."

I saw it rear its head and shoulders up above the shantytown, Kothrai fleeing from before it. The Pyreborn was a cloud of swirling sparks and black ash, bundles of cracked and calcified bones floating disjointed within. Its head was a deformed skull formed of carbonized shards, all floating atop an inner core of flame. Seventails staggered to my side, laughing, and we both watched as the Hmai's thrall unhinged its lower jaw, spewing a blast of incandescent death. Boats exploded, pitch igniting instantly. Kothrai warriors flashed to tumbling, rolling tangles of blackened bones, splashes of molten metal pattering onto the sand.

Our little band pelted across the shingle after the fleeing Kothrai, cutting them down as they ran. There was no room for mercy, quarter or honour in this fight – just butchery. By the time we reached the landing barges we were all spattered with blood. Kayan's Pyreborn waded into the sea, hissing and steaming, lifting an entire flat-bottomed craft up over its head as it ignited. Then a well-aimed boulder came crashing down through its chest, followed by a hail of arrows, and it fell, sinking beneath the water with a squealing, popping cry.

"That's got their attention!" shouted Harlaw, ducking down under the cover of an upturned barge beside me. He broke off to re-light his vile miniature cigar, then popped up, leveling his musket. Six shots rang out as he worked the handle, and I have little doubt that six Kothrai were neatly dispatched. "Looks like Vuhl's rolled out the welcome mat for us, Lamenter. Something mighty strange coming down on us, and it's brought its friends along too…"

I heard a great grinding and slamming of timbers, and risked a look out of cover, daring a rain of fire-arrows. And I saw the bloodied waters of Zamara's harbour lift in a tightly focused wave, bearing on its crest three galleys full of howling Kothrai. I lashed out with sorcery, felling the hulking captain of one of those ships, but it was something *beneath* the water which propelled them, and nothing could check their terrible momentum.

"Fall back!" shouted Seventails, "This surge will swamp the shore! Fall back to the fisher-town, and regroup!"

Silbern Chaar grabbed me by the shoulder, trying to pull me clear.

"He's right. You're no use to us drowned, Kuhal Moer…"

But I wasn't just mesmerized by the sight of that onrushing wall of water – by the sheer force which cupped three whole triremes in its palm and flung them at us like children's toys. I was watching Meracq D'avarian, who had clambered to the prow of a sunken landing barge, his sabre held out before him. His head was bowed in prayer. Suddenly he turned, and flashed me a reckless grin.

"Yours is not the only power here, Beast of Sarem. The Twins of the Calm and Storms are with me. Now – I will take the middle one. May I suggest that Lady Orsii takes the one on the left? The right, you may dispatch as you see fit, Lamenter."

The wave began to crest, jagged flotsam churning in its foam. Three galleys poised above us as the water was sucked away from around our feet, exposing the pallid corpses of dead Kothrai, already bring fought over by industrious crabs.

And, as the wave broke, as Meracq unleashed the power forged into his blade, and as Silbern, Seventails and Harlaw turned back, open-mouthed in shock, I opened my mind to Abyssus. I took up the mantle of his Herald, gatekeeper of the dead. And I *changed*.

It all happened at once. I felt a great weight settle across my shoulders, followed a heartbeat later by a redoubling of strength – of a cold, relentless will invading the mageblight in my bones. Through the sea – through the leagues and fathoms of cold, salty water which connected me to Abyssus, I felt the ancient creature's will. This first acolyte and father of the Aziphem, the architect of death, and of the stories we told to find solace in its shadow…

"Ahhhh. So you are my Dark Reflection, Kuhal Moer! You understand what the honorific means, at least. Very well. Let them

see Anghul, first of my children to walk Sarem's shores. He who crawled from the primordial swamps beside the first being capable of dread..."

The last glimpse I had of Meracq D'avarian was of him raising his sabre over his head, two-handed, the prow of the lead Kothrai galley coming down on him like a hammer of barnacle-crusted wood.

And as the foam washed over my head, I saw the tip of the blade cut deep, shearing through iron-hard timbers with a flash of sorcery. The ribs of the ship's hull snapped, clear along the length of its keel, carving it in two while the Saltmaster of the Eighth laughed, surrounded by a cloud of red-hot splinters.

Then the sea had me. I saw Silbern Chaar rush past, upside down, her armour dragging her across the shingle. I saw Seventails, collapsing and changing amid a swirl of bubbles, replaced in a heartbeat by the shape of a tusked crabcatcher seal. And I saw Kothrai bodies, nebulae of blood, coils of rope, sightless eyes bleeding pale green witchfire. Lost in the shock of Meracq's working, his unsplicing of their ship and their flesh...

I rose with them.

My horns broke the surface first – grown huge and tined like the antlers of a Stormwood elk, pierced with iron rings and carved with runes. Then the ghostly crown of Anghul, a nine-pointed diadem of bone shimmering like a heat-haze mirage. The bloodied water reflected a face which was nothing but a hollow skull, fanged and yellowed, teeth inset with silver and chalcedony. Hair hung from it in a ragged silver mane. My eyes burned in dark sockets, green as the aurora over the utter north. Then came the armour of bones, the cloak of spider-silk dyed midnight black, the weight of Cryptfeeder reborn, all glamours unbound, and once more the immense slab of pitted iron which Sothara da'Urgon Roege had used to work his slaughters...

So the Lich-King came to have his vengeance, bringing with him fear and bloodshed to herald his arrival. And the sworn men of Lord Grennen Vuhl despaired, for they knew that their wickedness was to be punished, by a force which knew not mercy or restraint...

A second Kothrai galley had been capsized in the flood, and it rushed toward me, rolling, scattering black-clad axemen, both living and dead. I laughed, feeling the bottomless power of Abyssus rising up through the water, through the soles of my boots... and I copied Meracq D'avarian's example, swinging my black iron battle-blade overhand. The ship burst like a rotten log, parting on either side of an invisible line twenty spans ahead of me.

"Oh yes. Oh, yes indeed. *This* is more like it! This is *delicious!*"

I raised my hand, palm upright, and a hundred corpses staggered to their feet. Seventails erupted from the water to my left, changing in midair, and a shaggy black bear landed amid the wallowing ruins of the Kothrai galley, smashing apart timbers and disappearing inside. Screams followed.

"Admirably theatric!" shouted Silbern Chaar, reaching my side. "But we must press our advantage now! If we can make their decks, it's but a short stroll from ship to ship, then on to the *Vengeance*. If not…"

"Then we won't have to worry about it, will we?" asked Kayan Orsii, miraculously bone-dry. A chain looped around her neck held a grisly harvest – ears, fingers and other scraps of flesh cut from Kothrai bodies. "Better them than us, though!"

The Hmai chantry were swarming over the last Kothrai ship, a blur of steel and darkness. They, too, bore bloody tokens of their victories, plucking them from the fallen with their bare hands. And with each one the Hmai seemed to move faster, strike harder…

"*Sagath Nu'tarim*. The Stolen Fire. Should we survive, I will teach you, Lamenter. Simply binding souls to dead flesh is only one of the mortal arts."

"I need my Cerebrex," I grumbled, flexing my bony fingers on Cryptfeeder's grip. Two hundred dead eyes (give or take the odd bleeding socket) blinked in unison with mine.

"Then let's go and get it!" shouted Silbern, clanging her visor shut. She was off before I could answer, running up the canted side of a galley's broken bows, then leaping to the deck of the next ship. The power of Abyssus had stolen into her as well – where she landed the timbers cracked and splintered, and a radial shockwave threw Kothrai warriors from their feet. Seventails erupted from below at the same time, his wolf-muzzle dripping crimson. I noted, with some detachment, that he was now roughly the size of an aurochs, and that the ragged shred he spat from between his teeth was an entire human arm.

I swept my blade forward, and my dead men lurched into a run through the knee-high water. They swarmed up the side of the galley, grim and silent, falling on the enemy with feral savagery. Amid the Hmai I caught a glimpse of Meracq D'avarian, his sabre hacking clean through the mainmast. Rigging fell like rain, bodies tangled up in it, jerking, struggling as they choked…

But I am the Lamenter, after all. Lord of the Desolation. Grandfather Despair.

I should have known it was too good to last.

I felt the thing rise up behind me, long before I heard the bubbling, sucking rattle of its breath. Shades of the Hanged Man – the way in which my daughter's pet demon had bound me up like a spider's supper, there on the hill of Oram.

This time I was quick enough to turn (so fast! So full of power, leeched from the countless dead!) - but not quick enough to do more than parry the stroke of its knife. It scored across the illusion of a skull which masked my face, slicing a line of white-hot pain across my cheek. The knife caromed away, slapped sideways by the bulk of Cryptfeeder, and I licked my bloodied fingertip, grinning.

"Fast, demon. Admirably so. But I hadn't forgotten that *something* had to have made that wave. You must be one of Vuhl's new coven. Eh? Another Nine for me to butcher?"

I looked up, and saw a hunched, dripping figure, wrapped in sackcloth bandages held in place by nails. Little strips of rune-daubed ribbon fluttered from the handles of countless dagger thrust through the thing's back in a thicket of steel, their points erupting from its chest. One of the Nameless one's hands was a bladed talon, but the other still had three human fingers – black-nailed digits which scrabbled at the perforated plate of steel covering its face.

"Lamenter," it sighed, bubbling like a punctured lung. "Or should I say *Rhul of Kaltensund?* Feurio the Drunkard's little friend." Those twitching, pale fingers found three of the holes drilled at random through the rusted metal masque. It tore the thing loose with a crusted, sucking sound. "Yes! I know you, Lamenter! Aemortarch!" It spat this word with utter contempt, quivering with rage. "That's why I joined him gladly! You, and your unholy spawn – both denied me my rest. But you – you broke your promise. Your holy book of lies..."

The creature straightened, and I found myself staring into a bloodless, sunken face – one cross-hatched with scars, its eyes cored out and replaced with tiny mirrors. Hooks peeled the flesh back from its lipless mouth, pulled tight by wires which cut deep into its waxy scalp and throat.

"You left me to die! And so I have chosen a new name, Kuhal! A new determination, a new fire, a new purpose, and to the scalding hells with *fucking Saint Acanthes!*"

I stepped back, shocked. I brought Cryptfeeder up to guard, feeling the power of Abyssus ebb away, sucking at my heels like an undertow. The story had shifted, and the terrible Lich-King's past had caught up with him.

Because the first of the new Nine – the right hand of Grennen Vuhl – was Paladyne Uveryn.

It saw the dawning recognition in my eyes. And it leered, socketing its hideous mask back into place.

"*That's right*. I am sworn to your rotten Tabernacle no more, Aemortarch. I will slay you in the name of Master Endsong. But first, I will grace you with the title I have been given."

I watched, mesmerized, as a brace of those impaling knives screwed themselves loose from the flesh of Uveryn's back with a sound like tearing meat. They hovered in the air around him, a halo of flensing steel.

"You may call me *the Betrayed*" sneered Grennen Vuhl's creature.

And then it launched its storm of daggers at my throat.

"The sages say that every time we make a choice, a whole new universe is born, in which everyone and everything we know goes blithely on, with the echoes of that choice changing all creation. Except, of course, in those universes where it chooses not to..."

Master Alchemist Solune,
Guild of Chains Academic Scriptoria

TEN BLADES CAME hissing in toward me, arcing out and away from the thing which had once been Paladyne Uveryn, then pulling together, closing like the fingers of a fist. I have mentioned before that sorcery is of little use against a storm of metal. But, unlike the elemental arts, at least *my* discipline is based on muscle and bone.

A trio of dead Kothrai erupted from the bloody water in front of me, slack-faced and dripping. Ten daggers thumped home into their pallid flesh, and they stumbled backward, moaning. I could count the points as they dimpled the backs of the Kothrai's surcoats... and I saw each one flash red with sorcerous fire as the Betrayed screamed, tearing them loose with a jolt of power.

Kothrai pieces sprayed wide. One of the wights fell, all but blasted in half, but the other two advanced, still smoking, craterous wounds gouged from their chests and bellies. Blackened sections of ribcage and spine showed through – but they hefted their axes at my command, slogging through the knee-high water to work my will.

Behind me I could hear the screams of the dying, the clash of steel, and the rending and popping of timbers as my friends tore into the underbelly of Grennen Vuhl's fleet. I risked a glance across the harbour toward *Sorrow's Vengeance* – and I smiled as I saw that the wards still held, and that the Tarkhanden were rallying around my daughter's ship, forcing the Kothrai away from the docks. There were soldiers there, but there were far more Zamaran citizens, armed with boat-hooks and marlinspikes, fishing nets and clubs.

"Your gambit may yet fail, Sir Paladyne," I said, as I watched the Nameless call back his knives, sending them singing through the air to unsplice my ghouls. No matter – the harbour was choked with corpses, and already more were staggering from the waves, hands groping in the shingle for weapons. "It seems that Grennen Vuhl is not the strategist he needs to be... at least when he's not conquering unarmed peasants."

"*Conquest?*" The Betrayed was laughing, its hunched body heaving with mirth. "And you think this is Grennen Vuhl's idea of a war-fleet?" A complex motion of both hands, and more knives pulled free from the steel thicket on his back, swirling and looping to pierce heads and hearts. Popping detonations flared all around me, and a spray of blood pattered down across the surface of the ocean.

"This is no *conquest*. A mere diversion… now that our attempts at diplomacy have failed."

I scowled – quite an impressive feat when your face resembles a time-ravaged skull.

"The peace faction. You knew?"

"We wanted you taken alive, of course. Crippled, perhaps. But we are happy enough with the end of Rasq T'ukallinat. No – this day of death and suffering is all *your* fault, Lamenter. Another slaughter laid at your feet. We are here to take the soul of the Herald… and of course, you have so conveniently taken up his mantle."

I didn't bother answering. Instead I pushed my mental fortitude to its limits, throwing twenty dead men at him in a rush. Axes swung, and pale fingers groped for purchase, but a storm of flying knives ripped them ragged, looping and whirling through flesh like a tailor's needle through silk.

Behind me I heard shouts, and then a concussive detonation. One of the Betrayed's daggers was plucked from the air by a musket ball, then another – I risked a glance over my shoulder and saw Harlaw at the rail of a great logjam of Kothrai ships, Silbern Chaar at his back. She held off a horde of reavers with great double-handed swipes of her broadsword, while the master gunner lined up another shot with his blackpowder musket.

I shouldn't have looked. The Nameless followed my gaze, then grinned, raising his open hand. A halo of spinning knives floated above it, glowing red-hot.

"Weakness *weakness WEAKNESS*, Aemortarch! To care is to know sorrow! *They die first!*" His laugh was unhinged as he sent a humming blur of steel scudding across the wavetops, but I was quicker. I raised my fist, and I felt the wards around the *Sorrow's Vengeance* buckle outward from within. Something hard and cold tore through, a needle-point puncture which wove together in its wake. An arc of pale green light sliced like a razorcut across the sky, trailing black smoke, and I answered the Betrayed with a frankly insane laugh of my own.

"But there are so many dead already," I said, as my new Cerebrex slammed down into my palm, shedding a rain of ash and sparks. "*Let's meet them.*"

There is power in places at the edge of things. A *boundary state*, the philosophers of Ghuram call it – or, as the witches of the high Hiledoran used to say, 'the lightning before the storm'. When mortal souls die, they fall through our reality into the Unmanifest, that place of the Aziphem and their mad, fragmented Father. Each little deadlight is a flickering candle, a sutured wound in the world. Through which the anguished come back as ghosts – and the chill of the Shard of Death bleeds into reality.

Alone, each one is a weak and feeble thing. Enough for hedge-witches to frighten the peasantry with, perhaps. But within the Cerebrex I held the souls of six thousand, four hundred and forty two men. That number swelled beyond comprehension as I inhaled, opening the wardings, stilling the rotation of the spiked spheres of iron and gold. Thick skeins of witchfire burst from the water, slaking the core of preserved tissue locked inside.

"*Aligning the seal of the Black Gate. Balancing the vitae flow to the seven cardinal sigils. Cerebrex bindings locked by the praxis of the Horned Eye, with restraint now unlimited to the second level...*"

I spun, holding the great metal ball out before one palm, and let loose a concentrated blast of all that edge-born power. Unfinessed, barely focused – it manifested as a solid rod of darkness, as wide as my outstretched arms, hissing across the surface of the water and annihilating all it touched. When it caught up with Uveryn's wheel of knives they were a heartbeat from slicing through Silbern and Harlaw. But at that moment the leading edge of the beam split open into a whirl of filament tendrils, binding the blades solid with shadow. The outpouring of energy from the Cerebrex flickered away to a thin line, strobing with stuttering detonations. And then it was gone, taking the Betrayed's daggers with it.

I turned to face the Nameless, Cryptfeeder bursting into guttering flame in one hand, the Cerebrex Incantus in the other. All around me dead men were rising from the churned and bloody wrack, hands groping for the light, burned and maimed and broken things hefting whatever weapons they could grasp.

"On second thoughts," I rasped, the mageblight burning cold and fierce inside my bones. "Why don't you just give up and *join* them?"

The Betrayed was still laughing, a sound muffled behind its lopsided mask. It wrapped its arms around its chest as though it was about to burst. Then it convulsed, snapping forward, its spine arching far beyond the bounds of mortal physiology. I watched, horrified, as a whole new crop of knives tore their way through the skin of its back and shoulders, steel grinding on steel. More now, and larger. Some, perhaps, even qualified to be called swords.

"Oh, you are *ready*. Ripe! Just as he said. A conduit for power. Resurrectionist of dead Gods. All that pretty knowledge in your head...."

The hunched figure looked up at me, mad eyes burning behind its mask.

"NOW! Enact the Rite, Lord Endsong. The trap is sprung!"

I was probably supposed to be terrified. Angry, at least. But all I felt for this once-human creature was contempt. That, and a terrible weight of sadness. The ire of Paladyne Uveryn was as hopeless a a prisoner trying to bludgeon his way through granite with his forehead, and just as painful to watch. Worse – Dirge's creature was a mockery of those horrors which I had faced so long ago. An insult to my own pain.

All of this sleeted through me in an instant, as idiot laughter bubbled up from behind the mask of the thing which called itself *Betrayed*.

Betrayed! Even that was a conceit – for had I *asked* to be worshiped by credulous fools? Uveryn had betrayed *himself* when he gave his life to Deacon Fell.

I advanced on the Nameless, snarling, trying to kindle righteous anger in my mind. All I found was disgust. Dirge was playing the same old game, raising demons for me to break, and this would be as cruel, sordid and pointless a death as drowning a maimed puppy...

Then I noticed the flames boiling away from Cryptfeeder's edge. I looked at the blade, and in its reflection I caught a glimpse of the muzzle-flash from Harlaw's gun, slowed to a silent bloom of smoke and sparks. The flames were *congealing*, solidifying with a sound like frost forming on glass. Ripples on the surface of the bloody sea crawled to a standstill. Specks of spray hung like jeweled constellations in the air.

"What?" I breathed, as the air turned cold. The light itself seemed to dim, becoming red as sunset. Looking up, I watched cracks skitter across the vault of the heavens, widening and multiplying. Little pieces of the sky flaked away to reveal a heaving, chittering darkness.

"Yes! It comes!" crowed the Betrayed, falling to its knees on the shingle. Water splashed up, then froze, glittering crimson in a halo around it. "The Untime of the Aziphem! What use is your dead flesh now, Aemortarch?"

I reached out, and realised that the Nameless was right. My horde of Kothrai and Tarkhanden dead were poised like grim waxworks, axes hefted high, lifeless eyes glassy and unfocused. All motionless, and cut off from the web of my will.

"Impossible! Grennen Vuhl cannot contain such power!"

"Indeed. *But Grennen Vuhl is not here*, Khytein. This little expedition is under the command of Lord Endsong himself – and his masters, of course."

The Betrayed's raw-rimmed eyes turned skyward. What hung above us now curdled men's minds like milk in the summer sun. But I was certain that the undead thing was far past madness already, and four sails to the wind.

The Dwellers in Darkness filled the sky from horizon to horizon, infinite and tiny, mighty and crippled, forms both foetidly organic and coldly mechanical conjoined in an endless, murderous bout of auto-cannibalistic copulation. A fecund, rotten, joyous tangle of eyes and teeth and penetrative, barbed appendages – all dimensions skewed so that the infinitesimal were mere parasites on the vast, who were in turn preyed upon by their hosts. An insistent sussurrus blurred in behind this nightmare, accompanied by a sense of cold which cut bone-deep, making me shiver. Only twice before had I laid eyes on the truth behind the veil of the world, and each time I had left a part of myself there. This was the reality to which Dirge had sworn all of Yrde.

"The music stops, Aemortarch. Now it's just those touched by sorcery, with all distractions put aside. You, your Hmai witch, the skinchanger, and the two aboard your daughter's ship. I think… Yes. We should deal with that pair of harlots first."

I forgot that the Betrayed was even there, as that voice raked its claws across my mind. A voice I'd forgotten for centuries, but one which I'd heard again not so long ago, issuing from between the lips of a dead man.

Dirge came striding out of the throat of his sorcerous vortex, stepping from ship to ship amid the cold and creaking hush of the Untime. The harbour was all crimson and shadow, galleys logjammed tight, the spray of their collisions hanging in veils around them. Coils of rope traced filigree through the air. Tarkhanden cannon-smoke, whole red-hot chains and swarms of shot… all hung motionless as a painted fresco, while storms of fire-arrows winked overhead like scattered stars.

Dirge had manifested as a raggage of skin, stretched over a long-limbed, impossibly tall scrawl of fire. His face hung lopsided on a head like a candle-flame, tapering up to that ultimate conceit – a crown of floating crystal shards, aflicker with lightning.

Each stride took him from one pitched deck to the next, shouldering aside masts and canvas. Where he touched the swarming Kothrai their frozen bodies cracked and collapsed, brittle as ashes.

"Do you like him, Kuhal? A thoroughly pragmatic man, dear Paladyne Uveryn. When he realised you couldn't save his immortal soul, he decided to find someone who would at least have a use for it…"

"I think I preferred him dead," I said, leveling the Incantus in my hand. My fingers were trembling where they wrapped through the outer iron cage. Too many memories. And from the black gem, I could hear Makara's heartbeat, fast and stuttering. A match to my own, if that withered chunk of meat in my chest was more than just dead weight.

Dirge reached out with his long, attenuated fingers, then swarmed up the sky like some great crippled spider. He hung over the frozen harbour of Zamara, legs folded in a pose of meditation, fire dripping from between the gashes in his skin.

"I am not here to fight *you, barbarian,"* he said, with a dismissive gesture of one hand. *"We want you alive, after all. No – I am here to witness the suffering of those who foolishly call themselves your* friends. *My gift to you. You will be able to know their pain quite intimately when we have you tied down to the rack."*

"Spare me the villainous prattle, Dirge. We both know how this ends."

"Oh, indeed," he nodded. *"It ends when those things above us devour this sordid little world. But in between now and then, I intend to reign for quite some time, Kuhal. You're going to help me. Just like your daughter did. Do you like my new form, by the way?"*

Self-control has never been one of my strong points. I clenched the Incantus until my knuckles were white, then screamed a Word of annihilation. No dead flesh, this side of the Untime. But ragged soul-stuff, ghostlights and frayed memories… all could burn. All were fuel for the fire of my hatred.

And hatred it was. An emotion so pure that it earthed itself through me like lightning. Stronger, indeed, than the echo of love which had kept me devoted to Makara's memory for all these centuries. The force of it blew away any guilt I might have felt. I hated Dirge, Sinder, Endsong with a passion I had almost forgotten existed, and it felt *good*.

Barbed black lightning erupted from the Cerebrex, a single bolt as wide as a Kothrai galley's hull. The water around me was pushed down into a popping, sparking bowl, revealing gravel and corpses. The air was ripped apart, reeking of ozone and oily tin.

But Dirge slapped the bolt aside, almost casual in his disdain.

"Really, necromancer! I am only as real as nightmares, here and now. A little trick your daughter discovered for me. Hoping her usefulness will stay the blade, I suspect. Such a fine brain. It will be a shame to pry it from her skull!"

The second blast was as ineffective as the first. Dirge laughed.

"Take him, my Betrayed. Alive doesn't have to mean all in one piece."

I snarled like a beast, swinging the Incantus around, the seething eye of it searching for the Nameless One's masked face. But the damned thing was faster than I had imagined – faster, indeed, than it had let on. It must have been simply playing with me…

A pair of blades came hissing in, plunging through my flesh at both shoulders. Their sharpened points crossed deep in my chest, bursting out on either side of my spine and throwing me off-balance. I saw a deep, furrowed wake come churning across the water, sliced behind a blur of darkness. I had barely time to throw up a wall of spirits, weaving them into a pathetic shield.

Then the Betrayed struck me with the force of a cavalry charge, throwing me bodily through the air. Even as I spun, helpless, I could see it springing from rock to rubble to shattered deck below me, readying another brace of knives.

Fast! So fast! Had the Devouring Wind been this quick? Had the Eyeless used its hatred to push itself so far beyond human limitations? I honestly could not remember.

I concentrated, shaping the web of soul-stuff around me into an arrowhead. Not a second too soon… for I ploughed into the side of a frozen Kothrai warship a heartbeat later, shattering timbers, staving in the whole straked side of its hull. Splintered beams whirred through the air, slowing in their hectic tumble as the Untime took them.

I shook my head, clearing it of purple starbursts. There was no pain – not yet. Most of my nerves were calcified threads of mageblight, after all. But the mind remembers. Just as mine remembered to roll aside, narrowly avoiding the Betrayed's fist as it hammered through the timbers where I had lain.

Aching. Joints afire. Bones singing with 'blight. I rallied my ghosts, and formed them into a spiraling gyre, just as I had done so long ago aboard Jerrold Sinder's mighty War Keel. I took to the air, pulling free of the wreckage even as the Nameless One wallowed and raged deep in the ship's belly.

There was something else about the spirits of the dead I wanted to share with him. Something known by those hedge-witches and petty dabblers back in Sarem. They called it the *poltergeist* – the mischievous soul of a dead child, who could tip over tankards and levitate dry leaves. Here, in the shadow of the Outer Dark, I commanded *thousands* of souls. And their combined power was enough to move far more than trinkets and twigs. Muttering words in the runes of old Sothara, I imagined a pair of huge, immaterial hands…

There!

I tore a cannon loose from the hulk of a Tarkhanden man o' war, half sunken and skewered on the ram of a Kothrai raider. I swung it like a club, battering Uveryn loose from the hold of the ship, down to the seabed. Knives spun and glittered in the deep red water, falling with him. The cannon broke the surface, then hammered down again, like a pestle into a mortar, pistoning down to crush the Nameless One's head. And indeed, it must have been loaded by some conscientious Tarkhanden seaman, for as the witchfire crackled and raved around it the great gun fired, spitting out a red-hot cannonball.

Of course, it couldn't be so easy.

I watched from high above, cloaked in swirling spirits, as the Betrayed split the iron cannonball in half, erupting from beneath the broken-backed ship in a fury. For an instant the thing disappeared inside the gaping bore of the gun, but no Nameless could be so easily trapped. The solid breach of the cannon peeled open like some twisted iron fruit, scattering shards. Knives whirled toward me in a dizzying storm. Kothrai sailors and warriors were cast aside, shattered, as Dirge's creature ripped their vessel in two.

And it *leaped*, taking to the air with me, eyes flashing madness behind a mud-and-blood-smeared mask.

"Endsong will have your soul, Kuhal Moer!" screamed the fallen knight. *"But I will have your flesh!"*

"Have *these*," I suggested.

And I emptied the Cerebrex, sending countless filaments of soul-stuff spearing down. To the left and the right of the onrushing demon, his hands opened like claws, long blades spinning in figure-eights around him…

I felt every vertebra pop, up the length of my back. My shoulders sagged, then bore up under the strain. I swear I heard the very bones of my skull creak, flexing along fracture-lines fused solid in my infancy.

And I hefted an entire Kothrai warship in each spectral hand, raising them from the sea dripping, anchor chains jangling, frozen statues of black-clad axemen toppling into the brine. Slowly at first, clawed back down by gravity… until the geas of the Untime took them, and the sorcery woven through their timbers freed them from reality.

Then they were just weapons, gripped in hands woven from thousands of souls. I brought them up and around, brought them *together* in a crushing detonation, smashing them to kindling from bow to stern.

The Betrayed was right between them.

The Untime took the explosion of timber, sailcloth, flesh and iron as it radiated away from the point of impact, leaving a jagged star hanging above the harbour. From up here, I could see the whole frozen tableau of Dirge's working, all the way from the flames hanging in veils above Zamara to the shattered towers of the gates, pried open by the shadow of Abyssus.

That was where I needed to go. Something deep in my soul – coiled around my blighted bones – dragged me toward that dark and gelid mass like a lodestone to iron.

Why did Grennen Vuhl want the mantle of the Herald? Because without it, his bindings on the great beast's shadow were fragile, thread-thin things.

Cryptfeeder would slice them through.

I let the Incantus float free for a second, pulling the two blades from deep in my shoulders. There was no pain – in the Untime I had become nine parts legend to only one part withered flesh. That legend was one of a skull-faced revenant, a tyrant from the grave, and such things, we are told, do not bleed.

I should have been more careful.

The first indication I had that the Betrayed was still alive came from above me. A shadow falling out of the sun….

Both of the thing's fists were locked together into an axehandle blow, and it caught me unawares, one of its own knives still in my hand. The blade seemed to be an unforged shard of iron, *grown* into the shape of a dagger. I was musing on this when pain exploded through me, a concussive, collarbone-fracturing crunch.

I was hammered down, hard. A blur of red and black; then I was under the water, impacting in a flat spin.

Corpses, ropes, ragged sailcloth and tiny bubbles swirled past me. The whole chill cauldron of Zamara's harbour was tainted red, shot through with blood. Some of it – despite my aemortal state – was surely now mine. *The bastard had broken my ribs!* Soul-stuff sutured them up, promising pain in my none-too-distant future.

I remembered the cannon, and I started to swim. Not a heartbeat too soon – for whole spars and bowspirits came hissing down behind me, impaling spikes sharpened and thrown by the wrath of the Betrayed. The black hulks of Kothrai galleys flickered past above me… but my foe could not possibly track me. The fool must have known that I didn't need to breathe.

But I could see the Nameless. It lit up the Dark Sight as a twisted knot of filaments, a sucking wound in reality.

And it had forgotten about my Incantus, left behind me when I fell.

They aligned, like the sun, the moon and Yrde at the moment of an eclipse. Putting the Betrayed directly between my hand and the Instrumentorum. And yes… the damned demonic thing was absolutely *full* of iron.

This was Corvo's art; the storm-magick born of the high and lonely Hiledoran. The memory of how that old sorcerer had been torn apart fueled my anger as it wove it.

One of the Nine had taken him, there on Urzen's bloody doorstep. A thing which was kin to the beast above me…

Just as in Oram, I may have overcompensated.

I bit back the pain in my shattered shoulder, and spat out the Words in a storm of red-tinted bubbles.

"Mach'tarii Salcathan'ei! Ko's'kthaa Daresch!"

Detonation.

The thunderbolt which pinned Uveryn to the sky was a colour beyond white, and it spiraled the water away from around me, flash-boiling a quantity of it to steam. Not one drop touched me – I stood on the dry seabed, hands outstretched, tendrils of power crackling from each fingertip, then weaving together into a pillar of raving light a span or two above.

The Betrayed screamed.

There was a grim balance here. The Incantus contained the patterned memories of Corvo the Ontohki, but it burned just as sweetly as the flesh of my foe. Piece by piece, the last vestiges of the old Stormcaller fell away from my mind, as gold and iron creaked and expanded, glowing hot.

But his swansong, through me, bought a kind of vengeance.

The sheer heat of the blast was enough to char the Nameless One's flesh, but it was the knives which doomed it. Heating to cherry red, then blazing orange... the creature tried to force the sizzling metal from its body, but the peculiar sorcery which had given it life would not set it free. More blades grew from the flaw inside Uveryn's chest, already nearly molten as they were forced through the focus of power, twisted out of shape. Soon a storm of hot iron whirled around the spread-eagled form of the Paladyne, the colour of autumn leaves. The metal erupting from his back was little more than attenuated tendrils, curling and dripping as he howled, his eyes boring into mine until they burst behind his mask.

Bright blood spattered. The Incantus whirled faster and faster. Cracked, cooked muscles split, spewing rivulets of molten iron into the gyre around the Betrayed. Bones snapped and charred.

Then the cages of the Cerebrex seized. The beam stuttered and faded. The sphere of trapped souls fell, smoking, to the surface of the sea.

All trace of Corvo was gone, save for the merest shadow of his face, the sound of his name.

The waters around me, thrust aside by the blast, were trapped in the grip of Dirge's Untime. They failed to crash in over my head as I watched the final moments of the thing which had once sworn its soul to me.

Some critical tipping point had been reached. The streams of molten metal had stopped, but the sheer heat was no longer coming from my pillar of white lightning. It was coming from within, where the sorcerous flaw which animated the Betrayed was unraveling.

"I repent!" screamed that blackened husk, curling in on itself amid a storm of hot metal. Things which had once been knives collapsed to liquid, running together like quicksilver. And all in whirling, ceaseless motion, englobing the wretched remains of Paladyne Uveryn.

"I repent, Aemortarch! Forgive me! I... was weak. I should never have faltered.... in your faith. They... they fear you. They..."

A spasm wracked the Nameless, and it bent backwards with a crackling, popping sound, until the back of its skull almost touched its heels. A scream was wrung from its throat, ascending through pain and into glass-shattering agony.

"My Forgiveness," I said, hearing the capital fall into place, as it would on the page of a holy book. "Is *hugely* overstated."

Then every drop of molten metal streamed outward from Uveryn in a great sorcerous explosion. A starburst of silvery needles reflected the red sun, under a sky of madness.

"Please..." he managed, as titanic forces twisted what was left of him around the knot in his soul.

The focus collapsed. All those ten-span needles came together at once, with a sound like a hammer on glass.

And the Betrayed was obliterated, becoming nothing but a spiked ball of iron, a mace-head which plunged to earth just as my Incantus had done. The splash it made hung glittering in the air as the Untime froze it.

I looked up at dirge, squatting on the sky. There was no way to read that mad and ruined face.

"One down, Pontifex." I said, reminding my fellow Aspirant of his old, old title. I chuckled. "Such a waste! Does dear old Vuhl have the balls left to curse you?"

"A better question, Moer! Do you still hold to that absurd sense of chivalry? The one which you thought made you more than a savage?"

I rose toward the apparition of my foe, knowing that he was as real as a fever dream. Wanting to gut him anyway. A *savage*, was I? I would show him savagery!

"I have," I said "An overwhelming urge to kill you again. The only – *only!* – good thing about hating a vile, deathless piece of shit like you, Dirge... I get to enjoy wringing the life out of you over and over and *over* again."

The Angan sorcerer counted on his fingers.

"Let's see. Once, Gernish Maudrin saved you. Then, you dropped a Keel on both of us. Then... oh yes, I'll give you that one. But seeing as I came back stronger, I'll forgive you as well. After that, it was your pitiful dead witch, then Zael Kataphraxis. You've actually fared pretty badly against me, Kuhal. It's your friends and loved ones who pay, of course." He leered. *"And the tally is about to rise..."*

I felt the whole intricate working of the Untime skew, staggering sideways. The great incantation was wheels within wheels, rolling cogs of meshed fire. And it failed for just an instant as two great powers were forced through it and into the world – into the null space which Zamara's harbour had become.

As flawed as the Betrayed. But greater. Stronger. Without the hairline fractures of mortal memory to mar their equilibrium. True demons of the Nameless.

"The Hungering Tide. The Duke of Chains. My children. And now you choose, Kuhal Moer. Your daughter's friends… or the Hmai. Such sweet ladies all. And all so very, very dead. Unless you stand in the path of one of my pets."

They descended from the sky amid ragged swirls of shadow – indistinct, puppet forms robed in black. One directly above the *Sorrow's Vengeance*, shattering the wards with a gesture. One above the heart of the Kothrai fleet, where Kayan Orsii had made her stand.

I had quite forgotten the Nine in all their power. They were as compassionate as an icicle through the heart, and as relentless as winter. These two were of that old breed, and I wondered just how long ago they had been created, sleeping dreamlessly in their black sarcophagi until Dirge saw fit to unleash them.

The mad Aspirant's laughter echoed in my head. But it seemed far away.

He was right, damn him.

The Incantus was dead weight, a boulder swallowed up by the silt of the seabed. Abyssus was outside the Untime, and Anghul was perilously weak.

I would have to choose. And no matter which choice I made, death would follow.

"The Grand Chirurgeon of the Guild of Chains, Manfred Ormis Vendire, has concluded in his masterwork, the *Liber Bio-Logicae Humana*, that we are over seventy percent water; and indeed, that the fluid within the Ghurami fruit known as a 'coco-nut' is remarkably similar to blood plasm. While we must commend the research undertaken by such an inquiring and brilliant mind, we cannot help but feel sorry for those who had to clean up after Lord Vendire's experiments...

Nolphis Voye,
sub-Redactor of Saradrim

CHOOSE, HE'D TOLD me. Supposing, for an instant, that I could. Silbern Chaar, Harlaw and Kayan Orsii on my left. *Sorrow's Vengeance* on my right, with so many more of my allies aboard. Agonizing indecision wracked me for a few precious heartbeats, and Dirge laughed, savouring every moment.

"It makes no difference, of course. All will perish. It's just that you can prolong the suffering... at least for a handful of them. Go on! Time may be stilled, but it's running out, Khytein"

He was right, damn him. I had stopped the Betrayed – but at a terrible cost, burning my new Incantus down to wreckage. There would be no more annihilating lightning, even if one of these Nameless was fool enough to place itself between the blackened iron sphere and my hands.

My eyes flickered left, then right. I caught a tiny movement, a shadow in the ratlines above the *Sorrow's Vengeance*. There *was* a way I could be in two places at once, but it would shear my remaining power down the middle...

My will unfolded behind Sei's eyes as he skittered to the deck, right between Issara and Kell. Looking up, I saw the shadows around the Nameless One shatter, letting it fall with a splintering crunch, collapsing the Sorrow's forecastle. It was a malformed hulk wrapped entirely in chains, mummified in steel. Baleful red eyes burned between the links stretched tight across its face, cutting into burned and scarred flesh.

At the same time I threw myself down toward Kayan Orsii, who stood surrounded by her honour guard of Hmai. The demon which descended upon her – and on the frozen forms of Harlaw, Silbern and Meracq D'avarian – was nothing but a tattered, empty robe, seething with darkness. I flew into its path, bracing Cryptfeeder in both hands, and I snarled a word of command, letting the memories of a hundred dead Zengaji take control of my flesh. The steel became part of me, balanced and ready for murder. Even so, I knew I could only stay the Nameless for mere seconds.

That was all it took for the chained one to wreak its ruin. All I could do, as it transpired, was *watch* – even as the second Nameless manifested a black iron broadsword, hacking down at me with a chittering hiss.

Aboard the *Vengeance*, that lopsided figure shouldered aside the wreck of the forecastle, sending chains looping out from its arms and chest. They slapped Kell Du'ath aside with effortless contempt, wrapping around Issara's neck and hoisting her from her feet. The blood-mage could barely scream as she clawed at the sorcerous iron, tearing her crimson nails to splinters.

Kell could scream, however. And the sound she let loose was all out of proportion to her tiny frame – a howl of fury shot through with murderous power. The timbers between her and the Nameless charred and erupted, red-hot splinters flying skyward. Chains snapped taut as the scream alone forced it backwards, metal glowing red-hot.

And then the tiny seeress struck, nimble and quick, faster than Sei himself as she unleashed a flurry of kicks and blows, hammering at the demon's defences. It's chain-wrapped neck snapped sideways as mageblight-heavy fists and feet hit home – ten times, twenty, a hundred, in a crystalline blur. Little pops and starbursts of white light exploded all around the thing as it was driven to its knees. But it never let go of Issara's throat, and now the poor Rasuuli countess was kicking and choking like a hanged man, her perfect lips turning blue.

"*Issara!*" screamed Kell, leaping backward to land on her tip-toes, poised. Sei almost collapsed into a pile of bones as she drew down power, staggering the wheels of the Untime as they ground behind reality. The Dwellers in Darkness wavered in the sky, buckling and warping like a mirage.

Then the ancient, fey Ythean unbound her hair, letting it fan out around her head. Each tiny filament left a razor-thin contrail in the air behind it as she propelled herself toward the Duke of Chains, silent now, mouth set in a grim, determined line…

Crystalline threads wove themselves through the chains. All the way down to the thing's ruined flesh, its cored-out bones. And the detonation, when it came, rocked the *Sorrow's Vengeance* to its massive keel, grinding it up against the Zamaran docks with a splintering crash.

Issara's body was flung through the air, end over end. She struck the mainmast with a sickening crack, her eyes rolled back to bloodshot whites.

Chain links parted. Whole blackened lengths of iron flew wide, coiling and twisting against a sphere of white fire. Deep in the heart of it, I saw the true form of the Duke – a flayed and wretched thing, chains pierced through its raw muscles with hooks. But I saw something else, too.

Like Slaughtermaw, the Doom of Oram, the Duke of Chains was an *occultiphage*. An eater of magicks. And now it had Kell Du'ath locked in a death-grip.

The light faded, leaving Sei dazed. Through his eyes I saw the Nameless kneeling on the deck, smoking, its hideous, fleshless grin stretched tight. A hundred ensorcelled chains held up the Ythean seeress by her hair, while others wrapped around her arms and legs, all but tearing her in two. Mortal flesh would already have given way, but Kell was mageblight through and though.

More the pity. For now the Duke of Chains drank her dry.

The oracle convulsed as the demon hunched over her, ribs protruding from its sunken chest. The pale light within her flickered and faded, guttering down to a single candle-flame of white inside her head. One last creak of corroded iron, crushing wrists and ankles, and I saw that flame waver…

Issara heaved herself upright, calling down power. But the blood of her enemies was frozen in the Untime, slow and thick as syrup. I saw the veins stand from her skin as she burned up vitae, summoning a blast of raving red force.

"Pick on someone your own size, wretch!" she screamed, her teeth all jagged and predatory. "Or at least someone who knows *size doesn't matter!*"

The blast knocked the Duke sideways, but its grip never faltered. Indeed, the vile thing staggered to its feet, leering, drooling, heavy with stolen power.

A spare chain licked out, whipcrack fast, its tip flaring red with lethal energies. But it never reached Issara. Because at the last instant

Seventails was there, erupting from the deck of the ship in a fury of splintered wood and rage.

This time the skinchanger had not taken on one of his primal forms. No – he was all of them and none, a hulking, bestial shape as tall as Rasq had been, but bulging with muscle, layered in fur. His belly was armoured in draken scutes, his shoulders bristled with the mane of a timberwolf, and his hands were wrecking instruments, black-clawed and long-fingered, reaching out to punch through the Duke's ribcage in ten places.

But it was his face I'll not soon forget - not this side of nightmares. A human face, contorted and stretched into a predator's muzzle, ragged with mis-matched teeth, tusks and fangs. I doubt he could have closed that nightmare mouth without lacerating his own lips, but he didn't intend to speak. Instead he snapped his jaws around the Nameless One's head, engulfing it in a single bite.

All this in an instant, as Kell Du'ath's dying scream echoed across the glassy tableau of the Untime. The chains which held her crawled with lightning for an instant, before the seeress cracked and shattered, collapsing into a cloud of glittering crystal sand. But in that instant the Duke's chains had been spread wide, and Seventails was quick enough, in his monstrous form, to pounce upon the raw meat of the Kothrai demon.

He lifted the Duke over his head, bones creaking between his talons. Snapping and slathering, he tried to pop the damned thing's skull between his jaws. Ribbons of muscle and flesh peeled away. Blood sprayed, pattering across the skinchanger's scaled chest and belly.

But it was not so easy to kill one of the Nine. Not even one of Grennen Vuhl's imitations.

The chains hooked and skewered through the Duke's flesh moved as quick as cobras, closing in to cocoon both Seventails and his prey. They clattered and slid shut, whipping around and around themselves, sealing tight…

In a deadly embrace.

For as Sei watched, those chains began to *tighten*, constricting the bucking, howling shape within. A charred smell began to hiss from between the links as they rasped against each other; the chains were glowing hot, cooking Seventails alive as he was crushed, bones splintering, the breath forced from his lungs in a final despairing moan…

There was no gloating. No words of victory. The chains just kept *tightening*, even as blood and grease rained down between their blackened links. Soon only the misshapen form of the Duke remained – and Seventails had been utterly consumed. The thing allowed itself an oily chuckle of laughter.

As it took a step toward Issara, though, the Nameless was unsteady on its feet. And the chain-wrapped ball of meat which was its head seemed deformed, crushed flat on one side.

All of which slowed it down enough for the Rasuuli witch to claw herself upright, leaning heavily on the mast. Bright blood dripped from the corner of her mouth, and she cuffed it away with the back of her hand, leaving a smear of crimson across her knuckles.

"It's the hard death for you, then," she slurred, smiling. "Was going to make it easy. No time for games. But you… you deserve some sweet attention. And I've seen what's under all that ironmongery. You're *meat*, same as the rest of them."

The demon stopped. Two loops of chain rattled down from its hands, coiling on the deck. It was waiting for a blast of sorcery – fuel for its inner fires. But it had not seen the huge and silent shape looming up behind it, murky and indistinct within the frozen, glittering cloud of Kell's disintegration. Issara didn't need to kill the beast. She just had to throw it off balance…

I nudged Sei in the right direction just as the blood-mage's shadow flared dark and jagged, huge spectral wings unfolding behind her. There was nowhere else to draw the *vitae sangre* from – not under the curse of the Untime. So Issara fed upon herself, burning away her youth, draining the vitality she had stolen - were the stories true - from a thousand butchered virgins.

The fearsome Countess withered up before my eyes, her skin grown leathery and wrinkled, her blue-black veins coiling up arms and legs like gnarled old roots. Eyes sunken, teeth yellowing, fingernails grown to brittle claws… she went from succubus to crone in a handful of heartbeats, building up a sphere of force between her hands.

The Duke of Chains leaned forward, its stance planted, the slithering steel peeling back from its chest and face. A lower jaw, split like an insect's mandibles, creaked open, revealing a throat lined with spiked copper plates. *No wonder the Nameless couldn't speak…*

"Watch my hands, you foul bastard," cackled Issara, now looking every one of her two hundred years. "Watch… and learn."

The Duke spread its arms wide. A hissing, popping sound bubbled up out of that nightmare throat.

Issara threw the sphere of power up over its head, arcing high. A seething mass of red tendrils flew, catching the sun, and the demon's head tilted back, watching its curve, eyes bright with hunger…

And Issara attacked, faster than she had any right to be, a desiccated thing all tendons and spite. I heard bones break as she caught the Duke a solid right cross to the jaw – all four knuckles splintered to ruin at once.

The blow would have caved in the face of a mortal man. But the Duke of Chains had given up mortality long ago. Instead of spraying teeth, the heavy, chain-wrapped creature simply tottered backward a step.

And caught up against Sei.

For an instant the Nameless hung there, on the edge of balance. The ball of roiling sorcery was falling now, out over the starboard bow, but Issara had the Duke's full attention.

"To all hells with it," she muttered, letting her broken hand hang at her side. "I never much liked the idea of being this old, anyway."

Then she struck the Nameless One with a second savage sucker-punch – an uppercut which sent the Duke crashing down to the deck in a clattering, oily heap.

"Don't make this meaningless, you little fool," she said, staring into Sei's eyes. Issara looked past my familiar, to someone – or something – in the deep shadow of the wheelhouse. "And you… you know what to do now. Time for redemption. Aye. Perhaps for both of us."

Then a coiling lash of chain whipped around her waist, squeezing tight. A violent convulsion, and the steel snapped taut, all but shearing Issara in half as she was thrown from the deck. Sei spun around, hissing, as the Duke of Chains tried to rise. But it was no easy task. The heavy, iron-bound demon was as cumbersome as an upturned beetle.

It was only a matter of time, though…

And all I could do was watch.

Oh, later, of course, when there was time to lick my wounds and count my scars, I had the privilege of guilt. I had to watch all three of them die, and there was nothing my little familiar could do about it. Not when I had so badly misjudged the other demon of the Nine which Dirge had thrown against me – a thing all ragged black silk and leather-gloved hands, its sword a rusted blur as it hacked and chopped at my defences. It took all of my remaining power to keep it from simply slicing me to ribbons. But that time allowed the Hmai chantry to spool in power, feeding it to Kayan Orsii, who – if the prickling at the back of my neck was any indication, and the pressure inside my chest as well – was trying to shatter the Untime itself.

I could only watch through Sei's eyes as five massive fingers reached down and grabbed a handful of chains across the Duke's chest. A huge hand – one which was tattooed with spirals of ancient knotwork. Whose fingernails were shards of granite.

"I know I killed them. I didn't want to. It were the voices! Lost Gods, lost souls, all in my head. I was so hungry! **So very hungry!**"

Gryst, the self-avowed pacifist, was clad in his leather apron and iron-shod boots – and he was dripping with gore from head to foot. The hand which effortlessly plucked the Nameless One up into the air was crusted with crimson, and in the other the ogre held a notched and pitted cleaver, scraps of skin and hair plastered to its blade.

"Now it's all happening again! Now I'll have to run again, and hide, and I might change even more! The voices got inside me! *They* made me into this!"

Gryst threw the cleaver aside. He held the Duke of Chains at arms length, then slammed his fist forward into its lopsided face, sobbing with each blow.

"I. Don't. WANT. TO. *REMEMBER!*"

This time something gave way within the Nameless. It screamed, chains looping out to strike. Energy crackled across the steel, promising death…

But Gryst simply shrugged it off. Mountains don't feel the lightning. And a weeping, distraught, five-hundred-pound ogre can part steel like paper.

That's just what Gryst did. The huge creature wrapped a double turn of links around each of his fists, then kicked the Nameless One in the stomach, sending it snapping back into the air. The chains arrested it, with the double pop of dislocating shoulders.

"I had *friends*, damn you! They let me believe I was something else! Not… not a *murderer*. Not a *monster*. But you had to kill them. You had to LET IT OUT!"

The ogre reversed his swing, blurring the Nameless One through a savage arc to slam into the ship's deck. Timbers shattered clean through. But Gryst wasn't done. *Touched by sorcery*, Dirge had said – those with the blight of the Aziphem were the only ones unaffected by the Untime. There was elemental power in Gryst, this tortured soul who had become a monster. And he seemed to double in size as it flowed through him, ancient and cold as those lightless caverns where water trickles between eternities of stone.

The chains snapped back. A fist with the heft of a millstone caught the Duke a terrible blow, launching him horizontally out over the water. Gryst smiled, dropping his shoulder and spinning. The Nameless One, helpless, was smashed bodily through a whole row of Kothrai warships before it was hauled back in to the ogre's embrace.

"Look what you've made me do!"

Bones cracked in that terrible, two-fisted grip. Black blood began to drip from between the chains as the Duke convulsed. Gryst brought his hands out, cruciform, chains sizzling hot across his knuckles, and the Nameless demon screamed, a terrible, inhuman sound. Those hooks went deep, and they weren't about to pull loose now. Grennen Vuhl had built his slave well.

Gryst tore him apart with ease.

Chain links popped and scattered as the ogre's shoulders heaved. Slabs of tectonic muscle bunched and coiled. And, with one last howl of rage, Gryst tore the Duke of Chains in half, splitting it from collarbone to crotch in a gush of hot black fluids. Tubes and bones, metal rods and hand-blown bulbs of glass spilled out, along with a slew of stitched-up organs. The last I saw of the Nameless was Gryst kneeling amidst its wreckage, weeping, his hands blistered and dripping.

But then, I had problems of my own to attend to. Problems which no amount of muscle and meat could easily dispatch.

Steel ground on steel, hacking at Cryptfeeder's edge. In my desperation I had switched the immense battle-blade to my right hand, and drawn the glass sword of Aerik Stormsong with my left, holding it in a reversed grip, Zengaji fashion. Sparks skipped and guttered as glass and metal chimed, faster than human eyes could follow.

But the thing I faced did not possess human eyes. Oh no. As I was about to discover, it was far from human… even by the standards of the Nameless.

Behind me, Kayan Orsii's spell was building, sending shivers of power up and down beneath the illusion of my clean-picked spine. Not much longer now, and Dirge's Untime would be shattered, freeing the Tarkhanden to rally, freeing them to sow chaos amid the Kothrai.

And freeing us to make our escape. For that was surely our only goal – to salvage what remained of our hope by casting aside conceits like honour. We would flee… and live, I hoped, to fight another day.

The Nameless had other ideas.

I spun in the air, wraiths bearing me up, concentrating their spectral power behind my arm to redouble my strength. A mighty blow – one even my brute father would have appreciated. Cryptfeeder came down like a hammer, shattering the demon's broadsword to splinters. At the same time, the glass blade came up and under, ripping it open from waist to sternum. I wasn't feeling merciful. I twisted the blade, snarling.

But it wasn't loops of steaming entrails which burst from the dark thing's belly. It was a seething, hissing swarm of insects. You can imagine my surprise.

I remembered the Eyeless, then – that creation of Urzen the Mad, aswarm with many-legged worms beneath its skin. No blade could stop it. It had taken a staggering amount of sorcery to tear the soul from its empty shell.

And now this. The Hungering Tide, it was called.

It lived up to its name. Ragged silks shredded as black scarabs poured from its cowl, its sleeves – from the gaping gash I had carved in it. They blew past me in a chittering cloud, each one marked with a tiny deaths-head. Coiling streams of them plunged down toward the deck and Kayan Orsii screamed, her incantation faltering.

For the stuff of this demon swarm was hungry indeed. They came ravening in their thousands, carrying the stench of long-forgotten tombs.

The Hmai warriors of the battle-chantry were overwhelmed at once, writhing and collapsing as tiny bodies engulfed them. Hooked claws dug into exposed flesh. Piercing mouthparts punctured eyes and veins. Hideous, slippery masses of insects forced their way down the Hmai's throats, choking them where they stood.

Crypt Scarabs. Eaters of the dead, from dark old Ghuram legends. Oh, Grennen Vuhl knew his nightmares…

I plunged toward the ship's deck, a hail of chitinous bodies cracking against my hands and face. Despite being the surrogate flesh of a Nameless One, these things could not fight their instincts. And I – hanging onto the thread of a story by my teeth – wore the illusion of polished bones. They would devour me last, which seemed, at the time, a small mercy.

I landed next to Kayan, throwing up my crossed swords.

"Aerik!" I shouted. "If you have power enough for a warding, weave it now!"

The disembodied Warbard chose not to answer. Instead, the blade which trapped his soul began to glow with fitful light, spreading tendrils through the air around us. Discordant notes, plucked on an invisible lyrecaster… I fancied I could hear him muttering curses under his breath, as he'd done while tuning his 'caster in the summers of my youth.

"Kuhal…" The Hmai witch was wild-eyed, sparks of power crawling through her hair. There was only so much longer she could balance the forces she had woven to shatter the Untime. "There! The heart, damn you! Destroy the heart, and the rest will fall!"

I spun on my heels, confronting the core of the swarm, and I saw what Kayan saw. A sphere of black iron hung above our ship, inset with green gems in the form of a faceted insect eye. Long copper skewers were driven through the sphere in a spiked profusion, sliding in and out, rotating as the mind within controlled its tiny thralls. It was some kind of twisted Cerebrex – a ball of preserved brain tissue, snarled up with loops and jags of witchfire.

There was precisely nothing left for me to throw at it.

"The Untime!" I managed, as I felt Aerik's wardings begin to weaken. Insects were blattering against the dome of light now in their tens of thousands, flaring and crisping as they struck. But sheer numbers would soon drain Aerik dry. "Can you break it?"

"Not yet. A few more minutes, were my chantry still alive. Now, though…"

She gestured at the tumbled bones and empty leather armour strewing the deck. Thank the Divine, I thought, that the Hungering Tide seemed utterly disinterested in the frozen waxworks of Harlaw, Silbern and Meracq.

A storm of oily black scarabs whirred around us, obscuring the demented sky. Above us, Dirge laughed, reveling in his mockery of godhood.

The glass sword cracked. Fractures skittered along its length.

"Don't die on me now, you old bastard!" I raged, watching whole strata of voracious insects settle on the dome above me. Millions of tiny, jeweled eyes stared back at me.

Then the ocean shivered. A sound came up through the ship's timbers, like slabs of iron clapped together, fathoms deep.

And a hand broke the surface, just off the starboard rail.

Not surprising, you may think – there were any number of hands floating in Zamara's harbour that day. Many of them were not even attached to bodies.

This hand, however, dwarfed the mighty stone fists of the Colossus of Faeros. It opened fingers the size of guard-towers, dripping with red and pink foam, exposing a palm shot through with splintered timbers, coils of rope and dead flesh.

An arm followed. Then the crown of an immense head, translucent as it obscured the dim glow of the sun. A liquid body, made of salt seawater and blood, drawing in the waters of the Eternal Harbour until the keels of three hundred Kothrai raiders scraped the stony bottom.

It was Issara.

"Blood in the water…" purred a voice like liquid night. **"Blood enough, little aspirant. Not so much the God now, hmmm?"**

She reached out to Dirge with one immense finger, refracted rainbows slithering across the surface of her skin. The Angan skittered away, long-limbed and frantic as a spider fleeing a candle flame.

"Impossible! You were meant to *die!* I have seen it! All of you! He must *despair*, damn you! He must be weakened, until I can hammer him into shape!"

Nonsense, I supposed at the time. The babbling fear of a power gone rotten.

Issara turned her huge and empty eyes toward us, reaching out with two fingers to grip the core of the Hungering Tide. It hissed as her liquid flesh touched it, sizzling with baleful light.

"So much *power*, Kuhal Moer. We come from the waters, and water is our blood. Nine months we swim in warm, hidden seas of it. And when we die, water takes what is left of us down to your new patron, who crafted life and love and death in the deeps. Blood and water, Kuhal, are *interchangeable*. But not for very long…"

I saw.

A threshold, a tipping point. *The blood of countless Kothrai and Tarkhanden, mingled and threaded through a vast, crushing tonnage of ocean. She held it together with the last of her will, focused on the drowned body she had fled, floating pale and serene behind the forehead of her new form.*

The cerebrex at the core of the swarm shattered with a tiny, glassy popping sound. Insects dropped from the sky like black rain, pattering to the decks, twitching on the slick and muddy seafloor.

"Now. Break this fool thing's working, Hmai. I will sweep away the rest of this filth. At least I can say I died doing something I

enjoyed!"

I let the warding drop. The light within Aerik's blade guttered and died, leaving it as nothing but a long, knapped tongue of glass in my hand. I let it clatter to the deck, then took Kayan Orsii's hand in mine.

"Are you ready?" I asked, staring into her eyes. The reflection of a hollow, yellowed skull stared back at me.

She nodded.

And together, we shored up the remains of our power to finish the incantation.

The sky shrieked, wavering like a mirage. The whole great dome of madness – Dirge, his masters, the darkness in which they dwelt – screwed itself around by ninety degrees, half-imagined facets and planes of it blurring to chaos.

"*She dies for this, Moer!*" howled Dirge, as the sun seemed to pop and explode, appearing in ten places at once. Stars and jagged pieces of moon wheeled across the heavens. The rolling mesh of fire which made up the Untime unraveled, stray chains of sorcery whipping down across the towers of Zamara, shearing them off like broken stumps of bone. "*Your precious Stormreaper dies! And there's nothing you can do to stop her suffering!*"

Then came a sound like stones shattering underground. A sensation of immense weight and cold. The smell of freshly fallen snow, and the taste of oily tin.

Time came back with all the force of a chain-mailed fist, and I caught Kayan as she fell, her eyes rolled back to bloodshot white. A pitched battle raged all around us, as Silbern Chaar, Meracq D'avarian and Harlaw took the fight to the Kothrai. To them, the Untime must have seemed like a mere flicker of darkness, a shadow flitting across the sun.

"... The *Vengeance!* Make for the ship!" bellowed Harlaw, his pistols flaring with sparks and smoke. On either side of him a black-clad axeman was plucked away, a spray of blood and scorched flesh pattering to the deck.

"Never mind the ship," said Silbern, cold dread in her tone. "What in all hells is *that?*"

I looked up, following the gore-slick point of her sword. Many of the Kothrai did too, pausing in mid-swing to stare at the pillar of bloody water rising above the harbour.

And then the other one. *Legs…*

"Balls of Abyssus, Sarem'ec!" breathed Saltmaster D'avarian. "Now *that* is some damned *sorcery!*"

Issara lost all semblance of human form – indeed, lost all surface tension as time came crashing down on her. But she retained enough control over the water bound up by her will to turn it into a cresting wave as it fell.

The shadow of that foaming wall fell across the bulk of the Kothrai fleet. In the throat of Dirge's bridging spell, oars clattered and men screamed, trying to back away, to sail clear before…

It was all but hopeless.

The wave came down like the flat of some sea-God's palm, wiping out hundreds of galleys at a stroke. Timbers sundered. Keels snapped clean through. Men were swept away to their deaths, ground and pulverised against the bottom, crushed between the disintegrating hulks of ships. The pride of Grennen Vuhl's raiders, churned to mincemeat by a maelstrom which rebounded from the hooked points of the island and came rushing back, lifting what remained into bobbing motion.

We were swept up by this backwash, the deck canting wildly. The ship we were on was flung up against the Zamaran docks, shattering along one side. I held on to Kayan Orsii, hunkering against the rail, my other hand clenched tight around the grip of Cryptfeeder. Some misplaced instinct had caused me to drive the great battle-blade into the timbers of the deck, giving me a handhold.

After a time, the ringing stopped. The tilted, blurred horizon settled, and I felt Silbern Chaar tugging at my shoulder.

I looked down at my hand. Flesh again – skin and arcane rings, tendons and veins. I was no longer the illusion of an all-powerful lich-king. In fact…

"… for the *Vengeance* while we still have time! The Tarkhanden are rallying, and they're going to kill their way through anything that doesn't look familiar!"

I felt a remote, warm pain in my forehead. I looked up at Silbern, and saw her stoop to pick up something from the deck. It was a sharp-tined curve of ivory.

"Worry about how you look later, Lamenter!" she growled, lifting me to my feet. "Now go! Run! Follow that insufferable Saltmaster, and don't stop. There's still a few of these Kothrai dogs with some fight in them…"

As if to punctuate her words the Ontokhi maiden spun on one heel, parrying an axe blow.

"Sloppy," she commented, trapping the haft and twisting the weapon from her attacker's hands. A swift, brutal head-butt shattered his nose. "Go! You can watch me kill these wretched sods any time, Kuhal!"

Another Kothrai came in, screaming. She disdainfully ran him through.

And I dragged Kayan Orsii over the rail with me, limping up onto the Zamaran docks with one broken horn and a head full of echoes.

The less said of our flight along the docks the better. The multiple piers, jetties and bores of the city's harbourfront had acted like the tines of an immense rake, and the wreckage of ships piled up between them in a jostling, creaking, screaming mass. Battle still raged around this charnel breakers-yard, but it was a one-sided affair. The people of Zamara were having their revenge on the Kothrai who had survived Issara's assault, and it was far from pleasant to witness. The Hmai sorceress draped across my shoulders was a dead weight, and on more than one occasion Harlaw had to fire over the heads of the Tarkhanden mob, clearing a path toward the beached hulk of the *Sorrow's Vengeance*.

For she was grounded indeed – high and dry on the strand, her massive sterncastle cradled in the wreck of a sailors' tavern.

"How in the hells are we going to float that thing?" asked Meracq, staggering up beside me. I refrained from commenting that we still had an ogre at our disposal; even with Gryst's prodigious strength, it seemed a hopeless task.

Then Kayan Orsii stirred, taking a little of her own weight. She groaned, staggering upright and proceeded to be loudly and violently ill in a very unladylike fashion. Silbern Chaar grinned in approval.

The Hmai witch planted one hand on her knee, then straggled a tangled mass of blood-red hair from in front of her eyes. She breathed in deeply, seeking some kind of equilibrium, then she rose, hands on hips, and smiled.

"We don't have to float it at all, you idiots," she said, grinning in a way which should have sent any sane man scampering for cover. A little thrill of terror gripped me, and I remembered how I had first seen the *Vengeance*, scudding through the storm over Oram.

"That's a *soulharp*. Thaumaturgical resonance. Elemental sorcery weaving, through applied harmonics."

Harlaw looked on intently. He may have fallen in love at that moment. Meracq blinked, open- mouthed. Silbern scowled at a little band of billhook-armed fisher-folk, skulking in our wake.

"She means that she can make it fly," I said. Kayan beamed.
"I mean," she corrected. "That I intend to *try*..."

Part Five

Scar of the Betrayer

"There are those antiquarians - and I know for
a fact that at least two of them are drunkards,
and another addicted to the poppy's-blood -
who insist that the draken of the Hiledoran are
sentient. That indeed, these brutes once possessed
a civilization far in advance of our own. Claims
have been made that the great beasts (who are most
closely related to the toad, the sand-adder and the
possibly mythical Ghurami 'crocodile') still retain
a measure of cunning, and that wanderers in the
high mountains often discover weathered, cracked
statues of armoured draken in almost human poses.

Such nonsense is, of course, nothing more than
the ravings of madmen, or worse, the lunacy of
professors who see notoriety as the best route to
tenure. The superstitious tribesmen of Rasuul
may believe that there are cairn-marked highlands
where the draken herd their cattle, and that
humans straying there are spared, so long as they
leave those herds untouched. But rational men
should remember that the Rasuuli also believe in
the blood-drinking Witch-Countess of Spirefend,
a fairy-tale monster as real as a dockland whore's
smile..."

Malachiros the Younger,
Chairman of the Oram Circle of Cynics

It was a lumbering, halting ascent – riven with dissonant chords
from the soulharp, sending the bulk of the *Vengeance* crabbing across
the sky. We lifted off with a creaking, splintering cacophony, dragging
the keel of our vessel from the ruins of Zamara's dockfront. Kayan
Orsii cursed and laboured below, in the open core of the *Vengeance*,
her hands a blur across the shining wires of my daughter's instrument.
The rest of us held on – and prayed, for what it was worth.

We flew.

It must have seemed a wonder and a horror to the Tarkhanden –
this great fortress of wood and copper, hanging like a thundercloud

over the ruins of their once-proud harbour. The sea between Zamara's tapering horns was now a stew of shattered timbers, floating corpses and ruin. Down there, below the bloody waves, lay countless souls. I felt them being drawn in by Abyssus, squatting in the heart of his Maelstrom and I smiled. We were free, and soon I would unlock that power. Armies of the drowned would rise from the seabed at my command, marching dark fathoms beneath the waves, their barnacle-crusted bones driven on to slaughter.

To Grennen Vuhl's dark tower. To the cold lands of the Kothrai themselves.

But there were other considerations first.

We pierced the veils of geomancy, sailing over the chasm and back into Sorath. Outside the Sunrise Gates chaos reigned, as the Eighth Fleet milled in confusion, locked out of their home port by Dirge's great working. His bridging spell had collapsed, but in doing so it had toppled one of the high white towers, and set the other afire.

Meracq D'avarian's men were doing what they could to aid Zamara's guardians… and so they were quite unprepared for the vision of a flying ship, bursting out through the veil in a blaze of thaumic lightning.

Mere moments before every cannon, ballista and catapult aboard the mighty war-fleet tore us from the sky, Meracq unfurled a red banner from our bowspirit, bearing the crossed anchors of the Eighth. He stood there at the very prow of *Sorrow's Vengeance,* a vainglorious fool in his admiral's finery, striking a heroic pose with his sabre raised high. Although I'll grudgingly admit, he likely saved us all from the mother of all broadsides.

Explanations flickered by semaphore. Rope ladders were thrown down. The captains of dreadnaughts with names like the *Wavehammer,* the *Great Kraken* and the *Reaping Blade* were hauled aboard, to hear from their Saltmaster the fate of their capital. Oaths and curses were the order of the day, framed with exquisite foulness by some of Tarkhand's finest sailors.

Diplomacy prevailed. I nursed my broken horn and sipped fiery Zamaran rum, looted from the hulk of the tavern we had destroyed. Only one of my daughter's fine blown-glass goblets had survived the assault, and I guarded it jealously, brooding over what had assuredly become Elion and Meracq's carnival.

It transpired that, once cut loose from the bonds of gravity, it was easier for Kayan Orsii to let the *Vengeance* drift above the Tarkhanden fleet than to let it settle back into the waves. And so we spent a tense and hurried few bells ferrying men and munitions, stores and supplies aboard by crane, while Master Gunner Harlaw marched up and down the rows of Tarkhanden volunteers like a Ghuram horse-trader, all but checking the poor men's teeth.

Elion Morekh almost scared his own band of bravos out of their wits – for it seemed the Tarkhanden had their own legends about the Ghost Captain and his ship of the damned, cruising in the lightless depths. The vision of my old friend in his tattered, centuries-old seafaring garb, his face a horror of scars and stitches… it must have seemed like something from an ale-house ghoul-story. But I'll give the men their due. Only a handful fainted, screamed, or ran. One particularly callow youth jumped over the side, and had to be fished from the waves by his laughing compatriots.

We were re-crewed by, I was assured, the cream of the Eighth Fleet's sailors and marines.

And none too soon.

Siara's thralls had been decimated. Those few who remained wore the fish-eyed stare of the newly dead. In my Dark Sight I could see that their souls were barely tethered to their flesh, and that if I broke the spell – if, indeed, I was able – that they would live on as hollow husks, nothing more. It seemed a cruel fate for men with whom I had no quarrel – and doubly cruel when I saw that many were tattooed or branded with the sigil of the Guild of Chains. I called on Abyssus to aid me, and with a touch to the forehead I set their souls free, coming as close to weeping as a Dark Lord is able.

There was no time for idle sentiment, however. I marked the corpses as Raw Materials; fodder for a new, more powerful Incantus Instrumentorum. Harlaw brought me the knives, and not a word was needed between us.

As to our destination – there was no argument. The map Siara had sent me was nailed to the wardroom table with daggers, and a more detailed sketch was prepared by Elion and Meracq, wrangling long into the night over a cask of Zamaran rum. Like so many other mythical pirates and fools, we were headed for the isle of Dath N'kaal, final resting place of the Void Heart. A weapon which Zael Kataphraxis had brought into being three centuries ago, to strike down the Akhazi serpent known as the Coldblood. It was quite a legend.

The difference, of course, was that I knew it as no mere campfire tale. No imaginary goblins or elves were involved in the forging of that blade. It was a fragment of some other reality, beyond even the seething Darkness where Dirge's masters dwelt.

And it must never fall into the hands of Grennen Vuhl. The living hand of Dirge's dark ambition. Grennen Vuhl, the slave-king of the Kothrai nation.

Oh, that grisly old bastard had been on my mind, all right. And not just in the fevered depths of my dreams, where my subconscious sharpened up the torture knives. A part of me wanted to make an exception to my rule. A dark, ancient part, certainly… but it made a convincing argument.

Which was why, on the day when the Eighth Fleet weighed anchor and set out under a storm-wall of white canvas, I set aside the tools with which I was repairing my Incantus, and went to seek out Urmokh.

I found the Skyborn Zengaji down in the depths of the hold, where a vast nest of blankets, straw bales and bedding had been constructed for Scarwing's recovery. The place stank of draken; indeed, the beast was curled up here like a gargantuan housecat day and night, recovering from its terrible injuries. For those unfamiliar with the smell, imagine a mixture of naptha, brimstone, oiled leather and cinnamon.[20] It lingers for days, even if one bathes like a Ghurami courtesan.

There are few things which make me nervous, but coming so close to a cramped, irritable monster is one of them. Scarwing bared a double row of butcher-knife teeth as I entered the dimly lit hold, hissing what may have been a greeting or a warning. The bladed ridge of scales down his back clattered as they rose.

"Easy there!" I said, raising my hands in front of me. "I'm here to talk to your soulbound. I… I hope your recovery proceeds apace?"

Very few other people would have attempted to make polite conversation with a Hiledoran Draken. But I had known the Archaeon, back in the madness of my youth. I knew that once, long ago, these creatures had been *civilized*, had wrought stone and built cities, had been scholars and sorcerers. The Archaeon itself had enacted the working which destroyed their minds, a sacrifice to erase their belief

---

20. There are some fools who believe that the draken could only exist if they were inherently magical. These are the same brain-damaged taxonomists who insist on depicting the great beasts with tiny little bat wings, connected to barely enough muscle to make them flap inanely. The genuine article is a hollow-boned, lithe, almost emaciated reptile, warm blooded like a hawk or a condor, with immense gliding wings and the same deep-chested, narrow-waisted profile as a Ythean hunting hound. Hence the traditional Drakenslayer's lance - for all their size, the apex predators of the Hiledoran are very, very light and fragile beneath their scales.

in a mad God.

So I was less surprised than perhaps any other man in Yrde when Scarwing replied.

"My flesh, Kuhal Moer, is already healed. We would have flown for you during the battle of Zamara. But the mind of Urmokh Zso… he has taken my pain, you see. To speed my recovery. And then, when the Untime was woven, he tried to seek out the Archaeon, alone. He succeeded. But raw contact with the mind of my entire race… well, you know full well that there is only so much a human brain can endure."

The voice of Scarwing was like the hissing whisper of a blowtorch. His words appeared in my mind without recourse to my ears at all, and as he spoke the great beast folded one of his wings back, revealing the prone figure of his Soulbound.

Urmokh looked as frail and haggard as a living man can possibly be. Even his knotwork of tribal tattoos seemed pale and lifeless, while his eyes were milky, focused on nothing.

"How…?" I asked, kneeling to place one hand on the Skyborn's chest. Urmokh was barely breathing – in the Dark Sight I could see the web-tangle of his soul pulled taut against his bones, twisting to escape. Siara's thralls had been in better condition.

"How do I speak? How do I think, when our Allsire burned us down to beasts long ago?" The draken chuckled, spraying a few droplets of sizzling acid. *"What the Archaeon has done, he can undo, Kuhal. My living egg was quickened by his own power. For the first time in millennia, a draken of the First Spawning lives. Conditionally, at least."*

The huge beast sighed, its charnel breath washing over me.

"Conditionally?"

"Oh, aye. My sire fears some bone-deep memory. The name of the Fractured One must never be spoken again. And it's there, he says – imprinted in my flesh, behind my eyes. Hence my binding, and Urmokh's foolish bravery. Half my mind is his, and half his mind is mine. Half of the name of a long-forgotten mad god, it seems, is not enough to shake the pillars of reality."

I groaned, massaging my temples. This is not easy to do when equipped with horns – even when one of them is a broken stump.

"The stupid, noble idiot," I said. "*Why?* Could the Archaeon really have broken the Untime?"

"Would he really have needed to? You have seen what my Sire can achieve, Kuhal Moer. You have seen more than most any man alive. If my Soulbound had been able to rouse the Archaeon from his torpor,

Dirge and all his Kothrai slaves would have been utterly destroyed."

I remembered watching the Archaeon's assault on the Urexian plain, all those centuries ago. A plug of rock torn from the crust of Sarem, blasted into the air by an immense fist of geomancy. Molten lava falling like rain as it flipped in midair, crashing down to create a thousand-span caldera men called the Hellmaw.

"And us with it?"

The draken shrugged, rustling the leathery membranes of its wings.

"What is our worth, weighed against the defeat of the Dwellers in Darkness? I am not here, Kuhal Moer, for the Tarkhanden, no matter how noble their cause. I am not even here to liberate Sarem from the Doom. I am here for the Void Heart, because my Sire desires it. And because it is the only thing which can slay the Fractured One, should he arise again."

A prickle of dread ran the length of my spine. Not just for the thought of Zamara's harbour boiling, molten stone spuming skyward…

"You are not the only scion of the First Spawning, are you?" I asked. "He has made more. He would rekindle your race. But…"

"Three hundred and twenty seven eggs, at the last count. You have seen the crystal spines which pierce the Allsire's skull?"

I nodded, remembering the man-length quartzite spears with which the great Draken had purified his own mind.

"The Void Heart can be broken. Pieces of it bound to bone and flesh. We will guard the gateway behind our eyes, that the Fractured One will never again escape from the Outer Dark."

"I thought there was no coming back. For those dead Aziphem… it is madness, or oblivion. Both."

This time the Draken's laughter was rueful, filled with pain.

"What of our friend Dirge, then?"

"What indeed. He has always been… persistent. A man of single-minded hatred."

"This much you should know, human. Those little Gods of yours are flecks of light, cast by the shards of the divine's shattering. They are parasites in the Outer Dark, feeding on a living corpse. The product of the first fragmentation. The first rift which split the Divine in two. Before the Shards, there was the Fractured One. And he abides. What do you think your petty dead Aziphem are parasites on, Kuhal Moer? And do you think such a thing could ever walk Yrde again without tearing it asunder?"

A sobering thought. Even besotted with drink, I would not like to dwell too long on its implications. And now I had no time for them.

"Deep musings indeed. But no amount of metaphysics will help me with what I came here to ask you, Scarwing. If that is, indeed, your real name."

"*To pronounce my real name, human, you would need several more sets of vocal chords… and a lot more teeth. Suffice to say that I carry the name Scarwing with pride. Scars are earned, after all.*"

I nodded. I had more than a few of my own.

"Enough games, then. The Eighth Fleet sails for Dath N'kaal. They mean to take the Void Heart and use it against Grennen Vuhl."

The draken snorted. Tiny licks of purple flame erupted from his nostrils, along with the smell of crumbled brimstone.

"*Then they are like children playing with their fathers' knives. All they will be able to do is slice their own fat little fingers off. Vuhl knows how to use the Void Heart – they do not.*"

"Or more likely, *Dirge* knows how to use the Void Heart, and he hasn't seen fit to tell his slave."

Scarwing nodded.

"*We are in accord, then. There is only one of us who can heal my soulbound brother. And only one of us who has studied the book of the black blade. Your daughter, Lamenter. Siara Anvhaur.*"

Now it was my turn to smile ruefully. Draken are known for their cunning, and that is *without* the intellect they sacrificed to starve their God.

"You propose a deal then, I take it? You'll carry me to Vuhl's tower, in exchange for… what?"

The twinkle in Scarwing's immense, yellow-irised eye was curiously human.

"*Why, we will make sure Dirge cannot use the blade, of course. Do you think he keeps Grennen Vuhl around for his wit, or his handsome looks? No. He needs a pair of hands, Kuhal. We will bite them off at the wrists. And then, when you have used the Void Heart to slay your old friend Dirge, you will deliver it to my Sire.*"

I felt another frisson of terror. Could I really agree to the resurrection of the Draken race – a power which would eclipse all the human kingdoms in the shadow of the Hiledoran? Would the people of Ontokh and Rasuul curse my name for centuries hence? I chuckled to myself. Of course. They already did.

"You have a deal, wyrm. Just don't expect me to spit on my palm to seal it. If you did the same you'd burn my hand down to a stump."

Scarwing shifted, rattling the scales across his back.

"That was the easy part, human. Now you have to convince the rest of your kind that you aren't flying to your death."

Predictably, the draken was right.

Meracq D'avarian tried to forbid it, until I pointed out that *Sorrow's Vengeance* was not part of his command. Dark words about the number of cannons which *were* under that command were muttered. Darker ones about necromancy, and Harlaw's opinion of the Tarkhanden gunnery crews, their mothers, and their sexual preferences followed.

Elion Morekh noted that fighting among ourselves was just what Grennen Vuhl wanted.

Silbern Chaar countered that having our chief necromancer, Herald of Abyssus and nominal leader fly into the gullet of an obvious trap was as strategic and tactical as dropping a live scorpion into one's codpiece. Unless she went along with me.

I replied that trying to *stop* said necromancer, along with a sixty-span fire-breathing monster, from doing exactly as they pleased, would be no easy feat. And that while I appreciated her gracious offer, there was a limit to the weight which even a full-grown draken could carry.

Maps were brandished. Ale cups were drained. Bickering turned to wrangling, and hence to argument. Which, by some alchemy, and after the candles were burned down to stubs of tallow, became *diplomacy*. I began to realise just why my father had hated such concepts, preferring the simple arithmetic of adding steel and subtracting heads.

I never heard the final decision of my crew. Dawn was painting the eastern horizon peach and crimson as I cinched the brass buckles of Scarwing's saddle tight, and the wind carried with it the scent of salt and woodsmoke. The last stars of the evening flickered above me in the deep blue canopy of the heavens, obscured by wisps of cloud streaming out of the north. It was going to be cold up there, in the slipstream of the draken's flight.

That was why I was robed in coarse wool, a scarf bound across my face, leaving only a slit for the smoked-glass lenses of Urmokh's flying goggles. I carried the Incantus on my back like a mollusk's shell, and Cryptfeeder slung diagonally from my shoulders. None of which made mounting up any easier – but as it was, this was only a feat I had attempted in the long-ago days of my youth.

It's true what they say, though. Drakenriding, like the art of horsemanship or drawing a bow… it comes back to you. Your muscles remember what has become blurred and pale in your mind.

For a moment I was lost in a reverie of three centuries past. Of flying above the moonlit clouds on the back of my undead draken mount, the cities of Anganesse slipping by beneath the belly-scutes of the great beast, all dreaming fitfully in terror. Makara had been there beside me, aloft on wings of sorcery and twisted wire, my demoness…

I gritted my teeth and took the reins.

They were a mere formality – Scarwing was in command here, and I felt his immense muscles bunch and flex beneath his scales as he turned on the *Sorrow's* foredeck.

"Do you think they'll realise we're missing?" I asked.

"Before they come to a decision? Doubtful. You always were a race of keening, squalling apes, Kuhal Moer."

Scarwing couldn't disguise the gentle mockery in his tone.

"And you were always, I suspect, a pack of smug, self-satisfied lizards," I replied. "Nonetheless…"

I felt a tug on the reins, in that instant before Scarwing threw himself from the deck and into the sky. The draken felt it too, and he paused, huffing impatiently.

It was Kayan Orsii, wrapped up in red and green silks, a circlet of jade holding back her crimson hair. For an instant her hand slipped down the rawhide trace of the rein and touched mine.

"I thought you should know. They've decided to let you go. Mainly thanks to Gryst, who threatened all manner of mayhem if his mistress the Stormreaper was not brought back alive."

I recalled the ogre's wrath unleashed, battering one of the Nameless to pulp. My allies had chosen wisely.

"How gracious of them. But as you see…"

"You were about to cut through that knot quite cleanly." Kayan smiled, her lips twitching up into a grin. "Sorry. It sounds much better in Hmai. But I had to say goodbye, Lamenter. And to tell you…"

Her hand fell away. For some reason, something brittle snapped inside me at that instant, as clear and sharp as the fall of an icicle.

"Kayan…"

When she looked up at me, she was all determination. An agent of her Emperor, a sorceress, a tool for the shaping of powers in the world.

"I will guide them to the Void Heart. I will ensure that it eludes the Kothrai, by whatever means necessary. But you must promise me, Kuhal Moer. Promise me, despite what villainy Grennen Vuhl has in store for you…"

She took a step back, frightened, perhaps, by what she saw in my face. Even scarified, even horned – it must have been the most human I'd appeared in centuries.

"Don't get yourself killed, you noble, saga-story fool," she said, averting her eyes. "We have unfinished business, you and I. There are things I have to tell you…"

She stopped herself, biting her lip. Whatever secrets Kayan Orsii carried, they were not for tonight.

It took a great effort for me to turn and grasp the reins again. Even when I did, I could feel her gaze burning into the back of my hooded robe.

"If you're quite finished?" hissed the disembodied voice of Scarwing.

I nodded. Even without words, the Draken sensed my will.

A pair of wings like vast, leathery sails spread wide, pulled taut over long fingerbones tipped with claws. A sudden, thunderous downbeat, and we were catapulted up into the sky, muscles and bones pistoning beneath the saddle as I held on for dear life. The smell of cinnamon, leather and brimstone filled my nostrils as chill streamers of cloud twisted by.

When I finally turned back to look, the *Vengeance* was adrift like a matchstick against the pewter-sheened sweep of the ocean – a tiny, toylike thing hanging suspended above the paint-fleck scatter of the Eighth Fleet's sails.

I hunkered down over the padded saddle-horn and gritted my teeth. The wind clawed at me, cold and merciless.

I was coming, Grennen Vuhl. Dirge. Siara.

I was coming to do what I should have done long ago…

Much can be achieved by stealth which cannot be encompassed by brute force alone. But when caught in the lantern light, silence and subtlety are useless. It's at that point when the very best assassins remind their prey... *we are masters of brute force as well.*

Kholruun Sath'hura,
Master of the Cyvenne Chamber of Night

THE WIND-CHILL WAS vicious, clawing at my tightly wrapped woolen robes with icy fingers. Up here, floating above the moonlit sea, the only sound was the riffle and crack of air shearing off the back of the draken's wings. But I could see for miles in every direction – down to the endless ocean of Sorath, picking out a chain of islets which straggled south, lit by the candle-flame twinkle of watchtowers.

We had entered the kingdom of the Kothrai, and so we flew high and stealthy, careful not to cast a vast and bat-winged shadow across the moon.

A *kingdom*, I called it, but in truth it was nothing more than conquered ports and razed ruins, a chain of shattered trader-harbours following the curve of the Ulmoaz Archipelago as it thrust south into the Sea of Storms.

Grennen Vuhl's people were not conquerors, for they cared nothing for dominion. Spoils and chaos, loot and pillage – such was the way of raiders everywhere on Yrde. My own tribe had been little different, and there was no shame in it. Look in your mirror, and you will see that for all our conceits, we humans still have canine teeth.

Hardly as impressive as those of Scarwing, I noted.

As we followed the step-stones of the island chain we passed by the limping remnants of Dirge's fleet – a mere handful of galleys and dromons making headway south. I fought hard to suppress the urge to swoop down on them, unleashing the draken's fire... but there seemed little point.

And in any case, seeing those pitiful few vessels below us hashed in the bones of my plan. Vuhl's forces were divided – here, a splintered and jury-rigged remainder of his master's failed gambit. There – somewhere far to the north – the main bulk of his black armada, bending all sail toward Dath N'kaal. Where, wind and tides willing, Elion Morekh and his Eighth awaited them.

309

If the Saltmaster and my allies could snatch the Void Heart from under Grennen's nose, they would wheel about and trap the Kothrai between the hammer of their vengeance and the anvil of the Tarkhanden's seapower, sailing from Lormiir, Tarkand, Ironrock Harbour…

Messenger gulls had already been cast loose by Meracq D'avarian's captains, and the massing of that great fleet would cover the ocean from horizon to horizon.

A good thing, too, for it seemed that the Kothrai had reserves of their own. We swept over the craggy, volcanic ridges of the island of Yeerath, scudding between thunderheads, and saw below us a fleet of great, square-sailed barges, bobbing at anchor in the ruins of the old Tarkhanden harbour. The silver moonlight picked out the savage runes of Akhaz daubed on their banners, and hinted at the huge shapes of raptor-lizards snapping and squalling on their decks. The Coldblood, it seemed, was eager to be in at the kill, and had sent its own slave-fleets east across the chasm to assist.

At last – after what seemed a frozen eternity, up under the vault of stars – I saw a light on the horizon. We had covered leagues, Scarwing and I, all the way from the Zamaran Reach down to the cold lands where the Kothrai made their home. Low, rugged islands flickered by below us, with fishing villages huddled by the waters edge. Glowering, black stone keeps dominated the headlands – the seats, I supposed, of Grennen Vuhl's jarls and warlords.

And now the source of that light was revealed, rising up over the horizon atop a pillar of shadow. A flaming beacon, set atop Grennen Vuhl's imitation of my own dark tower – a claw of granite upthrust from the ocean, built even higher by the sacrifice of countless slaves. Though barely half the height of my own spire, it seemed crooked and vile, its geometries all wrong. Set off to one side stood the lesser laboratorium tower on its spur of rock – the place where Siara was (I fervently hoped) still held captive.

There was no place on that needle of stone for a draken to land. But I had prepared for this eventuality. I unstrapped the Incantus from my back, clutching it in front of me, and I reviewed the necessary runes and incantations again in my mind.

Silence. Shadow. The arts of the Zengaji. Levitation. Stealth. When it came to swords in the night – as I knew it would – I hoped to have already raised an army.

The prickle and flare of power wakening the Incantus brought with it a mewling, growling fit from Sei, bundled up under my robes. The little skeletal cat wriggled his way loose from his pouch, eyes gleaming, and made his way daintily to my shoulder, his tiny claws digging in through the wool of my raiment.

"There was no way I was going to leave you behind, little friend," I said, rubbing one knuckle against the smooth bone of his skull. Sei purred, arching his spine. "You're the only one who knows his way through Vuhl's labyrinth, after all…"

"And I take it you'd still like me to provide a distraction?" rumbled Scarwing. The Draken seemed more alive than ever, up here in his element. All those weeks of cramped confinement had been shrugged off like a shroud, and the great beast was literally salivating with anticipation, little drips of phosphor falling away in our slipstream.

"I would be more than grateful," I said. "Although a mere distraction is, I fear, the least of what you'll be to these poor fools."

"They harmed my soulbound brother, Kuhal Moer. They have earned what is coming for them."

Rarely have any words sounded so grim. I almost pitied the Kothrai who were to be incinerated.

Almost.

"Then good hunting, my friend. Scour the north walls – the landward side of the keep. I will drop to the east, and may havoc follow after us both!"

The draken huffed, tucking his wings in and diving. Of course – there was no need for a reply. Havoc followed *everywhere* a battle-tempered son of the Archaeon chose to go.

We fell for a handful of heartbeats – enough for the ringing in my ears to crescendo with a sharp, painful pop. And then we were skimming the scrub-forest which cloaked Vuhl's island, following a cobbled road which led up the slope toward his keep. It was bigger than it seemed – a stout, foreboding pile of masonry, built without ornamentation but with war alone in mind. Dark walls climbed terrace upon terrace to a scraggle-toothed line of turrets, armed with trebuchets and crude cannon.

No time for misgivings, old man. No time to reconsider…

Just before Scarwing announced his presence – filling his immense lungs in preparation for a blast of flame – I took hold of my Incantus and *leaped*, propelled outward by the arc of the draken's flight.

Behind me, the night erupted with red and yellow fire. Splashback scorched the woolen robe across my shoulders as I spun upside down, out over the cliff's edge, a tiny mote of sorcery, flesh and bone hanging over the ocean.[21]

Screams followed. Horns rang out as I plunged down, parallel to a cliff-face all carved with gargoyles and narrow windows, archer's slits and the barred pits of war machines. Drakenfire is by no means sorcerous – it is a chemical brew which combusts some few heartbeats after being expelled from the creature's mouth. Scarwing, like all his kind, was adept at expectorating the vile concoction in either a stream, a mist, or a boiling cloud, which clung in sticky droplets to all it touched.

A score of Kothrai defenders were roasted alive in their armour before I even glimpsed my target – a narrow stone pier jutting out from the cliff wall, all but hidden among a maze of oyster-crusted rocks. Waves surged and foamed about these black pinnacles, and to miss my mark would be as sure a death as flaying.

But I carried an Incantus with me; a cerebrex infused with the souls of the dead. Tendrils of witchfire speared out all around me, turning the metal sphere into a spectral dandelion-head – thankfully invisible to mortal eyes. I drifted the rest of the way down in utter silence, gently bending the shadows around me and muffling the splash as I entered the water.

There were two Kothrai guardsmen on the pier – a greybeard and a young fool whose black chainmail barely fit him. The old reaver likely had more than a few slit throats tallied on his sword grip – I felt no remorse for him. The young one… well. I had been just like him once, and the thought of what I would have to do almost made me pause.

But this was the nature of fate. I silently cursed those Aziphem who were watching, and rose from the water, cold and silent, a black-robed phantom with a soot-blackened dagger in either fist.

I swear the young guard never even felt the knives; a mercy, considering the fact that the old one did. I took the first Kothrai's dying confusion and focused it into a spike, driving it into the greybeard's head with a hiss of effort. It was as I had suspected – his heart stopped cold, and I was able to cradle him down to the salt-caked flagstones next to his companion. Silent.

---

21. Many sages have wondered why wool contains lanolin in such vast amounts - and why this substance is so amazingly resistant to fire. The answer, of course, lies with the draken of the Hiledoran. For, when a species is preyed upon by a fire-breathing foe, only the least flammable survive to give birth to lambs. This is also why drakenriders wear lanolin-smeared leather or coarse wool when in combat.

One of them would have to stay here. There were men above us, watching from the narrow slit windows of the keep, and they would notice if the guards outside were not huddled around their brazier. I let the Incantus float beside me and gripped the young Kothrai by the temples, binding his soul back to his flesh. Before he could come gasping up into unlife I quickly drew the knives from out of his back, tucking them into my sleeves. The old man followed, and we left the youth behind, a blank-eyed ghoul staring sightlessly out to sea. Two ragged gashes below his shoulderblades dripped blood; a meal for the spiny crabs which were already scuttling around his boots.

Black is a good colour for villainy. The night - and a good, serviceable cloak - can hide many sins. I was glad that Grennen Vuhl was so clearly bent on wickedness, because the uniform of his guardsmen was all coal-dust and midnight. My own dark raiment blended in seamlessly as I sent Greybeard ahead of me, twitching a finger to have him fumble the keys from his belt. An iron-banded smuggler's hatch blocked our path.

I concentrated. A clammy dead fist pounded against the rusted iron - once, twice, thrice.

"Is that you, Marlach?" came a drink-slurred voice from within. "I told you, there's no more rotgut in 'ere. All gone. You an' young Pox-face will have to think of other ways to stay warm!"

My thrall groaned something in reply, but the drunkards in the guardroom weren't listening. At least not until I burst through the door behind their former comrade, Cryptfeeder lashing out at head height. The man sitting across the table from me was splashed with warm arterial spray as his friend's neck was severed clean, and before he could scream I had stuffed the dead man's soul down his throat, constricting it to the width of a reed.

He clawed at his own lips, choking, while Greybeard methodically chopped through the third, hacking off his upraised arms and splitting his skull to the jawline. He was pleading with the old man even as the bones in his wrists were butchered through, his voice sucked away into sorcerous silence.

Sei jumped nimbly up atop the table, scattering greasy cards and coins. The cantrip of stealth I'd tethered to him had rendered the whole slaughter in an awful hush.

Soon three more wights rose shakily to their feet, hefting weapons. The decapitated one tucked his still-dripping head under one arm, gripping it by a hank of hair. Now we were five, and I sent my undead creeping up the spiral stair and into the water-gate barracks, pale figures swathed in black. The moonlight glistened off fresh blood and white, unseeing eyes as they fanned out, standing over their sleeping comrades.

A chopping motion of one hand, and the steel went raping in. Bellies and necks, eyes and gullets – my dead thralls knew no compassion. Men awoke from one nightmare to another, before passing swiftly into a third – the soul-bound servitude of my will.

The Incantus was warming up now. We were ten, and not a single sound had alerted Vuhl's men to our presence. Little surprise, when a mad draken was scourging the keep above! Down here, layered beneath three hundred spans of solid granite, the water-gate guard had no idea of the chaos Scarwing was sowing.

Then again, neither did I. I only hoped that the Archaeon's son knew enough to stay clear of their siege artillery. Not even scales and scutes could protect a draken from a ten-span iron arrow trailing a sharpened chain…

There was no time for me to worry. The great beast was armed and armoured far more effectively than I, and next my little band would have to creep through Vuhl's dungeons and torture pits, laboratories and workshops, forges and kitchens. All without waking the whole immense keep (for the place was nearly as large as the whole city of Oram) to our presence.

The dungeon levels were just as vile as I remembered them – a charnel-house of lightless oubliettes, half-flooded cells where rotting limbs dangled from chains, and countless iron-barred cages were stacked one atop the other. The prisoners we found down there… suffice to say that none were hale or sane enough to join my little band of their own free will. Expediency (and no small measure of compassion) forced me to cut many throats that night, but these – they were the dross and cast-offs of Grennen Vuhl's experiments, used to perfect his craft. Things which made Urzen's creations look pure and whole.

They joined me in death. *Things half-flayed and stitched together wrong, things with metal tubes and pipes impaling them, with armour bolted to their bones, whole limbs replaced with skeletal steel…*

I supposed he had let them live as a warning to others. But then why leave them down in the stinking dark? No – it was more likely that these test subjects were cherished enemies of the Kothrai warlock, and that he hoarded them to feed his own cruel self-satisfaction.

Sei scrabbled at a blood-caked wooden door, and I kicked it down to find the lumpen, flabby butcherman I had crept past in my dream. I took a certain savage satisfaction in twisting Cryptfeeder as I ran him through, watching the light go out in his porcine little eyes.

Now we were a legion of horrors indeed. Scraping, shambling, all under the geas of terrible silence which Sei carried before us. There was no room for mercy in my plan – and indeed, with the Incantus stretched to its limits by the binding of a small army, no way I could temper the cold spite of my ghouls. Bakers and cooks'-boys, turnspits and quartermasters… all were murdered in their sleep. I knew the spreading contagion of my presence could not go undetected forever.

Behind the seething webwork of my will, I prepared the second phase of my assault, releasing the bindings which would burn up souls to empower me.

"Aligning the seal of the Black Gate. Balancing the vitae flow to the seven cardinal sigils. Cerebrex bindings locked by the praxis of the Horned Eye, with restraint now unlimited to the second level…"

It was well that I did. For as my flock of ghouls came staggering up from the castle's kitchens, we finally met resistance.

The men who had been left behind here were hardly the cream of the Kothrai nation. Those I'd encountered below, at the water-gate, were the very dregs of Vuhl's army – ancients, drunks and cripples, along with one addle-brained recruit. Dirge had commanded the true hammer of the Kothrai horde in his ill-fated assault on Zamara, and the anvil – the men of the shield wall, the reavers of the line – were sailing north, plowing a broad wake toward Dath N'kaal.

The men I found arguing around the long table in the warlock's great hall were a rabble. Cowards, too, it seemed, for the thrust of their argument was how best to flee incineration on the walls. But they were over a hundred strong, and their weasel-faced leader had worked them up into a state of near rebellion.

"….is what we get for overreaching ourselves, right boys? Bloody Sarem'ec monster like that, could gobble up a shoal of skarne for breakfast! We weren't signed up to fight creatures like that! That's sorcerer's work, so it is! Let old Vuhl face it down. Him and his… his *things*."

The crowd muttered a drunken assent. Many shot shifty glances left and right, as if seeking out hidden spies. They didn't see my dead men clinging to the shadows, shuffling into position along the tapestry-hung walls.

"I mean, all right. The Tarkhanden. They've kept us down for centuries. Made us slaves. *They* have to go. But they are flesh and bone. Men with treasures, and women, and blood we can spill! Now our Lord has us fighting nightmares from beyond the chasm… things like this Deadlord, this skeletal king with his bloody great lizards and his crew of demons. That's not *right!* In a fight like that, we're just worm-food, lads, and all but fools know it!"

"Talk like that'll get you killed, Temmun," growled a voice from the crowd. "Or worse!" chimed in another. Temmun glowered, pointing one crooked finger.

"And what happens when the bloody necromancer comes here? Your bones gonna dance to his tune, Naith? Garwyn? Or do we make for the ships, tonight, and go back to free reaving? A better life, that was, than all this black armour and no grog and bloody *draken* coming down on our heads!"

I crouched in a cold, black hearth – one large enough to roast a span of oxen. And I grinned, for the sheer irony of what I was about to do next. With a pass of one open palm across my face I masked myself with the image of a yellowed, time-ravaged skull, my pale white hair hanging down between a pair of horns – one curving and sharp, the other a broken stump.

Gods help me, but I was enjoying this again.

We fell on them in silence, blades sweeping out and hacking down. Ghouls leaped up atop tables, hurling themselves bodily into the mass of Kothrai. Axes, chair legs, meat cleavers and at least one re-purposed chamber pot swung wild. Screams of horror and alarm were muffled by Sei's sorcery as he scuttled up to my shoulder, and I strode into the press of bodies hefting Cryptfeeder in a two-handed grip, chopping left and right with grim precision.

Cowards they may have been – but these men were no fools. Free reavers, Temmun had called them, and like their Faeroan counterparts they were seasoned pirates all. Scimitars and boarding axes bit deep into dead flesh. The living rallied behind their weasel-faced leader, kicking over tables as barricades, fighting back to back as teeth and broken fingernails tore into their comrades…

I had found the cold place again – the meditative calm at the heart of battle, where the light itself shifted toward cerulean blue, and time seemed to slow down. The slaved tissue within the Incantus was linked to my mind, and my own flesh was pushed beyond mortal restraints by force of raw sorcery.

To the Kothrai, I must have appeared as a blur of black and witchfire green, my blade parrying axe blows in a shower of sparks before cleaving through spines, severing arms and legs, hamstringing frantic warriors as I spun.

One may gather that our slaughter was an easy matter. It was anything but. When the living face the dead, the advantage goes to those who still have heartbeats – so long as they know how to fight. A ghoul is fiercely strong, but clumsy. And a swift swordsman can use this to his advantage.

Commanding such an assault, for me, was akin to playing chess and sparring at the same time. My mind was stretched tight across a shimmering, invisible web of witchfire, from the Incantus to my aching skull, commanding the dead to advance, to outflank, to close in from all sides on Temmun's last few men behind their barricade of tables.

A score of my dead warriors went down, hacked to ruin by Kothrai blades. The reavers used that overturned board like a shield-wall, each man guarding the next man's left, and at the last I was forced to press the assault myself, shattering the table in two with a sorcerous blast. Splinters and ashes blew wide as my ghouls clawed their way over the barricade, hungrily ripping into those who tried to flee.

I hoped against hope… But we could never have captured all of them.

Even as Temmun himself was shuddering his way into unlife, bucking against the blood-slick stones like a fresh-caught salmon, I heard the horns ring out. Shouting from above – bellowed orders, the crash and rattle of armour -

"Ware! Intruders in the keep!"

"We are assaulted! Call the guard! Rouse the legions!"

They were coming.

"No time for skulking now, little friend," I whispered to Sei. I unbound the rubric of stealth from inside his hollow ribcage. Then I held out my hand, letting the skeletal cat scurry up my arm and to my shoulder. "I hope that big lizard of ours has the wits to know the game has changed. It's us against an army now…"

At least, that's what I hoped. There were only two ways this gambit could play out.

Firstly, the entire garrison of Grennen Vuhl's keep could descend on us like a frightened herd of aurochs – more than twenty thousand men, all told, less those who had been bathed in drakenfire. Otherwise the grisly old bastard would come for me in person. Was he vainglorious enough to match wills with me, now that I possessed the mantle of the Herald?

Perhaps. But I was betting on his cruelty rather than his hubris. That, and the fact that an army whipped into subservience will always charge first, and wait for orders later.

Grennen Vuhl's men were definitely of that character. A nation of reavers and pirates promised freedom, then led along the path to tyranny? They would be terrified *not* to blindly attack, for strategy had the hollow ring of cowardice. And cowards ended up as fodder for the Master's little hobbies…

They repaid my faith. My far-sight flickered with images of bawling, cursing sergeants, of crossbows loaded, of axes gripped in hairy-knuckled fists. They came on as a roaring, undisciplined, vindictive mob, pouring down the stairways and corridors – some half dressed, half-armoured, wielding a motley ironworks of weapons torn from armoury walls and war-chests. The dregs of Vuhl's armies, I had called them, and I was right.

But they numbered in their thousands. My gathering of ghouls was one hundred and fifteen strong.

I quickly plucked Sei from my shoulder and set him atop the Incantus Instrumentorum.

"Follow me as best you can. We're usurping Abyssus for a little while, but the hoary old mollusk shouldn't mind."

Sei tilted his head to one side, little flares of light twinkling in his eyesockets.

"Oh, I saw what you did with that carrion gull. You've *always* known more than you let on. Just let the damned thing follow me, and try to keep up. Any problems… well, you know what we've practiced."

I hoped it wouldn't come to that. The thought of a domestic cat – even one with all the cunning and guile of three hundred years behind its eyes – wielding such power…

There was no time for second thoughts. A cresting wave of flesh, iron and mail crashed into the great hall, tearing the wide double doors from their hinges. Ghouls screamed, bellowing a one-note song of slaughter. The stench of rawhide, shit, sweat and fear assailed my nostrils. And the dying started.

I slipped a hand down the front of my robe, pulling loose a slim leather trace. It held a small ceramic bottle, marked with certain runes in old Khytein.

Notably, one was a blank-eyed, grinning skull.

I popped the cork, and I almost reeled backward from the chemical stench of it. Alchemy is all fine and good… but I remembered the headache from the last time I had sampled this hell-brew. A word of advice. There are those who will tell you that natural, herbal medicines are all sweetness and light, bluebells and sunshine.

They are fools.

The infusion of hellcap and bonebark slithered down my throat like a live thing – just like the blood of Sothara da'Urgon Roege.

Indeed, I mused, before the elixir of the Touched took me – the old Bone Collector's blood must have been mostly alchemist's piss by the time he finally died…

There are no pretty words for the unbinding of the restraints to the first level.

Just a scream which goes on and on, bestial and wild, a roar of hunger thrown against the night…

It was my own - at first. Sheer raving power cracked the top of my skull open – or so it felt – and poured in the white light of the Aziphem. When I had been a boy I had watched the Touched accept the spirit of Theyr or of Ciermakh in this fashion. They had been utterly possessed, their minds scoured away to madness.

A three-century-old necromancer is slightly more durable. The balance of my bones was mageblight, after all, and the crystalline filaments were marbled through my flesh like veins of quartz through stone.

I let Anghul in. I felt the looming presence of Abyssus behind him. And beyond that – as if glimpsed through a swirling mist, across a vast gulf of distance – the crazed, tortured face of my own Shard, the divinity of the Aemortarch.

I threw it all behind the edge of my sword, and *charged*.

"Any man who says that women are weak, and lack the spirit of a warrior, has never seen a lioness defending her cubs. Or met my second wife when she's drunk."

Elion Morekh,
Lord Admiral of the Faeroan Conclave of Captains

I HAVE NO idea how many fell before my blade that night.

Once, above the Urexian plain, I had gutted an entire War Keel of Anganesse while under the thrall of the black potion. It had seemed, afterward, like the nightmare of a mad berserker, a dripping red hell of severed limbs and burst entrails, of screams and pleading.

The rage of Anghul closed over my head, and my world became so again.

I stormed ahead of a tide of ghouls, things stitched together by witchfire where my steel had taken them apart. The Incantus followed at my back, levitating in a haze of sorcerous heat. Its inner cage of gold twisted this way and that, aligning webs and traceries of soul-stuff, snaring the slain and driving them onward.

I was dimly aware, as I swung Cryptfeeder through rank after rank of mad-eyed, panicked Kothrai, that my legion was growing. *Eight hundred, nine hundred, a thousand...* they rode the wild surge of my anger and ecstasy. They became mere beasts, ravenous for flesh, scrabbling on all fours as they burst through doors and swarmed torchlit galleries, hunting down the heat and hammer of human hearts.

Atrocities ensued. Fractured images piled up like bloody snowflakes, burying reason...

But it was I, the lich-king, who inspired the darkest dread.

A figure in black, the image of a grinning skull floating just above my face, white hair dripping crimson. My hands were crusted claws, matted with scraps of skin and worse - splinters of shattered bones and teeth. Cryptfeeder was four feet of unholy ruin, its guard choked with macerated flesh.

Where I walked, death followed. I believe I screamed Siara's name as I worked my butchery... but it could just as easily have been an incoherent howl. Doors charred and burst into storms of tinder as I cast them down. Stones grated and splintered at my tread, as the ancient rock of the underkeep remembered its molten birth...

And soon the Kothrai weren't making an ordered advance, or forming shield-walls at chokepoints, stairwells and gallery doors. No. They were *running*, clawing at each other, trampling the wounded as they fled.

Cowards, all of them. And dead before they knew it.

I wielded Cryptfeeder in one hand, the black iron singing as it tore through tendon, muscle and bone. With my other hand I bled power from the seething heart of the Incantus, sending jagged sheets of black fire roaring down corridors, burning men to charcoal and bones as they fled. Red-hot armour clattered to the flagstones as their souls were torn from a haze of smoke, fed into the furnace of my wrath.

There are those among you, I suppose, who would wonder why I did not simply sup on the black potion daily; why I had not unleashed the Bindings of the First Restraint to slay the Nameless Ones, or to overthrow the Council of Seven in Zamara.

I could fool myself, and argue that the herbs required were rare – that the method of their preparation took many long and tedious hours. But the truth is darker still. *I dared not.*

This dreamlike state, where I watched my body rave and hack and slaughter… It was horror and ecstasy combined. A hair's width too far, and old Anghul would have my flesh – an act of possession made all the easier by the mageblight coiled through my bones. In this killing trance the stuff grew faster than fingernails or hair, making me more potent and less human by the heartbeat.

And there was something else, too. My strategy – if such a word could be applied to such extremity – was to break through to my daughter, set her free from Vuhl's restraints… and then rely on her to complete our escape. After the fury of the black potion faded, I would collapse like wet parchment, spent. And the Kothrai warlock himself was yet to put in an appearance…

I knew where I would find him. The villain *always* waits until his last grand soliloquy.

The black potion was failing as I dragged myself up the final flight of stairs and out onto the hanging bridge. It was just as I had seen it though Sei's eyes – including the blackened starbursts of soot against the stone where Vuhl had hurled his sorcery, missing us by inches. The door of the outer tower was ajar, and flickering red light spilled out into the night. I breathed deep, feeling the power dropping away. Just a little further…

There was no hint of dawn, even after my long night of slaughter. A cold rain had begun to fall, and as I stepped out between the shark-headed gargoyles and onto the bridge I looked up, hoping to see Scarwing's shadow against the clouds. Fat, blattering raindrops carved tracks through my mask of blood.

There was no sign of the great beast. I hoped that the Archaeon's son had not been overconfident – a draken pierced by a Kothrai harpoon would be hard pressed to fly, after all.

Behind me the keep echoed with the sound of steel on steel. Screams and groans issued from a thousand barred and slitted windows. But ahead of me…

The door crashed open as I reached the centre of the bridge, revealing a wild-haired figure in black. Grennen Vuhl wore a roughspun tunic, a peasant fisherman's kilt and a thick leather apron, stained with old blood. A belt stuffed with surgical and sorcerous tools was slung about his hips.

And his arm was crooked around the neck of my daughter. A curved skinning knife was pressed to her throat.

"You disrupt my work, Lamenter," he sneered. A grin advanced across his face fitfully, in a series of disjointed twitches. It was as if the warlock had forgotten any reason to smile. "A shame. She really would have looked just like her mother. I already have the wire mechanisms perfected… all we needed was a cut here, a slice there…"

He turned, and the red light picked out a tracery of black across Siara's skin. Thick, black lines, made by the same kind of wax and charcoal marker butchers use to plan out cuts of meat.

Vuhl giggled, turning his head to almost whisper in the Stormreaper's ear.

"Such fun we could have had, with the master away. Oh, how I would have loved to see the look on his flayed face! He could never perfect Urzen's art. Not even when he stole all the plans, all the tools. Power without genius, Kuhal Moer, is like a ship without sails. Directionless. *Useless.*"

Vuhl Turned to look me in the eye, and I saw once again the ragged gouge which defined one entire side of his face. The eyeball floating in that grisly hollow burned with slow-motion flames, purple and blue.

"I won't tell you that you have even the slightest chance of walking out of here, Kothrai," I said. "But if you let her go now, your suffering will be shortened… to merely centuries."

The warlock laughed, a mad sound torn away by the wind. Rain came hissing in across the sea as we stood there facing each other, washing over the Kothrai fortress like a wave.

"You think you're the only one who commands the dead? Fool! We were ready for you and that bloody Incantus of yours…"

Grennen Vuhl lifted the knife from Siara's throat, leaving behind a thin red line where the edge had nicked her skin. And he crooked the fingers of that hand into a claw, pointing past me…

"Sa'durach Nal Kasiim!"

A weaving of power unleashed. It spun by me, a shield-sized snowflake of glittering witchfire, curving in to strike the Incantus Instrumentorum. The gold and iron spheres locked, their rotation stopped.

"A'kruin! Deshanthar S'sath…"

I recognized the words – the old speech of Khytein. It made sense. The first Incantus – the prototype for all my others – had been built by Sothara the Bone Collector, the old tyrant buried beneath the black pyramid. And I recognized their intent.

Grennen Vuhl was trying to steal my army.

I snarled, brandishing twin handfuls of power. Vuhl had woven his spells long before, waiting for my arrival. I would have to counter them with sorcery far less subtle.

I bypassed the seething hub of the Incantus, leaving it sparking and twitching in midair. My mind fragmented as I reached out to my ghouls, tasting the hot iron of blood in their mouths, feeling the dull throb of their ragged wounds…

I cut them loose. Like puppets severed from their strings, thousands of dead men fell. I caught a blurred glimpse of survivors staggering backwards, disbelieving. Saved, I supposed, in the last instant before they were slain.

"Not so easy," I slurred, struggling up out of the trance. I had just felt myself die over ten thousand times at once – not a feeling conducive to good cheer. "You may be a cunning bastard, Vuhl, but I've got a few surprises left for you yet."

Siara elbowed the warlock savagely in the solar plexus, twisting in his grasp.

"Kill him! Do it now! He can't…"

The knife settled back against her throat as Vuhl retrieved it from its chain.

"Hush now, precious. Your daddy was just about to die for us. Then we can get back to our games…"

"Grennen," I said. "I don't think you should do that…"

The Kothrai sneered, his floating eyeball blazing. "And why not? I've eradicated your army. I've driven off your bloody draken. I've got a knife to your daughter's throat! What can you do to *possibly* threaten me, you dried-up old corpse?"

I rolled the kinks out of my neck. I planted Cryptfeeder between the stones in front of me, then laced my hands together, cracking my knuckles.

"This," I said.

I raised both hands to the heavens. Twin bolts of lightning stabbed down out of the clouds, twisting columns of green shot through with emerald sparks. I brought them together, even as I saw Vuhl's lips shaping a bellowed counterspell. But he was too late. The power flared into a sphere of witchfire, cupped in both my hands. And, with a roar of sheer defiance, I thrust it down into the pommel of my sword, down through the hilt, down the fullers, and into the stone itself. Actinic light blazed from between each roughly mortared block for an instant, and then it went flickering off across the bridge, seeking out a secret Sei had shown me.

For an instant there was no sound but the hiss and patter of the rain – the rumble and grind of fading thunder.

And then Grennen Vuhl's great fortress fell apart.

It began with a sharp crack, like an axe cleaving an ironwood stump. Zig-zag fissures skittered across the rain-lashed face of the keep, toppling gargoyles into the sea. Then an entire tower sheared off at its base, grinding and juddering sideways. It twisted as it fell, smashing into another, scattering blocks of stone like chaff. A whole section of the curtain-wall caved inward, crushing the kitchens, collapsing the barracks…

Booming, grinding sounds echoed up from below. Other towers tottered and toppled, some plunging end over end into the raging sea. Men clung to the battlements as they were shaken loose, falling into a growing cloud of rock-dust and ruin.

It was like watching a glacier calving, high on the slopes of the northern Hiledoran. Less than a minute, and it was all over. The fortress which had dominated the headland was nothing but a wreck of riven stone – a makeshift tomb for thousands of Kothrai.

And how many were innocent? A terrible little voice inquired in my head. *How many poor damned peasants, servants, slaves, prisoners…*

He has a knife to her throat! Howled a much louder voice. **"My blood! My Kin! Makara's! KILL HIM!"**

I thought that Grennen Vuhl was about to rip that knife sideways at any moment. The look of horror in his one human eye was only there for an instant – only until his composure slipped back into place like an iron mask. *But it was there.*

"How…?" he croaked.

"How many died to build it? Yes – I *know* about people like you. And I know your superstitions, Vuhl. When you entombed your masons and slaves in the walls, you did it for good fortune, yes?" I smirked. "How's that working out for you?"

That little glimpse of humanity should have made the Kothrai warlock less of a monster – less frightening. It did the opposite. He tugged his own madness over his frailty like armour, determined to match my infamy, no matter the cost.

"What should I care for the death of a few slaves?" he asked, staring back over the bridge to what had once been a mighty bastion. Now the span ended with a jumbled heap of stone. "I can always enslave more. Or free them. It's rather the same thing, in the end."

This little *bon mot* seemed to amuse the Kothrai no end. I assumed, at the time, that he was simply mad. I drew Cryptfeeder from between the flagstones with a grating crunch.

"And what would you know of freedom, Vuhl? Puppet of a flayed monster? Did he let you keep your shriveled balls when he enslaved you?"

"Hah! You think that all of this was Endsong's doing? And how *dare* you talk of freedom, you vile old hypocrite. Tarkhand is to my people what Anganesse was to yours. I am a *liberator!* I have brought the Kothrai back to glory!"

I twitched my head back at the smoking ruin of the keep.

"A glorious fate indeed."

"They will be remembered as martyrs. Victims of the true monster here today. The lich who had *better not take one more fucking step, lest I open his daughter's throat!*"

I was close enough to see the flecks of spittle in his beard. Close enough to smell the alchemical balm on his breath. The warlock's one good eye bulged from its socket as he raved.

"You think I care for empire? For dominion! You idiot! I am YOU. Sorath's answer to the same damned imbalance." His face fell, suddenly creased with sadness. "Don't tell me you had it easy. Don't deny the choices you had to make were hard. He… he helped me, is all. He told me all about your path. And I… I didn't think I could make it on my own."

Siara took this momentary weakness as a chance to drive her elbow hard into Grennen Vuhl's stomach. He bent almost double as she struggled free, and the knife fell from his hand. I was already raising my blade, lining up a killing stroke, when that empty hand filled up with flames.

The Kothrai flung himself backward, dragging my daughter behind him. He twisted her arm up her back, brandishing his fistful of sorcery.

"This kills just as surely, Lamenter!" he hissed. "Try me!"

"I really don't think you should do that, Vuhl," I said.

"*And why not?* What is it this time? You're out of tricks, Kuhal Moer, and mine have only just be…"

He heard the clink and rattle of chain, and stopped. His single eye followed the chain from Siara's steel ankle-shackle, all the way across the floor of the laboratorium, to the place where it was earthed to a silver ring in the floor.

Or where it *had* been. Sei sat next to the ring, head cocked to one side, the locking pin clenched between his teeth.

"Oh, damn it all to…"

That was all he managed.

Siara Anvhaur must have been leaching power from every tome, device, jewel, blade and stone in Vuhl's entire sanctum, the whole time she was imprisoned there. A little each day, balanced by meditations which took the place of sleep… the concentration required must have been staggering. But the result was a cataclysmic. Raw sorcery erupted as halo of silver flames, blazing a full fingerlength from her skin.

It burned Grennen Vuhl's fingers to the bone. He recoiled, screeching, his inhuman eye blazing red.

A backhand slap from my daughter didn't just put the warlock down. It drove him through the open doorway, tumbling head over heels. I didn't see him strike the far wall of the tower, but I heard the stone crack and shatter. The whole claw-shaped edifice trembled beneath our feet.

"Ohhh, that feels so much better! Father, I'm sure you have so much to tell me, but there are some things in there we must take with us. Come on! Before the Kothrai bastard shakes it off!"

I have never been one for physical contact. In fact, I had never even known the slightest affection from my own sire, now just a smear of greasy ashes up in far-away Kaltensund. Nevertheless, something made me take a single faltering step forward, then another, almost collapsing on top of Siara as I threw my arms around her.

I hadn't counted on feeling anything, either. Not for someone I barely knew. But that uncanny resemblance to Makara was there, and a huge surge of relief that I had not let the one and only strand of my bloodline die. For her part, I think Siara Anvhaur was one part astonished to nine parts horribly embarrassed. Not that our host was in any condition to laugh…

For a moment I felt her tense, the black jewel at my throat burning hot between us. Then she reached up, laced her fingers behind my back, and squeezed.

"You are a sentimental fool, Father," she said. "And I appear to be hugging a blood-soaked skeleton. But… thank you. I knew you would come." She broke away, smiling sadly. "Now we just have to plunder Vuhl's laboratorium, and find some means of escape. One little death-blow like that won't keep him down for long."

I followed her through the door and out of the rain, probing the feeling of goodness and contentment as if it was a rotten tooth. Face it, I told myself – after three centuries of deliberately cultivated evil, being a good father won't come easy. Necromancers don't spend their dotage on a bench outside the local tavern, drinking cider in the sun with the other old men. Necromancers *always* go down in flames.

Now it was Grennen Vuhl's turn. Time to summon the draken.

I tried to reach out to Scarwing with my will, but the roiling clouds above were fractured with lightning, and the great Draken was likely high above them, avoiding a fatal jolt of power. I watched Siara methodically gather a few tomes, a jeweled knife, some rolled-up scrolls and a fist-sized globe of jade into an altar-cloth, tying it into a bundle. Then she took down her bone-handled swords from their place on the wall, along with a two-span rod of black wood, carved with runes.

"I'm the granddaughter of a blacksmith. You…you saw him. Or at least what he's become. The Void Heart may not be made of steel, but when Zael used it was a sword, he gave it the *nature* of a sword. Something like that, from *beyond*… it has to imprint on this reality. So it's a blade. And this is every scrap of information Dirge and Vuhl collected about how to reforge it."

"Reforge it?" I asked, trailing one hand over the chain-hung frame which had held my flayed old nemesis. "Why?"

Siara shouldered her bundle. The swords hung at her hips, the staff clenched tight in her hand.

"An armoury full of blades which can slay the Aziphem. In the hands of an army of Nameless Ones. Backed up by the power of the Dwellers. Sound about right?"

"He… he's going to war against the Gods?"

"Have you ever known Dirge to lack ambition?"

I shrugged.

"Oh, no doubt. It's just that…"

I may have had a good point. I don't honestly remember. Because about that time, the roof of Vuhl's tower was torn off.

It was the shadow of Abyssus – a great, gelid fist of darkness, closing tentacular fingers around the stone until it splintered. Four levels above us were shorn clear off as the shadow recoiled, hurling a storm of masonry out into the rain-lashed night. The chains on Dirge's empty rack clattered in the wind.

And I looked up- and up, and up again – into a looming tidal wave of darkness, of water stained black by the stolen shadow of Sorath's death-god. Grennen Vuhl stood poised atop the tip of the wave, a great two-handed staff clutched in his hands. And inside the wall of water burned the ghost-lights of demon eyes, blood-red and malicious. There were hundreds of them.

"Leaving so soon?" cackled the Kothrai. I saw that Siara's powerful blow had shattered his collarbone, but that he had bound himself up again with necromancy. "I heard your little supposition, child. An army of Nameless. Indeed. Nine so far, but many more to come. Why do you think we make war on Tarkhand? Their priesthood will make perfect fodder for my flesh mills. These, however… well. There have been accidents. *Mistakes.* Some of my children failed to live up to my standards." He leered. "You must know how that feels, Kuhal Moer."

The sun must have risen behind the walls of cloud, because a grainy grey light painted the laboratorium. It illuminated the reason I was hardly listening to the Kothrai – villainous last-stand speeches, in my opinion, being cheap currency.

When Sei had come here before, it had been a dark and red-lit vault, seen from the eye-sockets of a dead cat. I had missed the fact that it was, in truth, a great shrine.

To me.

When Grennen Vuhl said that I must know shame for my children…

"Just as *you* have failed to live up to *mine.* You. *My father!* This girl-child beside you is not of your flesh. She is spawned of sorcery, just like me! The only two necromancers born in a thousand years, you and I. Fated to liberate our people from the crushing weight of empire! Guided by the hand of the same ascendant!"

I was stunned silent. *All those statues. All those paintings. Framed, glass-cased artifacts from my old life.* The life before I encysted myself in a dark tower, cocooned away from the world.

Grennen Vuhl was mad. Mad, mad, mad. Not just raving and foaming like a proper, hate-filled villain. His mind was twisted up in ways which made simple murder seem clean and wholesome.

"All I wanted to do with Jerrold Sinder's hand," I grated. "Was hack it off."

"Ahh… but he *made* you. He shaped you. As he has done for me. And now that I, your Son, have become your Lord – we will rule all of Yrde together!"

And what a happy family we would make, I thought. The father, the son, and a mad godling, making war on each other while ripping into the underbelly of the Divine.

"One problem," I said, drawing in power as I did so. Dirge's vile force had leached into the metal of the rack, and I drew it out like poison from a wound, coiling it through the layered steel of Cryptfeeder's blade. "I *disown* you, you insane, pathetic little abortion. Siara Anvhaur is my only child. I have *no son!*"

Which was eminently true. But which also had the desired effect. It pitched the Kothrai into a paroxysm of rage.

"Very well! You prove as worthless as my father of flesh and blood! *So you can share his fate!*"

The wave of shadow flared up, tapering into a pillar of spikes. At the same time, black flame boiled up from around Vuhl's floating eye. Instinct picked it. There was the key. *Take the eye, and claim the Shadow.*

"Meet your grandchildren, Kuhal Moer. Those who were too weak to become Nameless. I call them the Unmade. But you can just scream while they take you apart. They'll understand."

I turned to Siara as the wave began to split open, unfurling like a curtain.

"You take care of these wretched by-blows. I'll go for Vuhl. The eye…"

"*Commands the shadow.* I'm not completely stupid, Father!" she smiled, a fragile little gesture. And then she slid and locked the staff in her hands, making it snap out to double its length. A curved scythe-blade hinged open at each end with an oily little click. "I never much wanted a brother anyway, if it's all the same to you."

"He's too ugly to take after his mother. Too mad to be any blood of mine. Well…" I squinted. "Perhaps."

Then the lightning flared. The wave crested and broke, becoming a raving rush of dark tentacles. Grennen Vuhl raised his mace-headed staff and leaped down toward us, killing light flaring from between its blades. A hundred crippled, red-eyed demons threw themselves into battle, howling in equal parts bloodlust and agony.

We met them as equals. As *family*.

I cast out a half-dome shield of witchfire before us as the lashing tentacles struck. And the power of Abyssus drove back his shadow, making them recoil. Those which so much as brushed the barrier smoked and split, dripping night-black fluid. At the same time Siara drew back her arm, raising her double-scythe high. A throng of broken things staggered and lurched across the exposed tower-top – Nameless Ones who had failed. Each was more hideous than the wretches I had slain in the dungeons below, and it was obvious from their empty eyes and grey, sagging flesh that they had been raised from a watery grave.

Before they could burst through my witchfire shield Siara loosed her blade, sending it spinning up into the sky with a sound like draken wings. The rhythmic thud and whir cut the air as it arced out into the rain. At the top of its trajectory lightning flared from the clouds around it, making the whole wood-and-steel weapon blaze with blue fire. Then it curved back in again, returning to my daughter's outstretched hand.

Between her and the weapon stood a horde of horrors.

There was a brief, sizzling interlude of raving power and burning flesh, accompanied by a sound like tearing parchment. Then the rune-carved handle slapped into Siara's palm, and two score of the Unmade fell apart, the light going out in their eyes.

Things part artifice, part rotting flesh shuddered and sparked amid their own blackened blood. I saw faces driven full of nails, jaws replaced with lamprey-toothed feeding tubes, open chest cavities alight with arcane gems…

A single focusing of the will blasted them to ashes. The runes on that black staff glistened red, like the embers of a dying fire.

"Impressive," I said, bringing Cryptfeeder up to guard. "I thought you said you were more of a warbard than a warrior?"

Siara grinned. Gods, at that moment it was as if my poor doomed love was standing beside me again!

"There's a reason," she said "Why they call me the *Stormreaper*, Father."

Grennen Vuhl landed in a crouch, flanked by a legion of his arcane experiments. Half-human, broken things scrabbled and keened for blood.

"Come on then, girl!" he shouted. "Just as I promised you! Come here and *end this!*"

The butt of his mace-staff struck the flagstones with a concussive blast of force, sending us both sliding back, our hair streaming out behind us in a nimbus of sorcerous sparks. But neither of us faltered.

"You heard the man," I said.

And we both charged at the same time.

The Unmade were fiercely strong - as strong as only half-demons re-animated through sheer hatred can be. Gods grant that you never face even *one* such monster, let alone a whole mindless pack of them. Were it not for the outrage of Abyssus, his soul calling to his shadow, then the terrible after-sickness of the black potion would have left me defenceless before them. As it was, I watched from outside myself as I ran forward, screaming, the blade of Cryptfeeder slicing in a great blurred figure of eight.

I hacked down one rank of Vuhl's 'children' at the knees, a second at the waist, a fourth across the chest, and a last through a dozen lifeless necks. Heads popped like the corks from magnums of sweet Ghurami wine.

Siara spun her double-scythe with lithe grace, turning as we plunged into the ranks of Vuhl's creations so that a shimmering double-wheel of death surrounded her. She let the runic staff spin from hand to hand, rolling it across her back as the Unmade closed in, then sending it hissing out in a deadly spiral, flensing copper and iron from flesh and bone. Not even the unnaturally tough spawn of the warlock could survive its edge. They were macerated, scattered on the rain-lashed wind, and the broken tower-top ran slick with gore.

Grennen Vuhl tried to bring the hammer of the Shadow down on us, but a hastily flung shield twisted his fury aside. I pelted across the red-stained granite, utterly focused. Waist-thick pillars of shadow punched through the floor around me, through tables and workbenches, splintering bookcases and tangled glass alchemical apparatus as they went. Not one came close. And now I was ahead of Siara, letting her turn to face the resurgent Unmade.

I saw Vuhl's single eye widen with shock as time slowed down. Cold blue light flickered from every airborne raindrop as I locked my knees and slid across the flagstones toward him, a shield woven above me by one hand, Cryptfeeder swinging in the other.

I heard a sound like pheasants rising from an autumn wood, and I felt my daughter's double scythe come whickering past overhead, the rain washing a film of crimson from its blades. They seemed to turn so slowly in that interminable instant, catching the reflected flash of lightning far out at sea.

Vuhl saw them too, and he jinked left in time for the reaping wheel to pass him by. His mace was spinning, *bending* with the force of the blow he had aimed to stay my blade, stop my charge, drive me back. His teeth were gritted, his beard jangling with iron rings as he put his whole body into the strike…

But my attack was merely a feint. Mace-head and sword blade came together with a concussive, grinding crash, and as they did we collided chest to chest, both of us stunned by the impact. There was no time for words. No time for even the most animal growl of hatred.

Only time, in fact, for me to drop the shield from above us, thrusting my hand deep into the gory cavity in Vuhl's head.

My fingers closed around the eye, and I felt a terrible, burning cold slither up my arm to the shoulder. The Kothrai screamed, collapsing to his knees. Gelid pillars of shadow reared up as his mace clattered to the ground, and he spread his fingers wide…

No time to control it. No time to rip it loose. But that whirling pair of blades would be reaching its apogee about now, and when it came back to my daughter's hand it would punch clear through the shadow. It would tear Grennen Vuhl in half, burying a span-long claw of steel in his back.

I held him at arms length as he bucked and clawed, fingers scrabbling, lips moving soundlessly…

There. A tiny flash of light, as the storm spent its final energy against Siara's flying blade.

It came rushing back, quick as spite. I fought the ice, fought the pain, and *twisted*, hearing something shatter and crunch like dislocated bone.

The double scythe seemed to move so slowly. So slowly. End over end, upright now, almost lost to me as its killing edge lined up.

So I didn't see the blades retract. I didn't hear the snick and slide of hidden mechanisms, closing it down to a mere hardwood staff two spans long.

All I saw was Grennen Vuhl's smile, his teeth red with his own blood.

"… end this." he croaked.

Then the staff stopped spinning.

Its coin-sized, hardwood end rushed up on me, slicing through the air over Vuhl's shoulder.

It struck me full in the middle of my forehead, and the world flickered, black and red.

I looked down, what may have been only a heartbeat later. My hand was still clenched inside the warlock's head, and the 'blight, as far up as my elbow, had stained my skin midnight black.

Siara's staff clattered to the ground as I blinked, my eyelids as heavy as stone.

The next shock I felt was both my knees hitting the cobbles. Then the world tilted sideways, and a hand of cold stone slapped the side of my face. Rain pattered down on my upturned cheek. A straggle of hair lay across my vision.

I saw a pair of boots. I saw a small, pale hand, gripping a bone-hafted sword.

Saw it rise up.

Blinked again. Slower this time. Harder to open my eyes…

"I'm sorry," said a far-off voice.

Then something slammed into my temple with the weight of colliding worlds, and darkness took me.

"Soul, mind, and flesh. Three parts to the whole. A trinity, just like mother, father and child. Like the Divine, his Aziphem, and the race of Man. The three fit together into a circle, and a circle closed cannot be broken. But we can flip the tiles. We can slide and shift the fragments within it. And, with careful manipulation, we can perform sleight - not just of hand - but of spirit and intellect as well."

Aucharic Scavagne,
coven-master of the reborn order of the Blinded Seers

ONCE, LONG AGO, I had been captured by Jerrold Sinder – in those far-off days when he had been a mortal man, possessed of flesh and bone, and a name which wasn't Dirge Endsong.

I had expected to wake up chained to some gruesome rack, but instead I had awoken on silk sheets, in the palatial heart of the Angan governor's own Keel.

I opened my eyes – one swollen shut and crusted, the other merely sore. Pain had dragged me up out of sweet unconsciousness, and now it clawed at my wrists, ankles and throat.

Ahh, yes. This time it was the rack I had expected.

I twisted my head to the left, and saw cruel iron shackles stretching my arm out against a frame of blood-stained wood. Right, and it was the same. A loop of iron pinned my neck to the boards, while a half-mask clamped down across my mouth, making it hard for me to breathe.

Not, of course, that I truly needed to. I had been functionally dead for centuries. But the body has its own memories, and in straits like these, the urge to scream and curse is a strong one.

I had been betrayed.

Oh, of that I was certain. By my own flesh and blood, no less! If – and here, a slithering paranoia reared its head – if indeed Siara Anvhaur was my daughter at all. The resemblance, the mannerisms – all could have been taught, crafted, wrought by Dirge himself as the sweetest kind of trap.

What weapon sneaks into even the most secure fortress, slowly undermining the will of the most powerful tyrant? *Loneliness. Emptiness.*

If hope was the bait, then here I was, skewered on the hook.

I could barely move anything except my eyes as I took in the room. No dank and dripping dungeon, this – after all, I had collapsed several mountains' worth of stone on top of Vuhl's slave pits. No – this was a replica of a room I had seen before, long ago and far away. Urzen's high aerie in Korisal.

This was far from pleasant news. The blue-white flames of gas lamps reflected from an arc of curved mirrors above me, and behind them the shadows were filled with the gaunt, skeletal outlines of machines. Three hundred years would have been long enough for Dirge or his minions to salvage the mad artificer's creations from the wreckage of his keep, or at least to craft exact replicas.

And that meant only one thing.

They were going to make me one of the Nameless.

"He's awake," said a cold, clinical voice behind me.

Siara.

I strained at my shackles, summoning up every ounce of power… but there was nothing left. Even when I arched my back against the boards I could not pull them from their mountings. My eyes burned with rage as she stepped out in front of me, a sardonic little smile on her lips.

"Pleasant dreams, Lamenter?" she asked. She was dressed in a floor-length butcher's apron over her leather armour, and her hair was bound up in a twist of black cloth. Apparently things were going to get messy. She patted my cheek and looked past me, into the dark. "Oh, I'm *sure* they were. But just to set your mind at ease, I'll tell you *why.*"

Now I heard the rattle of surgical steel, and the shuffling footsteps of someone checking all of those alchemical and sorcerous engines. Grennen Vuhl's voice reached me at the same time as his salt-and-baitfish stench.

"See? She really *is* your daughter. Can't resist a chance to pontificate! Hurry, girl! He's coming. *Now.* If all is not in preparation…"

"You'll have to get used to us being equals, Grennen dear," sighed the Stormreaper. "Didn't that beating we gave you convince you as much?" She turned back to me as the rack swung down through ninety degrees, becoming a flat table. Now I could see great seething globes of preservative balm, trays of hooked knives, tubes of swirling witchfire caught between crystal globes…

"With you out of the way, the Doom will fall. Sarem will be in disarray. Just the right time for someone to appear out of the

Desolation, hmmm? A witch-queen, who will sweep away the impotent Tabernacle to become the *living child of their God*. Convenient, yes?"

A hefty clunk of metal on wood. I twitched my eyes left. It was a two-handed bonesaw, and my gaunt face was reflected in its blade. Vuhl grimaced.

"The witch gets Sarem. I will rule Sorath. Our agents in Akhaz are poised to strike when the Coldblood is removed from the situation. We thought… perhaps your friend Kayan Orsii would like Hmai. Tsargon Urd is a poor emperor, and not made for such times as these."

Once again, the pair of them loomed over me, haloed by gaslight. All I could do was focus my hatred at them both.

"Ohh, I know what he's thinking. What about the Dwellers? What about Dirge Endsong?" Grennen Vuhl smiled, and blue sparks popped and seethed around his sorcerous eye. "His place is not in this world. He knows something about the Outer Dark which you don't, see? He'll become a hunter of Aziphem, slayer and usurper of Gods…"

I heard the creak and boom of a huge, heavy door. The temperature suddenly dropped, making frost bloom on every glittering blade.

"But who, out of all those here, has the power to resurrect *them?"*

My two attendants froze, bowing their heads. And Dirge came stalking into the room, robed and hooded, his voice all honey and steel. He came to stand at the foot of my torture-table, his hands gripping its edge as he leaned over me.

"*You*, Kuhal Moer. Forged and refined flawlessly into a vessel of power. A conduit between the darkness of the Shards and our flimsy little world. I *felt* what you did with Kharnath. With Aesurn. With the rotting scraps of Anghul. With that power, I will raise the Aziphem I slay. I will bind them, and bend them to my will!"

He actually had fingers, I noted. And a skull upon which to hang his pale and riven face.

As Dirge pushed back the hood of his robe I saw that he had been artfully wrapped and draped around the body of a thrall – a still-living man enslaved to his will. The slick, bloody folds of the Angan's flayed skin had been pinned into place, and only an occasional twitch and whimper from the poor wretch beneath betrayed the fact that my host was still bodiless.[22]

---

22. The worst of it is, no matter how vile and obviously unnatural a master, or how self-destructive his creed, there will always be someone who volunteers for this kind of thing. The world is never going to be short of martyrs in waiting - and they are never the sick old men who keep their hands on the holy books. And the gold.

"Had you not spent centuries keeping Zael and Esau chained, you would be useless to me, barbarian. As it is, I can only call your continued existence a delightful co-incidence."

With a brisk nod, Dirge set his cronies to work. I saw his mask of flesh slip, and caught sight of the terrified eyes of the slave beneath for a second, before a pale, slim-fingered hand teased the bloody skin back into place.

Siara clamped an iron halo to my head, tightening the screws. A long skein of braided mageblight filaments – like Kell Du'ath's hair – looped from this device to a twisted hourglass creation, in which pale liquids bubbled. There was something in the lower bulb, clamped in a tiny brass claw...

It was Makara's jewel.

"We are not monsters, no matter what you think," said Siara, kissing me lightly on the forehead. "You will be with her forever. It was what you always wanted. And this way, you can step aside gracefully. In my new age, you will be revered as a legend."

Now I really tried to burst free of my chains. I thrashed and bucked, feeling the steel cut into my wrists and ankles. But it was no use.

"Now, now!" giggled Dirge. "There's no need for such profanity. Why, perhaps your little jewel will become the centrepiece of your daughter's crown." He looked sharply at Vuhl. "Well? What are you waiting for?"

The Kothrai winced, holding up a handful of long, barbed skewers. Each one was tipped with a faceted red gem.

"First... my Lord... we will enact the binding. There will be a brief moment during which you are vulnerable, but as you can see," he grinned "your greatest foe is at your mercy. Then you will have his flesh, and the unique structure of mageblight which makes him so... instrumental to our purposes."

With that he plunged the first steel spike into my shoulder. I won't pretend it didn't hurt. But there was a panic rising beyond the pain as I watched Vuhl methodically skewer my flesh. I saw their purpose, now.

Dirge was going to possess me. Take my body. And my mind would be trapped in the black jewel...

Siara spun out a thin filament of 'blight, clear and slim as spiderweb. With it she wove an intricate pattern between the gem-tipped barbs, criss-crossing my chest like the geometries of a summoner's circle.

"It will all be over soon," she whispered, as Vuhl lifted a heavy black medallion from its velvet wrappings. Tiny hooked teeth seemed to flex and writhe on its lower side.

"The wardings we have woven snuff out his power. Through this, you will usurp his flesh."

The Warlock lifted the dark medallion high. Dark triumph blazed in his eyes – one human, one utterly alien. Siara's smile was almost pitying. And Dirge…

Began to unravel.

I was blurring out of consciousness as the world grew dim around the edges. But I saw the pins slide out in a thousand places across Dirge's stolen form. I watched as his flayed skin peeled away, with a slick, sucking sound, leaving his thrall's naked body dripping red. The coils and ribbons of him peeled away and hung in the air above the rack, a score of ragged ends drifting like kelp in an offshore swell.

His face leered down at me, one eye burning white, the other a bloodshot orb.

"Hush, now. A moment's pain, and then you will be gone. It will all be over. Your suffering, your guilt…"

Grennen Vuhl pressed the black medallion into my chest, over my dormant heart. I felt a sharp spike of pain as filaments burrowed into me, filling my chest with sharp wires. Then I felt the caress of flayed-skin ribbons, tightening around my arms and legs. A swirl of bloody red, gore pattering down across my face, and the world blurred red.

"An interesting process," I heard the muffled voice of Vuhl saying. "For an instant, souls and minds, bodies and power are all in flux. Then one forces the other out."

I heard Siara agree, while trying to will the tendrils of Dirge out of my nose, away from my clenched teeth. I would have to breathe soon, and then he would have me. Wrapped up in the usurper's skin from now until he brought about doomsday! At least my oblivion would be with the one I loved.

At the edge of the darkness, I saw her face. Just like in my abyssal dream – but this time her eyes blazed with rage.

"Don't you dare give up, you bastard! Don't you dare! *If you think you know our daughter now, then you never knew me at all!"* I opened spectral arms to her, imploring. A backhand slap brought the taste of blood to my tongue. *"You don't* get *to give up, Kuhal Moer! There are machinations here, below the surface…"*

Phantom pain awoke something primal in me. I didn't want to die. Not here, and not now. Not without a fight.

Despite the arcane shackles cutting me off from death's Shard, I still possessed my own will. Strong enough to raise the spirits of dead Gods, if Dirge was to be believed. And certainly enough to strike back at the decay which was worming through my flesh and spirit.

Witchfire green scourged into the red. I felt as if my mind had been turned inside out for a moment, a sensation of falling, weightless…

Then I heard Dirge's scream. It was more outrage than pain, but it made me redouble my efforts, carving into his naked soul with blades of hatred.

"No! You can't resist me! I will have your flesh, Khytein! All the precious architecture of your blighted bones!"

My eyes opened behind a tangle of flayed-skin ribbons, whirling and knotting like the coils of a jellyfish. Through them I saw the shadow of Grennen Vuhl rear up, backlit by flaring sorcery.

"You want his power?" snarled the Kothrai. A jagged blade flashed in his hand, and his fingers stabbed down through the gyre of flesh, gripping the medallion on my chest. "You want to *Ascend?* To betray my faith, and leave me behind?" Steely fingers bit deep. I felt a tangle of wires pulled taut inside me, binding up my spine, coiling around my ribs. They creaked as Vuhl heaved, ripping the sigil of iron from my breast.

"Then I will have yours!"

The knife came down in a hissing arc. It sheared through the wires with a sound like a lyrecaster thrown into a furnace. And, as the tattered whirlwind of Dirge Endsong tried to pull loose, to rise and reform, Grennen Vuhl thrust the medallion deep into the gaping side of his head.

There was a flash of utter darkness. For a heartbeat, we were among the Dwellers themselves, lost amid a crazed topography of twisted angles, drowned in the mad, insect chittering and screaming of their endless, orgiastic feast.

Then something cracked, all the way down to the heart of Yrde. I was struck, as if by a hammer-blow, by the image of something huge and scaly, rough and half-formed, turning over in its sleep down there.

The bloody tangle of Dirge was torn away from me, with a sensation like hooks tugging at my skin. The manacles and loops of iron burned hot where they bit into my flesh, and I smelled the wood of the torture-table beginning to char.

Then the whole room shifted to the right, sinking with a rumble and a groan. Gas-lamps wheeled and spattered burning fuel. Mirrors cracked, crazing my reflection.

The entire edifice – a lower level of Vuhl's tower, I assumed – was trying to screw itself around in a circle, centred on the Warlock himself. I caught a glimpse of Dirge's face, stretched out like a carnival mask and screaming. His whole flayed form was drawn in, flaring wide…

And then he wrapped around Grennen Vuhl, the touch of his bloody skin burning the clothes away from the Kothrai's flesh. Wool combusted in an oily gout of smoke. Leather crisped and charred. And the two vile things… *merged*.

The tower lurched again as Vuhl convulsed, clawing at his face with both hands. Strips of pale white skin bound him in a suffocating grip. The floor beneath his feet tried to twist clockwise, shearing beams, breaking arches, shattering keystones…

The last I saw of him was a distorted hulk, eyeless and malformed, limbs twisting and popping from their sockets as the power of Dirge took him under. Then the floor gave way, and half of the room simply fell away into the sea below us. Vuhl and his master were lost in a rumbling cataract of stone and wood, cast down as the grey light of day spilled in with a blast of rain.

But, lost as he may have been, there was still time for Dirge to enact one final infamy.

Grennen Vuhl had said that all was in flux, as the sorcery of Urzen bound souls and flesh together. And I was the fulcrum – the pinch in the hourglass. Just as the Warlock's scrabbling hands disappeared into darkness, I felt something squeeze past me, pushing my mind aside as it slithered by. It was akin to the sensation of two eyeballs forced into one socket – a liquid, pressurized pain which made me slam my skull back against the boards.

The iron halo bolted to my brow crackled with witchfire. The skein of mageblight sizzled.

And I heard the echoing laughter of Jerrold Sinder, freed from his prison of cursed flesh.

Freed… into the black jewel.

I twisted my neck until the iron sawed into my throat. I tried to scream, but the half-mask wrapped tight around my face choked the horror in my throat. The essence of my foe poured into the blown-glass bulb, wrapped the gem in fingers of fire… and then it was gone. The glass crazed and shattered as the smooth black jewel fell from its mounts, smoking hot.

Once again, the building heaved beneath me. For the moment, at least, I had problems more pressing than Dirge's survival.

Such as my own.

For a moment, the heavy torture-table I was pinned to balanced on the edge. I was certain I was going to fall into the smoking abyss behind whatever the Angan and his Kothrai slave had become.

Then I felt hands tugging at my restraints. Bolts loosened, and metal bands clattered away. Through the dust and smoke of the disintegrating tower, I made out the face of my daughter, the Stormreaper.

"Before you try to kill me," she said, worrying at the neckbrace which still held me down. "You'll have to admit that my plan was a good one. Hopefully they kill each other before we get clear of this place."

I tore the leather straps apart, and cast down the half-mask which had gagged me. My mouth tasted of tomb-dust and oily tin.

"*All of Sarem?* Gods and demons, child. At least you didn't sell me out for less!"

Siara offered me a bright smile, heaving me to my feet.

"These two play for high stakes, father. But while they thought they were weakening my will, all those long days of imprisonment… I was weakening *theirs*. It wasn't hard to drive a wedge between them."

"Grennen Vuhl," I winced, rubbing some life back into my hands. In a manner of speaking. "Has some *serious* family issues. And, I'd take it, a deep aversion to licking anyone's boots."

I swung my feet off the bench, and held my head in my hands. When I was certain that my body blocked what I was doing from Siara, I reached out and palmed the black jewel from amongst a sad little drift of broken glass.

"*Serious family issues.* Huh! And quite a pair we make too, Lord Lamenter."

"You could have told me what you had in mind, girl."

"And *you* could have ruined it all by knowing. Dirge doesn't just feed on your suffering, father. It's like a fine wine to him. He *savours* it. Poor playacting would have tasted like a goblet full of piss."

We staggered together to a row of hardwood cupboards, which Siara threw open. She shucked off her apron and belted on her pair of swords, taking up her double-scythe staff. I had barely enough presence of mind to shrug on a woolen robe, then attach Cryptfeeder's scabbard across my back.

"How do I know this isn't some elaborate doublecross?" I muttered, fingers fumbling at the leather traces of my sword-harness.

"Apparently, if I die, the Doom goes with me. Incentive enough, even without a continent to rule…"

"It's *already* an elaborate doublecross. Vuhl and I made a deal. He takes Dirge, while I…" She gave an apologetic little smile. "Well, I'm supposed to have slit your throat already. He's gotten what he needed from you in any case – the pattern of the Mageblight inside you. He'll alter himself until he can work your little trick with the dead Aziphem."

"Won't that hurt?"

"He'd carve his own eye out with a spoon for power. Oh… wait a second. He already *has!* Grennen Vuhl only looks sane and manageable by comparison to Dirge, you know. But, in this fight, a sane enemy may be more dangerous than that ancient lunatic of yours."

"So…" I asked. "What's our plan if they *don't*, by some good fortune, tear each others throats out?"

We took the stairs to the broken tower-top two at a time. The grinding, roaring crash of dying masonry echoed up behind us.

"I found the ritual which Vuhl wanted, buried deep in Urzen's Scrolls of Binding. He copied *those* from the *T'zolmec Ch'aa* of the Blinded Seers, before the Ythean Empire era. The vitae flow…"

"Short version," I grated, searching the sky for Scarwing. The clouds had broken apart into tangled grey skeins, harried by a cold south wind.

"He'll be weak after the fusing. Just as the Undying One of the Blinded was, after the ritual sacrifice. We take the Void Heart to him, and chop! No more problem."

"The Void Heart, eh?" I said, tasting sea-salt and smoke on the air. But no stench of chemical drakenfire.

"You know. A sword, quite large, black, filled with stars?"

My will was a feeble candle-flame. So much lost. So much…

"We don't have it," I croaked, unable to sense Scarwing anywhere. No lingering hint of the great wyrm's death, no tiny spark of his mind battered unconscious – nothing.

"But you're *here!* You got the note I sent with Sei!"

Another little mystery. My bone familiar was nowhere to be found either. It wasn't like either he – or the Archaeon's own son – to slink away as cowards.

"Aye. And blood called me here in any case. Tarkhand's last honest Saltmaster, our friends, and a Hmai witch named Kayan Orsii have gone after the blade. I… I couldn't let you die."

"*Orsii?* Damned fates, father! She and Vuhl have been in conclave for weeks! It wasn't for love that he offered her the throne of the Cold Land! That bitch has *secrets*, and I can't pry them out."

I thought about those amber eyes. That small, pale hand in mine as I gripped Scarwing's reins.

We have unfinished business between us, you and I...

"Then let us hope she plays the same twisted games you do, daughter. By now, their fleet must have made landfall at Dath N'kaal."

"She... she would have told me. I used the skrying mirror too. We talked when Vuhl was gone. She said..."

"She might think," I chuckled. "That you would give the game away by knowing."

She scowled. Even that, damn her mother's memory, was desperately pretty.

"Not fair, father. Not even *remotely.*"

The tower shifted again beneath us – sharply this time, a row of shattered window-frames falling away with a sickening lurch.

"So... we don't have the Void Heart. Another of the Kothrai's allies sails at the head of our fleet. And your bloody draken is missing, leaving us stranded on this tottering pile of rocks. How, may I ask, do we get *out of here?*"

I heard the laughter first.

Sick, rasping laughter – the kind which you'd expect to hear from the throat of a hanged man. It didn't stop, but grew louder, unhinged and wild, as something scrabbled its way over the parapet.

Something far too large, surely, to be a human hand?

"Oh – you *don't*," said a voice all gristle and spite. "No no. No no no. You get to stay, and play, and keep me company. The little traitor girl and her dear, departed *daddy.*"

I watched, horrified, as a second set of fingers curled around the blackened stone. Each one was as long as Siara's forearm, lashed up with tendons like steel cables. The skin which covered them was mottled, heavy with ripe, full blisters.

"You couldn't just have brought the damned sword, could you?" swore Siara, snapping her double scythe open. "If those Blinded Seers were right, this is *not* going to be pretty..."

"Isn't it a bad idea," I asked, "To take aesthetic advice from blind men?"

I was already backing away. My attempts to muster some remnants of power were fruitless – a mere pop and flicker of witchfire around my fingers.

Then Grennen Vuhl heaved himself up over the parapet, and I knew we faced our deaths.

The Kothrai had been changed out of all proportion by the warping influence of Dirge. Centuries steeped in the Outer Dark had done things to the Angan sorcerer, and when he took Dirge's power into himself Vuhl had laid his own flesh open to those blasphemies. Now he was drawn out tall and thin, roped with lumpen, misplaced muscle. Naked, he was a nightmare of weals and scorches, scars interlocked across his chest and belly. The shape of a pair of flayed hands scrabbled toward his throat… Dirge's, at a guess. And the whole lumpen mass of him was burned – still steaming, raw and red, blistered and broiled.

But it was his face which held me. The tangle of his beard was still there, depending from a chin and jaw half-flayed and dripping. Iron rings still clattered amid the thicket of black, but they were melted and distorted, the runes carved into their surfaces all out of shape. From the lower lip upward, there was nothing left of Vuhl's face. A dome of scar tissue, ridged like a fingerprint, pale as an eggshell. It was cross-hatched with a grid of wounds, and bored through with two ragged holes – bloody craters for eyes. Inside them moved the seething, chittering flesh of the Dwellers in Darkness. It dripped like molten wax down Vuhl's bony cheeks, evaporating into twists of smoke.

"I feel – rejuvenated. Vigorous. *Young*. But ohhh…" and now that eyeless gaze locked on us, and a red, pointed tongue licked out over a row of yellowed teeth. "I am so, so *hungry!*"

One last trace of Dirge Endsong coiled around Vuhl's head. That scarified dome of a skull was haloed by a dozen ribbons of flayed skin, spreading out from the nape of his neck and hovering over all like a nest of cobras. Bereft of eyes, the Warlock used these tendrils to follow us as we backed away.

"Sweet damnation," whispered Siara. "He's a *monster…*"

I believe I was prepared to die in that instant. I dragged Cryptfeeder from its scabbard, spitting on the shattered flagstones. Oh yes. I was my father's son, and I would die like a Khytein savage, with a blade in my hands.

But then a shadow flickered over us. Something immense, angry, and trailing a mephitic stench of sulphur crashed down atop the tower between us and Grennen Vuhl. A blast of hot wind drove us to our knees.

I caught a glimpse of leathery wings spread wide, heard a hissing, roaring challenge –

"No. *That's* a monster," I managed – before I wrapped my mind around what was coming.

And then I tackled Siara to the ground, clamping one hand over my eyes and the other over hers.

Because drakenfire is one thing. But drakenfire backed up by the immense upwelling of elder sorcery I had just felt moving below us…

That was quite another.

The rumbling, spitting roar went on for what seemed an eternity. The stone trembled, growing warm beneath me. Even through closed eyes, behind tightly locked fingers, I could see the raging inferno of Scarwing's breath, tempered by his Sire's will into a lance of absolute destruction.

It could have rendered mountains of iron down to slag. It could have blasted whole mighty forests to ashes on the wind.

But when it tapered off, and I staggered to my feet, Grennen Vuhl was still standing.

I will admit – he *was* smoking. His skin was stripped raw, and his beard was still on fire in places. But damn the Kothrai's horrendously tough hide if he didn't just shake off the clinker and soot of the blast, leveling one clawed finger at the Archaeon's kin.

"Very nice, beast. Are you ready for *my* turn?"

Scarwing reared back on his haunches, lashing out with claws like butcher's knives. Vuhl leaned backward, grinning. He spread his arms wide.

"Get aboard! Come on! Before this all goes directly to the Hells!"

The draken's voice echoed in my skull, louder than reason. It got me moving, bundling Siara up the ladder of spikes which was the great wyrm's tail.

Then Vuhl called down power, and the world crumpled up around us like parchment.

It was no poetic turn of phrase. I felt reality spindle and stretch, warping along invisible fault lines, my body twisted through degrees which should have been impossible. I screamed, but the sound came out wrong, distorted into a glassy cascade of notes, spinning down into darkness.

The focus snapped back. Vuhl stood before us, his fingers sunk knuckles-deep in a core of night. Little flickers and filaments of purple lightning danced a fingerlength from its surface.

"Tell your precious Fractured One he will see me soon enough. Tell him to make peace with the Divine…"

Vuhl raised the sphere up over his head, his teeth locked in a rictus grin. Another instant and we would have been blasted into a thin and greasy film across the Sorathi sea.

But in that instant, the war-keel *Sorrow's Vengeance* dropped her wardings and veils above us, knifing in through the clouds with all her guns run out and ready. I saw Harlaw at the rail, and Meracq D'avarian at his side, both armed with massive, shoulder-mounted rifled matchlocks. Below them, a single broadside of one hundred and forty guns smoked with their tapers lit, aimed by a hand-picked crew of Tarkhanden marines.

And I had thought the drakenfire was loud.

Scarwing scrabbled backward off the tower top and into free-fall as the guns spoke, a sound like acres of tearing calico shredding the sky above us. The draken's wings snapped open as we fell toward the whitecaps, and my daughter and I hung on for dear life – or its equivalent – as we barrel-rolled through a cloud of spray, rising again on the far side of the airborne warship.

It isn't easy to withstand a blast of white-hot flame, tempered and interwoven with sorcery. That he had done so, in what Siara told me was a weakened state, was testament to Grennen Vuhl's toughness.

But to stand against a hurricane of chainshot, shrapnel, ball-shot and explosive shells…

Well, that was simply impossible.

Even if – and I fervently prayed – Vuhl had not been torn to mincemeat by that dire barrage, then his tower had been. As the gunsmoke cleared, the whole claw-shaped upthrust of stone gave one final heave, and collapsed into the hungry waves. Only a pall of dust and smoke remained where once the Kothrai's mightiest fortress had stood.

Siara leaned her head back against my chest, looking up into my eyes.

"That won't be the last of him, father," she said, with wry resignation. "A thing like that…"

"Oh aye. Keeps coming back. You know, I half expected Dirge to be the one who won that little tussle. He's been behind me for *far* too long."

Now the deck of the Vengeance was beneath us, and Scarwing hovered for a moment, picking a clear space between the coils of rope, barrels, casks and crates.

"Neither of them won. That's the nature of such a bargain. They both lost."

Sails cracked and bellied out as Elion Morekh bellowed orders from the wheelhouse. Down in the pit of the Soulharp I caught sight of the tiny figure of Kayan Orsii, her hands a blur across the strings.

"And unless we move quickly..."

I nodded, watching the deck rush up to meet us.

"I know, child. *We will too.*"

In battle, as in life, it is not the size of one's
opponent. It is not the disposition of their forces,
nor is it their numerical advantage. It is the visceral
will of the animal to tear out the throat of its prey
which will bring you victory. Anyone who tells you
otherwise is a fool, and soon to be a corpse."

Master Militant Gresh Navayne,
Guild of Chains operational commander during the Akhazi incursion.

THERE WAS NO time to confront Kayan Orsii then – not even when
my daughter evicted her from the well of the Soulharp, cracking her
knuckles and muttering about 'showing them what this tub can really
do'.

And after that, there was little to do except hold on. Even Gryst
and Elion Morekh looked seasick as the sails were furled, the hatches
battened down, and the *Sorrow's Vengeance* made ready to run silent
and swift. Siara whipped the wooden Keel north like a scalded
thoroughbred, plowing a furrow through the clouds. Ghostly discord
echoed in our wake was we spanned the Coldfathom Ocean, propelled
by a storm of sorcery.

Sorcery which seemed familiar.

But it wasn't until Siara staggered away from the harp, exhausted,
that I was able to find out why. By then we had traveled further than
I had rode on drakenback, and the lights of Quaziir lit up the belly of
the clouds off our starboard beam.

That was when Silbern Chaar carried my daughter to her cabin, a
tiny black ragdoll in her armoured hands. Elion Morekh threw on all
sail – sky-rakers and topgallants snapping in the wind. And those who
remained of our little company met in the galley, there to contemplate
our strategy.

Of course, there was the sword.

A heavy black blade, it seemed – levitating above Elion's map-table
like a hole cut into the world. It was smaller, now, than when the mad
Aziphem Zael Kataphraxis had summoned it into being. Then it had
been the length of a castle tower, big enough to slice the Coldblood
in two. Now it took the form of a tapering triangular broadsword – a
crude design, but one which sucked at the edges of my vision until my
eyes were fixed on its starry firmament.

Siara had said that such a thing took on the form we gave it. But

348

when I saw how the Void Heart had been crafted…

"I was *wondering* how you were going to wield it," I said, taking in the peculiar design of the blade's haft, grip and pommel. "Even more, really, than how you were going to *find* it. But I see that our friend and patron has been playing the long game…"

"It was Siara's intent all along." came a dry, sardonic voice. It appeared directly in my mind, right behind my eyes – but there was no question where it was coming from. The hilt of the Void Heart was of crude Khytein design, and the base of the blade, a full two handspans across, was tangled in inset coils of grey glass. "Your Hmai friend only did as your daughter would have wished…."

"And the fact that you now hold the power to slay Gods, Aerik Stormsong? Just another sacrifice you've had to make?"

I couldn't disguise the bitterness in my voice. Trusting the deathless Warbard was not something I would ever find easy again. If Aerik told me the sky was blue, I'd wait for a second opinion.

"Oh, stop being so damned *paranoid*. It's egotistical, and it's beneath you. Do you think I truly wanted to spend three centuries trapped in a prison of glass, just to end up bonded to this… abomination? You have no idea of the *cold*, Kuhal Moer. No idea. It's like being trapped under ice, being part of this thing. Cold, suffocating, and numbingly uncomfortable."

"There was no other way," put in Kayan Orsii. She had pinned back her hair with silver and jade, keeping up a brave facade. But I could see that she was desperately tired, and I didn't need the Dark Sight to note the tightly wrapped bandages peeking out from the hem of her robe at the shoulder. "The first of Meracq's sailors who found it tried to take it from its plinth. The bones on the floor all around it should have warned the man, but…" she shrugged. "Suffice to say he joined them. I think they were some kind of religious order, trying to study the thing. At least, their temple was full of traps. The sword was just a much better one."[23]

---

23. The temple of the Thirteen Angles on Dath N'kaal almost deserves its own account, aside from my own. Suffice to say that seekers after dark knowledge, in those days between the fall of Urexes and the events here told, were often given the name of an unspeakable cult, the Brothers of the Black Blade. These acolytes taught that the Void Heart, in their keeping on the dread isle, was but one aspect of a sword which spanned realities in the service of Primal Chaos. Scrolls which Kayan found indicate that, in other places and times, it had been known as, variously (and in other tongues, of course, hard to translate into Guildspeil) - Terminus Est, the Zanpakuto, Frost-of-Mourning and the Bringer of Storms

The Saltmaster was loath to discuss the expedition to Dath N'kaal. He spoke of a temple, all skewed and distorted. Of cyclopean blocks reared up against a yellow sky, of poisonous vapours which made the mind reel in horror. And of the final chamber, where the Void Heart was held in the hands of a great sandstone idol, surrounded by the bones of richly robed acolytes.

"I don't know what they wanted with the thing. But I know this much. Its presence had poisoned the world. Twisted that island into something *wrong*. If we have to use it, aye – we will. But then it must be destroyed. It's a curse, and your Warbard friend will lose his mind inside it."

"If he hasn't already…" I muttered, looking around the table at the faces of my friends. I saw fear in their eyes – but no small measure of determination, too.

"The real question," said Meracq D'avarian, leaning his forehead on his hands, "is where we go from here. We may have a mighty weapon against… well, whatever Vuhl has become. But how do we deploy it?"

At that moment the doors crashed open, letting in a swirl of icy mist. Every head turned toward the sound, and I felt the tension of sorcery prickle in the air. Then a hollow voice spoke out of the shadows, and a figure staggered forward, supported by another, larger form.

"Kayan Orsii knows. Ask the Hmai what plans our enemy holds."

Everything happened in a blur as Silbern Chaar and my daughter stepped into the lantern light.

The Hmai sorceress raised her hand and spoke a Word, sending her chair skittering backwards. She was on her feet in half a heartbeat, a shield of power flickering from her rune-etched palm.

Siara was quicker. Her working skewed the entire room like light through a prism, and when the after-echoes of magick receded she held the Void Heart in both hands.

"Silbern," she rasped, holding the great black sword out to one side. "Deal with this traitor, will you?"

The Ontohki snapped her skeletal visor shut and gripped the Void Heart's hilt in one armoured hand. Its edge flickered like the halo of a gas-lamp flame, all blue and purple as she made a couple of deft passes, limbering up her wrist.

"Wait!" shouted Kayan, her eyes seeking out mine. I could tell that she was terrified of the black blade – hells, even *I* recoiled from its menace, and it wasn't aimed at my throat. Yet.

"And what could you possibly say in your defence?" asked Siara. "I know you were talking to Grennen Vuhl. I heard what he offered you. An empire, for just a little knife-work? Seems a worthy trade."

The Hmai graced me with a lingering glance, then threw back her head and stared Siara in the eye.

"Precisely the deal he made with *you*, Stormreaper. And for a time, even your father was convinced." I rubbed at the raw mark on my neck where the shackle had pinned me down, and I nodded. "How else were we going to find out his plans – after he had destroyed you?"

Silbern stepped forward, blade held high.

"Enough words. Mistress, shall I end this thing?"

Siara held up her hand, slumping forward against the table. Meracq D'avarian, ever chivalrous, came to her aid, settling her into a chair.

"I should have guessed," she said. "And that was his scheme all along? To have me there as backup when he swallowed Dirge…"

"And to devour you thereafter," finished Kayan. "*Of course.* A working of power such as he has wrought – it has left him drained. Spent. His mind boils with thoughts of conquest, but he is, as yet, still weakened."

I thought back to the monstrous creature we had faced atop the bastion. Of a thing which could weather sorcerous drakenfire and laugh…

"*That* was *weakened?* Gods and devils, what would he have become if he…"

"Had devoured you both? Think on this, Lamenter. He has taken the power of your old nemesis. But he wants *you*. He wants to be able to raise dead Gods – to bring lost Aziphem back from the Outer Dark. Do you think they will be even *remotely* sane? Do you think, indeed, that Yrde can contain such power?"

Kayan dropped her shield and bared her throat.

"Strike if you will, Silbern Chaar. Or accept that your mistress is not the only one who can deceive a madman."

For a heartbeat, the black sword held steady. Then Silbern lowered it to her side, popping the clasps which hinged back her visor. There was a look of disgust on her face.

"If, indeed, he is yet a man at all," said Meracq D'avarian.

"Tell us then – what does the bastard intend? Exactly how will he try to take my father?"

I shuddered, more than a little chilled by the thought of Vuhl's attentions. I had grown into the power of communing with the Edge Gods – those Aziphem who kept a tenuous hold on reality. But to bring such beings back from the darkness…

I suffered a terrible vision, then, of countless shadowed idols. Faces of stone and wood and gold, stretching back in endless ranks, down into the dark. Every God humanity had crafted out of fear and superstition. Every mask the fragments of the Divine had worn, had breathed unspeakably powerful life into…

A legion which would make the Nameless seem like children. Black-winged angels, with as much regard for human life as we have for the fate of insects.

"Abyssus." said Kayan Orsii. "Lord of the Drowned. Kuhal Moer is his Herald, for better or worse. And that means they are connected."

"And Vuhl already wields his shadow," sighed Siara. "Do you really think he can…?"

"Do you want to stake this world on the chance that he cannot?"

Gryst's huge, hairy fist crashed down on the table, flipping the central boards on hidden axles. Underneath was a tiled map of Sorath, and it rotated and clicked into place, glittering with precious stones.

"I swear that chart was aboard the *Ironheart*, last I saw it," growled Meracq. Elion and Gryst shared a private chuckle.

"Must be a coincidence," rumbled Gryst. The edges of the chart, now I looked closely, had the look of being freshly torn from their mountings and nailed back in place.

"You wouldn't think the very elite of Tarkhanden seapower could be bribed with, say, a couple of crates of cider…"

Meracq ignored the Faeroan, tracing a line across the map with his dagger. He jammed the thin blade in between two tiles, just off the coast of Qauziir.

"That's us. Heading north by northwest, about – what? Fifty chains per bell?"

Elion nodded.

"Fifty-five, with a good tailwind."

"Then we reach our destination three days hence. Here." he stabbed down with one finger, pointing at a ring of inset amber stones, surrounding a circular slice of lapis.

"The Maelstrom," grunted our tame ogre. "Should 'ave guessed it. Even the ocean wants nothing to do with that place…"

"Now we know why there were no Kothrai blockading Dath N'kaal," said Morekh. "Their whole damned fleet must be on the move."

"Aye," spat the Saltmaster. "And in numbers my Eighth cannot match. You haven't seen them, Sarem'ec – black sails from horizon to horizon. Even if every ship under the red banner were to reach the Maelstrom before us…"

"A moot point. They won't. It's up to us to hold the line, Tarkhanden. Feel like asking for a little Faeroan help yet?"

D'avarian grinned, but it was a bitter thing.

"Whatever you've got, cousin. We will still be ten score ships against three thousand."

"You're forgetting something, Saltmaster. We've got the Beast of Sarem with us. I saw him take down the city of Urexes. Don't underestimate the lad."

The last thing I needed at that moment was the unquestioning faith of a man I'd left for dead. I groaned.

"And you're forgetting something too, Morekh. This time I'm not the monster."

I looked into my daughter's eyes. Then Kayan Orsii's. The message was clear. We could afford no more betrayals.

"This time - I'm the *prey*."

And with that, it was time to trim the lantern wicks and make a mockery of sleep.

Gods. Dead gods, forgotten gods, lost souls and madness. Such thoughts weighed on my mind as we sailed the skies, ever northward.

We flew toward a battle we could not win, our shadow scudding over the silver-grey ocean like an omen of doom. Skarne broke the surface with a snap and shimmer of membranous wings, arcing in shoals away from our path. Their tiny black eyes were rimmed with white. Panic radiated from the Stormreaper's Keel like a crackling penumbra, clouding my Dark Sight.

Even the predators could sense the growing tension and unease which wreathed the *Vengeance*. It was centred on the wheeldeck, on a figure wreathed in a robe of black sailcloth – a sad, rather pathetic figure, if you want the truth of it.

I couldn't help it. It's hard to look dark and regal when you're wallowing in grief. Even the cracked and slightly bent smoked glasses, the stub of my shattered left horn, and the tattoo-black stains curling up my forearms were not enough to paint a picture of grim determination.

But deep inside me my sorrow was turning to rage. Beat out on the anvil of my heart, in a grim mockery of the name of our vessel. For in one fist I clenched a gem – a smooth, flawless cabochon of jet. And I could feel – even through my white-knuckled grip – the twist and knot of two souls within. Of Makara and Dirge Endsong.

I sat there for a full day and a night, as squalls of rain blattered against my makeshift cloak, and Elion Morekh stood tall and silent at the helm, his dead eyes locked on the north horizon. Below us, the Eighth Fleet plowed through the worsening swells, their sails taut and their timbers creaking.

I didn't watch the racing wrack of clouds, or see the sickle moon wheel overhead.

People came to talk to me. To remonstrate, I supposed. Some left shaking their heads in bewilderment. Others shouted, but I could not hear them. The power around me deepened with my despair and my rage, until a teardrop-shaped swirl of shadows blurred the world away.

The storm worsened. Lightning crazed the sky as another night drew in. And beneath it all, my will ground relentlessly against the black gem, seeking for a way inside.

I didn't want to find one. Rationally, I knew that there would only be pain for me there. But it was my duty. I had to witness the depth of my failure. The failure of a nineteen-summer-old fool made ancient before his time. The failure which a whole worthless tome of holy scriptures called wisdom, but which I knew now to be nothing but petulance and denial.

I had failed *her*.

With the image of Makara's face it came. Reality fractured, and I sank into myself, my spirit coursing through a fractal tangle of crystal, down the long bones of my arm, into the maze of 'blight which webbed my blackened carpals…

Into the gem. And into the past.

The village where I had grown up was a sordid little place, in the grander scheme of things. Now that I had seen Urexes, Zamara – even benighted Oram – the huddle of longhouses with their crossed wolf's-head ridgepoles and their mossy thatch seemed crude and primitive. The square between them was nothing but hard-packed earth, surrounding a central fire-pit and the carved wooden totems of our Gods. Chains of fingerbones and painted scalps were nailed to the god-poles, tributes from my Father and his ilk.

Here in the dream-world both a dim, mist-shrouded sun and a leering crescent moon hung low in the sky. The Stormwood, where it crowded up around the encircling palisade, was frozen in the riotous amber and gold of autumn. Literally frozen – for leaves hung motionless on the air, and curls of smoke were scrawled out sideways from the chimneys of the feast-hall and the forge, smudged across the sky.

Of my people, there was no sign. The entire village had the ghostly aspect of a necropolis – and I, for one, was well accustomed to such lifeless places.

The only human beings in this grey-tinted landscape were Makara and a white-clad child, sitting on the ring of stones around the central fire. Gone was the black armour, the sigils and incisions with which Urzen had decorated her body. Instead, she wore a simple acolyte's robe, belted at the waist with braided leather and copper rings. She was bent over a lyrecaster of antique design, wringing a low and sad melody from its silver strings.

The child sat with his back to me, entranced, idly scratching in the dirt with a length of willow.

"I wondered how long it would take you," said Makara, letting her song trail off to echoes. "We've been waiting, of course. Nothing much else to do in a place like this."

I tried to run to her, but managed nothing but a clumsy stagger. It was only as I collapsed to my knees beside her that I noticed the little child's face, all serious and severe under a cap of white-blond curls.

"How…?" I asked, while Jerrold Sinder studiously sucked his thumb. "I felt the power of that bastard. I thought you'd be…"

Makara's smile was thin and cold.

"Tortured again? Imprisoned? In need, perhaps, of some heroic rescuer? *Please*, Kuhal Moer. For the love we once shared, put aside such foolishness. I am not what I was, and I have been trapped in here for *much* longer than he has. I made plans."

She helped me lean up against the ring of flat-cut hearthstones, carefully putting down her 'caster.

"It's a snare, isn't it? You built this place from my memories, so it would be sustained by my power. And he… damn it, Makara! How *did* you make him into a little boy again?"

"I'm not *little*," said Sinder gravely. "I'm six and three moons old. So there!"

"He's the part which Grennen Vuhl didn't want," explained the warbard. "His *humanity*. This is the age when he first began to lose it, I suppose."

It shouldn't have been possible for me to feel sorry for Jerrold Sinder, later to become Dirge, Lord Endsong. But, looking at that all-too-serious little face, I wondered just what had robbed him of his innocence. It cut something loose inside me, and I had to force myself to scowl.

"I… I'd feared I could never set you free," I began. "With him in here I thought… the two of you would be bound up. Bringing you back would bring back the monster."

I felt her hand on the back of my neck, stroking my hair.

"You always needed a monster, didn't you? Something worse than yourself, just to keep the balance. I was the same. But… we did terrible things, didn't we Kuhal? We got lost in the story. The blood, the vengeance… the old tale, from after the fire goes out. I may be just a shadow, but I know we should be judged. It's just… by whom?" she folded her hands in her lap, and nodded at the child, busily scratching pictures in the dirt. "He's told me things, you know. Things which I've come to believe." She grimaced. "His human side doesn't seem to be capable of lying. All that… the trickery, the rage… became part of Vuhl."

I thought back to Cyvenne, burning. Of avenues of the crucified, of red-fingered ghouls snapping and scrabbling over piles of headless bodies…

"The Divine can judge us, perhaps. But no mortal. Not… we were *justified*, Makara. Three hundred years of peace, dammit."

"He can't, you know."

It was Sinder. His voice was thin and piping, but his words carried a grim certainty, as if he was reading them off rune-carved stone.

"The Divine is mad. He was a mirror, once. But now he's just the Aziphem, broken, and they are like little drops of quicksilver."

I looked up at him, blinking. Too-big grey eyes stared back at me.

"That's why the Archaeon wants rid of them. 'Human madness, and human stories', he said. Mother fed me his blood, and he talked to me. He told me that we were a disease, and that if our stories stopped poisoning them, all those little drops would roll back together again…"

I reeled back, as if slapped. The Archaeon? The same great sire of Draken who had worked with my cabal to overthrow Urexes?

"This is the kind of thing he says," said Makara. "He knows far too much, and when it spills over… well, this business with the Archaeon is only the start. His mother was apparently part of some Angan cult, the Sons of Brimstone, and they *worshiped* the damned thing…"

I thought of Scarwing's admission, as we set our course for Kothrai. *A whole new generation of the Allsire's spawning, waiting under the Hiledoran in the dark. Draken rekindled to intellect, to ambition – and bound with shards of the broken Void Heart.*

"Tell me," I said, reaching out slowly to take Sinder's tiny pale hand. "What did the Archaeon want with you?"

"Kuhal, we don't *know*. He might have been driven mad by the binding process. He might be a shadow, created to confound us. You can't…"

"*Tell me*," I demanded, staring into those wide and guileless eyes.

And he did. Jerrold Sinder, six and three moons old, sat down in the dust with his willow-branch, and he told me a tale of treachery which staggered me to my core.

It was all the worse for the fact that it tallied neatly with things only I had seen, and only I could know.

He told me of the Fractured One, the two-faced deity of the dawn age, worshiped by the Draken at the height of their hubris. Of the wars of sundering, when the cults of his two images waged a bitter struggle for supremacy. Of the vast hordes of the Coldblood, overthrowing their Draken masters, casting them down into bestial warfare. Of a God, a reflection of the sleeping Divine, driven insane, forced across the threshold into the Real…

Sinder spoke of continents displaced. Rains of molten stone. The sky grown black as night for decades. Yrde could not take such power. And while Abyssus himself lamented giving complexity to life, the Archaeon enacted the rite which would sever the minds of all thinking beings.

All but three.

The Coldblood took refuge in a million-year slumber, a torpor which lasted aeons.

Abyssus dug deep into the seabed, his rune-warded shell already thick enough to turn aside that most dire of workings.

And the Archaeon, of course. Willing to sacrifice all but itself. Sharp spines of crystal erased the Fractured One's true name, and the great beast began its lonely vigil, crawling into a cave at the heart of the Hiledoran to await the rise of Man.

Who it saw as a disease.

A sickness, but a necessary evil. Who else but another thinking, frightened, superstitious race would feed the guttering flames of the Aziphem? Who would build them up into raging bonfires of belief and faith? And, when the Outer Dark was filled to bursting with those quicksilver droplets, it would come time to undo the great working, sending them rushing together again…

I thought back to Scarwing's cryptic words, and shuddered.

"Before the Shards, there was the Fractured One. And he abides. What do you think your petty dead Aziphem are parasites on, Kuhal Moer? And do you think such a thing could ever walk Yrde again without tearing it asunder?"

I saw in my mind an image of the Outer Dark united, those chittering, screaming multitudes working as one, a vast inhuman face arising from the stew of soul-stuff. Of the Archaeon's children, guarding the threshold, caging the titan, bleeding its colossal power…

Humanity would not be able to stop them. We would be incinerated like moths in a bonfire. Oram's fall would seem quaint and clean compared to that holocaust unleashed.

"The Archaeon was there at the founding of Anganesse. The knowledge of how to bind Esau came from the Sons of Brimstone, who flourished even in the time of Zael Kataphraxis. The Archaeon not only *tolerated* Urzen's monstrous experiments, but actually *aided* in them, seeking a way to imprison the Aziphem, who fed on our stories, and became like us – fickle, capricious, unpredictable…"

"Oh aye. Like *us* indeed. But what of my part in this comedy?"

"It promised us power," said Sinder, drawing a crude stick-figure draken in the dust. "But we saw through it. So clumsy, really. Why *us*? Why Anganesse? Questions turn to doubt so easily, Kuhal. Away goes faith. Away goes honour… So we broke the pact. We sent men south. We told the Coldblood that its old foe was still alive, and where it could be found."

I picked it.

The church of Esau, monolithic and imperial – a trap for all that quicksilver. A killing jar where it ran together, ready to be harvested. But then came the twist of the knife. The power of the Coldblood, descending on the Hiledoran like a hammer, smothering the Archaeon's sorcerous fires. Zengaji sent out to slit the betrayer's throats – the Thearch's, Sinder's. But the Nine awaited them, and all perished.

Desperation. The formation of a new alliance. Honeyed words, promising freedom to a handful of the subjugated…

I was the knife the beast had forged. I was the instrument of its vengeance against those who had wronged it.

I was, to put it simply, a way to sweep the chessboard clean. New plans would be put in place to eradicate the human plague. New plans which hinged, now, on the unexpected presence of the Void Heart.

I looked up at Makara, my head churning with shame and fear. If what he said was true…

"Can we believe him?"

"I don't know," she replied. "If we do…"

I saw the trepidation in her eyes. I felt it too.

"What do we do about it?" I asked.

I thought for a second that she didn't answer because she couldn't. That the question of whether or not to trust a fragment of our ancient foe, to believe in such a world-changing deception… that it had all been too much. Makara's eyes flickered closed, and she sighed. Her shoulders sagged forward, and I reached out to catch her.

Then the tip of a blade stabbed out through her chest. A cold black tongue of metal, leaving a bloodless line as it burst through her skin.

Her eyes opened for the last time. Violet as the edge of lightning, burning into mine.

"You have your answer…"

Then the blade ripped sideways, a black blur, and my poor lost love was torn in half. She was only a memory in this place – a *shadow*, she had called herself. What spilled out as she flew apart was not blood, but coils of inky darkness, thick as censer-smoke. When she struck the ground she shattered, brittle as porcelain, and the light went out in those eyes.

The sword drew back, spun, cut down….

And Jerrold Sinder was sliced in two, bisected from shoulder to hip. The little child's face betrayed a look of bemusement as he fell apart, cracking and swirling away just as Makara had done.

I waited for the blow to fall. I was still on my knees, kneeling before a half-circle of crude pictures in the dust. Little Jerrold's willow switch clattered against the hearthstones, severed in two.

I looked up into the face of my executioner, and saw nothing but black folds of cloth – the tight-wrapped shroud of a Zengaji killer. Even through the eyeslits of the mask he wore beneath, the man felt the sheer intensity of my anger, and he paused.

Oh yes. There he was, armoured and strong, the unmistakable starry edge of the Void Heart in his hands. And there I was, helpless, on my knees. But can you guess who was shit-stained with fear?

The whole little memory we were in trembled. Cracks spread out from around me, crazing the sky, the Stormwood, those floating leaves…

"Aerik told me you should be spared. That… that you should be given a choice," said my assailant.

Said Makara's murderer. **Said a fucking dead man!**

"How nice," I managed. "How… fatherly."

Ice began to form all around me. Frost crept up the hearthstones, painting the carved totems of my tribe's dead Gods.

"I… I warn you. Scarwing stands over you, out in the world. Should I not return…"

He took a step back. I clenched my fists, and trees in the Stormwood around us exploded in the grip of utter cold.

"Tell me, Urmokh," I asked, slowly rising to my feet. "Did you ever meet a young assassin by the name of Clanbrother Zuris O?"

The Skyborn shook his head. This wasn't going at all as he had planned.

"Ahh, well. A pity. *You two are going to have so much in common…*"

Now, there's some battles yer just can't win. No shame in it - that's just how it is. But you c'n always get two things outta a good scrap, and those are as follows. First, you can get you some revenge. On the enemy, for all his sins. And if that ain't enough, on that officer in front of yer, who might just become a bloody 'heroic casualty', if yer get me drift. Or, failin' that, just imagine they all yer damned deadbeat daddy, yer ex-wife - matter o' fact, it kinda feels good when the steel goes in all red-like!

Second thing is loot. Loot is the name of the one true God, and don't you maggots forget it!

Now, sometimes the first thing you have to loot is a uniform from the other side, but that's the fortunes of war, lads - hit 'em hard, hit 'em below the belt, and when they fall down, have a blade ready to catch 'em. Any questions?"

The facts of life,
as explained by veteran Sergeant 'One Eye' Scallyg,
Tarkhanden Eighth Fleet Marines (and not a very nice person)

THE SORROW'S VENGEANCE was already falling as my eyes snapped open. It felt as if the whole great ship had been slapped sideways by the detonation of sorcery – the shattering of the dream-world inside the black gem. I looked down at my hand as I slid across the polished hardwood deck... an instant before I slammed up against the rail. Black sand blew away between my knuckles.

Then the howling, yammering brightness of reality snapped into focus, and I rolled to my left. Just in time for Urmokh to carve a chunk from the rail with the Void Heart. A part of me noted, with clinical detachment, that the starry black steel slid through timber like butter.

"Murdering bastard!" I shouted, tears whipped out sideways from my eyes. "You killed her! Why...?"

I tore my cloak away and threw it in the assassin's face, cursing as he heaved the sword free. The world spun faster. Waves and red sails cartwheeled by below us. I could hear Kayan Orsii screaming, my daughter too...

Sailcloth shredded and flapped, broken-winged as it blew aside.

"The shade spoke half-truths. Worse than lies. You… *she*… gave us no choice."

I saw the form of Elion Morekh slumped across the wheel, his hands limp, his head down. A pair of daggers were crossed through his back.

That made me angry.

And, as the heaving ocean rose up to meet us, I felt that I had little left to lose.

"There's *always* a choice, Urmokh. And there's always another truth…"

It was a crude working, but it caught the traitor Zengaji full in the face. It manifested as a snarl of barbed tendrils, witchfire raving and snapping from my fingertips to his eyes and throat.

He howled – but more in surprise than pain. The Zengaji are potently warded against all forms of sorcery, and my shredding roil of fire did little more than bloody his skin. But it did throw him off balance. His wild swing with the blade went wide, snapping a trio of ropes behind me.

It bought me enough time to do two things.

Firstly, to undo the bindings of the second level, sharpening up my speed and focus. And secondly, to see the liquid cliff-face of a wave looming up below us, white foam dancing on its crest…

"You fool! You should have joined us! Aerik said you were *smarter* than this, Lamenter! This way we destroy your nemesis, free your people, reclaim all of Yrde…"

"Aerik should know," I grated "That I've heard such hogshit before."

We struck.

Thousands of tons of wood and steel came down hard across the crest of the wave, almost breaking the back of the *Vengeance*. Timbers groaned and squealed in protest. Nails were driven from the boards by the sheer force of our impact, and I heard the strings of the Soulharp cut loose, a bass thrumming sound behind the snap of some titanic whip.

I already had my forearm wrapped around a length of hawser – but Urmokh was not so fortunate.

The shock almost toppled him from his feet… but it was the sluicing sheet of water which followed which finally threw him over. Zengaji to the core, he turned his near-vertical plunge down the canted deck into a tuck and roll, holding the Void Heart out beside him as he came, bringing it up into an impaling strike.

I looked into his snarling face as time slowed down, painting the edges of everything blue and purple. Droplets of spray were still airborne from our impact. Iron nails spun end over end as a slew of broken casks and crates followed after Urmokh, carried on a wash of salt foam.

One man and a magic sword. Oh, how right my daughter had been. The time of such conceits was passing. Soon we would all be nothing but fireside stories, told by drunkards to warm the few wits left to them. The long dark beckoned. The cold sea gnashed and slobbered at my back, hungry as Abyssus himself.

But Urmokh, brother of Scarwing, wasn't the only fool aboard this tub with a magic sword.

Cryptfeeder came bursting up through the deck timbers in a spray of incandescent splinters, spinning on its long axis and haloed in flames. The Zengaji avoided being spitted on its length only by the most deft and timely of contortions. Even so, it tore a line of crimson across his back as he spun, lithe as a predator.

I moved at the same time, and I was just as quick. To anyone watching we would have seemed a blur – a dance of steel and flesh too fast to follow. I gripped Urmokh's arm with both hands and heaved, continuing the draken-kin's momentum even as the *Vengeance* slid crabwise down the face of the wave, wallowing into its trough.

An instant, and he was out over the rail, hanging above the cold, grey ocean. I let go with one hand, digging in with the nails of the other. I held out my empty palm, and the grip of Cryptfeeder slapped into it with utter certainty.

"I suppose you expect me to give you the blade," he said, his toes dangling above several fathoms of brine. He looked up at me with utter calm – his one drakonic eye glowing amber.

"No. I expect you to take it with you. To the bottom. The world will be well rid of the accursed thing – and Aerik Stormsong with it!"

Of course, there was no way that a Zengaji would give up and drown. Urmokh arched his body, swinging back against the side of the ship, and pushed off with his feet. In a heartbeat he was above me, upside down, my blackened claw of a hand still tight around his wrist. The assassin's feet hooked into the rigging, and the tip of the Void Heart hovered before my eyes.

"Let go. Now. Or join your witch in oblivion."

A poor choice of words. I snarled, bringing the point of Cryptfeeder up to Urmokh's throat.

"Drop the sword. Or you can go to Abyssus with one less hand."

I squeezed. Anger quickened the mageblight in all those little bones. It must have been like the grip of a blacksmith's tongs. And beneath the surface…

"Don't be a damned fool, Moer!" came Aerik's voice, slicing into my head like a flurry of ice crystals. *"You need me to slay your bloody demon! You need me, or humanity falls! My way, the Khytein and the Skyborn survive. We go back to the old ways, the ways of the Dawn Age. We… we can bring back our gods."*

"And Makara? Can you bring her back as well?"

The voice from the sword was silent for a breath or two.

"I didn't kill her, Kuhal. Neither did Urmokh. The memory you keep is far more real than the shadow we just banished. Damn Sinder! I needed time to explain! I needed you to hear the rational side of…"

"Of destroying civilization wholesale? Of the rule of Draken? Come on, old man! Where's the rational side to that?"

"You don't hear the madness of the Gods, boy," he whispered, as threads of mageblight slithered and coiled under my skin. As Urmokh regarded me coldly with mismatched eyes. As the *Sorrow's Vengeance* spun end on end, Tarkhanden warships tacking aside to avoid collision. *"You don't* hear. *Ciermakh. Theyr. All of them. Weeping and raging, even in my sleep…"*

"I don't hear their madness. No. *But I hear yours.* And I have the solution."

I felt a sharp stab of pain as I willed a long, thin filament of mageblight out through the taut skin of my wrist. A fragment of Kell Du'ath's sorcery, Gods rest her. The creeping infestation of the Divine had not turned me to a living statue like the little Ythean oracle. But three hundred years had webbed enough of the crystalline 'blight through me to coax out a thread as pale and fine as a strand of her hair.

Its tip was needle sharp. I focused my will, and sent it spearing into the back of Urmokh's hand, imagining the tangle of winter branches against a grey sky. *Imagining the similar rootwork of veins in his living flesh…*

Many sages, scholars, and ale-house philosophers have questioned, down the ages, how we in the necromancy trade can animate dead bones. *After all,* they ponder, *a fresh cadaver must be easy* – still possessed of rotting muscle and ligaments. But skull and bones, ribs and femurs – what makes them *move?* How do they hold together, swing swords, heft shields, march on their living foes?

The answer hinges on two simple facts.

Firstly, that the mageblight grows quickly in bone. And secondly, that the soul-stuff of the dead, the witchfire which quickens those bones – is *pure sorcery.*

What happened inside poor unfortunate Urmokh, then, was simply a magnification of what happens to any grave-cold skeleton in my thrall. But the power which drove that unfurling of crystal tendrils – the energy which kicked back up my nerves to set my brain jangling in my skull – *was no less than the Void Heart itself.*

Urmokh screamed as a series of gristly cracking sounds traveled up his arm, splitting his radius and ulna. Spikes of bloody crystal tore through his flesh, twisting like thorns. I watched the wriggling tips of a thousand mageblight roots following his veins, up to the shoulder, into his chest…

His spine locked. His face bulged out in a grimacing death-mask, before a twining branch of crystal forced its way out through his left eye, sending pale white creepers writhing across his cheek.

Aerik fought back, trying to stem the flow of power from the blade. But it was too little, and far too late. Already a clublike cyst of filaments had burst from the Skyborn's hand, fusing it to the sword. I pulled free, with the sound of a single snapping hair, and watched Urmokh swing in the rigging, held in place by the tangled 'blight.

He couldn't speak. But the traitor's head turned toward me with a grating, grinding sound. His one remaining eye burned into mine. And the voice of Aerik Stormsong roared through me like a winter gale, making me drop Cryptfeeder and clap my hands over my ears.

"You simply cannot *be such a fool, Kuhal! You* need *me! To slay that abomination! Aye, even to slay the Archaeon himself, if that is now your wish. But more…"*

I didn't want to hear. I fell to my knees on the pitching deck, hearing the sounds of voices coming closer, of heavy footsteps on the gangway…

"Consider this, as well. Your soul-seed, kept for centuries. Given to Siara Anvhaur as her birthright. Do you not think I could have done the same once before? Do you truly believe that Hurik, that oaf, was your real father?"

There were hands on my shoulders now. Cradling me back, wiping the sweat and blood from my brow. I didn't want to hear. But the voice ground on.

"Sothara Roege, boy. The Bone Collector. Do you think that Gernish Maudrin and I would let that flame go out forever? A monster he may have been, but power is power. *Do you think any* but his own son *could have even entered the black pyramid?"*

Aerik's laughter was as sharp and cold as the glass he was woven through. And now I saw the armoured form of Silbern Chaar, sleepwalking across the deck toward Urmokh, a long dagger in her hand.

"Sweet cursed Divine! What has he *done?"*

My daughter's voice. Still so hesitant, so tired…

"Whatever it was, it nearly killed them both. Poor bastard. He must have finally tried to pry that damned jewel from your father's fist…"

Kayan Orsii. I looked up, as if from in a deep chasm, as she stared into my eyes, checked the stuttering pulse at my neck.

"He's in pain," said Silbern, taking another step toward Urmokh. "Must… end his suffering. So cruel. Would be a comfort."

They weren't listening. And they couldn't hear Aerik, still raving in my head.

"Yes! One step more, girl! When she takes the sword, she's mine, *Kuhal. Explain all you want, but I was the one who raised your daughter. Your words will sound like madness, and sure defeat. Throw me away? Send me to the bottom of the ocean? Please! And I know you will never be able to strike down mistress Chaar in cold blood."*

His power was a terrible weight on the world. My limbs were leaden, my bones brittle as chalk. Aerik Stormsong turned close on one thousand years of relentless will on me, and I sagged beneath the burden, barely able to breathe. I held out a trembling hand toward Silbern, croaking a wordless warning…

And Scarwing, first of the prime spawning, made it utterly irrelevant.

The great beast was the length of a Kothrai longship, but he swept down with the grace of a swallow, skimming the wavetops with his claws. A mist of toxic droplets flew from between his scaly lips, perfectly aimed, and we all scrabbled back as they settled, kindling to chemical flame…

Urmokh caught the brunt of it. But he was already gone. The assassin laughed as fire consumed him, charring and snapping the rigging around him. And when the draken's talons plucked him from the blackened webbing he took the Void Heart with him, still fused to his ruined hand.

Tarkhanden sailors threw frantic bucketfuls of seawater. Steam and smoke hissed skyward after Scarwing's ascent. One massive downdraft of those leathery wings, and he was higher than our masts. Two, and the backdraft swirled the smoke into choking clouds, filled with sparks.

I watched the Void Heart getting away. *Aerik Stormsong* getting away – that gnomic, twisting old manipulator! I thought again of an army of Draken, their terrible Fractured One behind them…

"The sword…" I croaked, raising one blackened finger. A pitiful fizzle of witchfire sputtered from its tip.

Kayan and Siara looked down at me. There was nothing they could do.

But Gryst…

Well, we had underestimated the hulking great pacifist before.

Whatever the ogre had been before his transformation, now he was a force of pure rage. I had thought that at sea he would have been cut off from the geomancy of rock and stone which shaped him. But apparently not. For now the huge creature leaped from the deck in an explosion of raw force, spinning in the air so that his immense boots crunched into the mainmast with an audible crack of timber. His chef's toque went flying as he used the whip-spring of the mast to launch himself froward, bending the very tip of the foremast almost halfway back to the deck. I looked on, astonished. Those great spans of timber were Stormwood-hewn, the trunks of single ancient trees. Gryst left twin boot-prints in the foremast as it flung him up and back, his apron torn clear, his huge muscles bunching and writhing around nodules and spikes of granite.

Then his fingers gripped the crow's nest – the very apex of the mainmast. Nails shrieked – but held. Wooden joints creaked and howled as the whole hundred-span mast bowed back like the arm of a mangonel.

He was altering his mass. Bending and shaping the laws of creation with sheer power. And it was all instinctive, *all veiled behind a thunderhead of rage…*

The mainmast snapped back. The ogre disappeared into the clouds like a stone fired from some mighty siege-engine. And we all waited for the crunch.

I don't think any of us believed for an instant that Gryst would miss. There was a sense that something had gone whipsawing through the whole ship, as soon as he leaped. That the Aziphem were watching, and this was a *story* now, the stuff of legends. In legends, the last, desperate gambit always comes to something. In legends…

And now.

The sound came back to us from on high – the meaty thud and crack of a fist against a drunkard's jaw. But magnified, amplified… and followed by an inhuman shriek of rage and pain. The clouds lit up orange and red as Scarwing vomited gouts of flame. But the Draken of the Hiledoran, for all their ferocity and grandeur, are lightly built things. Hollow bones, in my estimation, do not stand well up to the impact of several angry tons of muscle and stone.

They fell like a meteor out of the boiling sky. Talons gouging, fists and feet swinging, massive jaws snapping and teeth slashing… a writhing mass of hate and flame. More than once Scarwing unloaded the full force of his sorcerous fire into Gryst's face, but the ogre was built from the bones of mountains. Fire was his birthplace, and magma his blood.

At least, so long as the story lasted.

And that was just long enough for the pair of them to crash down, sundering the spine of one of the Tarkhanden dreadnaughts.

Sailors screamed and cursed. Wood crunched and metal squealed. The ships to either side spun in, sails snapping and billowing, to bear up the weight of the stricken behemoth. Fires kindled within its copper-clad hull, and I saw men frantically pitching blackpowder kegs overboard, some slicing loose the stays of whole bombards and cannons to send them to the bottom.

It was little use. A series of massive explosions tore out the belly of the dreadnaught, ripping upward into the sky. Sailors manned the pumps aboard the two supporting men o' war, filling the wallowing hulk with billows of steam.

Then came silence.

It took next to no time to remove the daggers from Elion's back – they had skewered him through, pinning him to the wheel, and the sigil of the Dead Zero had thrown him into torpor. Once our captain was hale and well, it was a matter of barely a quarter-bell before our skiff was up against the smoking hulk of the Tarkhanden dreadnaught.

Meracq D'avarian went up the ladder first, followed by Siara, then a very protective Silbern Chaar. I followed behind, trailed by Harlaw. Kayan Orsii had elected to remain behind, supervising the re-tuning and calibration of the Soulharp.

This was the scene which lay before them, then, as I tried to explain what had happened. As I tried, indeed, to come to terms within myself with the enormity of such treachery.

Makara was dead.

The reason I had clung to life for three centuries – blown away as dust. Now I haltingly tried to lay out the pieces for my friends, all the while watching them intently, sniffing out the scent of betrayal…

The dreadnaught was built tough, armoured and massively ribbed. The heart of it had been cored out by flames, but bulkheads sheathed in metal had stopped the conflagrations rushing fore and aft, sealing the radius of destruction.

Scarwing and Gryst lay curled around each other against the blackened ribs of the hull, having thrashed and burned their way down through no less than seven decks to the bilges. The foul water there may have helped to extinguish them – but neither would ever rise again.

The great draken's neck was broken in five places, twisted and almost knotted in on itself. Gryst's arm was jammed down Scarwing's throat, his fingers clenched tight around the suppurating glands which gave birth to the draken's fire. Blowback into the creature's lungs had charred them from within, and I could see the great blackened rents in his belly where that detonation had wrought its ruin. Coils of steaming intestines looped out amid a scattering of broken scales.

But it was not the terrible natural weapons of the Archaeon's son which had undone Gryst. Even the fire seemed to have washed over him, burning him hairless and pale, with a sheen like moonstone. His great heavy features were set in anger, his free hand gripped tight around the blade which pierced his chest.

The Void Heart.

The grey-glass tangle of Aerik's prison had melted away, and the crude bone handle of Khytein design had been reduced to ashes. What transfixed the empty shell of our former friend was a sliver of starry night, constellations alien and malign winking from within.

He had brought us back the blade. He had cut through the knot of choices, allegiances, fates and fortunes. And it had cast his soul adrift in that alien gulf…

We all stood there at the rail for a time, while soot-smeared, bleeding Tarkhanden stopped their labours to watch us. My words seemed brittle, hollow as the calcified ends of Scarwing's broken bones.

"So, even if we win, then…" said Meracq, hanging his head. His voice was raw, thick with horror.

"Even if we win. Aye. Dirge fought for humanity all along. The

Kothrai, the Coldblood – they all think us part of the Archaeon's madness."

"Then why fight at all?" asked Silbern, turning away from the grim scene below us. Breakermen were picking their way through the ruin now, long hooks on polearms ready. Others came behind them with cleavers and saws. "Why waste our time on Vuhl, when all of Sarem…"

She looked gravely sick for a moment, as pale and haggard as I.

"Dirge is gone. The Doom has fallen. The fools will be *rejoicing*, Lamenter. Rejoicing. Praising your holy fucking name."

All that power, flowing into a Shard still fractured. Still contested. And there was her answer.

"That's why we must destroy Vuhl. Or whatever he has become. That's why – if the fate of all those we have lost is not enough. We will need the Lord of the Desolation, soon. We will need His Dark Reflection. Not me. Not merely Kuhal Moer. And right now, that power descends to an empty throne, in an empty tower."

"Not empty," said Harlaw. From somewhere the Master Gunner had produced another of his vile, slightly bent cigarillos, and now he lit it with a phosphorous match. "If I recall, M'lord, you told us there was one left there to keep the balance. A *placeholder*, you said."

"He's right," whispered Silbern. Zuris O. But he's not…"

My eyes widened. I gripped the rail hard enough to splinter the blackened crust of the burnt timbers.

"He's no sorcerer." I said. "But he *is* Zengaji. Kin to Urmokh. Perhaps even…"

"And of course, there's always *that*," said Harlaw cheerfully, puffing away on his stick of blackened tobacco." I followed the direction of his yellow-stained finger, even as the horns began to bellow, and the bells began to clamour.

It was the maelstrom.

There on the horizon – a wall of cloud, inky black and purple, shot through with ragged ropes of curdled white. A permanent flickering halo of lightning crowned it, and it *rumbled*, rotating with the bulk and ponderous vastness of a War Keel's millstones.

We must have been drifting toward it all this time, hurried along by the current which fed into its craw. I could see islands just outside of the gyre of cloud – jagged fangs of rock bursting outward like ribs, pointed and bladed.

But it was nothing so natural which Harlaw had been pointing at.

Between us and the Maelstrom lay the black fleet of the Kothrai.

Galleys in their thousands, swarming on the salt-wracked swells like insects. Great dromons and triremes, battle-barges and dreadnaughts, all painted midnight and shadow, all with their sails filled and bearing down on us. The wind out of the storm drove them forth at an angle to us, but nevertheless, there was no outflanking such a force. We here were mere hundreds. They were a nation mobilised on the face of the deep, a horde whipped on to slaughter by a madman.

And how had they reacted to Grennen's transformation, I wondered? Had they welcomed him with open arms, this unspeakable thing which had forged itself from ambition and hate?

I chuckled, despite myself. Did it matter, really? Would any dare dissent?

Now all those choices trickled away like the black sand from between my fingers. Now I felt the world go into frantic, heaving motion around me as I gripped the rail, staring into the Maelstrom.

We went forth to vanquish a foe who fought to preserve our very species. We went, for the best of reasons, to abet a race of monsters who saw us as a disease.

There would be no victors in this battle. No glory.

But – and I swore this by all the damned Aziphem who rode behind us, hungry for a tale of blood and sorrow – there would be time enough for vengeance.

I would whet my appetite on Grennen Vuhl.

And then… the Archaeon was next.

Part Six

The Eye of the Maelstrom

Battle at sea is a terrible business. You get all of the horrors of land warfare - the hacking and bludgeoning in close, the smell of the blood and shit on your boots - but there's nowhere to run. Not when a horde of madmen with cannons are right below your feet, trading iron with a similar bloodthirsty pack just a few chains distant, and all intent on blowing your temporary battlefield to matchwood! In the end, it's only the sharks and the skarne that love a good naval engagement. Us old sailors don't have peg legs and hook hands for the sake of *fashion*, you know!

Boarding Marshall Tarleck Halsen,
Master-at-arms of the Tarkhanden dreadnaught 'Wavehammer'

Now CAME THE rush of spray. The bellowed orders and the ringing bells, as the deck heaved and canted beneath my feet. Elion Morekh spun the wheel, and the ponderous bulk of the *Sorrow's Vengeance* came around, sails bellying taut as we rode the swells.

Around us, the Tarkhanden Eighth Fleet formed up into a line astern, two great dreadnaughts – the *Ironheart* and the *Skarne's Maw* – taking point before us. Lesser craft huddled in behind the arrowhead of our assault, their captains reading the flickering semaphore flags which relayed Meracq D'avarian's commands down the line.

Before he left for his flagship, the Saltmaster had clasped my hand and wished me well. He had spoken in hushed tones with Elion Morekh – a conversation which had ended with wild grins and slaps on the back for both parties. Then he had bowed low to Siara, Kayan and Silbern Chaar – favouring the last with a knowing wink – and stepped over the side to his waiting longboat.

This formation was known as the Chain and Anchor, and it relied on the superior gunnery of the Tarkhanden sailors. We would try to punch clean through the enemy fleet, raking them with a merciless procession of broadsides, then peeling the upwind half of their divided force away, closing to ram and grapple them down. Meanwhile, their allies caught downwind would have to tack against the storm to reach us – by which time we would have whittled down their numbers.

A fine scheme, if we had been outnumbered merely three to one. The

375

reality was sobering. We faced no less than eleven thousand Kothrai men o'war, and we were but two hundred and sixty three strong.

That was, until Kayan Orsii scribed a triangle in charcoal and ocher on the wheeldeck, and my daughter adorned it with mind-bending runes. The storm building behind us flowed into the eternal gyre of the Maelstrom as they worked their preparations, and fat drops of rain came hammering in flurries as I looked out beyond them, to the heaving scrawl of black sails and snapping pennants which was our foe.

"Are you ready to try, then?" asked Kayan Orsii, smoothing down the font of her salt-crusted sailor's greatcoat. "This is as good a time as any to even those odds."

"Are we close enough?"

The Hmai sorceress grimaced.

"I can feel them below us, Kuhal Moer. Grennen Vuhl might command his shadow, but Abyssus promised you the dead..."

She was right, of course. Sorathi legend claimed that all the sunken ships, all the doomed wrecks which had ever been claimed by storms... all sailed beneath the waves in darkness, bearing their drowned crews here to the threshold of the Maelstrom. Abyssus himself had told me that some chose to sleep rather than face oblivion.

"The circle is ready," said Siara, coming to take my hand. "Father... it's time."

I sighed, reaching out to take her proffered hand. Kayan took the other, and the two of them led me to the centre of the rune-etched deck.

The Void Heart hung suspended there, its wicked point hanging above the timbers. Our working would have no shortage of power, of that I was certain.

I felt the seething webwork of it as soon as I stepped back to take my place. To my left, Kayan skeined in force from the starry sliver of night, hammering it out into necromantic vitae to course through the runes below our feet. Siara ran her fingers across the strings of her lyrecaster, waking shimmering echoes, and I felt the power quicken, intricacies building one on another until the music itself took on the complexity of a ghost Incantus. I stood at its centre, feeling that great immaterial sphere expand, letting my will sink into the song.

Tendrils of green fire bloomed and unfurled. A constellation of motes filled the air, and razor-straight lines of light snapped between them, picked out as the rain fell through. *Now it was the size of my outstretched arms... now the size of the summoning circle itself... now rushing out to encompass the entire ship...*

I felt the cold weight of the ocean press down on me. I felt the suffocating darkness of the seabed. And I saw, in a Dark Sight now expanded to the proportions of near godhood, the wrecker's yard we were sailing over.

It was the ancient city beneath the weaves – the one from my dream. When Makara had brought me to the centre – to the great pit at the heart of the temple, where Abyssus dwelt – I had only witnessed a tiny fraction of courts and precincts. Now it was spread out below me, fathoms beneath the swells, and it was all but buried beneath the bones of ships. Canted ziggurats and towers served as moorings for a drowned fleet. Hulks with ragged, weed-encrusted sails hung weightless in the gloom, straining against rusted chains.

Here was an armada of the dead – the watchmen of Abyssus, waiting for his Herald to raise them to war. Here was a force fit to smash Grennen Vuhl's fleet to matchwood.

I was eager to oblige.

But at the first flare of sorcery, the Kothrai's warlocks and shamen retaliated. From some far-off chantry barge, nestled in the heart of the black fleet, came a building surge of power. I felt the insectile chitter and hiss of energies woven, and remembered – almost too late – the workings of destruction which had risen from the mage-towers of Urexes.

A bolt of darkness leaped skyward from behind the wall of black sails. Traceries of purple lightning haloed its crown as it burst against the cloud-base, building into an inky, roiling tumour of sorcery.

Then the Kothrai let it go, and the bolt hammered toward us, breaking my concentration, bending the world around it as it decapitated the wave-tops.

Meracq's acolytes held it. Mere spans ahead of the *Ironheart's* plunging bowspirit, the sea itself rose up in a vertical wall, saltwrack crawling with pale blue fire. The priesthood of the Twins commanded potent anti-magick, and their warding shattered the Kothrai assault, splintering it into streamers of greasy smoke.

"Concentrate!" snarled Kayan, as I felt her snag those traceries with her mind, lensing them around the weight of the black sword and feeding them back into our working. "There's worse to come, but D'avarian's Sanctified will hold. The Twins are strong here, and we have work to do!"

My daughter said nothing. Her eyes were closed, and her fingers were a blur across the lyrecaster strings. With each chord she bound the strands of soul-stuff from below to the massive, deep resonance of the harp – its finger-thick silver wires now thrumming with energy.

It was my task to release it. To send all that woven force spearing down into the brine…

I took a deep breath, clenched my eyes shut, and reached out for Abyssus.

The next thing I recalled was the taste of blood in my mouth. *Reeling, black starbursts exploding silently behind my eyes. Pain clenched its fists around my throat. I heard Siara swearing over the resonant hum of the song, and Kayan cursing in Hmai, struggling to balance the power of the sword.*

For Abyssus was there, his imminence distorting the world – but so was something vile. Where the Ancient One should have been a burning core of light, bound to a million souls…

"Too late! Too late, my Herald! What *is* this creature who has forged my shadow into chains? The darkness… *consumes* me!"

It was true. Grennen Vuhl's presence squatted behind the fury of the Maelstrom, chewing into Abyssus like a leech. Chains of solid night lashed and raved from the core of his power, pulling taut around the girth of the Elder One's shell. In other places they pierced clean through, burrowing into soft flesh.

Vuhl was winning. Wrestling the Elder One down. *Impossible* – but it was happening right before me.

"It's never too late," I said, holding out my will to Abyssus like an open hand. "There is time enough to free you. Time enough to slay this upstart, and erase his filthy soul. All I need is what you promised, Elder One. The sleeping dead. Your guardians. If you cannot raise them to battle… *I will.*"

I felt stones shift and crack, down in that deep well on the seabed. Great runic slabs shattered as Abyssus struggled against his captor.

"So… weak, Kuhal Moer. And the Maelstrom itself turns against me! Flee, you fools! I cannot perish, lest the world breaks. But what I may become…"

A surge of elder magick came boiling up out of the deep, almost driving me to my knees. My eyes snapped open as the runes scrawled on the deck burned crimson, charring the timbers. The ghost incantus flared bright, and I felt Kayan and Siara wrestling the power down, hammering and shaping it into the wild song they had built.

"Now! Do it now, father… we can't hold this forever!"

I flicked a glance sideways at Kayan Orsii. She was grinning savagely, hands seething with light.

"Come on, you old fraud! Show them what a godslayer can do…"

I raised my hands above my head, framing an incantation in the tongue of old Korisal. No better language exists for collapsing complex formulae into pithy commands.[24] Then I brought both palms down, fingers splayed, and arched my back against the massive outpouring of power.

I knew it was going to hurt. Indeed, I knew that it would be a pain worse than any I had felt since my death beneath the ruins of an Angan cathedral.

For once, I was sorry to be right.

Ten white-hot bolts of force speared out from my fingertips, while a spire of counter-discharge erupted from above my head in a burning halo. I could feel the mageblight in me shifting and re-weaving, adjusting to accommodate a sheer excess of sorcery – a fraction of the power of the Divine himself. Perhaps, I thought, in that glacially slow moment, *this* was what set me apart. The twisting strands of 'blight formed connections within me like those in the tissue of a living brain. *Never twice the same, encoding layers of memory and feeling…*

But this was no time for philosophy.

The ocean *heaved*.

Never mind the storm which came rushing up behind out fleet – this was a lurching drop, as tons of water shifted out from under us. Filaments of fire branched through the jade-green depths, licking out to caress the hulks of dead ships. Inside, bones stirred, clattering together amid shoals of bubbles. Frightened fish darted away as light kindled in empty eyes.

And my fleet of the drowned rose up to meet me.

It began as a v-shaped wave, erupting ahead of the onrushing Tarkhanden Eighth. Ahead of the bow-wave of the *Ironheart*, where skarne leaped and snapped amid the spray, a churning line of white spread out, hundreds of spans to either side. Then the tips of rotted masts began to break the surface, growing like a thicket of petrified trees. Weed-draggled rigging and sodden rags of sailcloth followed, and there were dead men clinging to the ratlines – hollow-eyed ghouls with barnacle-crusted bones, gripping weapons more rust than steel.

---

24. Use courtly Rasuuli, or poetic Ghurami, say, and you could be there all week just getting the average animated skeleton to pick what used to be its nose.

The Kothrai chantries were in full flight by now, and a hail of sorceries came down on the dead fleet. Jagged bolts of purple, spheres of bubbling darkness, smoking missiles trailing insane laughter… all crashed against the hastily wrought wardings of our own cadre. I could see the translucent panes of pure force which they cast up, each one the size of a mainsail, moving through the air to intercept the Kothrai's fury. Some slipped through, but most shattered into sparks and ashes against the power of Silan and Suramaei.

Where the warlocks' barrage struck home, rotten timbers burst into sickly flame. Whole ancient galleys and carracks were sundered, masts collapsing, the hungry sea gurgling in. But for every one of the dead fleet sent back to the bottom, another rose. They were a wave of salt-rimed, reeking doom, bearing down on the Kothrai fleet like a hammer. Behind them, the guns were run out from countless firing ports, as the Tarkhanden made ready to press home that advantage.

The storm intensified around us. The unleashing of so much wild magick fed into the charged atmosphere, painting scrawls of lighting above us. The rain began to lash down in earnest, and the swells picked us up, throwing us toward the Kothrai line as it came on. Where the storm-wind met the breath of the Maelstrom strange eddies and currents clashed, drawing down waterspouts from the skies.

For a moment I let myself see it all from the vantage point of Sei, perched in the crow's nest atop our mainmast. Gryst's huge handprints were still stamped into the metal lip of the lookout platform.

Ahead of us loomed the first rank of the Kothrai fleet. Almost within spitting distance – a wall of spiked rams, toothed wheels, cannons and grapple-throwers. Lesser shamen, not attached to Vuhl's dark chantires, stalked the forecastle decks, preparing to loose a hail of killing sorcery. The creak and groan of timber and hawsers, the clank of armour, the drunken war-songs of the axemen who waited to swarm our rails… all rose up behind the grumble of thunder and the incessant blattering of the rain.

Now I looked through the little cat's eyes at the blow about to strike this wall. A mere handful they seemed, my dead fleet – though they were, in truth, hundreds strong. Vessels from every age, from every nation, drawn in to this doomed place by legends. Now great sharkskin drums beat out the cadence for rowing skeletons. Now the waves rose up beneath a double rank of holed and worm-riddled hulls, promising one last glorious assault. I looked out from behind a galaxy of dead eyes, and I picked my targets.

For an instant it held – this image of doom about to be unleashed. Two walls of wood and iron, tossed on the churning sea, coming together with knife-swift urgency, balletic grace….

The dead fleet struck home with a grinding, crunching detonation, and I felt it in my bones as the horrorworks of the Kothrai's ramming gear ran them through. Spikes under the water gutted them. Millstone-sized wheels, toothed with ploughshares, bit deep into saturated timber. Ballistae spat iron shafts, and fire arrows arced high, raining down like sparks from a bonfire.

The sunken hulks could not take such punishment. The first rank were wrecked down to raggage by the fury of their own assault, spewing timbers skyward as ribs and keels sundered. But none of this slowed down the dead. They swarmed aboard, bones scraping against anchor chains, hideous grinning skulls rising up over the rails, some with the obligatory dagger clutched between their teeth. Others were content to use those teeth alone.

They were dead sailors all, and they took to butchering the Kothrai with wild enthusiasm. Rusted scimitars swung, spears and tridents reamed in through mail, axes hacked and splintered spines, ribs, collarbones…

I barely had time to concentrate as the second wave of undead ships piled in, some veering aside at the last moment to slip between the Kothrai. I watched one ragged-sailed frigate shoot the gap, a ghoul in a rotted tricorne spinning the wheel and laughing. Gun ports crusted solid with coral cracked open, and cannons poked out like fingerbones, their fuses hissing green…

Spectral fire tore into the Kothrai ships on either side, punching deep into their bellies. To port, a doomed black ship's magazine was ruptured, and detonations broke its back. To starboard, ghostly chainshot raked the decks, ripping through the tight-packed raiders and letting their soulless bodies drop as it passed through them.

Now there was a breach. Elion Morekh squinted up at the signal flags, almost torn from their ropes in the gale.

"We're going in, Kuhal!" he shouted, both hands on the wheel. "Brace yourselves for impact!"

I don't think he had been so happy in centuries. "There! We'll slide in slick as butter, then give 'em a taste of Harlaw's guns!"

I had barely enough time to wonder exactly what I was supposed to brace myself with… then the *Ironheart* struck.

Meracq D'avarian was no coward, and he'd chosen as his mark a huge twin-hulled barge of the Kothrai's second rank. He aimed to plunge his line of warships deep into the wound opened by the dead, and being a grandiose Zamaran nobleman, he presumed to accomplish it with style.

The *Ironheart's* immense ram took the form of a bladed screw, turned by oxen walking an endless treadmill. These beasts had been whipped into a near stampede as the ships came together, all their energy stored up in a great stone flywheel. Now the Saltmaster let slip a pair of brass levers beside the ship's helm, letting the screw churn the foam. It bit into the starboard hull of the Kothrai barge with a rending, cracking sound, pulling the two ships together. At the same time, the fore-mounted cannons which clustered around the flagship's figurehead thundered, shredding a fair remainder of its superstructure. I directed a score of undead sailors into the breach alongside D'avarian's marines, and soon the crack of flintlocks and the chime of steel on steel echoed amid the gunpowder smoke. Through the blue-tinted haze came a flash of cerulean light, and a massive split carved its way across the Kothrai's decks – Meracq's sword-boy had handed him his sabre, and he unleashed the Way of the Tempest with considerable enthusiasm.

He was not about to fight alone, however.

The *Skarne's Maw* grazed the port side of the barge as it came through, crushing a dozen men between walls of salt-crusted wood. Its ram was a solid brass blade, etched with the face of a shark, and it took its mark across the bows, shearing deep. It seemed for a moment that the blade was stuck fast in the Kothrai quinquireme, but it was not to be. The entire ram was mounted on steel rods, socketed into a brace of cannon barrels. Men loaded powder, lit fuses, ran with their fingers in their ears…

The resulting detonation flung the *Skarne's Maw* backward – but her bladed prow carved right through the doomed Kothrai ship, sending it to the bottom. Heavy chains reeled the brazen ram back into position as the *Maw* maneuvered, tacking and heeling over to present her broadside.

We came into the breach behind that stuttering roar of cannonfire, and we sailed in to a vision of hell. The Kothrai chantries had left off trying to sink the dead – a futile task, it seemed. Now they saw our aim, and were desperate that the *Sorrow's Vengeance* should not punch through their formation. We would be the needle, drawing a thread of cannon-bristling men o' war behind us.

For a frenzied hundred heartbeats my companions and I had to let the summoning ritual falter, as we poured all the power of the Void Heart into the wardings.

The world rang like a bell as glassy shields cracked and shattered above us. Onion-skin domes of flame flickered and turned to smoke, one by one. Falling stars of purple and black descended on us, trembling the ocean to its depths. Crimson bolts sheared away, howling, to punch clean through other ships of the line, setting them ablaze. I caught another glimpse of Abyssus, as the storm of sorcery raged. Those chains were pulling tighter, sawing into the mosaics and gems crusted on his shell. The water itself was bleeding darkness, lit up from within by crawling filaments of fire.

"Do not falter, my Herald! I can endure. I.... *must*...."

A Kothrai chantry's assault flew wide, plunging down into the deeps. A temple avenue on the seabed ceased to exist, as a miniature sun dawned in the green-tinted darkness. And still the rain of destruction fell.

The *Vengeance* shuddered from stem to stern like a live thing, the sea literally boiling around her. But our wardings held. And then we were through the gap, water choked with flotsam on either side. To my left, I watched the *Skarne's Maw* coming about, weathering a storm of arrow-fire and shot. From my right came a titanic crack as the Kothrai battle-barge split in two, both hulls shattered below the waterline. My dead men rode it down, still hacking and stabbing at their foes as the lower decks flooded with icy brine. But Meracq D'avarian's marines had already swung clear on ropes, scrambling back aboard the *Ironheart* as she made headway. With a hiss of spray we were past them, and through.

Now it was Harlaw's turn.

The little engineer had been waiting for this moment. Because he hadn't been content with the rows and rows of black iron cannon which studded the flanks of our craft. Oh no. Having seen what the Guild of Chains had accomplished in Oram, he had been driven to improvise.

Now six great wooden hatches rattled open on hidden cogs – three to each beam. Rotary cannonades like those devised by the half-mad Artificer Quenlon nuzzled their ugly snouts through, tasting the smoke-heavy air.

And as we slipped past Meracq's flagship, into the heart of the Kothrai line, they came roaring to life.

Aside from those grim new armaments, the *Vengeance* was still equipped with over two hundred conventional guns. The crews which fed them were the cream of the Tarkhanden navy, hand picked (with much grumbling and cursing) from among Saltmaster D'avarian's own command. Now those men took aim and fired, macerating Grennen Vuhl's formation on both sides. Even the storm of sorcery faltered as a hail of iron shot shredded through one of the chantry barges, turning warlocks and their thralls to dripping mincemeat. Timbers shattered, sending splinters scything through the low-slung underdecks of the Kothrai galleys, where there was no escape. Fires blossomed, greedily clawing for pitch-soaked wood, canvas, hempen rope…

Now the wound was ragged and bleeding. The red sails of the Tarkhanden Eighth Fleet came through, pulling up into a wedge which stuttered with cannonfire behind a fog-bank of smoke. Still the black ships perished, with only a sorry few scoring decisive blows back against our number. The dead were among them too, scaling the sides of galleys, dripping with seaweed and gore, their corroded blades reaping a terrible harvest.

Elion Morekh did not need to see the signal flags snapping at the *Ironheart's* masthead to know what happened next.

"Hard a'port!" yelled the undead captain, a savage gleam in his milk-white eyes. "Come on, you scurvies! Bend your backs to it, or I'll flay 'em raw!"

The *Skarne's Maw* led the way, slicing through the waves as the rain lashed down. A boulder from some Kothrai mangonel punched clear through her sterncastle as her sails luffed, then bellied full again – but the old warhorse kept going. Another broadside spat death back at her tormentors, and she came about, flames billowing from the broken stained-glass windows of her transom. The *Ironheart* was next, and then Elion spun the wheel hard, taking us in behind the northern arc of Vuhl's fleet.

I realised, then, what a hollow victory our attack had been. Behind us, forty black ships sunk slowly to their long rest, corpses, axes, mail and gold following them down into darkness. A handful more were reduced to guttering hulls filled with fire and bones. Of our line, we had lost perhaps five men o'war – with not a one of us unscathed barring the *Vengeance* herself.

But the Kothrai were legion. Though those downwind of us would be harried by the gale, having to tack against it to engage, even those upwind were too numerous to count. I gritted my teeth and reached below for more hulks, more skeletal ghouls to crew them…

"I… I'm fading, Kuhal Moer. I can feel him drilling into me. The mindflesh. The blood of memory… The Dwellers… oh, their pain, Khytein! Their *suffering!* I cannot free them. I cannot help them! I…"

Then the voice in my mind shifted, shot through with memories of toothache, corpse-rot and darkness. The hot, busy darkness at the heart of a midden.

It was Grennen Vuhl.

"He fails, *Lamenter. Just as you will. This maelstrom of his… it is a* gateway. *Like the gulf between Sorath and Sarem. But we can change it. It can go…* wherever we choose."

I was sure I had heard it. A sing-song disharmonic in the Kothrai's voice… like the sound of someone mocking him behind his words. *We.* An interesting choice of words. Vuhl hardly sounded like entitled royalty.

But I had nothing to say to the monster. Indeed, all of my concentration was focused on keeping hold of Abyssus, clutching for his power as it trickled away between my fingers.

Another handful of sunken ships broke the waves, their ragged sails flapping in the storm like broken wings. South now, barring the path, holding the line for those who still lived. I feared there would be no more.

Then I heard Kayan Orsii scream – a sound which she almost choked on. Siara, too had felt something, and the working faltered, lines of force shearing away, motes of fire winking out all across the ghost incantus.

"Well, Khytein," spat our captain. "There you have it. Feel like making a valiant last stand with me?"

I clenched my fingers into fists and looked up – up to the wall of clouds which ringed the Maelstrom. A wall which was even now parting, wisping away to shreds and rags around two great shapes as they bulked through.

"I'd like to say not today, Morekh. In fact, I'd like to say *never.* But those *are* what I think they are, aren't they?"

He simply nodded. The flux and arc of sorcery around those prows of stone sent lightning skittering across the sky in a whole slew of unnatural colours. Eagle-winged wolves graced their bows, carved leaping with their jaws wide.

"In that case, Elion of Faeros, I would be honoured," I answered, folding up the remnants of the working, and tucking away the residual power in the rings on my fingers. The dead, after all, could take care of themselves. We had bigger problems.

Because, gliding through the sky in defiance of every natural law – and each one the size of a bastion fortress, a sliver carved from the face of a mountain – came our doom.

Two war Keels of ancient Anganesse.

Arrowhead-shaped ships of stone, an order of magnitude larger even than the *Sorrow's Vengeance,* and built entirely for domination.

And that wasn't all.

Perched on the bows of one great stoneship were five figures in black. Robed, hooded – yet I knew them intimately. Grennen Vuhl had aped the Coven of Nine at the whim of his master Dirge. Three had been slain, at a terrible cost. Now the remaining demons of the Nameless came to avenge their siblings.

I cracked my knuckles and drew Cryptfeeder, preparing the bindings of the second level. But even the feel of a sword-hilt in my hand did little to comfort me.

As valiant last stands went, this one looked destined to be shorter and bloodier than most.

Behind the storm, I could hear the mad discord of Grennen Vuhl's laughter…

"We are all sinners. All have fallen short of the grace of Esau, and of his beloved earthly son, our Thearch. So, is it not a blessing that we should be shriven of our sin through pain? Is it not a benediction of the highest order he bestows, when the Thearch calls upon the dead to serve him? As you die, then, think of what your suffering will achieve before you are judged pure enough to enter paradise. Your bones inscribed with holy writ, ensconced in hallowed glass... you will carry forth the Keels of Esau's order militant. You will bear his faithful on your backs, as he bears your sins upon his cross of pain. And, after long servitude, you may yet be absolved, and join our Lord in his realm eternal..."

Prayer for those consigned to the Ossuaries -
Old Angan scripture relating to the making of the Keels.

THE GRIEVING ONE. *The Ravener. Deathknell. Bonesplitter. The Lightless.*

They were names which had already brought horror to the lands of Sorath. The Tarkhanden settlements of the Million Isles knew the creatures of Grennen Vuhl's coven, in the same way that dark legends grew up around Urzen's original creations. With the Betrayed banished, the Duke of Chains torn in half, and the Hungering Tide exterminated, there were yet five more of the vile things left to kill. Five out of nine – because Vuhl himself was counted among the demon host. Even Urzen, despite his unfortunate name, was never mad enough to offer his own flesh up to the Outer Dark.

And that wasn't all.

The battle around us had turned. What was once an ordered assault had become a confused, storm-lashed slaughter. Ships heeled and tacked in every direction, shrouded in swirling banks of cannon smoke. The crack and stutter of blackpowder fire combined with the shattering concussion of ball-shot striking timber, of masts snapping and of men dying. Here and there ships ground together, or rammed home to spin amid the swells, sailors and marines swinging across from deck to deck as boarding parties charged, pistols and swords against shields and axes.

Elion Morekh steered a course through the insanity. Steady at the wheel, he brought us through into clear water, between the bogged-down Eighth and the churning cloud-wall of the Maelstrom.

Where the Keels waited for us.

I did not even care to speculate how Vuhl had found such engines of war. No doubt Dirge himself had entombed these relics, keeping their bindings and soul-ossuaries quickened with blood for three hundred years. The sheer toll in human suffering was staggering. But it paled before the sight of those immense arrowheads of granite looming over us, ancient bonepowder cannons dripping jade fire from their belly-ports and broadsides.

Elion Morekh grunted.

"We're dead in the water, Khytein. Have to get this thing airborne."

I turned to look at Siara, who was still ashen-faced and reeling from the breaking of our ritual.

"Can you do it? Can you make this bastard fly? Because if we don't…"

The Keels provided us with an object lesson. A glassy, cracking sound split the skies as their batteries of guns spoke, spitting runic shot. Four ships simply disappeared beneath the hammer of that assault, their deaths heralded by the soul-scream of hundreds of doomed men.

"Oh, yes," replied Siara. "We can fly. But one poor imitation against two Keels of the line? We would be sorely pressed to survive, let alone fight back…"

Elion visibly bristled.

"Girl, you might be the most feared power since your father first raised a corpse. But when it comes to war at sea, you are still, as we say in Faeros, wet behind the ears." He pointed up at the Keels, which lumbered clear of the Maelstrom wall, slow and heavy. "I've fought those things in their heyday. Stoneships crewed by the Nekrologist priesthood of Urexes. The Thearch's own. And these specimens… well, suffice to say they aren't so lively-looking. I'd wager Vuhl's tried to train his Kothrai to sail 'em, but they're out of their depth. A couple of warlocks each to balance those big millstones, and another handful to steer… but they've got all the finesse of a one-legged drunkard. We'll fly rings around 'em. And Harlaw will do the rest."

I was not so certain. Even if they were crewed by drooling madmen, two Keels were a dire threat. All those Kothrai had to do was keep the millstones at the heart of each war-engine turning, and the guns firing. We would soon be reduced to a greasy slick of sharkbait.

"Get me close enough," said Kayan Orsii. "And I can bring one of them down."

I stared in disbelief. Gutting a war Keel while Unrestrained was one thing, but…

"Oh, spare me your condescension, Moer," she grinned. "You forget that I'm your most accomplished student. Barring, of course, dear devoted Grennen. I've read all about the war above Urexes."

I raised an eyebrow.

"Then you know it took an undead Draken to defeat the Thearch's Own. We don't even have a live one… more's the pity."

"But we *do* have the power to slice those ossuaries apart," she replied. "One strike in the right place, and the Void Heart will crack Vuhl's pretty toys in half."

The embers of all those things I felt for this strange Hmai were kindled afresh. She was out of her mind, certainly. But… *Gods, to be young again!* Only guilt and grief stopped me from kissing her at that moment.

"Leave some Kothrai for me, witch!" cautioned Elion, with a smile tugging at his stitch-marked lips. "And don't put your back out trying to carry that cursed blade."

She dragged the black sword free of its place in the circle of runes, struggling to heft its weight.

"Once the first of them die, I'll have strength enough to swing the damned thing," she said, as Siara opened her mouth to protest. "And in any case, I won't be using it to reach the chantry hall. Stealth will serve me far better than force."

"Stealth means sorcery," frowned the Stormreaper. "And that's never advisable aboard a Keel. *Balance.* They are flying rocks, and it doesn't pay to remind the world what's happening."

"You have a better idea? If we sit here and do nothing, we'll all drown together."

A figure loomed up out of the drifting cannon-smoke behind Kayan Orsii. It was at least a head taller than the sorceress in her ragged greatcoat and leathers – a thing with a skull-faced grin and shoulder pauldrons bristling with spikes.

"I say stealth went out the window long ago," said Silbern Chaar, reaching down to pluck the Void Heart from Kayan's grip. "Now it's time to show them what they truly face. You, Lamenter – you told me we should leave mercy behind us. Are you ready to practice what you preach?”

I nodded hesitantly. The Ontokhi sword-maiden lifted the Void Heart in one hand, as though it was light as a Ythean rapier. Once again, I wondered just how much she had been changed by the fall of Oram. Would prayers to her sainted ancestor feed power to her soul, even here?

“I must admit,” mused Siara, “An all-out attack is the last thing they will expect…”

“Because it’s *stupid…*” coughed Elion, into the back of one leather glove. We both pretended not to hear him.

“And it’s all we have.”

Behind us, the battle reached a new pitch of slaughter. The grapples were out now, as the Tarkhanden sought the dubious safety of close quarters. The Keels above would not fire into the heaving, creaking deadlock of ships and men for fear of slaying their own. Or at least, that was what Meracq D’avarian and his captains hoped…

“Then let us fly,” I said. “The Nameless are mine. Kayan, you and Silbern Chaar make for the chantry hall as soon as we can get you close enough. Siara – the Soulharp is yours.”

My daughter made a very undignified sound of disgust.

“Ram that sideways, father! My place is where I can kill the most Kothrai! Once the harp is in tune, I’ll slave it to the ship’s wheel. I spent too long as Grennen Vuhl’s guest not to pay him back in kind.”

Well, there was no doubt left in my mind. Wild, impetuous, foolish – and with a vengeful streak wider than both horizons. Siara Anvhaur was *definitely* my kin.

“Then see to it. Those cannons are reloaded, and we definitely have their attention…”

This time we didn’t just rise.

The whole immense bulk of the *Vengeance* leaped from the water like the skarne which rode her bow-wave, heeling over as she flew to prune the topgallants from a dozen Kothrai ships. Our copper-sheathed keel and steering fins trailed canvas and ropes as we ascended, soaring above the battle in the rain. Harlaw didn’t miss his opportunity to pour down shot from this new vantage, picking his targets amid the swirling chaos. The long guns spat fire, sending twelve-pound balls of iron flying in precise and deadly arcs. Here a Kothrai ship was holed beneath the waterline, breaking its back. There, and a black-clad captain simply ceased to exist, his severed hands still gripping the wheel as his crew howled in dismay.

But it was not the madness below us which held my attention.

"The Nameless are mine," I'd said. Oh, such hubris!

If my daughter and her merry band were to have any chance at all, I would have to face all five of the demons at once. Alone.

"Abyssus!" I called, striding toward the bows. "If you have power left to spare, heed your Herald! Abyssus! Shaper of the Aziphem! Let me be your vengeful hand!"

The reply from deep beneath the Maelstrom was wracked with pain. It came in like a storm of razors, tearing into my mind so that I staggered, reeling against the rail.

I spat blood. I clenched my teeth. I took the pain, and swallowed it whole.

"Almost… almost gone, Kuhal Moer. The shadow consumes me, even now. Human thoughts… all failing me. Fading. Tears beneath the ocean… But still. Yessssss. There are things which crawled here to die long before your race arose from the mud…"

I saw. And a terrible smile was the first thing the hooded coven saw of me as I walked out onto the bowspirit – a figure in ragged black rising up to challenge them.

"Filth! Unclean creations! You things shat out of Grennen Vuhl's madness! I enact the rite of the crucible! I call on the living to bear witness!"

We were between the Keels now, still rising, the *Vengeance* flying like an arrowhead beneath a cloud of sail. I looked back down the decks to where Silbern, Kayan and Siara were making ready, and threw them a reckless salute. Perhaps, I thought, I'd never see any of them again. Perhaps I would never have the chance to know my only child, or to slice through the uncertainty and pain when I looked into Kayan Orsii's amber eyes…

I crushed those thoughts and feelings – the hopes of a living man – up in one skeletal fist. And I threw down my opening gambit to the demons who stared up at me, their blank eyes blazing.

I had watched carefully when Meracq D'avarian had worked his Way of the Tempest.

In the Dark Sight the sorcerous strike was a subtle weaving and bending of forces, focusing them on the edge of his sabre. Now I wrought the same pattern of layered power, using the wellspring of magick which came seething up from Abyssus.

It was wild, and old, and brutal – the soul-stuff of beasts rather than men. But it folded and hammered down in the same way as the sorcery of the Twins, lighting up Cryptfeeder's edge with green fire.

I leaped from the bowspirit, the blade held high in both hands. The Nameless spread out as I fell, moving to entrap me. They supposed that I had chosen one of their number to slay with this single terrible blow. But they were wrong.

As I fell toward the Keel I reversed my grip on the sword, then unleashed the razor-sharp pressure-wave in front of it. I swept Cryptfeeder around in an arc, sending a whipcrack of green flame licking out across the deck of Vuhl's stoneship.

It missed every one of them. Now cowls and capes were being thrown back, and a mismatched horrrorworks of faces was revealed. Those who still possessed lips and tongues were laughing. But not for long.

The Nameless had gathered at the very tip of the Keel's arrowhead-shaped deck. And my slicing blow had cut diagonally across it. A fine spume of powdered rock puffed out from the flank of the stoneship for an instant, and as my feet touched down I heard a rending crack deep inside.

"Ladies and gentlemen," I purred, rising from a crouch with my blade held at guard. "Welcome to the domain of my lord Abyssus. Now, in so very many ways – *you're going down.*"

I'm not entirely sure if there were ladies among them. Gentlemen either, if one wished to wax anatomical. A thing with a pair of metal-toothed shark's jaws for a face snapped and hissed at me, raw tendons straining. Another was simply a pillar of whirling darkness in which a spine, brain and eyes floated.

But I was right. The crack I had heard was the ancient granite of the Keel giving way. I hoped D'avarian would be proud of me, for I'd sheared through its entire bow with one stroke.

We stood there, hatred crisping the air between us. I tried to think of some witticism - the kind of thing Elion Morekh would throw in his enemies' faces. But there was nothing. Then, with a rumble like a collapsing mountainside the deck fell away, and we were in free-fall.

I was glad to have saved my breath.

Things flew at me in a blur, hammering at my defences as I tumbled end over end. Steel hooks, flashing before a face that was all teeth. A single great crustacean claw, whole daggers bolted and drilled into its wicked edges. Lashing tendrils of icy black water, spattering droplets which felt as heavy as lead. Hells, even a red-hot anvil or two, swinging in through the rain behind a spiral corona of steam.

They assailed me from all sides as we fell, not bothering to activate the cantrips of levitation I was sure Vuhl had carved into them. Beneath our feet, an ungodly weight of stone crashed down through a raft of interlocked ships, sending the lot of them to the bottom. Kothrai and Tarkhanden drowned together, drifting lifeless toward the sunken city below.

I looked down, and picked my landing spot. Cryptfeeder spun in a series of figure-eights, fending off a barrage of blows from a thing split down the middle from crown to crotch, its halves held together by a web of white-hot wires. I noted, as I came down on the wheeldeck of a Kothrai man o'war, that someone had sewn its eyes shut, then added a wreath of them around its forehead.

Tempest strike. A second folding and layering of force, swept across the length of the black ship.

I landed clean on the shoulders of a Kothrai axeman, driving him through the deck with the bulk of his bones shattered. He was the lucky one – he never saw it coming. The line of witchfire I had unleashed bisected the masts, sliced the wheel in half, carved through a snarl of taut hempen ropes… and cut every sailor on deck off at the waist. The shockwave spun off over the sea, followed by a haze of bloody mist.

I was already airborne, leaping from collapsing mast to collapsing mast, when the first of the Nameless came down behind me, powering clear through the doomed ship in a spray of broken timbers.

It was the thing with the lobster claw – a mismatched, oversized pincer which distorted the entire left side of its body. Bio-sorcery had been used to add layers of tendon and muscle, distorting the wretched thing into a horror. Its lumpen face was partly human. But the rest was plated with pale chitin, studded with rough protrusions and knobs of horn. A pair of black, oil-drop eyes focused on me, as its lips parted in a gash of a smile.

This was the thing known as Bonesplitter, and I could see why. Not content with merely giving his creation a five-span claw, Vuhl had equipped that limb with blades, making it living guillotine.

And it was *fast.* I barely managed to parry the first snapping lunge of Bonesplitter's weapon, feeling those two spiked lobes hinge closed around my blade. Steel creaked and squealed in agony.

The Nameless had leaped the length of the Kothrai ship, and the sheer force of its impact drove me backwards, slamming up against the bow rail. I snarled, pushing back, my face inches from that of Vuhl's creation. It smelled of rotting bait, rusted iron and shit.

"…. Like a Faeroan outhouse," I gasped, weaving death-magick through the 'blight in my arms and shoulders. A twist of Cryptfeeder, and the claw creaked open by an inch. "But I'd serve you up with sweetlimes, if that's what it took…"

The power of Abyssus came up through the water beneath me. The ragged soul-stuff of creatures as old as the Coldblood, drawn here in the same way that the great beasts of the tundra go to hidden valleys to die, leaving drifts of yellowed ivory in the snow. I felt something huge and powerful smash up through the deck beside me, metal hooks glistening. I heard the sound of steel shark teeth grinding together.

"Raw! Prefer eat you RAW!" said a voice in my mind, jangling the nerves deep down in my brainstem. I clenched my eyes shut, fingers closing on the ragged edge of that power.

And I saw, beneath the waves, what this ancient city had been built around.

Ribs were buried under the silt, connected to vertebrae the size of tombs. Eyeless skulls with far too many teeth, tusks splayed in strange directions, limbs fused and warped into paddles, claws, hooks…

The remains of things from the dawn age, when life had taken strange forms. Things which had known, as their bloodlines failed, to crawl back to the demigod who had cursed them with the stirrings of sentience. The knowledge of their impending doom.

It was interesting, from a scholarly perspective. Taxonomists and scribes would re-write whole tomes from the evidence of these four great skeletons.

But all that mattered to me – now, with a mage-spawned horror scrabbling for my eyes with mandibles of brass and chitin – was that they were *dead*. And that I was a necromancer.

I spun loose from Bonesplitter's grip, feinting left as the thing called the Ravener snapped at me, hooks hissing through the air. Down, and those hooks bit into timber, trapping the creature. I hit the deck and rolled, my sword lashing out at ankle height to carve a slice through the demon's hamstring. It howled, but there were *wires* corded through that slab of tissue. It staggered, but failed to fall, catching up against its brother in a tangle of spiked limbs.

It bought me enough time. The bisected, seething Nameless called the Grieving One saw me win free, and its twin halves cracked apart, wires glowing hot within. A flat pane of sorcery sizzled through the air between us, punching down through the ship and instantly setting it aflame. I aimed a blast of my own back at the thing, swatting it from the air to crack up against the mast of another vessel – this one a Tarkhanden line-breaker.

Now to the working. I let my mind fragment, sending my will spearing down through the cold, dark ocean. Bestial fury welled up in me, the echo of the things Abyssus had entombed. And, as I bound up their bones with witchfire, they shrugged off millennia of seabed muck, rising in a roiling pall of silt toward the light.

The Grieving One kicked off the ship's mast, flying back toward me with a scream like a ruptured steam-pipe. The Ravener tore its hooks free, whirling around with its vast jaws grinding. Bonesplitter's wound was already healing, grey-green blood pooling the deck as it stood. And the Lightless was among us too – that pillar of boiling darkness which I now recognized as pitch-black water. It filled a hooded cape which otherwise contained nothing but a disembodied pair of eyes, a brain, and a spinal column.

The ship gave a lurching crack, and I heard muffled screams from below. The fire had cut something loose, and we were sinking. Around us the battle raged, as the Tarkhanden marines tried to repel ten times their number of raving Kothrai.

It all faded into a background haze, as tawdry as cheap stage-dressing. Here, in this little world of smoke and sparks and the salt stench of drowning – here there were only the four Nameless and I.

I sheathed my sword, holding my hands out in front of me.

"Now, now, fellows. Wait. Can't we just talk about this?"

I looked from face to face. One was a grinning pair of shark jaws. One was a globe of dark water. Another was an expressionless mask of flesh and chitin. While the last was burned and scarred eyeless, sawn down the middle as if with some huge serrated blade.

I took their chattering, hissing, bubbling and rasping as a definite 'no'.

"Do you really want to serve that madman who spawned you? Do you really want to kill the only one who could set you free?"

I didn't expect a different answer. But then again…

"Very well," I said, hanging my head in what seemed like defeat. I moved my fingers, feeling the puppet-strings of force piercing the timber, the iron, the salt sea… "If you won't talk to me, perhaps you'll talk to my *friends*."

My fingers crooked. I reversed my hands, palms-up, and *heaved*, the 'blight in my bones creaking with sorcerous force and leverage.

And the ship was torn in two. A thing five times its length and twice its girth came churning up out of the depths below, shattering the vessel's spine between a set of antediluvian jaws. What is was, I cannot say – all bone, it looked like the bastard son of a lizard, a seal and a meat grinder. Far too many pairs of legs flashed by before a desultory flick of its tail snapped across the deck, catapulting the Grieving One up into the air. Then the behemoth crashed down, breaching belly-full across a pair of Kothrai galleys. Wallowing them under.

Before the severed bows of the ship could sink, a second monster surfaced. This one was serpentine, crested like a draken, with a pair of gracile claws which put Bonesplitter's to shame. Its coiling, thrashing body powered it up and over in an arc, capsizing an entire war-barge before it opened its jaws and engulfed the Lightless, shearing off another few spans of decking as it went under.

I drew in power from the souls of the dying. The air was feverish with sorcery now, and the essence of a thousand butchered men flared around me, carrying me up into the storm. For a handful of heartbeats I looked down on the churning wrack of ships and smoke, wreckage and corpses. Above me hung the Keels, one wounded and listing from my strike, the other floating rudderless as muffled explosions shook it from stem to stern. My ladies were working their slaughter…

The Nameless would have tried to follow me, if they were able. But the great beasts I had summoned were a dire threat, and now all four had broken the surface. Here, a long and sinuous neck bore up a head like an arrow of bone, jaws gaping as it savaged loose the masts of a Kothrai trireme. There, the ocean boiled up around a dome of chitin, as a crab the size of a small island gutted a pair of ships with its claws. The spined serpent writhed in knots, constricting and crushing a doomed timber hulk. The reptile-thing, all teeth and rage, wallowed amid a spreading slick of blood.

And the Tarkhanden were quick to press their advantage. Ships cut loose their grapples and disengaged, flying before the storm wind and leaving my pets to their frenzy. For Meracq's captains had all seen what now crested the eastern horizon, and chains of pennants were run up the masts, trumpets sounding amid the rumble of thunder.

It was a wall of red sails – the might of the Tarkhanden fleet, drawn together to pursue what had seemed a fleeing foe. Suddenly we were not outnumbered, and I felt hope thrill through the hard-bitten veterans of the Saltmaster's command. To the south, my dead men had held the greater part of Grennen Vuhl's armada for as long as they were able. Bludgeoned back down to soulless bones, they sunk back beneath the whitecaps – but their purpose was fulfilled.

The broken Keel crabbed around in a wide arc, unwieldy with its bows shorn away. The acolytes aboard must have seen the Tarkhanden fleet too, and now they moved to engage, ponderous and slow. A pity; I had hoped they were mad or foolish enough to pour witchfire down on my monstrous thralls. The bolts from Angan guns would do nothing but make them stronger, after all. Elion Morekh followed, closing the distance as he threw on even more sail.

But I only had eyes for a smudged fleck of darkness, touching down light as a mote of ash atop the second Keel. It was the last of the Nameless, and stories whispered by the crews of the Eighth had told me all I needed to know about its provenance. Those stories also told me of its intent, here and now.

It was going after Siara Anvhaur. It was a weapon designed purely for her destruction.

Necromancy is not an art in isolation. To command the dead, you must share their death-agony, feel their yearning for justice, vengeance, or absolution. Now the soul-stuff with which I wove was shot through with feral urges – huge, glacial slabs of emotion which remembered the minds of beasts. The last gift of Abyssus cut both ways. There was a *purity* to it – all plots and counterplots shorn away, all motives laid bare.

An evil thing was bent on hurting my child, and I would crush it to pulp or die trying.

Below me, the Kothrai fleet was in disarray. The great dreadnaughts at the centre of their formation were caught up in the struggle between my ancient beasts and the Nameless – little more than collateral damage as sorceries flared, claws snapped and ripped, and teeth bit down on unnaturally tough demon-flesh.

I left them to their slaughter. The instincts of predator and prey are strong, and it took little of my mind or my power to keep those horrors awake. Instead I alighted on the Keel's foredeck, following the thing called Deathknell.

An eerie silence permeated the stone chambers of the Keel, for Elion had been right. The Kothrai simply did not have the numbers trained to fly the war-engines of old Anganesse, and their warriors still superstitiously clung to the old ways of axes, shields and ships. That was not to say that these barracks, bastions, and corridors had always been so empty. Oh no. Charred smudges painted across the walls showed the outline of screaming faces and warding hands. Blood dripped from ceilings, and shreds and scraps of armour lay in sad little crimson slicks and pools. I shuddered – because there was far too little dead flesh strewn in the path of my daughter and her allies. Many and more, I knew, would have been sucked into the hungry darkness of the Void Heart, cursed to drift eternally in emptiness.

I wondered if one would – or even *could* – die there. How long would it take to go utterly mad in a place where even *up* and *down* were meaningless? Then I hardened my heart. These Kothrai did not deserve to bear their stories back to the source. If the Aziphem were tainted by human madness, it was the madness of men like these.

I followed Deathknell. It was easy – the thing was burning hot, and carried the stench of some infernal forge. Hot iron and sulphur were my guide as we made our way deep into the Keel – toward the great ossuary well at its heart.

I did not have time for subtlety. Not when I saw that Deathknell had simply walked *through* the ornately wrought doors of the chantry chamber, melting them half from their hinges. Deformed eagle-wolves spun through the air as I lashed out with Cryptfeeder, finishing the job. The clangour of tumbling iron was swallowed up by the huge, green-lit vault of the room beyond, where millstones the girth of castle keeps ground out the grist of souls. Between them winked the brass-capped tubes of glass which lined the ossuary well.

The coven who balanced the stoneship's forces huddled around a mirrored obelisk, on an ornately carved plinth fenced in filigree and gold. Lecterns held open tomes, and the Kothrai magi were even dressed in a crude semblance of the Angan priesthood's cassocks and sashes. They were not having and easy time of it – the air was thick with the oily scent of sorcery, and should that balance fail, the Keel would be nothing but a vast slab of stone hanging in the sky.

My daughter faced them. She stood at bay, slightly crouched, her double-ended scythe gripped in one hand, a Zengaji throwing knife poised in the other. Kayan Orsii was at her right, twin slim sabres crossed. And guarding their left stood the grim figure of Silbern Chaar, spiked and bloodied, her visor snapped closed and the Void Heart held up above her head.

Between them and the chantry stood the last of Grennen Vuhl's demons. It was huge and hunched, clad in a chain-mail apron which was stapled and riveted to its sagging flesh. Cords of wire, tubing and muscle burst from crudely stitched gashes in its hide. It was hooded in a cowl of brass scales, but I could see the jointed pipes which fed into its mouth and neck, pumping with some vile alchemy. And where its arms had been, those muscular shoulders simply ended in steel-capped stumps, hammered down over raw flesh and bone.

Its new hands were anvils. Four of them, levitating in a cloud of sparks. The things were red hot, mottled with slag, and they seemed to be *watching* Siara, Silbern and Kayan, turning slightly in the air to keep their flat ends facing them.

The old, primal wrath rose up in me, until I could taste iron and bile at the back of my throat. I had to force myself not to lash out with raw force, sending us all on a death-plunge into the Sorathi ocean.

"Deathknell!" I roared, feeling more wild, free, and *alive* than I had for centuries. "*M'hartha nuan gamek har, t'thot! K'thar'ech tu salkar Khytein'i ganak sulan!*" Translated, it is a crude call to battle. "Hey, pig-rapist! Let me pleasure your sorry arse with good Khytein steel!"[25]

Siara turned at the sound of my voice, a look of horror on her face. "No! Father! You can't…"

"I know, " I growled. "*No sorcery.* I'll finish this puling half-demon the old way, and grind his sorry bones between those millstones."

"Lamenter!" bellowed Silbern. "That's not what she…"

I saw the reason for their warning too late. Doors slammed open, and hissing, clanking figures stormed into the chantry hall, metal reflecting green fire. There were scores of them – brothers and sisters of the Unmade. Grennen Vuhl had fashioned a whole cadre of the damned things for war.

"They are yours, Lamenter", bubbled the voice of Deathknell. "A gift from my master. The one who will be *your God* hereafter. This place is the perfect killing ground for one such as you. I will see to the shriving of your flesh – then Lord Grennen will see to the torment of your soul."

I looked around at a thicket of spikes, of hands welded to axes and blades, of helms bolted and riveted to crusted bone. Pain stared back at me. Pain, and the will to share it.

"I don't need to raise the dead to end you, *abomination*," I spat. "And neither does my daughter."

Deathknell laughed. I have heard the full gamut of evil mirth, from the deranged giggle of a sadist to the bellowing lunacy of the slaughterborn. This was more vile than either.

---

25. There's a kind of pun in there – '*gamek*' for 'domestic swine' sounds a little like the old Khytein for 'tempered steel', which is '*ganak*'. The Khytein do have a sense of humor, under all their dour warrior bluster. It's just not a very refined one…

"*Your* daughter? *Yours?* Please, Kuhal Moer. Were you there for her first steps? Were you there to comfort her when nightmares plagued her sleep? Were you there..." and he chuckled, sick and wet "When the Doom came to her village, and she had to *watch?* Oh no..."

The thing raised itself, with some considerable effort, to its full height. Hidden gears clicked and strained, and those four red-hot anvils began to circle, slow and ponderous.

I saw its face. *And I knew it.* I had seen it before, once, through the eyes of Sei, in a tower which was now a broken stump...

"My little girl knows better than to disobey," grated Deathknell – Garald Ninefingers, smith of the little Kaltensund town of Cross Corners. Siara's grandfather, the man who had raised her. The ghoul who had eaten her mother Tessira alive.

"Now, be good, come to your grandsire – and *die.*"

"Oh, we can bring them back. I could do it myself,
given enough raw Materials. Flesh, tendons,
muscle, meat, guts... the whole slop-bucket, if you
will. Raise a dead man, and all he wants is his soul's
last wish. Revenge, justice - call it what you want.
Redemption, the priests would call it. Hah! But
a thing like me... a thing with a whole mind, well.
That's something other. I could return to life,
after a fashion. The meat and blood are not the
problem. It's the 'blight. Belief. When thousands
of puling little thralls believe you're a lich-lord,
it's hard to persuade enough of them that you're
not. Fear keeps me on the throne here - but fear
keeps me dead. I've had to just learn to live with it
- if you'll pardon my use of the word."

Sothara Roege
in his discourses with the wandering bard Alexyi Samardan

THEY WERE A motley accretion, this new coven of Nine. Sea-salt
crusted, bloody, bubbling and hissing. Things which came from the
Kothrai's dark legends, and from the hands of a sorcerer whose mind
had gone to shit.

I suspected that one or two were actually the creations of Urzen...
unfinished wrecks dug out of the mad Clockmaker's sarcophagi.
Dirge had no doubt wielded the shovel. Others, like the Ravener and
the Betrayed, were clearly the poppy's-blood nightmares of Grennen
Vuhl. And while all of them had been forged with a cruel purpose,
Deathknell was something different. It had been made to terrify, and
then to destroy, one person alone.

The Stormreaper. Siara Anvhaur.

Dirge must have known all about her, even before he worked the
Doom. Now, the instrument of his vengeance was upon us, four
hissing anvils swinging in as a tide of the Unmade followed in their
wake.

Fish-hook and gaff fingers clenched, creaking. Harpoon tongues
jutted obscenely from peeled-open trachea. They came on grim and
silent, leather boots scuffling on marble, eyes red as funeral fires.

I couldn't lash out with sorcery. Not here. Though the wellspring of

401

death-energy was vast, boiling up from the battle below like smoke from a burning city, to express such power was to invite destruction. The acolytes sweating at their pulpits would be unable to balance the millstones, and all those ossuaries would shatter, sending us to the seabed as ashes. Better to light a match in the powder-hold of one of D'avarian's warships…

But I could contain the power. I could focus all that terrible necrotic magick through the lens of my rage, distorting my own bones, turning my muscles cold and hard as twisted bowstrings…

And that was the worst of it. My anger was misplaced. Here and now, these petty horrors were not my greatest foe. The traitor who had killed Makara, who had stolen what was left of her soul… well, I was still numb with the shock of it. Only later would I have time to grieve, and even then, it would be more for my own pain than for hers.

Now, Deathknell and his pitiful trap were nothing but a distraction. Even Grennen Vuhl himself was just an obstacle to be swept aside. The Archaeon would pay.

But first…

"Aligning the seal of the Black Gate. Balancing the vitae flow to the seven cardinal sigils. Cerebrex bindings locked by the praxis of the Horned Eye, with restraint now unlimited to the second level…"

The art of the Killing Strike unfolded as the light drained to icy blue. Leering Unmade charged at me, their malformed fingers bristling with steel, and I parried and sliced, ducked and rolled, came up behind a rank of them swinging, the edge of Cryptfeeder tearing through meat, muscle and metal like paper. All expressionless. All my anger hidden behind a mask of bone. To those watching it must have seemed that I became an anemone of branching, ghostly limbs, infinitely ramified. The blade of Cryptfeeder was a blurred cage of steel around me, its edge everywhere at once.

They were wasting my time. Deathknell was the one who had to die, not these abortive dregs. *Then this Keel, then Grennen Vuhl…*

'Fuck it all.' I thought, quite clearly. 'If it's time for killing, let's do it wholesale…'

"Diverting the primaris vitae mortis. Opening the forbidden interlocks. Aligning the bindings of flesh and spirit by the sigil of the Chasmic Architect, with restraint now unlimited to the first level…"

The memory of a chained and locked gate, standing in a field of bones. The smell of freshly turned graveyard earth in the rain. I blew apart the interlocks, peeling my soul raw, calling down the mind of a

God to share my pain.

It was Anghul who came to me – the Antlered One, my dead people's image of mortality. The Khytein may have been long dead, but he lived on in children's tales and Kaltensunder superstitions. He was a nightmare, a storybook villain. But this close to the Maelstrom the *vitae mortis* saturated the air like an abattoir stench. And I was an evil faery-tale myself.

"Come on then! You, who gnawed on the bones of my fathers! Shall we show them the old dance? Shall we teach them the lesson of Winter's King? The sacrifice, the blood on the snow, the knife all steaming and red?"

Had he not been so diminished, the old butcher's scream would have torn me to raggage. As it was, I heard my bones creaking, felt tendons tearing loose, felt my skin split and stretch and *reform* as Anghul possessed me. My mind reeled, and I was suddenly looking down on myself from above, watching with a dreamlike detachment as I bulked out, my broken horn budding and growing into a six-tined antler, my face turned to a grinning death-mask…

"I should never have turned my back on you, little human," sighed the Aziphem, in a voice like the breath of tombs. "Old Sothara was a pious and tedious fool, and I feared his spawn would become another tyrant, binding me to dreams of empire. But you… you have slain many. You have fed me well. And you have asked nothing for yourself."

I caught a flash of vision – a moss-hung and thorny skeleton, seated on a throne of granite. Its eyes blazed as it rose for the first time in centuries, creepers and briars tearing loose as it drew forth a huge and rusted sword.

"Let us finish these upstarts. May their doom be a warning to our common foe."

It made me clinical, this detachment from reality. Cold, like the hands and hooks and bladed stumps which came scrabbling for my throat. But it also allowed me to shape and twist the *vitae mortis* like an artist, sculpting it around my bones and marbling it through my flesh.

The Unmade came on like a tide, driven by Grennen Vuhl's will. From out of the green-tinted gloom came a hoarse battle-cry, and then two words in Khytein.

"Father! *Down!*"

I modified my backhand swipe with Cryptfeeder, watching the

veins all along my arm swell to the size of hosepipes. Spectral muscle distended my skin, and the edge of the blade was patterned with a corona of unlight – a black feathering of frost. I ducked down, sliding on one knee into the press of malformed bodies, casually twitching left and right to avoid the strokes of blades…

Above my head I heard a whir like game-birds breaking cover, and I knew what to expect next. The Stormreaper's double-ended scythe moaned hungrily as it came mowing through the Unmade, lopping off limbs and heads, carving through grey, necrotic flesh and grinding on steel. Where it met resistance the blurred wheel of death caromed away, a controlled ricochet sending it flashing and spinning across the room.

A score of ghouls fell as the scythe slapped back into Siara's palm. She looked up, from behind a curtain of straight black hair, and she smiled, cruel and passionate.

"Too proud to ask for my help, father? No matter. This is a close to playing children's games as either of us will come…"

I followed through, into the empty gaps torn into the Unmade's ranks. Anghul was laughing as I hacked them apart… this was likely as merry a time as the old God had enjoyed for centuries. For a moment I felt the exultation of Sothara Roege, the Bone Collector, echoing down from antiquity. Proud of his great-great-granddaughter.

This is how peace is won. When the slaughter is so vast that it can never be countenanced again. When the price is so high that it dwarfs the pride of kings. When the example you make is enough to wake a plague of nightmares…

I didn't realise I had reached the far wall of the chantry until my blade bit deep into stone. I turned, snarling with borrowed bloodlust, and caught a glimpse of myself in the mirrored obelisk of the Focus.

The spreading, chain-hung antlers. The skeletal, sharp-toothed face. The empty eyes brimming with green witchlight. *Oh yes…* for a time, I was utterly possessed. But even through the haze of power I knew two things.

Firstly, that the Unmade were *terrified*. Those who remained cowered back from me as I brought my great horn-heavy head up, scenting the air like a predator. Bloody drool dripped from between my teeth, and I pointed one clawed finger at them in wordless promise. *You're next.*

But it was the second revelation which made me howl as I powered back across the chantry, my blade a black blur. Its edge cut the air to ribbons, leaving a sizzling blue trail behind it. Its tip carved an inch-deep curving groove in the marble, spitting sparks.

Things had changed within me. The mageblight feeds on belief, and we were a long way from Sarem, where people prayed to my deathless corpse. The force which had shaped me - which had begun to change me - was closer, more urgent. It was the belief of my allies, my friends – my family. And it had undone three centuries of isolation. Perhaps, in some twisted way, Makara's death had been the final lock to shatter. *Perhaps*, whispered a terrible, insidious part of my mind, *holding on to the shade of my lost love had been a* weakness.

For, as I came slamming into the Unmade's hastily wrought shield-wall, I could taste the iron and salt of blood in my mouth. I could hear the steady, tectonic thump of my heartbeat, pounding in my temples like subterranean drums. Blades sliced past me, tearing through my skin, and I *hurt*, for the first time in decades. Pain turned to anger, and Cryptfeeder screamed, resonating like a tuning fork as I worked my butchery.

I lived again. Blood and sweat and shit and muscle and rage. Teeth-grinding, wide-eyed fucking *exultation*.

The Unmade fell left and right. Black blood spumed, dripping from the ceiling. Siara's scythe came whickering through the press of flesh, curving to ricochet off the millstones themselves in a spray of sparks. The Kothrai mages at their lecterns quailed, losing focus, letting the forces slip…

We lurched sideways in the air. I felt my feet leave the floor for an instant before gravity slapped me down.

"Hold it! Hold it, damn you! Remember the meditations! Brace the balance!"

The master of the Chantry held his great Angan tome in white-knuckled hands. The thaumic mandalas which hovered above the lectern were in flux, cut as sorcery shivered through the air. His coven clutched at their heads, fingers scrabbling wet, and we lurched again, spinning, staggering above the ocean.

Beyond them, Kayan Orsii and Silbern Chaar fought the last of the Nine.

Deathknell's glowing anvils carved contrails through the air as he fought, hunched and avid beneath his hood of mail. His terrible, cored-out eyes wept a patter of molten metal as he came on, parrying Silbern's every swing of the Void Heart. He sent a single one of his thralled anvils looping over to intercept Kayan as she blurred in to strike.

Off to my left, I heard a gristly, ripping sound, and my daughter's cursing. The last of the Unmade fell, and now those great blood-crusted blades of hers hinged away, back into the recesses of her staff. I looked up at her, my death-mask flickering and fading.

"Is that truly… who it looks like? Your mother's father?" For I had seen Dirge tear himself open to birth Siara's deepest fear into the world, and if this was just another copy…

"Oh, I'm *certain* of it," replied Siara. "Nothing but the best for me! I've been the ruin of Dirge's plans all over Sarem, while you slept. But there's more to that story than you know." She kicked a sliced-through Unmade cranium away with the toe of her boot, coming up to stand beside me.

"And you, Lamenter? Should I be calling your tame Aziphem 'grandsire', perhaps?"

I huffed, cracking my knuckles.

"Close enough. Sothara Roege wore this face too, and from what I've heard…"

She nodded.

"Are you ready, then? Shall we take this thing?"

Siara grimaced.

"Dirge knows less about the nature of fear than he'd like to think. Aye, this is the face from my nightmares. But for a very different reason. I watched Garald eat my mother, it's true. But even then, I knew that he was already dead. The Doom is not something you need to explain to children. *He was gone, and his eyes were blank, and I took the hatchet from the woodshed, and I…*"

We spread out, stalking around the fiery loops and swirls which traced the anvils' path through the air. The coven could only watch, following us with frantic eyes as they tried to keep the Keel aloft. Enemies or no, one slip of concentration and we would all die together.

"You what?" I asked, shifting into a wide stance, ready to attack.

"I became the Stormreaper," she said. "I grew up. Fast." There was a hard loss of innocence behind those words. Something I remembered from my own bleak childhood, and its violent end.

The anvils hung poised in the air. Deathknell turned its scarred and eyeless head toward us, in a peculiarly birdlike gesture.

"Come now, child," it purred. "None of us *ever* grows up. Somewhere inside you are still that snot-nosed, weeping little thing who put a hatchet in the back of my head. But I forgive you." It smiled. "So long as I can return the favour…"

The double snick of blades cut his laughter like a twist of ribbon.

"Wrong," said Siara Anvhaur – and hell erupted on all sides.

Deathknell was quicksilver fast for all its bulk. The spinning blade which would have taken off its head caromed off a flying anvil, while a second red-hot mass of iron flew toward me, trailing sparks. I spun aside and it clipped the hem of my robe, instantly setting it afire. I shrugged it from my shoulders and turned, just fast enough to parry the same anvil away with the flat of Cryptfeeder. Even with the might of Anghul, the shock of that impact sent tremors all the way up my arm to the shoulder.

And Deathknell was far from finished.

Metal nails, pitons, brackets and screws ground their way out from the stone of the walls. A stinging cloud of them curled in to orbit the demon's head, each one waking to a lambent orange glow.

"Somewhere inside *doesn't have to mean your mind,* little one! I have made an *art* of unsplicing meat! I will make your suffering last just as long as we have been apart!"

I saw Deathknell for what it was, now – the same kind of occult creation as the Devouring Wind. Even the iron in my blood was twitching to the call of its manic dance, as it raised a gyre of red-hot splinters. Waves of wyrd force made the atmosphere shuck and writhe, throwing up curtains of haze.

Kayan Orsii came in low, swinging her swords in a scissor cut to hamstring the demon. But it was too fast. Though she slid around its anvil strike with feline grace, a storm of red-hot steel drove her back, forcing her to conjure a sorcerous shield from her palm. The Keel rocked again, dipping and canting as the acolytes swore openly in Kothrai.

I parried a flurry of metal shards, Cryptfeeder grinding along the slag-mottled flank of another anvil. Siara snarled, moving in, her spinning scythe deflecting a hail of iron.

But it was Silbern Chaar who struck most decisively.

The Ontokhi maiden was armoured from head to toe, and the strange resonance emanating from Deathknell at first pulled her off her feet, sending her crashing to the deck. The Nameless One barely spared a chuckle for her, so intent it was on the object of its hatred.

But slowly, painfully, Silbern rose again. Something of her sainted ancestor must have leached into her, for no mere human could have resisted Deathknell's love of iron. She braced herself, as if against a winter gale, down on one knee, the Void Heart gripped in both hands.

Metal screeched and groaned as every spike and rivet tried to unscrew itself from her armoured form. The tips of those spikes began to glow, and the stench of burning hair rose up from behind that impassive skull-faced helm.

Too late, the Nameless turned, scenting pain and defiance in the aether. Its empty eyes widened as it brought all four anvils around, forming a wall between it and Silbern Chaar…

The Ontokhi let go.

At once the twisting, iron-hungry force took her. She spun in the air as she was drawn in, the edge of the Void Heart licking out, starry and cold, to shear through two of those hovering anvils with a sound like a tolling bell. Deathknell reeled back as one of his metal stumps burst, tubes vomiting black and grey. Green flames clawed at his flesh.

The other two anvils tried to hammer together in that instant, but they were simply too slow. Siara's double-scythe was already airborne, and it slammed into the gap as neat as you please, keeping them apart. Silbern completed her pirouette as she slipped through. Then she brought the Void Heart howling down in an overhand strike, fit to reave the demon's soul from its carcass.

Oh, but the creature was *quick*.

It saw the starry edge swinging, and it threw itself backwards, the tip of the greatsword missing it by a hair's whisper. Indeed, a floating hank of pale grey hair was sliced away by the otherworldly blade, disappearing into nothingness with a slithering pop.

Deathknell leaped backward, poised to land on its toes and spring forward…

But Kayan Orsii's blades were there to skewer it.

They went in with a sound like parchment being torn in two, pushing out from those empty eyes in a spume of black blood. The sizzling furnaces within Deathknell's skull fused them cruciform, and the thing's convulsion tore the grips from the Hmai witch's hands, their leather bindings smoking.

Silbern recovered, as two cooling anvils slammed to the ground behind her. And, as I gripped a fistful of the demon's hair, baring its throat, she swung the Void Heart in a merciless arc, taking the dead thing's head from its shoulders.

A plume of blue-green flame erupted from the stump. Deathknell's body fell to its knees, burning from within with a fierce heat, until nothing remained but blackened chainmail and bones.

I held up the slack-faced head, staring into those empty eyes.

There was something behind them, packed into the dome of Garald Ninefingers' skull…

That was when I saw that its lips were still moving. That they were, in fact, counting in Kaltenspiel. Counting in reverse.

The dying Nameless winked at me as I realised what was hidden in its hollowed-out cranium. A last, desperate ploy to erase my daughter from the world. A thaumic detonant.

If there were rules for war, such things would be anathema. I have seen the remains of places which were scoured with such weapons during the Kinslayer Wars, before the age of Anganesse. I have walked on glass beaches, where the tortured shades of whole villages writhe as shadows in the broken shards, burning…[26]

I caught the Kothrai acolyte-captain's eye as I cast about for a place to throw it. His face was a mask of horror and pleading. But, really, there was only one thing I could do.

I spun on my heel and heaved the old bastard's head out between the millstones, into the ossuary well. Then I waited for us all to be blown apart.

In the hot, heavy silence which followed, I felt something dripping down my cheek. I reached up with one finger and cuffed away a drop of blood, from a tiny cut at my temple. One of Deathknell's little shards must have clipped me.

"You…. you're *bleeding*," said the Kothrai captain, in thickly accented Tarkhanden. "We thought you were a lich-lord. But you are just a man?"

I looked down at that tiny red droplet, feeling, for a second, a strange kinship with this enemy of mine. *This pressganged fool got up in Angan whites, with hands more used to holding an axe than a tome of sorcery. Not even my true foe at all. Not part of the Archaeon's grand manipulation…*

But there was no time to answer. The detonant cracked the ossuary in half at that instant, a silent explosion making the world flare green. Flickering, jade-lit hell raved all around us as we were thrown back against the chantry walls.

The whole Keel spun like a sycamore seed. The millstones juddered, grinding down with a sound like metal on bone. As we were severed

---

26. The Kinslayer Wars came before the establishment of the first Ythean Republic, when the brother kinds Reythan and Sorvald contended for their father's legacy - the now sunken island of Abaaz. Why it is sunken, and why some of the Ythean shore is now haunted glass, comes down to the pair's lack of restraint.

from the sky, bolts of witchfire came stabbing out from the well, bending at eye-watering angles, reaming through the bodies of the Kothrai at their lecterns and lighting them up from within like paper lanterns.

"You fool!" bellowed the captain, as the man beside him flared and arched and died. "You've killed us all! You'll not raise my bones, you stinking Sarem'ec charlatan!"

He was right. A skein of soul-stuff slammed into his chest even as he spoke, filling him to bursting with raw power. For a second I could pick out every bone of his skeleton from within, as his flesh stretched and split, illuminated…

Then he was gone. Erased. And the Keel was out of control.

I was pinioned to the wall by the sheer force of our spin and tumble. It was blind luck that none of those bolts of witchfire found me, for where they struck they blasted men's souls to dust. I turned my head, looking down the rune-carved stone to where my daughter was similarly trapped. For a moment our eyes met, and we both saw the ocean reflected in each others' fears. The certainty of impact…

Which never came.

Something massive whipped around the Keel before we could plunge into the cold ocean. Something took up the strain as we fell, grinding and cracking against the stone, shearing off towers and hanging embrasures, scattering cannon and chains and blocks of masonry.

We hung there, suspended, in a mountain-sized arrowhead of stone. I tried to think of what unholy amount of vitae it would take to bear us up with sorcery. Without the millstones grinding out the suffering of ten thousand souls…

"Father… what *is* this? How are you…"

Even as she spoke, Siara saw realization dawn in my eyes. She returned my look of horror.

"That's right," grated Kayan Orsii, sliding down the steeply angled wall to the floor. A deep, bone-marrow crack sounded from all around us, as that unthinkable force began to twist and rend. "It's *him*. Lord of the Drowned. Vuhl has taken him."

Damn fate, but she was right. And I didn't need the dark sight to prove it, as the tip of a gargantuan armoured tentacle came questing in between the millstones. Plates of nacreous shell slithered and overlapped as it hooked into the stone, followed by another, then another. Abyssus could feel me, His Dark Reflection – and the one who rode him would shuck me out of this Keel like a grub from a rotten log.

"Run," I hissed, as those great, tree-trunk-thick hooks began to strain. "It's *me* he wants. Go! Back to the fleet. Silbern – finish the Nine. Kayan – destroy the Kothrai chantries. Siara. *Stormreaper.* You belong with your ship. The Vengeance may be the only way to save what's left of the Tarkhanden…"

Stone screamed and splintered. Hideous daylight came bursting in, through a crack in the great hall's ceiling.

"I won't leave you, Father…" began the Stormreaper, clenching her knuckles around the haft of her scythe. "We have the Void Heart. We can destroy this beast, and Vuhl with it!"

I laughed bitterly. Such bravery! Such fire! I was filled with overwhelming pride and sadness at that moment.

As the Keel was torn in half.

As the cyclopean bulk of Abyssus was revealed.

His pockmarked and craggy shell was a nautilus the size of a citadel. Whole fortifications, coral reefs and temples were perched atop its whorled ridges. From within the bell-shaped lip of this accretion burst countless segmented, armoured tentacles – some merely the girth of towers, others larger still. Spined and jointed appendages speared down into the water, or sunk their claws into the jagged islands which had ringed the Maelstrom.

Had… because the wall of cloud had been blown apart. The ravenous maw in the sea was gone.

Now the God-beast had arisen from his chasm of stone, and he cradled our keel in a tangle of armoured whips, peering down inside with a galaxy of pale, articulated eyes.

I thought back to what Abyssus had said, when we had met in my fever-dream. *Of how he was the keystone of the arch, the pinch in the hourglass of life and death.*

"We can't kill him. We… we don't know what would happen. We could all drop dead on the spot. The Divine could awaken, and splinter Yrde itself. Hells, the Aziphem themselves could die. Imagine the feedback! All that power, swelling the Outer Dark…"

Siara shuddered. Kayan spat, making the sign of the Dead Zero.

"I can break this possession," I said, staring up at a creature which disappeared into the clouds. "I can pry Grennen Vuhl loose from the old bastard's hide. But not if I have to worry about you three. Now – promise me! You *run*, and you don't come back for me!"

I tried to fill my shout with all the rage, bravado and spit I could muster. Could I truly do all that? Perhaps. And the Aziphem were watching. Behind the shadow of Anghul crowded all the poor diminished shades of Death's Shard, putting their backs to the wheel of my power. Lending what little they had left to their final hope.

"Gods speed then, Father," said the Stormreaper, as all those abyssal eyes turned and narrowed at once. As the tentacles tightened their grip, shuddering the Keel as it was ground to pieces. A single tear cut a track through the stone-dust and grime on her face.

She and Kayan linked hands with Silbern Chaar, who had slung the Void Heart over her shoulder on its hooks. Only the Hmai looked back as they blasted away from the deck, a cantrip of flight unfolding around the trio like a shimmering bubble.

That look said a lot. More than anything, it said 'come back alive'. There was heat behind it which I hadn't felt for centuries.

I cracked my knuckles. There, perched halfway up a spiked ridge of bone, stood a pale figure, chains of darkness splayed out from its fists. Mollusk-flesh hissed with cold beneath his feet.

He saw me.

He laughed. Abyssus spasmed, grinding out a long bellow of pain.

And as the Keel was torn apart I prayed to the shades behind me, begging them for the last of their power. I remembered Urexes, as the ocean came up to meet me. I remembered a statue walking, a storm of bones, fists like wrecking engines swinging in…

Cold. Cold and dark. Silver bubbles shoaling up, toward a light tinted with red. Corpses floating, or falling below me, shadows with pale faces. Great, mast-thick tentacles spearing down, questing, probing… all silent. All rendered in silver and deepest blue.

I spooled the power in. I felt the death-energies of two more Nameless, tangled up with the brute souls of monsters.

Holding my breath, clutched in the cold womb of the ocean, I began weaving. A thousand skull-faced dying Gods looked over my shoulder, and *grinned*…

"They say, in their wisdom, that every end is a new beginning. Tell that to the condemned man, in the shadow of the axe."

Chief Magistrate Olpharis Lorn,
Scion of the Judicial Archive, Cyvenne

Start with Abyssus.

A creature which was ancient before the human race was even so much as slime. A thing so encysted and marbled with the 'blight, the touch of divinity, that it's whole armoured shell *(stretching above me like a living island, piercing the clouds with the temples and towers built on its back)* was of the same crystalline stuff as Kell Du'ath. A thing which had created new life after the fracturing, to speak to the Aziphem, to shape them… to avoid the coming of another entity as crazed and potent as the Fractured One.

His armoured tentacles were spiked and gnarled pillars three chains long. Eight of them supported the unholy bulk of that inlaid and accreted shell, the lip of which was a thicket of bony thorns, interspersed with the jointed, articulated stalks of giant eyes. Whips of chitin and long, twitching feelers burst from within the shell in a bizarre profusion. Other, smaller tentacles *(Smaller! Hah! The length of anchor chains, the girth of ship's masts…)* lashed in the air, tipped with pincers, hooked claws, and – horribly – what appeared to be human hands, wrought on an immense scale.

I was feared as a necromancer. But not even an army of the dead could stand against such a thing – a creature so huge and powerful that a nimbus of pure vitae curdled the clouds around its thorny crest, waking sheets of boreal fire.

Lucky, then, that Abyssus was not my true enemy.

And, as it transpired, *neither was Grennen Vuhl. Not anymore.*

Dirge, the Song of Ending for All Things Under Light, stood proud atop a ridge of creamy-coloured shell, chains of darkness clenched in both fists. The Kothrai warlock was *gone.* Subsumed. Even beneath the final transformation of his flesh, I could tell that the mind which hunted for me was wrong. It clicked and whirred like clockwork carved from ice, like oiled glass, serrated and sharp with poison.

There was no delicate way to describe his hideous new form.

Dirge had returned, his features pushing through the blind, burned ruin of Grennen's skull. Naked, he was sexless and hairless, a full-body

413

scar. Runes had been tattooed in dark green ink across every inch of his skin.

But he had also been *cubed*.

It was as if a gridwork of slicing wires had lashed him clean through, gristle and bone, leaving him cross-hatched with bloody lacerations. Still the size of two men, still pale and twisted with layers of fused muscle, knots of cartilage… But precisely butchered. Painstakingly taken apart. All of those cross-sectioned cubes of flesh floated, slick and bloodless, over a core of busy darkness. The manifestation of the Dwellers, boiling beneath the skin-and-muscle husk of Dirge's new flesh, leaking out through his eyes.

The pieces *moved*. They rubbed up together, greased with clear plasm. His face was a squared topography, little segments of cheek and eyebrow and forehead bulging and sinking, bulging and sinking as the darkness roiled beneath. Sometimes a whole gelid cube of flesh would slide out, a fingerlength or more, then *rotate*, slotting back in with an obscene little sucking sound.

A pair of lips which were sliced through in six places contrived to form a smile.

They parted, and a tongue like filleted meat licked out, wetting them with darkness.

"And so we come to the endgame, little savage," he purred, in a voice which seemed to whisper intimately in my ear. "And all the pieces on the board are finally revealed. Revealed, indeed, for what they are. I am not here to destroy you. Oh no. I am here to offer you a *choice*."

Under the water, weaving my working stand by strand, I could still see him. Radiant and cold, Dirge was a map of runic inscriptions, shifting and changing their meaning as the butchered segments of his flesh entwined.

I laughed, releasing a cascade of bubbles. My eyes were growing dim, sight blurring black around the edges, and I cursed my newfound need for breath.

Just a little more time. Keep the bastard talking…

"You know the Archaeon's purpose now, pawn. You must realise that I have been humanity's champion all along. *You* are the monster here, and the Aziphem you court will be destroyed by your hubris. So I offer you this. *Join me*. I am not your enemy, Kuhal Moer. I am your creator, the one who has shaped you for the war to come. I won't pretend to be sorry that I failed to take your 'blighted flesh. But here, now – you can put all your hatred aside. We can go forth against the draken together, and crush them. Would our rule together truly be worse than that of the Archaeon?"

For a heartbeat or two I faltered. A ghostly Incantus of thaumic energies shimmered in the water around me, waiting to be unleashed. But dammit, the old monster was *right*. He was not my true foe. There were powers abroad in Yrde which must be stopped, and humanity – even the debased, twisted humanity which Dirge represented – must stand together. Or risk a final holocaust.

Still his voice whispered in my ear, cajoling, seducing…

"With Abyssus under my command, and an army of dead Aziphem raised under yours, even the Sire of Draken will not be able to stop us. I ask you, Kuhal – not as my enemy, not as my slave – but as my *equal*. Join me. We will bring about an age of peace. Humanity will be spared, not just from the ravening of the draken, but from their own warlike folly. We will be free to study the higher Arcana, together – and who knows what we may unlock?"

The keels of warships criss-crossed the bloody foam above me, cannons sounding, bodies falling to float down amid the ruins of the old city. The Tarkhanden were dying, and the Kothrai too. With a word, I could make it stop. With a word, I could prevent the deaths of thousands, perhaps millions.

But damn me if you must, for I could not.

Trust Dirge Endsong? Work beside him? Wait for the knife to plunge into my back?

I thought about all the friends who had died because of him. I thought of the Doom, and Siara's birth-parents, now bones rotting under the Kaltensund sky. And that, too, was selfishness. For those shades and shreds of memory, I willingly damned all of Yrde to war. When the final toll is tallied, and I bring my tale back to the Divine, do you think I will not be judged for this? For placing my only true possession – my carefully nurtured hatred – before the lives of countless strangers?

No. I said, with all the force of my will. No. and *No* and ***No*** and ***NO***, the weaving collapsing in on itself, the salt sea boiling around me…

And there, deep in the primordial depths of my mind, was the final infamy. Reason, logic, strategy and mercy be damned. When I faced the Archaeon, and when I destroyed that ancient beast, I would do it *alone*. I would do it for Makara, and for her memory. Not beside the man who had cursed her to demonhood. Not for the soul of the Divine himself.

NO!

Geometric lines of power lanced out, down through the silt, carving ziggurats and temples in half. The seabed cracked, as probing fingers of force drilled down, piercing ancient strata, raising a roiling pall of muck and shell fragments. Sei was the key to this, and the little skeletal cat leaped from the deck of the *Sorrow's Vengeance* at my call, sinking toward me with his empty eyes twinkling blue. I caught him up, and held him to my chest as the ocean heaved. As those four primordial monsters fell apart, their souls stripped from their bones and folded in, *harmonised*, amplified, sent coursing through the murk and slime, down among the dark and pressure beneath the seabed.

Where their fallen kin were slowly turning to tar. Where the bones of countless things from the age of the Coldblood lay embalmed in a salty slurry, waiting for my call.[27]

Abyssus may have lost the higher parts of himself. But the low, bestial fraction remained. I insinuated my will behind the hooks and chains of Dirge's possession. Sei's feral little mind masked my own. Power shifted, seething through me, and the flagstone streets of the sunken city began to crack…

What arose from the water, shrugging aside dreadnaughts with tectonic disregard, was the stuff of nightmares. The sea boiled with foam as a broad and bony back hunched clear of the swells, sending ships spinning aside like children's toys. Water sluiced out from between a knotwork of bones, fish caught wriggling and flashing in the sunlight, ropes of weed, anchor chains, snagged corpses both Kothrai and Tarkhanden…

The deep blue-green of the ocean was paled by silt as I unfolded, my mind reeling in awe and terror. But I was unable to stop what I had unleashed. Myself, Anghul, all those other Aziphem who were Facets of death's Shard – we were transfixed by the brute animal will of Abyssus, that fugitive part of the God-beast's mind which still fought Dirge's infection. We were his vengeful hand. But it was a hand poised, suicidal, fingers tight around the blade.

I saw the waves heave below me as my composite spine straightened,

---

27. How can we know what races, species, forms and shapes of life rose up in the time before even the rule of Draken? And between, when the race of man was but one strand of the great re-weaving of life? All I know is that most of them - even by their bones - looked like the kind of things only seen in the nightmares of drug-eating libertines. To think of them bellowing and rutting, clothed in flesh… well, there are some things even a necromancer shudders to envision.

evolution unfurling with a series of cracks and groans. The ocean was milky jade, boiling with silt, the colour of the amulet at Kayan Orsii's throat, the pins which held back her hair. Below me, amid the tiny, smoke-wreathed hell which swirled around my knees, she was fighting. My daughter was fighting. Silbern Chaar swung her otherworldly greatsword, hacking into Kothrai mages' necks.

But my hands were too big to wield a blade. And my new form, wrought as it was from primal terrors, was unable to help them.

For the thing which Abyssus and I had wrought was *titanic*.

Misshapen, salt-caked and ivory pale, I had become a tangle of calcified monsters, ripped from their rest and woven into a mountain-sized golem. Coils of serpentine vertebrae wrapped a pair of arms as thick as the God-beast's armoured tentacles. My chestplate was the carapace of an immense crab; my claws were leviathan's ribs. A head cobbled together from skulls formed a rough and jagged mask, and the horns which bristled from my brow were those of trench-dwelling things alien to sunlight – bio-luminescent lures and whips were tangled among them like jewels in a diadem.

At the heart of the construct, pinioned within its chest, I could feel a web of mageblight piercing me. I was held like a marionette in the grip of 'blight and bones, Sei cradled in my arms. Here, the stench of salt, rot and sorcery was overwhelming. My head swum with the potency of it.

I raised my foot, and I felt Anghul take a step forward from his mossy throne. I felt a tangled stump of bones, a hundred spans across, torn loose from the sucking mud of the seabed.

One step, and my arms swung loose at my sides, ploughing through the sea in a burst of spray. Ships foundered and drowned in the eddies left behind as my colossal form took up a fighting stance. A mouth brimming with green witchfire cracked open along faultlines amid the bones.

I had meant to say something intelligent. Some witticism, to cut Dirge to the quick.

Instead I *howled*, a bellowing roar of defiance. Close enough.

"So…" chuckled Endsong. "This is your answer? The same tired old masquerade which lost you an empire?"

"I wasn't trying to *rule* Anganesse. I was trying to bring it down." The words came out as sharp-edged thoughts, unspoken. But he heard them.

"And just think of what the White Empire could have done for us now! Nekrology such as Yrde has never seen, fit to crush a nation of fractious lizards… oh well. Your dirty barbarian folk were always ones for slaying draken with swords and spears. Best find yourself some bearskin underthings and a magic blade, *hero*." This last word came laced with infinite contempt.

"I never claimed to be one of those, either. Just a better alternative than you. As I recall, you wanted to feed this world to the Dwellers."

"Those mad things could be *managed*," he hissed. "Do you actually believe I would let them rape the Materia and the Manifest, in their idiot hunger? No… it was the Shards for them. For the damned Fractured One. And for him, I needed a special Shard indeed. One collapsed down to only two facets. No longer a gem, but a *razorblade*. A mirror. *Death's Shard*, Kuhal fucking Moer!"

"But the Doom…"

"Ha! I won't say it was nothing personal. But your wretched cult was just another tool. We were close… so close to forging a trap for the Archaeon's bloody God. And then *you*…"

"You… you killed millions! You can't wax all righteous with me. Not with so much blood on your hands!"

Dirge's laugh was cold and tired. It echoed with all of his four centuries and more.

"And what of yours… *necromancer*? Son of Sothara Roege? I know his creed, as well as you do. '*This is how peace is won. When the slaughter is so vast that it can never be countenanced again. When the price is so high that it dwarfs the pride of kings…*' – look to your own hands first!"

I did. And they were wrecking engines of bone and chitin, studded with curving crab-claws the length of longships, clawed with the ribs of abyssal giants.

I may have been used by the Archaeon and his cabal. I may have thoroughly misunderstood Dirge's grand plan. And – damn the truth – he may indeed have been the last, best hope for the human race. But he was my enemy. My daughter's enemy. And he had tried to kill her. Those crusted, bony hands knew just what to do with such filth.

The first blow seemed to fall in slow motion.

I raised my arm, threads of mageblight tugging tight, and I stepped forward into the shadow of Abyssus – still towering over me, despite my gigantic form. Bones creaked and cracked as I tightened my fingers into a fist, and sent it crashing in. Those calcified knuckles hammered into one of the God-beast's armoured tentacles, pulverising chitin, tearing flesh…

The great creature staggered, uttering a psionic shriek. Tentacles lashed, splintering a dozen ships below us. And Dirge hauled on his reins of darkness, bringing his titanic mount up and around.

"You can't slay him!" shouted the Angan, panic twisting his butchered face. "You'll shatter the whole damn shard! Crack the Divine's damned prison!"

A second blow followed, fingers spearing deep into the wound I had opened. Claws sunk into gelid mollusk-flesh, and I *pulled*, bracing my feet against an upthrust of stone.

"Not him. He'll live. Might… even re-grow some of these limbs. But you… not this time. Never again."

I dug in deep. I felt the bones strain, witchfire musculature flickering and ghosting around me. The brute stubborn will of beasts long dead…

I twisted and tore and *ripped*, severing that tower-thick tentacle with a sound like hooks through wet leather. Where it struck the ocean ships foundered and died, their decks awash with blue and viscous blood. Waves curled over them, sending them to the bottom.

"So be it then!" spat dirge – disgusted, enraged… but not afraid. "You have forced my hand, Kuhal Moer. You could have been so *useful!*"

Abyssus screamed, the bleeding stump of his tentacle lashing. But there were hundreds more. Hooks and whips and spiked clubs of bone. And now the battle began in earnest.

There was no art to it. No agility, no grace. Just brute strength, wallowing and pulverising, fist and claw and coiling toothed tentacle pittted against each other in a brutal struggle. Abyssus hung above the bottomless well of the Maelstrom, far out of my depth. But the ring of jagged rock which circled him was my bastion and my shield. More than once I moved into the shadow of those oyster-crusted pinnacles, just as armoured flesh shattered them, raving and lashing, lacerating itself to ribbons.

We traded blows as the battle raged on around us. Ships rammed and grappled, cannons spitting fire, smoke drifting in pale, shifting veils. None of their masts even came to knee-height against the vast construct I had wrought.

I slogged in, weathering lashes and strikes, pounding my fists against the shell of the beast. Cracks ramified. Temples tottered and fell. A tentacle slammed into my chest, sending me flying back, hard up against a spire of rock. As it reared back to impale me I caught it with both hands, wrenching loose plates of armour, macerating flesh...

We battered at each other through the bells of the noon watch, while the fleets of the Tarkhanden and Kothrai ground themselves to flotsam beneath us. Red sails and black, burning, sinking, souls feathered away to nothing amid the cannon-smoke. Shattered bone and blue, ammoniac blood. Torn-off eyestalks glowing as they fell beneath the waves.

A *titanomachia*. Their gods were at war, and never mind that this sordid scrap was not part of any eschatology. Both sides howled their prayers of battle-worship, even with their blood bubbling between their lips. Fanaticism and fury soon made the sea-battle a logjam of grappled-together hulks, in which men swarmed like insects, killing and raving.

And even beneath the brute fury of my possession I could feel it. A mounting horror, as the witchfire burned low.

Every blow I struck weakened me. Every pound of flesh I tore from Abyssus drained us both. Soon we were clenched in mutual agony, like pitfighters in the fourteenth round. Whips of flesh tore sluggishly at my prison of bones, while my fingers pried and scrabbled. We loomed over the battle like some mad sculpture – the hero and the beast, locked in mortal pain.

I gathered up my will and pushed myself back, staggering in the surf. I scooped up a Kothrai warship in one hand, men plunging over the rail, screaming, and I slammed it into the face of Abyssus, feeling its powder magazines explode with a dull crump against my palm.

Pain lanced through me. My left eye swum with black and red starbursts, throbbing.

I snarled, and came in swinging, burning up the last of my power, landing blow after blow, left and right, driving the God-beast down, cracking its shell, heedless of its lashing, gouging whips, pummeling and wrecking, *howling* now, sick with pain and ecstasy, ravening like the tattooed madmen we Khytein had called the Touched.

And I was spent. Sinking to my knees in the wash of swells. Blue blood spiraling out, tainting the foam. Fractals like those amid the stars...

Abyssus tottered and fell too. A tidal-wave of bloody brine slapped as high as my chest. The tangled mess of ships around us heaved, tossing men overboard. A few feeble tentacles lashed the air, raked bloody against the rocks.

But Dirge Endsong… had reserves of malice yet untapped.

"I hope that slakes your thirst for blood, savage," he said. His voice was tight with pain, his breath ragged and heaving. "It will have to do, if you want a glorious final battle. There may indeed be sagas. Of how the cruel necromancer was slain, trying to *end the fucking world!* You… you *unspeakable imbecile!* Oh, how you deserve what happens next!"

I could not move. I was trapped with Sei in a tomb of bones, cold seawater licking at my feet. Threads of mageblight bound me up, like an insect in a spider's web.

But I saw the patchwork face of Dirge begin to stretch. The interstices between those bleeding chunks of flesh pulled apart, first just around his eyes and mouth, then across his whole face, his chest, his body…

The pieces danced. They whirled, runic tattoos in flux, individual cubes of meat spiraling and blurred around a stick-figure shape within. A man forged from liquid night. The body, I realised, Dirge *had built for himself in the Outer Dark.*

In a place where dead Gods could not keep their form; where they melted down in the furnace of their own madness and disgust… Dirge had built himself something *other.* With nothing but his naked will, he had torn loose from that living topography of cannibal lust.

And that, dear friends, is the heart of pure power. No wonder he had manifested again as nothing but flayed skin. The better part of himself – *this* part – could not walk the Materium unbound. It needed a potent, 'blighted body to inhabit. One which Grennen Vuhl had so kindly donated.

The shadow-man opened its eyes, and the light which shone from within them was not light at all. It was anti-dark, seething and primal. A mouth like a jagged wound cracked into a smile.

And as the storm of flesh swirled around it, this new, terrible Dirge sucked up the soul-stuff of the dead.

All of them. Anghul himself trembled, as he felt his grip on the world eroding away.

Dirge devoured ten thousand souls – the drowned, the hacked, the skewered and slain – like a fire drawing air down a chimney. Forge-hot, that negative darkness wrought a working like a tangle of hooks.

And the pieces snapped back together. The last – a cubic fragment of an eyebrow – slotted into place just as Dirge pointed his finger at me, for what he intended to be the last time.

"Weak enough, Khytein. Weak enough – so I can finish you. This is where your story ends!"

And thunderclap. And blast. And ozone stink, vision gone, sound collapsing, feeling nothing but agony. Burning bones scattered like chaff, a storm of them splintered, ripping through flesh and sailcloth, friend and foe alike.

I felt the beam of force snapping and arcing between us. Between that accusatory finger and my chest, shattering my construct, blowing the minds of those ancient beasts away as filaments of fire.

For a fraction of a heartbeat I held it back through sheer will, seeing the purple-white sphere of force pushing in toward me, seeing my terrified reflection in its hellfire meniscus…

Then it all collapsed.

And my world was blown apart.

The thing with the end of the world, see, is
it happens all the time. Every day. Whenever
someone's dying, and they close their eyes for the
last time, that's a world ending, right there. For us,
it all goes on, of course. But for them… it's a quiet
little apocalypse.

Kulain the Blasphemous,the Mad Monk of D'arvonne

I DREAMED, AGAIN, of fire. Heaving cataracts and waves of it – an ocean of flame at the heart of our shattered world.

I dreamed of the Shards. And I saw what Dirge was building, at a place where art, philosophy and engineering intersected. A prison. A cage for a mad God. A place for the Dwellers to coil, like a tapeworm in the belly of creation, bled for power by the new lord of the Materium. Their conquering parasite, Lord Endsong.

It meant the death of the Aziphem. But Dirge knew how to slay them. Take away belief first. Faith, then wonder, plucked aside like puzzle pieces. Imagination, then dreams, then hope…

He would rule over a race of dead-eyed automatons. Things like the clock-men of Korisal, the drudges of Urzen and his ilk.

I had seen the machines in the deeps beneath the Demonspine Mountains. Headless torsos turning cranks. Bodies slaved to thick, dripping cables and tubes, caught in a loop of pointless motions as they rotted alive.

Oh, humanity would be saved. But it would become less than human. Less than the most mindless insects. Less, even, than the corpses I had summoned from their graves.

Somewhere in the dream I realised that I was not yet dead.

I blinked, and I saw a hand reaching down through the ocean of flames, fingers stretched out to save me. I scrabbled for those grey and black-clawed things, feeling a moment of fear as the abyss yawned beneath me, suddenly real.

Another blink, and the flames had turned to water. The play of light and shadow was nothing but burning oil and timber, atop a blood-stained sea. The hand reaching out to me…

Was Anghul's again. Flames boiled around him as he hauled me up, eyes streaming, through a burst of acrid smoke and into his own realm.

There was the thorn-choked glade, the bubbling marsh-pools with their drowned skeletons. The chain-hung throne all covered in moss.

"Not yet, son," said the antlered God, the robes which draped his right arm still smoking. **"When it's time for you to go, *I'll* be the one who takes you. Not *him*. Upstart! I was sowing terror when he was still pissing in his swaddling clothes!"**

In another time, and another place, I felt my head strike the salty timbers of a ship's deck. I saw a fleeting blur of faces above me… Kayan Orsii. Meracq D'avarian.

"Don't you see?" I laughed, staggering past the old Aziphem to the throne. I slumped down on it, feeling the rough-hewn runes carved into its back. "We've *lost*. What can we do against that kind of power? He's come back prepared to face the Archaeon, and I can barely face my next breath."

The yellowed skull inclined itself to one side, quizzical. Chains clattered and chimed, hung with feathers and charms.

"But he has his pride, yes? Like all fools. And that blast which sent you under – it was crafted to scourge the dead."

In that other place, strong hands hammered at my chest. I clenched my eyes shut, coughing, spewing up a double-lungful of brine. Silbern Chaar rolled away, and Kayan cradled my face between her palms.

"He doesn't know that you're *alive*, boy. Alive and kicking. So, while he's just spent a vast part of his power, Abyssus has managed to slip free. Not all the way. Not even enough to twitch one of those hoary great tentacles. But enough to start gnawing at the knots. Pulling loose the hooks. You see?"

I blinked, head back against the throne. Cold stone under my hands. *Ragged sails bellying taut above me. Kayan's eyes, filled with worry…*

"Nothing left to help him, though," I slurred, tasting blood and salt on my tongue. "Even without Abyssus. Even Dirge alone. I can't…"

"Then perhaps your daughter can," said Anghul, his voice flinty. **"She'll try, you know. Even if you manage to claw your way back to the Manifest and tell her not to. Her, and your Hmai witch, and that foolish Ontokhi. They believe in heroes, I'm afraid. Worse – they believe in *martyrs*."**

I heard the threat behind those words. I tried to focus, and I felt the granite under my palms turn to wood, for the briefest instant. The cold mist around me turned to cannon-smoke, reeking of alchemist's powder.

"I knew Kharnath, long ago," said Anghul, walking toward me.

He loomed like the edge of night, suddenly huge and immediate. His shoulders hunched like the folded wings of some carrion bird, mantling me in darkness. **"I pitied him, and I mocked him too. Poor threadbare old thing. Tied to his bloody stones. A power in my youth, such as it was… now swept away. Do you wonder, Kuhal Moer, why your enemy keeps asking you to *choose?*"**

I gritted my teeth. *WAKE UP!* The smell of graveyard earth and fungus filled my nostrils.

"Some fates only unfold at the victim's choosing. Sometimes the prey has to *decide* to die, to submit, to bare its throat. Just as you gave Kharnath a choice. Just as Aesurn chose. I like to think, at that moment, that the willing sacrifice is granted a vision of the whole vast web, of doors slamming shut, of futures collapsing in toward the real…"

A blink – a flash, and I croaked out a mouthful of smoke I had never breathed in. A jolt of sorcery gripped my heart, setting it beating again. A tear fell from Kayan's eyelash, hanging in the air like a jewel…

"So I have come to *choose*, Kuhal Moer. What you asked of Kharnath, back on his hilltop in Oram. I do not want to become a mumbling old shade, lost in the shadow of another God's holiness. I want to let go. So she can live. My great-granddaughter. Through Sothara, to you, to her. In that instant, I will see what wonders and terrors she works upon the world."

Too late, I looked at the old butcher's hands. They came together, and with a flicker of blue fire they drew apart again. Now they held a little stick-figure doll – the kind of gravestone fetish my tribe had tied to trees and ridgepoles to honour the dead. A soul-catcher. This one was crudely finished with white straw hair and a scrap of black rag as a cloak.

It was me.

"Take this gift. Take the Void Heart. Strike him down. The Khytein have no need for a God of Death. Not anymore…"

Anghul held up the little doll of twigs, his eyes flaring green above his permanent, post-mortem grin.

"Now they have *you.*"

He snapped the thing in half.

This time I sat up, screaming. Blood-and-salt-crusted faces stared down at me, smeared with soot, haggard and gaunt. *My friends. My allies.* They rallied around, holding me up, strong arms lifting me to my feet amid a ruin of tangled rigging, broken timber and smoke.

"God's bollocks, Lamenter – we thought we'd lost you. You valiant, stupid, awesome *bastard!*"

That was Meracq, his gold brocade in tatters. Most of the blood on him must not have been his own, or he would already have been a corpse.

"Sarem'ec are hard to kill, Sorathi," chuckled Silbern, cuffing him on the shoulder. Her armour was half gone, dented plates lashed on with rope and strips of rawhide. In one hand she held the Void Heart, and in the other a notched Kothrai war-axe.

The logjam of ships pitched beneath us as I scanned the ring of faces surrounding me. Kayan Orsii didn't speak, but her tiny smile spoke volumes. Elion Morekh had a crossbow quarrel through his forehead, but his grin was wide and gold-toothed, all the stitches torn away.

There was one missing.

"Where is she?" I asked, wiping the blood from my face with the back of my hand. There was a tingle of power in my fingertips, a slow unfolding of force thrumming in my bones. Whatever Anghul had done…

They couldn't look me in the eye.

"Where is she?" I asked, sharper this time. Colder.

Kayan raised a hand toward me, but I pushed it aside.

"No. *Siara*. Where has she gone. Don't tell me…"

It was Silbern who spoke first, and she still couldn't meet my gaze.

"When we dragged you from the ocean, she was the one who knew where to find you. But you were *cold*, Kuhal Moer. Gone. No heartbeat, no breath, pale as a week-old corpse. She thought…"

Elion finished it for her, as the Ontokhi's voice straggled away into grief.

"She's gone to kill Dirge. For *revenge*. Gone to where Abyssus fell. None of us could stop her. She was like… well, like *you*, Khytein. Like you."

Stubborn, and brave, and stupid. *Like father, like daughter*. Oh, I knew.

"It's ships the whole way, Lamenter," said Meracq D'avarian. "The Maelstrom may be gone, but the currents have dragged us all in together. Every Kothrai, every Zamaran, the whole damn Tarkhanden fleet – we sink or sail as one. The Stormreaper just set out north, and all she'll have to do is kill her way from ship to ship until she reaches him."

"Then we follow. *Fast*. No turning back for those who fall behind. I swore to end this, and I will. But she is not going to pay for my pride. Not in this lifetime."

I held out my hand, and Silbern Chaar didn't even waste her breath with arguments. The Void Heart felt right as I clenched my fist around it, feeling the utter cold of the blade send tendrils of frost up my arm to the elbow. Cryptfeeder in my right, this sliver of alien sky in my left.

And we ran.

There are songs, they say, about that mad, pelting flight across a city-sized ruin of ships. Saga poetry of the most base and violent kind, appealing to thugs who swill cheap ale in tavern-hovels, picking their scabs and crushing fleas between their fingernails.[28] There is much talk of fire, of surging waves, of black-clad axemen and furious mages, whole chantries gone mad with the loss of Grennen Vuhl. Of sword-gristle, butcher-cleaving, hardscrabble heroism. Of gore-slick timbers and burning sails.

All of it is true. We carved our way across the slowly spinning slick of shipwrecks, leaving horror behind us. And one by one they fell away. Elion Morekh, turning to face down a whole squad of Kothrai berserkers. Meracq D'avarian, two arrows in his side, grinning red as he flicked the blood from his sabre and leaned up against a trireme's broken wheel. Kayan Orsii, throwing a wall of sorcery up behind us, while waves of unnatural fire assailed it, faces boiling and howling amid the flames...

I never saw her go. She turned, at the last, or so I'm told – turned, as the fire rained down, and the cracks began to skitter across her wardings. But I was not there. Her amber eyes filled with smoke, and saw nothing but a shadow marching away, into darkness, obscured by drifts of sparks.

Even Silbern Chaar fell behind. My last companion, she stopped as we vaulted the rail onto the last ship before open water. Half sunken, it had once been the *Skarne's Maw*. Now it was a wallowing ruin, awash with bodies and burning lamp-oil.

"They're coming," she said, pushing back her skeletal mask. "They can taste the blade. They know your purpose."

"How many?"

Silbern shrugged.

"*All of them.* As many as can walk, or hold an axe. I think one of their demons survived, too."

------

28. You know who you are.

As if in confirmation I heard a cracking, rending scream from back amid the press of ships. A distant stick-scrawl of tangled masts toppled, billowing flames.

"Someone has to watch your back, Kuhal Moer. And I'm supposed to be your bodyguard."

I smiled. The *Skarne's Maw* nuzzled and bumped up against the shell of Abyssus, a wall rising up into the smoke.

"I wouldn't presume to stand behind a lady, would I?"

Silbern hefted the pair of axes she had looted from Kothrai corpses. Her spiked armour glistened red in the firelight.

"If I was a *lady*, would I tell you to hurry up and do your fucking job?" Her usual snarl lacked teeth; it was laced with sadness. For no good reason I thought of Feurio Zahfrey, the lights of his soul sinking into Kharnath's black monolith. The void Heart weighed heavy in my hand.

"Goodb…"

"Don't say it," she said, snapping her visor shut. "Bad luck. We'll meet again, Lamenter. Even if your afterlife is as much of a fraud as your holiness."

What could I do but go on? I turned away, stepped over the rail, and walked on the skin of a God.

Battle raged behind me. I ascended through clouds of smoke, following paths and footholds – clawholds, aye, and tentacle-hold as well – carved into the nacreous shell of Abyssus. Past the wreckage of temples, across whole canted bas-reliefs inset with gold and jewels. Dirge's power drew me in like a lodestone.

And rising now, pushing through the clouds into pale sunlight, I saw that I was too late.

There stood my enemy – crosshatched with bleeding wounds, his face a patchwork mask of horror. His left hand was heavy with smoking black chains, spearing down into the shell beneath us, hooked deep into God-flesh which heaved and shuddered, resisting them.

But his right…

Siara hung in the air at the end of a coil of shadow, chain-links wrapped tight around her so that only her head and shoulders were visible. The bladed end of the chain hovered over her like a cobra, slithering back and forth. Her double scythe lay broken. There was blood on the pale shell of Abyssus, crimson against opal.

She saw me. And the look of terror on her face must have alerted her captor, for Dirge turned as well, his head writhing around without recourse to his neck. Indeed, it was nothing but a slick sliding of cubed flesh – his face rebuilt on the back of his skull.

"Does your idiocy know no bounds, Moer?" he chuckled. "And is it, as it seems, *hereditary?* Here we have your lovely daughter – and what a firebrand! – just about to join my cause. And now *you.*"

I had no words for the monster. Rage suffused me, and I brought up both my blades, teeth bared in a savage grin.

Void Heart. Cryptfeeder. One the bane of flesh, the other of souls.

Dirge laughed.

"You trite little barbarian! Haven't you suffered enough? I'd thank you for bringing me the black blade, but your intent is probably less than generous…"

"On the contrary. *I'll give you both of them.* One in the belly, one in the neck."

"Pithy. I like it. Perhaps you have some more saga-song nonsense to spit at me before you perish?"

He gestured with his fingers. The chains tightened, clenching around Siara.

"No! Father… remember what I told you. Don't let him take…"

Her voice was a strangled croak. Dirge cut it short with a Word – slapping a cantrip of silence over her mouth.

"Let us *negotiate*, peasant. A wasted effort, I suspect, but we civilised folk must at least try…"

He turned, and I could see the cubed slices of his chest pulled back, stepped one upon the other to reveal a terrible gash of darkness.

"Let her go, and I'll kill you clean," I said. "I'll use Cryptfeeder to hack off your head. Not the Void Heart."

He arched one hairless eyebrow, amused.

"Not really familiar with bartering, are you? Woman's work, was it? Oh well. Here's my opening offer." He clenched his knuckles tight. This time I could see Siara screaming, see the blood bright on her lips. But all in silence. *"You or her.* Choose."

And of course, it was no choice at all.

My shoulders sagged beneath the weight of it. I looked up into her violet eyes, saw the horror there, the realization of what I was about to do.

"No!"

Her lips framed the words in silence. But her face – so like Makara's, so like mine – was beaded with crimson. That was what I heard. The call of blood to blood…

I sheathed Cryptfeeder. Reversed my grip on the Void Heart.

"Done," I grated. The edge of the blade up cold against my throat. Such an edge… it would slice through clean. I would fall into the void, and take the instrument of my death with me.

There have been very few times, in our long and thoroughly unpleasant acquaintance, when I have seen Dirge panic.

This was one of them.

"*No!* You stupid, honourable fool! Take that way out, and I swear by the Dwellers *she will follow you!* I don't want you *dead*, Moer. Not with all that precious mageblight in your bones. Not with all your centuries of study. I want you with me when the Archaeon comes. *I want you in my coven of Nine.*"

There was horror there. It burned behind the shock as I stepped back, the cold edge of the Void Heart falling away from my throat. But there was a traitorous part of me which whispered hope. *Siara would go free.* Silbern, Kayan… all of them. Oh, Dirge knew that they would fight the Archaeon in their own way. That his unwilling allies would help his cause. But this way, I would be able to protect them nonetheless. Prime demon of the Nine, as potent as That Which Walks… *I would be a black angel watching over them. So long as Dirge kept my leash long, and my obedience tight.*

My eyes came back to that wound in Dirge's chest. The seething nightmare-stuff inside was in constant flux, dripping and twisting. Reaching out hungrily toward me. For the first time, I wondered exactly what the Angan had been doing when I arrived…

Dirge caught the direction of my gaze. He ran one finger around the edge of the wound, a horribly erotic gesture. Pale clear plasm dripped from his black fingernail, hissing as it pattered to the ground.

"Well might you wonder at it," he said, his voice just above a whisper. "*This* is how I will ensure your loyalty, Khytein. You have given yourself to my service. Your mind is defenceless. And you have seen what I can do with this power. *Oh yes…*"

I remembered the thing which had been shat out into the world, through Dirge's flayed skin. Siara's greatest fear, given horrible form. I remembered, too, the look of abject, craven subservience on Grennen Vuhl's face… right up to the moment when he turned.

"Once I know your fear, I can unlock your mind. Fear is the scalpel, and it will help me peel you back to something I can work with. *Regress* you. Take you back to your sordid little childhood, your dirtscrabble stain of a village… oh, the fun we will have! Now.. look into the darkness! Let us see what. Comes. *Out!*"

His voice was hypnotic. And so was the swirling gyre within, shot through with filaments of unlight. Bubbles rose, swelled, burst. The edges of that wound in Dirge's chest stretched further apart, and a tendril of ink coiled out, hungrily seeking my face.

"Yes! *Oh, yes!* Let it out, Kuhal Moer! Let us see where your sorry little mind goes to scream at night! Let us see the terrors which beset a fucking *necromancer!*"

The sky creaked like glass about to break. My mind blurred, hashed with visions – faces eaten away to skulls, Anghul's black iron oven door clanging shut, ice and maggots, the towers of Urexes burning…

Something was *reading* me. Something was clawing through my memories, in the same ragged places where Zael had torn me apart.

But something was happening to Dirge as well.

The wound in his chest had all but split him in half. Cubes of flesh fell away, as the boiling darkness within budded like crystal, forked like lightning. Spikes stabbed out from it, ten spans long, then collapsed back in. Jets of inky night burst like blood in water, then were sucked back in.

The Angan's birth-ecstasy turned to horror.

"*What have you done?*" he pleaded, turning to me ashen-faced. "How…?"

In the next instant he was torn asunder.

The darkness unfolded in a complex flurry of interlocking planes and angles. It burst free from Dirge's flesh, all jagged and razored, a flower of night half a chain across. Tiny cubes of meat haloed it, the runes carved into them glowing as the chains which bound Abyssus – which bound Siara – dissolved. Power rushed past me, making my hair sizzle with sparks.

And my greatest fear stepped through into the Materia.

I caught only an impression of *weight* and *distortion* as it unfurled. A thing which was less a hand, and more a tangle of geometric heresies scooped me up, Abyssus falling away as the air congealed, shimmering like smoked glass. I was pinned in the centre of that vast unfolding – lines of force encircling me like a pentacle, then *piercing*, bone deep, coursing along the channels of the mageblight. I was held, trapped, at the heart of an expanding cloud of runic angles, black lines scored across reality, facets of power multiplying and growing solid as my fear took on a face.

Dirge snapped back together as a last afterbirth of force slithered through. He staggered, shaken, looking up at the thing which he had created.

And he knew fear. Oh yes.

My terror was his terror, and that of the entire world.

I saw it from outside, of course. From within, there was no encompassing the thing which I had nurtured in my soul for three centuries. My greatest fear.

Sei saw it rise up, billowing like ink in water, glassy facets painting it across the sky. My little familiar had been blasted clear when the construct fell, landing atop the shell of Abyssus. And now he saw the coming of something which matched the God-beast in sheer size.

It was a tattered robe as tall as the arch of heaven – a hooded, cowled thing with its hem in the ocean and its crown amid the clouds. And it *was* crowned, this abomination – its brow encircled by a floating diadem of iron, hammered from out of countless swords, axes, and blades. Great skeletal hands hung inside its sleeves, ringed with bands of steel, and its face was a ghostly flicker of images – of gap-toothed skulls, mummified screams, rotting horrors dug fresh from the earth. All in tumult, and all at once.

The thing unbowed itself, stretching up to its full height, and behind the ribs of its chest – each one a curving sweep of ivory, chains long – spun the very Shard of Death itself. A titanic gem, grinding on its axis in place of a heart.

The logjam of ships below seemed to move around it and *through* it at the same time, as if this impossible apparition existed on multiple planes at once. But its finger, pointed down at the tiny form of Dirge, was real enough.

"What… what have you wrought, Kuhal Moer?" he screamed, spooling in power. Abyssus denied him. His fingers sparked with failed sorcery, embers skipping and dying. "What *is* this thing! It was supposed to be your *fear!* It was supposed to *break* you!"

It was not my conscious mind which answered him. But the voice which issued from that deep and haunted cowl was definitely my own.

"This *is* my fear, Dirge. I have lived with it for three hundred years. I have made it my own. Do you know what I'm afraid of? *Do you?*"

The thing held out its hand, palm open. A bolt of lightning cracked the heavens, plunging down into the waves. For a heartbeat it snapped and raved between sea and sky, then it *solidified*, settling into the creature's grip. It was a staff ten chains tall, writhing with power.

"Perhaps you thought I would see Makara, enslaved as one of your demons. Perhaps my daughter. Perhaps even some trite fantasy of my father's disappointment. But no. *This* is what I fear, Dirge. I fear what I could become, *if I was anything like you!*"

The Angan took a step backward, poised to flee. He shot a glance at Siara's unconscious form, and I knew he meant to scoop her up and make his escape.

But not this time.

"I have to live with this fear every day, Dirge. That in ten years, or a hundred, or a thousand, I might actually begin to *think like you.* That people are just cattle, or worse, just *toys.* That power is its own justification. And then death would wear a fucking crown. Oh yes. Then they'd worship the reaper, the harvestman, the Antlered One on his graveyard throne. Then they'd have *no choice!* And what would I be then? No better than you! A shallow, petty, insane piece of *shit!*"

Now a storm of dead souls came spiraling up that stave, compelled beyond either my will or theirs. My fear, after all, was death enthroned – death become the Divine. It burned up human memories like coals in a forge.

"This is just its shadow! I have faced my fear, and I have hammered it down, and I control it! There are no terrors lurking in the back of my mind, Dirge. They are all right out in *front!*"

A great, sky-spanning blade hinged open as I raved. A hundred thousand souls made up its glassy plane – and the Void Heart was its edge. Stretched out thin as wire, the black sword had become a filament of stars, sharper than reason.

"No! Please! All I've done… was for *humanity*, Moer! For our fucking *species!* The Archaeon will end us, without…"

He may have been right. But that part of me which ruled here, in the naked shadow of my fear, was implacable. I spoke the words which the Tarkhanden would write down in their histories – which the Kothrai, in their exile, would call the Verse of the Pariah.

"Any genocide that starts with you, Dirge, is better than a peace which lets you live."

My eyes grew wide. Pupils dilated with power.

I saw Kayan Orsii, charred and soot-grimed, looking up at me in horror from the deck of a burning ship.

I saw Silbern pause, the end of a blood-soaked bandage clenched between her teeth. She sat on a pile of mail-clad corpses, and she nodded her approval.

I saw Meracq D'avarian snap off an arrow at its fletching, then look up at me and throw an ironic salute.

And I saw Siara's eyes flicker open. She looked up at me, and the first emotion which crossed her face was utter, agonized fear.

That was enough.

This would never be me. This was just a phantasm, ripped bloody from the Outer Dark.

With that realisation, I felt my shadow form begin to crack. In that last instant I brought the scythe back, up over my shoulder, tearing a gash through the clouds. Lightning raved and danced.

"I have faced my fears, Jerrold Sinder," I said. "Now… *it's your turn.*"

My terror swung the blade.

The contrail behind it was a sheet of witchfire aurorae, snapping like a banner in the wind.

And, as it sliced into Dirge, then on, down through the shell of Abyssus, down into his unspeakably ancient heart, I realised that my terror had no restraint.

There was a moment of reeking, busy darkness.

There was a taste of oil and ozone.

There was a flat, colourless explosion, angles sheared and skewed, reality collapsing in on itself.

And my story ended.

Epilogue

The Calm Between Storms

Interlude One - Nowhere

IN A TIME outside of time, I floated weightless.

As white and vast as a sea of mother's milk it seemed – as warm, as depthless.

This was the place where souls went, when they were taken. Ushered through the gates by the hungry, scythe-grinding psychopomp of their choosing – some jackal-faced, some stony, some haloed and feminine, some insects or snakes or patterns of stars.

I had taken the soul of Abyssus.

And he had taken mine.

I knew that the Source was behind me. I could feel it, raising the phantom hackles on what would have been my back. The Divine still slept, but he was fitful. The thing before me was most of the reason – the ghost of a God-beast, hazed and many-limbed, forgetting its flesh as it began to bleed into the whiteness.

I could not look behind me. Whatever was reflected in the articulated opal eyes of Abyssus was not meant for mortals to comprehend. Hells, it could only see *itself* through the warped mirrors of the Aziphem…

So –

"You cannot pass," I said, in fool defiance. A tiny stick-scrawl mannikin, a lick of fire in the void. Facing down a mountain. "Go back. Keep the balance. Heal yourself."

There were no words from the great, ramified kraken-thing. A writhing knotwork of tentacles may have picked out cursive runes. But I felt the impact of its thoughts.

```
+ Cannot +
+ Broken +
+ Powerless +
```

It was right. Back in the Materium, in the Manifest, it was just a titanic lump of carrion now. Cells collapsing, organs decaying, grave-stench and worms…

But what held the rest of us together? What made all those countless tiny cells work toward sentience, toward reason?

Only the ancient, ancient artifice of Abyssus. And without him…

A world gone cancerous. The slough and collapse of life back into a primordial broth.

Nevertheless, then –

"*You cannot pass.* You cannot go back to the source. *We are not done.*"

+ How? +

And I knew.

Thousands of sailors, Tarkhanden and Kothrai, had witnessed the birth of a new God. The Lord of the Drowned had been usurped, in their minds, by the thing which had slain him. The great reaper. The Beast of Sarem.

Me.

And that belief was *potent*. It was powerful enough to raise Abyssus, if we could only hammer the story tight around it. Powerful enough to gift him a huge and unclaimed Facet of Death's Shard, now that Dirge was gone…

I tried to order the images in my mind. They slipped away from me, slithering through fingers which were no longer there.

This would have to do. This was all I had left…

I turned my face toward the burgeoning light of the Divine, and I *believed* for it.

Interlude Two - The Northern Sorathi Ocean

"...HOLD ON! IT's going under!"

Silbern tackled me to the deck as a tentacle the girth of a ghostwood tree lashed down across it, claws and armoured spikes raking the timber to splinters. The weight of her pressed down on me as I coughed up brine and blood, my ears ringing with cannonfire echoes.

"Bloody great beast! I can't believe you left it so *long*, you saga-hero fool. You and Siara both..."

I turned, looking out under the rusted chain-mail beneath Silbern's arm. Through that aperture I saw Abyssus sinking, tentacles slithering and coiling, bubbles boiling up around his fractured shell. Sinking – but *alive*.

"You almost didn't make it."

"Dirge," I croaked. "Endsong. Where..?" I groaned, fighting for breath. "And do you think, milady, that you could see your way clear to getting the hells off of me?"

Silbern rolled away, cursing, and I looked up for a moment, through a tangle of rigging, to a sky underlit by fire. A shadow fell over me.

A pair of violet eyes narrowed.

"*Gone.* You faced him with the Void Heart in one hand, that ludicrous sabre of yours in the other... then things went... strange. Something blurred across the sky. Dirge just *disappeared*." It was my daughter, the Stormreaper – and she had assuredly seen better days. It broke my heart to see those cuts and bruises. But I was proud of how she'd earned them.

"Then Abyssus started sinking, and you were dead weight... we're both lucky Silbern here came after you."

"*Disappeared?* Seriously? No blood, no sorcery – just... gone?"

There was look of confusion on Siara's face, passing across it like the shadow of a cloud. Ahh, yes. She *had* seen something else. But to remember it now would be to unweave the world.

"He... something happened to my eyes. I blacked out. The chains, perhaps. Cutting off my air. When I shook it off, he was there... but *not there* as well. A ghost, in two places at once. He held up his hands, like there was something awful in the sky, coming down on him... and then he fell to pieces. *Disappeared.* Like smoke."

"But the Kothrai haven't."

This from Meracq D'avarian, his arm in a crude sling, his tunic ripped and bloodied.

"Your sorcerer may be gone – and I'd wager it was Abyssus who took him – but we're badly outnumbered. The rest of the black fleet have arrived, and they're reaping a swathe across this floating hell of ours. Axemen, berserkers, archers… we are *sailors*, Lamenter, not knights. This is turning into a land war, and that gives the advantage to Vuhl's men."

"Not Vuhl's anymore," I said, tottering to my feet. "Though you may be right. If the possession broke, then Abyssus could well have taken Dirge under. That beast's hospitality is more than he deserves. Though the darkness, the pressure…"

Siara wanted to believe. I could see it in her eyes. But Kayan Orsii had heard it all too, and she was less convinced. I looked across at her, feeling old and tired, and I caught a sparkle of mischief – of *understanding* – in those amber eyes.

Oh, indeed. She had always been one for secrets…

"I have heard of such things. The possessor can so easily become the possessed. If Dirge over-reached himself, then Abyssus would own him, body and soul. The torments that creature must have in store for him, down there in the dark…" she shuddered.

Siara nodded.

"It… it must have been. The feedback was likely what blinded me. And you, father – it must have struck you like an axe-handle to the skull. What with the mantle of Herald, and all…"

"I think that may be over now, child," I said, attempting a smile. It *hurt*. In fact, I hurt all over – a bruise from head to foot. "My erstwhile patron has fled. But our peril has not. If we can't fight our way free of this floating ruin, we'll burn and drown with it. We have to reach the *Vengeance*, and get her airborne…"

Something inside me had gone quite mad. It insisted that none of this – *nothing at all* – had existed only a few scant minutes ago. A few hundred heartbeats from the beginning of time, yet my memories went back so much further.

Siara and Kayan felt it too.

But…

"Or we could simply wait," said the Hmai witch, pointing back over my shoulder. Off behind us all, out to sea. "Wait for *them*."

I turned, and I saw them.

Another whole nation, it seemed, ploughing the ocean to foam. Great barges like ziggurats of wood and copper, pulled by leviathenes and wyrms. Sails as vast as entire fields upended, marked with the figure-of-eight ouroboros in purple and green. Their decks thronged with siege engines – with riders on their prancing lizard-raptors, with black-skinned warriors in feathers and golden mail.

The fleet of the Coldblood. The Akhazi Empire, mobilised for war.

I had seen those great war-barges, anchored amid the southern isles. I had flown above them on drakenback, reckoning them too far and too few to stop our mad flight to the Maelstrom. But here they were, and they brought our doom with them.

"Ready to sell your lives as dearly as possible?" asked Meracq. "Gods bugger me, I wish we had that ogre with us now…"

"If we die today," said Siara, "then at least we can say we cleansed the world of Dirge Endsong."

"Aye – and who will tell that saga? The Akhazi don't take prisoners, you know. I've heard that their women are even more fierce than their men."

Elion spat on the deck, drawing his cutlass.

"I've fought these devils before," he rumbled. "And you're right. If it comes to being captured or killed, throw yourself on their blades…"

Kayan Orsii started laughing.

We all turned to her in surprise, but this was no mad hysteria. She tried to stop herself with one hand over her mouth, but the demure gesture made her laugh all the harder.

"I'm sorry. Sorry. 'Their women are even more fierce than their men…' Gods, the tales we tell each other…"

Siara's eyes narrowed.

"What in the hells do you mean? Have you gone *mad*, woman?"

"What I mean," said Kayan, stretching out her arms to encompass the whole churning, flashing spectacle of the Akhazi fleet, "Is that these are *my* people. I am the ambassador to Zamara, yes… that much is true. But not from Tsargon Urd of Hmai. *From the Watchful Masters.* The ones who hold the chains of the Coldblood. The rulers of Akhaz."

A quartet of sword-points were at her throat in an instant. Siara. Morekh. Silbern. D'avarian.

But the witch simply laughed again, looking not at her captors – but past them, at me. Those amber eyes seemed to fill the whole horizon, hectic with sparks.

"You and your Gods-damned *secrets!*" hissed Siara. "You owe us a tale, traitor. And you had better make it worth the telling…"

Kayan nodded, that same playful little smile on her lips.

"After it was defeated, on the Urexian plain, the Coldblood was mortally wounded. It fell into torpor… a hundred-year sleep. And that was all the slave-caste were waiting for. My ancestors stormed the temples, throttled the Ecclesiasts, gutted the Vivisectors, drove the Aeternals from their high balconies. *We chained the beast.* Our God. In the same way you have chained Zael Kataphraxis."

Those sword tips wavered, but didn't drop.

"The creature is pathetic in its servitude. Powerful, but puling. So eager to be fed…" she shuddered. "But still playing the very longest of games. Our war against Hmai was a distraction. Our true foes have always been Dirge and the Archaeon, in that order. He – our God's betrayer. A dangerous, mad thing. And that other – its name is a curse. We fight for humanity. And we knew the next blow would fall here. By your hand."

She reached out for me, and wrapped her fingers around mine. They were warm to the touch – far warmer than the corpse-cold hand of Anghul.

"I was the foremost scholar of the Aemortarch in all of Akhaz," she said. "When this mission was planned, I begged the Watchful Masters to choose me. I felt I already knew you – the man behind those dusty pages, those interminable psalms…"

Now, at last, the swords were dropped. I stole a glance at Siara, and she was scowling, her eyes dark. But there was no real passion to it. I think, in that moment, that she was more embarrassed than enraged.

"So I became an *ambassador*. To find you all. The Stormreaper, Dirge's bane. The fleets of Tarkhand, last bastion against Vuhl and his Kothrai. And the Beast of Sarem. Kuhal Moer. I have been given a message for all of you, from my masters of the Free Domain…"

The fleet was drawing closer now. War drums and great, low-bellied serpent-horns shimmered the sky. Bells were ringing, and the rhythmic chanting of the Akhazi swelled up beneath it, fraught with sorcerous harmonics.

"Join us against the Father of Draken. Let us go forth, together, and prepare for the day which we know is coming. We are the tribes of Man, and we will not be ruled by his kind again!"

The music swelled up around us, just as heavy and urgent as the Wild Song of the Khytein warbards. Far away, someone was laughing – whether in madness, relief or simple mirth I will never know.

All I could think about was the steady pulse I felt through Kayan's hand. A double pulse, counterpoint to the Akhazi drums, synchronized, vital…

Hers and mine.

In that instant we were both alive. And I was certain she knew my answer.

Interlude Three - Kaltensund

SUMMER WAS SHORT in the North – a brief season of warmth and light squeezed tight between what seemed like eternities of cold. But it was all the more glorious for its brevity, and on a day like this, it was hard to even imagine the ice-flurries of winter, only a few months away.

Barad knew they were coming. He could taste them in the air as he swung down from his saddle, tying his hardy little Kaltland pony to the single tree atop its wind-blasted hillock.

Below him, the plains stretched north into the distance, capped by the dome of an ice-blue sky. Wildflowers nodded in the breeze as he sat, resting for a while on a fallen obelisk. Behind him milled a herd of shaggy, long-horned Nordeskine cattle, lowing and nuzzling the short grass.

Barad was angry. He had been left out again, sent out of the circle of wagons with the other young folk to hunker under canvas and furs while the men argued.

But it was *his* decision too! This was his future which they were wrangling over – his, and that of their entire people.

An emissary had come from the Witch-queen yesterday. Another one. And the message was the same.

It wasn't safe. These lands, north of the mountain passes, were abandoned for a reason. All hands were needed in the south, in those teeming hives with names like Cyvenne and Almerre and Rothkilde. The Witch-queen was preparing for something – for war, most men said, according to her arcane celestial timetable, scribed in stone atop the Dark Tower.

But there was nothing for him there.

Oh, he was a believer. He kept the New Faith. He knew that the Queen was the daughter of a god – a divinity who had abdicated his throne back in the Dead Times. He had read – at the behest of sad, pale-skinned old Father Sarwen – about the great rebuilding, when the fleets of king Meracq of Sorath had crossed the sea to save a Sarem crippled by plague, and littered with the unburned dead.

But he was only a tiny child then. Stories could not replace the truth he had lived.

His father, and the other men of the nomad caravans – they were *loyal*, dammit! They paid their tithes, and kept no Gods, and were true to the Witch-queen's laws. So what if they burnt little twig-and-grass idols to the Antlered One and the Deadfather? It was just for luck –

a superstition, really. Nothing more. And was not the Queen herself part of that very family?

No. This was about *land*. Good, open, fertile land, and healthy herds, and room to breathe.

Let others slave over the iron machines which the Queen and her allies built.

Let others raise their walls and towers in the South, against a threat which the powers themselves would not even talk about.

"The day will come," said the catechism – but the only thing Barad was worried about was the coming of winter. They would have to turn soon, leave the Abandoned Lands north of the Hiledoran, drive their herds south again, through the high passes before they were choked with snow.

Indeed. Let the Queen fret about magic, and prophecies, and other high, far-off things. For the nomads in their wooden wagons, life was about open fires, good wine, warm women, and far horizons. He had heard stories of the great cities, and he had no wish to see the barracks and warrens, rookeries and factories squatting under smoke.

Barad peeled an apple with his boot-knife, stuffing juicy wedges of fruit into his mouth.

Her own father had left it behind. Aye, him, the Deadfather – the God who Failed. Was his exile any different, any less deserved a respite than their own?

The shadow of a cloud slid across the herd, as Barad lay back against the sun-warmed stone, daydreaming. Yes – this was the life for him. A free man, son of the steppes, maybe one day to have cattle of his own, and a girl like Uthren's daughter Eyva to ride beside him…

It was only as he smiled, thinking of Eyvas' red-gold hair, her shy little smile, that Barad remembered the cloudless vault of the sky above him.

His eyes opened. He looked up, as that shadow wheeled and turned, wings opening, a shape out of primal nightmare cast stark and black across the sunlit plain…

It would be nice to say that the last thing he ever saw was the shape of it. *Long-necked and gaunt, wings flared wide as it prepared to stoop.*

But no.

The last thing he saw was the fire.

*If you enjoyed this story then please leave a review
and tell others what you thought of it.*

Other books by Drew Bryenton from

sci-fi-cafe.com

Elysium Burning

Chains of Tartarus

Soul Crusher

Available from AMAZON and other good bookstores